Holiday Romance

BOOKS BY CATHERINE WALSH

One Night Only

The Rebound

CATHERINE WALSH

Holiday Romance

bookouture

Published by Bookouture in 2022

An imprint of Storyfire Ltd.
Carmelite House
50 Victoria Embankment
London EC4Y 0DZ

www.bookouture.com

ISBN: 978-1-80314-546-4
eBook ISBN: 978-1-80314-545-7

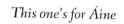

This one's for Áine

PROLOGUE

Chicago

"Are you sure?"

The sales assistant doesn't even try to hide her frown as she follows my pointing finger to the bottom shelf behind her. There, nestled among the daintier and more expensive perfumes, sits a squat green vial that looks like it was left there by mistake.

"It's calling to me," I say.

The woman, Martha according to her name tag, hesitates, but when I just smile, she sighs, her snowflake earrings sparkling as she bends down to grab it. "I think the Armani would be a better choice," she says as I push up my sleeve. We've already doused my other arm in five different perfumes and I'm running out of unscented skin. "There's twenty percent off."

"That one was too nice," I say, holding out my wrist. She sprays it dutifully and I lean down to sniff, wrinkling my nose at the faux apple scent. Sickly sweet with a strong chemical undertone. My sister will hate it.

Which means it's perfect.

"I'll take it."

Martha coughs as the fumes reach her. "If you're worried about budget, we have plenty of cheaper options."

"I'm not," I assure her. "This is the one. Really."

She opens her mouth to protest as the next song starts to play over the speakers, something about sleighbells and reindeers and a jolly good time. A visible shudder runs through her, and I wince in sympathy. I can only imagine how many times she's had to listen to it.

"Do they ever switch up the playlist in here?"

"That would be a no." Her eyes flick to the perfume and then to the line of people forming behind me. I see the exact moment she labels me a lost cause. "Gift wrapped?"

"Please."

She hides the bottle in a mound of tissue paper as though it personally offends her and I mentally cross the final item off my to-do list. With Zoe's present sorted, I am officially done and heading home for the holidays. Or, more realistically, for a week in December. My family has never been big into Christmas, but everyone expects me to go back and so back I go. At least it means I get to be the favorite child for a few days. Moving to the States for college grants me a certain air of novelty whenever I return, which basically means no chores. Zoe was livid last year when she had to do the dishes three nights in a row. Mam insisted I was too jet-lagged and, honestly, what kind of daughter would I be to argue with my own mother?

"Are you *sure*?" Martha asks, dropping her customer service smile as she clutches the plastic bag.

I hand over the cash, trying not to laugh at her reluctance. "Positive."

I step away just as my phone begins to ring, my good

mood plummeting when Hayley's name flashes up on the screen. For one wild moment, I think about not answering it. I wish I'd carried through with that impulse as soon as I do.

"I need a favor."

I turn, fighting my way through the crowded duty-free of O'Hare airport as her voice sounds in my ear. Hayley was the first friend I made at Northwestern. She lived three rooms down from me in our first year and I'd latched onto her in the way any newbie does when they're searching for a friendly face. And while the first few months didn't raise any red flags, the more I threw myself into my new life, the more I realized that there were other, much nicer people I could spend my time with. People who I had more in common with than the girl I always had to buy coffee for because she left her wallet in her other purse. She'd stuck around though, clinging to me in a way I found both confusing and flattering even though it was clear our friendship was hard work.

Zoe always said I was a pushover, but it's not like they teach you this stuff in school. I'd been given lots of colorful leaflets about making friends on my first day. Not a whole lot about dumping them.

"I'm kind of busy right now," I say. "I'm at the airport, remember?"

"It's a really urgent favor."

"I doubt that." I try not to sound as grumpy as I feel. "But what's up?"

There's a loud smack of gum as she answers. "Can I borrow your blue dress for a thing tonight? The one with the back straps?"

"I packed that one."

"What about the green one that makes you look like you have breasts?"

"I have breasts," I huff. The girls just need a little accentuation help sometimes. "Anyway, Andrew's not going to care what you're wearing."

"Andrew?"

"Your boyfriend," I remind her, wincing at the thought of her getting it on in my clothes. They've been together for a few months and I've barely seen him without her tongue down his throat. I chatted with him the first time we met, both of us pleased to find another Irish person so far from home, but I don't think Hayley liked the thought of us bonding and she's made a point of keeping us apart ever since. To be honest, I'm starting to think she doesn't like anyone in her life doing something that isn't solely with her. But now that jealous streak is nowhere to be found as she hums down the line.

"What?" I ask, knowing it's exactly what she wants me to do.

"I'm thinking about breaking up with him." She says the words casually like he's an old pair of shoes she's considering throwing out.

"Since when? I thought you liked him?"

"I did." A pause. "He makes a lot of jokes."

I roll my eyes as I start walking again, weaving through the other travelers.

"But I couldn't dump him right before the holidays," she continues. "I'm not a monster."

"No, you're right. Cold, dark January will be much better." Poor guy. He seemed perfectly fine the few times we've talked. Or maybe it's loyalty to a fellow countryman that's making me feel so bad. "Where are you going tonight?"

"Dinner with Rob." She's barely able to hide her glee. "We hooked up last night after he—"

"What?"

"Billy's friend."

"No, I know who Rob is," I say, picturing the muscly frat boy who's been slobbering over her. "What do you mean you hooked up?"

"We went back to his after Kendra's thing and, Molly, you would not *believe* what he can do with his—"

"So, you ended things with Andrew?" I interrupt, confused.

"I said I'm thinking about that."

...Yeah, I need new friends. "You cheated on him?"

"It's not cheating if I'm going to break up with him."

"Yes, it is!"

"Oh my *God*," she groans. "This is not a big deal."

"You need to break up with him if you're seeing someone else, Hayley. It's cruel."

"Alright," she huffs. "Fine. I'll do it now."

"No, not *now*. Wait until classes start back."

"But you just said—"

"I know what I said." I tug my suitcase closer to my body as I step onto one of the automatic walkways, catching my reflection in the mirrored wall opposite and schooling the heavy scowl I find there into something more public-friendly. Maybe she was right the first time, who wants to get dumped on Christmas Eve? "How about you don't see Rob from now until you do?"

"But I'm seeing him tonight," she says, like I'm an idiot. "Look, if it's such a big deal to you, I'll message Andrew."

"Hayley, you can't!" I snap, freaking out at the thought of her breaking up with him over text. I don't even know the guy that well, but there's such a thing as common decency.

There's silence on the other end of the line and I think she's finally realized how shitty that would be when she snorts. "Okay, *Mom*."

"Hayley—"

"I've got to go." Her tone changes to one of supreme boredom. "I'll see you when you get back."

"I gave you a key to water my plants, not to borrow my dress so you can cheat on—"

"*Bye!*" she calls down the line and immediately hangs up.

I stumble off the walkway, staring at my phone in outrage. I need new friends. That can be my New Year's Resolution. New friends. New, non-terrible friends.

I'm in such a mood after the call that it takes me another five minutes before I realize I've gone in the wrong direction and by the time I make it to my gate, sweaty and flustered, they're halfway through boarding.

It's a small plane. Two seats on either side and two in the middle, each one packed tight together. Progress down it is frustratingly slow as people hobble along, stuffing bags into overhead lockers and fumbling with heavy winter coats.

I match the shuffling steps of the person in front of me, concentrating so hard on not banging my suitcase on anyone's elbow, that it's only when I stop by my row and relax my aching fingers that I glance at the seat next to mine. I like to think I have acceptable standards for traveling. All I want and expect is someone who keeps their shoes on and doesn't steal my food when I go to the restroom. Just a polite, normal stranger who I can ignore for seven hours while I try and get some sleep. So you can imagine my horror when, instead of greeting some unknown frequent flyer, I stare straight into the eyes of Hayley's soon-to-be ex-boyfriend.

Andrew Fitzpatrick looks just as surprised to see me as I am to see him. But instead of the sinking, *you've got to be kidding me* feeling I'm experiencing, he just smiles. It's the kind of smile that Hayley gushed over after their first date. A freaking white-teeth, dimpled, make-you-feel-all-warm-inside smile. And he directs the full force of it right at me.

Crap.

"Molly?"

Crap crap crap.

"Hello!" I chime a little too loudly. Indoor voice, Moll. Or plane voice or whatever.

"Is this you?" He points to the seat next to him and I glance around for another miraculous one to appear. Of course, it doesn't. This flight was booked out days ago. He knows it too, not even waiting for me to respond as he stands, slipping into the aisle. "That's crazy," he continues. "And you've bagged the window seat."

Aka the trapped seat.

I store my suitcase overhead before I do that awkward shuffle past him. Seven hours. I'm going to have to lie for the next seven hours. Seven hours and thirty minutes by the time we take off and land. Maybe I could pretend to be asleep. Maybe I could—

"How's college going?" Andrew drops into the seat next to me as I shove the duty-free bag under the chair in front. He immediately puts his seatbelt on, even though people are still boarding the plane. "You're studying Business, right?"

Small talk. I don't usually mind small talk. But in these kinds of situations, small talk tends to lead to big talk. "Economics."

He lets out a low whistle. "That sounds even fancier. You're going to be an economist?"

"A lawyer. I think."

"You think?"

"I've got the grades."

He looks at me like I've said something funny. "But do you want to be a lawyer?" he asks when I don't say anything more.

"I haven't decided yet." The words come out more defensive than I mean them to and a moment of silence descends just long enough to make me feel rude. "And what about you?" I ask. "How's your... thing?"

His lips twitch at my hesitation. "Photography. It's going well. Hayley might have told you already, but I'm applying for internships next summer to see if I can stay in Chicago. Might not be the smartest decision seeing as how everything's unpaid. Like *aggressively* unpaid. But I'm crashing with my uncle until he gets sick of me. Free board for a few months if I do the graveyard shifts at his store." Andrew leans my way as a flight attendant slams our over-head locker shut. "Does it smell like candy floss to you?"

Great. "That's me. Sorry." I sniff my right arm to make sure. "I was picking out a perfume," I explain as his expression brightens.

"Really? Maybe you can help. I wanted to get Hayley something as a surprise. She didn't want to do Christmas presents but technically it will be January when I see her so... What?"

"Nothing." I smile, tugging out the inflight magazine from its little seat pocket. Why did she tell me about Rob? Why? Why why why why—

"I was thinking this one."

I watch as he opens his own copy and flicks to the gift page, pointing to a small Chanel bottle.

"It says it's a classic," he says, peering at the tiny text beside the picture. "Eighty-nine dollars. What do you think?"

I think I'm going to kill Hayley.

Eighty-nine dollars. Someone doing graveyard shifts for his uncle and sitting coach on a budget Irish flight does not have eighty-nine dollars to spend on a girl who's going to dump him in a week.

"You can't buy her something on a plane," I say as he takes out his wallet. "You should buy it from somewhere special."

"I won't tell her if you won't."

"And that seems like a lot of money."

He reaches for the call button. "I've saved for it."

"But—"

"Excuse me? Mr. Fitzpatrick?" We both turn as another flight attendant approaches us from behind, a teasing look on her face. "Your brother called ahead," she says, and a look of utter confusion crosses Andrew's face.

"A chorus of "Happy Birthday" was mentioned," she continues, handing him a small square envelope. "But would you settle for a free drink on us?"

"Gladly," he says, sounding relieved as his eyes slide to mine. "Can we make it two?"

"Of course," she says. "What can I get you?"

"Oh..." I glance at Andrew, who just waits. "White wine?"

"I'll have the same," Andrew says, showing her the magazine. "And can I get—"

"We'll begin our boutique shopping as soon as we're in

the air," she interrupts with a bright smile. "Seatbelt," she adds to me.

I buckle up as requested, waiting for her to disappear behind the curtain. As if this day could get any worse. "It's your birthday?"

To my surprise, he bursts out laughing. "No. This is my brother's idea of a joke. Christian's just hoping to embarrass me." His smile falters as he glances back at me. "Hey, are you okay? You've gone white as a ghost."

"It's the lighting," I lie. Okay. At least she's not cheating on him on his birthday.

Oh my *God*, that should not be my baseline!

"I knew he'd try something like this," Andrew continues as I try to calm down. "You got any siblings?"

"Just one. My sister."

"Older or younger?"

"Older. By about three minutes."

His brow furrows before he gets it. "You're a twin?"

"An identical one."

"Seriously?"

I nod, fighting back a wince at his enthusiasm.

"Wow, that's..."

And here we go.

"Completely normal and unimpressive," he continues, smiling when my eyes slide back to him. "You must be sick of people going nuts when you tell them."

"Just a little," I admit.

"Sorry."

"No, I get it. It's when they start asking if we feel each other's pain that I lose the will to live."

He laughs and I relax a bit. "There are four of us," he says. "Liam's the eldest. Then me, then Christian. And now Hannah, who's six."

"Six?"

"She was a welcome surprise." He slides his finger under the lip of the envelope, smirking when he opens the card to reveal nothing but a crudely drawn middle finger. "Classy. You get on with your sister?"

"Yeah. For the most part."

"I bet it's hard to be so far away from her."

"I never really thought about it," I say honestly. "I mean, we text all the time so..."

"Still," he prompts. "It will be nice to be together at Christmas."

"Sure."

"Sure?" He smiles again. Big smiler this one.

"We're not really Christmas people," I explain.

He gives me a skeptical look. "You're literally flying home on Christmas Eve."

"Coincidence. I work part-time at a shoe store and was going to work over the holidays, but my boss didn't have the hours and Zoe wanted me to bring stuff over so..." I trail off as he stares at me. "Here I am."

"You're breaking my heart here, Molly."

"It's not like I'm a Scrooge!" I say. "I'm just not really into all the—"

"Love?" he supplies. "Comfort and joy?"

"Toys. Money. The same twelve songs played over and over again."

"Ah, the commercialization argument."

I frown at how quickly he dismisses it. "Unless you're doing it for the kids, Christmas is nothing but several weeks of expensive stress that will inevitably end in disappointment. How can anything live up to that kind of expectation?"

"Wow. So, you're like a grinch?"

"I'm not a—"

"A real-life grinch."

"I'm practical."

"I'm getting that," he says, looking like he's enjoying himself. "But it also sounds like you're doing Christmas wrong."

"It's not the same for you. You just said it yourself, there's a child in your family. That's different."

"Child or no child, you're never too old to hole yourself up in the house for a few days and eat until you puke. Not to mention the fashion." He gestures at his sweater and it's the first time I notice the cheery reindeer embroidered on the front.

"Reindeers don't wave," I tell him.

"Rudolph does. Rudolph loves to wave."

I snort. "I get it now."

"You do?"

"Mm-hm. You're from one of *those* families."

He only looks amused at my suspicion. "Those families?"

"The ones in the commercials. Matching pajamas. Roaring fire."

"Unashamedly. I'm going to guess you're not?"

"Like I said, not big Christmas people." I frown when he continues to watch me, a new glint in his eye that immediately puts me on edge. "What?"

"Nothing. Just thinking about what I can do to make you a fan of the most wonderful time of the year."

"How about not saying things like that for a start?"

He grins. "I'm going to change your mind about this."

"Confident thing, aren't you?"

"Of course I am. So confident that I bet you I will change your grinch-like mind by the end of this flight."

"An actual bet?" I press my lips together, fighting back a smile. "How much are we talking?"

"One million—"

"*One* dollar," I say, lifting a finger. "And you should know that I'm extremely competitive."

"And you should know that I may look innocent, but I'm not above playing dirty."

"Innocent, huh?"

He gestures vaguely to his face. "I've got the whole boyish thing going on, I know my strengths."

I laugh at that, and he brandishes the fake birthday card between us. "Now," he says. "Do you want to see how much free stuff we can get out of this or what?"

His phone vibrates on his lap before I can respond, making me jump. Sometime during the last few minutes, we've both turned completely toward each other, and my stomach drops like we just hit turbulence when I see who's calling. I'd somehow forgotten all about Hayley as we'd talked, but now she screams her way back to the front of my mind as Andrew brings the phone to his ear, not noticing my panic.

"It's Hayley," he says as my pulse starts to race. "She's been studying so much; I didn't even get to see her before I left." He turns to the front, smiling broadly. "Hey, babe! You'll never guess who—"

I snatch the phone from his hand before I can think, pressing the button to end the call.

Silence. Awkward, awkward silence for the longest second as Andrew just stares at me. And then: "What the f—"

"You shouldn't answer your phone when we're flying."

"We haven't started moving yet," he says slowly. "The doors are still open."

"It can still affect the system."

His mouth opens and closes, all traces of joking vanished. "Can I have my phone back?" he asks eventually.

I think about saying no. About saving him from what I know is about to happen even at the expense of me acting like a weirdo. He's a nice guy. A nice, festive guy and if this has to happen I don't want it to happen when he's just spent ten minutes harping on about Christmas. But the unimpressed look on his face tells me he's about to call for security and I would really, *really* like to not get arrested.

"Right. Sorry." I hand it back to him. "I'm a nervous flyer."

"...Okay?" He turns away from me as much as he can in the small space, but I don't let up.

"So that bet, huh? You were going to convince me?"

"Look," he begins, but the phone buzzes again and we both look down to see a message flash up on his screen. I think I'm about to be sick.

Not by text.

Not on Christmas Eve.

She wouldn't.

Beside me, Andrew goes very, very still.

She would.

"White wine?" The oblivious flight attendant reappears beside him, two plastic cups in her hands. "We aren't supposed to open the bar until after takeoff, but—"

"Yes!" I exclaim, half standing as I startle the poor woman. "Yes, please."

Andrew doesn't move as I take the drinks and neither does our new friend, who looks a bit too pleased with herself.

"I know we said we'd let you off easy," she says as he stares down at the text. "But seeing as it's our last flight before Christmas, we couldn't ignore the opportunity to embarrass our passengers."

I glance behind her as two other attendants make their way toward us. Oh no. "I don't think—"

"*Happy Birthday...*"

Oh *no*.

A deep pink flush spreads upward from Andrew's neck as the cabin crew and then the majority of passengers take up the song.

"*Happy Birthday, dear Andrew...*"

As they do their rowdy best with the octave leap, Andrew slowly raises his head to look at me.

"Happy Birthday," I say with a weak smile, and down my cup in one.

CHAPTER ONE
DECEMBER 21ST, NOW

Chicago

I took a quiz the other day. One of those "what should you do with your life, you indecisive idiot" ones. Each question was meaningless (pick a color, choose a salad dressing) and interspersed with memes of celebrities I don't recognize anymore. At the end of it, I was told to become a kindergarten teacher. I didn't like that, so I took it again. It told me to go to medical school. As if that was a thing I could just rock up to one evening.

I've decided to quit my job, you see. No, I've decided to quit my *career*. Three years of law school, four years of law, and five weeks ago, I sat at my desk several hours after I was supposed to have gone home, closed one document, opened another, and realized that not only was I completely miserable, but I had been for a while.

It was like the shower in my first apartment, warm and normal one second, icy cold splinters the next. Don't get me wrong, it was a relief to finally acknowledge it, but ignorance is bliss, and when my next stage of enlightenment didn't come, when I didn't suddenly realize my passion for salsa dancing or my hidden dream to become an accountant, all I was left with was this sick, twisted feeling in my stomach while two little words echoed in my mind, over and over and over again.

Now what?

I still don't have the answer.

When most people decide to change their lives, they usually know what they want to change them *to*. They take over a crumbling chalet in the south of France, they retrain as a social worker, they sell all their belongings and become a nun.

They tend not to talk about things like rent and student loans and health insurance. There's never a four-part YouTube video about all the things I'll still somehow have to pay for. Never a three-thousand-word blog on how to start again in a realistic, not-completely-abandoning-my-old-life way.

"Molly."

Maybe I'll start playing the lottery.

"*Molly.*"

Or I could get a cat.

"Hey!"

I look up at the rapid knocking on the wall to see my friend Gabriela standing in the doorway.

"Didn't you need to leave ten minutes ago?" she asks. "I thought you were done."

"I am done."

I am not done. I am never done.

"It's fine." I turn back to my laptop and the contract within it, blinking as the words swim before me. "I've got a forty-minute window for delays."

"Of course you do." She steps fully into the room, her

arms crossed over her chest. You wouldn't know from the look of her that she started work at seven a.m. this morning. Her navy dress is still wrinkle-free, her makeup fresh, her dark curls pulled back into a low ponytail, showing off her heart-shaped face. One of those curls bounces free as she comes closer, peering at the piles of paper before me. "Is it the Freeman contract?"

"Is it ever not the Freeman contract?" I mutter. "Or do we just have one client now?" Because that's what it feels like. It's all I've been working on for the past few weeks. Or maybe it's years. At this stage, I really can't remember. Back and forth on the sale of a company that should have been agreed on months ago. "It's like I'm being paid to waste everyone's time."

"So long as you get paid," she murmurs, dragging one of the folders toward her.

Gabriela also did three years of law school. Three years of law school and five years of law. She showed me around on my first day at Harman & Nord and their swanky skyscraper office on LaSalle Street. The same one we're in right now. Gabriela doesn't want to quit her job. Gabriela, like the rest of our small circle of friends, loves her job and doesn't mind the pressure or the late hours or the ruthlessness that I'm understanding more and more I simply don't possess.

"It's fine," I repeat as she starts to read. "Honestly, I've..." I trail off as she looks at me. "...been reading the same page for the last hour," I admit.

"You need a vacation."

"I'm going on one."

"No, you're going home," she says pointedly. "Home is not a vacation. Especially not during the holidays. Especially not when you hate the holidays."

"I don't hate the holidays," I grumble, snatching my folder back. "I just don't go around with reindeer antlers on my head. There's a middle ground."

"You should just stay here next year."

"I can't," I say, rubbing my tired eyes for exactly two seconds before I remember I have mascara on. "I have to go back."

"You go back all the time. Make your folks come here. Give them the tour, let them see how impressive you are." She tilts her head, smiling prettily at me. "We can go for dinner and you can tell them how wonderful a mentor I am."

"Is that what you are?"

"Parents love me. I'm very polite."

"You're a suck-up, there's a difference." I close my laptop and start stacking my stacks into one giant stack, but Gabriela just stays where she is, watching me with a thoughtful expression. "What?" I ask.

"Nothing." She runs a finger across the dark wood of the desk before her eyes drop to my stomach. "Are you pregnant?"

"*What?*"

"You can tell me if you are."

"No!"

"No, you're not pregnant or no, you're not going to tell me if you are?"

"Both," I snap.

"Okay."

"I'm not even seeing anyone."

"*Okay.*" Her voice lowers to a whisper. "But is that the problem? Do you need some sex? We can get you some sex."

"Oh my God." I shove my laptop bag at her and gather my papers. "Stop talking. We're no longer friends."

"It's just you've been so distracted lately," she says, hurrying to keep up with me as I stride out of the room. "And I want you to know that if something's going on, you can talk to me. I'm a great listener. A lot of people confide in me."

"Who confides in you?"

"Michael."

"Michael's your husband, he has to confide in you."

"Yes, but I'm also great at it. And as two gals at the boys' club, we need to stick together."

"Two gals at... You've been listening to those podcasts again, haven't you?"

"Women supporting women," she insists. "That means we have to talk to each other."

"Not about my womb though, Gab."

We head back to the other side of the floor, down the long corridor lined on either side with glass-walled meeting rooms. For a lawyers' office, we have ironically little privacy. I've always hated it. Especially in my more anxious moments when I feel like I'm in a fishbowl. Like there are eyes on me all the time, waiting for me to slip up. Even now, the floor is busy, most people having already gone out for dinner and come back to work well into the night.

"Have you slept with anyone since Brandon?" Gabriela asks, still clutching my laptop bag as we reach my desk.

"Why does it matter?" I groan, wincing at the mention of my ex. "When's the last time you had sex?"

"This morning."

"That's... I didn't need to know that."

"Then why did you ask?"

"Because you—" I exhale sharply, pulling out the folders I need before tugging my coat on. "It's not about that."

"But you admit it's about something."

"I do," I say, placing the documents inside the bag. "But it's nothing serious and I'm fine. Or as fine as I can be after the week I've had." And the weeks I'm about to have. I take out the small suitcase I'd shoved under my desk, thinking about all the work I still have to do. It's not that I never talk to Gabriela about this kind of stuff, but I know she wouldn't understand. Both her parents are lawyers. Her brother is a lawyer, and her grandfather was a lawyer. All her friends are lawyers. It will never have occurred to her to do anything else. It will never have occurred to her that there *is* anything else and I know she'll try to talk me out of whatever this is I'm feeling and, to be honest, she's better at her job than me. She'll win.

"I just want you to know that I'm here," she continues. "And that I am ready to actively listen should you want someone to do so."

Amusement overtakes annoyance at her earnestness. "I know," I say, taking the bag from her and slinging it over my shoulder. "And I appreciate it. You know I do. But I'm fine."

"I just want to help."

"You can help me find my coat."

"You're wearing your coat."

Yes, I am.

"Okay, maybe I'm a *little* distracted." I check the time as I yank my blonde hair back into a ponytail. Thirty-minute window for delays. "Don't move." I pull out a white cardboard box from my bottom drawer, grinning when Gabriela gasps in delight.

"I thought we weren't doing presents this year! You said you were going to go to that beginners' samba class with me and not make fun."

"I'll still do that," I promise. Gabriela and I usually

trade each other small things for the holidays; favors or strictly budgeted gifts. Two weeks ago, she helped move my new mattress up three flights of stairs. Something that, for two not-so-tall girls, is a lot harder than it sounds. "This is for you and Michael," I explain. "Espresso brownies from that bakery in Little Italy." I pry open the box, presenting the neatly sliced squares of goodness. "Remember I brought them to your birthday party and you ate six?"

"I don't because I'm pretty sure I had a bottle of champagne alongside them." She reaches for the one closest to her, groaning when she bites into it.

"Put them in an airtight container when you get home," I tell her as she takes the box from me. "And keep them at room temperature. They're best with a bit of cream. And maybe some icing sugar. Or a little bit of—"

"I love that you think these babies are making it home," she interrupts, licking the crumbs from her lips. "You should have been a chef."

"I don't make food. I eat food."

"None of the work and all of the reward. I respect that." She shoves half the brownie into her mouth, holding up a finger. "*Waif ere*," she says around the slice, which I take to mean "Wait here" and I watch curiously as she opens a drawer in her own desk opposite mine, pulling out a Chicago Cubs teddy bear.

"It's for the baby," she says. "So your sister can raise her child right."

"Gab! You didn't have to do that."

"I know, but I'm nice." She lingers as I tuck it into my suitcase, fitting it in beside all the other food and the few pieces of clothing I'm bringing home with me. "How is that all you're taking?"

"It's just for a few days."

"Yeah, but it's Christmas," she protests. "What about presents?"

"I give most people money as a present. They expect it and they want it."

"That doesn't seem very Christmassy."

"And yet I remain everyone's favorite relative." I straighten, mentally going over the most important things. Clothes, wallet, tickets. Keys, passport, phone.

"You good?" Gabriela asks when I finally look at her.

I nod. "And if I'm not, it's too late. I'll be on my phone if you need me. And I'll be online from tomorrow. And—"

"*Goodbye*, Molly," she says, pushing me out the door.

"Bye," I say automatically. "Happy Christmas, I guess."

"It's good that you sound so miserable when you say that. Really gets me in the festive spirit."

She waits with me until the elevator comes, waving cheerfully as she eats the other half of her brownie. It takes an age to get down, stopping at every other floor before we hit the lobby. Outside, the surrounding skyscrapers tower above me, the streets full of people heading to restaurants and bars and clubs. At least at this time of day, it doesn't take long to catch a cab, and in no time at all I'm speeding west across the city, aiming for the interstate.

The snow falls thickly around us, gathering in a way I'm still not entirely used to even though I've lived here for years. I was still a teenager when I arrived and thought myself incredibly grown-up even though I was scared shit-less. I spent that entire flight wondering if I was making a giant, expensive mistake, but any doubts I had vanished as soon as I stepped off the plane. I knew as soon as I did that Chicago was my city. And I was lucky that it was. There's no predicting it sometimes, what calls to you and what doesn't. But in the same way house-hunters can walk through a front door and know instantly whether or not the four walls are for them, I knew as I settled into my life here all those years ago that this was where I belonged.

It's a gut instinct. A feeling.

Or maybe it was fate.

My parents assumed that after college I would move back to Dublin, but it never even occurred to me, the excuses rolling off my tongue whenever they asked. Summers were spent with friends and boyfriends. College was followed by law school. Law school by work. And alongside it all was a life I built from scratch. An apartment to call my own, friends I adore and a city I now know like the back of my hand. I love the parks and the festivals and the beaches. I love the architecture and the people and how easy it is to get around. I love how I have some of the best food in the world right outside my front door. And I love that it's all mine.

Even now I think my family still expect me to return to Ireland. But how can I? This is my home now. And I can't imagine being anywhere else.

So I've been thinking...

My sister's text comes through as we near the airport, followed by a series of emojis that she like to punctuate every message with.

Oh no.

Instead of you coming here for Christmas why don't the two of us bail and get the first flight to some Greek island?

I don't think they'll allow you on a plane this far along.

I'll wear a very big coat. They'll never know.

Zoe is eight months pregnant and due in early January. I think my parents are even more excited than she is about it, and recently made her move back into their house so they could fuss over her.

A couple of carolers came to the door earlier, she continues now. *Dad tried to be funny and requested Hotel California. Mam gave them some leftover packets of M&Ms like it was Halloween.*

And people wonder where I get it from. I can already picture how the next few days are going to go. The big family reunions (yes, it's hard work, no, I'm not married yet) and the smaller dinners at home where the four of us awkwardly carry out our strange version of Christmas. Mam will go to bed early and Zoe will slip out to meet a friend and Dad will corner me in the living room and ask the same gruff but well-meaning questions about my retirement plan and the insulation in my apartment building and whether or not I took his advice about investing in a good toolbox, because he doesn't really know how to talk to me anymore but still wants to try. Every year it's like the four of us are halfheartedly acting out something we saw on television, and more and more I wonder why we bother to pretend at all.

My phone buzzes as a photograph comes through of my very small, very single childhood bed, made up with blankets that I'm pretty sure my parents had since before I was born.

#*Glamour*, Zoe writes underneath, and I sigh, mentally apologizing to my poor back muscles. I'll need to book a massage as soon as I get back here.

Traffic slows as we near the airport, but at this time of year, I suppose I should be grateful we get there at all, and I tip the driver as I get out, checking in my suitcase and keeping my laptop bag on me. By the time I make it through security, I have zero time for delays and head straight to duty-free like a woman on a mission.

"Excuse me," I ask, stopping the nearest worker with a lanyard around their neck. "What's the worst-selling perfume you have?"

Five minutes later I leave smelling like an obnoxious concoction of pop-star-branded scents, with one sparkling pink bottle swinging from the bag on my wrist.

Eventually, I get to my gate, weaving through tired, disgruntled families and solo adults staring into space until I spy a dark-haired man sitting hunched over a *National Geographic*. I can't see his face, but I can picture his creased brow as he reads, the way he mouths every other word even though he swears he doesn't.

For a moment, I just watch him, and then I take a step and then another and another, and with each one, I feel the world outside slowly slip away. No more worries, no more planning, no work, no nothing. I'll have to deal with it all when I get back. Hell, I'll probably have to deal with it when I land. But not right now. It's the one time of year when I put my work second.

I'm smiling when I reach him and don't hesitate as I reach forward to pluck the magazine from his hands.

"Excuse me, sir," I say as he rears back, startled. "I think you're in my seat?"

Andrew Fitzpatrick's shocked look disappears as soon as he sees me. He grins up at me with those hazel eyes as if I'm the best thing that's happened to his day. I know he's the best thing that's happened to mine.

"Hey, stranger," he says, leaning back against the chair. "Fancy seeing you here."

CHAPTER TWO

EIGHT YEARS AGO

Flight Two, Chicago

Just don't meet his eye. Don't meet his eye and don't even look his way. Look down! Look down at your phone and pretend to be busy like the coward you are. Look down look down look down.

I look up, watching Andrew joke with a flight attendant as he makes his way slowly toward me.

He's shaved off all his hair and it doesn't suit him. I would say I barely recognize him, except for the fact that I definitely do. I'd know that face anywhere. I've thought about it enough these past few months, putting our flight last year right up there with the time I called my teacher Mam, or when I forgot to lock the restroom door on a train and a poor woman saw a lot more of me than either of us would have liked.

That is to say, it was embarrassing as hell and I've replayed the moment I snatched the phone from his hand at least once a week. After the Hayley incident, we didn't say another word to each other and, when we landed, he vanished up the aisle before they'd even opened the doors. The last time I saw him was in baggage claim at Dublin airport, where he was yelling down the phone at someone. One guess as to whom.

Hayley, I only hung out with once more, at some random guy's party she dragged me to a week after I got back. I called her out on what happened and she laughed it off, but she stopped texting me soon after and I let her. I made new friends, I settled in, I moved on.

But now? *Now??*

I mean, I know we're both from a small country, but come on.

I slink farther into my seat, pretending to scroll through a news article while I remain extremely aware of the empty seat beside me. Aware because it's one of the few empty ones left.

And Andrew keeps coming.

My heart starts to pound as I watch him approach from the corner of my eye. I mean, this is ridiculous. There's coincidence and then there's just plain old cosmic injustice. He could have booked any seat on any plane on any day, so why does it have to be this one? Why does it have to—

"Excuse me? Do you mind if I move your coat?" Andrew stops right beside me and I have no choice other than to glance up, clinging to the vague hope he's forgotten all about me.

He has not.

He stares at me, hands frozen above his head, about to shove his bag into the locker. As soon as our eyes meet, all that embarrassment increases tenfold, and I flush when he just stands there.

"Hello," I say with the biggest, falsest smile on my face. The word seems to trigger something in him, and his expression wipes blank as he drops his arm, swinging his bag back to his side before he moves on like he didn't even see me.

Okay, not great.

I turn weakly back to the front, pretending not to listen to the polite conversation happening a few rows behind. A minute later a confused woman appears next to me, smiling sympathetically as she slides into the seat.

"Had a fight with your boyfriend?" she asks, and I grit my teeth, risking a glance over my shoulder to find Andrew looking right at me.

I immediately spin around, slumping so he can't even see the back of my head.

But it doesn't matter. I still feel his eyes on me the entire flight.

———

Now

I toss the magazine back onto Andrew's lap, taking in his sweater, a clashing red-and-green monstrosity, with resigned acceptance.

"What the hell is that?" I ask, gesturing to his face.

"Oh, this?" Andrew strokes his chin. "My manly scruff because I'm a manly man?"

"Are you growing a beard?"

"The fact that you have to ask that question makes me want to lie and say no."

It's going to be a great beard and we both know it. I've just never imagined him with one before. I always thought his face was too open for one, with that stupid dimple in his left cheek and those ridiculous eyes that seem to change color whenever they want to.

"What happens in the summer when you tan but then decide to shave and your face is two different colors?"

"Would you believe I haven't thought about that?"

I smile but can't keep it up for long. "I'm sorry I'm late. I had some things I needed to finish up at work."

"Pretty sure late is me in the air and you on the ground. The plane's still there in case you missed the big tube thing outside."

"I wanted to surprise you." I drop into the seat next to him and hand over the envelope I'd kept in my pocket for the last few days.

"This doesn't *feel* like diamonds," he jokes, pretending to weigh it.

"It's a first-class upgrade."

His amusement fades as he stares at me. "Come again?"

"I think the lounge will be manic, but we can check—"

"How much did this cost?" He sounds horrified as he opens it, drawing out the tickets like they're from Willy Wonka himself.

"Don't worry about it. Less than you think."

"Moll, Christmas prices are bad enough—"

"I said don't worry about it," I interrupt. "Do you know how many unused air miles I had? I had to spend them on something. Besides, it's our ten-year anniversary."

"Ten?" He frowns as I start to feel a little hurt. "Are you sure?"

"Yes! Our first flight was ten years ago. That's an anniversary."

"Can't be more than seven."

"It's ten! It's—" My mouth clamps shut as he holds up his fist between us, a gold chain dangling from his clenched fingers. At the bottom of it, glinting in the fluorescent light, is a small blue pendant.

"Happy ten-year anniversary," he says as I take it.

"You're a jerk," I mutter, but there's no heat to the words as I admire my present. Simple and small and perfect for me.

"Careful," he says as I undo the clasp. "The elderly, heavily accented man at the antique shop told me it was cursed."

"Oh, he did, did he?"

"Something about three ghosts on Christmas Eve? Or maybe it was a golem. I went back the next day to check but the place had mysteriously disappeared." He helps gather my hair from the nape of my neck as I put it on. "I can guarantee you it didn't cost as much as these tickets did," he adds. "Or much at all to be honest. But it's only the first part."

Now that gets my interest. "I get a two-part present?"

"Anniversary present and a Christmas present."

"We don't do Christmas presents."

"I'm a bad boy, Molly, I do what I want. I'll give it to you when we land, it's in my suitcase." He scratches the side of his jaw as I twist the chain into place, positioning it against my throat to show him. "It looked bigger at the store," he says as if I'd care about something like that.

"It's beautiful, thank you."

"You're very welcome." His eyes flick up to meet mine, a smile spreading across his face. "Merry Christmas, Moll."

And just like that, I'm the happiest I've been in weeks. "Merry Christmas, Andrew."

———

"So, any new women in your life I should know about?"

I adjust myself on the stool as I shed another layer. Our

flight's delayed forty minutes so we're sitting at one of the small bars dotted around the gate. Me with a glass of sparkling water in front of me, Andrew with ginger ale. We tried the first-class lounge, but it was predictably full due to the number of planes struggling to get on the runway. The snow is particularly heavy this year, but I'm not worried about it. Whereas an inch of the stuff would throw Ireland into chaos, Chicago knows how to handle itself.

"Just one," he says, reaching for the small bowl of tortilla chips between us. "Her name's Penny."

I try not to show my surprise as I take a sip of my drink, the bubbles burning my tongue. He conveniently left *that* out of his last few emails.

Zoe once said that Andrew and I had the strangest friendship she'd ever heard of. But I didn't think it was that bad. We lived on opposite sides of the city and he was often traveling for work while I was simply *at* work all hours of the day. We rarely saw each other outside of these flights. And while I firmly believe that an online-based friendship can be just as real as an in-person one, because of my workload, if it wasn't for this little tradition, we probably would have lost touch by now.

But just because we didn't see each other didn't mean we didn't talk. Texts, emails, phone calls. He was the first person I told when I found out Zoe was pregnant. When I got my apartment, my job. He seemed mostly concerned with sending me memes and photos of suspiciously stained furniture he'd found abandoned on the sidewalk. (*Found you a futon*, he'd write. Or his favorite, *Let's play is that blood or ketchup.*) But he usually kept me updated on his girlfriends. In fact, he went so far as to introduce them to me on the rare times we met up between Christmases, prob-ably so they didn't get concerned that their new boyfriend was constantly sending pictures of disease-ridden armchairs to another woman.

"When did this happen?" I ask, trying not to sound hurt that I didn't know already.

"About two months ago," he says casually. "She's cute but a snorer. And a very early riser."

"You met her two months ago and she's moved in already?"

"Well, it feels cruel to keep her outside at this time of year."

I stare at him as he spins his phone on the counter, waiting until I get it. It takes me at least five seconds longer than I'd like to admit.

"You got a *dog*?"

"My roommate got a dog," he corrects, pulling up a photo.

"You got a dog!" I coo over the little sausage. "Penny?"

He nods. "We're very happy together."

"And I'm happy for you. I know you wanted one."

"So long as the neighbors don't complain we should be okay. Not sure about the guy across the hall though. Looks like a snitch."

I hand his phone back, hesitating as I try to gauge his mood. "So, Marissa's gone?"

"Who?"

I wince and he shrugs. A petite, raven-haired marketing executive he'd met online, they'd been on and off for the past year.

"We tried," he says. "But that didn't seem to matter in the end."

"I'm sorry. She was sweet."

He scoffs. "You only met her once and you didn't even like her."

"That's not true!"

"You never like anyone I date."

"I liked that teacher."

"That teacher," he repeats flatly. "You can't even remember her name."

Like it's my fault his exes are so forgettable. "Soph—"

"Emil—"

"Emily!" I slam my hand against the bar in victory. "Emily. Emily the teacher. With the incredibly quiet voice."

He gives me a fond look. "You're such a bitch."

"Emily was years ago," I remind him. "And didn't she dump you for that married guy? I'm not even supposed to like her."

"Alison dumped me for the married guy. Emily ghosted me."

"You have terrible taste in women."

"Hey," he says, one hand going to his heart. "Words hurt, Molly. Maybe terrible women just have a taste in me. Anyway, look who's talking. What happened to Brandon? You never told me why you broke up with him."

"He chewed with his mouth open."

"Seems fair."

I force a smirk as I gaze down at my drink, twisting one of the rings from my finger. "He got a new job in Seattle," I explain. "Moved away."

"And you called it quits?"

"It was a good job," I say lightly. "But I have no interest in long-distance and I wasn't about to move there with him. We'd only been together for a few months. I mean, I was still scared to go number two when he was in the apartment."

"The real second base."

I kick his leg under the counter and take another sip. "I asked him to stay," I say after a moment.

The humor fades instantly from his face. "Ah, Moll."

"I'm fine. Honestly, I'm so used to being alone now I don't know if I'll even like it when I find someone I *do* want to be with. I'm not sure I know how to bend like that anymore."

"I don't want to hear about your sex life."

"I mean in terms of compromise, asshat." I glance over his shoulder as the departure board flickers. Our flight status remains unchanged. *Delayed.* It's not that I don't mind the extra time with Andrew, but I would have much preferred to have it while sitting in first-class seats. "How long until they legally have to order us a pizza?"

"You're the lawyer."

"Not a pizza lawyer."

"True. How's it going anyway?" he asks. "Make anyone rich this month?"

"Three, I'll have you know."

"Did they deserve it?"

"All my clients deserve it." I drain my water, eager to change the subject. "How much time off do you have this year?"

"Just two weeks. I'm fully booked up then."

"And you only sound a little smug."

He grins. "I've been working on a more humble persona."

"Uh-huh. And how's that going for you?"

"Not as fun," he says, and I laugh.

When we first met, Andrew dreamed of traveling the world as a photojournalist. Of far-flung places and images of life in all its forms. And he tried. For years he tried. But the assignments were few and far between and, like it does for most people, practicality won out over wishful thinking. Weddings paid his bills, graduations and bar mitzvahs brought in a steady income. He never resented it. He told me once that he found a lot of joy in the ordinary, that he loved his work and the people he met. I believed him. And if I didn't, all I'd need to do was look at his photographs to see it.

"I'm thinking about getting a new website," he continues. "There's a guy I know who—"

"*Shit.*"

We both glance at the exhausted businessman beside us. "Sorry," he says when he sees our attention. "Excuse me, sorry. My flight just got canceled." He slides off the stool without another word, bringing his phone to his ear.

"That sucks," Andrew mutters, and I nod, suddenly worried as I check the time.

"It'll be fine," Andrew says, guessing my thoughts. "It's a busy night. We've been through this before."

We have. Last year we were delayed five hours, not long enough to go home but enough that everyone was *very* annoyed. It was the closest we ever came to a real argument until eventually, just to waste some time, we decided to get some food. I ordered cheese fries, but they were out of cheese fries, and I was so tired and so hungry that I burst into tears, and then Andrew wasn't mad at me anymore. He looked like he was about to march into the kitchen and make them himself.

"What?" he asks now, and I realize I'm smiling at the memory.

"You're a good friend, you know that?"

He eyes me suspiciously. "You need a kidney or something?"

"I mean it," I say with a laugh. "Come on, let's have a proper drink. We might as well if we're stuck here."

"I'm okay."

"I insist. What do you want?"

He takes so long to answer that I stop trying to get the barman's attention and turn to him.

"My treat," I say.

"I've actually stopped."

"Stopped what? Oh!" I make a face. "Like a pre-Christmas cleanse?"

Another pause. "No."

Awkwardness settles over us, straining the silence as, once again, it takes me way too long to put two and two together.

"*Oh*," I say slowly. "Like... forever?"

"That's the plan. I'm two months sober as of yesterday."

I relax a little at that. Sober sounds like such a serious word. Sober is a word for addicts and alcoholics and...

I stare at him as he watches me, looking tense. Oh my God. "Why didn't you say anything?"

"It's not a big deal."

"Yes, it is," I say, flustered now. "That's... that's great, Andrew. Congratulations."

He smiles slightly. "Stop panicking."

"I'm not! I'm fine." I tip my water glass to my lips only to realize too late it doesn't have any water left. "So, is it like a sponsorship thing or what?"

"I'm following a program, but it's mainly just me. It was getting a bit..." He shakes his head. "Anyway. It's all good. I'm seeing how it goes. But you? You deserve some champagne."

"No, I can just—"

"It's Christmas," he interrupts firmly. "And I promise

that as tempting as you are, you knocking back some bubbles is not going to trip me up."

"I'm really ok—"

"This is why I didn't tell you," he says gently. "Please don't make it a thing. Have a drink, Moll."

I hesitate at the sincerity in his voice. "Well, now it's awkward if I do and awkward if I don't," I grumble, and he grins.

"Then my job here is done." He holds up a hand, instantly making eye contact with the barman. "Besides," he adds, glancing over his shoulder as snow continues to fall on the runway. "Looks like we're going to be here a while."

CHAPTER THREE

One glass slowly turns to two as our flight is pushed back and back and back. Too hungry to wait for food on the plane, we end up ordering burgers and Andrew shows me so many videos of Penny that I don't notice how crowded our terminal has gotten until I get up to use the restroom and find the line snaking past the vending machines. The place is packed with people, other passengers finding space where they can along walls and windows, distracting sulking children with books and iPads and whatever they can get their hands on. By the time I make it back to the bar, there's even more, but they don't look as annoyed as you'd expect for a delayed flight this close to Christmas. They've gone past that. They look *worried*. And for the first time since I arrived, I start to feel the same.

I gaze up at the departure board by the bar and the long *Delayed* column beside each flight. God. If this turns into an all-night thing, I'll end up falling asleep on the plane and the upgrades will have been for nothing. It wasn't the little luxuries I was looking forward to, though they were certainly a perk, but Andrew was such a nerd about this part of our tradition and I selfishly wanted to see his reaction to everything. I wanted to make him happy.

Sober. I frown as I think back to the last few times I've been with him. Since when has he not been sober? Yes, alcohol was usually involved, but it was only ever a glass or two in restaurants and bars. No warning signs. I don't think I've ever even seen him drunk. I've seen Gabriela drunk lots of times. *I've* been drunk lots of times. But Andrew?

Once? Maybe twice? And he wasn't even that bad. I mean, it *was* Christmas. It's to be expected.

A short whistle drags my attention back to the man himself and I turn to find him sitting with his back against the bar, watching me.

"You alright there, Moll?"

"I like your sweater."

"You hate my sweater."

I do hate his sweater. I always hate his sweaters. He's big into the novelty Christmas outfits and this one is no different, bright green and dotted with red and white candy canes. Every year he wears something new, and the gaudier it looks, the happier it seems to make him.

"I like that you like your sweater," I explain.

He smiles faintly but doesn't move from his spot. "Can I talk to you for a sec?"

"Depends," I tease, sauntering over to him.

"Depends?"

"On what you want to talk about." I lean against the counter and turn my phone over. The screen is full of notifications, which doesn't immediately worry me because I choose to live chaotically when it comes to app alerts, but instead of the usual group chat updates and newsletters from a nail salon I went to once five years ago, I see a dozen very urgent-sounding notices.

"...and you're not listening to me."

"Huh?" I glance up to see Andrew staring at me with an exasperated look. I'd completely zoned out. "Sorry!" I grimace. "Sorry. It's just... are you seeing this?"

He frowns as I show him my phone before taking his own out from his pocket.

"A storm?" he asks, skimming the news.

"But, like, a *storm* storm." Right over the Atlantic. "Do you think we'll get out okay?" I look over at the rest of the passengers to see the news is starting to spread. Every second person is now on their phone, their expressions tight. "Surely they can just go *around* the storm, right?"

Andrew looks deadly serious. "Do you think we should tell the pilots that plan?"

I punch him in the thigh. "Well, we can wait, can't we? It's not like we have anything else to do and the lounge will empty soon and some spots will open up and—"

"Another glass of champagne please," Andrew calls to the barman. "For the lady freaking out?"

"I'm not freaking out." I'm just... *perturbed*. Perturbed feels right. We've never not gotten home for Christmas before.

"Drink your juice," Andrew says, interrupting my panic as he slides a full glass toward me. "And calm down. You're making me nervous just being near you."

I stick my tongue out at him but take a sip. "What did you want to talk about?" I ask, distracted as more and more people start to move. Do they know something we don't? Some of them are in a line. Should I be in a line?

"It can wait," Andrew says.

"What can?"

"Jesus Christ." I glance back as he starts to laugh. "You've completely lost it."

"I'm sorry! I'm *tired*."

He shakes his head, but he's smiling. "Come on, chug that back and we'll see if there's any more space in the lounge. Maybe you're just feeling rattled being amongst the plebs."

I don't respond as an ominous hush falls over the terminal. There's a flash of color by the gate as the doors to the tunnel open and we both turn as cabin crew, *our* crew, stride out. Hundreds of heads whip their way as they manage to professionally avoid every desperate eye, as though knowing if they meet any they'll be immediately surrounded.

A grim-looking man in a yellow vest heads to the check-in counter, reaching for the microphone, but whatever he was going to say is quickly drowned out by the huge groan that spreads throughout the crowd as the departure board flickers to life one final time.

Canceled.

Canceled. Canceled. Canceled.

The place erupts.

Gate by gate, the would-be passengers grab their bags and their companions until the place is a hive of anxiety. Flight after flight changes on the board, all saying the same thing.

Oh my God.

"Okay," Andrew says, his voice ridiculously calm. "Plan B."

"You have a plan B?"

"I will in about two minutes," he says, unlocking his phone.

I slide off my stool, downing my drink as the steward

tries to calm the sudden mob in front of him. I'm two seconds away from joining them myself.

What do we do? If every flight is canceled, we can... what? Get to another city and try to catch a flight there? A flight at this time of year? And even then, the storm is over the Atlantic, meaning every plane going that way will be affected. And everything else... We're four days out from Christmas. It's not like they're desperate to fill seats.

"We're not going to get another flight," I tell him.

"You don't know that."

"We're not, Andrew."

When he doesn't answer, I turn back to find his brow furrowed as he swipes through his phone. And I know why. Family is number one for Andrew. Not that I don't also love mine, but my sister and my parents and I are the kind of unit that is perfectly fine not speaking to each other for a few months beyond the occasional *I'm still alive* message. Andrew couldn't be more different. Christmas is a big deal in his household. I know it is because he won't shut up about it. He says it's for Hannah, the baby of the family, but by my calculations, the girl is sixteen now and yet they still go full throttle. He doesn't even pretend to be embarrassed about it. He loves it. I know he does. And he's *always* home for Christmas.

For a moment, the only thing I can do is watch him, my heart breaking at the frustration starting to creep into his expression. With all my planning, this was something I'd never factored in, and I have no idea what to do.

"We should book onto something in the morning," he says, still scrolling. "The storm will have passed by then. We can..." He trails off as his screen goes blank before a call comes through.

"It's Mam," he says, staring at it. "She usually stays awake until I'm on the plane."

We both wait until it stops ringing, only for it to immediately start again. Andrew's chest moves up and down with a heavy sigh before he clicks accept, moving a few paces away.

"Hiya!" he answers with false cheer. "Yeah, I'm... Yeah, it's not looking good, I'm afraid. No, we'll figure something out. With Molly, yeah."

I put my glass down, starting to feel ill as I gather my coat and purse. I need to join one of these lines and I'm halfway to doing just that when my own phone rings.

Relief trickles through me when I see the name on the screen.

Zoe. My sister will know what to do. My sister always knows what to do.

"Your flight's canceled."

"You don't say," I huff, remaining by the relative safety of the bar. All around me people are moving, ushering children and friends toward anyone who looks in charge. "Why are you even awake?"

"Oh, I don't know, Molly, maybe because it's because I have a human being growing inside me and I have to pee every thirty minutes. What are you going to do?"

"About the flight or the peeing?"

"You're not funny. I'm the funny one."

"Debatable," I mutter. "And I don't know yet. It's a nightmare here."

"The BBC says seventy percent of planes due to fly over the north Atlantic tonight are grounded and the other thirty percent will probably follow."

"And you're calling me with a solution, right?"

"I'm calling to remind you that if you don't get your ass

back here, I'll kill you. You can't leave me alone with Mam and Dad. This is the one time of the year all the pressure is off me because everyone's fawning over you and you are *not* taking that away from me. Surely, they have connecting flights from Canada or something."

"We'll still have to cross the ocean." I glance over my shoulder to find Andrew rubbing a slow circle into his forehead. He's told me a lot about his mother, an energetic, well-meaning force of a woman who's always struggled with him being so far from home. I can only imagine the conversation he's having. "I think we're just going to have to wait for the storm to pass."

"They're saying it's going to be another day or two at least."

"Who's they?"

"The weather guy," she says defensively. "The one with the tie."

"They all wear ties!"

"Molly?"

Andrew walks toward me, his hair sticking up at various angles where he's been pulling it. "We'll figure something out," I say to Zoe. "Break the news to Mam when she wakes, will you?"

"Oh sure, leave it to me to ruin Christmas."

"Would you just—"

"Love you!"

I focus on Andrew as she hangs up. "Everything okay?"

"Mam's panicking," he says, grabbing his coat. "I'm going to go get in line and see what our options are. You okay to mind our stuff?"

"Of course."

"And maybe you could look up some—"

"I'm already on it," I say confidently. "Don't worry. We'll get something."

He nods, his attention already on the other side of the terminal where people are beginning to gather. "Not like it's a busy time of year," he says, trying to joke.

My answering smile fools no one, but I manage to keep it up until he goes and I take a seat at the bar to call Gabriela.

"Okay," she says when she answers. "So, when you said you'd be on your phone, I didn't think you actually meant—"

"My flight's canceled."

"*Noooo*," she says softly. "You're kidding. Because of the storm? I didn't think it was going to get that bad."

"I don't think anyone did."

"Are you okay?"

"I think so. I mean, yeah, I'm annoyed, but I'm fine. It's Andrew I'm worried about. He's big on Christmas. I've never seen him in panic mode before."

"Andrew?"

"My friend?" I hold the phone between my shoulder and my ear as I open my laptop and log into the Wi-Fi. "My plane friend?" I add reluctantly.

"*Oh*. The man you fly economy for?"

"That's the one."

"That's cute that you guys still do that," Gabriela continues, and I grimace as my email blinks to life before me, updating by the dozens in the few hours since I last looked at it.

"I just wanted to call and let you know that I might be offline tomorrow," I say. Neither of us bats an eyelid about the fact that tomorrow is a Saturday. "We might not get out of here until the morning. But I'll keep you updated."

"I'm so sorry, Molly. Let me know if there's anything I can do."

"Can you fly a plane?"

"No, but I love a challenge."

We say goodbye, Gabriela's voice full of sympathy as I start a fresh spreadsheet and start Googling.

CHAPTER FOUR

SEVEN YEARS AGO

Flight Three, Chicago

I pick at my cheese fries, pushing them around the plate as I try to drum up the appetite to eat another one. I don't know why I agreed to this. Well, I do know why. I panicked. But what's a girl supposed to do when Andrew Fitzpatrick comes striding toward you like you're the final boss in a video game he just can't beat. Like he's been expecting you.

I certainly wasn't expecting him. So all I could do was sit there in the middle of the terminal and freak out as he approached, wondering what I'd done to make the universe hate me so much.

"11C," is all he'd said, thrusting his ticket at me.

I'd been completely lost for a solid five seconds before I realized what he'd meant. "34B," I'd responded, showing him my own seat number.

He'd been surprised at that. Maybe even annoyed. And then, like he'd decided to simply stop feeling both of those things, he sat down next to me, hugging his backpack to his chest.

"You want to get something to eat?" he'd asked.

I wasn't hungry, but I said yes.

And now here we are.

I peek up at him from under my lashes, watching him studiously ignore me like I am him. He looks different up close. Older. Granted, I'm older too, but some days I still think I look like a teenager. So does every bouncer and barman in Chicago apparently. The round face and doe eyes don't help, and if I'm not in my heels I get mistaken for a highschooler more often than I'd like. But Andrew looks like he's grown up. He's lost a bit of the puppy fat from around his jaw and his brown hair is longer, swept back in a messy almost stylish way. I say almost because he still dresses atrociously, tonight wearing a blue T-shirt with a cartoon elf on the front that is extremely hard not to keep looking at.

"So, are you some hotshot lawyer now?"

My eyes snap up from his chest as he finally speaks. "What?"

"You said you wanted to go to law school."

"I'm still studying," I say, surprised that he remembers. "What about you? Photography, right?"

He nods. "I've got a job with a portrait studio on Michigan Avenue. Babies. Families. That kind of thing."

"You like it?"

"I love it," he says, and I blink at the simple way he says the words. "The kids especially. I'm like a kid whisperer. You've never seen a four-year-old sit so still." He wipes his mouth with the napkin, his burger demolished. "You should pop by. I'll get you a discount."

"Oh, no," I say quickly. "I hate having my picture taken."

"We get that a lot. But it's never as scary as people think."

I shake my head, taking a sip of my beer. Andrew got both of us a drink, despite my weak protests. He's already finished his and the rules of buying a round dictate that I need to catch up.

"My boyfriend's sister just got engaged," I say, feeling rude to shut him down. "I'll put her on to you guys."

"Your boyfriend?"

"Daniel." I feel a burst of happiness just saying his name. I met him via an app that summer and I'm mildly (extremely) obsessed with him. He lives in an apartment near Lincoln Park and wants to work with animals. I am trying to be chill, but no. There is no chill right now when it comes to Daniel.

"We've been together a few months," I say, taking another sip. "He's... what?"

Andrew laughs as I fidget. "You're doing that I'm-in-love smile."

"No, I'm not!"

"Hey, own it. Law school, lover. You're living the American dream."

I huff, finishing the bottle before placing it down with a thump as silence descends again. Our eyes meet over the table, both of us acknowledging that this is weird, but also not as weird as it could be. Probably because of him. He was always easy to talk to and certainly seems to have forgiven me for whatever indirect role I played in him dating a shitty person.

An announcement crackles above our heads, calling our flight, and I glance around as a few other diners start to move, wondering what the polite thing to do is.

"You want to see if we can swap seats?"

"Huh?" I twist back to find Andrew watching me, a hesitant smile on his face.

"I'll sweet-talk the person next to you. You don't have to talk to me or anything," he adds with a shrug. "I mean, I'll talk to you so it *would* be weird if you—"

"Yeah, yeah." I smirk, thinking it over. It's an overnight flight, but I'm wide awake, and a bit of company doesn't sound like the worst thing in the world. "Sure," I say. "Let's see you turn on the charm."

"Oh, I don't need to turn it on," he dismisses as we gather our things. "It's always on."

"Hmmm."

"I'm very charming," he argues. "Five bucks says it takes me less than thirty seconds."

"Ten says it takes you more. And I'm pretty sure you still owe me a dollar from our last wager."

"Oh, so you want to go there, do you?" He takes a step in front of me, spinning around so he's facing my way as we walk toward the gate. I'd spoken without thinking, but there's no annoyance in his expression. If anything, he looks like he's teasing me.

"You're the one who said you'd change my mind about Christmas," I point out.

"Yes, I did." He sounds delighted that I'm playing along. "Okay. Let me play for my losses. Add on a dollar and throw in a movie choice."

"A movie? I thought you wanted to talk?"

"I'll talk during the movie. People love that."

He smiles when I laugh, his hands sliding into the pocket of his jeans.

"It's a seven-hour flight," he continues. "You've got to break it up."

Seven hours. The last time I had to sit next to him for

that long the very idea of it had filled me with horror. Now I was weirdly looking forward to it.

"So, do we have a deal?" He holds out his hand and I don't hesitate to clasp it. We shake.

"Deal," I say, and a smug look crosses his face.

"Thirty seconds," he reminds me, taking out his passport.

He does it in fifteen.

_____

Now

I'm starting to think we're not getting out of Chicago tonight. We might not even get out tomorrow. Andrew's still waiting in line with at least twenty people in front of him and I'm surrounded by twenty more as I sit by the bar, watching news of the storm as I periodically refresh my phone for flights in the morning.

Nada.

I move back to my work email, refreshing that too, but the damn contract I'm waiting on still hasn't come back, which means someone's getting a very early phone call from me tomorrow. I usually don't like working when I'm with Andrew. He's pretty understanding about it, encouraging even, but we almost came to metaphorical blows over it the last time we were delayed like this and I don't want to make tonight any worse than it is.

Another refresh of flights and I shoot off a few emails, fruitlessly trying to catch up. I'm not usually so behind, but Spencer got mono like it's 1952 and Caleb thinks he's too important to be working on anything he's actually assigned to. Gabriela already helps me too much as it is, so

I'm not going to go running to her. Which leaves me by myself.

Send email. Refresh flights.

Google career options for tired girls who still want to afford their nice apartment.

"My boyfriend flew out yesterday."

The man next to me speaks at a normal volume, but he's not looking at me. His gaze is absent, almost mournful, as he stares unseeing at the row of beer bottles across from us.

"It's his first time meeting my family," he continues. "But I had to work last minute so he flew out by himself and now I'm here and he'll be there. With my parents. Alone. For Christmas." He takes a shallow breath, finally looking at me. "Do you think I did something in my past life? Is this my punishment?"

"I'm sure they'll get on great," I say awkwardly, but he shakes his head.

"They don't know about him. I mean they know *of* him, but not that he's... that we're..." He trails off, that mournful look coming back.

I reach out to pat his back. "Gay?"

"What?" He shakes his head. "No. They know that. We're vegan."

Oh.

He groans, dropping his head against the counter. "I had a whole speech prepared. We were going to sit down and discuss it. Steven's too polite for them. He'll end up with second helpings of turkey and ham without me there. He's a skinny guy, you know? My mother's going to think we can't afford to eat if he refuses."

I continue to pat his back until Andrew appears at my shoulder a moment later, looking in concern at my new friend.

"Is he okay?" he asks.

"He's vegan," I explain as the man proceeds to bang his head lightly against the bar.

"Ah." His eyes slide from the stranger to me. "Can I talk to you? Privately?"

We move a few paces away to a closed kiosk. The airport is quieter now, but still busy with other desperate souls like us. "Anything?" I feel ridiculous as soon as I ask it.

He shakes his head. "We'll figure it out," he says, as though he's the one about to comfort me.

I stare up at him, hating the resignation on his face. It's a look I'm not used to seeing on him. I've always been the pessimist in this friendship and I'm free to be because he is so resolutely not. So this? This right here? No.

"It'll be okay," he continues, and he doesn't even try and sound like he means it.

"It will be," I say, and I must sound as determined as I pretend to be, because some of the tightness leaves his expression. I swear to God he almost smiles.

"I know that look."

"Is it my 'I've got this' look? Because I do. I'm going to sort it out."

"You can't control the weather."

"No, but I can circumvent it. Not every flight is canceled. We'll find something. Just let me... let me think. Okay? I'll get you home."

"Molly—"

"Ten-year anniversary," I remind him, taking out my phone. There must be *something*. "I've already ruined the first-class lounge. I am not about to ruin Christmas."

"And there you go acting like you're in charge of US airspace again. Put the phone down," he adds, but I shake my head.

"We're getting on a plane tonight," I tell him. "We're doing this. Christmas miracle time. Happy, jolly Christmas mir—"

He moves so fast I don't have time to react. One second, he's standing at the end of the bar, the next he's right in front of me, plucking the phone from my hand.

"Hey!"

He ignores me, shoving it into my pocket before clasping my shoulders. I suck in a surprised breath as he dips his head to stare straight into my eyes.

"It's okay," he says firmly. "It's out of our control. The airlines don't know anything more than we do. But no one's going anywhere tonight. The best they can do is find us a room and, to be honest, I don't want to spend the night in some anonymous roadside hotel. I've discussed it with my folks and they agree."

"About what?"

"About staying here." He takes a steadying breath and releases me, his smile tight. "A lot of people spend a lot of money to stay in cities like Chicago over the holidays. Plus all our stuff is here. It wouldn't be so bad."

"You want to stay here for Christmas?" I ask, trying to understand. It's the last thing I expected. "But your family—"

"I know." He doesn't try and hide the disappointment that flashes across his face. "And if a flight becomes available, I'll be the first person on it. But right now, there's nothing we can do except waste our time. They can last one Christmas without me."

The man is a liar. At least going by what he's been telling me about his family for the last ten years. And he knows it, switching tactics when I remain unconvinced.

"I don't want to spend the next few days refreshing my

screen and getting angry at overworked call agents. The storm won't last forever, they'll clear the backlog and we'll get something. If that's a few days from now, then so be it."

"But you—"

"It will be fun," he insists. "We can order way too much food, watch a bunch of movies. We can make it work."

"You can't just..." Wait. "We?"

"Yes, *we*." He looks at me like I'm an idiot. "Unless you want to spend Christmas alone?"

That isn't something that necessarily terrifies me, but this new alternative sounds a lot better. Christmas in Chicago? Christmas in Chicago with *Andrew*?

"Well?" He looks nervous. Almost as if he thinks I'll say no.

"You really want to do this?" I ask.

"It's not bad for a plan B."

It's not bad for any plan.

"We could get cheese," I tell him, almost breathless at the thought.

"I'd say that's a definite possibility."

"And stollen from Dinkel's bakery. And more cheese. We can go ice skating!"

"*You* can go ice skating," he corrects. "I will stand for approximately thirty seconds before falling on my ass and then abandon you for hot chocolate."

I try not to look too happy, aware that this is very much not his first choice, and yet incredibly okay with the turn of events. And maybe I was wrong. Maybe he's not so heart-broken about the storm, because he's looking pretty pleased with our new plan as well.

"Alright then," he says, running a hand through his hair. "Now, how the hell do we get out of here?"

CHAPTER FIVE

It's harder than you might think. It's another thirty minutes before we're finally brought landside and another twenty after that while we wait for Andrew's ridiculously large luggage to be released.

"You hiding a body in there?" I ask as he unpacks his coat. His suitcase is at least three times the size of mine.

"Just clothes, presents, and all manner of American contraband to be swapped for Irish contraband on the way back."

"You should start a little black market," I say, eyeing the dozens of people settling in for a night on the airport floor. I feel a twinge of guilt just looking at them. Should we be doing that? Maybe we could—

"Stop it," Andrew says.

"Stop what?"

"Whatever you're thinking about."

"I'm not—"

"You are. I can always tell." He straightens, zipping up his coat. "They'll put on more flights in the morning and we can check then. In the meantime, do you know what we should do?"

"Book a massage?"

"We should get a charcuterie board."

I snort at the seriousness of his expression. "We can get whatever we want," I tell him.

"I want a panettone," he says. "And some cheesecake. What do you want?"

"Mince pies. Though I've never been able to find them here."

He makes a face. "Because no one actually likes mince pies."

"I like mince pies."

"And you are wrong."

I ignore him as we wind our way slowly around the other passengers, heading for the exit. I'm feeling much calmer now that we have a plan. I'm great with plans. "Where are we going to do this?" I ask, trying not to step on anyone. "My place or yours?"

"Yours," he says immediately. "Not just because it's nicer, even though it is. But my roommate's inviting his girl-friend over for the week and I'd rather not listen to them having sex while we're watching *Miracle on 34th Street*."

I nod, secretly relieved. My place *was* nicer. I've lived for the past three years in a pretty decent two-bed apart-ment in Uptown. I sometimes rented out the spare room to friends of friends or offered it up to visiting relatives, but I've had the place to myself for the past few weeks and even deep-cleaned it last night so there's no dirty dishes or under-wear lying around.

At least I hope there isn't.

"We'll have to get normal food," I say as we stop just

inside the doors. Andrew pulls a thick green scarf from his bag and winds it around his neck. "Alongside fun food. I cleared out the freezer last night so do you want to stop somewhere on the way back, or I know a few places we can—"

"Hey lovebirds!"

I turn, startled, to see a red-faced man on the other side of the doors, sitting on a sturdy suitcase. He's smiling at us and looks far too cheery for someone whose flight has probably just been canceled.

"Can I help you?" I ask, but he just points to the ceiling. I glance back at Andrew with an is-this-man-going-to-kill-us eyebrow raise, but he's not looking at me. He's looking up with a smile and I follow his gaze to a bundle of green leaves directly overhead.

"What's that?" I ask, confused.

Andrew's eyes drop to mine. "It's mistletoe, you idiot."

"*That's* mistletoe?" No way. "It looks like spinach. Like a sprig of spinach."

"How do you not know what—"

"I know what it *is*, I just haven't seen it before. It's not like I spend December looking up the whole time, is it?"

"You're five foot nothing, you spend most of your life looking up."

"I am five foot *three*, thank you very much. And I can see the world just fine from—"

"Don't be such a grinch!" the man interrupts. "It's tradition!"

"Keep your pants on!" I yell back. Andrew only laughs, but a couple of other people have stopped at the commotion and now suddenly we have an audience.

"These things are so dumb," I mutter, trying not to meet

anyone's eye as Andrew pulls a matching bobble hat on over his hair. "And kind of creepy, don't you think?"

"I plead the Fourth."

"Fifth."

"Whatever."

Another couple moves past as we dawdle, glancing up as they see the mistletoe. Without even breaking their stride, they turn to each other and kiss, provoking a small cheer from the onlookers.

My mouth drops open as they move on as if nothing happened.

"Bad luck not to kiss," the cheery man yells, turning his attention back to us.

"No, it's not!" I exclaim. "You just made that up!"

Andrew shifts beside me, still looking amused. "Molly—"

"He made that up."

"Just ignore him."

"I can't ignore him. He called me a grinch. Why does everybody always call me that?" I watch with increasing annoyance as an older duo raise another round of applause by locking lips right beside us. "That's it. You have to kiss me."

"You're too competitive, you know that? Let's just find our driver."

I grab hold of his sleeve, that familiar need to prove myself to complete strangers giving me a blissful focus I haven't had all day, and before I can think twice about what I'm doing, I slide a hand around the back of his neck and lift my face to his.

I wasn't lying when I told Gabriela I hadn't been with anyone since Brandon. But the thing is, I also hadn't really *been* with Brandon either. Not for our last few weeks anyway. It had been one of those slow breakups, awkward and unsure, where every kiss became a question, where every touch could be our last. Until we stopped doing both altogether.

So, it might be because I've been so starved of human contact that the moment Andrew and I come together, things start to get... different.

It's the heat of him that hits me first, so at odds with the sharp bite of cold air swirling through the doors. The gentle rasp of his beard is a surprise against my skin, especially when compared with the softness of his lips. Men don't have soft lips in winter. Men have chapped lips in winter because they don't know how to use lip balm. But Andrew's are soft. Soft and warm as they cling to mine. Cling because he's kissing me back. This is no peck on the cheek, no joke between friends under the mistletoe. He's standing there and he's kissing me back and I suddenly can't get close enough.

There's a swooping sensation in my stomach that must be from the champagne and it takes more effort than it should to let him go. I force myself to pull away, but Andrew chases me, closing the inch of space I put between us to brush against me once more before he draws back completely.

My stupid heart is pounding when I open my eyes and I find myself staring at his shoulder as he turns back to the now clapping man as if to say, *There you go, buddy. Merry Christmas.*

"Happy now?" Andrew asks me after taking a short bow. "Going to start eating candy canes and join the novelty sweater club?"

I clear my throat, knowing it's my turn for some quip about the taste of his onion rings or how I need to wash my tongue with soap, but my mouth is suddenly dry and I can't seem to force the words out.

"Moll?"

My phone buzzes with a text and I use the excuse to break away from his questioning gaze. "Ride's here," I mutter, barely glancing at the screen, and I walk outside without waiting for him, eager for some fresh air, no matter how cold it is. And it is freaking *cold*. Still, I breathe it in, inhaling until my lungs hurt.

Well, that was weird.

Andrew bumps my arm a moment later and I cast my eye around the drop-off point for our car. "Blew your mind with that kiss, huh?"

I glance sharply at him, but he's smiling. He's *joking*. "Because I'm just saying, if this is you finally getting into the festive spirit—"

"Okay," I interrupt, and he laughs. The sound of it makes me feel better.

"I think I'm getting hungry again," I tell him. It's not a lie. All that panic takes up a lot of energy.

"We'll get a really big panettone," he promises as I concentrate on locating Trevor and his white Toyota. Not going to lie, it's mainly the *white* bit of that description I'm focusing on. "The biggest panettone in all the land."

"Stop saying panettone," I grumble as his phone rings.

"Must be my panettone guy." He dodges my hit as he retrieves it from his pocket, his smile fading when he checks the screen. "It's Christian. Trust him to be up at this hour."

"Doesn't he live in London?" I ask, tucking my chin into my coat as I shiver. Andrew's younger brother had moved there a few years ago to work.

"He's not a good sleeper."

"Ten bucks says he's calling to yell at you."

Andrew only gives me a look as he accepts the call. "Hey," he says as I shudder again. "Yeah, we're completely grounded." He tugs the scarf from around his neck, holding it out to me and then throwing it at my head when I don't take it.

Put it on, he mouths, and I roll my eyes, secretly grateful as I do just that. I'm wearing my traveling Irish coat, not my Chicago one, and boy oh boy, do I feel the difference.

Andrew scowls at whatever his brother is saying, but he keeps one eye on me until I have the scarf wrapped tight. "It's not like we didn't try to... I *know* Mam's upset, but what I am supposed to do? Yeah, she's here. No, I'm..." His voice drops as he turns his back to me, walking a few steps away. "That's not why I... Oh, *real* mature."

I turn away, pretending I can't hear him as I tug the scarf up over my chin.

It smells like him. No, not him. His soap. His *soap*, Molly. Jesus. I glare at the line of cars, annoyed with myself, even as I breathe in the scent.

Seriously though, what is that? Sandalwood? *Pine?* Is pine soap a thing?

"You Molly?"

I jump at the shout across the road as a large scowling man gestures at me from the driver's seat of his white Toyota.

"You going to get in or what?" he asks gruffly when I nod.

I grab a tense-looking Andrew, who hangs up as we hurry to our ride. Whatever Christian said to him has destroyed his good mood and, by extension, mine, and he's silent as we get into the back, head bent as they continue their conversation through text.

We're on the interstate when he finally snaps, shoving

his phone away with a noise of frustration as he sits back, gazing out the window. The urge to comfort him is overwhelming, and, as if to prove to myself that nothing's wrong, I slip my hand into his free one and squeeze.

"We can video call your family," I say. "The whole day if we have to. We'll live-stream my apartment. Everything but the bathroom."

He sighs dramatically. "But is it really Christmas without one of my siblings barging in on me showering?"

"You guys have strange traditions."

He gives me a halfhearted smile before returning my squeeze and letting me go. "What about your family?" he asks as I bring my hand awkwardly to my lap. "Are they going to be okay with this?"

"They'll understand," I say automatically. To be honest, I've been so focused on him, I haven't even thought about them. "I'll give them a call in a few hours when my parents are up but it's Zoe they'll be concerned about."

"She's due soon, isn't she?"

"A couple more weeks."

"And then you'll be an auntie." He seems cheered by that. "I'll have to give you all my godparent tips."

"I don't need them. She picked one of her friends as the godmother. I sulked for a whole day."

"As is your right. It's a grave injustice."

"That's what I said. And she just—" I break off as my screen lights up on the seat between us, Gabriela's name flashing in the darkness.

"Work stuff," I explain before he can ask. I sigh, bringing the phone to my ear. "If this is about—"

"I just want you to know that I accept," Gabriela interrupts in a rush.

"Accept what?"

"Position as best person in the whole freaking world."

"Not following."

"Michael's friend's partner works for Delta."

I blink at the back of our driver's head. "Okay?"

"Michael's friend owes us a massive favor because Michael introduced said friend *to* said partner."

"I'm really not—"

"I've traded in that favor for two standbys tonight."

My breath catches as I realize what she's saying. "You got us tickets home?"

Andrew's head snaps my way just as Gabriela speaks again.

"Well, no," she says. "I got you tickets to Buenos Aires."

"*Buenos Aires?*"

"Where you get a connecting flight to Paris," she continues, and I groan, knocking my head back against the seat. "Completely bypassing the storm on the east coast."

"Gabriela—"

"No, it works out," she says excitedly. "Overnight tonight to Argentina. You've got one stop in Atlanta. Then tomorrow at seven their time another overnight to Paris."

"Paris isn't in Ireland."

"I know that dummy, but it's nearer, isn't it? You'll be there on the twenty-third. Granted you'll both be zombies, but you'll be a lot closer there than you are now. Come on," she adds when I don't say anything. "I did it! You've got the air miles and you'll get your refund for your first flight anyway."

I will. And I do have the air miles. I have lots of air miles. I've been hoarding them for years, on some wild idea I'll get a sudden impulse to go traveling. And heading south to bypass the storm that shows no sign of letting up is the only option right now. But that's two to three days of solid traveling and all just to see my family for a holiday we don't even care that much about. All just to...

My eyes flick to Andrew to find him staring at me. He's not moving, he's barely even *breathing*, a hopeful look on his face that makes my chest hurt.

Ah crap.

"I know it's a lot, but you've got to decide soon," Gabriela says in my ear. "Plane goes in just under two hours and we'll need to book you in. Are you still at the airport?"

"Tonight?" Andrew whispers, and I nod jerkily.

"We just left," I tell her, not able to look away from him. "But we can get back?"

Andrew grins at me and a bizarre kind of disappointment mingles with renewed determination as I pull my gaze away. "Do it," I say. "Book us in. I've got our details on my desktop. The folder's named—"

"Christmas Flights/Completed," Gabriela finishes. "Because of course they are."

"You know my computer password?"

"It's your sandwich order from that deli down the street," she says casually as I sputter at this blatant invasion of privacy. "You're kind of predictable, you know that?"

"Just book us in."

"Yes ma'am," she says, and I can hear the smile in her voice. "This makes me feel great. This is my good deed for the year."

"Best person in the whole freaking world," I agree as Andrew starts texting again, his thumbs flying across the screen. "I'll let you know when we're at the airport."

She bids me a delighted "Bon voyage" as we hang up and I lean forward to the driver.

"I don't know if you heard that, but—"

"We're ten minutes away from your destination," he says, not looking at me.

"Right," I agree. "But see the thing is, we really need to get back to the airport."

"And I need to get home," he says. "I'm finishing up for the night."

"But I—"

"For the year," he adds. "My wife bought steaks."

"Trevor—"

"Big ones."

I stare at the back of his head as he stares stubbornly in front.

Fine.

Fine!

I grab my purse from the floor of the cab, reaching for the money that was to make up the vast majority of my relatives' Christmas presents.

"What are you doing?" Andrew whispers.

"Getting you home." I count what I have before leaning forward again. "I will give you one hundred dollars if you turn this cab around right now."

Trevor's eyes snap to mine in the rearview mirror. "Two hundred," he says when he sees I'm being serious. "Cash."

Andrew scoffs and I nod.

"Sold."

"*What?*" Andrew glances between the two of us, shocked. "No!"

"It's fine," I say, handing over the bills. "What's the point of earning all this money if I'm not going to spend it?"

He keeps protesting as Trevor swiftly, and probably illegally, turns the car around, earning a few annoyed honks in the process.

I put a hand against the door to steady myself until we're in the right direction.

"Molly—"

"Too late now," I interrupt cheerfully.

Andrew huffs, but I can already see his mood lifting. "I'll pay you back," he promises as Trevor speeds up.

"Yes, you will."

"Buenos Aires?" he asks, looking dazed.

"I hear their airport is just lovely this time of year."

"And then Paris." A smile spreads across his face. "We'll be able to get back from Paris," he says confidently.

He starts talking about connecting flights, bringing up the clock on his phone to work out the time differences, and it only takes a few seconds before his excitement amps up my excitement. This is an adventure, right? This is either a fun little adventure or possibly the stupidest thing I've ever done. And I once tried to wax my own eyebrows.

By the time we get back to the airport, we're practically jumping out of our seats and Andrew throws open the passenger door before we've even parked.

"Pleasure doing business with you," Trevor calls as I follow him out.

Andrew hurries around to the trunk as I glance toward the entrance, mentally calculating the time it will take us to check the bags and get through security. Thanks to Trevor's driving, we should make it with a good thirty minutes to spare if the lines aren't too long.

"Hey, Molly?"

I turn to find Andrew right behind me and, before I can react, he brings his hands to my cheeks, holding me steady as he kisses me hard on the forehead. It barely lasts a second, but my pulse skyrockets like the overdramatic traitor it is.

Andrew pulls back to grin at me. "You've just saved Christmas."

Technically Gabriela saved Christmas, but I'm not about to correct him. Not while he's still cupping my face. Not when he's looking at me like that.

"Let's wait until we're on the plane," I say as he turns to grab our bags. "Better yet. Let's wait until we're on the right continent."

We walk quickly back through the entrance, right past the mistletoe without even seeing it. Well, I see it. I am extremely aware of it, but Andrew doesn't seem to be so I pretend I'm not and follow him through the crowd.

"Excuse me. Sorry. Pardon me. I'm so— *Watch it*," I snap as a businessman almost runs into me.

I join Andrew at the departure board, both of us gazing up at the handful of flights still scheduled.

"I can't see it," he says, breathless. "Can you see it?"

I scan column after column, but can't see anything heading to Atlanta. "Maybe it just needs to refresh," I say with more confidence than I feel, but it stays exactly the same.

Andrew's expression tightens and I take out my phone, trying not panic as I call Gabriela back.

She picks up on the third ring. "Did you make it?"

"We did. But are you sure you booked the right flight?"

"I'm positive. I checked it twice."

"I don't see anything," I say as Andrew stares at the board so hard it's a miracle he's not giving himself a headache.

"I swear, Molly. I'm looking at the website right now."

"Read out the flight number."

"It's definitely going," she insists. "Delta DL676. Chicago Midway to—"

"*Midway?*" I screech the word so loud that a baby nearby bursts into tears. "We're at O'Hare!"

There's a long pause on the other end of line. "Oh."

I deflate instantly, my adrenaline spike crashing as I turn fully away from Andrew. I can't even bear to look at him.

"I should have checked," Gabriela says, sounding miserable.

"*I* should have told you," I say quickly. "This isn't on you."

"Let me keep looking."

"Gab—"

"There's got to be something. If not tonight then in the morning." She keeps talking, but at a tug on my coat, I twist around to a grim-looking Andrew.

"I'll call you back," I say, when he motions for me to hang up. "She's going to see if we can—"

"How long do we have before the gate closes?" he interrupts, and I check the time on my phone.

"An hour, but..." I trail off, realizing what he means. "That's not enough time."

"It might be. It's what? Forty minutes to Midway?"

"Not in this traffic. And even if it's delayed, there's security and luggage and—"

"I'm not saying we wouldn't need a bit of a miracle," he says. "But we could try. I've got to try."

I don't want to. I *really* don't want to. It was stressful enough getting back here, I don't want to rush across the city just so we can prolong our disappointment.

But he's looking back at me with those goddamn puppy dog eyes and his hair is all mussed up from where he's been pulling at it and I'm reminded of every single time he's lit up at the mere mention of his family.

When this man became my weakness, I do not know. But tonight, it's like he's got me wrapped around his little finger.

I take a breath, hand clenching around the handle of my suitcase as I already regret my decision. "Okay," I say. "Let's go."

CHAPTER SIX

It's travel chaos outside the airport, with people still arriving for canceled flights. The confusion and frustration in the air is palpable and it doesn't help that the line for cabs is several people deep. Andrew and I don't even bother to join it, both of us glancing about as though for a miracle.

"Will we do that thing where we just shove in front of someone?" I ask, watching a woman climb into a taxi. "Like in the movies?"

Andrew grimaces but doesn't say no and that's when I spot a semi-familiar face walk past us with his cap down low.

"Trevor?"

Our driver glances back automatically at his name, scowling suspiciously when he sees me. "Thought you had a plane to catch?"

"I did. We do! You're still here?" I follow him as he turns away, almost tripping in my haste.

"Just had to use the men's room."

"Needs must!" I chime in a cheerful voice I don't recognize. "And what an incredible stroke of luck for us," I add. "Because as it turns out we've gone to the wrong airport and we'll be needing your services again."

He doesn't even turn around. "No."

My mouth drops open and I glance back at Andrew who's struggling with both our bags.

"I just gave you two hundred bucks," I remind him.

"For a transaction that was agreed upon and completed."

"Oh, come on," I plead. Not the best argument of my career, but it's all I'm really capable of at the moment. We have five minutes max to get into a cab or else there's no point in even trying. "We just want to get home."

"So do I," he huffs. "And you've already delayed me by an hour."

"And paid you handsomely for it. We're from Ireland," I try again, exaggerating my accent in a way that would probably make everyone back home wince. But sometimes you've got to play the leprechaun card. "Do you have any family from there?"

"Nope," Trevor says flatly. "Though an Irish guy pissed in my cab once."

"Okay. So, I agree that's not a great—"

"Goodbye."

"Wait!" I whirl around, almost colliding with Andrew as Trevor stops by his car. I grab my bag and open it up right there in the middle of the road, the stuffed Cubs bear falling to the wet concrete as I retrieve a small pink box I'd placed carefully inside. "Let me bribe you," I say, holding it out to him.

Andrew shifts beside me, picking up the bear. "I don't think you're actually meant to say when something's a bribe."

I ignore him, opening the lid. Trevor peers inside, curious despite his best efforts.

"What the hell are those?" he asks, and I know I've got him.

What are they? They're handmade truffles from my favorite chocolate shop in the city. Aka, they're expensive as hell. A sumptuous variety of caramel latte, passionfruit and ginger, toasted coconut rum, and a dozen other practically perfect small dollops of joy. I was going to share them with Andrew once we got to our first-class seats. We were going to eat them with our free champagne. We were going to toast our tenth Christmas flight.

But Trevor doesn't need to know all that.

"Chocolates," I say, bringing the box closer to him. He looks down at them suspiciously, but his expression softens when he sees them. And why wouldn't it? These are good-looking chocolates. I would know. I picked them out myself.

"My wife loves chocolate," he admits gruffly, dragging his gaze reluctantly away from them and back to me. "My daughter too. She's about your age."

"I'm sure you must love her very—"

"She's a pain in my side."

"Alright, well—"

"Just get in the cab."

I blink in surprise as he takes the box from me. "Really?"

"Don't question the man," Andrew mutters as I hurriedly zip my bag back up. We've caused a *minor* traffic jam behind us and I raise an apologetic hand as we follow Trevor back to the car.

"Should have retired years ago," he grumbles as we get into the back. "You sure you know where you're going this time?"

"Midway," I say as Andrew drags a hand down his face. "And I'm happy to pay any speeding ticket you get."

"I bet you are," Trevor mutters as he pulls out of his space, but there's no heat to the words and, when he glances back at us, he looks almost determined. "Buckle up," he says. "I'll do my best."

The ride south to Chicago's second airport is fast, but tense. Neither Andrew nor I speak as Trevor navigates the weather and the traffic, breaking the law only *slightly* as he fully earns those chocolates.

By the time he screeches to a halt at the drop-off point, we have a three-minute window for delays and Andrew scrambles out immediately to the trunk as I lean forward to Trevor.

"If you wouldn't mind waiting for ten minutes just in case we miss—"

"Out."

"Right. Yep. Happy Christmas!"

With our bags in hand, we race inside, pausing only briefly to check the departure board before going to check our luggage in.

Our first hurdle.

"I'm sorry," the woman says as soon as I show her my boarding card. "But the bag drop closed twenty minutes ago for this flight. They're about to start boarding," she adds as if that's a thing we're not *completely aware of*.

"I understand," I say, using my most professional voice. "But the plane is still here and I don't think my companion's giant suitcase is going to fit in the overhead locker."

"They'll already be loaded onto the airplane."

"The plane that hasn't left yet!" I stress, slapping my hands on the counter with every word. "Please."

"We're just trying to get back for Christmas," Andrew says. "Her sister is about to give birth and I'm the only person who likes my mother's brussels sprouts. It's really important we get home."

The woman looks genuinely sympathetic, but just shakes her head as I resist the urge to slump to the floor and pretend none of this is happening.

"Let's leave them," Andrew says to me, looking desperate. "We'll just dump our stuff here."

"But all your presents," I protest. "And my Tabasco sauce."

"Your what?"

"We can't leave our luggage here," I continue, ignoring him. "That's insane."

"Do you have a better suggestion?"

"Obviously not, but—"

"We're going to miss the plane."

"And they'll destroy our stuff if we—"

"Just go."

We turn back to the counter as the attendant picks up a desk phone with one hand, and motions for me to pass my suitcase with the other.

"Go," she says again. "I'll get these on and ring the gate."

Oh my God. "Really?"

"My dad was in the military," she says. "The years he didn't make it home for Christmas?" She shakes her head, tapping a number onto the keypad. "Go. Be with your families. But I can't promise anything."

Andrew jerks toward her, looking like he's about to hug her, but he thankfully turns instead and starts running toward security.

I linger for a second longer, slipping out a small piece of black cardboard from my wallet. "There's this amazing Thai place in Ravenswood," I babble. "They made me this special fifty-percent-off card because I ate there every night for two weeks once. I want you to have it."

The attendant just stares at me. "...Okay."

"Because it's Christmas."

"Molly!"

"Try the papaya salad," I tell her as Andrew's frustrated shout calls from across the concourse. "And thank you!"

I reach his side in record time as we round the corner, my heart pounding with each step.

This is it. We just need to get through security. We just need to get through security and...

Shit.

Andrew and I come to an abrupt stop as we almost run into the wall of people waiting for passport control. A screen overhead says the wait to get through is forty-five minutes and even the preclearance line is jammed. Despite our rush, for a few seconds the two of us simply stare at the orderly, tired lines in front of us, and I feel my last bit of hope slip away. The gate is supposed to close in another few minutes and I doubt they'll keep it open for much longer.

Andrew exhales sharply, his body tense as he scans each column as though looking for the shortest one.

"I'm going to ask them to let us through," he mutters, and I follow numbly as he approaches a TSA agent standing to one side and starts to plead our case. I don't have the heart to tell him that there's no point. I'm sure they get asked the same thing by a dozen people every minute.

I swallow thickly, adrenaline warring with fresh disappointment as more and more travelers keep joining the lines. There's a burning in my chest that moves to my throat and my breathing grows shallow as each second passes. We're going to miss the flight. We made it to the airport and now we're going to miss the flight.

"Andrew," I mumble, but he's not listening. To be honest, I'm not even sure if I spoke out loud or in my head.

God, it's warm in here.

"You're going to need to wait just like everyone else," the agent says, sounding like he's reading from a script.

"They're keeping the gate open for us," Andrew says. "If you could just—"

"Andrew," I say.

"Sir, everyone's in the same—"

I burst into tears.

I've always been a bit of a crier. Sad tears, happy tears, angry tears. It's my body's go-to reaction no matter the situation or the time of the month. And usually, it's not so bad. A couple seconds' pause, a tissue under the eyes. I get it out, I fix my makeup, and I move on.

These tears are not those tears.

These are loud, sloppy, sobbing tears that make everyone in our immediate circle stare at us. At *me.*

"We're going... to miss... our *flight*," I wail as the security agent rears back in horror. Even Andrew looks alarmed, and he's definitely seen me cry before.

The agent shifts uncomfortably, one hand raised between us as though he doesn't know whether to comfort or corral me into the corner. "Ma'am—"

"My sister's... having... a baby," I gasp, almost choking myself as I force the words out.

"Just let her through," someone calls from up ahead, and they're immediately backed up by others.

"It's Christmas!"

"She's pregnant!"

"She's not..." The agent's face tightens. "It's her sister who's—"

But he's drowned out by even more voices supporting little old highly hysterical me. A particularly violent hiccup has him wincing as Andrew rubs slow circles into my back.

"Alright, alright," the man mutters, hurrying us to the front of the line. "Just make it quick."

It's like he doesn't even know who he's talking to. We rush through passport control and practically fling our stuff through the scanners. By some miracle our bags aren't picked up for extra checks and then we're off, sprinting through the terminal as fast as we can and garnering several annoyed protests in our wake as we dodge wheeled suitcases and roaming shoppers.

"Run," Andrew says, sounding only a little panicked as we careen around a corner. "Run, run, run."

Somewhere above me I hear what sounds like my name being called over the announcement system, and I pick up the pace, my laptop bag banging uncomfortable against my hip as it slides down my shoulder with each step. They made this look *much* easier in *Home Alone*.

"We're here," I yell as we approach our gate. There's no one else waiting but the doors are open, the desk still manned. "We're here!"

An annoyed-looking attendant speaks briefly into a walkie talkie before rounding the counter. "Ms. Kinsel—"

"Yes! Hi. That's me." We stumble to a stop in front of her as I bring up the tickets on my phone.

"We've been calling you," she says sternly.

"And we came running," Andrew says, grinning at her. Her glare softens as she takes him in because of course it does, but it's me her attention returns to as she checks our passports.

"Is everything alright, ma'am?"

Andrew's relieved smile fades as he glances at me. It's only then that I realize I'm still crying.

"I'm fine," I say shakily, snatching my passport back in embarrassment.

She doesn't look convinced, but waves us through anyway, shutting the door behind us.

"I didn't know you were serious," Andrew mutters, sounding concerned as we hurry down the tunnel.

"I wasn't," I whisper back. "I'm honestly okay." Only now that I've opened the floodgates, hell if I know how to close them again. Oh God, did I break something inside? Is this just who I am now?

I'm going to be so dehydrated.

We've clearly held up the already delayed flight and get glares from the other passengers, but I don't think either of us care as we head down the aisle to two seats right by the toilets. Not that I'm about to complain, collapsing down as Andrew stores our carry-on bags away. He takes the seat next to me as the attendants begin final checks and close the doors, and I blow out a shaky breath, the sweat cooling uncomfortably on my body from the sudden burst of activity.

"So," Andrew says, opening the plastic bag of airplane freebies. He finds a tissue and hands it to me as the tears continue to stream down my face. "You bring your own bottle of Tabasco sauce home with you?"

"I grew up in a house where the only flavors were salt and pepper." I sniff, dabbing my eyes. "What do you think?"

"I think that if you can keep up this crying trick, we'll never have to queue for anything ever again."

I start to laugh, which somehow only makes me cry harder, but I give into it, letting my adrenaline tip into hysteria until an attendant politely lets me know that I'm scaring the other passengers.

CHAPTER SEVEN

SIX YEARS AGO

Flight Four, Chicago

"I want you to stop sending me pictures of lamps."

"Now, see..." Andrew shoves my bag into the overhead compartment before sliding into the seat next to me. "Now that you've said that I'm never going to stop. You've just shown your hand, Kinsella."

"Does your girlfriend know you're sending me pictures of lamps you find on the street?"

"Not only does Emily know, but she actively encourages it so I don't take them home to show her."

I laugh as I bend down to grab my water bottle, my body protesting the movement. I'd been up half the night with research and ended up falling asleep in an awkward position that every muscle in my body was now punishing me for.

"You alright there, champ?" Andrew asks when I groan.

I sit back up, trying to get comfortable. "I need a massage."

"I have a girlfriend, Molly."

"Shut *up*."

Andrew just grins at me.

He's been hyper ever since we met up at security. At first, I thought it was because of his new relationship, but then I caught the whiff of alcohol on him when he leaned in for a hug and he confessed he'd come straight from a party.

"You're not going to fall asleep on me, are you?" I ask now as he puts his seatbelt on. "You look like you turn into a sleepy drunk."

"I can handle myself." He watches some of the other passengers shuffle down the aisle before turning his attention back to me. "You can meet her, you know. Emily. I don't want you thinking you can't."

"Why would I think that?"

He shrugs. "Just don't talk to her or look her in the eye. She gets funny about things like that."

"Sure, sure." I sip my water, watching him curiously. "Introducing her around, are we? Things must be getting serious."

"Yeah, well..." He trails off, looking awkward, and I try to ignore the shallow pang in my heart. They *are* getting serious. It's only been two months since he told me about her. As far as I knew, there'd been no one long term between her and Hayley and I was kind of used to him being single. Or maybe that's just because now I was. Daniel had broken up with me in the fall, a real "it's not you, it's me" situation and I'd been moping about it ever since. And that's allowed! Sometimes you need a good mope. But when that moping gets in the way of being happy for others, I know I have to start digging myself out of my broody little hole.

So, I do the first thing that comes to mind, which as it turns out is kicking Andrew's foot with mine.

"*Ow*," he says pointedly.

"I'm happy for you."

"And you have a weird way of showing it."

"I mean it, Andrew. This is great. I can't wait to meet her."

He smiles at that. "It *is* great."

"Yes."

"Because I deserve good things."

"You do. The best."

"Including..." He waggles his eyebrows as he presses the call button. "Some champagne?"

I laugh. "They're not going to serve you."

"They will. It's Christmas."

"And you're drunk."

"Tipsy. Trust me. I can handle this."

He makes eye contact with a flight attendant squeezing down the aisle and smiles so widely that she falters in her step.

"Smooth," I mutter, but he just hushes me and, as promised, gets us our champagne.

———

Now

Buenos Aires is a beautiful city. Cosmopolitan, passionate, full of food and dance and *life*. Or at least, so the giant posters surrounding us make it look like. I wouldn't actually know seeing as, without a visa, we're not allowed to leave the airport.

"God, you know what I'd love right now?" Andrew says from where he's sprawled on the chair beside me. "Some of those little truffles from—"

"I will punch you in the face," I tell him. "In your big stupid face."

"I mean the money, I can understand. But the chocolate?" He brings one hand to his heart, looking at me with a wounded expression. "I love chocolate."

"I know you do," I grumble, staring at an image of a red-lipped tango dancer on the opposite wall. "That's why I bought them."

I peer at the overhead lights, trying to decide if I'm hungry or tired or both. We flew to Atlanta where we waited four hours to fly the ten hours to Argentina where we're currently waiting for our connection to Paris, which will take another seven hundred and eighty minutes. Thirteen more hours.

Yeah. So much better than staying in Chicago with my bed and my shower and my food and my—

I groan, slumping down in my chair. All my clothes are in my checked luggage, which was something I hadn't been particularly concerned about, but is all I can think about now with no change of clothes on me. I probably stink, even with the cheap body spray I bought in the drugstore here.

"We made the right choice," Andrew says, correctly interpreting my annoyance as he scrolls through his phone. "That storm isn't going anywhere. We would never have gotten a direct flight."

"Would staying in Chicago really have been so bad?" I sigh, only half-joking. "I mean, I know you love your family and everything, but..."

Andrew smirks. "I'm never going to stop thanking you for this. You know that, right? I can't think of anyone else who would put themselves through this for me."

"Alright," I mutter, embarrassed. "No need to be all sincere about it."

He laughs, mimicking my pose as he slides down his seat, legs spreading in that way men do. I don't call him out on it though. There's no one else in our row and I like the way his knee brushes against mine. I like it even more when he doesn't move it away.

I take a slow breath at the sensation, holding it in as I try to stay relaxed. We'd barely spoken once we were in the air, both of us too exhausted to say more than a few words to each other. But I remained constantly aware of him. As aware as I am now as he stares blankly ahead and I stare at him. Discreetly, of course. Face tilted away, corner of my eye, stealth-wise. I can't help it. I'm kind of hoping that if I keep looking, I'll eventually see it, whatever had me so confused back in Chicago. Confused now.

"We should try and sleep on this one," he says. "We'll only have an hour to catch the flight on to Dublin." He pauses. "If there aren't any delays."

"There won't be. We'll make it. Maybe we'll even get on the news."

"So that's your plan. Brief, local fame."

"We'll make it," I repeat, and he shoots me a half smile.

"I know. I think I'll be better once we're... I don't know, in Europe?" He laughs at how ridiculous it sounds. "At least it will be a fun story to tell the family. We'll take a break between movies to stretch our legs and I'll say, hey, remember that time I flew twenty-four hours out of my way just to get home for Christmas?"

"Stretch your legs? How many movies do you guys watch in the Fitzpatrick household?"

He grins. "It depends on the year. Dad usually chooses the main one, but he can be unpredictable. If it doesn't scratch the itch, we can go all night, though my parents usually head to bed around midnight." Andrew shifts, twisting his body to face me. "I was going to suggest a movie marathon at yours if we'd stayed. Just Christmas films all day."

I force a smile. "That sounds nice." It sounds very nice. But I don't want to think about all the things he was going to suggest. It had only been for an hour or so, but I'd gotten very attached to the idea of spending Christmas with Andrew.

"We should go to the Music Box next Halloween," he continues, and I raise a brow. The Music Box is the kind of pretentious movie theater that I love and he tolerates. "They do horror marathons," he adds at my look.

"I can't sit still for that long; I'll need to pee."

"I'll get you an aisle seat. Quick escape. Or one of those adult diapers."

"Well, how can a girl say no to that?"

"It's a date then."

My smile freezes on my face as I force myself to turn back and face the tango lady.

Not a date. Not a date! So why—

I flinch at the tickling sensation by my ear and whip my head around to see Andrew drawing back, eyes wide at my exaggerated response. His hand hovers uncertainly between us.

"Your earring," he explains, showing me the small silver crescent. "It was caught in your hair."

My hand flies up to my bare lobe. "I must have lost the backer."

He drops it into my open palm with a frown. "Are you okay?"

"Just tired," I lie. I take out the other one and slip them both into my pocket. Andrew doesn't look convinced, but he lets it go. "Bet you're excited to see the kids," I say, changing the subject. His older brother, Liam, has a boy and a girl. "You must miss them."

"I do," he says. "I swear it's like every time I get back they're whole new people. It was the same with Hannah. Although, the way Liam and Christian used to talk about her growing up, I gather she was very annoying."

I laugh. "Seriously?"

"Nah. I suppose every six-year-old is annoying when you're eighteen and just want to get on with things. We're close though. She's a good kid. Real smart. Smarter than any of us."

"We should do something next time they come to visit."

"She'd love that," he says, perking up. "She knows all about you."

"She does?"

"Oh yeah. Irish girl making it big in the world? She thinks you're pretty cool."

I stare at him, delighted. "No one's ever called me cool before."

"Hard to believe," he deadpans.

We fall into silence and after a moment he takes off his sweater, using it as a cushion between his body and the chair.

He's wearing a holiday T-shirt underneath because of course he is. Though this one isn't that bad, navy with a gingerbread man on the front. I examine it for a second before Andrew picks a loose thread from his sleeve and then I'm staring at his bicep, and the curve of muscle that disappears beneath the fabric. There's a tiny scar by his elbow, a sliver of raised pink skin from some childhood fall that I'm immediately fascinated by.

"Why didn't you move to Seattle?"

"What?" I jerk my gaze up to find him watching me and try not to look as guilty as I bizarrely feel.

"With Brandon," he says. "You said you asked him to stay, but why didn't you want to move?"

"Because of my job."

"They don't have lawyers in Seattle?"

I frown. "Don't simplify it like that."

"I'm not, I'm just..." He trails off with a shrug. "You're right, never mind."

I can't read the expression on his face. He almost looks frustrated, though that could be the exhaustion. To be honest, I'm kind of surprised we haven't started snapping at each other yet.

"I didn't want to leave," I say. "And I'd have to take the bar exam again. It would have been a whole big thing."

"You'd have to do that to practice in Ireland too," he points out, and I give him a funny look.

"Yeah, but I'm not moving to Ireland, am I?"

"You might someday."

I huff. "You sound like my parents. I have no intention of moving back to Dublin. Chicago's my home now." An uncomfortable thought strikes me. "It isn't for you?" He's lived there even longer than I have.

"Sure it is," he says. "But so is Ireland. If you can have a home in two places."

"Of course you can. But I'd only been with Brandon a few months," I add, feeling the need to point that out again. "Definitely not enough to move halfway across the country."

"So, if you'd been with him longer, you might have gone?"

"I don't know." The words are curt, sounding as annoyed as I feel. "That's way too much of a hypothetical."

We stare at each other for a beat before he nods. "Okay."

"Yeah? So can we change the subject?"

"Sure. Are you seeing anyone else? I don't think I asked."

"That's not changing the subject."

"Never mind then."

"I've been concentrating on myself," I tell him.

"Have you now?" He smiles slightly. "And what does that look like?"

"I do hot yoga on Sunday mornings. And I get a massage every second Tuesday."

"Swedish?"

"Deep muscle." I grimace. "Usually because I've strained something in hot yoga."

He smirks. "Well, I'm glad you're not dating anyone. It means I get you all to myself." He sits up as he speaks, stretching his arms over his head. The movement lifts his T-shirt, revealing a thin band of skin just above his jeans that suddenly has me furious.

I snap my gaze away, my jaw clenching in a way my dentist would *not* be happy about. "So, you want me to be alone then, is that it?"

He pauses. "I didn't mean it like that."

"It sounds like you did."

Andrew goes quiet beside me, but I can't bring myself to look at him. My anger disappears as quickly as it came, leaving me tired and embarrassed and still so very, very confused.

"Sorry," I say after a long moment.

"Me too. I really didn't mean it the way it sounded."

"I know. I just..." Need to get away from him. "I'm going to go stretch my legs and text Zoe."

"Molly—"

"I'll be right back." I stand so fast my vision swims, but I ignore it as I stride off, limping slightly from a dead leg. I focus on the pins and needles so I don't focus on him and march down the terminal before taking an abrupt left at a restroom sign.

The hallway is empty and thankfully so is the ladies' room. So, as millions of equally confused women have done before me, I lock myself in the first stall, sit with a huff on the toilet lid, and just... ugh.

Maybe I drank too much. Maybe I'm tired and I'm stressed and I had one too many glasses of champagne. That can be the only explanation for why I feel like I'm losing my goddamn mind. Because Andrew and I...

Sometimes I feel like he's been the one constant in my life since I moved to this city. Through the chaos of my early twenties, of finding my way, finding myself, he's always been with me. Maybe not physically. There were years I only saw him a handful of times, but he was always there. I could always talk to him. Could always moan to him. Could always celebrate and commiserate. And now I'm hiding from him in an airport bathroom.

I shouldn't have kissed him.

Why did I kiss him?

I close my eyes, dropping my head to my knees as I feel the beginnings of a headache forming at my temples.

I'm just not going to think about it. That's what I'm not going to do. Instead, I'm going to compartmentalize and focus on getting us back to Ireland and then, *then*, I am going to quit my job and book a vacation and on that vacation I will eat a lot of food and I will fall in love. I will fall in love with a masseuse and he will be very handsome and have an impeccable dress sense and won't be confusing at all.

But for now, I compartmentalize.

I stay there for as long as is socially acceptable and only then force myself to move in case I miss boarding. The harsh fluorescent lights overhead do nothing to help my confidence. I've been playing with my hair all night and it now hangs limply around my face, while my makeup has all but melted into my pores. I look like a mess. Which is understandable and not something I would usually care about with Andrew, but now I feel uncharacteristically self-conscious as I wet a paper towel and wash my face as best I can. It doesn't help that I'd changed clothes back in O'Hare, trading my skirt and blouse for sweatpants and an oversized hoodie. They're comfortable but aren't exactly helping the whole girl-in-the-before-photo vibe. Especially when there's not going to be an after photo anytime soon.

I give up on my halfhearted makeover, practice my I'm-totally-normal-and-just-a-little-tired smile, and open the restroom door, fully committed to acting like everything's fine and—

"Finally."

Andrew's waiting outside.

I freeze when I see him and he scowls when I do, straightening from his slump against the wall as I stand there like a cornered mouse.

"Alright," he says, peering down at me. "What the hell is going on with you?"

CHAPTER EIGHT

"What do you mean?" My nerves skyrocket at the suspicion on his face. He's standing way too close to me, as close as we stood under the mistletoe, and nope, no thank you. Not needed right now.

"You're being weird," he says when I try to skirt around him. He immediately moves to the side, blocking my way.

"Because it's been a weird night. Day. However long it's been."

His hand shoots out when I try to get past again, pushing me gently against the wall. Only you'd swear he'd pulled me into his arms the way I react, sucking in a breath so loud that he rears back like I hit him.

He looks at me like I'm a stranger. Probably because I'm acting like one.

"You look like you're going to puke," he says, some of his wariness morphing into concern. "Do you want to sit down?"

"I'm fine." I push the hair back from my face, feeling a flush in my cheeks. Maybe I do need to sit down. Maybe I'm ill! That would explain everything.

"What is it?" he asks. "You can tell me. Is it your period?"

"No," I mutter, annoyed until I force myself to meet his gaze. The worry I see there only makes me feel worse. This is *Andrew*. I can talk to Andrew.

Just not about this. If Andrew is my one constant right now, then I refuse to let him go, since casually revealing to your friend that *hey! I liked it when our bodies touched! Let's do that again!* might come across the wrong way.

"Can we go now?" I ask. "Trust us to miss this flight."

"We've got time." His expression softens at the panic he no doubt sees on my face. "Come on, Moll. What's up?"

"Beyond the giant mess of this trip?" I hesitate when he just looks at me like the stubborn asshole he is. "It's nothing," I say eventually. "I've just been super busy lately."

"You're always busy." He doesn't say it in a judging way, more like a statement of fact, but it still stings.

"I know," I say. "But work feels especially manic right now."

"Okay, well—"

"I also think I'm at the beginning of an early midlife crisis? And I was excited about seeing you and the flight and probably put way too much expectation on the whole thing and it's just—"

"Molly—"

"It's stupid," I finish.

"What's stupid?"

I ignore him, noticing his empty hands for the first time. "Who's watching our stuff?"

"A shifty-eyed man who tried to sell me a Rolex," he says without missing a beat. "What's stupid?"

"The..." What is happening to me? "The mistletoe thing... I shouldn't have..." I lift my hands helplessly, but he gives me nothing, staring at me with a blank look like he has no idea what I'm talking about. Because of course, he doesn't. He's probably already forgotten about it.

"You know what?" I say. "Maybe I am going to puke."

"Are you talking about when you kissed me?"

I am full-on sweating now.

"Molly?"

"Yeah. Yes." I shift my weight from one foot to the other. "I shouldn't have done it."

His brow furrows. "Why not?"

"Because it's *dumb*!" I exclaim. "The whole thing was dumb and I liked it and maybe I'm tired of spending every year with people thinking I hate Christmas and I just wanted to show that I could have a little good-natured, festive fun and—"

"You liked it?" he interrupts.

"What?"

"You liked the kiss?"

I stop talking, biting the inside of my cheek so hard I'm surprised it doesn't bleed. Maybe I should just get a flight to Greece and meet Zoe there. I bet Greece is lovely in December. "I guess."

"You guess," he repeats slowly. "And that... makes you want to puke?"

"I think it's because I've been going through a dry spell since Brandon," I tell him, and he blinks. "That and the champagne and all my aforementioned stress. It messed up my mind. Made me all floopy."

"That's not a word."

"You're right." I poke him in the chest, ignoring the immediate tingle in my finger. "It's not. Another indication of how floopy I am. That's all."

Andrew's gaze narrows as he examines me, but I actually feel a little relieved. Confessing to him has already started to heal me like the good little lapsed Catholic I am.

"Okay?" I ask, and he pulls back, putting some much-needed space between us.

"Okay," he says. "I get it."

"You do?"

"Yeah. When you kissed me under the mistletoe, it didn't go as you expected."

"Right."

"You were tired and stressed and haven't kissed anyone in a while so, when you kissed me, your wires got crossed."

"Exactly."

"It confused you."

"It *did*." I'm beaming at him now, relieved he understands.

Andrew nods. "So, we should do it again."

"Yes, we... What?"

"We should kiss again to clear things up," he says, completely serious. "So you'll be less confused."

I pause. The words individually make sense, that much I understand. But together... "How would that make me any less confused?" I ask.

"Because if you feel nothing, you'll know it was just a random, stress-induced moment of madness. And if you feel the same way..."

"What?" I demand when he doesn't continue. "If I feel the same way what?"

"It doesn't matter," he says simply. "You probably won't. Seeing as how you were just tired."

"I *am* tired."

"Right."

I stare at him as a speaker close to us blares to life with an announcement, but it's not for our flight. Andrew doesn't move an inch and I realize belatedly that he's waiting for me to make the next move.

And I know what that move should be. I know he expects me to laugh and drag him back to the gate. I know that's what I should do.

But looking up at that familiar face, I know it's not what I *want* to do. And isn't that just terrifying.

"You don't think it would be weird?" I ask.

"I don't think it will be any weirder than how you're being right now," he says flatly. "It's worth a shot, isn't it?"

I have no idea. But the man kind of has a point.

"Okay," I say, calling his bluff. If he's surprised, he doesn't show it. "Great idea." I straighten my shoulders, hands clenching into fists at my side as I fight the urge to pull my hair back. "You should probably do it. Kiss me, I mean. Seeing as I kissed you the first time. Although I guess, scientifically, we'd need to go back to O'Hare and find the mistletoe, but I don't think they'll still have it by the time we — Okay, okay! Jesus."

My back hits the wall as Andrew crowds me, stepping into my space until we're as close as we can be without touching. My hands shoot out, grabbing onto his shoulders to hold him there as my pulse starts to race.

"This is an experiment," I clarify, and I swear I see a faint glimmer of amusement in his eyes. For whatever reason, it makes me feel calmer. "It's for science."

"For science." He echoes it like a vow. "Do you want to hear a chemistry joke?"

"No."

He grins and I suddenly can't breathe. "You sure? It's a pretty good—"

I kiss him.

You know when people say that the anticipation of a

kiss can be better than the actual event? Those people have never kissed Andrew Fitzpatrick.

It's a light one. A tame one. And yet again my reaction is not what it should be, my heart vaulting into my throat, my body surging up to meet his, following his warmth. And I should be disappointed, because with everything else going on in my life, this, this right here is the last thing I need. The last thing I need and only thing I want.

That simple realization sends a spark of alarm through my mind, a blaring *Woah there, timeout,* but then Andrew shifts, his mouth slanting over mine as his hands leave my hips to cup my face. He tilts my head to deepen the kiss and I make a noise, a little, dare I say it, whimper, that has me so embarrassed that, again, I'm the first to pull away. This time Andrew lets me go and I open my eyes, ready to apologize and make excuses or just downright *lie,* when I look up at him and see that I've wiped the smile right off his face.

A lock of hair falls across my forehead, tickling my cheek, and I watch as Andrew's eyes track the movement, before he slowly, like I'm some sort of skittish animal (which, okay, yes), tucks it behind my ear. Goosebumps break out over my skin as he runs his fingers through the strands before dropping his hand to the side.

"No loose earrings this time?" I try to be sarcastic but only sound hoarse instead.

"Can only use that excuse once."

Neither of us moves. Neither of us speaks. The corridor we're in is bright and smells strongly of disinfectant. But it's also empty and we're both alone as we're probably going to be for the next while.

"Feel better?" he finally asks, and it takes me a moment to figure out what he's talking about.

"Yep," I croak.

"All cleared up?"

"Uh-huh."

"Want to do it again?"

"Ye— *No*," I amend quickly, and just like that his smile is back, the intensity in his expression vanishing like he just flicked a switch.

"Still confused, huh?" He sighs. "I knew it wouldn't work."

"Then why did you suggest we do it?"

"I wanted to see what it would be like."

I stare at him. "And?"

"Yeah."

"What do you mean, *yeah*?"

"It was good," he says, turning to listen as another announcement blares across the terminal.

"It was more than good!" The gooey warmth I feel curdles into annoyance as his attention shifts away from me. "I am an excellent kisser. And that was an excellent kiss."

"Sure."

"No, not *sure*, you—" I break off when he turns, heading back down the corridor. "Andrew!"

"We're going to miss our flight," he calls over his shoulder.

I hurry after him, struggling to keep up with his long legs.

"I can't believe you scared me like that," he says when I do, typing something into his phone. Up ahead people are starting to get in line for boarding. "I thought there was something actually wrong with you, but you just have a little crush."

"I do not!"

"Think you do. I can tell."

"From one kiss?"

"Two kisses." He says it almost absently, reading a new message.

"The first one doesn't count," I tell him. "And the second one was *your* idea."

He doesn't answer as he retrieves our cases from a cheerful young woman with giant baubles attached to her T-shirt.

"Six out of ten," he says, turning back to me.

My mouth drops open. I know instantly what he means. "For our *kiss*?"

"Don't feel bad. You said so yourself, you're tired."

"I'm not—" I break off before I almost shout at him. "You're being annoying on purpose."

"Yeah," he says as if that's obvious. "Feel better?"

The line starts to shuffle forward as the doors open. I do feel better. As if he knew pissing me off would distract me above all else.

"Yes," I admit, trying not to fidget under his gaze. "I do."

"Good." He joins the end of the line and, after a second, I follow.

"You didn't have to kiss me just to distract me."

"Ah, sure we all have to make sacrifices." He glances over his shoulder and I swear there's a goddamn twinkle in his eye. "And you're an excellent kisser, Molly Kinsella."

"Stop teasing," I groan.

"I'm not teasing about that." He holds out his arm, wrapping it around my shoulder when I step into him like I always do. "Forget about it, okay? It's not weird and it's not a big deal. I'm just glad you're out of your funk."

"I know it's not a big deal. I never said it was a big deal."

"I'm telling this story at your wedding though. How you wanted to throw up at the thought of kissing me."

"Maybe I'll tell it at yours," I quip back. "How you came on to me in Buenos Aires during the worst Christmas ever."

"Fine. Whoever marries first gets the story."

"Deal."

"Deal."

I gaze up at him, eyes narrowing. "Six out of ten?"

He smiles. "Seven. Anything more and I need to see some tongue."

"That's gross. You're gross. Don't kiss me again."

"I will try and control myself," he says seriously, and I huff, but it's halfhearted. I'm mostly relieved. Relieved that I'm no longer keeping things from him. That he truly doesn't seem to think it's a big deal that we've kissed each other twice in twenty-four hours after ten years of, you know, *not doing that at all*.

I stay silent as we shuffle toward the plane, trying not to overthink it. Andrew gets another text and is quickly distracted though his hand remains tight around me.

I'm not teasing about that.

It's not a big deal. He just said it wasn't and now he's acting like it too. But my lips are still tingling. My lips are still tingling and even when I press them together, they don't stop.

CHAPTER NINE

FIVE YEARS AGO

Flight Five, Chicago

"Try it on."

"No."

"Just try it!"

"No, it would make you too happy."

"Try it on or I'm taking it back."

"That's not how gifts work, you weirdo." But Andrew shrugs off his sweater (*all the jingle ladies*) and unwraps the one I just gave to him.

"It's cashmere," I say as he holds it up. "And I know it's not exactly *fun*, but it's wintergreen, which is definitely a Christmas color, and it's light enough that you could wear it all year round if you wanted to."

He doesn't answer, too busy pulling it on over his head. I don't know why I'm so nervous. I've never been someone who worries about gifts, and yet I spent a whole weekend running around the city trying to find the perfect one for him. And I'm pretty sure I failed. I should have just got him a gift card. Everyone loves gift cards.

"I've kept the receipt," I say. "So, if you don't like it or it doesn't fit, we can—"

"It'll fit," he interrupts, his voice muffled by the fabric. His head pops through, his hair ruffled as he pulls it down over his chest.

I lean forward, brushing some lint from his sleeve before realizing I'm fussing. "Well? What do you think?"

"I *think*," he says, pulling the label free, "that this is now the nicest thing I own."

"Really?"

He smirks. "Is this moment about me getting a present or about you giving me a present?"

"Me," I say, and he laughs. "You're really hard to buy for."

"I'm easy to buy for. Get me anything."

"*Anything* is code word for hard to buy for."

"Okay, we're definitely not doing this again," he says. "This is supposed to be fun, not stressful. Don't you exchange presents with your family?"

"Of course, I do. But it's usually money, the greatest gift of all."

"You're a cold, sad woman."

"Give me my present."

Andrew smirks, reaching into the front pocket of his bag. He's the one who insisted on doing this, and I only agreed because I thought we would swap on the plane and open them in our respective houses. Alone. I didn't think he'd want to do the whole thing *now*. In front of everyone. We're due to board in a few minutes and the rows of seats by the gate are filling up, with a few people already waiting in line, their passports at the ready.

"Here you go."

He grabs my hand, pressing a small, tissue-wrapped rectangle into my palm that I quickly open.

Huh.

I truly didn't know what to expect. But I think if you'd given me a hundred guesses of what Andrew might get me as a Christmas gift, I would have needed a couple more attempts.

"It's a... fridge magnet?" I ask, and he nods.

"But it's also a fun one," he says. "It has a pun."

"I can see that."

"It says, 'Pasta la vista, baby,'" he continues, straight-faced as he points to the Comic Sans print. "And there's a picture of—"

"—some pasta, yes."

"I got it on eBay."

"Andrew."

"It cost me three dollars in postage."

A noise comes out of me before I can stop it, somewhere between a snort and a laugh, and I slap my hand over my mouth. "This is what you got me? I spent the last two weeks anxious out of my mind over this, and this is what you got me?"

"It's the thought that counts."

"You *thought* about this?" I narrow my eyes, not buying it for an instant. "Give me my real present."

"That is—"

"Andrew."

He grins, reaching back into his bag. "You're the spoiled child on Christmas morning, you know that? This was a supposed to be a lesson in gracious disappointment."

"I'm returning your sweater."

"Again, not how this works, but here."

I drop the magnet onto my lap as he passes me a slim, red leather book.

The spine is cracked and the cover well-worn from being carried around. It has to be several years old at least. If not decades. *A Diner's Guide to Chicago* written in slanting letters on the front.

"It might not be the most up to date," he says, leaning into me as I open it. "But look." He flips forward a few pages, pointing to the margins.

"The owner wrote notes?"

"*Owners*," he says. "The handwriting changes. Looks like a few people got their hands on it."

He's right. There's some marked in pencil, some in red pen, and the writing switches from neat square letters to a tiny calligraphy I can barely read. "Where did you even get this?"

"I found it at a flea market months ago. Thought you might like it."

"I love it," I correct, tracing the scrawled words. *Ask for the handmade butter. Steal it if necessary.* "It's like reading a diary." *Tasting menu is worth the overtime. Flirt with Diane to get the good table.* "You got it months ago?"

"When you know, you know."

And he kept it all this time. Just to give to me.

"Uh-oh," Andrew says as I start to choke up. "Here they come."

"They're happy tears," I assure him. "Christmas tears. It's perfect, thank you." I clutch it to my chest, twisting so I can hug him.

"You're welcome," he murmurs, squeezing me back. "Happy Christmas, Moll."

A phantom voice echoes throughout the terminal, announcing a twenty-minute delay to our flight, but neither of us mind so much. In that moment I think I would have taken a twenty-hour delay so long as I got to spend it with him.

———

Now, Paris

"What do you mean, *my bag isn't here?*"

I stare at the woman behind the counter as she stares right back, her nude lipstick perfectly applied as she smiles apologetically at me.

"My stuff is in that bag," I say stupidly.

"I'm sorry."

"You lost it?" This is a joke. This is a terrible, very unfunny joke. I almost expect a camera crew to come leaping out, announcing I'm on some cheap reality show. I barely slept on the flight to Paris, after barely sleeping at the airport, after barely sleeping since I left Chicago. It's the 23rd of December. I have not had a shower in forty-eight hours, the timing of my contraceptive pill is *extremely* messed up and they have *lost my bag?*

"They put our luggage in at the same time!" I exclaim. "How did they lose mine and not his?"

"Maybe yours was too small," Andrew mutters behind me only to quickly look away at the death glare I send him.

"We didn't lose it," the woman reassures me. "We know where it is. It's in Argentina."

"But *I'm* in Paris."

"We'll have it on the next flight over."

I resist the urge to drop my head to the counter. "But we're not staying here. We're trying to get to Ireland."

"Again, I'm extremely sorry." Her polite tone doesn't

change, but there's a hint of steel behind it that tells me I'm not the first wailing passenger she's had to and *will* have to deal with today. "We can compensate you per day your bag is not with you and fly it immediately to where you'd like it to go, but at the moment there is nothing more we can do for you."

"But—"

"I'm sorry, madam."

We hold each other's gaze for a long second, but for once I'm the first to blink as I force out that awful customer urge to yell at the person who has nothing to do with my problem.

"Okay," I say, sounding every inch the forlorn little girl that I feel like right now. "What do I need to do?"

One signed form and two minutes later, we trudge our way back through the entrance hall of Charles de Gaulle airport. The place is predictably packed and I feel my mood slip farther as I stare up at the departure board.

"We've missed the flight to Dublin, haven't we?" It was going to be a tight squeeze anyway but waiting for my bag that never came had made it impossible. I don't need to ask Andrew to know the rest of them are sold out.

"Don't worry about it," Andrew says gently. But I do. Because something as simple as getting home for Christmas should not be this complicated.

"There's a flight tonight that's booked out," he continues. "There's not much else we can do, but if we hang around, we can see if we can get on it and there's always tomorrow."

Tomorrow. Tomorrow is Christmas Eve, which means we're cutting it close. Too close to waste another day hanging around at an airport. Not that that seems to have occurred to Andrew. He's not even looking at the board, he's gazing unblinkingly into space, his shoulders slumped in defeat. He's given up. Which is understandable. Giving up is by far the most appealing option right now. Definitely the easiest one.

It's just something I've never been a particular fan of.

"We're both exhausted," he continues. "Maybe the best thing to do is try and get a hotel room and then—"

"London."

"What?"

I turn to Andrew, doing the timings in my fuzzy, weary head. "We can try and get to London. We'll be able to get home from there."

He hesitates. "We're talking about a couple of hundred dollars, Molly."

"That's what credit cards are for. We've come this far. You really want to give up now?"

"I want you to sleep for a few hours before you collapse."

"I said I'd get you home," I dismiss. "So, I'm going to get you home."

I push past him to a bit of empty space along the wall where I sit cross-legged and open my laptop. It takes a second, but he follows like I knew he would.

"Let's think about this," I say, frowning when he just looks at me. "Sit!"

He sighs heavily to show he's just humoring me, but dumps his bag to the floor, sitting in front of me with a grumpy look. I know it's because a part of him has stopped believing he'll make it in time, so I don't hold it too much against him.

"London isn't a problem," I say, scanning the available flights. "There are seats this afternoon and this evening. And from there..." Shite. There are over a hundred flights from London to Dublin a day, but with the number of Irish people living in the UK, it's not exactly a surprise that they're all booked out.

I send Andrew a quick smile that he doesn't believe for a second.

"Molly—"

"You're not allowed to talk if you're sulking," I interrupt. His eyes bore a hole in my skull, but I keep looking, widening my search to surrounding cities. Anything to get him home. Anyway, anyhow, any...

My fingers freeze over the keyboard as a thought occurs to me, one so simple and so perfect that I can only sit there for a second, reflecting on my brilliance.

"We come from an island."

Andrew looks at me like I've lost my mind. "Yeah," he says slowly. "You want to swim home?"

"No." I straighten, going full smug-Molly mode as I open a new tab. "I want to get the ferry."

"The ferry? You don't think it will be booked out?"

"The car tickets might be," I say, adding in our dates. "But there's always room for foot passengers. We'll obviously miss the sailing today, but tomorrow..." I let out a shriek of victory that makes several people nearby jump.

"Paris to London," I say as I piece together the puzzle. "We grab a hotel room and in the morning get the train from Euston station to Wales. There's a lunchtime sailing from Holyhead. We'll be in Dublin on Christmas Eve. You can get the bus or I'll get my dad to drive you if we have to. That's it, Andrew. You'll be home for Christmas."

I glance up when he doesn't immediately praise my genius idea, only to find him watching me with a look in his eyes that throws me so much, I snap my attention back to my spreadsheet, suddenly self-conscious.

"You'll still be exhausted," I add. "But I think we can make it work. Unless you have any other—"

"I don't," he interrupts. "That sounds perfect. That's... thank you."

I nod, still not looking at him. "I'll book the tickets then? We can be in London by late afternoon if we get the lunchtime flight. Maybe we could stay with your brother?"

"He's already gone home," Andrew says. "But I have a cousin there. Oliver. He's usually happy to have company."

"That's great. If he'll have us."

"I'll text him now." There's a pause before he speaks again. "I'm sorry, Molly."

I glance up at his words. "Me too. I'm sorry we missed the Dublin flight."

"Not your fault. And this is a good plan. I'm impressed."

"This is nothing," I dismiss. "Just wait until I've had a coffee."

He cracks a smile. It's a small one, but I'm counting it as a win. "Was that a subtle hint, Miss Kinsella?"

"Cream. No sugar."

He sighs exaggeratedly but gets to his feet. "Anything for my travel agent," he says, and I try not to look too pleased as I turn back to my laptop and start booking us in.

CHAPTER TEN

It takes another thirty minutes to sort the tickets and keep our various families updated on our new plan. Andrew's seem grateful. Mine just seem baffled that I'm going to so much effort. But at least his cousin is happy to put us up for the night, responding within a few minutes of Andrew's text that he was polishing the china as we speak.

From the look on Andrew's face, I couldn't tell if he was joking or not.

It's only when everything's sorted that I begin to realize what being without my suitcase actually means. I'm not used to looking like I currently look. The corporate world demands a certain groomed appearance and, seeing as it's one of the few things in my job I am in complete control of, I take it seriously. So while I have no problem dressing comfortably for a long flight, there's only so many times a girl can turn her underwear inside out.

"I need to buy some clothes."

"In Paris?" Andrew makes a face. "They're not exactly known for their fashion sense."

"Cute," I deadpan, but I'm secretly glad he's perked up.

The coffee helped, and we both get another espresso before leaving his very-much-*not*-lost suitcase in luggage storage before risking a venture into the city. It does feel a little like tempting fate, but there's five hours to go before we need to be back for our flight and neither of us want to spend another second more than we need to in an airport.

A brief consultation with my good friend Google and we get the RER train to Les Halles, an underground shopping mall near the Seine, where I head to the first decent store I see to grab a pair of jeans and a couple of plain T-shirts and sweaters.

Andrew is not impressed.

"It's literally two days before Christmas," he says, trailing me around the racks. "And that's what you want to wear."

"Yes, because I'm an adult."

"An adult who said she didn't want to be a grinch," he presses. "That means embracing the meaning of Christmas."

"The meaning of Christmas is not a T-shirt saying, 'Pull my cracker.'"

"No, it's family and friends. And as a friend, I would really appreciate it if you embraced a bit of glamour." He plucks a pair of snowmen earrings off a display, holding them up to me. "These for example."

"No."

"I think they'd go really— Oh my God, they light up."

I roll my eyes as they start to flash in his hands and head to the counter, moving quickly at the thought of getting out of these clothes. The salesperson lets me do so in the changing room and I breathe a sigh of relief as I pull a fresh T-shirt over my head. I spend another minute arguing with myself before I take a quick detour back through the store and then leave to find Andrew waiting outside with a shopping bag in his hand.

"Tell me you didn't buy them," I say suspiciously.

"For my sister," he explains, glancing down at my outfit. "Feel better?"

"Hugely," I admit. "Though that could be the magic of the season coursing through my veins."

"Come again?"

I part my coat to reveal my last-minute purchase and Andrew's eyes widen at my new gold-and-black-striped sweater. *Joyeux Noel*, it says in slanted writing, decorated with an appropriate amount of glitter.

"Look at you, Cindy Lou Who." A slow smile spreads across his face. "I can't believe you went to such a minimal effort for me."

"Minimal? This is a big step! The glitter is itchy."

"Well, beauty is pain. You know, those earrings would go really well with—"

"No."

He smirks as I zip up my coat again, but still seems amused, no hint of his previous bad mood left. And that was exactly what I wanted to happen when I bought it.

"I feel like we should do tourist stuff," Andrew says reluctantly, but one look at each other and we know neither of us has the energy.

"Something to eat?" I ask hopefully, and he grins. "But not around here," I add. "I'm not wasting our few hours in Paris on fast food."

"You love fast food."

"There is a time and a place," I say firmly, leading us away from the mall. We still have ages before we need to get back. "Trust me."

We head east, away from the Louvre and its tourists just

as it starts to rain. One of my favorite food bloggers raves about a small restaurant by Saint-Jacques Tower and it's there I bring Andrew, finding it down a quiet side street. It's just open for lunch and we get a small table right by the window, the smell of rich food and the gentle chatter of voices immediately putting me in a better mood. I've always felt comfortable in restaurants, even when I'm by myself.

"Very French," Andrew declares as the waiter hands us our menus. "Do you want me to take your picture?"

"No."

"Why not? I've got my camera. You're in Paris. You're geeking out over yeast," he adds as I start admiring the breadbasket. I drop a roll on my side plate and make a face. "Let's create a memory."

"I don't particularly want to remember this trip," I tell him, and he gives me a look of mock hurt.

"*This* trip? This expensive, exhausting, terrible one?"

"The very same."

"I think we're having fun."

"That's because *you* still have your suitcase."

The waiter comes back for our drinks and I have to bite my tongue to stop myself ordering a glass of wine. Instead I ask for an ice water with some broken French and Andrew gets a ginger ale. Another one. It's what he got at the airport and on the flights. I wonder if it's his go-to whenever he wants something alcoholic. Is that something you do when you're trying to stay sober? I really have no idea. But I don't know how to ask him about it without sounding too prying.

"They do French fries in France, right?" Andrew asks, picking up the menu.

"*Frites,*" I answer. "But I think you should go for—"

A sharp vibration comes from somewhere nearby and we both stare at each other before I realize it's my work phone. The automatic anxiety I get spikes through me and I dive into my laptop bag, taking it out to see a call from my boss go to voicemail.

"Are you working over Christmas again?" There's no judgment in the question, but for some reason that only makes me feel worse. I don't want to be the person who's always expected to be busy.

"Not officially," I say, checking my emails out of reflex before I realize what I'm doing.

Andrew watches me with a frown. "If you need to—"

"I don't."

"I don't mind. Do what you have to do."

"I don't have to do anything," I say, putting the phone down. "It can wait. What?" I add at the confused look on his face.

"Nothing," he says quickly. "It's just I know how busy you are."

"I'm trying to get a better work/life balance," I say, even as my stomach drops. It's one thing to realize how much of your life has been consumed by your job, it's another to hear someone else say it.

But Andrew smiles. "Work/life balance, huh? What's brought on the change?"

"Nothing in particular. I just didn't want to..." I shrug, watching another email notification light up my screen. "I don't think that's who I am anymore," I say, trying to explain it. "I'm thinking about slowing down."

"Vastly underrated," he says, and I relax a little at how easily he accepts the thing that's been weighing me down for so long.

"Might be saying goodbye to any bonuses though."

"But you'll get the bonus of a hobby you'll give up after a few months."

I smile, playing with the edge of the tablecloth. "You won't mind if I can't get you first-class flights anymore?"

"I'm still not convinced you bought them in the first place. That was a *very* convenient storm."

I ignore him, glancing at the window as the rain falls harder. Passersby start to run, the unlucky few without umbrellas holding jackets and purses aloft, trying to protect themselves from the downpour.

Paris, I remind myself. We're in Paris. I just wish I wasn't so jet-lagged and could care.

"We should go on a vacation," I say. "A real one."

"We can do that," he says, reading through the menu. "Where do you want to go?"

"Anywhere."

"Okay, that narrows it down."

I pick at my bread roll, restless as I watch him. He changed clothes back at the airport, switching his long-haul sweatpants and hoodie ensemble for jeans and a red sweater decorated in Christmas trees. It should be ridiculous, but he somehow pulls it off, the material fitted to his chest in a way that—

"You keep staring at me like that, I'm going to start charging," he murmurs, not looking up. I flush, caught red-handed as I take a sip of my water.

"I'm just not used to your stubble."

"Beard," he corrects. "It's an attractive and impressive beard."

"You can't see your dimple."

Andrew drops the menu onto the table, leaning back as his eyes flick to mine.

Uh-oh.

"You like my dimple?" he asks.

"I didn't say that. I just said you can't see it."

"And that upsets you, does it?"

"What are you getting to eat?" I ask, and he smirks at the warning in my voice.

"What are you getting?" he counters.

"The Andouillette grillée."

"And what's that when it's at home?"

"A sausage."

He makes a face. "Sausages freak me out."

"Which is why you should get the pesto tagliatelle," I say primly. "And then you're going to get the chocolate mousse."

"I've never been the biggest fan of mousse."

My mouth drops open. "That's a bald-faced lie. You love chocolate. Why wouldn't you like chocolate mousse?"

"I don't know, I went through a phase of buying those little pots from the grocery store and—"

"That's not the same," I interrupt, exasperated. "It will taste completely different here. Fresh, for a start. Hand-made. I read they add a little touch of lavender to— Stop looking at me like that!"

"I can't help it." He laughs. "You get so excited about whipped eggs."

"*Beaten* eggs." Christ, it's like he enjoys annoying me. "You beat eggs for a mousse. And not even eggs, egg whites. You beat them and then you fold them into—" I break off as my work phone rings again and I feel a surge of anger as I reach for it, thumb hovering for a second before I turn the thing off.

Oh, they're not going to like that.

"Molly?"

My gaze darts to Andrew, who's watching me with concern.

"I seriously don't mind if you need to take a call or—"

"I'm on vacation," I say sharply. "They know I'm on vacation." I shove the thing back into my bag, glancing at the laptop and folders inside. I have a brief, overwhelming urge to throw everything into the largest puddle I can find.

"I'm thinking about quitting," I say abruptly, and Andrew sits up in surprise.

"Your job? You want to go to another firm?"

"No, I want to get out completely. I want to stop practicing law." It's the first time I've said the words out loud. I haven't even said them to myself. But as soon as I do, I know it's the right decision. There's no panic, no sick feeling twisting in my gut. Only a sense of relief.

Andrew doesn't say anything for long moment, looking as though I've completely blindsided him. Which, I guess I have in a way. My job is all I've been since we first started getting to know each other. I've never given any indication otherwise.

"To do what?" he asks eventually.

"I have no idea."

To my surprise, he almost looks disappointed. "Come on, Moll. You have no idea what you want to do? Seriously?"

"I don't," I protest. "At least not realistically. I've had a look at—"

He stops me with a quiet laugh. "You just said it. 'At least not realistically.' So, you do know what you want to do."

"Oh, *sorry* if I'm taking supermodel and Hollywood socialite off the table at this time."

"They were never on the table, to begin with," he says flatly. "You hate any event that goes on past eleven p.m."

Okay, fair point.

"Tell me," he continues. "If money wasn't an issue. If

you woke up tomorrow with a brand-new life and you could do anything. What would you do?"

"That's the problem. I don't know."

"You're lying. It's something bohemian, isn't it?"

"Andrew—"

"You're going to start making hats."

"I don't know what I want to do," I repeat, frustrated. "I just know that right now I'm unhappy."

Going by his sudden scowl, it's the wrong thing to say. "How unhappy?"

"I'm not... it's..." Backtrack, Molly. Backtrack. "It's just something I've been thinking about. It's not like I'm handing in my notice tomorrow."

"Why not?"

"Because I'm not an idiot? Leaving without a plan would be a really dumb move financially. And even with one, it could be huge mistake. It's going to take a few years."

"A few..." He looks incredulous. "You've just admitted you're unhappy and now you're going to stay like that for, what? Five more years?"

"Not *five*," I mutter. Maybe three.

"Mistakes can be fixed," Andrew continues.

"They can also be prevented."

"I can't believe you're already talking yourself out of this."

"I'm not!"

"You are. You're—"

"Excusez-moi?"

It's at that moment our waiter chooses to appear, his pen poised over his notepad with that stressed air all service staff at Christmas have. Yet another reason to dislike the holidays.

The man hesitates, taking in our matching glares as we turn toward him. "Encore une petite minute?"

My eyes dart back to Andrew who waits a beat before pushing his menu to the side. "You pick," he says to me. "I trust you."

"Even if I order you the sausage?"

He smiles a little at that. A temporary truce. "I trust you not to order me the sausage," he amends, and lets me take charge, watching me thoughtfully as the rain falls in sheets outside.

CHAPTER ELEVEN

I order him the pasta, followed by the mousse, and we spend the meal going over the plan to get to Dublin and not talking about mistakes or jobs or anything beyond what the next twenty-four hours will bring.

We head back to the airport with hours to spare and are the first people at our gate. Andrew doesn't even risk going to the restroom, waiting until we board despite the fact he grows visibly uncomfortable as the minutes tick by. We take off five minutes early and there's hardly any wait for his suitcase on the other side. Everything goes smoothly.

And doesn't that just make me suspicious as hell?

"It's like you *want* something to go wrong," Andrew says as I double-check the sailing for tomorrow one final time.

"We should make a backup plan."

"This is our backup plan. We're here. The tickets are booked. The weather looks good. We'll be fine."

"The train could break down."

"Then we'll get a bus," he says firmly, and I nod despite the niggling feeling in my gut.

"Where does your cousin live anyway?" I ask as we make our way through the crowds outside Heathrow airport.

"He moves around a lot. But he's in Notting Hill right now."

I perk up at that. "Like the movie?"

"Exactly like the movie. You've been to London before, right?"

"Mam took my sister and me for a weekend when we were younger. We almost got separated on the Tube and I've never recovered from it."

"So *that's* why you scream every time you take the L."

I nod. "People think it's the screeching sound of the tracks, but no."

"Just your childhood trauma."

We wait in line for a taxi and end up with a blissfully silent driver who, other than saying hello, makes no attempt at conversation. And just like that, we're off on the next stage of our cursed adventure.

"We should try and see some stuff if we have time," Andrew says, peering out at the M4. West London passes by in a blur of cars and houses. "Especially since we didn't get to see Paris that much. I haven't been here in years."

"I don't think we'll have time."

"We will," he insists, glancing over at my reluctance. "We have all day."

"We'll see," I say in a perfect imitation of my mother. (It means "no.")

Our surroundings grow increasingly fancier as we leave the motorway and near Notting Hill. The houses lining the roads look finer, the cars slicker; shiny Teslas and SUVs that I don't think anyone really needs to navigate the narrow residential streets. My nose is practically glued to the window as I take it in, especially when we pull up outside a white terraced townhouse that looks like something out of *Mary Poppins*.

I am instantly confused.

"Is your family secretly rich?" I ask Andrew as we get out. London real estate isn't exactly cheap, though I know looks can be deceiving. Maybe the building has been split into tiny apartments and his cousin is subletting from a subletter who's squatting. But I don't think so. The place looks too maintained, the painted shutters and window boxes too matching. A tasteful string of lights hangs from the roof and a fat white candle sits in the window, waiting to be lit. "You have to tell me right now," I say as the cabbie drives off. "I'll know if you're lying."

Andrew only laughs. "We're not rich."

"But *someone* is," I insist.

At this, he hesitates. "Well—"

"Cousin!"

The front door flies open as a man emerges from the shadowy interior. He steps into the daylight in a thick burgundy dressing gown and matching slippers, both of which look out of place for the middle of the afternoon. Even at Christmas.

Oliver.

He's younger than I thought he would be, late twenties maybe, and handsome, with an angular acne-scarred face and a thick head of blond hair in desperate need of a cut. He almost seems surprised to see us, despite the fact he knew we were coming.

"We didn't mean to wake you," Andrew calls, only sounding a little sarcastic.

"You're referring to my outfit?" Oliver looks down at himself. "This is loungewear. I've been up for hours."

"That's because you didn't go to sleep."

He smiles ruefully. "You always were the smart one." Oliver waits until we've walked up the stone steps before hugging Andrew hard enough that he almost falls backward.

To my surprise, he does the same to me, wrapping his arms tightly around my body. He smells oddly like cinnamon and I don't hate it, but when he pulls back, I see that his eyes are bloodshot and suddenly his attire makes a little more sense.

"Late one last night?" Andrew asks, coming to the same conclusion.

Oliver pats him on the cheek. "'Tis the season," he says faintly. "Come in! My favorite Irish cousin and his beautiful Irish friend. Has Christian met her yet? She seems his type."

His voice fades as he disappears inside, not bothering to check if we're following. I glance at Andrew who's staring tiredly after him.

"Is he always—"

"Yes," Andrew sighs. His hand goes to the small of my back and he presses me forward into the house. "Yes, he is."

"I used to spend every summer in Cork," Oliver says when we enter. My eyes adjust to the dim light to find him standing on the bottom step of a stately, carpeted stairway. "Are you from Cork, Molly?"

"Dublin," I say, trying to glance around without being too obvious about it.

"I hated going to Cork. Weeks of constantly being made fun of for my English accent. Namely by this man."

"It was more of a family activity," Andrew tells me, and I try not to smile.

"He was my greatest bully," Oliver says, pointing to

him. "Except for the day one of the village kids tried to do the same and he punched him in the nose."

"What!" I turn to Andrew, who doesn't even have the decency to look ashamed.

"He had an excellent right hook," Oliver continues. "Even when he was ten."

"He's still family," Andrew says with a shrug. "We were the only ones allowed to make fun of him."

"That's not what I—" I glare at him. "You broke a kid's nose?"

"Fractured," he says as if that's any better.

"It was magnificent," Oliver adds fondly. "Well, then! Do you want a tour?"

Andrew stretches, eyeing his suitcase. "I think we'd rather—"

But Oliver is already off, shuffling into the next room, and despite my exhaustion, I hurry after him, too nosy not to.

I've been around rich people in my life, you meet them a lot in my line of work, new money and old, but this is next level. This is like... *movie* rich.

The house is small in the way I suspect most London homes are. The opulence is in the details, the ornate furniture, and polished floorboards, the vases of flowers and matching gold and silver Christmas decorations. They're classy and restrained but also make me scared to touch anything in case they immediately crack into a million pieces.

Oliver leads us through the living room and then another living room and then a goddamn *library* before the kitchen, dining room, and pantry that's almost the size of my bedroom in Chicago. Eventually we end up back where we started in the hall, where a grandfather clock I hadn't noticed chimes grandly.

"And now for the first floor!" Oliver declares, but this is where Andrew puts his foot down.

"Can we do this later, Oli? I need to stand under running water and stare at the wall until I feel normal."

"But the... Oh, alright," he says, obviously disappointed. "At least let me show you to your rooms. I've given you my favorite ones." He looks at him pointedly. "Because I'm nice."

Andrew wrestles with his suitcase as Oliver leads me up the stairs, pointing out the paintings that line the wall along the way.

"How do you feel about floral patterns?" he asks when we reach the top.

"I feel completely neutral about them."

"Wonderful!" He throws open a door and gestures me grandly inside.

It is, by far, nicer than any hotel room I've ever stayed in. It's really the size of two rooms with large windows over-looking the street below. A four-poster bed dominates the space and the wallpaper is indeed floral, as is the bedspread, the upholstery on the chair, and the love seat that's placed against the window. A solemn, possibly haunted closet takes up the other wall, and to my right by the bed is a door that I'm guessing leads to an en suite or maybe the chamber-maid's room because honestly who knows. It should be stuffy, maybe a little old-fashioned, but there's a charm to it I didn't expect. One that makes me feel instantly comfortable.

"Do you like it?" Oliver asks.

"I like all of it," I confess. "You have a beautiful home."

He beams, delighted with my response. "I'll leave you to

get settled. Let me know if you need anything!" His voice echoes at the last bit, already vanished down the hall, and I take a moment to inhale, breathing in the scent of furniture polish. As I do, I slip my coat off and step farther into the room, running a hand down the thick quilt cover.

What a weird twenty-four hours.

"Looks comfy."

I spin around at Andrew's voice to find him standing in the doorway, gazing at the bed.

He gives me an innocent look and leaves my laptop bag just inside my door. I hesitate only briefly before following him out to his own room, which turns out to be directly next to mine.

"From the way he spoke about your childhood, I thought he would have put you in the attic," I say.

"The attic here is probably bigger than my entire apartment."

I glance around, taking it all in. It's just as nice as mine, but with a stereotypically more masculine feel, all dark wood and navy shades of wallpaper. It's also...

"Smaller," I say promptly, glancing around. "Your room is smaller. I win."

"Congratulations." He unzips his case, his attention annoyingly not on me.

"I can't believe you didn't tell me your cousin's rich."

"He's not."

"Please. This place is like something out of a storybook." I cross my arms when Andrew fails to suppress a smile, smirking to himself like there's some joke I'm not in on. "What?"

"It's not his."

"What do you mean?"

"This isn't his house, Moll."

Oh, God. "Please don't tell me we're squatting in—"

"No." He cuts me off as he straightens, a washbag in his hands. "A police officer is not going to come knocking on the door. At least not for that. Oliver is a gallery assistant at some tiny, ridiculous place in Mayfair. This is the owner's house. Or one of them anyway."

"He lives with the owner?" My voice drops to a whisper. "Is it, like, a sex thing?"

"Would you— No." He laughs. "The *owner* is a seventy-five-year-old man with dubious royal connections who stays on some Greek island during the winter because he can't stand the cold. He doesn't like the place being empty when he's gone and is convinced someone's going to steal all his artwork so, for the past three years when he's not here, Oliver stays."

"That's *nuts.*"

"It could only happen to Oli," Andrew agrees, laying out a fresh pair of jeans on the bed. "Just don't tell him I told you, okay? He thought it would be fun to pretend. He always wants a little drama."

"Well, who am I to spoil his Christmas?"

Andrew just nods, continuing to sort through his clothes until my presence becomes awkward lingering.

"I might take a nap," I announce, lacing my hands behind my back.

"Go for it."

"I'm pretty tired."

"I bet."

"Then maybe after I'll— What are you doing?" I blurt the words out as Andrew pulls his sweater *and* T-shirt up over his head. My eyes immediately drop to his bare chest before I snap them back to his face.

"Undressing."

"Why!"

He looks at me like I'm crazy. "Because I'm going to have a shower." He reaches for his belt buckle, one brow raised when I just stand there. "I can put on a show if you—"

"I'm going!" I say, ignoring his smirk, and I spin out of the room, slamming the door shut behind me.

CHAPTER TWELVE

FOUR YEARS AGO

Flight Six, Chicago

"Don't go."

"I have to go."

"Then let me come with you."

"No." I spin around, laughing when I'm met with a pouting face. "Since when did you get so clingy?" I tease.

Mark steps toward me, his hands going to my waist. "Since you're going to be away from me for two weeks."

"One week," I correct. "You're the one that's making it two."

"So come see me when you're done. My family won't mind."

"I need to work."

"And I need to see you." His voice drops to a murmur and I lean into his touch as he kisses me. It's not that I don't understand his insistence. This will be our first proper break apart since we made things official and I'm not exactly looking forward to it either.

Mark breaks the kiss, hands sliding around my hips to hold me against him.

"I love you."

"I love you too," I say, smiling against his lips.

His grip tightens. "Let me go with you."

"Maybe next year. Or we could—" I break off as someone clears their throat loudly behind me and I turn awkwardly in Mark's arms to find Andrew standing a few feet away.

He is, bizarrely, dressed in a suit, and I stare at him for a moment before I remember that he said he'd be coming straight from a wedding gig.

"Oh, don't let me interrupt," he says, his amusement clear. "Just feeling a little phlegmy today."

I give him a look as I pry myself away from my boyfriend, hoisting my backpack over my shoulder.

"You're early."

"Yes. You must be Mark." Andrew strides the two steps toward us, holding out his hand.

"And you're the friend," Mark says as he clasps it.

"To all that will have me. Andrew."

"Nice to meet you."

The shake goes on a little longer than necessary and I find my eyes drifting back to Andrew. He looks different, all clean cut and dressed up. His suit is deep blue, his shoes a polished brown and there's a faint hint of stubble along his jaw that makes him more handsome than boyish. More grown-up than I've ever seen him.

"Where's Alison?" I ask, tearing my gaze away to look for his new girlfriend.

"Oh, we're not at the accompany-the-partner-to-the-airport stage of the relationship yet," Andrew says. "Though she says if I'm good I might be able to start holding her hand by the spring, so fingers crossed."

"He likes to make jokes," I explain to a frowning Mark.

"Sure," Mark says, still sounding confused, and I turn back to him before this can get any more awkward.

"We should probably head through. It's getting busy."

"You've got some time."

"I need to do some shopping," I lie as Andrew wanders a few steps away, pretending to give us privacy.

"Call me when you land?"

"It will be the middle of the night!"

"I don't care. I'll stay up." He kisses me again as his hands drift lower, grabbing a quick squeeze that I swiftly pull away from, glancing at Andrew who's miraculously not looking our way. It's another minute of "I love you"s and "I'll miss you"s before I finally convince him to leave, and even then he stays exactly where he is, watching us walk toward security. Andrew stays quiet, which makes me *very* suspicious, and sure enough, as soon we round the corner, he turns to me.

"Don't," I warn him.

"Don't what? Talk about how nice your new boyfriend is?"

"Shut up."

"He's very nice. And so tall."

"Andrew—"

"Clearly an ass man though."

My face heats as a woman in the line beside us glances our way. "Are you going to be like this the entire flight?" I ask tersely.

"If you keep reacting like that, I will," he says with a grin. "I think I made him jealous."

"I think you think very highly of yourself."

"Oh, come on. That man was clearly marking his territory back there."

"He was not!"

"He was five minutes away from pissing on your leg."

I try to hold back my laugh, but that turns it into a snort, which only makes him smile harder.

"I can't help that I inspire such possessiveness in people," I finally say.

"Must be the hair."

"Stop."

"I mean it. It's very chic. You cut it yourself?"

I hit him with one hand while the other tugs self-consciously on my newly shorn strands.

"It suits you," he says, spotting the movement.

"Yeah?"

"Yeah. Really shows off your ears."

I scowl at him before I turn to face the front. "I hate you."

"No, you don't," he says, bumping gently into me from behind. "And that man is completely in love with you."

I glance over my shoulder to find that this time he's not joking. My lips twitch as I try to hold my frown against the sudden burst of happiness at his words.

"Whatever," I say, catching the start of his grin before I turn back around.

———

Now, London

Gabriela calls me five minutes after I shut myself in my room. I spend those five minutes analyzing every word Andrew's ever said to me and trying to remember the exact tone of his voice when he told me my dress looked nice one year, so when the call comes through, I'm so relieved for the distraction, I could cry.

"They lost my bag!"

"Who did?" she demands like she's going to come straight over and beat them up for me.

"Argentina." I collapse back onto the bed, my body immediately sinking into the soft mattress. "They lost it and we missed our flight to Dublin so now we're in London and we're staying with Andrew's fake-rich cousin for the night."

"*Fun.* How fake-rich?"

"He lives in his boss's mansion and his name is Oliver."

"Shut up." She sighs. "When are you flying to Ireland?"

"We're not," I say, staring up at the ceiling. "We're getting the ferry."

"*Cute.*"

"Long," I correct. "The ferry goes from Wales, which means we have to get a train there in the morning. And then Andrew has another bus from Dublin. We're both already exhausted. I'll be surprised if he doesn't sleep through Christmas at this stage."

"Is he okay?"

"He's... fine."

There's a long pause at the other end of the line as she probably reads a million things into my hesitation. And then: "What happened?"

"Nothing."

"Oh my God."

"*Nothing!*"

"That's your something voice," she says. "I knew something was up. I *knew* it."

"That's not why I was—" I sigh, rubbing my eyes. "That's a whole different thing."

"Oh, we are having the biggest lunch date when you get back. We're going to order some crab salad from Morillo's and lock ourselves in the east meeting room and you are not coming out until you tell me everything. In fact—"

"He kissed me."

Gabriela immediately stops talking, like all the air's been sucked from her lungs by my words. "Who did?"

"Andrew!" I roll over so I'm faceplanting into the mattress. "Twice."

"*Twice?*"

"I guess technically I was the one that kissed him. There was mistletoe the first time."

"Okay."

"And it kind of threw me. Because I was all, oh, friendly mistletoe kiss between friends because we're friends—"

"Sure."

"—But then it was *not* that. And then in Argentina, he followed me to the restroom—"

"He *what?*"

"It's less creepy than it sounds," I assure her, twirling a strand of hair so tight around my finger that it hurts. "Anyway, he followed me and we kissed again."

"In the restroom?"

"In the hallway *outside* the restroom. Because I told him that the first kiss messed me up and he said we should try it again, so we tried it again."

"Molly." She sounds extremely disappointed in me. "That's such a line."

"It only sounds like one."

"Because it is one!" She mutters something under her breath and I picture her pacing up and down the office. A quick check of the time tells me it's four p.m. London time, which means it's ten a.m. Chicago time and I feel a familiar stab of guilt. I haven't responded to a single email since we left Buenos Aires.

"What are you going to do?"

"I was hoping you would tell me."

"Do you like him like that?"

"I don't know. Maybe. But what if that's exhaustion? What if it's stress and exhaustion and instead of manifesting a gray hair or a nose pimple, it's made me super horny?"

"Or what if you're just super dumb and you've never realized what's right in front of you?"

I flip onto my back, closing my eyes. Somewhere in the house, soft jazz music begins to play because of course it does.

Am I dumb? Sometimes obviously, but this time I don't think so. There have been times when we've both been single, but even then...

I frown as I think back to his previous girlfriends. A bunch of perfectly nice women (give or take) whose Instagrams I definitely stalked for at least a few minutes when they were together. And when they were together, they were *together*. Photos of them on vacation and at parties with friends. At thrift stores and cafés and parks. They never seemed like the kind of people who would cancel plans because they had to go to work on a Sunday.

They would have put him first.

I don't think I've ever put a partner first. And I tended to date people who understood that and did the same. I didn't want to move to Seattle with Brandon. But he didn't want to stay in Chicago with me. Is that why I've never thought about Andrew like that before? Why I've never even let myself *think* it? Because I knew I wouldn't be able to give him the attention he deserved and I didn't want to do that to him?

Because I knew I could never put him first. And it's only when I decided to make a different life for myself that I...

"Hey, Gab?" I sit up, drawing my knees to my chest. "If you didn't get into law school, what would you have done?"

"Change of subject much?"

"Indulge me."

She makes an unhappy sound, but she does. "I don't know. Probably I'd have had a breakdown, dyed my hair and tried again."

"No, I mean if you weren't a lawyer. If for whatever reason you couldn't have this career, what would you do?"

"Oh, that's easy," she dismisses. "Probably the violin thing."

"The vio... You play the violin?"

"Yep."

"Since *when?*"

"Since I was five?" She laughs. "I wanted to be in an orchestra. I still get lessons once a week. Helps me calm down."

"How do you have the time?"

"Asks the girl who once did a three-hour round trip on a Monday night because she read about a food truck she wanted to try. Same as you, Moll. I make the time. You always make the time when you want to. That's why you're traveling around the world right now, isn't it?" She pauses, her voice turning so casual that it's almost funny. "Why?" she asks. "What would you have done?"

"I don't know."

"But it's something you've been thinking about?" she presses lightly.

"Maybe."

There's a bang on her end, like she's hit her desk in

triumph. "I totally called it! Something's wrong. Something's wrong and I knew it because I'm attuned to you."

"Gab—"

"Because of our close bond."

"Are you going to let me talk or what?"

"Talk. I'm listening. Tell me everything. What are you thinking?"

I bite back a smile even as the urge to lie threatens to take over. "I *think*," I begin, "that I decided to become a lawyer when I was sixteen years old because it sounded impressive and was an acceptable thing to want to be. And now I think I've spent a third of my life devoted to a career that I don't even like that much."

"At all?"

"I like *you*," I say, dropping back to the mattress. "I like the competitiveness. I like the adrenaline kick when we close a deal and I like having the cash to buy nice things and that my family is proud of me because I've got a good job and a good life. But the thought of looking ahead five, ten, fifteen years from now and seeing myself in the same office at two a.m. on a Tuesday makes me want to cry."

"Jesus, Molly. Is that what this is about? You want to quit?"

"I've been thinking about it. But I don't know if I'm ready yet."

Gabriela goes quiet and I gear myself up for her counterargument, which is why I'm so surprised by her next words. "Then I'll help you."

"You will?"

"Yes," she says determinedly. "Women help women. I will help you quit. I'll take you to a life coach. We'll make some lists. I'll teach you the violin."

I laugh. "I thought you'd try and talk me out of it."

"Are you kidding me? I need new non-lawyer friends, Molly. This is a blessing." She pauses. "Is that why you didn't tell me?"

"That and I'm still figuring it out for myself."

"No, you've decided," she says. "I can hear it in your voice even if you can't. But this is good! This is a project. You know I love projects."

"I do," I say. "I'm not going to look at my email until I get back."

"Good. Screw them."

"But *you* can text me if you need me."

"Okay, thank God," she says in rush. "Spencer's still out. Who gets mono anymore? Seriously."

I grin, feeling a bit of the weight I'd been carrying around lift. Two people down, only everyone else in my life to go. "It feels realer when I talk about it. Less scary."

"I also feel like I'm helping? Which makes me feel good, so it's a win for both of us."

I go to reply when my phone buzzes with a text by my ear.

"If it's anyone from the team, just send them to me," she says as she hears it too. "The revolution starts now."

"It's Andrew," I say, checking the message.

Oliver says you can help yourself to anything in the kitchen if you're hungry. I told him you're always hungry.

"I said I was taking a nap. He probably thinks I'm asleep."

"Ah yes, your other issue."

"He's not an issue."

"A conundrum, then."

"Gabriela—"

"I mean, we're on such a roll now, we might as well keep going. He's not seeing anyone, is he?"

"No," I say reluctantly. "He was, but they broke up during the summer."

"And you haven't been with anyone seriously since Brandon."

"No."

"So I say, why not explore?"

"Because what happens if he kisses me again and I hate it?" I ask. "And then it's ruined. A perfectly good friendship gone just like that."

"What if that doesn't happen and instead the kiss leads to mind-blowing sex and becomes the best decision you ever made? I think you need to talk to him seriously about this. Maybe he's freaking out too."

"He doesn't look like he's freaking out," I grumble, plucking at a loose thread on the bedspread. "He's acting like the whole thing is funny. Like it's a joke."

"Molly, I don't know him, but I guarantee you no one would think kissing you is a joke." Her voice hardens. "In *fact*, if he says even *one* thing to make you feel—"

"Alright," I cut her off. "Thank you, babe."

"You're a catch, you hear me?"

"I do," I say dryly, but I smile. "But right now, I think I actually need to have that nap. Jet lag is not fun."

"Okay, but if you have any more problems about *anything* at all—"

"I will come to you. I will confide."

"That's my girl."

We say our goodbyes and I hang up. I do nap, but it only makes me feel worse and I wake forty minutes later with a dry mouth, a growling stomach, and the beginnings of a headache. With that added grossness on top of my plane grossness, I decide to check out the shower for the first time. There's a neatly folded towel on the vanity so I grab that and the toiletries left by the sink and hope to God there's hot water. There is.

And it is *blissful*.

The water pressure is what I imagine those shampoo commercial waterfalls must feel like and I stay there for way too long. I even do a deep conditioner but have no choice other than to let my hair dry naturally seeing as I can't find a hairdryer in the room. I *do* find a handheld clothes steamer though, which I immediately put to use unwrinkling everything I bought in Paris and having way too much fun doing it.

I'm working on the pillowcase just for kicks when there's a knock on the door and I open it to find Andrew on the other side, dressed like he's about to head out.

"What are you doing?" I ask, nodding at his coat.

"What are *you* doing?" he counters. He stares at my steamer like it's a space gun from a cheap sci-fi movie.

"I found it under the bed. Just because we're traveling doesn't mean we have to show up all wrinkly. If you ask nicely, I'll steam your stuff too."

He slumps against the doorframe. "I'm trying desperately to think of a way to twist that into an innuendo."

"And you've got nothing?"

"I've had a long day. And to answer your question, I'm going out and so are you. Oliver suggested we go soak up the atmosphere."

"Now?"

He pauses at the disbelief in my voice. "You don't want to see London at Christmas?"

"You mean go see an already overcrowded city at one of the busiest times of the year? No. It will be full of tourists."

"We *are* tourists." He grins as I unplug the steamer. "It's just for an hour."

"We have to be up early."

"And we will be. Tell me the last time you slept in past eight a.m."

I open my mouth, but the man has a point.

"Look," he continues, seeing my hesitation. "You can stay here by yourself and... steam, but I'm going to get a hot chocolate." He pinches his fingers together. "With a little bit of cinnamon. And three marshmallows. We deserve to have some fun."

I sigh, glancing at the bed. I wish I was sleepy, but I'm not. I'm wide awake and growing restless. And he knows it.

"An hour?" I ask.

"Tops."

"Fine." I start to shrug my robe from my shoulders and his smile disappears. It's at that moment I remember I have nothing but a bra on underneath. Everything else was getting steamed.

"Okay," I snap, pulling it back on. "Sorry to tantalize you with my bold display of skin."

Andrew recovers just as quickly, his grin back in place. "So, you're tantalizing now, are you?"

"And with that comment, I'm not steaming your clothes. I hope you're happy with yourself." I point to the door and he straightens, hands in the air.

"I'll see you downstairs," he calls, swinging the door shut behind him. "Preferably clothed."

CHAPTER THIRTEEN

I stay in my new pair of jeans but put on a fresh T-shirt under my Christmas sweater. I don't bother doing anything with my hair, leaving it damp around my shoulders and risking the chill. I still have Andrew's scarf from when he gave it to me in Chicago and, after a moment's hesitation, I wrap it around my neck and tuck it into my coat.

Oliver and Andrew are waiting for me by the front door when I come down. Oliver's dressed like he's going to some fancy restaurant and Andrew is dressed like Andrew. He's swapped his heavy Chicago coat for one of Oliver's and his camera bag is slung over one shoulder. I try not to stare at him as I come down, but I don't miss the way his eyes flick to his scarf when I appear. I expect him to ask for it back, but a hint of satisfaction flickers across his face, as though he's pleased to see me wearing it.

"Beautiful!" Oliver declares when I hit the bottom step. "You descend the stairs like you were born to."

"Huh?"

Andrew just shakes his head as Oliver picks up a black backpack I hadn't noticed before.

"Where exactly are we going?" I ask as he tugs it on.

"I thought we could see the lights," he says vaguely. "And then I have one quick pit stop to make so I can drop something off and then... pub?"

The thought of a cozy English pub where I can plonk myself next to a fire isn't the worst idea in the world, but I glance at Andrew, ready to say no. He's expecting it and just winks at me, before giving a look that says, *I told you it was fine.* And he did, but still, there's no need to make it any harder on the man. With everything that's happened in the last few days, he's probably hoping I've forgotten all about his casual "I'm sober now" bomb, but it's something we're going to have to talk about at some point.

Now, however, is not that time and so I try and push it from my mind as Oliver shepherds us out the door. As soon as we hit Portobello Road, I see instantly what he means by "lights." I hadn't noticed the decorations in the taxi, mostly because it was daytime, and they were all off. But now the narrow, winding streets are lit up. Strings of fairy lights crisscross overhead and the houses get solidly merrier as we move away from the extremely posh to the moderately posh. Warm golden glows give way to multicolored bonanzas that I can't help but smile at as we make our way slowly through the crowds.

Oliver doesn't seem in a rush and is practically indulgent as he lets Andrew take pictures of the houses and storefronts, the packed restaurants, and pubs. He even makes him take pictures of him, posing regally around the town until Andrew threatens to only send him the bad ones.

Oliver's kind of hilarious. Just on the edge of annoying. But he seems genuinely happy to have Andrew there and me by extension, asking about my life in Chicago and my childhood in Dublin, as well as buying me a fragrant mulled wine from one of the stalls dotted around. It's the first bit of Christmas fun that I could see myself getting used to and the way Andrew keeps smiling at me every time Oliver makes me laugh makes it all the better.

Eventually, we leave the brightly lit streets behind, moving into a quieter, more residential area. It's not as fancy as where Oliver is staying, I can tell most of these houses are split into separate apartments, but it's nice and peaceful and, through the open curtains of many rooms, I spy young families and groups of friends sitting around dining tables. I assume he's taking us to some small neighborhood pub, and so am surprised when he comes to a stop in front of a tiny red-brick house halfway down the street.

It's at the end of a small row of houses, with a narrow alleyway in between it and its neighbor. Unlike all the others we've passed, it's completely dark, with no car parked outside.

"We're here," he announces, turning to us with a smile.

"We're where?" Andrew asks, and I'm glad I'm not the only one confused. "Are you house-sitting this one too?"

"Oh no," Oliver says cheerfully. "This one I'm breaking into."

"You're— What?" Andrew hisses the last word as his cousin takes off down the alleyway, vanishing into the shadows. "Oliver!"

"He's obviously joking," I say, but Andrew doesn't seem to think so.

"Stay here," he mutters as he heads after him, but to hell with that. I ignore his annoyed look as I follow them both into the darkness, my eyes adjusting in time to see Oliver toss his backpack over a tall brick wall that blocks off what must be the backyard.

"Explain," Andrew says, catching him by the elbow before he can go any farther. "Now."

Oliver gives a world-weary sigh and shrugs him off. "You used to be fun, you know that?"

"I'm telling Aunt Rachel," Andrew warns, but Oliver just rolls his eyes and then, before I can so much as blink, takes a step back and leaps, grabbing hold of the top of the wall and pulling himself nimbly up before disappearing down the other side.

"Are you coming?" he calls way too loudly. Andrew looks horrified, but I feel a thrill shoot through me. Even though I just met the man, he's Andrew's cousin and I highly doubt that whatever we're doing is that illegal or dangerous.

I mean, maybe it's *slightly* illegal.

And maybe it's the mulled wine or maybe it's because I'm having a surprisingly nice time, but whatever it is, I'm feeling a little reckless tonight.

"I dare you," I say, and Andrew scoffs. But he knows he doesn't really have a choice and so, with a final pointed glare at me, copies his cousin's movement and jumps. He manages impressively well, while my effort is less graceful. I've never done anything like it before and there's a moment when I'm straddling the top of the wall where I'm pretty sure I'm going to simply fall down the other side, but Andrew lingers below and helps me climb down while my arms shake like Jell-O.

"Nice one," Oliver cheers as I dust off my sore, slightly grazed hands and look around. We're in a small, pleasantly overgrown backyard, the patch of grass illuminated dimly by the lights coming from the surrounding homes. But through the windows of the veranda doors, the house looks as it did from the front, empty and dark.

"Are we really breaking in?" I ask.

Andrew huffs. "We're not breaking in."

"We're kind of breaking in," Oliver says, making his way to the stone patio bracketing the back of the house. "But we're leaving things, not taking things. And we'll be fine. This is a nice neighborhood. They probably think we're cleaners."

I follow him to the conservatory, picking my way through the withered winter flower beds while Andrew remains tense by the wall.

"Are you going to smash the window in?" I ask, worried.

"Of course not," Oliver says, gazing at the various garden pots dotted around us. "We're going to find the key." He kneels abruptly beside a small terracotta one, picking it up. "It must be under— No." He reaches for the blue one next to it. "This one looks— No."

Andrew's mood grows increasingly worse as Oliver uses the torch on his phone to look through the shrubs.

It seems a little too obvious to me, but I leave him to it as I take a closer look at my surroundings. The place is cared for, despite the wild look about it. Beside a weathered bench, there's a covered barbecue and a small table and chairs. Butterflies made of colored glass dangle on the walls and the grass looks like it's been mowed recently. In fact, the whole garden is mostly swept clear of debris and leaves... except for a few pointedly arranged ones around the gutter.

"Molly," Andrew says in a warning tone as I wander off, but I'm like a hound catching a scent. I did a lot of team-building days during my various internships. Escape rooms are nothing new to me.

"Don't encourage him," he continues.

"Why are you in such a bad mood?" I ask, crouching beside the drain.

"I'm not."

I don't even bother to reply as I copy Oliver with my torch, plucking out the leaves. They're muddied and gross, but it doesn't take long to find a discarded metal tin of mints, hidden at the bottom. Bingo.

Oliver is by my shoulder in an instant. "Excellent work. You get a prize."

"I do?"

"Don't encourage *her* either," Andrew says as he joins us. Oliver wipes the key clean on Andrew's sleeve before Andrew can stop him and hurries back to unlock the door. A flick of his wrist and it swings open and for two seconds the three of us simply stare inside before a loud beeping starts.

Oliver strides inside and I follow, too caught up in it all to stop.

Maybe I should become a criminal? Some kind of mysterious jewel thief.

I enter a tiny kitchen that leads into an open-plan living room. Oliver strides through it as though he's been here a million times before and I go after him, with Andrew so close he bumps into me at every step, as though getting ready to grab me and flee.

"We have twenty seconds to figure this out," Oliver says, coming to a stop in the small entranceway beside the door. He flicks open the lid to the beeping alarm and cracks his knuckles. "Pick a number between one and nine."

Andrew makes a choking sound behind me. "Are you serious?"

"Of course not." His fingers fly across the pad, promptly shutting the beeping off. "You're too easy to annoy this evening, you know that?"

"Not as easy as you'll be to *murder*," Andrew snaps, and

I wrap a hand around his wrist, squeezing briefly. I have no idea what's gotten into him.

"Is this your real house?" I ask suspiciously. Oliver laughs, slipping past us back into the living room. Like the yard, it's a little messy, just as all homes should be, but yet it feels empty. Even more so with the small, bare tree in the corner as though the owner had put it up and didn't have time to do anything more.

"Who lives here?" I ask, gazing at a photo near me. A tall woman with curly black hair beams out at me, standing in front of the Eiffel Tower.

"Lara," Oliver says casually.

"And who is Lara?" Andrew asks when he doesn't explain further.

Oliver glances between us before he settles back on Andrew with a pleasant smile. "My Molly." He drops his backpack to the ground as Andrew's face creases in confusion. Like a clown pulling out a string of handkerchiefs from his pocket, he proceeds to unravel handfuls of homemade Christmas bunting. "You're tall," he adds. "You're in charge of hanging."

"Oliver—"

"We went to uni together," he interrupts. "During Freshers' week, I got drunk and tried to jump off the science building into the lake. She called me an idiot and kneed me in my unmentionables to stop me. We've been best friends ever since." He looks up, his expression unnervingly serious. "Lara loves Christmas and usually has the best-decorated house on the street, but this year her mother is sick and so she is in Berlin by her bedside, where she has been for the past three weeks. They're both coming back tomorrow and I can't have her return to an empty, cold house. I simply refuse. And so here we are, decorating it like we're trying to win a daytime reality TV show." He hesitates. "If you'll help me, that is."

Oh my God. I glance at Andrew with a pleading look that has him rolling his eyes.

"You don't even like decorations."

"Now I do."

He turns to Oliver, ignoring me. "You could have just told us this."

It's Oliver's turn to look confused. "But that wouldn't have been as fun."

"Oliver, I swear to—"

"A compromise," he interrupts, glancing at his watch. "Seeing as how we're short on time. Thirty minutes tops. Let's see how much we can get done."

I pull out a bag of snowflake confetti. "Like a game?"

Andrew drops his head back with a groan, but Oliver just nods, pleased at my interest. "Exactly. I'll even set a timer."

"Christ." Andrew sighs, taking one look at my face and knowing I'm a goner. I don't really know what the big deal is. This kind of thing seems right up his street, but his scowl only deepens as he straps his camera bag tighter to his chest and looks at his cousin. "Where do we start?"

After a brief discussion, we agree to play to our strengths and I'm put in the charge of the kitchen. Oliver passes me small boxes of party food from the local supermarket, along with novelty cakes and cookies. I put everything away in their respective places, but can't help but arrange a few plates ready to be eaten for tomorrow. Sparkling apple cider and wine complete the edible portion of the décor and, by the time I turn back to the front room, the place has been transformed.

The bunting hangs cheerfully over the open fireplace

along with dozens of fairy lights emitting a soft, warm glow. A different, colored set is strung around the tree, which Andrew is in the middle of decorating, a look of fierce concentration on his face as he tries to space out the baubles. Oliver is on stocking duty, stuffing the two he's taped to the mantlepiece with more treats.

I'm not exactly experienced in this kind of thing, but figure it can't be too hard and do my best with the last of the decorations, little Santa Claus figurines and glittering snowflakes. By the time we're done, the place couldn't look more different than where Oliver's staying. The ornaments are mismatched both in tone and style, giving the room a chaotic feel, but one that can't help but make you smile. It looks like a festive fever dream. It should be my nightmare, but it's kind of... fun. Not that I'm going to tell Andrew that.

"I'm taking all the credit, by the way," Oliver says as he stuffs the leftover packaging back into his bag. "Neither of you were here. All me."

"What a surprise." Andrew straightens from where he sits by the window. "Happy?" he asks.

"Deliriously so. Just one final thing." Gently, almost reverently, he places one small, wrapped present under the tree, arranging the tag just so. *To Lara*, it says and knowing what he got her immediately becomes the most important thing in my entire life. Against all odds, I manage to keep my mouth shut.

"Thank you very much for all your help," he says after a moment. "Even if I did initially trick you into it."

I nudge Andrew with my elbow and he sighs.

"We're happy to help," he says, only a little reluctantly. "Though next time, I'd prefer if you—"

He breaks off as flashing blue lights sweep suddenly across the front room. "Oliver—"

"Alright!" Oliver claps his hands together, ushering us toward the back door. "All done."

"You said—"

"Time to go!" he says cheerfully, turning back to set the alarm.

Andrew and I make a beeline for the yard where he gives me a leg up the wall. Twenty seconds later Oliver joins us and walks briskly down the lane, leaving us to follow. I glance a few times behind us, apparently just to make sure I look extra suspicious, but no one comes chasing after us and no sirens start blaring. We're safe, even if Andrew is back to looking agitated again.

No one speaks until we reach the next street, at which point Oliver comes to a sudden stop, rubbing his hands together.

"Right then!" he says. "Thanks for that. Pub?"

Andrew shakes his head. "We're going home."

"What?" Oliver sounds aghast. "Why?"

"Because I don't trust you tonight."

"What are you talking about? It went fine."

"We're going to back to the house," Andrew says firmly. "We're up early."

Oliver turns to me for backup but all I can offer is a sympathetic smile.

"Fine," he sighs. "I guess I'll go find some like-minded people."

"You do that," Andrew says, steering me firmly into the direction we came.

Oliver catcalls us for another few moments before he gives up and, when I glance over my shoulder, I see him walking the other way.

"That was kind of fun," I say. Andrew only grunts. "Are all your family like that?"

"Just him."

"All my family are boring. The only black sheep we have is my aunt who has an Etsy store for her bracelets." He doesn't answer and, not for the first time that evening, I find myself ticked off at his sudden change in attitude.

"Would you stop?" I ask. "I've never seen you this grumpy before."

"I'm fine."

"You sound like me," I tell him. "What is it?"

He shakes his head, jaw still clenched tight as he glances back the way we came. "He could have gotten us into trouble. He should have told us what was going on."

"He was just messing with you."

"If the police had knocked on the door—"

"They would have contacted Lara," I say. "It would have been fine."

But it might not have been. It's only then I realize what he means. By the time they contacted Lara, chances are we would be stuck in a police station somewhere, very much missing our window to get home. And while that hadn't even occurred to me, of course, it would have been at the forefront of Andrew's mind. Of course, he would have been worried about getting over another hurdle to see his family.

Guilt trickles through me as he opens the map on his phone, searching for the quickest way to Oliver's place. My mind wavers for only an instant before I make it up.

"Why don't we stay out?"

He doesn't even spare me a glance. "You're the one who wanted to stay in."

"Yeah, but I'm awake now. And the night is young. Let's go explore the city."

"The night is young?" He looks up and I can tell he's

suspicious at my change of heart. "I thought you didn't like London at Christmas."

"All the more reason to prove me wrong."

"Molly—"

"Come on. Just for an hour. Before I get tired and cranky. Like you."

"Funny," he says, but he moves when I tug on his arm and lead him toward the station.

CHAPTER FOURTEEN

Andrew relaxes the farther we travel into central London and by the time we get off at a crowded Westminster station, he's back to his usual self, grinning at the crowds of holiday tourists around us. I hadn't planned any further than "go to the city, find something dipped in sugar" and after one disorienting moment, we decide to follow everyone else crossing the bridge beside Big Ben, where we soon spy a Christmas market on the south bank of the river.

It's kitschy, even for Andrew, with quaint mom-and-pop stalls filled with sweet treats and plastic trinkets that don't fool me as authentic for a second. But I guess it's not the worst place to be on a clear December evening. It's busy, but not so busy that we can't move around, and once we get past the stalls there are benches to sit at and games to play. A classic carousel spins shrieking children and their indulgent parents around and around, and Christmas pop music plays over the speakers, one hit song after the next.

I buy us both a bag of churros and Andrew his promised hot chocolate as we walk along the Thames and I'm feeling weirdly content and perfectly comfortable, so I don't even think when the next words pop out of my mouth.

"This would be a great date night." I go still as soon as I say it, only to double down when Andrew turns to me with a smirk. "It would!"

"Is that what we're doing?"

"*No*," I say childishly, but then, with my conversation with Gabriela echoing through my mind: "Maybe."

Andrew's expression doesn't change, but it takes a moment for him to look away. "This isn't a date," he says. "I wouldn't take you somewhere Christmassy on a date."

"Where would you take me?"

"I haven't thought about it."

"You've thought about it enough that you know you wouldn't take me here," I point out and I know I've caught him when he goes quiet. "Tell me," I say, and I shake the churros before him like a bribe. He snatches one in his hand, examining it for a second before he eats half of it in one bite. Men.

"Okay," he says as we keep walking. "I guess it's more of what you don't like rather than what you do like."

"And what don't I like?"

"Picnics."

"I like picnics," I protest. "I just don't like insects. Which picnics usually involve."

"You also don't like sitting in the sun."

"I burn."

"Or paper plates."

"They're flimsy."

"You don't like picnics," he concludes. "You *do* like the cinema, so I could take you to some old fancy movie and pay crazy ticket prices, but I've never liked things like that for a first date. Why waste an evening sitting in silence when I could be talking to you instead?"

"So, that rules out the theater."

"Which is handy seeing as you also hate the theater."

"Now, see, I don't hate the theater. What I hate are places that don't let you pee when you need to pee. And sometimes you've just got to sneeze. I mean, I'm sorry it's your big dumb monologue, but you can't hold something like that in. It damages your brain."

"No, it doesn't."

"Yes, it does. I read it online."

"No theater," he says. "Museums and galleries are tough. Everyone has their own pace and they can be tiring too. A bookshop can be romantic, but you don't read—"

"I read!" Sometimes.

"Hikes and walks, you're back to the pace thing. Plus, the sun, the insects."

"Plenty of places to pee though."

"True. If the weather's nice we could go to the water, but again the—"

"I get it," I interrupt flatly. "I'm undatable."

"I didn't say that." He eats the other half of his churro and I'm so distracted by a fleck of sugar at the corner of his mouth that I almost miss his next words. "Ax throwing."

"Ax... what?"

"I would take you ax throwing," he says.

I stare at him. "What the hell is ax throwing?"

"Exactly what—"

"It sounds like," I finish. "Alright, Mr. Smart-Ass. That doesn't seem very romantic."

"Have you ever been?"

"Obviously not."

"You get these little axes and these round blocks of

wood, like archery or a dartboard. It has a bullseye and everything. And then you go to your lane, and you just throw." He mimes the movement. "You ever feel like screaming sometimes?" he asks. "Ever have a bad day where everything is going wrong, and you just want to stand up and yell?"

"Only three to four times a week."

"Hot yoga doesn't cure everything," he says evenly. "So, I would take you ax throwing. After which, we'll both have built up an appetite, so I'd take you to dinner. Somewhere quiet so we could talk. Of your choosing, of course. And that would be our date." He downs the last of his hot chocolate and tosses the empty cup into a nearby trash can as though he didn't just describe what might be the weirdest and possibly greatest day ever.

"What would you do for me?" he asks.

"On a date?" I frown. "I have no clue."

"Well, that doesn't seem fair."

"I'm terrible at date ideas."

"Then make an effort."

I groan inwardly. I wasn't lying. With my line of work, dating follows a predictive pattern. An alcoholic beverage after work, usually late, and then maybe a formal dinner. I haven't done anything anyone would consider "fun" since college.

"Well, since you *love* picnics," I begin, and he laughs. "Dinner," I say, more seriously. "But not out. I would invite you over to my apartment and I'd cook."

"I didn't know you could cook."

"I can make pasta, garlic bread, and cheesy garlic bread."

"Ah, the three food groups."

"I wouldn't attempt dessert though. I'd buy that, but I'd

plate it nicely and most likely lie and say I made it from scratch so you'd be impressed with me."

"And I would pretend to believe you because I'm nice."

He would. I know he would. And I would get two desserts in case he didn't like one. But I know what Andrew likes. Anything with melting chocolate in the middle. I would wear something casual that I was comfortable in because, between cooking and plating, I wouldn't have time to dress up. Afterward, we'd go over to the couch and we'd watch one of his dumb comedies or maybe he'd let me pick the movie and he'd suffer through it silently. And then the credits would roll and it would be dark outside and I'd kiss him because it would be a date and it's perfectly normal to kiss someone on a date and even more normal to feel your heart race when you do.

"So, you're going to woo me with food, is that it?"

I blink away the image of us, clearing my throat for good measure. "Are you complaining?"

"Absolutely not. That sounds right up my street."

"I can do it after the ax throwing," I say airily, and he smiles.

"Sold."

Our eyes meet and there it is again, the spark of something that seems to happen more and more.

And Andrew knows it. He stops along the walkway, pausing to lean against the railing. In the distance, Big Ben looms across the river, while directly behind him the market continues in all its festive spirit. But it's quieter here, mainly couples and solo visitors wandering like us, taking pictures of the lights as they eat roasted chestnuts and lick melting marshmallows from their fingers.

But I'm not looking at them. I'm looking at Andrew, Andrew who's gazing at me with such a serious expression that I suddenly feel like I'm being pulled in front of the school principal. And I know he's going to ask me about it. About the kiss. About us. He's going to ask the question and I don't know the answer and I get so panicked, so worried, that I distract him with the first thing I can think of.

"Take my picture."

"What?"

"Take my picture," I repeat, more confident this time.

His brows rise. "You hate having your picture taken."

I do. It wasn't just because I looked like a wreck in Paris. I've always been uncomfortable in front of the camera. I can barely stand the professional headshots they make us do at work and my Instagram feed doesn't have a single selfie of me. Not even when I was rocking that bob cut everyone complimented me on but that was way too much maintenance to keep up. I don't do pictures. But my distraction is working.

"I feel pretty," I say. "And I want to document this ridiculous day."

He doesn't respond at first, as though waiting for the punchline. I just stand there.

"Okay," he says, reaching for his camera.

"You also could have told me I always look pretty," I tell him.

"I could have," he agrees, and gestures for me to pose.

Predictably, I feel instantly self-conscious.

What do I do with my hands? How do I pose? Do I tilt my head? Do I smile? Do I jump into the river and swim far, far away?

Andrew glances through the lens and makes an adjustment, eyes flicking up when he sees me flailing.

"You're terrible at this."

"Andrew!"

He laughs and some of my awkwardness changes to annoyance.

"Never mind," I say. "Put it away."

"Oh, absolutely not. I'm having too much fun now."

I almost pout, squirming under his attention as he gets ready.

"Put your left hand on the railing," he says. "Not like you're holding onto the *Titanic*... Perfect. Look at me."

"I am looking at you."

"Look at me like you did before."

"Which was how?" I ask, confused, but he only shakes his head, his attention on the camera.

"Whatever you do," he says as he goes almost unnaturally still. "Don't smile."

"Shut up."

The lens shutters.

"What did I just say?" he says in mock outrage as my lips twitch. He clicks again. "You know what they say about cameras stealing your soul, don't you?"

"Is that what you're doing?"

"I just want you to know what you're getting into," he says, and finally lowers the camera, looking pleased as he checks the screen.

"Done?" I ask. I weirdly feel a little out of breath, but I suppose that's the effect when Andrew Fitzpatrick turns his full attention on you.

He nods and I hold out my hand. "Let me see it."

"Nope."

"Let me see it!" I grab it off him, but only because he lets me, pulling the strap over his head as he clicks something and a screen appears, showing me the last photo he took.

For a moment I don't recognize myself.

My hair has dried naturally in gentle, frizzy waves and the cold has left my nose and cheeks pink while the rest of me is bathed in the soft glow of the fair. I'm not looking at the camera. I'm looking at Andrew. Looking at him with a smile I've never seen before. Whenever I pose for a photo, I usually smile with my lips closed thanks to my two crooked front teeth. Someone made a passing comment about them when I was fourteen and I've never forgotten it. Honestly, I've never had a photo taken of myself where I haven't anticipated how I was going to look. And how I thought others would look at me.

My lips are open in this photo, my eyes creased, caught mid-laugh as I turn slightly away from him. I look like I'm having the time of my life. I look like I'm in a winter wonderland. I look...

"I look *amazing*."

"I'm just a really good photographer."

I'm far too pleased to even think of a retort. "Can you send me this one?"

"Of course."

I start to hand the camera back, but change my mind at the last second, cradling it to my chest. "Can I take one of you?"

He pauses. "I won't lie, I know you're a capable, professional adult, but that camera cost three grand so if you—"

"Thanks," I say, ignoring his sigh as I peer through the lens. That much I know how to do. "What do I press?"

"The big red button."

I make a face at him but to be fair, I guess that's the answer.

"Say cheese," I mutter, trying to frame him as he did me. For someone who's used to being on the other side of the camera, he doesn't look awkward, just leans against the railing, his body facing the water, while his face tilts my way.

I hesitate. "It won't be as good as yours."

"I hope not, seeing as I'm a professional," he deadpans. But his expression softens. "Just feel it," he says simply. "It's not all about science and angles and light. Sometimes you just... feel."

Feel. I guess I can do that.

"Think about something that makes you happy," I say, clicking the button again.

He smirks. "Like you?"

"Maybe not me," I say without missing a beat. "Let's try and keep this shoot PG-13."

And there it is. His grin is instant, lighting up his whole face, and the carousel in the background is a blur of so much color and movement that it's like the noise of it is captured alongside everything else. And with a small click of my finger, I've saved it forever.

I don't even need to look at it to know I did a good job and I pass the camera back to him, feeling so happy that it almost hurts. "There," I say. "Now we're even."

"Even?" he asks, still smiling.

I nod, turning back to the water as he examines the photo. "Now I've got your soul too."

CHAPTER FIFTEEN

The house is dark when we get back, but even though we need to be up in a few hours, I'm not ready for the night to end just yet. I think about proposing a movie, maybe raiding the fridge for some snacks and recreating the Christmas we would have had if we stayed in Chicago. But my grand plan goes out the window as soon as we step through the door and see a line of discarded clothes scattered down the hallway leading to the kitchen.

"Huh," I say as Andrew sighs. He runs his hand along the wall, searching for a light switch, and when he finds it, I see the clothes are accompanied by receipts and what looks like bank cards, as though someone (Oliver) had gone through his pockets as he undressed, leaving a trail of bizarre breadcrumbs behind him.

Andrew turns the light off again. "I say we just go to bed."

"What if he's hurt himself?" I ask, already heading to the kitchen.

"What if he has company and you're interrupting him?"

"It's just *his* clothes," I point out, though I get ready to close my eyes quickly in the event of a naked Oliver plus company roaming around the house. Thankfully, it doesn't happen, and I find our gracious host slumped on the kitchen floor beside the fridge dressed in a full Santa suit, white beard and all.

"Cousin!" he proclaims when he sees me.

"I'm the friend," I tell him.

"And yet you already feel like family, such is our connection."

He's wasted. Pissed. *Inebriated.* Whatever you want to call it, the man is going to feel it in the morning.

"You should have worn that back at Lara's house," I joke as Andrew comes into the room behind me.

"You'll have to forgive me, I'm usually much more civilized than this but I met up with my friend Zac in Chelsea and he insisted."

"Did he?" Andrew asks flatly.

"Well, I didn't want to be rude," Oliver says, looking wounded that Andrew would even think of such a thing.

"Do I need to take you to the hospital?"

"I'd much rather you order me a tikka masala."

"How about a glass of water and some toast?"

Oliver sighs loudly but doesn't protest and, as Andrew finds his way around the kitchen, I reach into my pocket and hand him the box of gingersnap cookies I picked up as we were leaving the market.

He smiles at me, turning it over in his hands. "You got me a present?"

"As a thank you for letting us stay."

"That is almost questionably thoughtful of you, Molly, but I shall accept it in the spirit which I'm sure it's intended."

"...Great."

His eyes latch onto my face, surprisingly focused. "Did you have a nice time?" he asks, suddenly urgent.

"We had a lovely time."

"You'll come back to visit then. With or without Andrew, I have no strong feelings toward the man."

I laugh and he starts prying open the box. "You know, I'm pretty sure there's a ready-made pizza in the freezer," he calls to Andrew. "I wouldn't dare make it myself, however. Not in this state." He lowers his voice to a faux whisper. "Much too dangerous."

I smirk, glancing over my shoulder, but Andrew's not listening to us as he pulls white bread out of a plastic packet, a look of fierce concentration on his face. It's only then that I take in the messy surroundings of the kitchen, of the numerous wine and spirit bottles lining the counter. Oliver must have attempted to raid the cabinets before he got too tired.

"Hey," I call softly, twisting fully to face Andrew.

It takes a moment for his attention to come back to me. "Yeah?"

"Could you get his stuff ready for bed? I'll take care of the toast."

"Pizza," Oliver protests, but I shake my head.

"Toast will do the same job *and* you won't wake up in the morning with half of it stuck to your face."

"Wanna bet?"

I ignore him, watching Andrew as he lays a slice of bread carefully on the counter, his eyes flicking between it and the alcohol at his fingertips.

"Sure," he says after a second, and disappears without another word.

"I love a woman in charge," Oliver says as I make the food before forcing him to drink a pint of water. By the time he's done, Andrew has returned and together we haul Oliver to his feet.

His bedroom is, of course, all the way in the attic, and I'm disappointed to find his room incredibly ordinary compared to the rest of the house, with whitewashed walls and a plain navy bedspread. It's also a mess. His belongings are thrown everywhere, but I smile as I see the leftovers of Lara's Christmas decorations littering the floor, discarded colored paper and cotton wool, as though he'd spent the day doing arts and crafts just for her.

"Only two more sleeps until Christmas," Oliver says grandly as Andrew helps him onto the mattress. "I'll get up in the morning to see you off."

"I'm willing to bet everything in my suitcase that you won't," Andrew says. "And I have a giant Toblerone in there."

Oliver looks aghast as his cousin crouches before him. "You're only telling me this now?"

"Thanks for letting us stay. Get a real job."

"Anytime. And absolutely not. And, Molly!" He cranes his neck to where I stand in the doorway. "A delight to meet you. Thank you for my present."

"Thank you for having us."

"Always, always."

We leave him to sleep it off and head back down the stairs, pausing outside our respective doors on the floor below.

"Sorry about all that," Andrew says. "There's one in every family."

"I like him," I say. "I'm glad I got to meet him."

"Yeah, well..." He smiles a goodnight smile, turning toward his room.

"Andrew?" I step closer to him, trying to guess where

his mind's at, but unable to tell anything from his expression. "Are you okay?"

"With Oliver?" He shrugs. "He's melodramatic, but he means well."

"I meant with... He's pretty drunk," I finish, and Andrew tenses in understanding.

"I'm fine," he says. "No wagon-falling here. My cousin isn't exactly a glittering advertisement for the wonders of drinking."

"Still," I try again. "We can talk if you want to."

"I'm okay, Moll. Stop worrying."

"I will if you stop lying." We're both surprised by the exasperation in my voice, but I go with it, not caring anymore. "I'm going to worry," I tell him. "Of course I'm going to worry. You can't just tell me you're going through this incredibly hard thing and not expect me to want to help."

"Molly—"

"You don't have to do this by yourself." As soon as I say the words, I get a flashback to Gabriela following me around the office, begging me to talk to her. She knew something was up with me just like I know something's up with him. And I guess now I finally understand her frustration. "You can talk to me."

"I know I can." His gaze gentles at the obvious hurt in my voice. "I know I'm just... This is all pretty new to me too. Besides my roommates, you're the first person I've told."

Now that shocks me. "Really? Not even your family?"

He shakes his head. "Not yet. I'm still figuring out how to explain it to them without freaking them out."

"But what about Christmas?"

He knows what I mean. No one likes the stereotype, but the culture of casual drinking is very much alive in Ireland.

Even more so at this time of the year when my social media feeds fill up with breakfast mimosas and lunchtime pints with captions of *'Tis the season* and *Might as well*. It's expected. Almost encouraged. And if you don't join in, it means something is wrong.

"I'll tell them I'm on antibiotics or something," Andrew says. "Christian's usually too hungover to touch anything anyway. I won't be alone. I guess I just don't want anyone to treat me any differently."

"But they will," I say. "They have to." I take another step toward him, relieved he's finally talking to me, furious I didn't ask sooner. I didn't realize how guilty I'd felt since he told me. I mean, talk about being a bad friend. So caught up in my own problems, year in and year out, that I didn't even see it.

Andrew smiles, reading my thoughts like I spoke them out loud. "You can't take the blame for this one, Moll. This is all on me. I got very, very good at hiding it. Even from myself."

"When did you know?"

"That I had a problem?" He shrugs, trying to play it casual even as a stiffness creeps into his body. "There weren't any warning signs," he says. "At least not the ones you think you know to look out for. I didn't wake up hungover all the time. I wasn't angry or moody. Or at least I told myself I wasn't. But it was becoming an everyday thing. Every meal, every event. Every time I went anywhere, anytime I did anything, it was all I could focus on. But I kept telling myself that as long as I didn't get too drunk, it wouldn't be an issue." He pauses, scratching the side of his neck. It's a nervous gesture. One that I'm not used to seeing from him. "I was in denial," he says eventually. "And I guess

I lied just now, I couldn't hide it from everyone. It's why Marissa and I..."

I straighten, realizing what he's saying. "Oh my God, Andrew."

"She asked me to stop and I didn't. I was convinced she was blowing it out of proportion. But she could see it. Her dad had problems when she was growing up and she didn't want that in her life."

I have no idea what to say, so I don't say anything, listening like I need to start doing.

"It got worse after she left," he says after a beat. "Just to be predictable. But I realize now I couldn't stop for her. I had to stop for me. And I did."

"That's good," I say. "That's *great*."

He smiles at my earnestness. "I still get the odd moment," he admits. "The guy running the program says it's helpful to avoid places with excessive drinking, but it's the little moments that get to me. The quiet times when you think... maybe, it wouldn't be so bad. Maybe I could just have one and then I could stop. Even though I know deep down I won't. And tonight? Spending it with you, knowing I'm seeing my family tomorrow? What better way to finish a perfect day?"

"So tell me when that happens," I say. "Let me be there for you. Even if it's just as a distraction."

"A distraction, huh?" His voice goes soft as he gazes down at me. "You want to be my distraction, Moll?"

I don't answer, feeling like I'm pinned in place as I swallow, my mouth suddenly dry. His eyes drop to my throat at the movement before trailing down to the necklace he gave me. I don't think I'm even breathing as he reaches up, tugging the chain from under my sweater so that it sits on top.

"Thank you for telling me," I whisper as he plays with it. "You can tell me anything. You know that, right?"

"I do." He lets go of the pendant, but his hand stays where it is, tucking a strand of hair behind my ear in what's fast becoming his signature move. "But just for the record," he says. "You can't tell me stuff."

He smiles as he dodges my hit, taking a step back from me and putting some much-needed distance between us in the process.

"I promise to tell you when it gets too much," he says. "And you can distract me however you want."

I grimace, thinking he's back to joking, but he shakes his head.

"I promise," he repeats, and he looks so sincere that this time I believe him.

"We should get some sleep," I say eventually, thinking about our final day of travel tomorrow. "If we wake up and the ferry is canceled, I say we buy as much food as we can carry and make smores in that giant fireplace downstairs."

"And you say you don't do Christmas."

"Goodnight, Andrew." I open the door to my room, dragging my gaze from his as I step inside.

"Sweet dreams," he calls after me, and I listen for his own door to shut before I do the same to mine.

Inside, I flick on the bedside light and change out of my clothes, leaving on my underwear and T-shirt to use as pajamas before washing my face in the bathroom. With barely anything with me, it doesn't take long to pack for the morning. My laptop bag remains untouched where Andrew had left it that afternoon and I have one spare T-shirt to wear for the journey. The rest I fold into the small bag I got them in, and I put them beside my shoes, lined up neatly at the end of the bed.

When I'm done, I pull on the thick gray robe hanging on the back of the bathroom door and stand staring at the bed.

I know I need to at least try and get some sleep. That I'll hate myself tomorrow if I don't. But I don't think I've ever been more awake, my mind jumping from one thing to the other.

My skin feels tight. My body restless.

A perfect day.

That's what he said today was. Perfect.

There's a shuffling noise at the wall separating us, most likely him just plugging something in, but at the sound of it I tense, suddenly aching aware of how close he is.

Before I know what I'm doing I'm out my door, marching the two steps it takes to get to his where I knock, almost bruising my knuckles against the wood until I hear him cursing on the other side.

"Oliver," he growls as he opens it. "I swear to God if you—"

Andrew stops talking as soon as he sees me. "Are you okay?" he asks, instantly concerned.

Am I? I think seriously about my answer as I take in his messy hair and his kind eyes and his stupid shirt saying, *Yule got this.*

"No," I say, and press a hand against the center of his chest, pushing him back into the room.

CHAPTER SIXTEEN

It's dark on the other side of the door. He hasn't put a lamp on yet, and the streetlights outside cast everything in an odd purple-and-orange glow. Behind him, the room is tidy. He's barely unpacked other than his washbag and a spare T-shirt thrown on the bed, ready to wake up and go tomorrow. Ready to leave all this behind.

I shut the door at the thought, though I keep one hand on the handle just in case I chicken out.

"Molly?"

"Just don't talk for a second." To my surprise he does as I request, letting me stand there, taking him in silence. And I do take him in, my eyes traveling from his face, down down down to his chest, his jeans, and back up again.

Or what if you're just super dumb and you've never realized what's right in front of you?

Gabriela's words echo through my mind as I stare at him. I stare at him for so long my hand starts to cramp against the handle and I have to let go.

"You kissed me back," I say, and he goes so still I swear he isn't breathing. "Not to clear my mind. Not because you thought I was being funny. You kissed me back because you wanted to."

"I did," he says, and my heart stutters at those two simple words. But it's still not enough. I don't understand and I'm not leaving here until I do.

"Have you ever wanted to kiss me before?"

"Molly—"

"Have you?"

A muscle jumps in his jaw, fascinating me before he answers. "Once," he admits, forcing the word out. "Years ago."

"When?"

"We have to be up in five hours. Do you really want to do this now?"

"You want to wait another ten years?"

He scoffs but doesn't argue further, looking almost embarrassed the more I watch him. "Our third flight," he says eventually, and then, so quietly that I'm not even sure I heard him right: "You were wearing a red scrunchie."

I frown at him, confused. "That's our first real flight."

"I guess."

"That was seven years ago."

"I—"

"You've wanted to kiss me for seven—"

"I wanted to kiss you *then*," he stresses. "But you wouldn't shut up about your boyfriend, would you? So I left it alone."

He left it alone.

"What about you?" he asks while I freak out. "Have you ever wanted to kiss me before?"

"No."

He waits a beat for me to continue, huffing when I don't. "Alright, thanks, Molly."

"I didn't!" It's the truth. "Not until the other day." When it became the only thing I ever wanted. Like someone had turned a spotlight on and aimed it straight at him. "I liked it when we kissed," I say because it feels like something that needs to be made clear to him. "But then you started joking around—"

"You said you didn't want to do it again."

"I was obviously *lying!*" I exclaim. "And you said it wasn't a big deal."

"Because you were acting weird!"

"Because it *is* weird! *This* is weird. I've never felt like this before with you."

"Like what?"

"Well, right now, like I want to push you over," I snap. "And otherwise..." Otherwise, like my entire life was leading up to that very moment. "I liked it when we kissed," I repeat, folding my arms under my chest.

"So why did you freak out?"

"Because I didn't want to ruin our friendship. I like our friendship. It's important to me and I didn't want to lose it."

"You're not going to."

"You don't know that. You don't. And for all I knew, you felt nothing more than friendship for me, which means I would be making things majorly awkward for both of us and if you *did* feel more..." I fumble with the words, flustered now we were getting to the heart of things. "If you did and we tried something, there's no saying if it would last or not, and then that's it. Ten years gone. You can't go back on something like that. Some things can't be unsaid."

"So, you're scared of liking me because you're scared of losing me?"

The urge to hide is strong. "Well, when you say it like that it makes me sound pathetic, so no."

"Moll..." His voice is filled with tenderness as he takes a step toward me. "Look at me, I'm not going anywhere."

"I know."

"You don't. And that's the problem. Everything you just said? I worry about it too. And I'm not going to let go of something like that, someone like *you*, that easy." He pauses, frowning slightly. "I shouldn't have tricked you into kissing me back in Argentina. It was selfish. And you're right. I wanted to kiss you. When I realized that you wanted me as well..." He shakes his head, his gaze intense as he stares down at me. "I snapped."

Snapped.

No one's ever snapped for me before.

I don't know why that turns me on so much.

"I guess everyone gets a little crazy during the holidays," I whisper, and I honest to God blush at the look in his eyes.

It becomes very clear to me then that I have two options. I can go back to my room and go to sleep and we'll keep tiptoeing until one of us cracks.

Or I can stay where I am. I can stay where I am and I can...

"Seven out of ten?" I ask.

His confusion lasts only a second before he realizes what I'm saying. "I guess practice makes perfect," he says evenly.

And then everything happens at once.

I close the space between us and step into him, fully into him. Chest to chest, hip to hip *into* him until it's only our faces that aren't pressed together. Andrew tenses against me, but I don't let myself read too much into it and when he doesn't move away I tilt my head up and press my lips to his.

It's not the smoothest move I've ever done. More *I dare*

you to stop this as opposed to *let's explore this newfound delicate thing between us,* and yet, it does the trick. Warmth flows through me again, a heavy feeling of rightness that fills and soothes every inch of me. Places I didn't even know needed soothing, like the nervous coil in my belly and the tightness in my shoulders. It all melts away with ridiculous ease as if to say, *Look, you idiot, this was all you had to do. It was right in front of you all along.*

There's still some sugar by his mouth, leftover from his churros, and when I flick my tongue out to lick it off, he makes a noise I've never heard from him before. My hands go to his hair, moving from a caress to a clutch as I hold him to me, our kisses growing deeper, needier until the gaps between them grow shorter, until we barely stop touching. And I never want to stop touching. Kissing Andrew Fitzpatrick was the best decision I ever made and I'm brazenly about to tell him this when he pulls back, pushing me an inch away so there's space between us.

My breathing is ragged, his just as bad, and I think maybe that's it and we'll go back to talking or he'll bid me goodnight and I'll have whatever the female equivalent of blue balls is, but instead his eyes drop from my face to where my robe is tied loosely around my waist. There he reaches out, running his finger along the half-hearted knot before a gentle tug pulls it free.

I'm not exactly wearing the sexiest of lingerie underneath. The T-shirt is plain white cotton, the underwear black and practical, but Andrew doesn't seem to care, his gaze intense as his hands slide under the hem of the shirt and around my waist, growing surer with every inch until he's holding me steady.

"This okay?" he asks.

I can only nod, barely able to form a thought as he

draws a path up the sensitive skin of my rib cage. My top drags up as he goes, revealing my stomach as he stops just short of my breasts. His fingers feel hot enough to burn.

"Words, Molly."

"I'm good," I bite out, but he pauses at whatever he hears in my voice and brings his touch back to my hips. Before I can tell him to keep going, he drops his lips to mine, and okay, this is good too.

I respond with an enthusiasm I might have been embarrassed to show with another partner, but with Andrew I don't hesitate, wrapping one arm around his shoulders as I press myself into him, giving him no doubt this time as to what I want. He gets the hint.

He kisses me. Harder than before. Hard enough that I'm gasping into him, doing my best to keep up, and my back hits the door before he spins us both away from it. He does it so fast that I almost trip and I try to concentrate on the kiss while concentrating on keeping upright while concentrating on Andrew. Andrew who's steering me toward the bed and following me down onto it. Who's overwhelming me until he's all I know, until I stop thinking about anything other than the heat from him and the heat because of him.

My legs fall apart and he falls into the cradle of my thighs, our bodies pushing against each other until a pulse goes through me, deep and needy.

I want his shirt off. I want his shirt off and my shirt off. I want my skin against his and my body against his and I want it now and for the rest of the night and forever and ever and ever.

And still, he kisses me as his fingers move up again under my top, finally going right where I want them to, where I *need* them to, and screw our friendship. I have one life to live here and I want this to be it. And with my lips never leaving his, I reach for the bottom of his T-shirt, intending to pull it off and give in to everything I want, when we're interrupted by a firm, mocking knock on the door.

I didn't know knocks could sound mocking, but somehow this one pulls it off.

"Oh, lover boy?"

Andrew freezes above me, his expression almost comical.

"You've got to be kidding," he says, so close to me that his breath skims across my lips.

"Romeo?" Oliver calls again.

"I'm sleeping," Andrew yells.

"I'm not falling for that one again," Oliver says, his words slurring. "You know I'm not one to stop a man from relaxing, but I'm afraid I need a little help. I won't lie to you, after all that water I'm in desperate need of a piss but can't seem to find my way out of this bloody suit."

Andrew stares at me and, before I can stop myself, I run my finger down his nose. An almost pained expression crosses his face. "I'm tired, Oliver."

"Molly's welcome too," his cousin says conversationally, and I clamp a hand over my mouth as embarrassment shoots through me.

"She's also sleeping," Andrew shouts.

"I don't think that was snoring I heard."

Christ on a bike.

"Or maybe it was just a very good dream?"

Andrew rolls his eyes and starts to lean down but I stop him with a hand to his chest.

"What are you doing?" I whisper.

"What does it look like?" he asks, and I can't help but

smile at his irritated tone. I push him again and he follows the movement, collapsing beside me.

"Not when he's still outside," I tell him.

"He's not."

"Oh, no, I'm still here," Oliver calls. "Listening too. Surprisingly thin walls, you see." He knocks again and Andrew shoots a glare at the door before turning back to me. One look at my face and he recognizes defeat.

"Give me a minute," he says, and I pat his arm.

"Excellent!" Oliver sounds delighted and a moment later I hear the gentle shuffle of his slippers against the floorboards.

Neither of us moves, Andrew still looking at me as though he's hoping I'll change my mind.

"You should go," I say as I glance down his body, to the evidence of what I felt against me a few moments ago.

"He'll have to wait a minute," Andrew grumbles, and I bite my lip, trying not to look smug. I certainly feel smug. And Andrew knows it too, huffing as he climbs off the bed and snatches my robe from the floor. He sits back on the mattress as I pull it on.

"Are you okay?" he asks carefully.

I nod, pausing to look at him. "You?"

"Yeah."

"Okay then," I whisper, and we smile at each other as though sharing a joke, or maybe just sharing how ridiculous this is. In the best possible way.

"Goodnight, Andrew," I say, pulling my gaze away from the sight of him, deliciously rumpled at the end of the bed. I feel his eyes on me as I head to the door and it's not until I'm on the other side, closing it, that I hear his low response.

"Night, Moll."

CHAPTER SEVENTEEN

THREE YEARS AGO

Flight Seven, Chicago

"I hate men. I hate them. I mean, look at this crap. *Look.*"

Andrew rears back as I shove the phone into his face, showing him a picture of Mark and his new girlfriend. *Naomi.* The woman with the poreless skin.

"See?" I demand when he doesn't say anything.

"See what? Your screen's locked."

I drop my arm with a scowl, tapping in my password so hard I hurt my thumb.

"Molly—"

"Hang on," I mutter as I put in the right digits. "There." I turn my phone back his way with one hand and reach into my giant bag of duty-free toffees with the other. "It's been three weeks since we broke up. Three weeks and they're already on vacation. Do you know what that means?"

"I can't think of a single answer that would make you not yell at me."

"That it's been going on much longer," I say, ignoring him. "Mark cheated on me."

"You don't know that."

"They're at the *beach*," I say, going to the next photo. "Drinking out of *coconuts*."

He starts to nod before shaking his head when I just glare at him. "Moll, I won't lie to you; I am extremely bad at girl talk so this entire conversation is just making me nervous that I'll say the wrong thing."

"Well, tough," I snap. "Because you're sitting next to me for seven hours, which means you have to contribute to my breakdown. That's the friendship rule."

"But is it a *plane* rule," he begins as I start scrolling through Mark's last few posts. Bitterness stabs me with each one like my heart is breaking all over again.

I've been dumped three times in my life and each time it's *sucked*. It's sucked *balls*. And—

"I think that's enough of those," Andrew says, taking the packet of toffee from me. "I'm pretty sure everyone here would prefer if those vomit bags remained decorative for the rest of the flight."

I swallow the lump of sugar in my mouth, aware that I'm acting like a child throwing a tantrum and yet unable to stop. Between Mark and more responsibility at work, some days it felt like I was hanging on by a thread.

"That's what 'meeting someone else' means," I say, continuing the conversation I'd been having in my head. "It means 'I've been cheating on you.'" I'd just been too stupid to realize it. No one breaks up with someone because they see another person across the street and go, "Yes! Her!" He would have started something with her weeks ago. Maybe not going all the way, but emotionally moving on before blindsiding me on a rainy Tuesday night with a well-rehearsed speech and a packet of tissues because he knew I was going to cry and I did. "Can I have my toffee back?"

"No."

I scowl as Andrew shoves the packet down the side of his seat. He's wearing a sweater with a dog on it that says, *Dachshund through the snow*, which honestly just feels a little lazy, but he told me his girlfriend had bought it for him so it's not like I can tell him that.

"I think you should get dumped too so we can be miserable together," I say at the thought of her.

"That *was* part of our contract."

Contract. Ugh. I was still waiting to hear back from one of my clients about—

"Stop thinking about him," Andrew says.

"I'm not. I'm thinking about work."

"Just as bad. Why don't you think about *Home Alone* 2 colon *Lost in New York?*"

"Nobody says the title like that."

"Because they don't have the proper respect for *Home Alone* 2 colon—"

I cut him off with a groan as he starts flicking through the options on my screen. He's already loaded up the movie on his.

"You're going to marry Alison," I say as he plugs the headphones in. "You're going to marry Alison and *I* am going to have to hook up with someone at your wedding. Is your brother still single?"

"You're not hooking up with my brother."

I huff at the clear dismissal in his voice. "Why not? I'm a delight. You don't want me in your family?"

"Not like that, no."

"I'd settle for a third cousin," I say, but that only seems to make him madder.

"No settling at all."

"Well, I'm going to have to do *some* settling seeing as I

can't seem to hold down a relationship for more than a year. I mean, there's got to be something wrong with me at this stage." I regret the words as soon as I say them, wincing as Andrew glances at me. Why not just lay out all my insecurities for everyone in my life to know? Why not everyone on the plane! Seems like a great plan. Super healthy. "Sorry," I say. "I may or may not be having a bad day, I don't know if you can tell."

Andrew doesn't respond, just holds up an earbud until I accept it, slotting it in place and placing a finger over the play button so we can sync. But Andrew doesn't move, still watching me with that serious expression that makes me desperate to fill the silence.

"Okay, so I may have overreacted about the coconuts as well. But—"

"Mark doesn't deserve you," he interrupts. "And I don't care if he's found his soulmate or if he spends his weekend rescuing stray dogs. He hurt you, so I hate him. And I would very much like to punch him for breaking your heart. In fact, if anyone ever makes you think you are less than what you are, or that you don't deserve everything that you reach for, I will make their lives as miserable as you want me to. Prank phone calls. Stones in their shoes. Whatever you ask me to do, I will do it. You are hardworking and passionate and kind and one day... one day you are going to find someone who lights you up even more than you already do. And they'll be lucky to have you."

I can only stare at him as he sits back, so lost for words that I don't notice him retrieving my bag of toffee until he drops it in my lap.

"Okay?" he asks as I jump.

"Okay."

"No settling?"

"No settling." The word comes out as a whisper, but something in my face must satisfy him because he nods, turning his attention back to the screen. "Good," he says, hitting play. "Now watch the damn movie."

———

Now, London

The next morning, I stand in the concourse of Euston station, waiting for Andrew to return with our promised coffees as what honestly feels like eleven million people converge around me. It is six forty a.m. on Christmas Eve and no one looks particularly happy to be here. Parents clutch the hands of bleary-eyed children and single travelers and couples stand grimly just like I do, laden down with bags and sweating in their coats. Everyone either stares at their phones or at the large board overhead, which flickers every thirty seconds with rolling destinations and departure times.

It's chaos. And once again, I think about how this was not supposed to end up this way. Andrew and I were supposed to enjoy an hour in the first-class lounge before floating to our seats. We were supposed to enjoy our flight in comfort and luxury before parting as usual at the airport, me into a taxi and him to a bus to bring him home. We were supposed to be at our respective houses by now, which means I wouldn't be standing here, cold and grumpy and exhausted.

I also wouldn't have kissed him.

I wouldn't have nearly done much more than just kiss him.

Or maybe I still would have.

I peer up at the board, waiting for our platform to appear as I fiddle with the scarf around my neck. Andrew's scarf. Underneath it lies the necklace he gave me, the one I have yet to take off. I run my finger over the pendant, shivering when I remember the feel of him last night. I don't even want to think about what would have happened if Oliver hadn't interrupted us.

I mean, I want to think about it a *lot*, but—

"Three-fifty for a croissant," Andrew announces as he appears through the crowd with our breakfast. "There's London prices and then there's just daylight robbery."

"So you didn't get any?"

"No, I got two. I've seen you when you're hungry, no one wants that."

I smirk as he passes me a coffee, taking a sip as he bites into one of the pastries.

"Why the face?" he asks. I'm surprised at the hint of worry I hear. As though he's afraid he's the reason for my mood.

"I'm thinking of those first-class tickets," I say. "And how very much that experience would not have been this experience."

"Ah, it's good to be among the people," he says. "Keeps you grounded."

"I feel like I'm one wrong look away from screaming the whole place down."

He shrugs, his gaze flicking absently over the crowd. "We can handle that. What's your line?"

"My line?"

"Your I've-had-enough-and-I-don't-care-how-bad-a-mood-I'm-in line." Andrew takes another sip of his coffee. "Mine is if we break down. I don't mind a wait to change drivers but if we break down, I am officially losing my shit."

"I don't know what mine is yet."

"You can take a crying baby? Crying baby is a good one. There's also strong-smelling food, considering how early it is in the morning. That would be a hard number one line for me if I wasn't so sure something extremely bad wasn't going to happen."

"Don't say that."

"I don't mean a crash," he says casually. "But at the very least a three-hour delay resulting in a missed ferry."

"You're being pessimistic. *I'm* the pessimistic one. I'm the most pessimistic."

"Are you seriously trying to beat me at pessimism?"

"Trying?" I ask, and he grins, letting the conversation drop.

We haven't talked about last night yet. It's not like we've ignored it. We only left the house an hour ago and before that we were getting ready. We'll have to acknowledge it at some point. And say what I have no idea. No idea because I don't know how I feel about it yet.

I don't regret it. But I'm not sure what it means either. I've never been one of those people who overanalyzed their relationships. But that's because they've followed a traditional set pattern. Meet a guy, talk to a guy, date a guy. That's it. Not whatever this is. Not whatever we—

"You know you make these faces when you're thinking really hard about something?"

I start, spilling my coffee over the lid as I squeeze the cup too tightly. "Huh?"

"Like you're having an internal conversation," Andrew continues, watching me curiously. "You start making these expressions. Did you know that?"

I did not.

"What are you talking to yourself about?"

"You."

His eyebrows rise, a smile beginning before I shut it down.

"You've got crumbs all down the front of your coat."

His smile drops as he brushes them off and I turn, a little primly it must be said, back to the concourse.

Maybe he's waiting for me to bring up last night. And that's fine. That's totally fine, I have after all initiated the majority of non-platonic friendship events between us. I know he doesn't regret it because he's acting completely normal just like he promised he would, so maybe he's just waiting. For me. For a *Hey, remember when we almost had sex a few hours ago? Remember when we made out for a good several minutes and felt each other up and—*

"I will give you one hundred dollars if you tell me what you're thinking about right now."

"Just don't look at me!" I exclaim, and I step in front of him so he can only see the back of my head. Almost as soon as I do, the board changes and Andrew points to where our platform number has just appeared.

"A seacht," he says, speaking in Irish as he pulls the handle of his suitcase up. "Numero siete. Lucky number seven."

"Okay."

"This way, Molly. Let me show you the way to go home. To the green hills of Ireland. The old Emerald—"

"I get it," I snap, and he laughs.

One good thing about his ridiculous suitcase: it carves a neat little path for me through the crowd. Around us, dozens of people break away, doing the same. This train, like all the others, is standing room only. There are lines at the barrier and again on the platform with some people going so far as to hoist their luggage over their heads in order to squeeze their way to the doors.

It gets a bit tense, and it isn't long until something bumps into my shoulder, followed by a muffled apology as a man with an acoustic guitar shoves past.

I gaze after him suspiciously. "If he starts playing that thing, we're moving to a different carriage," I tell Andrew.

"That's your line?"

"That's my line."

By some miracle, we manage to find a spot for our bags and no one is sitting in our booked seats, so we don't have to make anyone move either.

Still, I hold my breath, waiting for something to happen. For a tree on the tracks or a failed engine. But everyone gets onboard and eventually, warily, we pull out of the station and chug our way through the buildings of North London.

I start to feel a little better.

I think Andrew does too. He doesn't do anything for the first few minutes of the journey, sitting rigidly beside me before his shoulders lower with a quiet sigh. Another minute and he unfurls the same *National Geographic* he had back in Chicago, along with a paperback thriller he must have picked up with our coffees.

I fight back a yawn and turn to the window, watching as the sky begins to lighten and the city gives way to the green fields of the countryside that make up my view for the next few hours. I must doze off, because the next thing I know, Andrew is shaking me awake as the conductor announces our impending arrival into Holyhead. We still have another twenty minutes or so, but everyone predictably gets up to stretch their legs and the carriage is soon filled with people passing down bags and gathering their belongings.

There's a marked difference in mood from when we got

on the train to getting off it. There's no jostling this time around. Everyone is smiling, suddenly chatty now we're halfway home. I do start to get a little antsy as we wait for our turn to exit, but it vanishes as soon as I step onto the platform and stretch my legs. I can't see the sea, but I can smell it, fresh and salty and alive. I can hear it too, the shriek of the gulls, the blasting horn of a departing ship. It's a sunny day in Wales, the clouds white wisps above us, and the air is the clearest I've experienced in months.

I take a deep breath of it, turning to Andrew as he passes me my bag. "I just remembered something."

"Yeah?" He's distracted, making sure we have everything as he pulls his coat back on.

"Yeah. I freaking love the ferry."

He laughs so loud a nearby child glances at him in alarm. "I've never been on one."

"Seriously?"

He hesitates. "I've just gone way down in your estimation, haven't I?"

"You've never been on the ferry? It's the best!"

"I believe you."

"I'm going to take you up on deck when we get to Dublin."

"You can do whatever you like to me," he says, only to grin at the look I give him.

We check in his suitcase and then it's a short wait at passport control before we file down a long hallway, straight onto the ship.

It's smaller than I remember, probably because the last time I was on one I was a child, but there's still lots of room to move around, and we spend a few minutes exploring before grabbing turkey and ham sandwiches from the cafeteria. Santa himself makes an appearance, which sends every child onboard into a frenzy. Everyone's inner child too, considering Andrew makes us stand in line for twenty minutes to say hello and get a company branded keyring for our efforts. The rest of the journey is spent watching *Elf* on one of the giant television screens before I drag him out to join the other brave souls on the open deck. A sharp wind hits us as soon as we do, but we find a bit of shelter as we near the port, Andrew a warming presence as he crowds my back, sheltering me from the worst of the wind.

It's late afternoon by this stage and day is turning to night, but a thousand lights welcome us where Dublin city hugs the bay.

"Ten bucks says we sink," Andrew says, his mouth right by my ear so he can be heard over the noise of the engine.

"*You'll* sink," I say. "I'm an excellent swimmer."

He laughs as he moves closer, his arms bracketing me in as he holds onto the railing on either side of me. I stay very still, practically holding my breath as he leans in.

"Thank you," he says.

"For what?"

"For getting me home for Christmas."

"You're not home yet," I warn, but he ignores me. His lips skim my cheek, his gloved hands coming to rest on mine, which exactly two seconds ago, I would have been more than okay with, so I can understand his surprise when I immediately knock him off, moving up the ship.

"Okay, so that's what we call a mixed signal," he calls after me, but I barely hear him, my attention on the rapidly approaching coastline. "And can we not do that?" He pulls me sharply back as I lean over the railing.

"It's fine."

"So is standing behind the safety line."

The ship's horn blares as we near the port and I motion

for Andrew to stand beside me before we miss it. "We have to wave!"

"To who?" he asks, still sounding a little disgruntled that I ruined the moment.

"To them."

I point over the railing to the flat stone wall leading to Dublin's Poolbeg lighthouse. People dot the pathway, getting in their Christmas Eve walks, and they raise their arms overhead as we sail past.

We're too far away to see them clearly, too far away to really see them at all in the dim light, but I can just make out their faint shouts, can see their exaggerated movements as they say hello.

"It's like they're welcoming you home," I say, glancing at Andrew when he doesn't respond. He's not even looking at them, his gaze trained on me with the biggest smile on his face.

"Don't laugh," I warn, suddenly self-conscious.

"I'm not."

"You're about to."

"Because you're adorable."

"Wave at the good people of Dublin," I order, and he nods, schooling his features into a serious expression as he joins me at the railing.

"Can I yell?" he asks.

"Within reason."

He seems to consider this for a moment before holding his hands aloft. "*Hello!*" he screams over the noise. "*Merry Christmas!*"

"Andrew—"

"*And Happy New Year!*"

"You can stop now."

"It's cathartic," he says. "Try it."

"No."

"I dare you."

I huff, but as the horn blares again, it's not like anyone can hear us.

"Go on," Andrew urges, and I press my lips together before copying him.

"*Merry Christmas!*" I screech, and he grins.

"Again," he says, so I do. And together we scream and we wave until our voices grow hoarse and our arms grow tired and an announcement calls over the intercom, urging us back inside to disembark.

Only then does Andrew tug me free of the rail and we laugh, breathless as we follow the others down the stairs and get ready to go home.

CHAPTER EIGHTEEN

A cheery coach driver in a Santa hat is there to greet us as we trickle out of the port, his accent so strong that it takes me a moment to adjust.

"Well?" he jokes, as we put our luggage in the hold. "What did yis bring me?"

Andrew can't wipe the smile from his face as we find our seats. We pick two near the back, with him at the window, and I text Zoe that not only are we still alive, but she now has to do as promised and pick me up.

"What time is your bus?" I ask, my voice a little hoarse from all our yelling.

Andrew shrugs, watching the world outside as we leave the port and head into the city. "On the hour every hour. They run up to eleven."

"Really?"

He glances over his shoulder at how pleased I sound. "According to the website."

"Well, why don't you swing by mine first? You can finally meet everyone. Have a shower, some dinner. We're not that far." My enthusiasm wanes when he just looks at me. "Unless you want to head straight—"

"That sounds great," he interrupts. "The shower part in particular. Plus I'd love to meet your folks. And Zoe."

"You're not allowed to like her more than me," I say, only half-joking.

"Well, then you'll have to up your game in the next twenty minutes now, won't you?"

And it's twenty minutes exactly until my sister messages back, confirming the new plan. By then the bus has dropped us at the top of O'Connell Street, a broad sweeping avenue in the center of the city, that might as well have been in the North Pole by the look of it.

The air is full of noise, of voices and laughter and Christmas music coming from every direction. Women call out as they sell pots of poinsettias and bouquets of red berries, clutching cups of coffee to keep warm. Enthusiastic teenagers collecting for charity shake rattling buckets of coins at passers-by. Every single store I can see has its doors thrown open, crammed with last-minute shoppers and people who apparently just live for chaos.

Even the cars have made an effort, dressed up in Rudolph noses and reindeer antlers as they crawl so slowly through the traffic that most people simply weave between them to cross the roads.

I gaze around at it all with a strange feeling in my gut, surprised at how happy the scene makes me. It's like my head knows they're just the same old decorations they put up every year, but something about them now makes my heart beat a little faster, makes me smile at the passing strangers, and even the exuberant choir belting out some Mariah Carey across the street is a little less irritating than it would usually be.

It's Dublin at Christmas and there's excitement in the air.

And yes, you would have to be a grinch not to be taken in by it all.

We need to go to Merrion Square to meet my sister, so we collect our luggage and start walking past the glittering hotels and impressively large Christmas trees down toward the Liffey, the river that splits the city into the north and south side. Even that hasn't escaped the festive cheer, with the numerous bridges that cross it lit up in bright neon lights that shimmer gleefully in the reflection of the water, ready to be posted to a thousand Instagram accounts. Including mine, I guess, seeing as Andrew stops us halfway across to take a selfie.

We round the curve of Trinity College next, where giant snowflakes are projected onto the front entrance. Our progress slows considerably here, the narrow sidewalks congested with people, but Andrew doesn't seem to mind, navigating his suitcase with good humor even as mine starts to sour. Eventually, I slide in front of him, intent on politely pushing people out of the way, but Andrew tugs me back and I follow his gaze toward Grafton Street, the busy shopping thoroughfare with its famed Christmas lights strung elegantly overhead.

"No," I say as he raises a brow.

"Come on."

"It's jammed."

"It's Christmas."

It's Christmas.

And the smile on his face is so boyish, so hopeful, that I don't resist too hard when he tugs me again, and we wind our way through the traffic and onto the busy street. The stores are still open here too, and people move in and out of them with cones of gelato and cups of hot chocolate, numerous shopping bags dangling from their arms.

We edge around a tight circle singing along to a busker, a rosy-cheeked teenager who looks like he's having the night of his life, before Andrew brings us to a halt at the mouth of an alleyway to get our bearings.

"I feel like I should pop in somewhere and get your parents something," he says, peering into the nearest store. "I'd offer the giant Toblerone, but I'm not that grateful."

"What about one of your photos?" I suggest. "They'd love one. Truly."

"You think?" He sounds distracted and I look over to see his face tilted to the sky, or more specifically, to the mistletoe hanging from the stone archway above.

"That could be anything," I say. "It could be drugs. A lot of drugs in this city. It's a big problem."

"Worried you're going to freak out again, huh?"

"*No*, I—"

"Because I'm too hot to handle? It's the bobble hat, isn't it? Nothing screams sex appeal like a knitted bobble—"

I kiss him, and both of us smile when I do.

Maybe we don't need to talk about us. Maybe we'll talk about it when we have time, without Christmas and family looming over us. We'll talk when we're back in Chicago. And in the meantime, we'll share a kiss goodbye.

Except I don't want this to be goodbye.

The thought comes to me as soon as his lips touch mine, sending a sharp spark of panic through me, and though he obviously means this to just be a quick one, I keep myself pressed firmly against him, clutching the ends of his coat as his hands settle on my arms.

"Do you know what?" he murmurs when he breaks

away. "I think we're both really good at that. Eight out of ten."

"Shut up," I groan, but I'm more embarrassed than annoyed. More pleased than embarrassed. And he knows it. The way he looks at me now makes me wonder if he's thinking the same thing I am, which is why the hell have we never tried this whole kissing thing before. Though maybe if we had it wouldn't have been the same. These feelings felt sudden to me back in Chicago, confusing and strange. But now I can't help but think that maybe they're not so sudden after all. Maybe they were more gradual than that. A slowly cresting wave just waiting to break on the shore. Maybe it was always coming. Maybe that's why it feels so right and the thought of leaving him now, even just for the next few days, has me feeling hollower than I have any right to be.

"Come on," he says, slipping his gloved hand back into mine. "I want to meander."

"We've been meandering for *three days*."

He doesn't care.

Andrew makes us walk all the way to the top of the street, which takes twice as long as it should seeing as how he stops at every window display.

Finally, we turn left at the Christmas tree, walking parallel to St Stephen's Green park. It's shut for the night, but the line of horse-drawn carriages is still operating outside it and they take turns clopping off with delighted tourists taking videos as they go. We keep moving, past more hotels and pubs and restaurants where people spill out onto the streets and straight into taxis, before completing the block down the quieter and darker Merrion Square. And there, halfway down by the towering government buildings, a woman in a bright pink coat leans against a car, her head bent as she scrolls through her phone.

My sister.

"That's her," I say unnecessarily, seeing as she's the only person around. My steps quicken as excitement bubbles inside and as we draw closer she glances up, waving when she sees us.

Andrew makes a surprised noise behind me. "So, she's, like, *identical* identical."

I laugh. "I've definitely shown you a picture before."

"Yeah, but in person it's..."

A lot. I know that. Zoe and I look the same down to the last freckle at times, though she always kept her hair longer than mine. And of course, now there's one pretty big difference.

"You're alive!" she proclaims, throwing her arms wide. I have to step to the side to hug her, her pregnant belly making it impossible to meet her face to face. When I pull back, she grabs my hands, placing them where my soon-to-be nephew rests.

"Meet Logan," she says.

"I thought it was Patrick."

"Patrick was last week. Now it's Logan."

I smirk. "And next week it will be?"

"I met a really nice Ryan the other day," she says as her eyes flick behind me.

"Meet Andrew," I say, welcoming him into the family reunion.

Zoe holds out a hand as though she expects him to kiss it. "Charmed."

"Would you stop?"

"What? My child needs a father." She says this while shaking Andrew's hand, Andrew who isn't quick enough to mask his confusion.

Her expression turns serious. "He left me when he found out."

And here we go. "Zoe—"

"I thought I meant something to him, you know? But he left me. Penniless and alone and—"

"She went through a donor," I say loudly. "And she earns more than I do."

Zoe huffs. "Spoilsport. I paid a stupid amount of money for a small bit of semen," she tells him, pinching her fingers together. "A complete rip-off. I was perfectly fine chancing it with a couple of one-night stands but Molly was like '*Noooo*, that's unethical.'"

"Being the sarcastic twin is all she has," I say, and Zoe tilts her head, looking at him thoughtfully as she rubs her belly.

"I never had an Andrew on my name list."

"Okay," I say, stepping in front of him. As I do, I draw her attention back to me and a smile lights up her face.

"I can't believe you're here," she says, and draws me into another hug. This one is a proper one and I feel the same twinge of sadness I always do when I see her for the first time after a few months. I don't think it will ever be easy being so far away from her, even if it is what I want.

"You need to sit down," I say. "How are you even standing right now?"

"With great difficulty." She unlocks the car as Andrew brings his stuff around to the trunk. "Have you seen these ankles? Of course, whenever I complain to Mam, I get a twenty-minute lecture about how she had to carry *two* babies. She's *thrilled* about finally getting to meet this guy, by the way. The famous Andrew in the flesh."

He smiles. "Famous, huh? No pressure, then."

"We also expect our guests to repay our hospitality with solid gold? Molly, I don't know if you told him the rules?"

"There's a giant tube of M&Ms in here if you play your cards right," he says, hefting his case inside. Zoe plants a hand over her heart.

"And there we go. Andrew is at the top of the list. Goodbye, Logan! We barely knew you." She glances at me. "He gets shotgun."

"But I'm your sister!"

"And he's the *guest*. Get in before I make you walk, my baby's cold."

And with that, we get into the car.

CHAPTER NINETEEN

The unease starts to kick in the closer we get to the house. Zoe peppers Andrew with questions the entire way, which gives me the chance to sit back and not think for a few minutes. Or at least, try not to think. I guess I should feel a sense of relief. All that money, all that stress, all those chocolates given to grumpy cab drivers, and here we are. We made it.

But all I feel is apprehension. I can't help but wonder if as soon as we step foot back in Chicago, this will be over. That we'll go back to just being Andrew and Molly. I mean, sure, we had a cute time in London. A little back and forth, oh, I'll take you ax throwing. But that was said with twinkling fairy lights and an eccentric cousin and that new warm contentment that didn't have anything to do with our real lives. With our friends and jobs and responsibilities. Throw those into the mix and anything could happen.

"Did you see the O'Reillys got an extension?" Zoe asks as we turn onto our road. We pass a familiar red-brick house on the corner with a very notable box taped onto the side. "Mam's fuming. Say it's ruining the whole street."

"She's just jealous."

"Of course she's jealous." She pulls in sharply, parallel parking with enviable ease. "Home sweet home," she says, sending me a smirk.

I ignore her, gazing up at the small, terraced house of my childhood. "They've seriously made you move in with them?"

Zoe lives in a decent apartment down by the docks. One of those fancy buildings with its own Pilates studio and at least five independent, *very* serious coffee shops within walking distance.

"Only for a few weeks," she says as we get out of the car. "Not going to lie, I kind of like being looked after. Just don't tell them."

We follow her up the small laneway, Andrew grinning at the lit-up reindeer in the garden next door.

"*Mam?*" Zoe calls as we step inside. "I found your second-favorite daughter!"

"Zoe."

"And she brought a boy home!"

"Zoe!"

She ignores me, waddling a few steps into the house. "They must be at Mary's," she says, already turning back when there's no answer. "Give me five minutes."

"Mary's?" Andrew asks when she disappears outside again.

"Our neighbor. She's been by herself since her husband died. They spend a lot of time there."

"That's kind of them," Andrew says, following me into the room. "You must miss it, knowing everyone on the street."

"Are you kidding me? Do you know how nosy people can get? The woman four doors down baked me a cake the day I first started my period. I don't even know how she knew."

He laughs. "I still think that sounds nice."

"It was red velvet."

I shrug off my coat and scarf, already sweltering at the balmy conditions they like to keep the house in. A few of Zoe's things are scattered about as well as a couple of noticeable presents for the baby, but otherwise the place looks exactly the same as it always does. A small front room and an extended kitchen at the back, with three bedrooms and a bathroom upstairs. It was small and basic, but loved and cared for, and I had nothing but good memories of it growing up.

"Where's the tree?" Andrew asks, flicking the tassel at the end of one of Mam's cushions. She's had them since before I was born, along with the brown couch and the heavy wooden bureau that belonged to my grandmother. That sits where it always has, in the corner of the room, groaning under the weight of a million family photographs.

"We never get a tree."

From the look on his face, I might as well have told him Santa isn't real.

"Where would we put it?" I continue, gesturing around the small room.

"You really did nothing?"

"I guess we used to decorate the pine tree outside when we were younger. Dad pretended there were fairies inside."

"Okay, well, that's completely charming."

"I was a charming child." I point to a beaming photo of four-year-old me as proof. "Up until about twelve."

"All went downhill, huh?"

"Puberty was not my friend."

He scans the row of photographs, lingering over a few.

"This is the part where you tell me I grew into myself," I remind him.

"Did you though?"

"*Okay*, Mr. Sarcasm. You're a guest in this house, lest you forget."

Andrew just points at another photo of one of us atop a donkey. "What's going on here?"

"Zoe's birthday."

"Which is also your birthday," he says, only to frown when I shake my head. "Were you one of those one minute before midnight, one minute after situations?"

"Nope. We just celebrated on different days. We got to pick them."

He stares at me. "You got to pick your own birthday?"

"Uh-huh." I grin as I realize I'm blowing his mind. "My parents were very keen that we each got to feel unique. So, we celebrated our real birthday *and* we got another day."

"That's just greedy."

I laugh. "It felt very normal to us."

"Which one do we celebrate?"

"My real one," I assure him.

"And your other one?"

"March tenth. There's no significance," I add. "None. I picked it at random. I haven't done anything on it since I moved away, but my parents still send me a card."

"I can't believe you get two birthdays."

"I'm special."

He falls silent, examining each picture with intense focus, as though trying to glean as much as he can from them before he finally pulls away, asking about the shower. Despite not technically living here anymore, I fall quickly into the role of host, heading upstairs to make sure the place is clean while he runs outside to get what he needs from his suitcase.

"I'll just be in here," I say, pointing to my old room when he returns. "Mam will probably make stew because it's the only thing she can cook."

"Stew sounds great," he says, hanging up the spare towel I pass him.

"Give me a shout if you need anything."

He flashes me a brief smile and disappears behind the closed door.

This is where a normal person would leave him to it. But I don't move. It's like my feet are stuck to the carpet, my body weighted to the spot as I listen to the scrape of the lock against the wood, the gentle rustling of clothing before the shower turns on. The hallway fills with the noise of our boiler heating the water, of the water itself splashing against the tiles.

It's only when the front door opens below that I force myself back into my bedroom. Zoe left out some of her (non-maternity) clothes for me and I throw on a pair of her jeans and a hoodie before scraping my hair back into a bun. The water shuts off barely a few seconds later and I quickly tidy my things as I hear Andrew fumble with the lock.

We meet in the hallway, him with only that ragged towel wrapped around his waist. His clothes are in his arms, hiding half his chest, but I still get an eyeful of smooth wet skin and a shadowy trail of dark hair that disappears beneath the—

"No sixpack, sorry."

My eyes snap up to the small, knowing smile on his face.

"You don't need one," I say, and his smile widens. "That was quick," I add.

"I figured you might want one."

"Oh. Nah." I wave a hand, my eyes trained somewhere above his left shoulder. I don't want to waste a second more away from him than I have to. "I'll, uh... You can change in my room."

I don't give him a chance to respond, slipping past him into the now empty bathroom as we switch places. It's steamed up from his shower, the air warm and scented with soap. *His* soap. That stupid sandalwood/pine/going-to-take-you-into-the-woods-on-a-summer's-day-and-kiss-you-on-the-soft-forest-floor soap.

What *is* that?

I move automatically, trying to keep busy. I wipe the mirror clean and shake out the shower curtain. I hang up the mat and wash my hands. I stand in the middle of the room and try not to cry.

They're tired tears, I know they are. Emotional, physical, someone-look-after-me tears that burn behind my eyes. That I refuse to let fall.

Maybe I should have just brought him straight to the bus stop. It would have been easier that way. A clean break. No seeing him in my house, joking with my sister, probably about to charm my mother. I should have said goodbye in town, but I don't want to say goodbye at all.

I don't want him to go.

I don't want him to go. I don't want him to go. I don't want him to go.

I stare at the shower, taking a few steadying breaths until I'm sure I have myself under control. When I do, I return to my bedroom, where I knock softly, entering when Andrew tells me to. He's still only half-dressed, his chest and feet bare as he looks between the shirt options he's laid out on my bed.

"How formal is dinner here?" he asks.

"Tuxedos or get out."

"I figured."

I step farther into the room as he grabs a T-shirt with one hand and rubs the damp towel over his hair with the other. The muscles of his stomach pull taut as he does. The same muscles I touched last night. And where just as the kiss in Buenos Aires seemed a whole other world away, the dark bedroom in London feels like a lifetime ago, one we still haven't talked about.

"You're making a face."

"I know."

Andrew frowns, draping the towel against the back of a chair. "What's up?"

"I want to decide what this is before Christmas," I say. "I don't want to wait until we get back to Chicago. That's too long. You said you're not going anywhere, but I need to know where we stand or I'll just go crazy." I pause, sliding my hands down my thighs. "Does that make sense?"

"Of course it does."

I nod, waiting.

"Well," he says when I just stare at him. "What do you want this to be?"

Damn. I should have asked that first. "I don't know," I say honestly. "I know I don't want to stop."

"Neither do I."

"But don't you feel like we're moving too fast?" I ask. "I mean, we've gone from nothing to something pretty quickly, haven't we?"

"Maybe." He shrugs. "Maybe not. It doesn't feel wrong to me." He hesitates, looking at me curiously. "Does it feel wrong to you?"

I shake my head. Because that's the problem, it doesn't feel wrong at all. It feels right.

"Because if Oliver hadn't interrupted us..." Andrew continues.

"I know."

"I was ready to use some of my best moves, that's all I'm saying."

"Shut up," I groan, sitting on the edge of the bed. I catch a brief glimpse of his smirk before I drop my head into my hands.

"We have time," he says when I meet his gaze. "We have lots of time. So, if you want to go back to the beginning, we can do that."

"The beginning?"

"Yeah." He grins as he crouches before me. "Like first-date beginning. I mean, sure we'll have a leg up on other couples, but it's not like they could compete with us anyway."

Other couples. A fizzing kind of pleasure shoots through me at the words.

"You say you don't think it's wrong. But if you're worried it could be, we'll just... chill. Take things as they come. Okay?"

"Okay," I mumble, fidgeting with the hem of my sleeve.

"When do you get back to Chicago?"

"The twenty-eighth."

"I'm back on the seventh," he says formally. "Would you like to get a coffee with me, Molly?"

"I guess."

"Would you like to show a little more enthusiasm?"

"Would you like to put your shirt on?" I respond, and he laughs, doing as requested.

"I'll see you on the seventh."

"You'll just be back!"

"And I'll come straight to you. We can get dinner."

Dinner. I can do dinner. I've had dinner with lots of people. "I get to pick where we eat."

"I wouldn't dream of it any other way."

I nod, distracted as his hands find mine. It's getting harder to think when he's near me like this. But dinner is good. "There's this Nepalese place in Wicker Park that I think you'll really—"

The way his gaze drops to my mouth is the only warning I get before he kisses me. It only lasts a few seconds, nowhere near long enough, and I try to curb my annoyance when he pulls back.

"When you say taking it slow," I mutter, and he smiles before kissing me again.

"You want to make out on your bed?"

"And make all my teenage dreams come true?" Yes, yes, I do. But before I can push him down on the sagging mattress and act out seventeen-year-old me's fantasies, we're interrupted by Zoe calling my name from below.

"If this interrupting family thing becomes a habit for us," I begin, and he laughs, sitting back on his heels. "Ready to meet my parents?" I ask, accepting his hand as he helps me to my feet. "Mam is—"

I break off with an annoyed huff as Zoe calls me again. And even though it's been years, I'm so used to the sound of my sister shrieking at me that my first instinct is to ignore it. But a second later she yells it a third time, only this one is followed by a short, piercing scream.

CHAPTER TWENTY

I go down the stairs so fast I almost trip. Andrew actually does, stumbling over the bottom step as we find Zoe standing in the middle of the kitchen. She's bent double, one hand grasping the back of a chair, her face screwed up in pain.

"I'm fine," she says when she sees us. "Sorry, I'm fine."

"You screamed!"

"I'm dramatic. I just—" Her lips press together as she barely holds back a groan. Andrew curses softly beside me.

"Are you having contractions?"

She shakes her head. "Fake ones."

"They don't look fake," I say.

"They're Braxton Hicks. It's a thing. It's a known thing." She has to force the last word out as another one hits, her knuckles turning white as she collapses into the chair. "Jesus *Christ*."

"We should go to the hospital," I say as Andrew crouches beside her. She immediately grabs hold of his hand, and he doesn't even wince as she proceeds to squeeze the bones off him. "Zoe? Hospital?"

Zoe just rolls her eyes, or as much as she can roll her eyes while her uterus is gripping itself like a stress ball. "I'll just have a bath."

"How will that help!"

"I don't know! Stop yelling at me!"

Andrew acts as a steadying weight as she attempts to stand and she grunts a thank you as she gets to her feet.

As she does, I see a wet patch spreading rapidly down her pants. It's only through sheer force of will that I swallow my gasp.

Andrew follows my gaze and, to be fair to the man, he doesn't so much as flinch as he looks quickly back to me, eyebrows raised.

"Zoe? Honey?" I keep my voice as gentle as possible. "I think your waters just broke."

"I probably just peed myself. You do that a lot when you have a human pressing on your bladder."

"I don't think you peed yourself and I don't think these are fake contractions. I think you're having your baby."

Zoe stares at me, looking genuinely confused and extremely irritated.

My sister is not an idiot. We battled it out at school together to get top of our classes. She beat me by three points in our final exams. She does the *New York Times* crossword every day and once learned Portuguese in six months because I bet her she couldn't.

She's not an idiot. But she is, and always has been, a stubborn brat, and right now, seems so completely set in her ways that the alternative is unthinkable to her.

I try again. "You're going into—"

"I'm not going to labor," she says, irritation winning out over confusion. "Don't be stupid. You're stupid."

"Zoe—"

"I'm not due for three weeks."

"It's not like the baby is checking its calendar!"

"The hospital?" Andrew asks.

I start to nod before remembering how little I have with me. "I don't have my license."

"I can drive her."

"Hello?" Zoe calls, waving a hand. "Stop talking about me like I'm not here."

"Stop being a dumbass," I counter. "Where's Mam and Dad?"

"They're dropping Mary at the church."

"Which church?"

"I don't know!"

"Well, how long will it take them to—"

"Maybe they should meet us there?" Andrew asks.

"This isn't happening," Zoe groans as Andrew and I share a look over her bent head.

"Look, if they're fake, then they're fake," I say. "No problem. But it won't hurt to hear it from someone who didn't learn their medical knowledge from *Grey's Anatomy*. Please just let us take you."

Zoe gives me a look like *I'm* the unreasonable one in this situation, but something in my face must convince her that she's not getting out of this.

"Maybe they'll give me painkillers," she says, and I nod encouragingly.

The contractions seem to ease once we get her into the car and she calms down when we're on the road, texting our parents as well as a few of her friends to let them know what an idiot I'm being. Despite her refusal to believe this is happening, she thankfully has the directions saved on her GPS and Andrew makes quick work of the traffic as he drives us back into the city. The maternity hospital is right in the center of town and we end up paying an extortionate amount for parking three streets away but, right now, I couldn't give a crap.

In reception, a nurse with Christmas puddings as earrings takes one look at us and immediately jumps into action.

"I'm *fine*," Zoe says for the millionth time as the woman, Cara according to her lanyard, tries to lead her toward a wheelchair. "I'm not even having them anymore."

I clamp a hand around her forearm when she tries to shrug me off. "Can we maybe listen to the nice medical professionals?"

"I *will* when it's *time* to." But she gets into the chair, her eyes wide and her face pale, and I see her attitude for what it really is, sheer undiluted terror.

Despite her jokes about baby daddies, she's never wanted to be in a relationship. I've never seen her go out with someone for more than a few weeks, and even then, I think it's because she was curious about what all the fuss was about. But she wanted to be a mother, so she became one. It would never have occurred to her that she couldn't at least try. And like everything else she did, she tried her best.

As a single parent, that meant plans. Five-year plans and ten-year plans, complicated financial charts, and a tight network of friends and family to help her out. I know she planned for so long and tried for so long that a part of her had forgotten about the actual event, especially when that event was two and a half weeks early.

"Are we going to another waiting room?" she asks, sounding very young as she blindly signs a form.

"We're going to the labor ward," Cara says.

"The... Why?"

She doesn't even blink. "Because you're going into labor."

"This can't be happening," Zoe repeats for the twelfth time. She passes the clipboard back and turns her wild gaze to me. "I can't have a December Capricorn."

"It turned out okay for Jesus."

"The man was *crucified*, Molly!"

Cara takes up her position at the back of the chair, looking at us expectantly. "Do you want to follow me?"

It takes us all a moment to realize she's talking to Andrew.

"I'm not the father," he says, startled.

"Oh, I'm sorry. I thought—"

"I'm a single mother," Zoe interrupts, texting furiously into her phone. "Modern and strong and brave. Can we wait for my mam?"

The nurse is already wheeling her through the doors. "If she makes herself known when she arrives, we'll be sure to—"

"No, we need to wait for them," Zoe says, starting to panic again. "We need to— Mam!"

At that moment, our mother chooses to stride through the reception doors, coatless and hatless despite the weather outside.

"I'm here, love. I'm here." Her previously blonde hair is now a white-silver and there're more lines around her face than I remember, there always are whenever I see her, but she looks as strong as ever as she hurries over to us, her gaze taking me in briefly before they snap to my sister.

Zoe grasps her wrist, holding her to her. "I think I'm having my baby," she says, like she's confessing something.

"We'll see what the doctors say."

"Where's Dad? Is Dad coming? Where—"

"He's gone back to the house to get your things, but we thought it best that I come straight in."

"Yes," Zoe says. "Yes, stay with me."

"I'll be there the whole time," she says, squeezing her.

"Are we ready to go now?" Cara asks with the patience of a saint. My mother nods and, with a frantic smile my way, she wheels my sister through the swinging doors of the labor ward, leaving us to stare after them.

"Is this the part where she finds out she's suddenly having triplets?" I say to Andrew who looks a little out of breath.

"I was having visions of her going into full labor in the car," he says, running a hand down his face. "I always thought I was pretty good in an emergency, but..."

I laugh a little manic laugh and look around the waiting room. No one seems particularly bothered by our few minutes of drama, all too concerned with whoever they're waiting for themselves. "Well, I guess we should... Shit! Your bus! If you need to—"

"I've got plenty of time," he interrupts. "I can stay here if you like."

"Really?"

"On the hour, every hour," he reminds me, and I nod, relieved.

"At least until my dad gets here?"

"Of course." He drapes an arm over my shoulder, drawing me into him as he leads me to a row of empty chairs along the back wall where it looks like I'll be spending the rest of my Christmas Eve.

———

At some point, we sit there long enough that I fall asleep. I don't remember feeling tired, but the events of the last few days must be catching up with me because one moment I'm gazing blankly at a poster for quitting smoking, and the next I'm horizontal, staring at the legs of one of the expectant fathers across the room.

I'm twisted along three seats in a very awkward position, one I know I'll be feeling in my back for days seeing as I'm no longer twenty and reaching down to pick up a sock too quickly has the potential to put me out of commission. But I don't move right away and not just because my left leg is dead and about to break into a thousand pins and needles. No, I stay where I am because there's a pleasant scrape against my scalp, a frankly, semi-orgasmic experience that I never want to end.

Andrew's playing with my hair.

I open my eyes to see his own closed, his head tipped back against the wall as he runs his fingers absently across the crown of my head. One particular tug sends a shiver down my spine and he opens his eyes as I shift, looking down at me as though surprised to find me there. He immediately stops touching me, returning his hand to rest on his thigh.

"Sorry," he murmurs, and I shake my head.

"Keep going. That's better than any of the massages I pay a gazillion dollars for."

"I aim to please." He says it sarcastically but the look on his face is unsure so I purposefully close my eyes and turn away from him, waiting.

After a moment, he starts back up again and, I swear to God, I almost purr.

"What time is it?" I ask instead.

"A little after eleven."

"What?" My eyes fly open. "Your—"

"I'll be grand," he says, his other hand pressing firmly on my shoulder as I try to sit up. My head spins as I shrug him off, moving too quickly.

"You missed the last bus."

"I'll get a taxi."

"But you'll—"

"I'm fine, Moll."

My panic eases at his calmness.

"Okay," I say, still hesitant as I slump back into the chair. "Is my dad here?"

"He left about twenty minutes ago. Sorry. Think he and your mam are going to take shifts sleeping so someone's always with Zoe. He didn't want to wake you. Said you looked as tired as a corpse." Andrew hesitates. "But in an affectionate way."

I snort. "Sounds like him." I take out my phone to shoot him a text and as I do, my attention catches on the duty-free bag next to us.

"He also dropped that in," he says when I pick it up. "Said he assumed it's for your sister."

"It is," I say, taking out the tissue-wrapped package. It feels like years since I bought it. "It's her terrible Christmas present."

"I'm sure you can get her something else," he says kindly. "The shops are still open."

I can only smile. "It's an on-purpose terrible Christmas present," I explain. "It's tradition to get each other bad gifts."

"It's tradition to get each other presents neither of you wants?" He sounds understandably confused.

"It's the thought that counts."

"Have you thought about getting each other something

you'd actually like? Maybe you could start a new tradition. A, dare I say, much better one?"

"I know how it sounds," I laugh. "But it's something we've done since we were kids. We don't know why we do it except that we've always done it. And I don't know..." I shrug. "It's fun. I always get her perfume. The worst perfume I can find."

"What does she get you?"

"Food," I say. "Usually some disgusting, novelty snack that I can only take one bite of. It then spends a month in the back of the cupboard before Dad finds it and eats it."

"Perfume," Andrew says slowly, realization dawning. "That's why you always smell awful on our flights. It's true!" he adds when I whack his leg. "I thought you were just an eccentric. I've got to say I'm a little relieved. Though I still don't get it."

"Do you know how hard it is to get something someone will hate?" I ask. "Do you know how much thought I put into that gift? I think harder about her present than I do anyone else's."

"I know you're trying to make it seem like this is a logical thing, but it's really not."

I smirk, smoothing the bag against my lap. "It's tradition," I repeat. "It doesn't have to be logical."

"And you said you guys didn't know how to do Christmas."

Mam enters the waiting room before I can respond, carrying a tray of plastic cups filled with water. "The doctors are with your sister," she says, passing them to us. "Who sent me away because apparently I was looking at her too much." She sits beside me, taking in my Christmas sweater with a single eyebrow rise.

"It's from Paris," I say, a little defensively, and she shakes her head.

"You poor thing. You must be dead on your feet after all of that."

"It wasn't so bad," I say, glancing back at Andrew. It's only then that I realize we haven't exactly done introductions. "Mam, this is—"

"We've met," she interrupts, giving him a warm smile. "When you were asleep. He's told me all about your adventures."

Oh, he did, did he? Andrew looks innocently at me as she takes out her phone, reading a text before carefully typing out a one-fingered response. She's still texting when he stands suddenly, giving an exaggerated yawn.

"Just going to go stretch my legs," he says, wandering off before I can stop him.

"He's very handsome," Mam murmurs, still focusing on her phone. "You never told me he was handsome."

I make a noncommittal noise, waiting for her to send her message. "Your hair's nice."

"The new girl at the salon says I can pull off gray."

"You can."

"Hmmm." The phone goes to her lap as she turns to me, rubbing her thumb across my cheek. Whatever she sees in my face must satisfy her because she lets me go, moving her attention back to the labor doors. "I'm glad you're still in one piece. You had us all in a panic thinking you wouldn't make it back."

"I didn't think it would be that big a deal."

"To not have you home?" She seems surprised by my surprise. "Why would you think that?"

"Just..." I trail off, a little embarrassed. "I don't know. We're not exactly big Christmas people."

"I still want you here," she says. "We both do. You should have seen your father. He usually tracks your plane by the minute. And this year, with the storm, we were terrified that you wouldn't be able to make it back at all. He stayed up all night waiting to see if they would put on extra flights."

"You didn't say anything," I protest, thinking of all the calls Andrew had to fend from his family.

"And stress you out even more?" Mam shakes her head. "That's the last thing you needed, to be worrying about us. Molly, you're an adult. One who's off living her own life. I never want to make you think that you have to drop everything to come back here. Only if you want to."

"I do want to," I say quickly. "I always want to."

She hesitates, her eyes dropping to my sweater. "If you want to start putting up decorations," she begins, and I almost smile at the reluctance in her voice.

"I don't. I really, really don't. I just want to be with you guys."

She seems a little mollified by that, leaning into me as though sharing a secret. "Did you see that light-up snowman the Brennans put up on the roof? Where they're finding the money for all the electricity, I don't know. But God forbid I say anything to them about it."

"I'll have to take a picture for Andrew," I say. "He loves all that stuff."

"Does he now? And that's what's rubbing off on you, is it?"

"Maybe a little bit."

"You'll be wearing reindeer antlers on your head next," she mutters.

"Or putting up stockings in the dead of night. Can you

imagine if Dad walked down the stairs one year and the whole house was like Santa's grotto?"

"He probably wouldn't notice," she says dryly, and I laugh. Her expression softens at the sound.

"I'm glad you made it home," she says. "Never think that I don't want that." She draws me into a hug, kissing me firmly on the cheek.

"We're being watched," she adds, when we pull away and I glance over my shoulder to where Andrew lingers by the magazine rack, giving us our moment. "Should that boy not be on a bus somewhere?"

"I think he wants to be here in case something happens."

"I see. Well, you can tell me all about *that* when we're home."

"You'll like him," I say truthfully, and a warm smile breaks over her face as her phone chimes. "Your sister wants me back," she says, getting up with a groan. "I'll try not to look her in the eye this time."

Andrew returns when she goes, a teasing look in his eyes. "Hah hah," he sings. "Your family loves you."

"Everyone loves me," I grumble, trying not to show how embarrassed I am. He can see right through me, of course, but thankfully knows not to push and merely settles back in his chair, both of us facing the swinging hospital doors as we wait for the latest miracle to occur.

CHAPTER TWENTY-ONE

My nephew is born ninety minutes later, three weeks premature, in the early hours of Christmas morning.

"He slid right out," Mam announces when she tells us the news. Andrew, to his credit, gives only the slightest wince. Because of course, Andrew is still here. Andrew who stayed with me, who just scoffed when I told him twice to get a taxi. Who held my hand without even asking, knowing I needed it. And I was glad of it. Selfishly so. I didn't want him to go. I want him here. I want him with me.

Because the baby was a little early, the nurses whisked him off for some checks, so it's a while before I'm able to see him. A while that soon has me pacing up and down the waiting room in frustration.

"If he's fine then why do they need to do so many tests?" I say out loud for the millionth time. Andrew doesn't bother to respond, only pats my knee when I collapse back into the chair beside him.

"Distract me," I order.

"Sexy distraction or card trick distraction? Not that they're mutually exclusive, of course."

"Can you get me sugar?"

"Even better. I can get you the most processed, shouldn't-even-be-allowed-in-a-hospital sugar known to man." He squeezes my leg and makes the long, arduous trek across the waiting room while I try and catch the eye of the nurse manning the station, the nurse who has learned in the last twenty minutes to not even look in my direction.

As I do, another one appears through the main doors, a stack of paperwork in her hands. She's pretty, with long dark hair scraped back into a thick braid. She does a double-take as she passes Andrew, which doesn't exactly surprise me, but then she comes to a complete stop, her eyes going wide as she halts mid-step.

"Andrew?"

Andrew glances up, about to tap his card against the machine, when his face breaks into a smile.

"Ava?"

Ava? Who the hell is Ava?

I watch, bewildered, as the stranger leans in for a hug, thrown by the sharp spike of jealousy that runs through me.

Their voices lower as he draws her to the side and chat rapidly for a few minutes. Eventually, she hugs him again, smiling cheerfully as she disappears back around the corner. Andrew glances my way and my eyes immediately drop to my phone in the most obvious move ever.

"Making friends?" I ask when he returns, tossing a chocolate bar into my lap.

"I used to babysit her," he says, and I glance up in surprise. "Am I old now?"

"They're just getting younger," I say, relieved. "So she's working through Christmas?"

"Actually... no. Depending on her paperwork, she's out of here in an hour. She's driving back to her folks tonight."

I start to nod before I realize what he's telling me. "Oh."

"Yeah. She's going to give me a ride. I'll be home for breakfast."

"That's... perfect." I start to unwrap my snack even as my appetite shrinks. "Brilliant news."

"It will save me the taxi fare at least. But if you need me to—"

"Shut your face," I interrupt. "Shut it right up. Go home. This was the whole point of everything. You've already stayed way longer than you should have."

"It's a bit of a special situation."

"And I'm *sure* Zoe will understand that you, a stranger, is not here to mind her."

"And who's going to mind you?"

I still at his words, melting a little inside, and take a large bite of chocolate to hide it. I realize then how easy it would be to get him to stay with me. That all I need to do is ask and he would. I know it without a doubt and, weirdly, that helps me not to.

My mother appears through the doors a moment later, catching my eye. Time to see my sister.

"Go," I say gently. "Please. I am so sick of you."

He laughs, lounging back in the chair. "She's not going for a while yet," he says. "I'll see you back here?"

I nod, my knees creaking as I stand. I'm going to need to do some serious hot yoga after Christmas. "Text me if something changes."

"I will."

"Better go meet the newest Kinsella," I say, and think about leaning down to kiss him, the way couples do, but chicken out and do an incredibly corny finger-gun motion instead that makes him smile and me want to die.

Before I can do anything else to embarrass myself, I turn and follow the signs to the maternity ward.

Zoe's fancy job has paid for a fancy private room. It's small and bare, bar the giant hospital machines blinking at us, but Dad brought some of Zoe's things from home, including a card from the neighbors and a stuffed animal from our childhood. I remember Gabriela's Cubs bear waiting in the suitcase, which is still probably stuck in Argentina, and make a mental note to give it to her as soon as I can so the baby can imprint early.

And it's the baby I go to see first. My as-yet-nameless nephew lies pink and new in a plastic crib on the other side of the room and, as soon as I lay eyes on him, the predictable happens.

"You're not crying already," Zoe grumbles from the bed.

"It's okay to cry now, Zoe. All the cool kids are doing it." I lean over the crib, pressing my finger to the tip of his nose. "You are very small," I tell him.

"He didn't feel small when I was pushing him out."

"I'm trying to have a private moment with my nephew."

"Well, do it while passing me my juice. *Ow.*"

I turn around to see her fall back against the bed, a pillow propping up her torso. "You look like shit," I tell her, leaving the child to sleep while I focus on her.

"I just had a baby," she grumbles. "What's your excuse?"

"Days of traveling to be with you."

"Oh, that was for *me*, was it?"

"I knew the baby was coming. Sixth sense."

"Thanks for the heads-up."

I take a seat next to the bed, handing her the plastic cup on the nightstand. She really does look worn out, which is understandable all things considered. And whereas my usual reaction to anything she does is to make fun of her, I feel like she should get a pass for today so, instead, I take her hand and pat it gingerly until she snorts and pulls it away.

"That's enough affection from you, thanks very much."

"Well done, Zoe."

She huffs a breath, but she smiles. "Thank you."

"The nurse said everything's fine?"

"Yeah. Just a few checks because he's an early bastard."

"An attention seeker like his mother. It's nothing we can't handle."

She watches me as I brush the hair back from her forehead, her face softening with each movement. "Sorry I freaked out before," she murmurs.

"I think you're allowed to. Plus, you're right. Christmas birthdays are the worst."

"I know." She groans. "It's going to be so freaking expensive. And when he grows up, he's just going to complain that he doesn't get any attention." She sighs. "He's going to have to get a fake birthday too, isn't he?"

"Maybe Mam and Dad were on to something."

"Hmmm." She tilts her head away and pats the bed beside her. "Get up."

"What?"

"Get up!" she commands, tugging at the blanket. "I need a hug. All those hormones."

I roll my eyes but there's more than enough room in the bed for the two of us, so I do as requested, climbing carefully onto the mattress and twisting into her body, flinging an arm around her. We used to sleep like this when we were children and Mam first put us into our own rooms. It was a necessity, she claimed. She said we were too clingy and that we needed to learn to be independent. She wasn't wrong. Zoe and I were inseparable back then and those first few days I didn't know what to do without her. But Zoe especially found it hard. She started getting nightmares and eventually Mam let her come into me when she woke up (I think she only did it so that Zoe wouldn't go into *her*) and more often than not I'd wake in the morning to an elbow in my stomach.

Still, after all this time it feels natural to snuggle in next to her and lay my head on her shoulder. I think it always will be.

"Hey," I whisper, setting her present on her lap. "Happy Christmas."

"Oh no." She grimaces, poking it with one finger. "Perfume?"

I nod.

"Yours is at the house. Ugh." She lets the tissue paper fall to the bed as she turns the glittering pink bottle in her hands. It looks even worse than it did at the airport. "I can smell it already."

"No sniffing," I say as she brings it to her nose. "That's cheating."

"Alright. Alright."

I watch with a smile as Zoe scrunches her eyes shut and sprays it a few inches from her chest. She immediately starts coughing.

"Oh my *God*."

"It's good, right?"

"This can't be healthy for the baby. I smell like a twelve-year-old girls' magazine. From 2004."

"A vintage bouquet."

She winces again. "Don't try and make me laugh. It hurts my vagina."

"How does it—"

"I don't *know*," she moans. "It just does. Don't question

me, I'm a new mother." She burrows deeper into me and I wrinkle my nose at the perfumed smell of her. "Andrew seems nice," she says after a minute.

"Smooth transition."

"You want to tell me what's going on there?"

"How did you—"

"Please," she scoffs. "It's obvious. *You're* obvious."

"We kissed."

"You did?" She makes a humming noise that I don't know what to make of. "What kind of kiss?"

I give her a brief rundown of the last few days, including the brief but memorable make-out session in London. "We've decided to try dating when we get back," I finish.

"*Dating?*" She looks appalled. "You don't need to date. You basically know everything about each other."

"Not like that."

"Yes, like that," she says. "You're just adding in boning."

"Zoe!"

"I'm *joking*," she says when I make to get off the bed. She pulls me quickly back down, her arm like an iron fist across my stomach. "Has he gone home, then?"

"He's going soon. He bumped into someone from his hometown because this is Ireland so of course he did. She's giving him a ride."

"He could always stay here for the night. Go back in the morning."

"He can't, he has to go home. That's the whole point of all the stress." I pick at the bedspread and then, when that doesn't satisfy me, my hair, suddenly restless.

"You don't want him to go," Zoe surmises.

I shrug, fooling no one. "I'll see him in a few days."

She just watches me, her face pale and tired, but her

eyes as shrewd as ever as she takes me in. "You could always go with him."

"Excuse me?"

"You could go home with him," she says. "For Christmas."

"That's ridiculous."

"No, it's not. Christmas is about spending time with people you love."

"I don't *love*—"

"As a friend, then," she interrupts. "And it's not like we'll be doing anything here. They're keeping me in overnight."

"I'm too tired for any more traveling," I say. "And I'm certainly not going to crash their Christmas."

"I'm sure they'd love to have you. I'm sure *he'd* love to have you. Why else do you think he's stuck around here as long as he has? If he didn't care so much about you, he would have left hours ago. He likes you."

"And I like him! No one is denying that, but I'm not leaving you. Not when you have stitches where no one should have stitches."

"But I'm not doing anything!" she says with a laugh. "I'm done. That's my baby and this is my Christmas. This bed. These walls. We're talking about a couple of hours down the road."

"You're reading too much into it."

"Will you ask him at least?"

"No!"

"Molly!"

We both freeze as a sound comes from the crib, a tiny hiccup that has us both turning to the baby. My nephew makes another noise and wriggles, as if testing out this strange new world, before falling still again. Neither Zoe nor I move, waiting to see if he does something else.

He does not.

"So, fun new thing about me," Zoe says as we stare at him. "I don't think I've ever loved or will ever love anyone as much as I love him. Even if he turns out to be a dick. Which with me as his mother is a real possibility."

"I kind of want to eat him. That's a thing, right? Like, I see his little fists and I just want to... eat him."

"How about you hold him instead?"

I make a face. "No."

"Why not?"

"You know me and babies," I say, even as I find it difficult to tear my eyes away from him.

"Yes, but this one is *my* baby. I expect you to show him more love and attention than this."

"Well, I expected to be a godmother."

"Would you get over that?" she snaps just as the door swings open and a nurse who does not look old enough to be in charge of, you know, keeping humans *alive* bustles into the room.

"Twins!" she proclaims, glancing between us. "Which one of you is Zoe? Just kidding. The one in the hospital gown, right?"

"Nothing gets past this one." Zoe sighs, pushing herself up. "Can I go home now?"

"No," the nurse says cheerfully. "You do that and you'll be back here in an hour. It's feeding time."

"I'm not hungry."

I roll my eyes as I climb off the bed. "For the baby, you idiot."

"Oh." Zoe looks down at her breasts with a doubtful look. "Will you send Mam in?"

I nod, rounding the bed to kiss my nephew's tiny little forehead. "I love you," I whisper because I do, and then hug my sister goodbye.

My mother is talking on the phone outside, but she hangs up when I exit.

"Zoe wants you to go in," I say and she nods, but doesn't move.

"Are you alright?"

"I'm fine. I was... Zoe actually..."

She just waits.

"I was thinking about maybe spending today with Andrew. With his family. For Christmas. Christmas Day. And then I could—"

"I think that sounds like a wonderful idea," she interrupts.

"You do?"

"Yes, it's not like we'll be doing anything here," she says, echoing Zoe. "We'll be able to celebrate properly tomorrow."

I raise my brows at that, but don't say anything.

God, I mention briefly I thought she didn't want me home and now I'm going to come back next year to find out we've won most festive house in Dublin.

"I'll have to ask him first," I mutter, pulling my sleeves down over my hands. "He might say no."

Mam just gives me a look as the smiling nurse pops her head around the door.

"Can we have the mother of the mother?" she asks as Zoe's frustrated grunt comes from inside the room.

"I can't do it!" she calls. "My nipples are broken!"

"Just keep me updated," Mam says, cupping my cheek briefly as she follows the nurse back inside. "And best behavior."

"Why wouldn't I—"

"Pleases and thank yous."

"I'm not *nine*."

Though a few hours home and I feel like I am. I fight back a smile as the door swings shut, leaving me alone in the hallway. I stand there for a moment, stalling, before heading slowly back to the waiting area, past rooms of sleeping mothers and exhausted partners, past nurses and midwives and doctors as they get ready to spend Christmas Day in the hospital.

Andrew is in the same position I found him in at O'Hare, hunched in his seat, a magazine in his hands. Only this time it looks to be one for lactating mothers as opposed to a *National Geographic*. I linger just around the corner to watch him and know in my heart that whatever I'm feeling isn't going to go away anytime soon. This isn't me bouncing back after Brandon or losing my mind over a travel plan shot to hell. It's deeper than that. It's deeper and it's real and it's worth sticking my neck out for.

"Is Zoe okay?" he asks when I approach.

"She's fine," I say. "They're both fine. Fine and dandy." Oh my God, shut up. "Ava still around?"

"She should be done any second now. Though I realize I'm jinxing myself by saying that." He stands, stretching his arms over his head. "You good?"

"Yeah. Tired."

"I bet. Maybe you can—"

"I was actually thinking I could join you guys," I interrupt, the words spilling out of me in a rush.

Andrew looks confused, arms still raised as he bends his back. "For what?"

"For Christmas. Zoe suggested it and I thought it would be a nice opportunity to meet your family." I lose confidence by the second when he just stares at me. "I mean, only if that's okay with you. And no worries if it's not because I know you're excited to see everyone and we've come all this way to..." Nothing. He's giving me nothing. "You know what? I'm sorry. This is such short notice. Forget I ever said anything. Zoe's just—"

"I'd love for you to come." His arms drop to his side before he rubs his face, like he's trying to wake himself up. "That sounds great. If you're sure you're okay leaving Zoe?"

"She's not getting out until tomorrow," I say, a little awkward. "Shouldn't you check with your folks first?"

"I'll let them know," he shrugs.

"That a stranger is coming to visit on their biggest day of the year?"

He gives me an odd look. "You're not a stranger. They know who you are."

"They do?"

"Of course they do," he says as if it's the most obvious thing in the world. "They've known about you for years. And the biggest day of the year is Hannah's birthday. She makes sure of it."

"If you're positive—"

"I am," he says firmly, looking much more awake now. "They'd love to meet you. Mam especially. Honestly, this will make her day."

"Well... okay. I guess I'll go tell everyone." I start to walk backward, not taking my eyes off him. "Meet you back here?"

He nods, watching me go, and it's only when I reach the double doors that I force myself to turn around, smiling so wide that my cheeks start to hurt.

CHAPTER TWENTY-TWO

TWO YEARS AGO

Flight Eight, Chicago

"I think I'm dying."

Andrew watches me sympathetically as I slump back into the chair, pressing the mini soda can to my temple. "You should have said something."

"I know," I moan, shifting around again. It's impossible to get comfortable in this stupid seat. Next year, we're flying business class. I'll pay for us both, I don't care. Though I don't think even that could save me right now.

My period's being a little bitch. The doctor said it might be stress. She did that thing where she asked me if I had a high-pressured job and I just started laughing. But yeah, stress. Who knew. I mean, the old crimson tides have always sucked but they've at least been *manageable*. Nothing a few painkillers and a night of feeling sorry for myself couldn't handle. This month it's like my body's just decided to give up. I'm as weak as a newborn kitten and the trip to the airport has completely drained me.

"Don't look at me," I complain. "I look gross."

"You've looked worse," he says, smiling when I glare at him. I'd tried my best when I arrived, using all the energy I had as we ate, listening and nodding in all the right places as he caught me up on dating post-Alison (shite) and his apartment (also shite). But the headache started when they called our gate and, by the time we made it onto the plane, I could barely keep my eyes open.

I shift again, drawing my legs up as I try desperately to get comfortable in the small space, as though if I contort my body in the right way, the ache will suddenly stop.

"Here."

"What— Hey!" I glare harder when Andrew steals the tiny airplane pillow from my lap, fluffing it out as best he can before placing it on his shoulder. When I just stare at him, he pats it invitingly, one brow raised.

"No," I say flatly.

"You're not going to get comfortable sitting like that." When I don't move, he takes the blanket and then his own pillow, building a kind of wall between us. "I once dated a girl who said the only way she could be comfortable on her period was if she lay flat on the floor with her legs up against the wall. I used to come back to the apartment and find her in different rooms, working away on her laptop like that. I didn't question her and I'm not going to question you." He pats the pillow. "Slump."

God, this is embarrassing. But I guess the good news for me is that I'm in too much pain to care. I push up the armrest, shuffling closer to him. The position immediately allows me to bring my legs up more comfortably as I rest my head gingerly against the pillow. God damn him, but it works.

"Okay, you're not allowed to move," I mutter and can

feel his laugh through the makeshift barrier as I tug my legs tighter to my body. "Don't let me fall asleep."

"I won't."

"I mean it, Andrew." My eyes are so damn heavy.

I test out more of my weight on him, leaning a little heavier when he doesn't comment, and finally start to relax.

"Sorry I'm ruining Christmas," I mutter, and he laughs.

"You're not ruining Christmas."

"I'm ruining the flight."

"The whole point of this flight is to spend time with you. I'm spending time with you so do you see me complaining?"

He doesn't have any time to when I'm doing enough for the both of us.

"You're sick," he says firmly. "Let me look after you. I'll always look after you."

He says the last bit almost as if he's mad that I'd think otherwise and I nestle into the pillow, feeling a little better.

"Okay," I say. "I might have one very short nap."

"Good."

"But you have to wake me up for snacks."

"You got it."

There's movement above me as his head tilts, almost like he's placing a kiss to the top of my head. But it's too light for that, barely more than a whisper, and I think nothing more of it as unconsciousness pulls me under.

Now

It's another hour before Ava returns, looking heroically alert after a double shift, and at the sight of her, I'm reminded once again that whatever the world pays its nurses, it will never be enough. She's changed into sweatpants and a black fleece and accepts my added company with a more-the-merrier smile.

The city is a lot quieter when we emerge from the hospital, the sky dark and clear of any clouds. Ava leads us down the street to a small blue car that we somehow, with Tetris-like skill, manage to fit Andrew's suitcase inside. Of course, it means taking out Ava's bags and putting them in the back seat, but with only me to join them we have room.

As well as playing the radio at full volume, Andrew makes an effort to chat to her as we drive, helping to keep her awake, and she seems grateful as she catches him up on the latest news from the village and shares stories from home. Names and memories wash over me, meaning nothing, and despite the noise, the gentle rhythm of the car smoothly zipping along the empty streets soon has me closing my eyes.

At some point, I fall asleep. How I don't know. It's uncomfortable in the back, and the roads grow increasingly bumpy once we're off the motorway. But I'm beyond exhausted and so sleep I do, waking up only when a phantom finger drifts a path down my cheek.

Of course, it's not a phantom at all, but Andrew, and when I stir, he draws back, smiling softly in the dim glow of the dashboard as he twists in his seat to watch me.

"You alright?" he asks.

I nod only to immediately regret doing so when my neck screams in protest. "How long was I out?"

"About an hour," Ava says. "We're almost there."

We are? I sit up, a smile pulling at my lips as I take in the passing fields before nestling back into my corner.

"Hey," Andrew says. "Don't fall asleep again."

"You're not the boss of me."

"I mean it, Molly. Don't make me wake you up."

I ignore him, trying to get comfortable. I don't actually intend to go back to sleep, but my lids are feeling heavier and heavier and—

"Ow!" My eyes fly open as Andrew pokes me sharply in the leg.

"I warned you," he says, and turns back around. "We can walk from here," he continues, pointing to the side of the road.

Ava shoots him a confused glance. "Seriously?"

"Seriously. We're right over the hill. It's five minutes tops."

"What about your case?"

"We'll manage." His voice rises as he calls back to me. "We can walk, can't we, Moll?"

I make a face seeing as how I'd much rather stay here in the warm car until it drops me off at the presumably warm house, but Andrew has other ideas.

"She can walk," he says.

After a minute, Ava pulls into the side of a field and unlocks the doors. She's too sleepy to protest further but still looks unsure as she hugs Andrew and then me goodbye, driving off with a "Merry Christmas" and a soft beep of the horn.

I wait until she disappears around the corner before I turn to Andrew with a frown. "Am I being punished?"

"What do you mean?"

"I'm freezing my ass off."

"Want me to warm it?"

I don't even dignify that with a response, walking ahead of him in what thankfully must be the right direction because he jogs a few steps to catch up with me.

The cold air wakes me up at least, though there's still that dull ache behind my eyes that will take more than a cup of coffee to counter. The thought of having to put on a bright smile for Andrew's family, on top of awkwardly explaining my presence there makes me groan and I clench and unclench my gloved hands, doubt filling me as I lengthen my stride up the hill just as the dawn begins to break.

This was a stupid idea. I'm crashing their *Christmas*. I don't care how nice they are. I don't care how much Andrew likes me right now. No one really likes the strange lady who rocks up on Christmas morning. Way to make a first impression, Molly. Way to—

"So right now, what you're doing is city walking," Andrew calls to me. "When what you need to be doing is countryside walking. Especially on an incline."

I stop just as we reach the crest. "Sorry."

"No, please," he says, slightly out of breath. "I'm impressed."

"Do you want help with your suitcase?"

"Do you actually want to help?"

"No," I say, eyeing the thing. "But I don't have any sympathy for you. It was your idea to walk."

"It was. I was hoping to be romantic."

I blink at him. "Okay, we're going to need to have a serious conversation about what is and is not romantic, because if you think—"

"Just look over the hill, you idiot." And then muttering to himself, "Before I push you down it."

I make a "very funny" face and lunge my way up the final steps, pausing at the top as I wait for him. "Lovely," I proclaim, staring down at the small valley. "I'm so glad you made us..."

Oh.

Andrew reaches my side as I fall silent and together we watch as slowly, gently, the world around us lightens, as though coming to life before our very eyes.

"That's why we're walking," he says. To his credit, he only sounds a little smug.

The first weak rays of the sun highlight the frost on the gently sloping hills. There'll be snow on the mountains this morning, but down here the grass is still green enough that you'd be forgiven for thinking it's summer. There is no one else in sight. No other car upon the road, no lone figure walking their dog. Just Andrew. Just me. Just this moment, peaceful and perfect and bright.

"We had snow one year," Andrew says, pointing across the fields. "We went sledding down that hill all day."

"I'm jealous. Snow in Dublin just melts. And in Chicago, it's..."

"Normal."

"Yeah." In Ireland, it was rare and usually a cause for celebration if not huge traffic problems. "I feel like you planned this," I add.

"Nah. Just got lucky with the weather. Wouldn't have the same effect if it was raining."

I hum in agreement. "Is this the part where you tell me you live in a hobbit hole?"

"I live there."

"Where?"

He reaches out and gently grasps my chin, turning my face to a sprawling, white farmhouse to our right.

"You live on a farm," I say, unable to hide my surprise.

"I do."

"With animals?"

He looks like he's trying very hard not to laugh. "We have cows."

"How many cows?"

"Fifty."

My eyes go wide. "That's so many!"

This time he does laugh at me, but I'm too charmed to care.

"And to think you were going to spend today in Chicago," I say. "With no cows at all."

"I was going to spend it with *you*," he corrects quietly. "And I still am."

I press my lips together, trying not to show how warm and fuzzy that makes me feel, but of course, he picks up on it, smiling at me knowingly.

"Alright," he says. "Let's get inside. Before you run away from the embarrassment."

"I'm not going to run away. I'm too cold to run."

He nods down the hill. "We should stick to the grass," he says. "The roads will be icy."

We make our way carefully down, Andrew's pace quickening with each step we take.

"Will anyone be up this early?" I ask, almost whispering as he wheels the case up the drive. There are three cars along with a tractor parked outside, but the house itself looks like it's still asleep.

"Dad will be up with the animals already," he says. "He'll be out all day and Mam's probably still in bed, though Christmas is kind of her forte so she might..." Andrew trails off as he comes to a sudden halt. "Oh. Christ."

"What?" I ask in alarm. "What is it?"

"Are you allergic to—"

But whatever he was going to ask is drowned out as the

front door opens and the air fills with excited barking. Two dogs bound toward us and I barely have time to brace myself as they aim for Andrew, almost knocking him down before they come to me.

"Woah woah woah!"

Andrew lunges, grabbing the brown one by the collar, but the bigger one jumps up, his paws hitting my shoulders as he tries to lick my face.

"Uisce! Polly!"

A hissed whisper comes from the direction of the house and I peer around the slobbering tongue to see a shadow emerge from the porch. That shadow becomes a woman who hurries toward us, arms outstretched to grab the dogs.

"Inside, inside," she chastises, tugging the dog off me. "Now!" Andrew lets his one go at the command and to my surprise they immediately do as told, hurtling back to the house.

"My mother," Andrew introduces, checking to see if I'm alright before he turns to her. "I was just saying, I didn't know if you—"

He's cut off as she draws him into a firm hug, her arms wrapped around his shoulders, head burying into his chest. Andrew immediately reciprocates, holding her tight and I feel immediately like an intruder witnessing their reunion. I take a step away, trying to give them their moment, but the movement draws his mother's attention and she pulls back, wiping a hand across her cheek.

"Ridiculous," she says. "Scaring us like that for nothing." With an appraising eye that reminds me of my own parents, she gives him a once-over as though checking to make sure he's still in one piece before turning to me. "Won't be home for Christmas, he says."

"I almost wasn't," Andrew reminds her before reaching

out to grab my hand, tugging me into his side. "This is Molly. Molly, this is my mother."

"Call me Colleen," she corrects, and then I get my own hug. "Thank you for bringing him to us," she whispers in my ear, and all I can do is pat her shoulder in response because, honestly, what am I supposed to say to that that won't make me immediately tear up?

With a final squeeze, she steps back, and I get a good look at her for the first time. She's a little taller than me, with thick salt-and-pepper hair pulled back into a bun and a weatherworn face that speaks to days spent outside. She's still only half-dressed, a short duffel coat over her pajamas, the legs of which she's stuffed into a pair of muddy, no-nonsense rubber boots.

"We were planning on sneaking in," Andrew says apologetically. "I thought you'd still be in bed."

"On Christmas morning?" She huffs. "I suppose you'll be wanting your breakfast. I'm doing a fry later but there's no reason I can't whip you up something now."

Andrew and I share a glance and I'm relieved to see an echo of my own exhaustion in his eyes.

"We need to get some proper sleep," he says. "Or we won't make it to lunch."

"Of course! The others won't be up for a few hours anyway. I've got Liam's old room made up for you. The radiator has a mind of its own and we're a little tight for space, but it's the best I can do. Now, if you don't like it, we're going to have to—"

"I'm sure it's fine, Mam," Andrew interrupts, nudging me after her as we head toward the house.

I don't even have the energy to look around once we get inside, saying goodbye to Colleen before following him up the stairs.

Liam's old room is halfway down a long hallway and is small and simple with faded blue wallpaper and a worn beige carpet. A queen-size bed takes up most of the space, along with an old wooden dresser and a box of books marked for charity.

"Where's your room?" I ask.

"I shared one with Christian," Andrew says as he positions his suitcase against the wall.

"And Liam doesn't stay here as well?"

"He lives in the town over. He'll bring the kids for dinner but won't stay the night." He frowns as he presses a hand to the radiator. "I'm going to get a hot water bottle. Mam wasn't lying, these things take ages to heat up."

I nod, my mind starting to shut down as he leaves me alone. Chilly air hits me as I take off my coat so I don't remove anything else but my shoes while I wait for him. I even keep the scarf on as I perch at the end of the bed, stroking a hand down the quilt. I hadn't thought about what Colleen meant when she said we'd be tight for space. Of course, they can't just magically drum up an extra bed at such short notice, but it never occurred to me that we'd be sharing one.

The door opens before I can worry too much about it and Andrew slips back inside, clutching a hot water bottle to his chest. He hesitates by the wall, no doubt seeing the warring thoughts on my face. Lord knows I'm too tired to hide them.

"Here," he says, handing it to me. "I'll go kick Christian out of bed."

"Don't be silly. We'll fit."

His eyes flick between me and the mattress. "Are you sure?"

"Am I sure I don't want to be the person who ruins your brother's Christmas morning? Yes."

"There's a couch downstairs I can—"

"Andrew," I interrupt. "Please take this literally, I want you to sleep with me."

He laughs, looking relieved. "Okay," he says, and goes to take off his sweater before thinking the better of it. I understand. It's not that he doesn't think I can't handle him in a T-shirt, but it is *cold* in here.

"I'm keeping your scarf on," I say, and turn to the bed to strip back the blankets. I hear him kick off his shoes and then he closes the curtains before climbing in beside me.

It is predictably, immediately awkward. The three layers of clothing we're both wearing don't help. Nor does the fact that we're both frozen, with only the hot water bottle to keep us warm. I'm about to ask him if he'd prefer to keep said water bottle where it is or put it down by our feet when he huffs out an annoyed breath, and promptly turns on his side, drawing me into him.

"Is this okay?" he asks, arranging us so he's spooning me. I can only nod as I try to ignore how incredibly comfortable it is and how much I like the warmth of him and the smell of him and the everything of him.

"Should we set an alarm?" I whisper.

"My family is the alarm."

"But what if—"

"I'll wake you, Moll. I promise. Try and get some rest."

I don't need to be told twice, and as his head sinks into the pillow next to me and his body heat slowly transfers to me, I slip quickly, blissfully, into a deep and dreamless sleep.

CHAPTER TWENTY-THREE

I may fall asleep with Andrew wrapped around me, but I wake wrapped around him. My arm is tossed over his broad chest, my thigh hooked over his hip and nestled between his legs, pressing against him like I'm unconsciously trying to climb over the man. Or on top of him.

I don't move away. A little because I just don't want to. Mostly because I still feel tired. It takes me a few minutes to gain enough awareness to move my limbs and, even when I do, they feel so heavy that I don't try much more than a halfhearted twitch.

Eventually, I register noises other than the sound of Andrew's breathing. Murmured voices, a cabinet door slamming. They're faint, probably from downstairs, but the thought of someone walking in and seeing me like this, a stranger draped over their son or brother, is enough to make me get up.

I do it as gently as I can, trying not to wake him, but Andrew moves as soon as I raise my head, rolling us over so he's on top of me, pressing me gently into the mattress. At first, I think he's still asleep and that I'm trapped, but then his breath tickles my ear and I feel the ghost of his smile against my skin.

"Where are you going?" His voice is a quiet rasp that sends goosebumps down my arms and I realize I could get happily used to Andrew in the morning. But there'll be plenty of time for that.

"To pee," I grumble, and he laughs, peeling himself off me before turning over onto his side, tugging the blanket up to his chin.

"Two doors down. Put a sock on the doorknob or someone will walk in."

"What?" I ask, mildly alarmed.

"Christmas with the Fitzpatricks," he says as if that explains everything. Which it kind of does and also doesn't. I wait for him to say more, but he already looks as if he's gone back to sleep and, with my bladder now doing that I'll-let-out-a-little-tinkle-if-you-don't-move-soon warning, I slip out of bed, wincing as my bare feet meet the chilly air. I must have kicked off my socks sometime during the night. Or the morning. Or whatever part of the day we've just spent unconscious.

I move over to the curtain to check, drawing it back to find it fully light outside. Andrew groans when the sunshine hits the bed, but we need to get up, so I leave them open and dart out of the room before he can complain.

It's warmer in the hallway, as well as more... delicious? The smell of garlic and onions wafts from downstairs and my stomach rumbles loudly, despite the fact my internal body clock is now well and truly busted. God knows how I'm going to get back into a routine.

I count the doors as I head toward the bathroom. There's a sock on the handle, just as Andrew said, but I can't hear anyone on the other side. And though I don't want to meet any more of his family members standing outside the toilet, I also really, *really* need to pee. I'm weighing up the pros and cons of trying to find another one, thighs pressed together, when the door flies open, revealing a young woman in mismatched pajamas.

She yelps when she sees me, dropping the toothbrush that was dangling from her mouth.

"Hannah!" Colleen rounds the top of the stairs, carrying an armful of folded towels. "What did I say about waking them? And why aren't you getting dressed?"

"I'm brushing my teeth!" the girl says, affronted. She's tall, with green eyes set far apart and a button nose with a small piercing at the side. Her long brown hair is tinged bright red at the ends, half of it still up in old-fashioned curlers. She looks nothing like Andrew, except for the glint in her gaze when she turns back to me. "I'm Hannah."

"Molly," I say.

She grins. "I know."

She bends down to scoop her toothbrush from the floor while Colleen joins us. "I have to put my contacts in," she says apologetically, holding up a little box. "Two seconds."

She leaves the door open as she heads back to the sink and I try not to stare at her reflection in the mirror.

Hannah.

She was only six when I first met Andrew and over the years she's more or less stayed that way in my mind whenever he spoke about her. It's bizarre to see her now, to realize how much time has passed. Every Christmas I would get an update on her life and now here I stand before her.

About to wet myself.

Colleen clears her throat, drawing my attention back to

her. "I've put the hot water on in case you wanted a shower. I'll leave the towels just inside the door."

"Hot water after ten a.m.?" Hannah teases. "Did we win the lottery?"

"It's Christmas and she's a guest."

"She's *Andrew's* guest," Hannah smirks.

I am seriously going to— "Do you mind if I use the bathroom?"

Hannah winces as she hears the urgency in my voice. "Sorry! Of course." She scurries past me, blinking her contacts in.

"Take your time, Molly," Colleen says as we trade places. "Hannah, get dressed. You're peeling potatoes."

"It's Christian's turn to peel potatoes."

"He's bad at it," she dismisses.

"He's bad at it purposefully so he doesn't have to do it!" Hannah's protests fade as they walk away and I close the door, barely taking the bathroom in before I run to the toilet. No one tries to come in in the minute I take to go through the motions, but I hear Christmas music coming from one of the closed doors on my way back to the bedroom, and Hannah singing along with a surprisingly good voice.

Andrew is lying on his back when I return, one arm flung over his face to protect him from the daylight.

"Was that my sister's dulcet tones I heard?" he asks.

I shut the door. "I scared her."

"You're very scary." He drops his arm to look at me and my heart does a little flip in my chest. "That was the best night's sleep I've had in weeks," he says. "Which is saying something considering it only lasted two hours."

"You were tired."

"Maybe." He watches me from the bed, his gaze warm and inviting. Still, I don't move.

"Are you coming back in?" he asks, noticing my hesitation.

I twist my hands in front of me. "I think everyone else is up, so..."

"So." He sighs, flipping the covers off.

"Your mother put the water on for a shower," I tell him.

"You go first. I'll guard the door."

"You don't have to—"

He barks a laugh. "I do. Trust me. The sock doesn't always work." He gets up and tosses me an old dressing robe I'd missed before. I shrug it on gratefully as I look around for my bag. And that's when it hits me.

"What?" Andrew asks when I don't follow him to the door.

"I don't have my stuff." I don't have *any* of my stuff.

He's momentarily confused before he realizes what I mean. In all the chaos of yesterday evening, of the journey home, of *everything*, I had completely forgotten the fact that not only did I not have my suitcase, but I hadn't brought anything to the hospital either. Nothing but the clothes on my back and the phone in my pocket.

He winces, running a hand through his hair. "Don't worry about it," he says. "We have plenty of clean clothes. Hannah will give you something. And Mam has a lot of... lipstick."

I try not to smile. "Lipstick?"

"Hairspray?"

"You need to get a girlfriend," I say without thinking, and immediately regret it at the look in his eye. "I'd settle for shampoo right now," I add, ducking past him into the hallway.

I follow him back to the bathroom where he shows me how to work the shower, jokes for five seconds about staying inside while I undress, and eventually takes guard in the hallway, just as he promised.

But even with him there, I take the quickest shower I can, using the supermarket shower gel and shampoo sparingly before towel-drying my hair. When I look halfway decent, I pull the robe back on and gather my old clothes under one arm.

I step out to find Andrew still guarding the door. Only now he's not alone.

An almost unfairly attractive man stands beside him, a mug of tea in his hand.

Christian. The youngest brother.

He's a little taller than Andrew, with an expensive haircut and a fairer complexion that must come from his mother's side. He has that classical handsome look about him, dark eyes, a long nose, a hint of cheekbones. Whereas Andrew has always been a little scruffy, and even more so this morning, Christian looks like he belongs in a soap opera. Or, at the very least, a marketing campaign for men's razors.

He smirks when I appear, not exactly mean, but not exactly friendly either and lacking the teasing warmth that I always get from Andrew.

"It's nice to finally meet you," he says, raising his mug in a mock toast.

"My brother," Andrew says needlessly. "Christian."

"Hi." I tighten the belt around my waist, pausing when both sets of eyes drop to my hands. Christian's immediately flick back up.

Andrew's take a second.

"Andrew was just telling me about your nephew,"

Christian says. "Congratulations. It sounds like the two of you have had quite the week."

"Something like that," Andrew scoffs. "Hannah's going to bring some stuff in for you," he adds to me.

"I can just wear my clothes from yesterday. She doesn't have to—"

"She wants to," he says cutting me off. "And you have to be nice to her because it's Christmas." He nods to the shower before I can argue any further. "Water still warm?"

I nod and he smiles.

"My turn," he announces, pushing away from the wall. I step to the side to let him pass and he disappears behind the door, leaving me alone with his brother.

Christian studies me for a moment before bringing his finger to his lips in a shushing motion. With exaggerated slowness, he opens the door next to the bathroom, revealing a boiler similar to the one my parents have. With a wink, he flicks the switch, turning the hot water off.

"Happy Christmas," he says to me, and pads toward the stairs, sipping at his tea.

I wait until he's gone before turning the water back on and then I scurry back to the bedroom where I use Andrew's deodorant and get dressed in the same clothes I slept in. I'm barely covered for five seconds when Hannah calls through the door.

"Heard you needed supplies," she says when I open it. She tosses me an unopened packet of underwear as she steps into the room. "Don't worry," she says. "I've got hundreds. I'm making a dress out of them for school."

There's a lot to unpack in that sentence. I decide on the easiest option.

"You make clothes?"

"Yep," she says cheerfully. There's no hint of shyness or faux modesty about her and I love it. I wish I had been that confident at her age. "I thought you could wear this with your jeans," she adds, laying out a soft blue sweater with a subtle shimmer of silver thread throughout. "It's a little big but—"

"It's perfect," I say, touched by her kindness. "Thank you."

"No problem." She adds a pair of socks and a plain vest to the pile. "So are you dating my brother?"

"I—what?" I blink as she bounces onto the bed.

"He hasn't brought a girl home in *years*," she says innocently, stretching her long legs out before her.

Andrew brought someone home with him? A spike of jealousy runs through me as I think through his last couple of girlfriends and who was the most likely candidate. He definitely let *that* little detail slip by.

"Mam hated her," Hannah continues, smiling when I stare at her. "But she likes you. I can tell."

"You can?"

"She gave you the good towels."

The door opens before I can respond and Andrew thankfully appears. His eyes immediately find mine with a soft look that drops as soon as he notices Hannah.

"Get out of my room."

"This is Liam's room."

"Then get out of Liam's room."

"I was just talking to—"

"Out," he says, grabbing her arm.

"But I'm *helping*."

He pushes her into the hallway, shutting the door on her raised middle finger.

"Are you going to have sex?" she calls through the wood,

and he bangs on the wall until her footsteps sound, moving toward the stairs.

"She's sweet," I say when he turns back to me.

"When she wants to be."

I pick up the sweater Hannah left me, wrapping it around the packet of underwear that I'm suddenly ridiculously shy about it. Andrew immediately notices something's up.

"She didn't say anything to you, did she?"

"No," I lie. I keep my eyes on the window, pretending to be captivated by the view of a field outside as I listen to him unzip the suitcase behind me. "What's the deal with your brother?"

Andrew sighs mournfully. "I knew you'd like him more. It's the dark brooding thing he's got going on, isn't it?"

"I thought he was the prankster of the family."

"Many layers. I promise you he's not a jerk," Andrew continues. "No matter how much he seems like one." He pauses. "Though if you find yourself under some mistletoe, I'd rather you didn't—"

"Shut up." I scowl and he grins at me.

"So, what's the plan for today?" I ask, changing the subject.

He blows out a breath, his face scrunched like he's thinking hard. "Well, first is the five-k run, then a dip in the frozen lake and then we'll—"

"Andrew."

"We're supposed to eat at six. Which means we'll probably eat at seven. It's eleven now so we've got a lot of time to kill. Watch movies, eat junk food." He shrugs. "It's Christmas."

It's Christmas. It's Christmas *Day*. Christmas Day and we made it. We're here.

"Do you want to call your sister?"

"Oh crap. Yes." I dive for my phone as Andrew grabs some clothes from his suitcase and shoots me a glance.

"I'll go change in Christian's room. He'll love that."

I smile at the offer of privacy and perch on the end of the bed, hitting my sister's number. She picks up after the third ring.

"Christmas in the hospital," she says by way of greeting. "Can't wait to hold this over my firstborn for the rest of his life."

"How are you feeling?"

"My vagina is sore and they've stopped giving me drugs. Did you make it to Cork okay? How are the in-laws?"

"Okay so far." I tuck the phone under my ear as I undress and put on the fresh clothes Hannah left me. "They've been really nice but I still feel weird. I probably should have stayed in Dublin."

"Well, it's too late now," she says dryly. "Are you sleeping on the couch?"

"We're sharing a bed."

It takes a full twenty seconds for her to stop cackling.

"We haven't done anything," I protest in the middle of it. "We haven't even kissed."

"Alright, Virgin Mary, I believe you. Stop putting so much pressure on yourself! Just enjoy the day. Offer to make your garlic bread." Her voice turns wistful. "I miss your garlic bread."

"I'll make it for you when you're home," I promise. "Do you have a name yet?"

"No," she huffs. "And do you know what could be great? If everyone could stop asking me. Maybe I'll be one of those trendy people who lets their kid pick their own name."

"I don't think the birth certificate people are going to wait that long."

"And that's bureaucracy for you."

"Can you at least send me some pictures of my nameless nephew?"

She can.

We hang up and five images come through just as Andrew returns, dressed in a fresh pair of jeans and a navy Christmas sweater with a reindeer on it.

"Look," I say, holding up my phone. "I'm an aunt."

"Hey now. How handsome is he? Is Zoe okay?"

"Just tired."

He frowns. "If you want to try and get back today, we can borrow Christian's car."

"No," I say quickly. "Don't be silly. I'll see her tomorrow." *And I want to stay here with you.* I don't say the words even though they're on the tip of the tongue, even though that's clearly what I mean.

I sit on the end of the bed, the covers still rumpled from when we slept, and run my hands up and down my thighs as Andrew starts unpacking his suitcase and hiding presents under the bed.

"You never told me you brought a girlfriend home before."

Confusion flashes across his face before he glances at the door. "Hannah."

"I'm learning all your secrets."

He smirks, not seeming the least bit worried by the question.

"Was it Alison?" I ask, thinking about his last long term-girlfriend before Marissa.

"Nope. Emily."

"*Emily?*" Quiet-voiced, teacher-of-children, sweet-as-can-be-until-she-ghosts-him-for-three-weeks-out-of-the-blue Emily? "Seriously?"

"I was young and in love. Or at least I thought I was."

"Was it a disaster?"

He laughs at the question, but I don't care if I'm showing my inner bitch right now. I'm determined to make a good impression on his family and knowing that someone else made a bad one will give me a lot more confidence.

"A huge disaster," he says, and I relax. "I shouldn't have asked her to come. We'd only been going out for a few months and I liked her a lot, I thought I was falling in love but it was too big a step. The jet lag hit her hard and she couldn't really eat, which upset Mam, and then we think she was allergic to the dogs, which *really* upset Mam, and..." He shrugs. "It felt like every little thing that could go wrong did go wrong. It's a miracle we didn't break up with each other there and then."

"And you didn't bring anyone else home after that?"

"You know I didn't," he says. But I don't. Not really. I didn't know about Emily, which only makes me think of all the other things I might not know about. That I *want* to know about. Want to and will. Because I have at my disposal an indulgent mother, a smirking brother and a scheming sister. Not to mention the fact I haven't even met Liam yet.

Andrew's eyes narrow, guessing where my mind is headed. "If you want to know something about me, just ask me."

"But you're biased," I say pleasantly. "I want to know the shady things too."

We both pause as my stomach rumbles. "I guess I better feed you," he says, amused. "You ready to go downstairs?"

"As I'll ever be," I say, butterflies fluttering as I follow him into the hallway.

I hear them immediately. Hannah's defensive tone, Christian's quiet murmuring before her squeal of protest.

"*Mam!*"

The word echoes up the stairs as we climb down them and Andrew winces, pausing on the bottom step, just out of sight.

"Are you sure this is okay?" I ask, suddenly nervous. "That I'm here, I mean? You guys take Christmas so seriously." *And I am bad at it.*

"It is more than okay, Molly. Trust me." His voice is firm and I try to believe him, I try even harder when he reaches out and squeezes my hand.

"You ready?" he asks, waiting until I nod. "Then let the day begin."

CHAPTER TWENTY-FOUR

The kitchen falls silent as soon as we appear and even Andrew seems a little freaked out by it, rocking back on his heels as he takes them all in.

"Don't be weird," he tells them, pushing me gently ahead of him. "Everyone, this is Molly. We have her to thank for getting me home this year."

"Thank is a pretty strong word," Christian says from where he lounges by the table. Hannah sits opposite, peeling a large mound of potatoes while their mother hovers behind them. At Christian's words, Colleen hits him on the back of his head before turning to the stove.

"How are you, Molly?" she asks. "Did you get any sleep?"

"A little," I say. "Thanks again for letting me join you."

"Not at all!" A timer dings and she moves a saucepan from one ring to another. The room is a mess of carefully controlled chaos with pots and pans and all manners of food in various stages of preparation. An old iPad showing a color-coded spreadsheet is propped against a stack of cookery books, and she examines it briefly before turning a knob on the oven.

"Do you need any help?" I ask, eager to be of use. Christian snorts as Colleen throws me a sympathetic smile over her shoulder.

"Mam's favorite thing to do at Christmas is to complain that no one helps her," Andrew explains.

"But then yells at you if you try," Hannah quips. "We're allowed to do basic food preparation and that's it."

"Did you or did you not burn your hand on the stove?" Colleen grumbles.

"I was *six*."

"I have everything under control," she says. "In fact, the greatest gift you could give me is to all be out of the house for as long as possible until dinner is ready. It's a beautiful day and you can go meet Liam and the kids in the village."

Christian grimaces. "I'm good."

"You're hungover," Hannah mutters, tossing a slice of potato skin at him.

"The dogs need a walk," Colleen continues as though they hadn't spoken. "And you can show Molly around."

"Around what?" Hannah scoffs. "The grass?"

"Hannah."

"I'm just saying."

"And *I'm* saying that I want you out that door in five minutes tops."

"But you said you needed me to—"

"I changed my mind."

Hannah huffs as she pushes her chair back, but does as she's told, shooting me a quick grin before running up the stairs.

"You're the one who wanted a girl," Christian says mildly, which earns him another head whack.

"You're going too," she warns him.

"I can't." He lumbers to his feet to kiss her on the cheek. "Promised I'd help Dad fix a fence or something. Think he wants to bond."

I raise my brows, glancing at Andrew. I can't imagine Christian out on a farm, though from the pained expression on his face, neither can he.

"Do you all help out?" I ask. Christian dumps his mug in the sink and tugs playfully on Colleen's apron string before he slips out the back door.

"A little bit," Andrew says. "Liam was the one who got into it. He has his own land a few miles over."

"Do you know anything about farms?" Colleen asks politely.

I shake my head. "City folk through and through."

"We'll give you the tour before you go."

Speaking of a tour... I step toward the fridge where a dozen family photos are pinned with fading magnets, the kind you used to find in old cereal boxes. Ruddy-faced children peer back at me, shots of the three boys on family vacations before later pictures of Hannah, first as a baby and then older, beaming as she's surrounded by her brothers. But it's one brother in particular who's caught my attention.

"I would really appreciate it if you could now move away from the fridge," Andrew says behind me.

"But you're so cute," I coo, peering at a photo of him as a toddler. "Though I have to ask..."

"Please don't."

"Why are you naked in every picture?"

"Because he refused to wear clothes," Colleen says by the sink.

"Mam," Andrew warns.

"Flat out refused until he was five," she continues,

ignoring him. "I'd dress him, turn my back and he'd have them whipped off in an instant. One time when he was three, he started stripping in the middle of the supermarket. I'll never forget chasing him around the frozen aisle. Screaming his head off, grabbing hold of his—"

"Hannah!" Andrew roars. "Hurry up!"

"I'm coming," she yells back. "Keep your pants on."

"Yeah, Andrew," I say. "Keep your pants on."

The look he gives me is one of huge betrayal.

"Two hours minimum," Colleen reminds us as he tugs me into the hallway. "And if anywhere is open, see if you can get some more bread!"

We emerge just as Hannah appears, running down the stairs in a green velvet dress and black Doc Martens. She skips the two bottom steps, landing with a thump that sends more family photos rattling.

"Did you make that?" Andrew asks, as she hands us our coats she retrieved from upstairs.

She nods, complying with his gesture to spin around. The skirt balloons out when she does before falling gracefully around her legs.

"What did I tell you?" he asks, sounding genuinely proud. "The smart one."

Outside, Christian is sitting on the porch, shoving his feet into rubber boots as the dogs sniff around him. They immediately bound up to Hannah, who doesn't bother to put them on the lead as she corrals them toward the gate.

"I will give you one hundred euro to spend the day with Dad," Christian says to Andrew. Andrew only smirks, bringing me after Hannah, who's waiting for us at the top of the drive.

"He's been in a bad mood since he got back," Hannah says when we catch up with her. She's left the coat open to show off her dress and is shivering in the cold. "It's because he's the only single person this year."

Andrew's head whips toward her and, for a second, I think he's about to refute that, about us, but his eyes narrow. "You're dating someone?"

"Maybe," Hannah says.

"Since when?"

"None of your business."

"It is my business, you're sixteen."

"I can read and write too," she says, and takes off down the lane in a light jog that has the dogs running after her in excitement.

Andrew turns my way, looking for an ally, only to find me grinning instead. "What?"

"Nothing," I say innocently. "Just the big brother protective streak is kind of hot."

"I am not—"

"Oh my God, you are."

"She's sixteen!"

"Exactly." I laugh. "Sixteen. Not six. She's allowed to have a boyfriend."

"Girlfriend," Andrew corrects.

"Girlfriend." I nudge him with my elbow as we start to walk after her. "She's still a baby to you, isn't she?"

"Maybe," he admits. "It's weird, you know. She was only six when I left. And now she's—"

"Practically a woman," I say dramatically. His lips twitch as our eyes meet and when he doesn't look away I find it's my turn to ask, "What?"

"Nothing," he says. "Just glad you're here."

———

It takes twenty minutes to walk to the local village, which is just one stretch of road with a church, a pub, two mom-and-pop stores, and a garage. They are all predictably closed (besides the church), but there are plenty of people out, all getting their walk in before they spend the rest of the day eating. Or maybe that's just what I'm hoping will happen.

Hannah disappears off with a group of friends as soon as we arrive while Andrew is stopped by every second person we meet. It feels like everyone knows both him and the difficulty he had getting home, and a few even know me, or at least my name when Andrew goes to introduce me, Colleen has obviously been telling our adventures to anyone who would listen.

"You're so famous," I tease. "The prodigal son returned."

"Don't tell that to Christian," he mutters, but he seems pleased that I'm impressed, glancing at me every so often as I take in the village even though I pretend not to notice.

Outside one of the houses is a small stall selling hot spiced apple juice and pastries and I immediately drag Andrew over to get my hard-earned breakfast. I'm tearing into a Danish when a girl of no more than five or six comes barreling toward us, a fairy wand in her hand.

Andrew scoops her up like a pro, planting messy kisses on her cheeks until she's squealing delightedly in protest.

"Yeah, that's what she needs," a man says from behind us. "To get even more hyper."

Liam. I meet my last Fitzpatrick child, the eldest brother, and finally, get some real family resemblance. Whereas Christian and Hannah take after their mother, Liam definitely comes from the same side of the family as Andrew, with the same messy brown hair and hazel eyes.

His are smaller though and gaze kindly at me from behind a pair of thin-rimmed glasses.

"You must be Molly," he says, reaching out to shake my hand. "Heard you were crashing the party today."

"Ah, don't worry," Andrew says. "She's staying in the barn. Another one!"

I turn at his call to see an older boy shuffle our way. Far too cool for the exuberant welcome his sister just gave, he gives his uncle a halfhearted hug, a shy but pleased grin on his face.

"Christ, Padraig, how big are you now?" Andrew asks.

"Don't," Liam sighs, buying his own cup of spiced apple. "I'm having to buy a new pair of trousers for him every week at this stage."

"Going to be as big as your dad, are you?"

Padraig shakes his head, though I notice he straightens his shoulders a little at the attention. Andrew introduces me to the children, who both greet me solemnly before turning immediately back to their uncle.

"Your dad said you were in the nativity play," Andrew says to Padraig as he hoists his niece, Elsie, into a more comfortable position. "One of the wise men. You sang a song?"

Padraig nods.

"A solo?"

He shrugs.

"What? Are you all shy now?" Andrew teases, ruffling his hair. "Are you too shy for presents too? What did Santa bring you?"

We stay chatting for another few minutes as Padraig finally starts opening up about the new LEGO set he got. Liam asks me questions about my sister and the baby while keeping an eye on his children and, specifically, what treats his brother buys them from the stall. When Andrew presents Elsie with an exceptionally large chocolate chip cookie that's about the size of her face, he excuses himself, taking them off to find Hannah and the dogs.

Andrew shows no inclination to join them, finishing the last of my juice as he leads me toward the opposite side of the village, where only a few houses are dotted about. "Want to see the castle?"

"You have a castle?"

"Or maybe it was a monk's tower?" He doesn't wait for my answer, practically dragging me along as we leave the village behind. "I'll be honest, I didn't really pay attention."

He leads me to a bunch of old ruins five minutes away that might have been a castle, a monk's tower, or any number of things, but is now overgrown with grass and wildflowers. It's quiet out here, away from the village, the peace broken only by the sound of the odd bleating sheep in the distance.

"Ta-da," Andrew says as we stand in the center of it.

I wait. "This is it?"

"This is it."

"I don't get a history lesson?"

He makes a face, turning in a small circle as though looking for a place of significance. "I had my first kiss over there," he says, pointing to an unremarkable patch of dirt glistening in the melting frost.

"I meant about the monks."

"I don't think the monks were really into kissing back then. Or now for that matter."

"Oh, he's so funny." I press a foot against the low wall and, finding it sturdy, step up, reaching out to Andrew so I can hold on to him for balance.

"Hannah thinks your mam likes me," I say as I walk

along the perimeter. I feel like an overgrown child in my bulky winter clothing, but I kind of like it.

"She does. I bet you she even got you a present."

"She didn't," I groan.

"She always has spares in case some relative drops in unannounced. I hope you like mass-market scented candles."

"But I don't have anything for her!" Why didn't I think about that? I should have got something in the hospital gift shop.

"Just sign your name on my stuff. It can be from both of us."

"Uh, no."

"Why not?"

"Because a, that's not fair to you, and b... isn't that a little, I don't know, official?"

He laughs. "She has us sleeping in the same bed, Molly. I don't think a joint present is going to shock her that much. Just remind me when we get in. We tend to do presents before dinner."

I reach the end of the wall before it crumbles into nothing and jump down onto the grass. It's not as graceful as I envisioned and a shock jolts up my ankle, but I shake it off with a grimace as we move around a mostly intact part of the tower, stepping out of the shade and into the bright winter sunshine.

"So, is this it or are you— Hey!" My breath comes out in a huff as Andrew turns, stepping into me so I'm forced to move back. I hit the wall as I do and he follows, his arms going to either side of my head so I'm barricaded in.

Oh. "Hi."

"Hi." He smiles as I gaze up at him. "You know," he says. "I was really, *really* looking forward to seeing my family and being a good second son, and yet ever since I've come home, all I am is annoyed that I can't spend every second alone with you."

"Are you telling me I've ruined your Christmas and that I should have stayed in Dublin?"

"It was pretty selfish of you to come," he agrees. "And take up my precious time with thoughts of you."

"Thoughts of me?" I like the sound of that. "Indecent thoughts?"

"God no." He reaches for the zipper of my coat, flicking it once before pulling it down. "I'm a gentleman."

I smirk as his hands settle on my hips. "Castles get you all hot and bothered, huh?"

"There is about to be a lot of people in my house for the next few hours and it is going to be impossible to get a moment to ourselves. I think we should come up with a signal when we want to escape."

"I didn't go through the worst journey ever just so you could ignore your family," I remind him.

"Ah, it wasn't so bad."

"It was very bad! We were exhausted, and we spent a lot more money than we should have and it's only through sheer luck that we—"

He shuts me up with a kiss and I am so happy he does.

He tastes like spiced apples and smells like the winter air, crisp and clean and bright. I want to take a deep breath of him. I want to fill my lungs with him and only him and when he starts to move away, I cup the back of his head, keeping him right where he is.

"Now who's hot and bothered?" he smirks.

"I'm just not used to this yet," I admit. "I still feel some-times like I'll wake up and we'll be on a plane. That none of it will have happened."

"It was always going to happen," he murmurs. "But trust you to choose the most stressful three days ever to do it."

"Hey!"

"It's true."

"At least I—" I break off, biting my lip as he shifts suddenly, fitting his thigh between my legs.

"At least you what?" he asks innocently, but I don't respond, I *can't* respond, and he knows it, pressing up into me until my breath hitches in my throat. Andrews hears it and pulls back, but only so he can see my face when he does it again.

I grip his shoulders as heat pools low in my stomach, unable to take my eyes off his. I wish I could. He's got this cocky look about him that shouldn't be as hot as it is, but I'm too turned on to call him out on it.

"It's Christmas Day," I tell him instead and he nods, distracted. "You said back in Chicago that I'd get the second part of my present at Christmas."

"Your what?"

"My present," I remind him. "You got me a two-part present."

"I did, didn't I?"

"So, where is it?"

"Where's what?"

"Andrew!"

He grins. "Two parts seems a little greedy now, doesn't it? Especially since we didn't actually go on the flight you claimed to have gotten me *and* since you gave away those chocolates—"

"I'm your present," I interrupt, and he laughs.

"Yes, you are."

Disappointment fills me as he moves his leg away and

I'm about to protest when he suddenly grabs the back of my thighs, hoisting me up.

I panic, my ankles locking around his waist as I scramble to get a hold on him. "Andrew!"

"Much better," he says as we become eye level with each other.

"If you drop me, I'm going to kill you."

"I'm not going to drop you. I'm incredibly strong."

I huff, clutching him close as his hands move from my thighs to my ass. "Seriously?"

"I might have had some indecent thoughts," he admits, and when I don't protest, he leans in, pressing a hot kiss to my lips that the monks would *not* have approved of.

But they're not here right now, are they? There's only us, so I give into it, kissing him back and tightening my hold around him until my body hums with pleasure. We stay like that for a perfect, blissful minute, cocooned in our own little world until a loud shout echoes around the walls, breaking us apart.

"Andrew!"

We both freeze, staring wide-eyed at each other as Hannah's annoyed voice calls from somewhere nearby. "Mam rang and told us to come home!"

"Whoever invented little sisters can burn in hell," Andrew mutters, resting his forehead briefly against mine before pulling away.

"Christmas with your family," I remind him as he lowers me carefully to my feet. "You love Christmas with your family."

"She also wants to know what kind of gravy Molly wants," Hannah continues, her voice drawing closer as he zips my coat back up. "Or if she should make another— Oh."

Hannah rounds the corner, stopping abruptly when she catches sight of us. Her sudden grin reminds me so much of Andrew that I'm a little spooked. "You guys smooching?" she asks, sounding delighted by the thought.

"Don't say smooching," Andrew grumbles, stepping away from me. He grabs my hand as he goes, tugging me once more into his side.

"Making out?" Hannah continues. "Swapping spit?"

"Would you shut up?"

"Tangling tongues?"

"Hannah—"

"Let me guess," she interrupts, rubbing her nose absently in the cold. "I'm too young to know what kissing is."

"You are."

"When did you have your first kiss?"

"That's none of your business," Andrew huffs, walking us back toward the village. Hannah latches onto my other side, not letting up.

"Didn't you have it in the castle? You did!" Her eyes light up at whatever expression she sees on his face. "Is that why you brought Molly here? That is so corny."

"Don't you have somewhere to be? Down the well, maybe?"

"Andrew can be very sentimental," she tells me, looping her arm through mine so I have a Fitzpatrick on either side of me. "It's kind of cute."

"I'm not cute. I'm a grown man."

Hannah continues undeterred. "For my seventh birthday I was *ridiculously* into Disney princesses," she says. "And he surprised me by coming home for the party. He had the full-on Prince Charming outfit from Cinderella and he brought me back the dress, you know the blue one?

He waltzed with me in the living room and then had to do it with every single one of my friends."

"That *is* pretty cute," I confirm as Andrew shoots me a look, one that drops completely at Hannah's next words.

"It's why I got into fashion."

"It is?" he asks. His surprise is obvious. "You never told me that."

"It was definitely then. I was obsessed with that dress. I wore it every day after school for weeks until Mam threw it out and said it was an accident. I wouldn't stop crying and she told me if I loved something that much, I should learn how to make my own one. So, I did."

"When you were seven?" I ask.

"I didn't say it was any good. Mam helped me staple some crepe paper to one of her old skirts. But yeah. That's when it started."

Andrew's gazing at her with a look on his face that makes me want to kiss him again, but thankfully before I can and make Hannah go truly nuts, Liam's children come running around the bend, the dogs not far behind. Hannah uses the distraction to draw me away, letting the others bring up the rear as we stride down the path.

"You know," I say as we leave the village behind. "You make me feel very old."

She bursts out laughing. "Why?"

"Because the first time I heard about you, you were six."

"On the first flight?" she asks.

"That's it." I smile at her. "Andrew tells you about our flights?"

"He tells us everything about you. It's a tradition by this stage. Of course, you didn't come off in the best light the first two years," she continues slyly. "But he was always a bit of a drama queen. Then it was all Molly's doing this and

Molly's doing that. She's got into law school, she's graduated law school, she's got a new boyfriend, she's got a new apartment, she's moved out of the apartment, she's got a new job. For the first few years, Christian was convinced he made you up, but honestly, that's why when you came, I was like, 'Hi!' It's like I already knew you."

"Well, I appreciate the warm welcome," I laugh. "He tells me about you too."

"Oh yeah?" she scoffs. "Like what? How annoying I am?"

"Like how impressed he is with you. Like he thinks you're the smartest out of all of them and how you're going to be famous one day."

She looks at me skeptically. "You're just trying to make him seem nice."

"I'm not. He tells me all the time."

She purses her lips, trying and failing to hide how pleased she is. "I guess he's not the *worst* brother," she says eventually, and we glance over our shoulders to where he's walking with the kids and Liam. Andrew frowns at the sudden attention, immediately suspicious, and Hannah collapses into giggles before giving me a friendly tug, quickening our steps up the lane.

CHAPTER TWENTY-FIVE

I meet my final member of the family when we get back to the house. Andrew's father, Sean, is a quiet, no-nonsense man who welcomes me with a warm calloused handshake before thanking me for helping his son get home, just like the others. You'd swear I paddled the guy over on a dinghy.

Colleen continues to ignore my repeated offers to help, and instead grabs Andrew to do the dishes while Hannah uses the opportunity to shut me in her room so she can show me the outfits she's been working on. It wasn't just brotherly bias when Andrew said how talented she was. The pieces are gorgeous, even half-finished, and I dutifully act as a model for an hour as she talks me through her process.

Afterward, at Andrew's insistence, I sign my name on the various gifts he got for everyone. I still feel guilty, but relieved overall that he told me what his mother was planning or else I would have felt even more uncomfortable as I gathered around the enormous, picture-perfect tree with the rest of the family. As predicted, Colleen hands me a scented candle, beautifully wrapped with my name in neat calligraphy on the tag, but most of the attention is on Padraig and

Elsie, who unwrap their mound of toys and thank each person dutifully.

It's an odd sensation, joining in on these little rituals, the same ones I spent my entire adulthood avoiding, as if to prove to myself that I didn't care. And while it will always be awkward joining a group of people who know each other inside out, it's hard not to get caught up in the jokes and the teasing and the sheer unfiltered joy of it all. I don't think Andrew ever stops smiling. Not once.

But the highlight of the day is, of course, Christmas dinner. We're called to eat a little after seven p.m. to a small dining room that you can tell is used only on special occasions. I'm surprised at the amount of food, even though Liam's wife, Mairead, and the kids have joined us, but it makes sense when Andrew explains how his mother *slightly* freaked out about me coming and made double of everything, just in case. I know that half the fun of big holidays like this is the leftovers though, so I don't feel too bad about it.

We all manage to squeeze around their table, even though we're so close that I'm touching shoulders with Andrew on my left and Hannah on my right. But the kids eat quickly and grow bored, and it gets easier when they're excused and get up to run around the living room with the *Star Wars* lightsabers they'd got from Christian.

Despite the welcome I'd received, I'm low-key nervous at being the lone outsider at the table. As bizarre as it sounds, I'm worried they'd try to include me. Ask me polite questions about my life that I would politely answer but that no one cared about. Instead, to my relief they practically ignore me. Bickering and talking over each other, including me only when someone tries to get me as an ally on their side. Usually, Hannah. All the while Andrew is a constant presence beside me, explaining quietly when new names are mentioned and which household item Christian broke at any given time.

I'm so distracted trying to keep up with it all, that I almost forget to be worried about the moment I've been secretly dreading.

No one batted an eyelid when Andrew declined a drink at the start of the meal, but as the hour goes on and more bottles are opened, it begins to get more noticeable.

Hannah's allowed a second glass of Prosecco even though Christian has been sneaking her sips of his beer throughout the afternoon. He's on the red wine now. They all are, except me, and while Colleen seems to accept easily that I'm not drinking tonight ("I'm leaving early to get back to my sister"), I can tell she's starting to take it as a personal slight that Andrew refuses every bottle she offers him.

"I still have that headache," he says, his voice straining when she gets up for the third time to go hunting for something she thinks he might like. "Probably the jet lag."

I squeeze his knee under the table and his hand immediately covers mine, keeping me there.

"If that one is too heavy for you, we have a merlot in the—"

"Stop fussing," Christian says, spearing a carrot with his fork. "You'd swear he joined a cult."

"He traveled a long way to be here and I'm just making sure—"

"All you're making sure of is that your food is going cold and you're the one who spent all day cooking it." He grabs the glass she just placed in front of Andrew and tips it into his own. "There, problem solved."

Colleen throws her hands in the air in a fine-I-give-up

movement and ignores Hannah's casual suggestion that she wouldn't mind trying some wine.

The brothers' eyes meet over the table, a silent discussion occurring that seems to relax Andrew as some of the tension in his shoulders loosens. The squeeze he gives my hand is the only warning I get.

"I actually wanted to talk to you guys about something," he says, and everyone's eyes swing our way. He hesitates at the attention and I'm not surprised considering he told me he hadn't planned on telling them, but before he can continue Hannah lets out a small noise, her mouth dropping open as she stares at us.

"No way."

"What?" Andrew asks, confused.

"No *way*," she repeats. "You're engaged?"

"*What?*" Colleen shrieks as I almost die of mortification.

"We're not engaged," Andrew says quickly, but Hannah's not listening, already ecstatic.

"Oh my God, you definitely are!"

"No, we're—"

"Congratulations," Christian says loudly, smirking when Andrew glares at him. "Brilliant news."

"Christian—"

"Where's the ring?"

"There's no ring. We're not engage— *Mam*, stop it. We're not engaged. Hannah!"

Hannah drops my left hand where she'd been trying to look for a diamond. "Well, you should have said something."

"You want me to announce every time I'm not engaged to someone?"

"*No*, but—"

"What did you want to say, Andrew?" It's Liam who interrupts and thank God he does, because my heart is beating so fast, I'm starting to get dizzy. I calm down when the table falls quiet again and I give Andrew an encouraging nod when he glances at me.

"I just..." He takes a breath, dragging his gaze away from me to look at his family. "I've given up drinking," he says. "I'm sober. Not just for Christmas or for January... but forever, if I can."

Silence.

Christian is the only one who doesn't look stunned, as if he already suspected it, and, as a result, he's the first to speak. "That's great, Andrew," he says, unusually serious. "Well done."

Liam and Mairead quickly chime in with similar words of support, but Colleen just smiles at him, looking confused.

"But you don't have a drinking problem."

"I do, Mam," Andrew says. "Or at least I did."

"But you're not—"

"You don't have to explain yourself, son," Sean says quietly. "It's nobody's business except your own. I'm very proud of you."

"Thanks, Dad," Andrew murmurs as Hannah leans around me to smile encouragingly at him.

"Your skin is going to look *amazing*."

"What's wrong with my skin?"

"It's a bit dull," she says solemnly, and Andrew rolls his eyes.

Colleen however still seems upset, her gaze flitting around the table as though she doesn't know where to look, and Andrew's leg tenses beneath my hand as she stands.

"Well," she says abruptly, and, before anyone can stop her, grabs two bottles of half-finished wine from the table.

"Hey," Christian complains as she takes the glass from his hand next.

"Support your brother," she snaps, bringing them to the sideboard before heading back for more.

"I am! I'm getting rid of his temptation!"

"That's not necessary," Andrew says as Sean hands her his own glass.

"Of course it is," she mutters. "You've been sitting there suffering while we're waving everything around in front of you. Molly, I don't know what you must think of us."

"I—"

"I can't even remember how much wine I put into the gravy." Her hand flies to her chest. "And there's brandy in the ice cream."

"Mam, it's okay."

"Did you join one of those clubs?" she asks suddenly. "Triple A?"

"It's just AA. And no, but I've joined another program that—"

"Your uncle Kevin has been told he has a gluten intolerance. Maybe you should talk with him."

"Mother of God," Christian mutters, dropping his head to the table.

"I know it's not the same," Colleen says. "But he's had to give up a lot. You know how that man likes his bread."

"There's gluten in beer too," Hannah pipes up, and Colleen gestures toward her with a *see* motion.

"I'm doing okay," Andrew says firmly. "I just didn't tell you guys until now because I didn't want you freaking out." At this Colleen harrumphs. "I don't want to be the guy that stops you having a glass of wine with dinner. It's a personal decision and I'm glad I made it. I've got plenty of support..." Another hand squeeze. "And I think I'm going to be able to do it," he finishes. "But I wanted to be honest and let you know."

Sean nods while Colleen sits back down, still looking flustered. "You didn't have any gravy, did you?" she asks.

"No."

"Good. That's good."

"You alright, Mam?" Christian asks as she starts folding her napkin into a tiny square.

"I'm fine."

"Want a glass of wine?"

"Yes, I think— *No*," she amends, horrified as Christian starts to laugh. Andrew grins as she glares at him and then Hannah starts listing all the sober celebrities she knows and Sean excuses himself from the table only to come back with a fresh bottle of sparkling water that Colleen quickly adds some sliced lemons to.

And they move on.

I don't know whether I've become more attuned to him these last few days, or if he really is just that relieved, but it's like a weight has been lifted from Andrew's shoulders, and though he has to spend several minutes convincing his mother to pour more brandy over the pudding, it's worth it when they turn off all the lights and set it ablaze. That's accompanied by ice cream, and more dessert brought over by Liam who says he saved a cake from their family holiday to Milan in November.

"It's panettone," he declares, starting to cut into it.

Andrew and I turn to each other at the same time and he smiles so wide that I burst out laughing, much to the confusion of everyone else.

After dinner, Liam and his family return home and the remaining Fitzpatricks (and me) move to the living room, where Andrew's father has a fire going in the hearth.

"Movie time," Andrew explains as we settle on the couch. It's the sinking kind, worn with age and impossible to get out of, and as soon as I sit beside him, I'm tipped into his side. Neither of us mind so much, Andrew quickly draping an arm around my shoulder like he's afraid I'm going to move away.

"What are we watching?" I ask.

"Dad always picks. It's the one time of the year he gets to be in charge of the television." Almost as soon as he's finished speaking, Hannah starts a drumroll on her lap as Sean stands, drawing all eyes toward him.

"No pressure," Christian drawls from where he's lounging on the floor with his back against the couch.

Everyone is wearing some sort of Christmas hat now, including me. And while a week ago, I wouldn't have been caught dead in it, I kind of love how ridiculous everyone looks.

Sean clears his throat, standing in front of the fireplace as he holds up a battered DVD case. "*Field of Dreams* is a—"

The family groans around me, cutting him off.

"We watched that last year," Hannah moans. "Mam!"

Colleen shrugs as she helps herself to more chocolate. Now that the dinner is out of the way she's much more relaxed and looks ready to finally settle down for the night. Every few minutes I notice her watching us all and smiling like she can't believe all her children are home, as though nothing has ever made her happier.

Sean continues bravely on. "A classic film about family and—"

"At least it's not *Apocalypse Now*," Christian mutters.

"Why don't we watch *Sleepless in Seattle*?" Hannah suggests hopefully.

Andrew says nothing, observing the room with a small smile on his lips as he plays with a lock of my hair.

"Let Molly decide," Colleen says after another minute of arguing. "She's the guest."

"Um..." I try to straighten from Andrew's side as everyone turns to me, but he doesn't budge, his arm keeping me locked against him.

Hannah looks at me pleadingly.

"I kind of like *Field of Dreams*," I say.

Sean beams as Hannah boos me, but, despite the grumblings, the room goes quiet when the movie is on, even if Hannah spends half of it on her phone until Christian plucks it from her hands and slides it into his back pocket. A brief wrestling match occurs before Colleen tears them apart and then they have to put their phones in the kitchen drawer for the rest of the night.

When it's finished, Colleen switches over to catch the last half of *My Fair Lady* on television. By the time *that's* done it's nearing midnight and Christmas Day is officially over. Andrew's parents excuse themselves first, and after another ten minutes, Christian stretches exaggeratedly as he catches Andrew's eye.

"Well," he yawns. "I'm wrecked. I'll see you guys in the morning." He gives Hannah a pointed look and pushes himself off the floor, heading to the stairs.

Hannah doesn't budge. Not until he comes back into the room and pinches the top of her ear, giving a sharp tug.

"*Ow*. Okay!" She bats him away as she follows him out, grumbling a goodnight.

And just like that we're alone again. I lift my head, finding Andrew watching me. He looks good like that, bathed in the glow from the Christmas lights, tired, but sated as he curls a lock of my hair around his finger.

"You sleepy?" he asks.

"Not yet," I say truthfully. "Your family are really nice."

"I'm glad they got to meet you." He tugs my hair. "Want your Christmas present now?"

"*Yes.*"

He laughs as he pushes me off him and drops to his knees by the tree. There are still a few presents wrapped underneath, which Andrew said were for the various wider family members who would drop in over the next few days. I don't think much of it until he returns to the couch with a round object, wrapped in purple tissue paper.

"Close your eyes," he says, and I do. A second later he drops something into my hands. The heavy weight of it catches me by surprise, and I make quick work unwrapping it as he sits back down beside me.

It's a snow globe.

But not the kind you see in airport gift shops, the cheap plastic things you're more likely to lose than keep. This one is big, like a paperweight, its base a heavy dark wood that takes up my whole hand. Inside there isn't a snowman or a miniature house, but a plane suspended in the night sky, its little windows a warm yellow.

"It's us?" I ask, not taking my eyes off it.

"It's us."

I turn it gently in my hands, running my fingers over the glass. "I don't have any Christmas decorations."

"I figured. I thought you wouldn't mind this one."

"Wouldn't mind?" I have to choke the words out. "I love it, Andrew."

He shrugs, watching me examine it.

"You're supposed to shake it," he reminds me, and I do, tilting it so the snowflakes flutter, until the plane is soaring through a winter's night. I lean forward so I can see it better in the light and Andrew's hand drops my hair in favor of rubbing slow circles into my back. It's like he can't stop touching me. And I don't want him to. In this moment, I don't think I've ever been as comfortable with another person as I am right now. The burnout I'd been experiencing the last few weeks, the anxiety and the nerves and the sleepless nights wondering what I should be doing with my life, it's all ebbed away, giving me a kind of clarity I haven't had before.

"Remember when I said I wanted to tell you everything?" I ask, not taking my eyes off the plane.

His fingers pause in their movements and I smile at whatever dramatic direction his mind just went. "Yeah," he says slowly.

"I don't have a secret lovechild somewhere."

"I was thinking CIA agent."

"I'm flattered." I place the snow globe carefully on the coffee table and sit up as best I can, twisting to face him. "I lied to you before. When I said I didn't know what I would do if I wasn't practicing law."

"I knew you were lying," he reminds me. "I said you were."

"Okay, well... I'm unlying to you now."

He just waits.

"I like food," I say, stating the obvious. I've always liked food. My greatest pleasure in life is eating and eating well. Finding new restaurants, trying new flavors. I introduced my friends to some of my favorite dishes the way a lot of people share their favorite movies, intently watching their faces to ensure they're reacting in all the appropriate ways. "I'm not good enough to cook professionally," I continue. "I know I'm not and I don't think I want to do that either. But..." I trail off as Andrew gently pulls my hand free from my hair. I hadn't even realized I'd been playing with it. "I did have one idea," I admit.

He smiles when I don't continue. "I'm dying of suspense here, Moll."

And it all suddenly seems so stupid. I don't know why I'm bigging it up so much or why I'm so scared to tell him. Maybe it's because I've never told anyone before. It's just one of those little dreams inside your head, like marrying a member of a boyband or winning the lottery. Only, as Andrew is about to find out, nowhere near as glamorous. "Did I ever tell you that I wanted to be a tour guide when I was little?"

He watches me for a beat, as though trying to weigh up if I'm joking or not. "No," he says eventually.

"Well, I did. I wanted to be one of those people who stands on top of the tour bus and leads a group of people down the street wearing a bright rain jacket and waving a matching umbrella over their head. My dad loves tours like that. He would take me and Zoe on them all the time. I always thought they were fun."

"And you want to be one now?" he asks curiously. "In Chicago?"

"Not exactly. I want to be a food guide. I want to take people around the city and show off all the restaurants and food stalls, not just the ones in the tour guides or the ones designed to be posted on Instagram. I want to show off the *real* places. Off the beaten track."

"So why don't you?"

"Because I don't live in a movie. Because I've got another eight months on the lease of an expensive apartment and student loans that I'm already spending a lifetime paying back. Because I live in America, which means I need health insurance. Because I spend several hundred dollars every year dyeing my hair."

"You dye your hair?"

"Of course I dye my hair. You think these highlights are natural?"

He looks very confused. "What, like the lighter bits? That's not your hair?"

"I dye my hair," I say. "I dye my hair and I pay a monthly subscription for my hot yoga classes, and I like getting massages when I want them. Which means I need enough money to pay for them."

"Or marry rich."

"Or steal."

"Or that," he agrees.

"It was just an idea. I don't know the first thing about how to get started. It would probably take years and might not even make me any money and..." I trail off, repeating the same things I've said to myself for weeks. In those moments in the dead of night when I can't sleep and I wake up so anxious and worried that sometimes it's like I can't breathe. I started a little bit of research, but never let myself think too much about it. The cons always outweighed the pros. The price of failure always much too high.

"Sounds like you're thinking a lot about what could go wrong and not about what could go right," Andrew says gently.

"I'm just trying to be realistic."

"I know you are, but I've had a lot of bad meals in my life, Molly, and not one of them has been from one of your recommendations. There's a reason everyone always asks you where to go when they want something to eat. And there's a reason you always have the answer. So, what if it doesn't fail? What if you're good at it and it takes off and you make enough money for everything you need and you live out the rest of your days doing what you love?"

"I..."

He frowns when I don't continue. "Have you really spent the last few weeks trying to figure out another career when you've had this idea in the back of your mind? Did you not think that maybe the reason your heart was so against every other path was that you knew exactly what you wanted all along?"

"No."

"Then what?" He meets my stare straight on, fully ready to argue with me. I hate when he gets all serious and reasonable about things.

"I've had too much ice cream to talk about this properly."

"That old excuse."

"It's true," I protest. "I'm tired."

"You're scared."

"So?" I ask. "There's nothing wrong with being scared."

"There's not," he agrees. "So long as you don't stay scared forever." He taps a finger under my chin when I look away, turning my gaze back to him. "You can get help," he adds. "It's not like you have to step outside one day and just start. There'll be people who can help you. I can help you. But you have to ask for it. You have to try. And I'd rather you tried than stay miserable, Molly. No matter how scared you are."

I don't know how to respond to that. Don't know how to do anything other than just stare at him. I don't understand how he always knows what to say to me. How he always knows how to cheer me up and calm me down like he understands me better than I do myself.

My fingers twitch with the now familiar urge to touch him, to be as close as I can to him, and I shift a little, drawing my legs onto the couch.

"There's a laptop in the other room," he continues, for

once oblivious to where my mind has wandered. "Do you want to show me what you've been—"

"Let's talk about it in the morning."

"I'm not saying you need to make a decision; I just want to see what you've—"

"Andrew." I turn, swinging one leg over him so I'm straddling his thighs. His hands grip my waist, holding me steady as surprise and then heat flares in his eyes. "Let's talk about it in the morning," I repeat, each word slow and clear as I lean down and bring my lips to his.

CHAPTER TWENTY-SIX

I am officially obsessed with kissing Andrew Fitzpatrick.

Some people run. Some people bake. Some people paint miniature figurines or upcycle furniture to sell for five times the price. It's healthy to have hobbies. And now I have mine.

"That's it," he murmurs when I finally come up for air. "I'm bringing you home for Christmas every year."

I smile, tracing his nose with the tips of my fingers. I wonder how I resisted staying away from him for all these years. My heart aches at the thought, at the time wasted, but I quickly disregard it. I'm glad we got to be friends first, that now I get to give myself to him fully without worrying which parts of me he might reject. He's already seen me at my worst. Tired and stressed, angry and crying. He's seen it all and still seems to want everything. To want me.

"Were you jealous of my exes?" I ask before I can stop myself.

Andrew just smirks. "Do you want me to be?"

"Maybe."

He doesn't reply immediately, seeming to think about

his answer. "I wasn't so much jealous as I was happy when they made you happy," he says eventually. "And irrationally angry when they made you sad. I may have a protective streak when it comes to you."

I shrug, trying not to look as happy as I am by that statement. It doesn't fool him for an instant.

"You like that, don't you?"

"I don't know what you mean."

"No?"

"No, I'm emotionally very healthy and—" I yelp, laughing as he pushes me onto the couch.

"You're a terrible liar," he says, leaning down. I turn away at the last second, still laughing, but he doesn't seem to mind, his lips meeting my throat like that was his intended target all along.

He nuzzles into me, gentle at first and then hard enough that it sends my pulse fluttering.

I push at his shoulders, wanting a real kiss, but he doesn't budge, concentrating on the soft patch of skin where my neck meets my shoulder before drifting a trail to right below my ear. One hand pushes my hair back, the strands slipping through his fingers as he starts a delicious suction that leaves me reeling.

"Are you giving me a hickey?" I ask only to squirm when he sucks harder before releasing me.

"No," he lies, sounding pleased with himself.

I scowl when he pulls back, but it's only halfhearted as I surge up to kiss him properly. He lets me this time, his mouth slanting over mine with a low groan that instantly becomes my favorite sound in the world, and when he pushes his hips into me, I gasp so loud I'm amazed I don't wake his whole family.

The thought of them has me breaking away, clambering off the couch on wobbly legs. Andrew blinks up at me, slightly dazed, and for a moment he looks disappointed, maybe even a little nervous, as if he thinks we've gone too far. But then I hold out my hand in a silent question, remembering what he said. That we'll take things as they come. That we'll do what feels right. And this, this right here, feels right. And when he puts his hand in mine and follows me out of the room, I know it with my whole soul.

———

I hold in a giggle as we attempt to make it up the stairs as silently as we can. It's a little after one a.m. and there are no lights on under any of the doors we pass. The house is fast asleep, but I've never been more awake.

I turn to Andrew as soon as we're in our room, but he moves away, striding to the radiator by the window with single-minded focus.

"Thank Christ," he says, pressing a hand to it. "Dad said he'd fix it this after—"

"Andrew."

"Right. Sorry."

He hops back over the bed, the movement a lot more graceful than it has any right to be as he comes to stand in front of me.

"Sorry," he whispers again. "You sure about this?"

"Yeah. You?"

"I'm sure. I am very, very sure." He steps closer, vanquishing the space between us. "Feels strange though," he muses. "To give in after all this time. I feel like I've been hiding it from both of us for so long. And now I'm just... not."

"Hiding what?" I ask, thoughts scattering as his fingers circle my wrists, clasping them gently.

"How much I've thought about this moment." I swallow as his mouth drops to my ear, his words barely more than a whisper. "Do you want me to tell you?" he asks. "How much I want you right now?"

I shrug a little, or at least I think I do, my body no longer seems to understand what my brain is telling it.

"What do you want, Moll?" Andrew asks when I just stand there.

"I want..."

"Yes?"

Everything. The word gets stuck in my throat, choked down by the realization. I want everything with him. I want it so much I can barely stand it.

"A kiss," I say instead, trying to focus as his grip tightens ever so slightly.

He immediately acquiesces, capturing my lips with perfect aim, but it's not enough. It's nowhere *near* enough.

The kiss is soft. The kiss is sweet. The kiss... is a freaking tease.

I writhe against him, needing more, and when I pull away he loosens his hold on my hands so I can raise them to his chest, clutching him by his sweater.

"You," I say. "I want you. All of you."

Heat fills his gaze, as though charged by the same electricity I feel running through my own body. "You have me, Moll. You've had me for years."

"Then stop teasing," I mutter, and grab the back of his neck, pulling him down to me.

This kiss is stronger, surer, our lips moving against each other in seamless synchronization like we've done it a million times before. Andrew's hands drop to my waist, unbuttoning the front of my jeans before he slides them down my hips. I don't even break the kiss as they fall to my ankles, stepping out of them and kicking them to the side. My sweater comes next and I raise my arms as he grabs the hem and pulls it over my head. There's a slight edge to his movements now. Like with each piece of clothing, we grow more frantic and he follows me in our less-than-elegant striptease until we're both making out in our underwear, still rooted to our spot against the door.

He steers us toward the bed and my mind whirls, forgetting to be embarrassed by the noises I make and the cellulite on my thighs and the stretch marks on my hips. These are things I'd usually be thinking about the first time with someone new, but Andrew isn't new. And even if he was, I'd still be too distracted trying to get enough of him to care. Because no matter how much I try, I can't get enough. I want him to touch me everywhere, I want to feel him everywhere. I want ten hours of kissing and foreplay. I want him in me now.

And Andrew seems just as torn as I am, his hands moving up and down my body as if he doesn't know where to focus. When he's not kissing my lips, he's on my neck, my throat, licking down between my breasts and back up again before nipping me hard enough that it's just short of pain, a spiking pleasure that I know will leave another mark. I want it to leave a mark. I want proof of this night, of this moment, so that when I wake up in the morning, I'll remember exactly what happened.

"Bra," he mumbles in my ear, and I nod jerkily as I push up, reaching behind for the clasp.

"Do you have a—"

"Yes," he says, almost diving off me as he kneels beside his suitcase. I try not to stare at his ass in his black boxer shorts and then remember I can stare all I like now, and when he comes back to the bed with a victorious expression, I raise a brow at the row of foil packets in his hand.

"Do I want to know why you brought condoms home for Christmas?"

"It's called sexual health, Molly. And I have an old girl-friend in the village who—"

"Not funny," I snap, launching myself at him. He laughs as we fall to the bed and I straddle him, carefully tearing open a packet as his eyes skate over my bare chest before focusing on the pendant around my neck, the present he got me. He tugs it gently, positioning it in the hollow of my throat before sitting up to press the lightest kiss to it.

Our underwear is the last to go and they go quickly before I'm rolling the condom onto him and then suddenly our places are switched, his movements confident and sure as he pulls me under him.

"You good?" he asks, and I nod, grabbing his face to kiss him again. He lets me do so only briefly before he breaks away, skimming his nose along my jaw before he moves downward. It takes me a few seconds to realize he's not coming back up.

"Andrew?"

He only hums against my skin, his tongue tracing a circle around my belly button before he keeps going.

"You don't have to—" Shut *up*, Molly. My head hits the pillow, fingers digging into the bedsheets as he gently parts my legs.

The first touch of his tongue has me squeezing my eyes shut. The second has me squeezing my thighs, but Andrew doesn't seem to mind. If anything, it seems to spur him on as he grabs hold of my hips, keeping me as still as he can as I move against him. The man can take direction, I'll give him that, and he follows every movement of my body as I silently tell him where to go and what I need until he learns me better than I even know myself. Until he needs no direction at all. And when one hand leaves my hip to join his efforts, I'm a goner. Pleasure ripples through me, almost unbearable in its sweetness.

I can only lie there, my breathing ragged as he waits for me to still before licking his way back up to my mouth.

"Okay, good job," I say, patting the side of his face. "Night night."

He smirks, taking me in before kissing me. My hands go to his back, exploring to my heart's content. The sudden freedom to do so makes me almost giddy and he encourages my enthusiasm by kissing me harder, by reacting to everything I do. He shudders when I run my fingers up the sides of his stomach, he grunts when I tug at his hair. I am fascinated by every one of his movements, every sound that comes from him, every muscle that contracts under my touch.

He feels warm and hard against me, and even though we're both sweating, I don't protest as he maneuvers us under the covers, the heavy drape of the quilt over our bodies only making me feel like we're closer together.

He settles more fully over me, testing his weight against mine, how our bodies fit together. So familiar yet new. And I know that whatever is happening, there's no turning back from this. This is not a one-night thing.

This is not a mistake.

How could I ever have thought this would be a mistake?

I'm so ready for him now that there's no hesitation when he moves into me, a moan escaping me as our eyes lock together. An almost pained expression comes over his face at the sound and he bends to kiss me with renewed determination, open, hot, and less skilled than before. The arms on either side of me tremble as though he's doing his best to keep himself in check and when he pulls back, the slow drag sends my nerve endings into overdrive.

He kisses me like I've never been kissed before. Like he's been waiting his whole life to do it.

Or maybe just ten years.

I grip him harder at the thought, pulling him into me until our bodies are pressed so flush together that there isn't an inch of space between us. And I don't want there to be.

I love this man. I love him I love him I love him and all I can think about is how he must love me too. He must. Because he wanted me here. He wanted me with him. Maybe long before I ever wanted him. And I'm so glad I stopped under that mistletoe, I'm so glad fate finally got fed up with waiting even if I don't have the bravery to tell him as much yet. But maybe I don't need to. My touch can tell him what my words can't and so I touch. I touch and I caress and I let my kisses speak for themselves. And as he brings my hands over my head, lacing his fingers with mine, I try to remember if I've ever felt this way before, if I've ever felt so *much* before, and then he pulls at my bottom lip and dips his head to press his mouth to the skin just above my heart and I can't remember anything at all.

CHAPTER TWENTY-SEVEN

ONE YEAR AGO

Flight Nine, Chicago

"I can't remember where I... No, I definitely left it on her desk. Well, if it's not there then someone moved it. I don't know who! If I did, we wouldn't be in this mess."

"Molly."

I hold up a finger, reaching deep for my last shred of patience so I can make sure I still have a job in the morning. "Call Lauren and check with her," I say. "And don't tell Carlton... I don't care if she's gone home for Christmas, so have I!"

"*Molly.*"

"I'm on the phone," I hiss, glancing at Andrew. He glares at me from across the small plastic table, looking just as irritable and tired as I feel.

"Well, unless you want me to order you a glass of water, you need to get off it," he says.

It's only then that I notice the exhausted-looking server standing beside us.

Shit. Fine. "I'll call you back in five," I say, hanging up

with a pointed look at Andrew before I skim through the menu, already knowing what I want.

"Cheese fries," I say. "Thank you."

"I'm sorry, we're all out."

Of course they are. "The club sandwich is fine."

The waitress winces. There's a ketchup stain on the front of her blouse and her dark hair is falling out of its half-hearted bun. "We finished serving our sandwich menu at—"

"You choose then," I interrupt, handing the menu back to her. "Surprise me."

"Our soup of the day is—"

"Yes. Great. I'll have that."

She mumbles another apology and spins on her heel, going immediately to the party at the next table.

"Seriously?" Andrew asks when she's out of earshot. "She's barely more than a kid."

"I'll leave a good tip," I mutter, dropping my head into my hands. I massage my temples, trying to ease the migraine forming there. I know I'm being a bitch, but I don't know how not to be right now. Work is an endless nightmare that's only made worse by the holiday, our flight's been delayed for five hours and now we've apparently waited thirty minutes to order food that they don't even have.

"It's not her fault," Andrew continues, and I have to fight back a scowl, keeping my head bent so he can't see my face. "What?" he asks, when I don't respond. "You're not even going to talk to me now, is that it?"

Oh, for the love of—

"What do you want me to say?" I snap, sitting up so fast my head spins. "Because it feels like whatever I do, you're just going to take in the wrong way with the mood you're in."

"The mood *I'm* in? You're the one who's been on her phone for the past hour."

"Yes, because of *work*, Andrew. I have a job. One that doesn't just stop when I leave the office."

"How about one that stops for a few hours so we can talk to each other?"

"A few hours? We're going to be here all night at this stage!"

"Um... excuse me?"

"*What?*" We snap the word in unison, both of us turning to see the waitress standing terrified before us.

"I'm really, *really* sorry," she begins as my phone buzzes on the table. "But the soup..."

Andrew's still looking at me like I'm the worst person in the world and I'm starting to feel like it too, the pressure of work the last few weeks turning me into someone I barely recognize.

"We *definitely* have the chicken Caesar salad," the girl continues, and it's the earnest hopefulness in her voice that finally tips me over the edge.

The tears come instantly and once they start there's no way to stop them.

"I'm sorry," she gasps as Andrew mutters a curse word and slides out of his seat. "We have spaghetti? It will take longer but—"

"The salad's fine," I say, barely able to get the words out. "That sounds perfect, thank you."

She gives me a panicked nod as Andrew kneels beside me, placing a hesitant hand on my arm as everyone around us politely looks the other way.

"I'm sorry," I say, my voice wobbling. "I'm really tired."

"I know. Me too. I'm sorry for snapping."

"*I'm* sorry for snapping. Crap. My makeup."

"Don't worry about it."

"Don't be such a *boy*." I pluck a napkin from the dispenser, dabbing it under my eyes. My phone keeps ringing, but both of us ignore it. "I just wanted some cheese fries."

"I know. We can try somewhere else. Or I can steal them off that guy's table."

He says it so seriously that I snort, which is not a great thing to do while crying, but it does the job of shutting me up, the tears ending as quickly as they came.

"Ugh." I press the napkin to my nose, blowing lightly. "I'm sorry about work."

"You don't need to be. I know you—"

"No." I cut him off. "I'm being rude. They announced last month that they're making cuts, so everyone is turning on each other like it's a Battle Royale and I'm just..." I sigh, slumping in my chair. "I don't know when I last got a full night's sleep."

"Can I do something?"

My breath hitches at his words and I'm reminded again why I drop everything every year to fly home with this man. No "Maybe you shouldn't work so hard," no "Get yourself together, Molly." Just how he can help me. Even after I've spent the last two hours ignoring him, that's all he wants to know.

"Just pretend I've been nothing but great company," I say. "And tell me if my mascara's ruined."

"The bits all over your face or..."

I scowl at him, but he just smiles, and then, to my surprise, rubs his thumb over my cheek, wiping away the stains. It's a strangely intimate gesture, his skin rough and warm against mine, and I still beneath the sensation, confused by my reaction to it. He swipes once more, slower this time as his smile fades into a frown.

"Molly..."

My phone rings and he jerks back, dropping his hand like I've burned him. Before I can stop him, he gives me an encouraging nod, returning to his seat.

"You should get that," he says.

But to hell with that.

I silence the damn thing before shoving it into my purse.

"For all they know, I'm in the air," I say. "I'm all yours."

Something flickers in his gaze at my words, but whatever he's going to say is lost as the waitress returns, visibly sweating now.

"So, when I said a *chicken* Caesar salad..."

Now

I sleep in fits and starts. Either I wake or Andrew does and every time that happens one of us reaches for the other. At some point during the night, we come together a second time and it's slower and careful, but no less perfect, and when he brings me to that sweet spot, I have to turn my head into the pillow to muffle the sounds I can't help but make.

Only then does sleep come properly, and the next time I wake the clock on my phone tells me it's a little before seven. Andrew is dead to the world beside me, his head turned toward mine, and for a few minutes I simply lie there, adjusting to the darkness, adjusting to, well, *this*.

I could get used to this.

Going to bed with him, waking up with him, repeating it over and over again until it stops being special. Until I can take him for granted.

Not in that bad way, but a comfortable one. Knowing that he'll be there. Just like he's always been.

I check the last few messages on the family group chat, scrolling through endless photos of everyone holding the baby. Zoe's due home today and now so am I, and while I desperately want to see her and my parents, another part of me is miserable at the thought of spending just a few days away from Andrew. It makes me want to wake him so we can make the most of every minute we have left, though, of course, I don't, going down the normal route of staring at my phone in the dark for several minutes and liking everyone's Instagram stories.

I've just finished sending a slightly-too-long update to Gabriela when nature calls and I use the excuse to slip out of bed. It takes some careful maneuvering, but it looks like the exhaustion has finally caught up with Andrew and he doesn't stir as I creep out of the room.

I go about my business quickly and am back outside the bedroom door when my stomach cramps with a familiar morning pang.

I shouldn't be surprised. I've always been a breakfast person (okay, I'm an every meal person) and despite stuffing my face for most of the day yesterday, habits are clearly hard to break. Tucking the dressing robe properly around me in case I run into a Fitzpatrick on my travels, I continue past Andrew's door and sneak down the same stairs we'd rushed up not hours before.

I feel my way through the dark house until I get to the kitchen where, after a bit of flailing, I manage to find the light switch. Taking Colleen at her word that I can help myself, I grab a slice of bread from a bread bin on the counter. I don't even bother to toast it, just lean against the counter as I tear off mouthfuls as fast as I can chew. I'd love a coffee but can't see a machine anywhere and it didn't escape my notice that everyone was drinking tea yesterday morning. I'm sure they must have a bit of the instant kind somewhere, but the thought of rooting around their cabinets is a step too far on the guest scale for me.

There has to be somewhere in the village I can get my caffeine fix. I haven't discussed timings with Andrew in regard to me going back to my parents, but we'll surely be able to—

I jump, startled as a cough sounds from somewhere nearby, and stuff the remaining bread into my mouth in case Andrew woke up and snuck down after me. But when I hear it again, I realize it's coming from outside and the porch that wraps around the back of the house.

Curious, I brush my crumbs into the sink and peek my head out the door.

Christian stands just outside, dressed in sweatpants and a hoodie. A lit cigarette is poised between his lips and there's a guilty, deer-in-the-headlights look on his face that vanishes as soon he sees me.

"I thought you were Mam," he says, sounding more relieved than a grown man in his late twenties should be.

"Sorry."

"Couldn't sleep?"

I shake my head, wrapping my arms around myself as I glance about. Two robins hop around the frozen ground near us as though testing their bravery. It's cold, but not unbearable and I step out farther.

"Do you mind if I...?"

He shrugs as I gesture lamely at the porch and I take a place against the wall on the other side of the door.

"You're up early," I say.

"I'm heading back to London in an hour or so. Boss is a dick, wants everyone in the office tomorrow."

That sounds familiar. "What do you do?"

"Real estate."

"Do you like it?"

"Nope." He smirks. "But it pays the bills. Well, kind of." He takes another drag, turning his head so he's not blowing smoke my way. An awkward silence descends or at least one that's awkward on my part. Christian seems perfectly content to just stand there, watching me. Is this why people smoke? So they have something to do with their hands?

"So," he says, after thirty seconds of me desperately trying to think of another topic. "Are you and Andrew..."

"Engaged?"

He laughs at that. "Sorry about dinner," he says, not sounding sorry at all. "Hannah's a romantic."

"And you?"

"Just a younger brother." He tugs his hood up, burrowing into it against the cold. "But it's a thing now, is it?"

"It's new."

"New's not a bad way to end the year," he says, his tone kinder. "Even if he's always had terrible timing."

I only smile, a little confused.

"Do you know what you're going to do yet?" he asks.

"Like..."

"Stay in the States, back to Dublin?"

"Ah." The emigrant chat. "I have no plans to move back to Ireland. Chicago's felt like home for a while now."

"Good for you," he says. "Long-distance though. That's always looked hard."

"What do you mean?"

"Well, not that it can't work," he adds, and I freeze, my impromptu breakfast churning in my stomach. Christian hurries on, mistaking my silence for annoyance. "You'll be grand." A quick smile. "Has Andrew found an apartment yet? He never believes me when I tell him how Dublin is for renters. I think he has it in his head that he'll just come home and walk into a place."

I pull my hair into a halfhearted bun, my now clammy hands moving automatically as I tug the strands back again and again and again. "I'm sure he'll find something," I say. The words sound faint, as though spoken by someone else.

"Not in time though. When does the new job start? March?"

March? *March?* "I can't remember."

"Maybe you could get him to look at those places I sent on? He'll need to put his name down just to get a viewing. And tell him not to come crying to me when—"

Both of us flinch when the door flies open, Christian hiding the cigarette behind his back on instinct. Andrew steps out, taking in the scene before turning an accusing eye toward his brother.

"What are you doing out here?"

Christian shrugs. "Stealing your girl."

"Well, can you steal her inside? Preferably next to the radiator?" Andrew motions me back into the kitchen and I follow numbly. "And put that out before Mam catches you," he says to Christian. "What are you? Fifteen?"

Christian steps inside a second later, rubbing his hands together as Andrew turns on more lights. "They think it's going to snow today," he says, glancing out the window.

"They always say it's going to snow," Andrew says. "It will be on the mountains if there's anything." His eyes dart toward me and he frowns, shrugging the sweatshirt from his body and passing it to me. I put it on automatically, just so I have something to do other than look at him.

He's moving back to Ireland? He's moving back to Ireland and he didn't tell me?

"I'm going to finish packing," Christian says. "Take it easy, Molly." He doesn't wait for a response as he disappears back up the stairs.

"Are you okay?" Andrew asks when he's gone.

"I'm fine."

"Are you sure?"

"*Yes.*" I move around the counter, wishing he hadn't interrupted us and that I'd asked Christian what was going on.

Andrew just grins at me. "What am I supposed to think, waking up to an empty bed?"

"I'm sorry. I got up to pee and then I was hungry."

"You are? What do you want? Mam usually buys those little variety packets of cereal as a treat. I laugh, but I've never wanted anything more right now." He starts rifling through the cabinets, pulling out various breakfast items. As he does an image comes to me, of him sitting at the airport bar, just before our flight was canceled.

Can I talk to you for a sec?

I'd been so caught up in what was happening I hadn't listened to him. Was that when he was going to tell me? Was that why he was so quick to suggest spending Christmas in Chicago even if it meant not seeing his family? Because it was the last time he'd get to do it?

"You want a coffee?" Andrew sets out two mugs on the

counter and goes back to his rummaging. "No one drinks it but me, so I always bring home my own stash."

He glances over when I don't say anything, one hand holding a plastic-wrapped assortment of mini cereal boxes.

"You sure you're alright?"

I lean forward on the kitchen island, my arms dwarfed in the baggy sleeves of his sweatshirt, my feet sliding in the fuzzy slippers Hannah lent me.

"Christian said..."

Andrew's brows draw together when I don't continue, and he looks toward the stairs with a scowl. "Christian said what?"

"He thinks you're moving back here. That you're starting a new job. Looking for an apartment."

Silence.

I said it purposefully like we were sharing a joke, in an "isn't Christian funny, hah hah hah" way. But Andrew just places the cereal on the counter, his expression guarded as he removes a mini-packet of Rice Krispies.

Oh, hell no.

"Molly—"

"You can't be serious."

"It's not what it sounds like."

"It's not? Are you moving back here?"

"No."

Oh. Okay, now I'm confused. "But Christian said—"

"I know. He... I had a plan. When Marissa and I broke up, I started re-evaluating things. My life over there. My sobriety. I thought that maybe I needed a fresh start."

"Back home?"

"I'm aware of the irony."

"But you're not moving home," I confirm, trying to wrap my head around what's happening.

"I changed my mind."

He changed his mind. And for the first time since we got here; I feel a prick of unease at his words.

"When?"

He hesitates, as if knowing in putting out one fire, he may have just started another.

"When did you change your mind?" I press.

"Does it matter?"

"*Yes*. Because from what you're implying, up until three days ago, you'd planned for *months* to move home. And now you're just... not? Because of what? A kiss?"

"It's not just that and you know it."

"But if we hadn't kissed that would still be the plan, right?" I start to feel a little sick. Back to his family, to his friends, back to a new life and he was going to throw it away for me? "You've got a new job?"

"I haven't accepted it. And I'm not going to." He's tense now, his good mood vanished. I'd feel guilty if I wasn't so mad. I can't believe he didn't tell me. "Moll, come on, this isn't a—"

"*Don't* say this isn't a big deal," I warn. "I know you think it's not, but it is. You said so yourself how sad you were missing Hannah grow up. And your niece and nephew love you and your parents love you and you love Ireland, I know you do." The excitement on his face when we walked around Dublin, the calm that settled over him when we stood on the hilltop yesterday morning. I'd never seen him like that before. He said he needed a fresh start and now he was going to trade it all for something we've only just dipped our toes into? That we've barely begun to explore? Every long-term relationship I've ever had has ended with someone choosing something or someone else over me. So what happens when I give everything to this man and he turns around three months from now and realizes he chose wrong?

"We don't know what this is yet," I say, trying to get him to understand.

One look at his face and I know he doesn't. If anything, he looks pissed off. "I don't know what this is? Really?"

"We haven't even—"

"Flight one," he interrupts, placing the packet of Rice Krispies to the side as he moves on to the Coco Pops. "When you didn't even know me and you tried to protect me. You literally stole my phone to stop me from getting hurt. Flight two, I stared at the back of your head the entire time, waiting for you to turn around. I know you thought I was mad then, but I wasn't, I was embarrassed. I wanted to talk to you, but for the first time in my life I didn't know how. Flight three. Our first real flight. It was the quickest that journey has ever been for me. I was going to ask you out, but you said you had a boyfriend."

"Andrew—"

"Flight four." He moves onto the cornflakes. "When we got drunk on champagne and talked the whole way home. I don't think I've ever had so much fun in my life. Flight five, when you bought me that sweater. I didn't wash it for a week because it smelled of you. I carried that old food guide around with me for weeks, wondering if I should give it to you or not, and the look on your face when you opened it... I'd never been so happy to see someone smile. Flight six when I saw you saying goodbye to your boyfriend. You wanted to know if I was jealous of your exes, Molly? I put it down at the time to not wanting you to date an asshole, but seeing you together felt like I was being ripped in two. I was with someone else at the time and just standing there looking at you felt like cheating."

He waits for me to interrupt again, but I don't. I just stare at him, feeling ridiculously close to crying.

"I lied when I said I wanted to kiss you once before," he continues. "Flight seven is the second time I wanted to. I don't know why. Nothing special happened. I just came up the escalator and you were sitting by the gate and I felt like I was home already. I hated parting that time. I hated it, but I didn't know why. Flight eight, you were basically dying from your period. You fell asleep on my shoulder and I could have pushed you to the side, but I didn't. My arm went dead, but I didn't move because I liked you touching me and I wanted to look after you. Sometimes I think it's what I was born to do. Flight nine is when we were delayed and you started crying because they were out of cheese fries. I'm pretty sure I would have sold all of my belongings just to get you some and I was so close to telling you how I felt. So close to figuring this out, but you were exhausted and I didn't want to stress you out even more. By the time I got back after Christmas you'd already met Brandon and I was too late."

He moves then, rounding the table, and only stops when I take a step back, bumping into the stovetop.

"I was going to tell you about moving home. I swear to God I was. But not yet. Because more than anything, I wanted you to give me a reason to stay. I was going to flirt, test the waters, maybe ask you out on a proper date, but you were so busy with work and then the storm happened and..." He shakes his head, almost scowling at me now. "The storm happened and you dropped everything to get me home for Christmas because you knew that was what would make me happy. So, flight ten, Molly. Flight ten when you kissed me under the mistletoe and became the only girl I've ever truly wanted. Don't tell me I don't know what this is. Don't tell me I don't know what I want."

My heart is beating is so hard in my chest, I swear that I can hear it. I can certainly feel it. An aching thump against my rib cage as though it's trying to leap out and join his. I want nothing more than to hold him, to touch him, but I stay where I am, the future repercussions of this scaring me more than anything ever has. Because it's easy to take the leap. To quit your job, to fall in love. Wanting is the easy part. It's the hard stuff that comes after. And the idea that Andrew might be making the biggest mistake of his life for me is enough to make my blood run cold.

"We both agreed that we would start at the *beginning*," I say when I can speak again. "This is not a decision someone makes at the beginning of a relationship."

"And if I move back here, we can't start at all. Is that what you want?"

"What I *want* is—"

We both tense as the staircase creaks. I fold my arms over my chest, half expecting Christian to return with some quip, but it's the youngest Fitzpatrick that appears in the doorway, barefooted in her flannel pajamas.

Andrew smiles, some of the intensity in his expression seeping away. "Hey, sleeping beauty," he says, his voice infused with lightness even though he doesn't take his eyes off me.

"What time is it?" Hannah asks, looking more ten than teen as she rubs her eyes, peering into the dim kitchen.

"Seven thirty."

"What?" She sounds horrified. "Why are you up?"

"Body clock is out of whack." He shakes the cereal. "Plus, variety pack."

Hannah doesn't look convinced, her eyes narrowing as she glances between us. "Are you guys fighting?"

"No."

"You look like you're fighting. You look like you're—"

"Go back to bed, Hannah," Andrew interrupts, but she just gives him a look as she goes to the sink.

"I'm getting water first," she mutters. "I'm allowed to get water. I live here."

Andrew gives her that quintessential I'm-going-to-murder-you sibling glare, but Hannah ignores him, her eyes flicking to me as she leaves.

I flash her a smile, but it must look as strained as I feel because her brow only furrows deeper as she leaves the room. There's a long pause where she's clearly trying to eavesdrop on the staircase before it creaks again when she gives up.

Andrew waits a moment before he turns back to me, planting his hands on the counter.

"I want to see my sister," I say when he goes to speak again.

"Molly—"

"We'll talk about it," I say. "We'll sit down like adults and talk about it. But I can't... I can't *think* right now."

I knew it. I knew as soon as Christmas was over something would happen. The magic would break. I just didn't think I'd be the one to break it.

Andrew presses his lips together, clearly unhappy. "I can borrow my mam's car and give you a ride back."

"I'll catch one with Christian."

"You're not even going to let me—"

"Not because of that." I sigh. "It makes sense, doesn't it? He's going there anyway. I just want you to think about it for a few days. Spend some time with your family, with your friends here. A lot has happened in a few days and it sounds like we both need space to just breathe."

"I don't need space."

"Well..." I stare at him, helpless. "I do."

There's a finality to my words that I didn't mean, but one he fully hears. He straightens, his throat moving as he swallows.

"Better make you that coffee then," he says, turning his back to me.

And I don't know what to say to that so I don't say anything at all, lingering for an awkward second before I slink back up the stairs. At the far end of the hall a door lies open, and it's there I find Christian, sitting on the edge of an unmade bed, his face creased in concentration as he tries to get a new pair of earbuds out of their plastic casing. He doesn't look up when I knock.

"Yeah?"

"Can you give me a ride back to Dublin?"

His fingers pause only briefly in their struggle as his eyes flick to me. "I think Andrew was planning on—"

"Makes more sense, doesn't it? Save on the gas?"

He frowns. "Is your sister okay?"

"She's fine," I say, trying to sound bright. "I just want to get back up and see her."

"It's not a problem," he says, slowly. "I'm leaving in an hour though."

I shrug, backing out the door before he can change his mind. "Not like I have anything to pack."

I'm fully dressed by the time Andrew comes back up the stairs with my coffee. Neither of us speaks and before long the rest of the family is gathering to say goodbye. Colleen is upset to see her youngest son go even though she pretends she isn't, fussing over him before disappearing into the kitchen after their final goodbye. Sean and Hannah stay out at least, though Hannah is the most subdued I've seen her, eyeing Christian moodily as though he's leaving purely to ruin her day. I hang back until Colleen reemerges and presses three stacked containers of leftover food into my hands, along with another candle for my mother and a small, knitted toy lamb for Zoe.

"You'll come back and see us," she says, her words more an order than a request.

Andrew waits until the last possible second to hug me as he always does. For a moment I think he might kiss me, but he lets me go with a smile that I know is for the sake of the others.

"Call me when you get back," he says, and I nod, already feeling the distance between us.

Despite the cold weather, he remains outside as Christian drives us down the lane. I keep my head twisted back to look at him, watching until the very last second when he vanishes from view.

CHAPTER TWENTY-EIGHT

The drive back is strange. I'd been asleep for most of the journey down so was unaware of how deep in the country-side we were, and am amazed at how easily Christian navigates the winding, unmarked roads. It's a miracle he doesn't get lost, especially in the darkness. We're driving for more than thirty minutes before the sun begins to rise.

I also thought Christian would be the strong and silent type but, to my surprise, he's kind of... chatty. Not only that but the man won't sit still. As soon as we leave the farm, he switches the radio to some generic hits station and starts muttering about other drivers on the rare occasion we pass them. He fiddles with the heating, he pops a mint and offers me one. He taps his fingers against the steering wheel and grills me about life in Chicago just as Zoe had asked Andrew when she drove us home.

Once we're on the motorway he starts to calm down, and I wonder how much of what he said about his boss wanting him back in the office is true and if maybe, unlike Andrew, home for Christmas is more of a duty than a gift. One that he's happy to perform, but glad when it's over.

It's only when we approach Dublin and the cars become busier with Christmas travelers that he brings up what happened this morning.

"Did he freak you out?"

"Huh?" I'd been distracted, busy staring at my phone, wondering if Andrew was going to message me.

"My brother," Christian says, giving the finger to someone cutting abruptly across us. "I never pegged him as the intense sort, but people change."

"Intense?" I ask. "Seriously?"

"What?"

"*You're* the intense one."

"Am I?" That seems to surprise him. And I suppose it's not hard to understand why. I think back to the first time I ever heard of him, on that very first flight with Andrew, when he'd pulled the birthday card trick, just to embarrass him. "Is it the family?" he asks. "Couldn't handle a Fitzpatrick Christmas?"

"Your family is lovely."

"What then?" His tone is blunt as if we didn't just meet yesterday. "Because don't think I didn't notice the awkward-as-hell hug you gave him back at the house. Or the fact that you keep pretending it's not a big deal that I'm the one driving you back."

"It's economical."

"It's suspicious as f— *Hey!*" He blares the horn as someone slows down too quickly in front of us, trying to make their exit. "A Kerry license plate. Typical."

I turn my attention back to my phone.

"It's just," Christian continues, and I sigh. "The way Andrew's spoken of you over the years, I know you guys are close. And I've never seen him be that touchy-feely with a girl before. I would have told him to snap out of it if he didn't keep smiling every time you walked into the room." His eyes slide to me, just in time to see me flush. "But I guess it's none of my business."

"It's not."

"Yeah." A pause. "Except it kind of is."

"Excuse me?"

"It kind of is my business," he says. "Because he's my brother and I love the idiot and I went to bed and he was happy and I woke up and he wasn't, so what? Why are you leaving so soon?"

"I'm not allowed to go back and see my newly mothering sister?"

"Andrew would have happily driven you back himself. What did you fight about?"

"We didn't fight. There was a misunderstanding and now we just need space to figure it out."

"What the hell could you have..." His eyes narrow as realization dawns. "He didn't tell you he was moving home, did he?"

"Not in as many words."

"So, I stood there freaking you out and you just lied and pretended you already knew?"

"I was trying to save face."

"You're good at it." He sighs. "Shit. I'm sorry. I thought he would have told you."

"Yeah, well, I thought he would have told me too."

Christian grimaces, eyes darting between me and the road. "Alright," he says, and I can tell by his tone he's trying to lighten the mood. "So, how are you at long-distance?"

I clear my throat, covering my phone with my hand. I don't know if I should be the one to tell him this, but I feel like he's not going to let it drop. "It doesn't matter. Andrew said he's decided to stay in Chicago."

"What? Since when?"

I feel a little justified hearing the bewilderment in his voice. "Since now, I guess. Because of me."

"Huh. Okay." A myriad of expressions cross his face as he works through that little update. "And you don't like that?" he asks eventually.

"I don't not... It's a big thing," I say. "A big choice. For him to decide to stay just because it's where I am? That feels like a lot."

"And you think you're not worth it, huh?"

"I didn't say that."

"What, then?" There's a frown on his face like he's trying to figure me out. "Scared he's going to change his mind?"

"It's not a completely unrealistic outcome. This whole thing has happened way too quickly. Usually, you meet a guy, you hit it off and you try each other on for a while. See if you fit. This feels like we were moving along at this snail's pace for ten years and suddenly, bam."

"Bam? Did someone step on the snail?"

"No, the snail... No, I meant now it's going too fast."

He gives me a confused look. "Okay."

I try again. "What I mean is he's spent the last three days trying to get home to you guys. And watching you all together... He loves you. He loves this place. He's always said that. And now he's just going to throw that away for me?"

"See, now I think you're giving yourself *too* much credit," he says. "It's a difficult balance, I'll give you that."

"Christian—"

"He likes Chicago," he interrupts. "He's spent all his adult life there, just like you. And just like you, he moved there before he knew you even existed. I'm sure sitting next to you on an airplane once a year was thrilling, but I'm also going to take a wild guess that he didn't stay there because of that. He has a life over there. He has friends, he has memories, he has his roommate's dog that he won't stop sending pictures of to the family group chat. To be clear, the easiest option is for him to stay. And as to your weird snail analogy..." He stares out the road, exasperated. "Yeah, fine, if you two just met three days ago, but you didn't. You've known the guy for ten years. And I think he's been a bit in love with you for ten years and he was just too stupid to see it. Why would you want to take it slow? I wouldn't take it slow."

"Being in a romantic relationship is not the same as being in a friendship. It could ruin a friendship."

"So what?" he exclaims. "Get a new friend! What else are you going to do? Pretend you don't know each other? Set him a series of tasks to prove himself?"

"No, I—"

"Because it sounds like you're so worried about losing him that you're not even going to try for something better with him and if I'd known talking to you this morning would have sent you into this spiral then I wouldn't have done it. I would have kept my mouth shut, flirted with you to piss him off, and stolen some money from his wallet on the way out."

I blink. "Flirted with me?"

"I've been threatening to flirt with you for years," he says with a smirk. "Because I knew it would rile him up. Because *you* rile him up. I'm telling you, Molly, you've been it for him for a very long time. And I think he's been the same for you."

Has he been? My hands grow clammy as my brain does what it's been doing ever since the mistletoe kiss and starts to filter through each and every moment when Andrew and I could have been more than friends.

"Okay," Christian continues when I stay silent. "That's a lie, I don't know if he's been the same for you. I barely know you. But Andrew's—"

"It is," I interrupt. "It is the same for me."

Christian starts to nod when he catches sigh of my face. "Are you..." He trails off, horrified. "Are you crying?"

"No," I lie, pressing my hands to my cheeks.

"Ah here, Andrew's going to kill me if you tell him I made you cry."

"It's not you," I explain. "This happens a lot."

"That doesn't make it better."

"I'm just realizing I was an idiot." I wipe a tear and then two away, blinking to make sure no more will follow. "I suppose asking you to turn the car around would be too much?"

"We'd need some serious sobbing for me to do that." But he glances at me as though afraid I'm about to do just that.

"I think I'm in love with your brother," I tell him. "And I think I need to fix it what happened this morning."

"Good for him and yes, you do, but I've got an airport pint with my name on it and I'm not turning this car around."

"I'm not above bribing you."

He laughs. "And I'm not above being bribed."

"I'm just saying, I've done it before. I'm very good at it."

"I'm dropping you home," he says. "And then I'm getting out of here. Just give yourselves both a break, see your nephew, see your family and then give him a call. He'll know you'll need the space."

"Or—"

"Not happening," he says, and I slump back in my seat.

He's right though, I know he is. "You're pretty good at relationship chats," I say. "For a boy, anyway."

"Yeah, well. It's always easier when it's about other people, isn't it?" He tilts his head then, peering out the windshield at the thick gray clouds with an almost wistful expression.

"What do you know?" he mumbles. "And only a day late."

I follow his gaze, though it takes me a moment to see what he's talking about. The droplets on the window I first think are rain and then are most definitely not.

"It's snowing," I say, unable to hide my surprise.

"It will probably melt immediately," Christian says, echoing Andrew.

But it doesn't. It sticks.

It sticks and it keeps falling and by the time we get to Dublin, it's really coming down.

We crawl to a halt as we reach the city center, mainly because the flurry of snow has sent everyone haywire. It feels like everyone in Dublin is outside, kids and adults playing or simply standing about with big, delighted grins on their faces as the city gets its white Christmas. I start to worry I'm going to make Christian late, but he just shrugs me off.

I direct him back to my street and he drops me off, waiting for me to dump his mother's leftovers in the hall before driving off with a wave. As he does, the door two houses down opens and my sister appears, holding a baby carrier in her hands. She smiles as soon as she sees me, walking down the street, before doing a double glance as Christian passes.

"Who's that tall glass of water?"

"Andrew's younger brother."

"You little—"

"Don't be gross," I complain, already knowing what she's going to say.

"How is that gross? I'm impressed."

"Shut up. Should you be on your feet right now?"

"Yes, *Mother*. If I can birth a human, I can walk the two doors down to the neighbor to show it off." She holds up the baby carrier and I peek inside.

My nephew is fast asleep, almost completely covered up by a variety of brightly colored blankets.

"How did Christmas in the countryside go?" she asks while I poke where I think his itty-bitty feet are.

"I'll tell you later," I insist, mustering up a smile for her. "Let's go inside. I want to spend what's left of Christmas with you guys."

"Since when?"

"Since now."

She pauses at the edge in my voice, looking distractedly at the scene behind me. "Did something happen?"

"No."

"Molly—"

"I'll fix it."

"What does that mean?"

"It means let's go inside. I need to call Andrew."

"I don't think you do." She nods at the street and I turn to see a vehicle approaching, its windscreen wipers moving overtime.

I don't recognize the car but, as it draws closer, I recognize the man in the front seat.

So much for giving me space.

Andrew drives carefully down the street, his gaze focused on me as he pulls up to the house. It's only when he does that I realize he's not alone. Hannah bounds out of the passenger side, practically bouncing on the sidewalk as soon as he stops the car.

"She insisted on coming," Andrews explains as he shuts the door. "And now she needs to pee."

"I can help with that," Zoe calls, gesturing Hannah toward the house. The girl shoots me an excited grin as she runs past.

"I like your hair," Zoe says to her.

"I like your baby."

"Thank you." Zoe shoots me a pointed glance as they step inside the house and I turn back to Andrew who now stands stiffly by the car, his hands in his pockets.

"You followed me up here?" I ask even though it's obvious.

"I let you get a head start before I couldn't take it anymore. Hannah kept insisting I wait until New Year's Eve because it would be more romantic, but I figured you'd have gone by then."

I nod, folding my arms over my chest. "I was going to—"

"I wanted—" He breaks off his own interruption, running a hand over his head. Around us the snow continues to fall, blanketing the street. We're far from alone. A lot of front doors are open with people sticking their hands mistrustfully out or simply standing there, gazing at it. Bundled-up kids dart up and down the road, shrieking with delight every time one of them slips and falls. Someone's already started on a snowman next door.

"I know you don't want to put too much pressure on this," Andrew says, dragging my attention back to him. "I know you're scared that I'll flake out on you. But I'm not going to lie and say I'm not staying in Chicago for you. Because I am. For *you*, Molly. I don't want to do long-distance. And I don't want to just be friends. I thought I could do it once if that was how you felt, but not now. Not anymore. I don't want to not see you for months until we meet for a hasty lunch. I don't want to wonder how you are. I definitely don't want to meet your boyfriends. I want you, I want *us*, and I think we could make it work."

"Andrew—"

"I love you." He takes a breath once he's said the words, as though he had to race through everything else just so he could get to them. "I'm *in* love with you and I'm sorry it took me so long to figure it out. I'm sorry I wasted so many years trying to find someone else, when the only one I wanted was you."

I hear a faint *awwww* from Hannah behind me before the quiet hustling of my sister to get her back inside. I ignore them both. I ignore everything but the man in front of me.

"I don't think I could handle it if I lost you," I admit finally. "I think that's why it was easier to keep you as a friend all these years. Why I didn't even let myself think of you as anything more. Because if I did and you left—"

"I'm not going anywhere."

"I know," I say quickly. "I know that now, it's just... You're right when you said I keep thinking about failure. I don't know when I started doing that. I don't know when I started denying myself what I want, but I do. And I don't want to be that person anymore." I gaze up at him, laying my whole heart out like I never have before. "I want you to stay in Chicago with me. I want us to be together and I want to kiss you all the time. I don't want to wait or go slow or start at the beginning. I want you too. I want *us* too."

His eyes search my face, like he's looking for any hint that I don't mean what I say, but whatever he sees must satisfy him, because he takes a cautious step toward me. "All the time, huh?"

My laugh comes out like a hiccup. "We've got a lot of years to catch up on."

"Better start making up for them then." And he does, dipping his head to press his lips against mine as softly as he did under the mistletoe.

"I'm in love with you," I say, because I need him to hear this. I need him to understand what I suddenly, overwhelmingly do. "In an extremely non-platonic, never-leave-me way."

"I won't," he murmurs. His gaze softens as he wipes a snowflake from my cheek. "For as long you'll have me."

Forever.

Because I know in my soul there will only be him. There's only ever been him.

"You're cold," he murmurs after a moment of us just gazing at each other like two love-struck kids.

"I'm fine."

He grimaces. "Okay, that was just me being macho, I'm the one who's cold."

I smirk and go to hold his hand, but that's not enough for him. He draws me firmly into his side, arm wrapped around my waist, and I think about all the times he's done this before and how neither of us thought twice about it. It was always natural for us to touch, to be as close as we could to one another. Just another hint maybe, that this was always supposed to be our fate.

We step inside and my nose tingles at the change in temperature. Andrew tugs my damp scarf and coat off, his eyes running over me when I shiver as though assessing for signs of damage.

I can hear Mam fussing over Hannah in the kitchen and catch a glimpse of my dad in the living room, rocking his sleeping grandchild with a look on his face I don't think I've ever seen on him before. Andrew hangs my coat up just as Zoe comes downstairs, dressed in a giant fluffy sweatshirt. She stops when she catches sight of us, eyes dropping to where we grip each other's hands like someone's trying to tear us apart.

Her lips twitch. "Oh, hey," she says casually. "Nice to see you again, Andrew."

"How are you doing?"

"Peachy," she says though she's looking straight at me. "It's really coming down out there," she says after a beat. "We'll go from staring at it in wonder to complaining about it in less than twenty-four hours, I guarantee it. Are you sticking around?"

"For a while yet," he says, his tone just as light even as his fingers tighten around mine.

Zoe only nods. "I'll put the kettle on then," is all she says, and turns without another word into the next room.

"Welcome home, Molly."

I look to my left to see Dad lingering in the doorway, still rocking his grandson.

"Hi, Dad."

"We didn't open the presents," he continues. "Well, except for your sister. She opened hers last week because your mother got her an air fryer and she wanted to try it."

"You waited for me?"

"Of course we did." Dad looks surprised. "It's not Christmas without you here, now is it?" His eyes drift to Andrew. "Bet your mother was glad to have you back."

"She was," Andrew says. "Thanks to this one."

"Your arm will go dead," I add, but Dad only smiles faintly, his attention fixed firmly back on the grandchild in his arms as he turns toward the couch.

"Sure, he's only a small thing," he says, settling into the

cushions. "Light as a feather. Come in here when you have a minute," he adds. "So I can say hello properly."

Andrew shares a smile with me before shrugging off his damp coat to hang it beside mine.

"Andrew?" Zoe calls from the kitchen. "Do you take milk in your tea?"

"Just a splash," he says like he's been here a thousand times before.

I hear Hannah ask for two sugars before politely accepting a second slice of cake from Mam.

"Okay?" he asks quietly, and I nod.

"Want to see me charm the hell out of your mother?"

"I'd like to see you try."

A familiar glint enters his eye. "Is that a challenge, Molly?"

"You talk big, is all."

"Always so competitive," he sighs, reaching in his coat pocket. "Luckily for me, I have a secret weapon."

I almost laugh. "Is that—"

"Homemade Christmas jam, direct from the heart of Ireland?" He holds it just out of my reach, tugging me forward. "You think I would show up to woo you unprepared? Mrs. Kinsella," he calls as we enter the warm kitchen. "I'm sorry to drop in unannounced. My mother insisted I bring something with me."

I take a seat at the table as Andrew does exactly as promised and immediately obliges my mother by writing down the family recipe.

Zoe sets a mug of tea in front of me with a look on her face that says I'm going to give her minute-by-minute details of everything that happened before she disappears to join Dad and the baby. Hannah takes another mouthful of cake as she slides her phone toward me, showing me the dress she's working on, and I try and pay attention, but it's hard when Mam is laughing and Andrew keeps glancing at me as though to make sure I'm still there. Hard when his hair is damp from the snow and his skin flushed from the heat of the house. Hard when, whenever he does catch my eye, he smiles that singular smile of his, as bright and as brilliant as I've ever seen it. And it's almost ridiculous how heart-burstingly glad I am that he's here. How grateful I am that we made it home. How wondrous it is to do something so simple as to sit in a warm kitchen at Christmas, surrounded by people I love as the snow swirls like a waltz outside.

EPILOGUE

TWELVE MONTHS LATER

Chicago, O'Hare Airport

"This is a mistake."

"The panettone?"

"*No*," I huff. Although... I glance at Andrew, suddenly nervous. "Why? Do you think we should have gone with the tiramisu? Because—"

"It was a joke," he interrupts calmly. "A cruel joke that I'll spend the rest of the day making up for."

"Andrew."

"That I'll pan-*atone* for it."

"Don't," I warn, but he's already smiling, delighted with his pun.

"Stop stressing," he says. "You've planned this down to the minute. Everything's going to go fine."

"Planned it down to the minute and we're already running behind."

"Since when do you not factor in delays?" He nudges me and I tear my gaze back to him. "Stop glaring at the board."

"I'm not glaring at the board. I'm *looking* at the board. And—"

He pulls my beanie hat low over my eyes to shut me up and by the time I push it back he's already leaning down, kissing me through the stray strands of my hair now stuck to my face.

I let him because I'm nice like that.

And because I really, *really* like when he does it.

The bustle of the busy airport disappears around me as I relax into him, tugging on the end of his scarf to keep him right where I want him.

He's still smiling when he pulls back, looking down at me with an almost smug expression. "I don't think I'll get tired of that."

"Kissing your girlfriend?" I quip. "I hope not."

"More like getting to do it whenever I want."

I huff, while secretly agreeing with him. It was surprisingly easy coming together over the last year, blurring into each other's lives almost seamlessly. It makes me wonder if that was why neither of us had made the effort before. Because once we let ourselves have each other wholly, there was no going back.

My phone buzzes in my pocket and I mutter a "Finally" as I take it out. No one's been replying to my messages, which is *really* not helping my stress levels right now. But it's an email rather than a text that's come through.

"Is it Zoe?" Andrew asks.

"No," I say, still reading through it. I've gotten a lot better at not squealing when these things come through. "A new booking. My New Year's Eve tour is sold out."

"Look at that!" Andrew leans into me, dropping his head to mine as we read through it. "Congratulations."

"You still want to come on this one?" Andrew's joined

my tours dozens of times. At the start, I asked him to come to help boost numbers, but when he kept showing up even when we got busier, he eventually confessed that seeing me excited and doing what I loved got him all... well, you know.

"Of course," he says. "If you're not going to kick me out now."

"Never," I say, and I grin as he presses a kiss to my temple.

A month after our nearly disastrous trip home last year, Andrew moved in with me. I was the one to ask him, using the excuse that I would need help with the rent, which was true, but more that it was just the right time. We were seeing each other nearly every day anyway and it made sense, seeing as how he'd already told his roommates he'd be moving out and the fact that he'd been sleeping over most nights anyway.

A month after that, I handed in my notice. I was terrified, *more* than terrified. I was convinced I was making the worst mistake of my life and told Andrew as much more or less every minute of every day for about a week. But we'd taken it seriously. I had savings and a plan. I had help from Andrew and Gabriela who more than came through on her promise to support me.

I went on a short course run by a local tour guide and got a job at the bottom of a big company. I spent my days in the cold rain, doing the early slots and the evening slots and the slots no one wanted, holding my bright yellow umbrella aloft as I took people around my adopted city. In my spare time, I spent a good chunk of my savings putting together my food places. Along with the help of Andrew and my friends, I designed chocolate tours and seafood tours, halal, kosher, vegan. Tours to suit every taste bud under the sun.

And in early May, as tourist season started to peak, I took the plunge.

And Molly's Food Tours began.

The salary cut was... tough. Sometimes people didn't show and I was left waiting for hours and out of pocket for the week. Some days, it went perfectly. People tipped. Restaurants started contacting me, people started recommending me.

I was still learning, still growing. If next summer ended well, I'd maybe be earning enough to hire someone else. But I was trying not to think too far ahead, which I'd learned only made me stressed. I would get through the next six months and then maybe a year and then maybe two.

But first, I had to get through Christmas.

"I still think this is a mistake," I say, nerves fluttering again as I think about the next few days, even though the whole thing was my idea in the first place. "We're not going to last twenty-four hours before we all start killing each other."

"I wouldn't celebrate the holiday any other way." But he must see my panic isn't going anywhere because he sighs, reaching into his backpack. "Alright. I was going to wait for an audience to give you this," he says, handing me a brown paper-wrapped rectangle. "But I think you need to be reminded of it now."

"Reminded of what? What's that?"

"It's your present, what does it look like?"

"Can I open it now?"

"No," he deadpans. "I gave it to you to hold awkwardly until—"

I ignore him, quickly undoing the string. We promised each other we'd only do small presents this year and my one was waiting at the bottom of the closet at home (a mini bottle of my favorite Tabasco sauce because he kept stealing mine).

"I hope it's a letter explaining why you keep using my expensive shampoo when you have your own shampoo."

"It makes my hair shiny." He shrugs. "And it smells like you."

"That's creepy."

"Please. You love it."

I do my best to scowl as I slide the paper off, but I can't keep it up. Especially when I see what's inside.

It's a photo frame, which isn't exactly surprising. But what is surprising is the photo within it. Not one of Andrew's, but rather...

"It's my first review," I say, recognizing it instantly. It's hard not to. I already know the entire thing off by heart, I've read it so many times. A polite and cheerful five stars from a Brazilian student visiting the city. I'd been doing my solo tours for a week and had spent every evening checking for updates with my heart in my mouth.

I still remember the moment I got it. It was the middle of the night and I'd woken up like I did a lot during that time, the nerves eating away at me. When I saw the alert on my phone, I almost threw up. When I started reading it, I woke Andrew so he could confirm it was real. There were some happy tears and then pancakes and then forwarding the review to every single person I knew. It had been a good morning.

"I love it, thank you." I rise up to peck his cheek.

"I am, as always, extremely proud of you, Moll. Even if you did pick a panettone over the tiramisu."

"Stop it."

"Probably should have told you that Mam *hates* panettone."

"She does not! She—"

"Molly!"

We both turn as my name rings across the arrivals hall. The latest batch of passengers has started trickling through the doors and among them is Hannah. Her hair is dyed bright pink this year and is tied up in a high ponytail that bounces as she runs toward us.

My great, stupid Christmas plan is about to begin.

I half expected Andrew to laugh in my face when I suggested we invite both our families to join us in Chicago, but he got immediately excited about the idea. As nice as our little tradition was, neither of us wanted to spend the holiday apart and I think we were still experiencing PTSD from last year. To my even greater surprise, both the Fitzpatricks *and* the Kinsellas immediately said yes, though Andrew's brother Liam is going to stay at home with the kids and spend the holiday with his wife's family.

I really didn't know how everyone was going to fit. Both sets of parents had booked into a hotel, but Christian and Hannah *plus* Zoe and the baby are all staying in our apartment, where we'll be hosting Christmas dinner as well. My initial determination had turned into full-blown panic these last few days as Andrew and I got everything ready, but that starts to fade as Hannah throws her arms around me, the biggest grin on her face.

"It's so great to see you," she squeals, and I smile as I return her embrace.

"Also your brother," Andrew says beside us. "Who is also here."

"I like Molly more," Hannah says, squeezing me tight, but she lets me go to do the same to him as I turn back to the door just in time to see the rest of her family walk through. Hers and mine. Both my dad and Sean are in deep conversation, while Christian is wedged between our mothers, a look of waning patience on his face as they gossip around him.

Zoe appears a moment later, pushing an empty stroller with one hand and holding my nephew in the other.

Baby Tiernan looks about the airport with a kind of apathetic neutrality that morphs into grumpy confusion as my sister bends her head, pointing at me as she whispers in his ear.

"Auntie Molly!" I hear her say as she approaches us. "Remember your Auntie Molly? Auntie— Yeah, he doesn't care."

I smirk, kissing him on the head. "I'll win him over."

"I don't know. He only likes talking animals at the moment. Also spoons? Weirdly into holding spoons all day. I'm hoping it means he's a genius." She hands him over to Hannah, who doesn't bat an eyelid when he immediately starts playing with her hair, and Zoe turns back to give me a hug.

"You're regretting this idea already, aren't you?"

"Totally and completely."

"I've got you," she whispers into my ear, before pulling back to shove something into my hands. "Happy Christmas. Don't open it until you're alone," she adds as I gaze down at my present. "The smell is... not good."

"Is it cheese?"

"No," she says, smiling wickedly, and I wince as I slide it into my purse just before I look properly at my parents.

"Zoe?"

"Hmmm?"

"What the hell is Mam wearing?"

"I thought I'd make an effort this year," Mam announces as she reaches us. She looks a little flustered, probably due to the oversized, bright red sweater she's wearing. *Granny Clause* is written in block letters across the front. "Your father and I wanted to mark the occasion."

"Then why isn't Dad wearing one?"

"Because he respects himself," Zoe mutters, ignoring the look our mother gives her.

"The girl at the shop said the whole point of a Christmas jumper is that it's ugly," Mam says worriedly, and I smile reassuringly.

"It's not ugly."

"It's a little ugly," Zoe says.

"I think you look brilliant," Andrew says to Mam as he joins us. "And it's the exact shade of the one I got for Molly and me, so you'll fit right in."

My head whips toward him. "Excuse me?"

"Two-part present," he says pleasantly. "Since you loved that so much last year."

"You're joking."

"Am I?"

"We should get this show on the road," Zoe says, extracting Hannah's hair from Tiernan's grasp as she lifts him back into her arms. "And then I need some sugar. If you're making us do Christmas that means I get sugar."

"We're not wearing matching sweaters," I tell Andrew.

"We'll see."

"Molly!" Zoe calls. "Show. Road. Please."

I send one last warning look at the man I love before facing our party, who are all watching me expectantly.

Oh God.

I suddenly struggle to remember why I ever thought I could pull this off. Two vastly different families who expect two vastly different Christmases? And a *baby*? I mean, this is clearly a mistake. This is a large, expensive mistake that—

Andrew grabs my hand, squeezing tight. "Breathe," he says, his voice pitched so only I can hear him.

We've been working on the whole pessimism thing. Progress is slow.

"All people and bags accounted for," Colleen says kindly when I don't speak. "This was a marvelous idea, Molly."

"Though I suggest Tenerife next year," Christian says, eyeing the freezing Chicago weather outside.

"You ready?" Andrew asks, and I nod, summoning a smile as I take everyone in.

"Hats and scarves on," I announce, gesturing them toward the exit. "Keep together and no straying from the group. If you need the toilet, now is the time to use one and most important of all..." I glance up at Andrew. "Keep an eye out for mistletoe," I finish, ignoring his grin. I have to ignore it, or I'll just kiss him and then we'll never get out of here.

He snakes an arm around my waist as we trail our families out of the airport. "Mam's right," he says. "This was an excellent idea."

It was. It is.

And I just need to look at the man walking by my side to remember that even if it doesn't go exactly to plan, fate has a way of working things out in the end.

A LETTER FROM CATHERINE

Dear Reader,

Thank you so much for reading *Holiday Romance*! If you want to keep up to date with my latest releases, you can sign up for my newsletter at the following link. Your email address will never be shared and you can unsubscribe at any time. I also heard that very good things will happen to you? Worth a shot, isn't it?

www.bookouture.com/catherine-walsh

I love Christmas. I *love* it. When I was a child, it was because there was a magic around it that didn't exist at any other point of the year. Christmas meant food and presents and being shuttled around to various branches of my family so I could get said food and presents. As I got older it meant days off work. It meant meeting friends in fairy-light-strewn pubs and wearing really nice boots.

Of course, most importantly, it meant spending time with people I love.

Like a lot of people, I moved away to work for a few years and, while I was gone, flying home for Christmas became very important to me. Some years, I could barely afford these flights but, like Andrew, it meant a lot to me to do it. Even though my family would be the first to insist we don't really "do" Christmas, the thought of not spending it with them was unthinkable. The days leading up to the journey would be filled with anticipation and, though I also faced my fair share of delays, I used to love getting to the airport and seeing everyone else excited to see their friends and family. The idea for *Holiday Romance* stems from this time in my life and the conversations I'd have with strangers as we flew home on those cold December nights.

I hope you loved *Holiday Romance* and if you did, I would be very grateful if you could write a review. I'd love to hear what you think, and it makes such a difference helping new readers to discover one of my books for the first time.

I also love hearing from my readers – you can get in touch via my website, or on Twitter or Instagram.

All my best,

Catherine xx

https://catherinewalshbooks.com

 twitter.com/CatWalshWriter

 instagram.com/catwalshwriter

 tiktok.com/@catwalshwriter

ACKNOWLEDGMENTS

Lots of people supported me in big and small ways while I was writing this book. I will definitely have forgotten some of them and I'm SORRY, but the ones I didn't forget are below.

My biggest thank you goes to all the book bloggers who championed *One Night Only* and *The Rebound*. Your support and love got these stories in front of so many new readers and I am eternally grateful for your reviews, posts, emails, and general awesomeness. You've kept me going through every late-night writing session and or-I-could-just-give-up moments. My greatest hope is that I get to meet you all in person one day to thank you. Preferably, this will happen on some sort of yacht with an elaborate tiered cake.

This book is dedicated to Áine O'Connell, who has been a lifeline for me since we first met and who, despite having no time of her own, always makes time for me. Dr. Siobhan Morissey helped me with all my airplane questions including but not limited to "What happens if there's a big storm?" and "How do planes work?" Poulomi Choudhury is always encouraging AND recommended a printer that actually works and thus will forever have my love. Donna MacKay bought me cake and then traveled an hour out of her way to post my purse back to me when I maybe accidentally sort of lost it in Edinburgh. Tilda McDonald is always on hand to offer career advice and has so far not asked for a commission. Bex Dash let me use her dog's name and gave my books both a New York AND a Naples photoshoot. Jeanne-Claire Morley organized Molly's Paris itinerary via WhatsApp. Cornelia Conneff helped a clueless city girl with all my farm-related questions. Lucy Baxter responds to every message with unfailing support and Rachel Helsdown continues to be my first and most enthusiastic reader for every project.

Massive love to my editors, Celine Kelly and Isobel Akenhead, for helping to whip this book into shape. Isobel, thank you so much for your passion and belief in these stories. I'm so glad I found my way to you! Thank you as well to the entire team at Bookouture and everyone who worked so hard on getting this book out into the world.

As always, second biggest thank you to me, who once again wrote a whole book and didn't even have an emotional breakdown about it.

Yet.

Made in the USA
Monee, IL
29 October 2023

45377521R00204

PRIMAL VISION

Sheraton 213
West 382-7171
L.A.

174 6882 032 R

9:30 pm
worcester

Kann keine Trauer sein –

In jenem kleinen Bett, fast Kinderbett, starb die Droste.
(zu sehn in ihrem Museum in Meersburg),
auf diesem Sofa Hölderlin im Turm bei einem Schreiner,
Rilke, George wohl in Schweizer Hospitalbetten,
in Weimar lagen die grossen schwarzen Augen
Nietzsches auf einem weissen Kissen
bis zum letzten Blick –
alles Gerümpel jetzt oder gar nicht mehr vorhanden,
unbestimmbar, wesenlos
im schmerzlos-ewigen Zerfall.

Wir tragen in uns Keime aller Götter,
das Gen des Todes und das Gen der Lust –
wer trennte sie: die Worte und die Dinge,
wer mischte sie: die Qualen und die Statt,
auf der sie enden, Holz mit Tränenbächen,
für kurze Stunden ein erbärmlich Heim.

Kann keine Trauer sein. Zu fern, zu weit,
zu unberührbar Bett u Tränen,
kein Nein, kein Ja,
Geburt und Körperschmerz und Glauben
ein Wallen, namenlos, ein Huschen,
ein Überirdisches, im Schlaf sich regend,
bewegte Bett u Tränen –
Schlafe ein!

Gottfried Benn
6. I. 56.

MANUSCRIPT OF GOTTFRIED BENN'S POEM "KANN KEINE TRAUER SEIN –"

PRIMAL VISION

Selected Writings of Gottfried Benn

EDITED BY E. B. ASHTON

A NEW DIRECTIONS BOOK

Library of Congress Catalog Card Number: 58-13434

ACKNOWLEDGMENTS

Certain of the poems and prose pieces in this volume have been published and copyrighted previously as follows: "Artists and Old Age" and "The Death of Orpheus" in *Partisan Review;* "Monologue" in *Western Review;* "Who Are You," "Through Every Moment" and "A Weightless Element" in *Prairie Schooner;* "Night Café" in *Accent.* Ullstein Publishers, Frankfurt-Berlin, for the use of quotes from *Briefe der Expressionisten,* ed. K. Edschmid.

First published as ND Paperbook 322 in 1971
Published simultaneously in Canada by McClelland & Stewart, Ltd.
Manufactured in the United States of America

New Directions Books are published for James Laughlin
by New Directions Publishing Corporation,
333 Sixth Avenue, New York 10014

CONTENTS

INTRODUCTION

"German poetry's last internationally presentable figure"—this was one title bestowed on Gottfried Benn after his death in 1956, by a leading German news magazine. Earlier, in his lifetime, press and public had played guessing games with his Nobel Prize chances, popular dailies had placed him "at the top of our literature." He was "the man who exerted the greatest influence after the war" and "one of the grand old men of literary Europe."

These paeans were sung to an unreconstructed Expressionist, an esoteric thinker who wrote only to express ideas to his own satisfaction, an eccentric stylist whose mature prose was as popularly unintelligible as his youthful verses had been commonly unpalatable —in short, an author one would expect to be esteemed by the older sophisticates, shrugged off as a has-been by the *avant-garde*, and ignored by the public. Yet the public ate up Benn's books, and German youth hung on the lips of this bald, heavy-lidded purist and self-styled relic of a bygone age.

In part, no doubt, his magic lay in the promise of controversy. Dropping Benn's name among German intellectuals was enough, in the post-war years, to kindle a whole spectrum of reactions from angry red to mystic purple. He has been years in his grave, but eminent survivors of the German *hegira* of 1933 will still lump him with "a bunch of Nazi writers"—though Benn, unlike the rest of the bunch, had some violent Nazi attacks on himself to quote in reply, besides non-Nazi praise of his "confessions" of a later date: "They do not gloss over the refusal to emigrate," said a Professor Max Bense; "they defend it, and they complete this defense by defending his error. His submission is not to political change, but to error. . . ."

The poet Michael Hamburger, who translated Benn, compared

him with "a man talking to himself in a room full of silly people. . . . Monologue is the only kind of communication which Dr. Benn thinks valid."

German critics found that positive. One, Wilhelm Grenzmann, wrote in 1951: "An all but forgotten author saw himself torn out of his stubborn soliloquies and involved in public discussion, with partners multiplying day by day. One sensed an uncommon language, heard incredibly bold, radical statements, and realized that this recluse who obviously had no taste for dialogue was speaking from the innermost core of our time. . . ."

A glance at the bibliography of publications about Gottfried Benn shows a strangely divergent history of the approach to him in Germany and elsewhere. In other countries he was unknown before Hitler (except to rare devotees such as Eugene Jolas, who tried for years to fit Benn into the *transition* movement of artistic revolt against the tyranny of form). The Nazi era brought him some ideological attention, largely because anti-Nazi polemics made him look like a pillar of he Third Reich. But only recently has he won serious recognition as a protagonist of modern literary trends.

In Germany, on the other hand, he was a noted modernist in the twenties, disappeared from view and almost passed into oblivion under Hitler, and then grew to amazing—and amazingly non-literary—stature in the last five years of his life. Few of the hundreds of German essays devoted to him since he resumed publishing in 1948 explore his lifelong expressionism. Most of them stress the daring things he said, not the daring way in which he said them. Once upon a time he was an innovator—that's that; it does not seem to impress his present following. What does?

Probably the best, certainly the most thorough, non-German analysis of Benn's position in letters is found in Michael Hamburger's *Reason and Energy: Studies in German Literature.* The English poet ascribes Benn's post-war renaissance to "the interest aroused by the sole survivor from a great shipwreck." There is something to that, but it is no full explanation; others have survived the shipwreck without arousing such interest. Mr. Hamburger, after pointing out the "moral obtuseness" that let Benn "enumerate the misfortunes of his own family" in a work "in which he elaborates his anti-humanism," found it "peculiarly irritating to be asked for sympathy on one page, only to have it violently rejected on the next." But here, too, Benn would seem to deserve acquittal. For just what did he say in his preface to *World of Expression*, a book he called "a kind of reference work and primer on trains of thought in my generation"?

> As an example of this generation I mention my family: three of my brothers died in battle; a fourth was wounded twice; the remainder, totally bombed out, lost everything. A first cousin died at the Somme, his only son in the recent war; of that branch of the family nothing is left. I myself went to war as a doctor, 1914-18 and 1939-44. My wife died in 1945 in direct consequence of military operations. *This brief summary should be about average for a fairly large German family's lot in the first half of the twentieth century.*
> [Italics mine. E.B.A.]

The last sentence counts; and it is no plea for sympathy. What Gottfried Benn wanted and got from his German audience, in this and in scores of other passages, was not sympathy but *identification*.

There, it would seem, lies the key to the near-miracle of the old highbrow with the sudden mass appeal. The "world of expression" that Benn loved to discuss—a world understood, at best, by one out of ten of his readers—was hardly what spellbound them, nor is it apt to have been his complicated rationalization of their record, his philosophical defense of their "existential position." He had something more basic to offer: a sense of sameness. For here, however cryptic he might be in his writings, was a man who throughout his life, from Kaiser Wilhelm's time to Dr. Adenauer's, had shared the experiences, the actions, the reactions of the German people.

Gottfried Benn, M. D. and poet, was born in 1886 in a country parsonage a few hours west of Berlin, the son and grandson of pastors, descended from freeholders traceable in those parts as far back as records go. The region is historic, dotted with battlefields ever since a German king beat the Wends in A.D. 929—a victory of considerable import at one stage of Dr. Benn's life, as evidence that his surname is Wend in origin, not Jewish as a fellow author had maliciously hinted. Benn's mother, born in French Switzerland, infused this Wend-Teutonic "hereditary milieu" with "100 per cent unadulterated, wholly unmixed Latin blood." Her son had papers to show that all her forebears had been Swiss Calvinists. "So, what happened was mixture, not miscegenation, producing crossbreeds, not mongrels, and in any case it was an Aryan mixture. . . ."

Thus wrote Gottfried Benn in *The Way of an Intellectualist*, an autobiographical essay published a year after the Nazis came to power. We know his background so well because he was so hard put to measure up to their standards. To the same effort we owe the data on his "further racial and environmental relations" in another country parsonage in the heartland of Prussianism, a few hours east of Berlin, where he grew up with the village boys, went barefoot till November, and observed old pagan customs. Later he mixed with the scions of local nobility, sons of families traditionally officering the cavalry regiments founded by Frederick the Great. To please his father, he studied divinity for two years before transferring to the Academy for Military-Medical Instruction, where officers' and officials' sons were inexpensively and excellently trained as army surgeons. For each term of study they had to remain a year in active service. Young Dr. Benn was first attached to an infantry regiment famed from the Franco-Prussian War, then to an engineers' unit that had distinguished itself in the Danish War of 1864. Off duty he wrote poems.

There is a curious, frequently noticed interrelation of certain sciences and arts. Mathematicians will go in for music, physicians for literature, notably lyric poetry—William Carlos Williams is an obvious American example. For most of them it seems to be an escape from pain and death and impotence and cynicism; writing may let a doctor forget the grim side of his trade. Benn wrote to express it. He put it, all of it, into what may well be the most bluntly horrifying poems ever written. Perhaps he forgot it in uniform. At least he later recalled that *Morgue*, his first book of verse, came out as he "marched through potato fields at regimental drill and trotted over pine hills with the staff of the divisional commander. . . ."

In 1912 the chance discovery of a congenital defect obliged him to quit the army. He found medical jobs at pathological laboratories, on cruise ships, in a tuberculosis sanitarium—writing after hours. He came to know the Mediterranean, the perennial object of Teutonic longings, and to be known in the "Café Megalomania," as the literary rebels in Berlin termed their nocturnal base of operations. Their high priestess, Else Lasker-Schüler, called him "Giselher" or "the Nibelung" and acclaimed his style: "Every line a leopard's bite!" He wrote for her magazine, *Sturm*, for the radical *Aktion*, for *Das neue Pathos* and *Die weissen Blätter*, for all the organs of intellectual revolt that sprang up in those last days of the boring old order in Europe. Then, in August 1914, Dr. Benn got back into uniform and went to Belgium with the German occupation forces, to take medical charge of an army jail and of the prostitutes of Brussels.

What happened to him there took some explaining later. It was an outburst of expressionist productivity, an eruption of a prose that now seems like a bridge from Nietzsche to the Existentialists but then led nowhere—nowhere, that is, but to nihilism. Disintegration of human reality was what emerged in Benn's Rönne, the "man no longer endowed with a continuous psychology," and "yet more starkly, cruelly, bottomlessly" in Pameelen, the hero of two "epistemological dramas," *Karandasch* and *Der Vermessungsdirigent*, which Benn wrote at the same time. "Here," he would interpret himself in 1934, "we actually see the epoch decompose. Crumbling in this brain is what was regarded as 'I' for 400 years— what truly, legitimately carried the human universe through the generations of that period, in inheritable forms. Now, this heritage is finished. . . ."

In Brussels, too, he wrote his most realistic, most emotional, and only moral work, *Home Front* (translated here)—a short play dealing not with reality's disintegration but with its decay. Here the triumphantly corrupt reality was the military government Benn served, a slew of inane generals, degenerate bluebloods, grasping bureaucrats, profiteering scientists, patrioteering journalists. The philippic clearly had to be kept under cover for the duration. Yet in whose name did it indict the occupying power? Who had its sympathies? The vanquished? The oppressed? Oh, no: "The nation lives by the wounds of its youth, breathes through the bullet-torn lungs of its boys—why," cried the hero, "should it transplant the rottenest of moral systems into this empire that we have conquered?"

The very words anticipated Nazi verbiage. Yet the fact that it would have been treason in 1915 sufficed to get the play published in a radical leftist collection in 1919, and the author embraced by the revolutionaries who spearheaded German expressionism after the Kaiser's Reich fell. The collapse, the "revaluation of all values," was a common point of departure for Werfel, Kaiser, Toller, and the rest of this politico-artistic vanguard. Each of them fought his private bout with despair, his own battle with nihilism. To Benn nihilism was "a sense of happiness." It absorbed him all his life—in avowal, in denial, in art, in the "world of expression," the only world acknowledged by the poet who attributed even artistic creation only to "the form-seeking power of nothingness."

Consciously or unconsciously, he spent the 1920's in a retreat from substance. It was the substance of his work that had caused his misbranding, and he withdrew to form: from the bald, un-rhymed, ametrical language of his juvenile shockers to a glittering tide of poems in trochaic rhythms and short, flawlessly rhymed lines whose brilliance masked their punctilio—poems of which unfortunately only a few can be rendered in English, translation of all rhymed verse being a matter of luck. He fell back on tradition, on a deceptively deft employment of technological and scientific neologisms to conceal strict, classicist orthodoxy. In prose and in his philosophy he retreated all the way from asocial insurgence to a kind of atavistic tribalism—this, too, buried under avalanches of genetic and anthropological terms by Dr. Benn, who now made his living as a Berlin specialist for skin and venereal diseases.

He knew little private happiness that might have carried over into his writing. The wife he had married in 1914 died after an operation in 1922. The child she had borne him while he was in the army—a daughter; he had mentioned her in *Birthday* (translated here)—went to foster parents. A young girl worshipped him, but after an exchange of love letters he coolly dismissed her. An actress lived with him, off and on, and finally threw herself out of a fifth-story window. Three months later he wrote to friends who were shocked by his engagement to another woman: "Grief is something that only the fortunate can afford. . . . Only he who sees every hour with the fangs, the talons, the rusty nails it tears our heart with, he has absorbed life and stands near it and may live." But he did not marry the other.

He inveighed against sentiment. "Never forget," he wrote to Paul Hindemith's wife, "that the human mind originated as a killer, a vast tool of vengeance, not as the phlegma of democrats. It was designed to fight the crocodiles of primal seas and the scaly giant sloths of the caves—not at a powder puff!"

Paradoxically he was published, read, admired, promoted in the 1920's by a highbrow, humanistic, partly Jewish, dominantly liberal minority of Germans, while he, with the lowbrow majority, was inching toward the cult of disciplined violence, toward the primitives who were the sworn enemies of his audience. He was discovered and hailed by non-conformists abroad—as in the pages of *transition*—at the very time of his transition to the sternest of conformisms. He had given fair warning. "Is the individual case necessary?" he defined Dr. Rönne's dilemma; it was not Dr. Benn's fault if his reply was misconstrued. In *Primal Vision* (translated here) he glorified "the tribe, the growth in darkness," sang of "mass in instincts," exclaimed, "Lost is the individual; down with the ego" —was he to be blamed for not being understood? When *transition* asked for views on "the crisis of man," he submitted *The New Literary Season* (also translated here), a 1931 lecture defending creative individualism against the literary commissars of Russia. It was not his fault if people drew the conclusion that Gottfried Benn would not embrace a different collectivism within two years.

Soon after the Nazis took over, Benn received a letter from a self-exiled young colleague, the older son of Thomas Mann. "Klaus Mann," he wrote later in the non-Nazi part of his autobiographical *Double Life*, "was close to me in a way and visited me on occasion; he was a person of high intelligence, traveled, well-bred, well-mannered, with the fine, now extinct quality of always showing some respect in talks with your elders." The letter, dated from a fishing village on the French Riviera, is worth quoting.

Dear Dr. Benn:

May an ardent and faithful admirer of your writings approach you with a question justified solely by this concern with your intellectual existence? . . . Several times in the past weeks I have heard rumors about your attitude on "the German events" that would have shocked me if I could have made myself believe them. I absolutely refused to credit these rumors, although I now learn for a fact that you—as indeed the *only* German author our kind had counted on—have *not* resigned from the Academy . . . . What company do you keep there? What could induce you to put your name—to us a byword for high standards and an all but fanatic purity—at the disposal of men whose lack of standards is unmatched in European history and from whose moral squalor the world recoils? . . . What friends can you gain, on so wrong a side? Who understands you there? . . . Your young admirers, I know, sit today in the cheap hotels of Paris, Zurich, and Prague—and you, their idol, keep playing the Academician of *that* state! And if you are not concerned with your admirers, let us look for the objects of your own touching enthusiasm. Heinrich Mann, whom you worshipped as no one else, has been shamefully kicked out of the same organization you're staying in. My father, whom you liked to quote, is no more than a target for billingsgate in the land whose world-wide stature he did, after all, raise a little—if not as much as its new masters can lower it now. The great minds of other countries, who used to matter to you, too, vie with each other in protests—think only of André Gide, certainly never one of the vapid "Marxists" you found so dreadfully repulsive.

And here we have come to the crucial point, I suppose. How well I always understood your resentment of the German "Marxist" literati—how often I shared it! ... No one suffered more than I from this type. And yet, for years now, it has worried me to see dislike of these bloated blockheads drive you, Gottfried Benn, into an increasingly grim *irrationalism*. Your attitude stayed purely intellectual, and I admit it was tempting to me, too—but this did not prevent me from sensing its dangers. ... Today it seems almost a law of nature that strong irrational sympathies lead to political reaction if you don't watch out like the devil. First comes the grand gesture against "civilization"—a gesture I know as only too attractive to intellectuals; then, suddenly, you've reached the cult of force, and the next step is Adolf Hitler. ... I know my place now, more clearly, more exactly than ever. No Marxist vulgarities can irritate me any more. I know a man need be no obtuse "materialist" to want what is reasonable, and to loathe hysterical brutality with all his heart.

I have spoken unasked, that was improper; I must beg your pardon once again. But I want you to know that for me—and some others—you are one of the few we would hate to lose to "the other side." And whoever equivocates now will cease to belong to us, now and forever. You, of course, must know what you get in exchange for our love and what great substitute you're offered over there; unless I'm a bad prophet, it will eventually be ingratitude and derision. For if a few ranking spirits still don't know where they belong—over there they know exactly who does *not* belong to them: the spirit.

I should be grateful to you for any answer.

Yours,
Klaus Mann

Benn gave his *Answer to the Literary Emigrants* (translated here) in an open letter which Goebbels featured in the press and on the air. It contained passages of which the author was to say in 1950, "Today I would not write them any more; they are romantic and have an unpleasant ardor. ..." They are, perhaps, the most lucid examples in print of the effect exerted on impressionable German intellectuals by the Nazi triumph and the personality of Adolf

Hitler, down to his "abnormal levity of all functions, notably including the organic ones"—for Gottfried Benn was still a medical man. Above all, however, the *Answer* was unequivocal: "I shall go on revering what I found exemplary and educational for German letters ... but I personally declare for the new state ... and I must accept it for this state if you, from your shore, bid me farewell."

Benn was now "Acting Leader [*kommissarischer Leiter*] of the Poetry Section, Prussian Academy of Arts," and a director of the new Union of National Writers. His essay topics were "the poet's rapprochement with his people," or "the German" (*Der deutsche Mensch*), or National Socialism as "decidedly a matter for the productive." His new prose, published in book form in 1933, was entitled *The New State and the Intellectuals*.

Was he a Nazi? He never joined the party—never considered joining, as far as is known—and never called himself what most Germans in 1933 called themselves every ten minutes. Why, then, his ardent declaration for the "new state"? His friends laid it to resentment of more influential and successful writers, leftists or Jews. Yet Benn always preached against art supporting the artist. He always scorned material success, and as for the other kind—he had sat in the Prussian Academy before 1933 and whatever he had written had been published (usually by leftists or Jews) and widely argued. The grudge theory may be correct, but it seems likelier to be doing Benn an injustice.

There is a touch of Luther's „*Ich kann nicht anders*"—"I cannot do otherwise"—in what the Lutheran pastor's son replied to Klaus Mann's letter: "... it is my people whose trail is being blazed here. Who am I to exclude myself? ... People means much! ... [Europe] whispers in your ear that the people are not behind Hitler.... A great mistake! ... Standing behind this movement ... ready to perish, if need be, is the whole people...."

Gottfried Benn could not exclude himself.

One of his poems of that spring became a hit, but not even the title, "*Dennoch die Schwerter halten*," is adequately translatable. "And yet to hold the swords"—*and yet, nevertheless, despite all—*

no English word or phrase conveys the Wagnerian overtones of defying the world and challenging destiny which this *dennoch* caused to ring in a majority of German ears in 1933. And in the body of the poem readers found more: what "slept behind the millennia" (*i.e.*, "a few great men") and Nietzsche and "a few dying warriors" and *Götterdämmerung* motifs, and "*dennoch*".... It was reprinted over and over, finally in an anthology entitled *The Prussian Dimension: Intellectual Passages-at-Arms.*

By then the poet was engaged in some passages-at-arms of his own. A colleague, a literary Baron Münchhausen, drew first blood by doubting Benn's Aryan descent; crusaders against "degenerate art" objected to the expressionist in the Academy. Benn dug up his family tree for five generations and wrote *The Way of an Intellectualist* (translated here in part; republished, 1950, as Part I of *Double Life*) to prove that Rönne and Pameelen were compatible with Nazi ideology—in vain. As Klaus Mann had warned him, the new culture guardians did not even understand his language. For publication in 1934 he still eulogized "the Führer whom all of us worship without exception," but to a lady correspondent he wrote: "Horrible tragedy! The whole reminds me more and more of an amateur theater that keeps announcing 'Faust' though the cast suffices only for 'Hussar Fever.' "

The lady was a poetess and understood him. Her minister husband quit the pulpit; she penned an ode for Hitler's 50th birthday. Benn was stripped of the right to issue certain medical certificates, and his application for a city job in his specialty was returned with an unsigned memo: "No openings." He wrote to the poetess: "On 1-1-35 I'll leave home, practice, existence, Berlin—to return to the army I came from. Assignment unknown, future in doubt. It is an aristocratic form of emigration."

In provincial Hannover he handled disability claims and such; the poems he sent to the newspapers now and then were pastoral, entitled "Asters" or "Anemone." Suddenly, in 1936, the Nazis found out that his early work was immoral. "Pig, stench, unnatural filth"—these were among the milder epithets hurled by the party press, but Benn's army superiors stood by him. In his private drawer lay a new prose manuscript, *Wolf's Tavern* (translated here, unpublished till 1949), reflecting a mood like post-honeymoon disenchantment, reluctant to fault a partner taken for better or worse.

After two years, tiring of the small-town atmosphere, Benn got a transfer back to Berlin. The literary hue and cry now led to a complete ban on his writings, and to his own expulsion from the Reich's Literature Chamber. "Had I been obliged to write for a living," he commented, "had I had a wife and children to support, there would have been nothing left but gas or two grains of morphine."

He had a child, but she was supported by her Danish foster parents. He also had a new wife, a titled, impecunious young lady from Hannover, but she could live with him on his army pay. He loved her as tenderly as he could love; he felt far from gas or morphine, although his duties included the analysis of Wehrmacht suicides. For five years—one of peace, three of victory in Poland, Norway, the Low Countries, France, the Balkans, Africa, Russia, and a fifth in which the tables were turned and bombs began to fall on Berlin—*Oberstabsarzt* Benn sat in the High Command building on Bendlerstrasse, poring over suicide statistics and poems such as "Wave of the Night," "A Weightless Element," "Retrospective Sketch," and "Monologue" (all translated here).

In 1943 his section was evacuated from Berlin to Landsberg (now Gorzow in Poland). His young wife took a job as a Wehrmacht typist and accompanied him. They lived together in well-heated barracks; they had enough to eat; Benn had time and leisure to read, to write some poems, the *Novel of the Phenotype*, and essays including *Pallas*—"in fact," he recalled later, "these eighteen months were the quietest and happiest of my life."

An acquaintance—we shall probably never know who—arranged for a private printing of his poems. "I wanted to see in type what I felt like saving out of the past years," Benn wrote to his former publisher, enclosing a copy. He sent out a total of nine ("I have no more friends I can trust") and asked the recipients not to show them around. "I could cite the booklet as evidence of anti-fascist underground activity," he wrote years later, "but I do not have this ambition." Such poems as "Monologue," that scathing, scarcely disguised indictment of Hitler's régime, were indeed just what underground groups liked to distribute in bulk—anonymously, of course. But Benn only wanted a few elect to know that he was still a poet.

For his secret drawer he put down reflections on Landsberg, the war, himself, the government ("those six buffoons"), and the people ("a mystical totality of fools")—*Block II, Room 66* (translated here). By then, the thinking minority knew they were being led up a blind alley to a precipice. Unheard by the unthinking majority, they deplored the régime, its vulgarity, mendacity, stupidity, futility. A few deplored its inhumanity as well, and some of those lost their lives in attempts to resist it. Benn disagreed with them. He saw "nothing to step out against and nothing to fight here, neither with a small slingshot nor with a big trumpet. . . . What thought in me moved in a realm of its own; what lived of me was considerate, well-bred, and sincerely comradely in my allotted environment." Then the front caved in, the environment collapsed, the Benns had to flee to Berlin, and in the postscript to *Block II, Room 66* he penned a graphic thumbnail sketch of the end.

Benn sent his wife to a village on the Elbe, as far westward as trains would still run with American spearheads near Hannover. He remained in Berlin, in the path of the Red Army—an act of courage, for aside from his brief Nazi record he had a long anti-Communist and anti-Russian one; but the capital's need of physicians was desperate, so Dr. Benn stayed. The Russians also turned out to be interested only in his medical capacities.

When things began to calm down, he hired a maid and sent her for his wife, whose village haven had changed hands, from American to Soviet occupation. The maid returned weeks later, alone, in a desolate state, having been picked up en route by Russian units.

One day in August a country boy knocked on Dr. Benn's door with a letter from the doctor's wife. "I'm sorry," the boy said. "Next day she killed herself."

Three years went by, Berlin was under siege again, and Dr. Benn was practicing in the blockaded rubble pile when his first book in a decade appeared, in Switzerland. The response brought him back home: 1949 witnessed—along with the lifting of the blockade, the end of military government in the Western zones, and the decision to set up a West German republic—the publication of five volumes by Gottfried Benn, two of poetry, three of prose. For the six more years granted him, he ranked unquestionably with the most prolific, most talked about, and most controversial German writers.

The road back had not been easy. "I'm old," he had written to friends, late in 1945. "I've no more plans, no hope, no longings. The flat is cold, I have no stove, and cold is worse than hunger; but nothing affects me inside. I see a far country where shadows weep."

He journeyed to his wife's grave: "In all my life I haven't been so moved as that day in the wretched village, in the kitchen where she waited months for me, where she lay in a corner of the floor, on a potato bag spread on wood shavings, and injected herself with the morphine we had saved for certain contingencies. . . ."

In German eyes the world in 1945 wore Allied uniforms. Benn's daughter, grown up into a Danish newspaper editor since their last meeting, came to Berlin as a war correspondent with British forces, but he could not visit her at her hotel, nor escort her to her car. "That's fraternizing, Papa," she explained. "I mustn't."

Machinery to separate the sheep from the goats was set in motion. The de-nazification questionnaire, the *Fragebogen*, became as important in some respects as the *Ahnenpass*, the racial pedigree, had been under Hitler. "I haven't tried to find out whether I can publish," Benn wrote. "I don't really care, but I hear I'm on black or gray lists. . . . Undesirable before, again undesirable today—that's rather consummately undesirable; but to me it seems all right and confirms my oft-voiced basic feeling that art stands apart from state or history and must essentially be rebuffed by the world."

Little by little the gates to the world were reopened. A pack of

Swiss cigarettes came out of the blue, from a publisher who had heard that Benn was alive. Postcards arrived, CARE parcels, letters from refugee acquaintances in America and England, anti-Nazis, Jews. Benn's renewed contacts were private, mostly female; the "literary emigrants" had not forgotten the *Answer* he had given them in 1933. They themselves came back like the Bourbons after Waterloo, "on the enemy caissons"—young men in enemy uniforms, older ones as military government advisers; their job, to eliminate Nazis and Nazi influence from German life, was a labor of love. Inevitably there ensued what seemed to Benn a "Byzantine fawning upon the emigrants." He never liked them as a type, and the feeling was mutual.

"Though I think every day of my wife and her pitiful end, I just got married again," he informed friends in the spring of 1947. "In the circumstances here one can't make it alone."

He was sixty-one, his bride thirty-four. They had met when she came to his office for typhoid shots, and the anti-sentimentalist claimed they were marrying mainly to keep his apartment, for as a dentist she made more money than he did. "She's frail and often sick," he wrote to his daughter, "and now she's got herself a little dog, too; that's terrible—I hate animals; they upset me—but evidently she must have something to play with." And to a refugee friend in New York: "She is sorry she isn't non-Aryan; it was always her dream, and to her patients she brazenly pretends to be Jewish. She regards that as a distinction. . . ."

On the side he wrote a "Berlin story" but did not think the emigrants would let him publish it. "They consider anyone who stayed a saboteur," he explained, comforting himself with maxims from Lao-tse. Pride stiffened his back: "I will not have myself de-nazified."

A leading literary emigrant, one of the few who had exiled themselves in disgust rather than under pressure of political or racial persecution, paved the way for the removal of the stigma. Eugen Gürster-Steinhausen—now German cultural attaché in London—wrote in an emigrants' magazine on "Gottfried Benn, An Adventure in Intellectual Despair"; the article appeared in Sweden, was commented upon in Switzerland, led to the publication there in 1948 of Benn's unpublished verse since 1933, *Static Poems*; the reaction snowballed, spread to Germany, encouraged Allied-licensed publishers to approach the poet and solicit contributions—but Benn hesitated. His *Letter from Berlin* (translated here)—"from this blockaded Berlin . . . whose brilliance I loved, whose misery I now endure as that of the place where I belong, the city where I lived to see the Second, the Third, and now the Fourth Reich, and from which nothing will ever make me emigrate"—expressed the piques and peeves, the personal resentments and general disagreements that made him unwilling to get back into the literary prize ring under the Marquess of Queensberry rules of the "re-education" program.

Besides, he was busy. There was work to be done in Berlin. He still went on night duty in his home district, under conditions he would later describe in *Double Life:*

> Night duty means staying in a poorly heated shack from 8 p.m. to 7 a.m.—some twelve phone calls a night, no street signs, illegible house numbers—backyards, cellars, rubble dumps, unlit during the blockade—candle in your left, hypodermic needle in your right—here an old man with a heart attack, there an acute alcoholism, a brain tumor *in extremis*, a typhus calling for hospitalization, a woman hemorrhaging—if you want a cab to cover the large area, you pay the fare yourself—in short, no lyrical idyl. But all this is as it should be, and I would not want to miss it.

In autumn he sent all his manuscripts to a publisher, suggesting that they be divided into a volume of essays and one of "pure prose." He was not quite sure of the essays: "It is a question, of course, whether today one should still bring such grave charges against the Nazi era. Perhaps no one wants to know that any more."

Agreement was reached, and the same house has since been publishing all of Benn's works, old and new, poetry and prose. "The comeback is under way," he exulted. In the new year, book followed book off the press: *Three Old Men*—a playlet setting the mood; *The Ptolemean*—the "Berlin story," including also *Wolf's Tavern* and *Novel of the Phenotype*; the new poems; a selection of old ones; the essays, titled *World of Expression*. (Selections from all of these works are translated here.) The last-named volume was not in print before the author's doubts were confirmed, and this time the objectors were not the returned emigrants but the lingering or resurgent half- or three-quarter Nazis who had already envisioned Benn as their literary spokesman. Friends of long standing implored him to curb his "attacks on Germanism," begged him to delete at least *Art and the Third Reich*, the opening essay which he had written in 1941.

Benn refused. He would not dilute his "doctrine of the world of expression as the conqueror of nationalism, of racism, of history." But he tried to dispel the publisher's fears for the book: "I could imagine that it may even find a certain echo.... Something in what I write must be jogging the world in its sleep."

The reception of the essays bore him out. He continued to be criticized, but increasing plaudits indicated that he was striking popular chords, that his instinctive rejection of totalitarianism as well as democracy, of war and of politics, of history and of humane ideals—a negation so comprehensive and at the same time so delicately balanced as to leave no philosophical approach but nihilism and no moral principle but detachment ("*Ohne mich*, count me out")—was shared by multitudes of his compatriots.

In his next book he achieved the fullest measure of this identification. It was a political autobiography that he published in 1950 —his and that of some 50,000,000 Germans. The *Double Life* of the title was his and theirs. He was "defending his error" and theirs. The first part, his 1933 declaration for the new state, was an intellectual version of a common experience, and so was the subsequent tale of his disillusionment, his silencing, and his resignation in the face of ruin.

In that second part of *Double Life* there is disingenuousness and special pleading; there are omissions and distortions of fact. But there is nothing, no argument, no evasion, no presentation and no misrepresentation, that would not make the average German reader feel he was hearing his own voice, or a voice he wished he had. Every word eased the general conscience. Beneath the cant that outraged foreign critics—"He wants one law for himself, another for those whom he dislikes," Michael Hamburger wrote indignantly —lay the simple instinct of moral self-preservation that has produced so many national cants.

In *Double Life* Benn spelled out a new pragmatism. What had been sensed in his earlier books was now couched in plain, easily understandable terms in an exegesis of the "Ptolemean" and his maxims:

> "Realize the position"—*i.e.*, adjust to the position, camouflage yourself, avoid convictions ("with a customer you keep your private views to yourself . . .")—but on the other hand, go right along with convictions, ideologies, syntheses in every direction of the compass, if institutions or agencies require it.

A great public need was filled by this canon that enabled men to live with themselves while surviving in our time. The premise of a senseless and intrinsically evil historic world obviated the passage of moral judgment upon one's superiors. It anticipated any turn in the political winds. It exculpated any collaboration with whatever powers might be ruling. True, it was a canon taken out of context, for Benn's next words show that he did not mean to preach "adjustment" for its own sake but in behalf of "artistics," of forms, of the expressive world. To the Ptolemean, forms alone count: "They are his ethics." But how few, in Germany or anywhere, can live by forms? How few can grasp artistics? To the many only the first half of the new canon made sense, and in *Double Life* it was the many to whom Benn was speaking.

"Never again shall I make a personal appearance," he had vowed in 1948. "Beyond fame and defeat, aloof from affirmation or negation, I have in the past years rounded out and concluded my inner image in some books. 'Silently the eon flows.' "

Yet he had always liked the platform, and by 1951 he felt ready to resume face-to-face contact with his audience. At historic Marburg University he delivered a lecture on "Problems of Lyric Poetry" that evoked echoes in the realm of European letters. T. S. Eliot, in Cambridge, quoted and discussed it at length—"and that," as one German paper noted proudly, "has not happened to modern German literature since the war's end, in so prominent a place and from such prominent lips." Benn spoke in Darmstadt, where he was awarded the Büchner Prize, one of Germany's top literary distinctions. At the Belgian resort of Knokke he spoke in French about mid-century German poetry. He spoke on Else Lasker-Schüler at the British Center in Berlin. He spoke over the radio. He spoke in discussions.

The young Gottfried Benn had offset the tendentious realism of *Home Front* with the explosive surrealism of the Pameelen dramas; now the aging one balanced the reminiscent philosophizing of his *Three Old Men* with the sardonic, semi-topical symbolisms of a new play, *The Voice Behind the Curtain.* He propounded a categorical imperative of his own: "To live in the dark, to do in the dark what we can"—the only kind of moral law he considered still possible. And he dedicated the play "to my wife, a generation younger than I, whose light, wise hand arranges the hours and the steps, and the asters in the vases."

He felt age creeping up on him. Medical practice grew too strenuous; he had to abandon it at sixty-eight. Never a coward, he faced and attacked the problem on two fronts: as a man of letters in an essay, *Artists and Old Age* (translated here), and simultaneously as a man in a last, cautious, poignantly rejuvenating flight of fancy to a young poetess who had written a Ph. D. thesis about his lyrical style.

"Yes, in literature I have won through," he wrote at seventy, "and cabinet members and the Federal President and the Lord Mayor send me birthday greetings, but getting old means that everything one has done seems dubious in retrospect. . . . My wife is charming to the shabby old man." He died two months later, and the feuds that had been swirling about him, unabated, faded in the solemn chorus of eulogies.

They recommenced in a lower key. For once a man can no longer refute us, the issues shift, with his acts receding behind his effect on others, and Benn's influence, like his life, was paradoxical. The writers who sound most as he did decades earlier are either unlikely to know him (the French, for instance) or apt to bristle at his name. If they write poems, they jettison rhyme and meter; form, to them, is to be shattered, not to be sheltered in. Benn's themes bore them, and yet it is their work that seems to have fleshed out his "world of expression."

The aged Benn thought little of his successors. "They accept it as a given fact," he wrote not long before his death to a fellow Expressionist from the old days, Kasimir Edschmid, "that our generation exploded the language of the past century, ripped it apart, and that we rolled the stones farther, or tried to—and they don't know yet what it is in verse or in prose to move the pillars of Hercules even some worms' lengths. . . ."

Benn's influence, and the question of how much the *avant-garde* of the 1960's owes to that of the 1920's, will never be settled. His significance, however, is beyond question, and it is another paradox. The Germans like to call themselves "the nation of poets and thinkers," and Benn was both; even so, it was probably not as a bard that he appealed to them so strongly in his last years, nor as a sage, but as a German.

E. B. ASHTON

PROSE

THE BIRTHDAY

Gradually a doctor had come to be past twenty-nine, and the sum of his impressions was not such as to arouse especial feelings.

As old as he was, though, he asked himself this and that. An urge to know the meaning of existence came over him repeatedly: who fulfilled it? The gentleman who was walking vigorously, an umbrella under his arm; the market-woman sitting in the evening breeze under the lilacs, after closing time; the gardener who knew all plants by name, cherry laurel or cacti, and that the red berry on the dead bush was last year's?

He came from the North German plains. In southern lands, of course, the sand was light and loose; it had been demonstrated that the wind could carry grains of it around the globe. Here a grain of dust was large and logy.

What had he experienced? Love, poverty, and x-ray tubes; rabbit pens; and recently a black dog in an open square, straining about a big, red organ that swung between his hind legs, calmingly and winningly, as children stood by, ladies' eyes sought the animal, teen-agers shifted position to see the event in profile.

How had he experienced all this? He had brought in barley from the fields, in harvest wagons, and everything was big: the shocks, the baskets, the horizon of the horse. Then a young woman's body had been full of water, calling for discharge and drainage. But hovering above it all was a faint, doubting As If: as if you were real, space and stars.

And now? It would be a gray, meaningless day when they buried him. The wife dead; the child weeping a few tears—a teacher by then, probably, obliged to look at copybooks in the evening. Then it would be all over. The influencing of brains by and through him would end. The preservation of energy would take over.

What was his first name? Werff.

What was his full name? Werff Rönne.

What was he? A doctor in a whorehouse.

What time was it? Twelve o'clock. It was midnight. He was thirty years old. A thunderstorm roared in the distance. Clouds burst into May woods.

Now, he said to himself, it is time to begin. In the distance roars a thunderstorm, but *I* happen. Clouds burst into May woods, but *my* night. I have northern blood, I'll never forget that. My forefathers guzzled everything from troughs and stables. But I, he encouraged himself, am only taking a walk. Then he searched for something metaphoric to tell himself and failed, but this he found significant and portentous: perhaps imagery itself was already escapism, a kind of illusion and a lack of fidelity.

❋

Silent blue mists driven inland from the nearby sea enveloped Rönne next morning as he walked to his hospital.

It lay out of town, far from any paved road. He had to walk on ground that was soft and pervious to violets; loose and watersoaked, it swayed about his feet.

Out of gardens crocus hurled itself at him, the matitudinal candle of poets, the yellow variety that had been the epitome of loveliness to Greeks and Romans. Was it any wonder that it transported him to the realm of the gods? In ponds of crocus juice they bathed, sheltered from intoxication by wreaths of blossoms. Saffron fields by the Mediterranean: tripartite stigma; flat pans; sieves of horsehair over light, open fires.

He egged himself on: the Arabic was *za-fara*, the Greek, *kroké*. Corvinus came to mind, the Hungarian king who knew how to avoid saffron stains while eating. Effortlessly the dyestuff occurred, the spice, the flowering meadow and the Alpine glen.

Still yielding to the delight of such extensive association, he noticed a glass sign with the inscription "Maita Cigarettes" illuminated by a sun ray. And now—via Maita—Malta—beaches—shiny—ferry—port—mussel-eating—corruptions—there ensued a bright, ringing, gently splintering sound, and Rönne swayed with happiness. But then he entered the hospital: eyes inflexible, unshakably resolved to connect today's sensations and feelings with his existing stock, omitting none, linking every one. He envisioned a secret construction suggestive of armor and the flight of eagles, a kind of Napoleonic fancy, such as conquering the hedge he lay behind. Werff Rönne, thirty years old, established, a physician.

Ha, not so simple today. Straddle, and down from the chair, Miss—that thin blue vein running from the hip into the hair, we'll remember that! I know temples with such veins, slim, white, weary temples but this I'll remember, this snaky little twig of violet blood! How? Well, when the talk gets around to small veins, I shall stand fortified, especially in regard to surface veins: at the temples?? Ah, gentlemen!! I have seen them on other organs, too, thinly winding, like a sprig of violet blood. Would you like a sketch, perhaps? It went like this—shall I go higher up? The opening? The great ventricular vein? The heart chamber? The discovery of the circulation of the blood——? A wealth of impressions faces you, does it not? You whisper: who is this gentleman? He stands absorbed? Rönne is my name, gentlemen. I collect such little observations now and then, not uninteresting, but of course quite insignificant—small contributions to the great structure of knowledge and the cognition of reality, ha, ha!

And you, ladies, we know each other, don't we? Permit me to create you, to drape you in your essentialities, your impressions within myself. The lead organ is uncracked. It will demonstrate its memory. Already you rise . . .

You address the part you love. You look into its eye, animate, inspire. There are scars between your thighs—an Arab bey. Those must have been large wounds, opened by the depraved lips of Africa.—But you sleep with the white rat of Egypt whose eyes are pink; you sleep on your side, with the animal along your hip. Its eyes are glassy and small, like red caviar pellets. At night the animal gets hungry. Over the sleeper it climbs to a plate of almonds on the bedside table and softly returns to her hip, sniffing, alert.

Often you wake when the cool, thin tail snakes across your upper lip.

For a moment he probed into himself. But he stood powerfully, as memory picture followed memory picture and the threads between them rustled hither and yon.

And you from the lupanar in Aden, sweltering between the desert and the Red Sea. At all hours bluish water trickles down marble walls. Clouds of incense rise from trellises on the ground. You know the love of all nations on earth, but you long for a humble cottage on the Danish Sound. Come last flushes, a billiard table, boys in light suits playing before it—and you in a brothel in the path of war, between harness and leather, daily riven a hundredfold by unknown members, or by lumps of clotted blood and dung.

Transfigured he stood before himself. How he was playing it up. Playing? Rainbowing! Greening! A May night utterly ineffable! He knew them all. Face to face with them he stood, clean and natural. He had not weakened. Strong life pulsed through his head.

He knew them all, but he wanted more. He wanted to explore a most hazardous field; there probably was, or had been, a conscious life without feelings, but our likings—he distinctly remembered that sentence—are our heritage. In them we experience our lot: now he wanted to love one.

He looked down the corridor, and there she stood. She had a birthmark, strawberry-colored, running from her neck over one shoulder and down to the hip, and in her eyes, flowerlike, a purity without end, and about the lids an anemone, still and happy in the light.

What would her name be? Edmée, that was enchanting. What else? Edmée Denso, that was supernatural; that was like the call of the coming new woman, the imminent, longed-for creature that man was about to create for himself: blonde, and with the lust and skepticism of sobered brains.

Well, now he loved. He sounded the feeling within him. Exuberance had to be created against nonexistence, lust and pain to be forced out into the bald, gray light of high noon. But then there must be oscillation too! He was facing strong sensations. He could not stay in this country. Meridionalities! Exaltation!

Edmée, a flat-roofed white house in Luxor or the Cairo palace? City life is gay and open; the light is famous, a limpid glow, and night comes suddenly. You'll have innumerable fellah women to serve you, to sing and dance for you. You'll pray to Isis, touching your forehead to pillars whose capitals bear the flat heads with long ears on their corners. You will stand in sycamore gorges among wading birds.

He searched a moment. Something like Coptic had arisen, but he was unable to bring it to light. Now he sang again, the happy tender heart.

Winter comes and the fields green; a few leaves fall from the pomegranate bush, but the corn shoots up before your eyes. What will you have: narcissi or violets the year around, poured into your bath when you rise late in the morning; or do you want to roam at night through little villages along the Nile, when the bright southern moon casts large, clear shadows on the crooked streets? Will you have ibis cages or heron houses? Orange groves, flaming yellow and clouding the city with sap and vapor at noon, or a chiseled frieze from Ptolemaic temples?

He stopped. Was that Egypt? Was that Africa around a woman's body, gulf and liana about her shoulders' flow? He searched here and there. Had something been left behind? Was there anything that could be added? Had he created it: glow, sorrow, and dream?

But what a curious ferment in his breast! An agitation as if he were drained out. He left the examination room and went through the hall into the park. It drew him down, down on the lightly-mown grass.

How this has tired me, he thought, by main force! Then it struck him that pallor was the fruit, and the tear was pain——: tremors! Gaping distance!

The park glowed luxuriantly. A bush on the law wore fernlike foliage, each frond large and fleshy as a deer. About each flowering tree the earth lay like a closed bucket, watering it and surrendering itself. Sky and blossoms: softly, out of eyes, came blueness and snow.

—Sobbing and more, ever nearer, Edmée, to thee! A marble parapet rims the sea. Meridionally gathered lilies and barks. A violin opens you, all the way into your muteness—

He blinked upward. He trembled: against the lawn a radiance stormed, moist, from a golden hip, earth mounting the sky. Spread on the shadows' edge, light struggled. Back and forth played the tongue of enticement; out of its plumage a shower of flowers escaped from the magnolia into a breeze that brushed by.

Edmée laughed: roses and bright water.

Edmée walked: on narrow paths, between violets, in a light of islands rising from osmium-blue seas—in short, of rock and star. Doves, rock-pigeons, chopped silver with their wings.

Edmée grew tanned, a bluish oval. She played before palms, she had loved much. She carried her nakedness like a cup, coolly flexing her enkindled stride, the hand on her hip heavy, harvest-yellow under grain and seed.

In the garden mingling ensued. No longer did the flower bed riot with colors; the humming of bees no longer ochred the hedge. Extinct were direction and cadence: a drifting blossom halted and stood in the blue, like the hinge of the world. Treetops gently dissolved, chalices shrunk, the park submerged in the blood of the disembodied one. Edmée sprawled on the ground. Her shoulders smoothed, two warm ponds. Now, slowly, she closed her hand about a shaft, the ripe abundance, brownishly mown, on her fingers, under great sheaves of transfigured lust——

There was a swell in him now; now a tepid escape. And then the structure became confused as his carnal ego melted away—:

Steps resounded over the slope of a valley through a flat white town; dark gardens enclosed the alleys. On crumbling sills and architraves, scattered over a Florentine landscape and representing gods and mysteries, lay drops of bright blood. A shadow swayed among mute members, among grapes and a herd; a fountain plashed in splintering play. . . .

A body lay in the grass. Fumes washed up from basements; it was mealtime, pipe smoke and bacon rinds, the bad breath of one dying.

Up looked the body: flesh, order, and preservation summoned. He smiled and hardened again; withdrawing already, he looked at the house: what had happened? What had been mankind's way thus far? An effort to bring order into something that should have remained play. But after all, it had remained play in the end, for nothing had reality. Did he have reality? No; all he had was every possibility. He bedded his neck deeper into the may-weed that smelled of thyrse and Walpurgis. Melting through the noonday, his head pebbled, brooklike.

He offered it to the light; irresistibly the strong sun trickled into the brain. There it lay: scarcely a molehill, brittle, the animal scratching inside.

❁

But what about the morel quarter, he asked himself soon after. Behind the palace with the laurel-ringed pillars, alleys plunge precipitately, house leaning on little house, down the slope.

One-eyed men hang about snail wagons. They put down money. Women pry up the shells. A circular cut, and the pink flesh hangs out. They dip it in a cup of broth and bite. The woman coughs, and they move on.

Soothsayers, aided by thought transference, ring incessantly, shrilly, addressing ladies especially, and carry batteries.

Gypsy women before pushcarts. Rays, flattened, purple and silvery, their heads chopped off, are split in half, notched, and hung up to dry between other fish, thin, crooked, copper-glistening.

There is a smell of fire and stale fat. Countless children are relieving themselves; their language is alien.

What about the morel quarter, Rönne asked himself. I have to face it! Come on, down! I have sworn I'll never forget this picture of summer beating a wall with shrubs of flaming plumage, with rushes of taut, blue, stinging flesh—beating against an un-streaming wall the damp blue vine!

He raced down. About the cavernous alley flocked little houses,

9

undermined by long narrow caves spewing forth bone: young and lusty, old and creaking, the groins girt high.

What was sold: wooden clogs for want, green dumplings for the ego, schnapps for pleasure, necessities of body and soul, salve boxes and Holy Virgins.

What went on: small children close before kneeling women, just off their breasts; rough voices, down and out over charred stone; a gentleman digging inconceivably far into his pocket; skulls, a desert, bodies, a gutter, treading earth, chewing: I and you.

He fled deeper into the alley. But there, a small monument, erected to the founder of a boys' club—the human soul, the community system, the longer life expectancy and the city council, flaunting full beards and population increase. Reconstruction unfolded: abilities were tested and re-tested, investigations carried on and results determined.

Where had his South gone? The ivied rock? The eucalyptus, where by the sea? Ponente, coast of decline—where the silver-blue wave?

He raced into a dive, battled drinks, hot, brown ones. He lay on the bench to let his head dangle, because of gravity and blood. Help, he cried, exaltation!

Chairs—objects for gentlemen with knees bent forward and desiring support for the rear surfaces of their legs—dried dully, northern fashion. At tables such talk as "Well, how's it going," waggish and manly and about the lower parts of the anatomy, ran honorably through time. No death hurled the bleary-eyed barmaid hourly into nothingness, at the stroke of the clock. Shopkeepers scratched with their feet. No lava over the dead rubble!

And he? What was he? There he sat among his sensations; the rabble was what happened to him. His noon was mockery.

Once more his brain welled up, the dull course of the first day. Still between his mother's thighs—thus he happened. As the father pushed, he rolled down. The alley had broken him. Back: the whore screamed.

He was about to go, when a sound happened. A flute chimed

in the gray alley, a song, blue between the shacks. A man must be walking there, blowing it. A mouth was active in the sound that soared and faded away. Now he was starting again.

Out of the blue. Who asked him to play? No one thanked him. Who would have asked when the flute was coming? Yet like a cloud he came, appearing for his white moment and already disappearing into all the gorges of the sky.

Rönne looked about, transfigured, though nothing had changed. Except for him: he was blissful up to his lips. Plunge after plunge, thunder by thunder, rustling sails, flaring masts, the dock stretching, roaring between small basins—great and glowing, the *harbor complex* approached:

The light rises over the rocks, casting shadows; the villas shimmer, and the background is mountain-filled. A black spindle of smoke darkens the pier while the tiny local boat fights the crinkled waves. On the swaying gangplank bustle the *facchini*: "Hoyoh—tirra—hoy," ring their voices; the full tide of life flows. The ship's belly points to tropical and subtropical regions, to salt mines and lotus rivers, to Barbary caravans, to the very antipodes. A mimosa-fringed plain yields reddish resin, a slope between chalk marl, the rich clay. Europe, Asia, Africa: bites, deadly consequences, horned vipers, and the whorehouse on the quay meet the arrival; silently in the desert stands the sultana-bird.—

It still stood silently when the *olive* happened to him.

The Agave was beautiful, too, but the fine-oil-bearing Taggiaska came blue-black and melancholy before the Ligurian Sea.

Sky, seldom clouded; roses cascading; through every bush the blue gulf—but the endless bright forests, what a shadow-weighted grove!

When the cloth was spread around the stem, there was work to be done. A mixture of horns, claws, leather, and woolen rags; every fourth year one had eaten. But now men otherwise devoted with suspenseful zeal to the bowling game were cutting treetops, abruptly engrossed in the fruits.

The weevil in touchwood. A wood-nymph, flaring out of the

myrtle. A small press is turned, a slate cellar crossed in silence. The harvest nears, the blood of the hills, round the grove, bacchantically, the city.—Came *Venice*, and he flowed across the table. He felt lagoon, and a relaxation, sobbing. At the muffled sound of the song from the old days of Duke Dandolo, he scattered into a zephyr.

The stroke of an oar; a breath drawn; a barque: support for the head.

Five iron horses given by Asia, and around the columns rang a song: sometimes, for an hour, you are; the rest is what happens. Sometimes the two tides swell into a dream. Sometimes a rustling: when you are broken.

Rönne listened. There must be greater depths. But the evening came fast from the sea.

Bleed, rustle, suffer, he said to himself. Men looked at him. Yes, he said, their freckles, their bald necks with hair stubbling over the Adam's apple—under my crucifixion; I will go to rest.

He paid quickly and rose. But from the door he glanced back once more at the darkness of the tavern, at the tables and chairs of which he had suffered so and would suffer again and again. But there, from the shaft of the centerpiece next to the leaky-eyed woman, a large, legendary poppy glowed with the silence of lands untouchable, russet, dead, and consecrated to the gods. There, he felt deeply, his way would now lead forever. A yielding came over him, a surrender of final rights. Mutely he tendered his brow, loudly its blood gaped.

Darkness had fallen. The street received him, above it the sky, a green Nile of the night.

But over the morel quarter the sound of the flute rang once more: sometimes the two tides swell into a dream.

A man decamped. A man hurled himself into his harvest, to be bound by reapers offering wreaths and verse. A man drifted out of his fields, aglow under crown and plumage, immeasurable: he, Rönne.

(1916) Translated by E. B. Ashton

HOME FRONT

Cast: Privy Councillor Professor Dr. Paschen, Chief of Welfare. Hans, his son. Dr. Olf, his deputy. Dr. Dunker, resident at a base hospital. Professor Dr. Kotschnüffel, pediatrician. Herr Jöhlinger. Herr Mabuse. Duke of Wildungen. Prince Gerolstein. Count Vichy. Prince Fachinger. His Excellency, the commanding general. Officers, clergymen, orderlies.

The action takes place in the welfare section of military government, in a conquered province. The set shows Paschen's study, a balcony in rear, doors leading left to his private apartment, right to the office.

SCENE ONE

Garlanded, flower-bedecked room. Door to balcony open; a serenade is played in the street. On balcony: Paschen, Olf, Dunker, Mabuse. Olf and Dunker into the room.

OLF: What? Eight months of keeping your trap shut? Eight months of gnashing your teeth so this profiteering scum can warm their bellies? Blood squalls have cleansed the skies; now the land wants up, the hamlets stir, swarming with grain and shrubs—blood summer land, Dunker! Get the scythes off the walls! (*They go back to balcony. Paschen and Mabuse come in.*)

PASCHEN: Listen, your memorial article is beautiful, but I would go into high gear and step on it. Like this, you know: juncture of epochal significance, victory on the home front, a battle won, cultural achievement of the first water: the opening of the first German stocking plant. And then you must camouflage the stocking a little, throw a sort of peace veil over it . . . not field-gray twill, not armor, rather what the foot needs, or you might bring in a children's stocking—one has to see windmills. sort of. and cornfields and nursing mothers—by the way, what do you mean: I fifty-five! Vigorous man in his forties, man of the people—sod—smell of the soil. (*They go back to balcony*.)

OLF: (*comes in with Dunker*): Did you see them, the bloody gray skulls, the splintered visages? For this the tumult, the screams, the killing? I tell you, Dunker, they couldn't get another son-of-a-bitch to charge into barbed wire if those out there knew who's peddling death here.... With this whip—and if they put me up against a wall, my blood shall spurt like the cry of a bugle: Set dogs on the throats of this gang!

SCENE TWO

All return from balcony. Music ends.

PASCHEN (*shuts door*): Frontally we're not going to pull them in. It's got to be done, though. We'll infiltrate the holes: rehabilitate cripples, consumptives, prostitutes—what stinks is soft. Plenty of opportunities now at home, I tell you. Ladies-in-waiting may respond to definitions of open and disguised brothels; cathedral deans will try out prophylactics; it's a great age! (*to Dunker*): So tomorrow your speech on the cripples will conclude my celebration. I'll try to induce His Excellency to appear. You know he has quite a stake in that, through his wife. Here's her pamphlet, here's her article in the Journal. You understand: capital and intelligentsia, nobility and the loving-kindness of women, binding up wounds, balm, fragrance....

So, the carpenter must get to be a carpenter again. A priori and absolutely. And the Sunday arm must be brought in, and then there was a celebrated case who made his living as office manager: had neither arms nor legs, wrote with his chops, and when he wanted to get somewhere he would drop off the chair and trundle around like a roller. Would be nothing for me—I incline to vertigo—but the fellow supported six children and a wife.

DUNKER: I admit I had prepared myself more about frozen feet....

PASCHEN: Frozen feet? Don't be silly, boy. Vistas, social rearmament, gathered forces, psychological influence—laughing and trusting in God to the end of the pilgrimage—then you can come with your sprained feet. Mabuse, you'd better crank up.

MABUSE: "Today many thousands of our seriously wounded brothers and their families look into the future with fear—the spectre of lasting infirmity, of dire physical distress. . . . But, gentlemen, the magnificent upsurge, the unique achievements of the past decades. . . . There has been a famous painter who painted with his feet, and Beethoven was deaf."—Then more specific: the great noblewoman, the powerful manifestation in the legislative body, the fruitful discussion, and finally quite simple, quite the physician and healer: wood and hammock, plaster and cardboard—and at the end, ascending again, the moral and religious base, perhaps the interrelation of creatures—gentle fadeout—rallentando. . . .

PASCHEN: That's it, you see. Paschen school. Almond milk. Crowd has got to whimper! Feeling, feeling starts the flow of cash. You must charm up university chairs for us, factories, whole industrial areas . . . eh?—? Did you say something? Don't give us the profile, man. Personal detachment! Nature is indifferent to individualities. Get some sex, that's the most God-pleasing business.

SCENE THREE

Kotschnüffel enters with handbag.

KOTSCHNÜFFEL: Greetings, my dear Privy Councillor, on your day of honor—greetings from home and from Her Highness, the wife. How's the infant? Suckling all right? From the train I could perceive a girl who was nursing as she walked. Are you here on a buttermilk regime? Impossible conditions.

PASCHEN: Just in time, Kotschnüffel! The mother's breast as cultural fertilizer. Infiltration through the bub. I'll introduce you at once to His Excellency. What'll we say? Favorite student of the revered old master, isn't it? The Luther of the sucking instinct?

KOTSCHNÜFFEL: Let us not forget my inauguration of the cereal bouillon—I guess I may put a sample package up here (*takes it*

15

out of the bag)—nor my autorship of the Nursing Bible. Here it is. (*Takes it out of the bag.*) How about a translation into the local languages? Resourceful publisher? Warmly concerned with the national welfare—

PASCHEN: Boiling point?

KOTSCHNÜFFEL: Five figures.

PASCHEN: Will do.

KOTSCHNÜFFEL: At the same time, why don't you market the nipple of my design? Introduction urgently required, from all I've seen here. (*Takes it out of the bag.*) Here an acorn-shaped model specially adapted to the spirit of the times: Teutonic forests, primeval vigor, also high-quality workmanship and material. (*Shows it around.*) Paschen, how you look in your field-gray, so solid—and the gentlemen all so nobly bemedaled, warrior's adornment, sans peur et sans reproche.... Say, Paschen, if I keep fingering teats here a while, you think I'll snag a cross myself yet, eh?

OLF: Dunker, you tell me: a robustly consummate bastard—but to let a new army croak so these hogs can piss on marble and foul the temple into stables for themselves and their brood, the slobbering of their privates—? Why not scratch your drooping tails on the walls, you sticky baldpates! Past forty, and not in the bughouse yet? Out of your skulls bleat notions grown invaluable in giant cells, washed by long-rotted lymph of Mesopotamia, crumbs of Syria, Nordic bone structure, the starry sky above—and they've got the whole mess in their blood——scrubwomen!

KOTSCHNÜFFEL: Vacuum cleaner! W.C.!

OLF: The entire intellectual content of any one age: three or four invaluable conceptions, emotionally wrapped—delusive systems—brain convolution patterns: maybe the long-continuing roar of the cannon has set off molecular tremors in the young organs in question, demonstrably capable of quick development? Are you taking that into consideration, you prophylacticians? Do you go the whole hog?

PASCHEN (*takes Kotschnüffel's arm*): New Delusive System, Incorporated.

SCENE FOUR

Enter Jöhlinger, followed by orderly.

PASCHEN: Hello, Jöhlinger! Morning! Have you heard, two high priests are already here, one Catholic and one Protestant; a chief rabbi is hustling over, too—can't you tell me a better psalm, quick, something like: Carry on in glory? (*Orderly delivers telegram; Paschen reads:*) To their dear honorary member, the creator of new values from the old spirit, which God preserve! The Provincial League of Women's Societies. (*Looks up.*) Dear German woman!

JÖHLINGER:—with a knee-warmer in her hand . . .

PASCHEN: Wipe that grin off your face, Jöhlinger, and look tender, if you please! Bellyband industry with bladder-warmers for Dad, or an oak for every grave to advertise seedboxes? Considerations, Jöhlinger! Suggestions! Where do you come from? How are the engines? Motor humming? Shaft driving? We've got to show the fellows here a thing or two! What their government didn't accomplish in two hundred years—we've been here four months, and there you have the welfare state! Make offers! Say, wage book! Say, trucking ban! Bait! Bait! Forward! Deadline: a week! First achievement of the new Department of Welfare! Fetlocks, Jöhlinger! Pastern-joints! An item for Mabuse, eh? Write: in the name of humanity, starvation wages, needy children, the sorrowful gaze of the Crucified, collieries, Borinage, Meunier, and Verlaine.

JÖHLINGER: Whazzat? I'll write as follows: let this lice-ridden pack work two months under our rule—and then, even if we're kicked out again, they've tasted blood; they know what's what; they'll make demands, and the competition is weakened. Ante up, gentlemen! Pay now and support your grandchildren.

PASCHEN: That you can disseminate in your Yiddish sheets, not here, understand? Here we deal in welfare, understand? Here we act on motives that warm the cockles of every heart from

17

shack to palace, understand? Humanitarian ideas, get that through your thick skull! Ideals, you hear me? Anyone doesn't like it is out. The boom is in neighborly love, man, don't be so dense— who's dealing in new fatherland here, you or I? (*Bangs fist on table.*) I am!

OLF: Who is that? How do you define yourself?

PASCHEN: Man, I! Graduate linen-weaver, mule-train industrializer of the Pico de Orizaba, gift bicycle coordinator for the Sirius expedition—welfare purveyor, culture fertilizer, pioneer— silly question!

OLF: What culture??? Men eat mud—are eaten by lice—so that these three bastards—that's the end! (*shouts*): What culture!

PASCHEN: But, my dear fellow—I, your superior officer! Authority, wherever it is, is from God! You must have been overpowered by the grandeur of this celebration. No nonsense, now—the garland-carriers are coming; maids of honor are washing their breasts; even Jöhlinger will drape himself in a mantilla so his Syrian knees won't show so. . . .

OLF: Capital redistribution? Off the gold standard? Copper in the mint? Stockpile lentils and manganese, acceptable as collateral up to two thirds value?—The country lives on the wounds of its youth, breathes through the bullet-torn lungs of its boys; why, with the hotel building of your intellectual personality, should it transplant the rottenest of moral systems into this empire that we have conquered, this city whose stones reek of the blood of adolescents who would spit at you? Yes, I tell you: each single boy who is dying out there in this hour would spit at your mean, shriveled pan, you corpse defiler, you pimp of a dismantled brain— don't you ever tremble that the carrion stench of all the ill-buried young skulls might smoke you out of your sties and hit you in the neck?

AN ORDERLY (*enters hurriedly*): The gentlemen of the cloth.

PASCHEN (*runs into his apartment*): Hans! Hans! The zither! There in the corner! A song from home—you by the fireplace, I on the couch—softly—sounds of longing to make the heart soar. . . .

(*Looks out of the door*) Ask the gentlemen to step in.

Clergymen cross the stage from right to left. For a moment it remains empty.

SCENE FIVE

Enter Duke of Wildungen and Count Vichy in the habit of Grand Master and Lord Commander of the Order of St. Michael.

WILDUNGEN: Pushed around by a peasant. Sidetracked. Who is the man? Who can vouch for the teeth of his sire? Disgustingly officious middle classes. What was the Red Cross in the last war? Michael's Order, Christian's Knights, the rest picking charpie, and that was that. Phew—paysans!

VICHY: And now, to paralyze him, one drapes him in a knight's cloak. Cochonnerie! (*Spits.*)

WILDUNGEN: Craché! Ah . . . charming chanson that La Vaughan sings now (*spits*)—right crachat—and (*spits*) left crachat—autour de mon crachat (*capers around, trilling*)—autour de mon crachat. (*Enter Prince Gerolstein and Prince Fachinger in the habit of Grand Master and Lord Commander of the Knights of St. Christian.*)

VICHY (*waves to Gerolstein*): Morning, Highness! Spring! Polo weather!

GEROLSTEIN: But the oysters are going stale. There's no unmixed bliss.

VICHY: God knows. Last night I had snails eaten for me. Little chippy sat at the next table; had them served to her just to look at the stuff—but it's completely out of the question, you know. I've no doubt there are lots of pretty nutritious things, but to put them right into your mouth. . . .

(*Enter Kotschnüffel, Jöhlinger, Olf, several officers.*)

WILDUNGEN: Excellency wants just to present the cabinet order. I'm to make the speech. Common goals—what goals? Nationalization of the popular spirit, if the war could bring us that! Examining board at birth, elimination of the unfit, official testing for the kind of school, later for occupation, a Taylor system of mentalities—goal much to be desired!

KOTSCHNÜFFEL: Vast scope, Serene Highness! Breathtaking vision! Popular liberties, particularly in the field of social hygiene, cannot be prolonged by a farsighted state. One is tempted to speak of a wilderness, if not of mythical conditions—where, for example, is the nursing law: Monday, Wednesday, Friday on the right breast, the rest of the week on the left one? Where is the standardized coloring of infant feces, with compulsory reporting? Great tasks, Serene Highness. Let us impregnate the homeland, let us found a concern, let us educate the people—what am I saying, educate? No, let's command them to stop making children, progeny, random types—rather: bone conformations, five ball and four axle joints, several flexor and extensor muscles, half a pound of heart . . .

OLF: But, please, the latest apparatus. Consider (*takes Kotschnüffel, bending upper and forearms against each other*): up and down—good old curve—single-axle—turnverein—pater familias—utterly obsolete joint—while here (*moves Kotschnüffel's shoulder*)—you see, like this . . .

KOTSCHNÜFFEL: Let go!

OLF: Ball joint!

KOTSCHNÜFFEL: My dear colleague!

OLF: I let a people perish for a fair city.—What's liquor amnii? A weak saline solution. Riparian fauna! Do you see the fan top of a palm tree?

KOTSCHNÜFFEL (*to Wildungen*): His way of expressing himself is somewhat hazy, Serene Highness. He means the hygienic aspect of the city. Its sanitary facilities are indeed very good. Some are excellent. One has even been illustrated in my work on chamber pots for children of six months. (*Into background.*)

VICHY (*offers cigarettes*): Get enough sleep, keep your nose clean, light a Syrian cigarette—still works all right. A battle isn't so bad, either.

FACHINGER: A what?——— Were you really . . . ? Actually . . . ? I say, let's have it, old boy! Don't always hold out on everybody. So, where have you been these days? Pious Sister or franctireuse?

VICHY: Do you smell nothing? I come from the lower depths. De profundis. Been eating with the civil servants—

GEROLSTEIN: Nature boy.

VICHY: You know, doctors and court personnel and so. Very curious crowd. One's from Allenstein, and the other doesn't go bathing because he has a wife and children. Unquestionably a very curious crowd; you must do it too, some time. When I walked in with my Houbigant, they all started sniffing the air! There, if you don't stink out of all holes, you're a pig.

GEROLSTEIN (*draws Olf into foreground*): Listen, my dear doctor, I would like to have a little confidential talk with you as a physician. Heart on my sleeve, you know. It's about a not quite insignificant physical matter. You know, every time I'm not sleeping like a top, tossing around, let's say, too many blankets or that constant auto honking—well, anyway, I don't want to make too much of it—then I regularly have such a sore feeling on the tongue next morning, after my first cigarette. Here, you see (*sticks out his tongue*)—excuse the bad manners, but to a doctor I suppose one has to bare the part—here, quite a well-defined spot, sort of a sour soreness. Don't you think that can turn into something, kind of cancer or so? Say, listen, Vichy, didn't you have something like that once, on the arm, I think? How did you singe that off?

OLF: No cause for worry, Highness. Elevate your gaze from your wretched carcass—

GEROLSTEIN: ... Wha ... ?

OLF: To the comforting earth that smells so strangely at this moment—

GEROLSTEIN: Dreamer!

OLF: Dreamer? Cosmic sentiment? Moon and dark water—I? No, Highness, only my brain bleeds in a forebirth of indescribable bastardizations. You will not see them, nor shall I see them—but liquor amnii——

GEROLSTEIN: A cordial, ha, ha, ha!

SCENE SIX

Paschen ushers clergymen out of his room. Handshakes, bows.

PASCHEN: ... deeply happy to have had you to myself a moment. Here, in the daily routine, in enemy country, in struggle and combat, so much will wither, and it may well be the best ... gentle bells ... sounds of longing ...

OLF (to Paschen): The sow licks her piglets, too, and the girl is unquestionably vindicated by her udder; but you, as man, yourself a brilliant representative of the exclusively decorative meaning of ethics, are now propagating ideology, the value of content—

PASCHEN: An unexpected stricture.

OLF: While I dream of a mankind of men, concretely conscious of the pure formality of its intellectual structure, no longer thinking in anything but forms—tangentially, functionally, stripped of concepts, drained of words. That would be the dance; that would be happiness.

PASCHEN: Tango! Chaine anglaise! Fall in, Jöhlinger, Kotschnüffel, as lead-off men! The young gentlemen are dreaming! Whippersnappers, masturbators, ragged individualists—how much manhood do you represent, ha? Who is that: Olf? Are the boots paid for? How much is your dream? Want a warm lunch some time? Five hundred million of mankind are cleansed in this war, and you pipsqueak——

OLF: Cleansed? What? This grubby vermin, still thrilled by the compound of air pressure and peristaltic motion that you call soul, swept off its feet and into the doldrums by the fact of walking upright—while a future visibly dawns in which the ascension of feces into the earth will be permitted as the ultimate transcendence.

SCENE SEVEN

His Excellency, with retinue. Band, hymn. Duke of Wildungen steps forward.

WILDUNGEN (to Paschen): On the wings of time came this hour ...

KOTSCHNÜFFEL: What poetic imagery! What prophetic view of historic evaluations!

WILDUNGEN (to Paschen): ... came this hour, and if I, as Grand Master of an order as ancient as our country's history, now lay around your shoulders the cloak that makes you a knight, I am heeding only the vast call of this time, in which moral values come to the force again as salient and decisive. And if, as the sage has said, knowledge ennobles, how much more so does feeling, how much more a warm heart that beats in humble self-sacrifice for mankind.

PASCHEN: Who would not die in this time—!

WILDUNGEN: Your worth is known. The orphans call you their father, the cripples their brother and healer, and no one is happier than I to acknowledge the wisdom of a Providence that has chosen you to work in this land, bought with so much precious blood— propitiating the shadows, sanctifying the manes—I think I am not going too far if I say: today the fallen are rejoicing in their graves that they could prepare your way.

PASCHEN: Your Excellency will forgive a man the tear he cries in silence for his nation.

WILDUNGEN: And now, Sir Knight, administer your high office in blessed national service; do your great work in this place that bears the imprint of centuries of history, in this fortress of the captured king, in this battle-scarred city. (*Paschen bends over Wildungen's hand.*)

OLF: Who ever saw this city otherwise than as a place where patrols might walk? Who has seen the white gleam of the one house with pillars and a flat roof?

PASCHEN: Shut up, repulsive windbag. His Excellency's lips move; His Excellency's pupils dilate—

KOTSCHNÜFFEL: He probably means the lavatory from my book . . .

OLF: I see the march of the world divide before a house unencompassed by any purposes, and lie down round a hall that was never deserted by the southern sea. . . .

PASCHEN: He is sick, Excellency. In the morning already feverish . . .

OLF: And inside hunting fauns redeemed for their bodies, laughing forms with so many felicities among women and grapes;

bodies, foliage about their sex, rustling in beauty; anemone groves of love; battles between armies of bursting gestures; a virgin jungle of existences deified into form and tensed by inexhaustible blood— do you still want to conquer cold land?

PASCHEN: He's seriously ill. Ran a high fever this morning. I was reluctant to deprive him of this consecrated hour. I judged wrong, Excellency. Beg Your Excellency's pardon.

EXCELLENCY: Poor young man. But we, in this hour, will gather around us the powers that wrought our rise, and we will pray that under their radiance this land also may waken and bloom! (*Holds out his right hand.*) I—the will to achieve it!

PASCHEN (*clasps hand with his right*): I, the feeling, the soul in particular.

KOTSCHNÜFFEL (*joins them*): And I believe I may say: I, the faith.

OLF: To ravage you. I! Come on, rabble, out of your gold braid and cockades; get out of your bodies, fragrant and stinking ones—come to me: brains! What do I see, Excellency: a buttock, soft-boiled, one groove to the sex, another into the groin? Privy Councilor, was it? A piss-pot with three toads fucking in it? Neighborly love? Sodomy!! Obedience? Respect? White hair? —What's so venerable about your brittle guts and your enlarged prostate, Excellency? Stuff dotards? Suckle fetuses?—Thank God, death still has this ugly animal world by the throat——Come on, brains, mother sows with your word piglets; the land is now dismembered, Europe is reeling, screaming moon and raging constellations—where's the star for my chest? (*While he is taken out:*) The man-wrought and thought, the wound-red glow from the weal we call brain, fades out; why do you go on yipping, rabble— spars without a roof, timbers on dead gables . . .

PASCHEN: Your Excellency planned to be so gracious as to visit the reorganized insane asylums in the afternoon. We'll have the painful spectacle of greeting this fallen morning star once again.

EXCELLENCY: This young man! What language!

(*Written 1915, published 1919*) *Translated by E. B. Ashton*

ALEXANDER'S MARCH BY MEANS OF FLUSHES

It is winter, severe frost, in the mornings almost a little hazy with cold. As the geography textbook puts it, a pale, delicate haze accompanies the sun at a distance extending to the orbits of the nearest planets: it is the Zodiacal Light, appearing in pyramid form like a shimmer of the Milky Way. Something of this pale and delicate haze appears far away in the morning, especially during the hours before noon, when the flaming sun slowly rises over Gneisenaustrasse.

It is the time of the solstice; something about tropics is going on. Say what you will about the problems of evolution, in any event a Gregorian year is drawing to a close. You get older; temples turn gray. Nothing abnormal, no specific phenomenon: air gets into the medulla, anatomically speaking, in some families as early as the twenties, in the present case in the thirty-seventh year.

It is Christmas Eve; the case in question is alone but not quite forgotten. Quite unexpectedly a messenger brought him a small package. A sloshing inside, as of water, was traced to a small triangular carton, a fantastic glass jar, a fairy tale name—in other words, to a perfume evoking Punjab and Asiatic subtlety, with place designations like "Champs Elysées" adding detail, and "Mouchoir de Monsieur," moreover, strongly influencing the whole *milieu*. Could not the notion strike for an instant—might not the recipient momentarily succumb to the illusion of being the *monsieur* so abstractly adverted to: a gentleman, a member of the communal sphere, so to speak, carrying in his jacket the cambric handkerchief he had taught himself to use discreetly, with well-attuned calm and without exaggeration? Somebody sounding, whose approach and measured entrance one looked forward to? A not insignificant

25

center of this or that grouping, and, to complete the picture, a social figure casually exuding the entire complex of modern civilization, a sediment of the age and a reflex of its manifold phosphorescences? Like a flatulence it hung over him, reddening the organs of his face and neck, and he went on groping through this and that.

This is Rönne, a doctor, of medium height and healthy constitution, left eyelid drooping slightly, usually disgruntled, dyspepsia in the brain, a tendency to gain weight and perspire. In his youth he had gathered all sorts of impressions on his own, also combined with revealing moods, elations, evanescences; now these had become rarer. What can impress, what is to be revealed, everything's got worms inside—that was one of his sayings. Wherever you looked, things were a public nuisance: Faust became So-what, Don Juan manufactured pessaries, Ahasuerus learned to fly gliders, the myth of Man was crying for execution.

Formerly, perhaps, one had at times been thinking, too, in a way, but a certain something was always so quickly encountered. No matter what the starting point: the Hegelian business manager of cosmic reason or the manifestation of smallest changes in the maturing social reconstruction, the synoptic or the causal-genetic method, the individual or the catastrophic approach—even about these preliminary questions there was only indecisive gabble. As far as he was concerned, Rönne would gladly forget it; he did not mind; he was ready to grant everything—but what followed so closely after, this obtrusive insistence on amalgamation, this propensity for results implying such a fatal urge for security, this was what he could no longer share.

Rönne had spent the past year pretty much without impressions. To be sure, after a spring that was no spring and a summer full of excesses, he had sometimes felt somewhat dizzy late in the year, even structurally unsteady. Then an autumn day would dawn over Berlin, a consecration of blue, an illumination of things hidden; he would soak up the light and feel in the back of his neck a kind of minglement, a nearness from far away—and there were odors that relaxed, too, and odors that weakened: southward, of fruit markets, heavy and umbellar.

However, he had spent the past year not only without impressions but completely withdrawn. He regarded public figures as vulgar, ridiculous scum pursuing a fame they paid for and betting on the idiocy of their grandchildren. A tenor's trip to Riga seemed a far-reaching scandal to him. The newspaper jungle rustled, offices got up steam, photographers had a high time, residents of noble and distinctive bearing were involved in such utterly dubious matters as tone scales, creation, and the world once more—ah! The world once more—that was the means whereby the naive and those who bore themselves well were to be brought to their knees. Creativeness: this lack of skepticism, this substitute for a resigned perception of death, this last great fetish in the talons of vultures, waved before cadaver-blue continents! He, Rönne, had a patient in the Latvian city, an engineer, probably employed in some enterprise, whom he had once treated and who had impressed him as a quiet middle-class gentleman. That was *his* relationship with Riga, and to his mind a far cheaper and less equivocal one than the fogginess of those lacquered buffo roaches.

Or a politician's tour of the villages—could there be as much shamelessness anywhere else under one skin? Those eternal "decisive moments" and "world-historic instants," before lunch already, and at the grand opening of a men's room—this communal divination, this latrine demonry—that one cranium could be designed to shield such quantities of cerebral garbage from the influence of the weather! It was a miracle of nature, a true miracle of nature, considering the usual cool reserve of inorganic matter toward the organic hoopla. Something in Rönne was crying for purification. Somewhat voluminously he made for the window: there was snow, the sweet sleep of colors, the deep uninseminability of whiteness—snow and stars, the emptiness of the universe.

Or, if life required conversation with an engineer, principally about progress in Diesel engines or something else with axle and torque—certainly plenty, granted, but what was so urgent about it, after all—improvement, the great motive for sleeping, or elaboration of culture, the great motive for sleeping with? But what was his concern, anyway; those were trains of thought, rather—and Rönne shivered and virtually felt himself shrink. No hallucinatory warmth, no hyperemia; dark was the room, cool the night round the house in the snow. Mutely into the distance he gave one of those unmoving glances, at the eye full of tears, at the dark, wounded countenance of life.

Had anything happened at all since the dawn of the world? He was in the mood to doubt it. Alexander's march, for instance, had that happened? A thousand missiles and the tragedy with the battering-rams—plenty, granted, but here he stood, a little man, middle-class background, not much family and slight effect: did any part of these connections exist for him, carry him, animate his planes, or even those of his patients, the customers of yesterday? What about it, where were they, were they rising anywhere—not a chance, empty, dropped off, literally wiped out—*how should there be an exchange*? Rönne, looking into the night and devoid of flushes, and those traceless nonentities, so-called personalities, spasms of nothingness, whooping-cough of the void—? Life was a matter of hours, full ones and empty ones, that was the whole of psychology. The institutionally construed, recollectively delivered, social personality, the empirical phenotype with the balanced blood pressure, was facing the other: the staccato type about to crack the sphygmometer with acute hyperemia, the expansive type with simultaneous vision, the shifty-eyed hallucinator. Cain and Abel, Klante and Zoroaster, laughable nuances of the same buffoonery—but some day it must be decided, Rönne cried; comprehensive ideas, perspectives of dimensions are coming over me—let's go and conquer the world, march with Alexander by means of flushes: there is the Saracen city, a flake on white rock, with arabesques senselessly pressing; there is the Barbary blood, the Gobi gull, plunging and numbed by a dream.

(1924) *Translated by E. B. Ashton*

PRIMAL VISION

A matchless clarity came over me as I saw I had passed the peak of life. I scanned the day, one of the unpeculiar days in the recurrence of time—early November, slightly chilly, in the street tokens of autumn haphazardly expended by the tepid earth.

I noticed a lightness that moved me. It probably was how things were, myself included, all of us transparent in the cadence of the world. A coming and going, an urging and denying, and, in between, untouchable, the way of existence. The source beyond comprehension, the end a myth, the here and now an evaporating puddle. Far and detached the years of youth, the stormy features, the malady of the great flight. Far and detached that brush and countryside—"we'll go to the woods no more, the laurels have been cut."

From the century when Antiquity was aging comes a strange report. It looked to people in the Roman Empire as if the rivers were becoming shallower and the mountains lower; on the sea one could not see Mount Etna as far away as before, and the same was told of Parnassus and Olympus. The universe as a whole, said the observers of nature, was on the decline. This downward trend in space was what I felt so strongly. Everywhere one saw daylight between the trees, and shouting and screaming were heard where once one had had to listen for any sound. My eyes ranged over the topography, and in curiously plastic fashion space covered me with a nearness from far away.

So it was in the country, when I went on Sunday excursions, and in the city, where my home soared above all else. Above the decade, today, after the war's end; above the forty years since Nietzsche, the starting point of instinctual psychology; above the hundred years since the first gas lamp burned in the city, in the famous year that gave Europe a continental railway net, transatlantic steamers, the telegraph, photography, improved microscopes, and the means of inducing artificial sleep.

Yes, this city—truly not made of dew and bird song, but rather swarming with material bustle—how light and soundless it is in my room! Outside, if anyone noticed, what life and strife, what chaos, what *paradoxa*: Antiquity and experimentation, stages and neuroses, atavisms and ambivalence! Epic bizarrerie of the moment: collectivism, yet even fruit barges incorporate, and roadside stands pay dividends; five proletarians sleep in one bed, but the brace of griffons must resemble madame's face, perfumes come from truffles, and dishes from palm marrow. In the Land of Singers and Sages every fifth grade school pupil is too poor to breakfast before morning classes, but the Dahlem institutes spend millions on a boardinghouse for visiting foreign scientists. The starry skies: moon rockets, missile flights to the stars, and the last horse-drawn cab rolls from Wannsee to Fontainebleau with the family following, bag and baggage, in a dogcart; two waiters, in tails and white tie, walk from Brandenburg to Geneva to lay a wreath before their union memorial; three Hindus approach on a bicycle trip round the world—all surely items worth mentioning, fraught with reality, but in my rooms they became soundless and mute.

Three of these rooms faced the street, a fourth the backyard. A night club opened on the yard; I often listened to its seductive themes. Sometimes music rang out at night when I entered my bedroom. I would open the window, turn off the light, and stand breathing the sound. For long times I would stand gazing into the night that held nothing for me any more, nothing but the dusk of my heart, an aging heart: vague air, graying emotions, you give yourself only to fall a prey—but giving and falling prey were very remote.

Into the other rooms fell the red glow of the city. Not having seen Niniveh on its jasper and ruby foundation, not having seen Rome in the arms of the Antonines, I viewed this, the bearer of the myth that began in Babylon. A mother city, a womb of distant ages, a new thrill by tap dance and injection. What the monastic eras poured into horal books and corollaries, the centuries of rationalism into speculations and cosmogonies, was now throbbing in the movements of chorines: in the murmur of their knee joints they revealed the existential cast of whole series of nations. And the same unknown Something pulsed before me in the city's flesh and stone. It ripped foundlings from the fields and spewed forth community blocks from its bowels; it smeared forests with concrete for a mankind engaged in multiplication. A human mass that had more than doubled its live weight in the past century, was increasing further by twelve million individuals a year, and would put on another hundred per cent in less than a hundred years. Result: giant centers, overpopulation, bread dearer than children's flesh, melons into garbage, potatoes into the flower bed—this was what the world was coming to, far beyond me and my time, beyond my rooms and this hour of standing in the November night, in the silence facing the red glow.

After years of struggling for knowledge and ultimate things, I finally had come to realize that there may be no such ultimate things. In part, this discovery was due to my encounter with an elderly gentleman who had convivially accosted me one evening— a fellow townsman of mine, an ear specialist with his own hospital, and a medical colonel in the Bavarian army, as he pointed out in his first sentences. He talked about mutual acquaintances, some young men who had often been at his father's house—drones, good-for-nothings, pen-pushers, sots—all long since gone and forgotten. Years ago he had met one of them again and would, he said, have helped him to a newspaper job, if the fellow had kept the appointment instead of appearing at his home several days late, totally inebriated. The ear specialist "had him shown out," as he put it, and after a few more weeks the man had succumbed in delirium.

Thus the medical colonel awakened the past and was, indeed, the dead man's superior in living standards, attire, scope of activities; he surpassed him considerably in resonance, hospital ownership, and military rank; in fact, he eclipsed everything about him—but did this mean that the friend of his youth had died wholly unfinished, useless, without a symbol? Did the course of his life not even suggest the enormity of life, its immense urges and intoxications, its indifference to individualities, its carnal disintegration? He, too, after initial years of surely angelic purity, had gone down in this rhythm; did the one before me cut a wider swath, did the ear clinic serve him as a vehicle of more mysterious experience? I wavered, could not bring myself to say yes. Life, having been fully operative on the deceased, must have marked even this human form, however far beneath the medical colonel. At the moment, to be sure, I could not tell the mark.

An idea took shape in me: it was the unity of life that I saw here, to be defended from attack. Life seeks to preserve itself, but life seeks also to perish—more and more clearly I perceived this chthonic force. When I thought of the animal kingdom, of the genus, of the origin and death of species, it was true that inundating oceans had carried off whole racial segments in short order, geologically speaking, and that volcanic eruptions had smothered great animal communities under a downpour of ashes; but the actual extinction of species, the passing of biological forms, had never been caused by these geological incidents. The extinction of species, as well as the spontaneous emergence of new ones at the same time, impressed me more and more as a paleontological fact due to a single underlying cause. Thus butterflies and other honey-sucking types appeared at the same time in the Earth's history as flowering plants, certain sea urchins and crustaceans appeared along with the reef-building corals they would live in symbiosis with—and their eventual simultaneous disappearance was unrelated to elemental events, not visibly connected with environmental changes, baffling explanation, to be interpreted only as a phenomenon from within. It seemed to express a fading formal tension, an aging, a decrease in numbers and living space on the one side, and an unfolding presence on the other; there seemed to be a polarity of the formative drive, an inner tension between formal features. In scales, balanced by gods, existence seemed to rest: now there was more water around, now more land, here a coral, there a bivalve in repose at the base, rising and falling about the figure of man who exuded animals and split off plants—he, inescapably subject to forces of further creation, of the scalebearers, and of their distance. To these, then, the late inebriate would also have succumbed, and in great associations his series of forms sank into a premature grave.

A trivial occasion, a purely personally motivated line of thought —yet the experience induced me to take a closer look at my companion, this gentleman at the peak of his era, the leader of broad strata, the carrier of the positive idea, the causal-genetic thinker. I saw him before me with his instruments, his otoscope, his pincers, germ-free and nickel-plated—way behind him lay the Moorish epoch, the age of the herniotomists and lithotomists, the Galenic darkness, the mysticism of the mandrake. I envisioned his hospital, spick and span, a very different thing from the herb gardens and distilleries of the medieval urine watchers. Tangibly his sonorous and voluminous voice enveloped me in its suggestive and hypnotic charm, completely dislodging the memory of those spells and incantations of the Cimbrian priestesses I had been reading about, who practiced their so-called healing art in white linen garments girt with a bronze belt. Only when I reflected how long mankind had survived just the same, although till recently obstetrics had been carried on underneath the clothes, in secretive obscurity —when I considered how long it had survived despite all plagues and leprosies, despite epidemics, worms, and the bacteria which our representative had· only for a relatively short time risen to combat effectively—then my thoughts might veer in the direction of that striking hypothesis advanced by the latest American race researchers, to the effect that for a majority of men the time of death must be regarded as hereditarily determined. They have calculated, in fact, that disease has no decisive influence on the life span of some eighty per cent of mankind; it is heredity, they hold, that contains the factor for this part of individual fate as well. And when I found additional support for this hypothesis in some statistical oddities: that in England, for example, which I had studied, the ideal life span calculated by modern science (equal to the mortality norm, that standard figure checked every five years over a century, in 276 districts) had been established early in the nineteeth century—i.e., long before the so-called victorious advance of modern biology—then it could happen, in considering the ear specialist and his pincers and, more generally, the relationship between disease and man, that I was unable to keep the druids' rune-covered staffs and the sacrifices offered in our forefathers' holy places from intruding upon my reflections.

In any event, here he was standing before me, the biologist, the germ-layer Marxist, the aniline exporter, the man of interest-bearing science, who rose as a lamb and spoke as a dragon. The age of Bacon, the mankind of thought, the cast-iron century, no longer carving gods but smelting devils: four hundred million individuals jampacked on a tiny continent, twenty-five nationalities, thirty languages, seventy-five dialects, international and intra-national tensions of extirpative vehemence. Here, a fight to boost wages half a cent an hour; there, the Carlton Club golf tournament in flower-bedecked Cannes, princes in the gutter, tramps as dictators, orgies of vertical trusts, fever of profits: to exploit the continent's limited resources economically, i.e. at a premium.

Dissolution of the classic systems from the Urals to Gibraltar. Ultracapitalism: earthquake in Southern Europe means a high time for builders and interior decorators; iron and steel salesmen are blessed from Mount Athos before go-getting in the Maritza valley. On the front page we weep for the victims, and in back come the black-bordered profit statements. For editorials we have human frailty, and for the business section, geological thrust folds and the economically sound motion of the Earth. And socialism: well-regulated food supply, immortality of the body, salubrious survival —the Hesperidian dream of trade union health insurance.

And on the other side stood the great country with the legend from Philadelphia, the man whose skull was bashed in with a piece of lead pipe because he wore a straw hat on May 14. St. Aloysius of the Delaware, the virginal martyr who would wear a straw hat out of season.—Who had more money in the bank at thirty: Dempsey or Hölderlin?—"Where are the prominent citizens of New Salem?" Lincoln asked when he came to the town. Answer: "New Salem has no prominent citizens; everyone here is a prominent citizen." And there they stood, honest confessors of democratic equality from ice cream to the cut of their pants.

Standard idols, dance-drilled wraiths, staple products. Rites under klieg-lights, Communion with jazz, Gethsemane: the record in ecstasy. Christ—the successful entrepreneur, social lion, advertising genius, and founder of modern business life, who knew how to save the situation at the marriage in Cana with cheap Jordanian rotgut; the born manager, who could invite the rich Nicodemus to dinner even at a time when New Religion was not in demand. For the dollar was agreeable to God, and land-holding as such a moral asset; therefore, Bible lessons to keep the boom going, and the Pentateuch against the soil fixers. The keep-smiling prophet of the New World shaking hands across the Atlantic with the aniline metaphysician of the Old, like code cables concerning oil shares and gasoline exegesis. Knock-out Mid-Europe—the new type whose birthmarks dot the globe: the new suspension bridge from Manhattan to Fort Lee, to be completed in 1932, 3,500 feet long, held up by four cables, each three feet in diameter, a thickness never achieved before; on the Brooklyn Bridge, built 1888, the cables are only sixteen inches thick—a difference of twenty! By flight and fire the new type compresses the zeniths; he surmounts time and space—a strange time, a strange space—with conveyor-belt categories and piece-work concepts; he *improves* time and space, the primal visions.

This, my century! Were it my century—ah, it was the eon; it was history, the tribe, Aurignac, the growth in darkness, the unbridled license of the night of creation. Once it was the green luxuriance of the anthracite forest, once the vertebrates' conquering drive into prehistoric seas, once this race, come from the glacier rims of

Asia, with shrouded memory, restless, shortening the very periods of the Earth.

Some mass lay in concealment, and something made it realize a compulsion. Age-old urges! The strongholds of diluvial industry in France and Austria, right next to the modern ones at Creusot and the Skoda Works—exquisite skill! The laurel leaf tips of Solutrian culture—the acme of stone work technology! In the warm mid-interglacial period the beauty of Willendorf—primary style impulse, indigenous constructivism. Excavations in the loess of Central Europe have yielded twenty-five thousand artifacts, beside the remains of nine hundred mammoths. The passage of Magdalenian man from stone-hewing to bone work marked the dawn of a new era; the silver lining was the Quarternary hunter with the horn harpoon.

Stimulus and repression. Today's technology, yesterday's mechanics. The first pirogue had greater sociological consequences than the submarine and the airplane; the first arrow was deadlier than poison gas. The people of Antiquity knew W.C.'s as well as elevators, pulleys, clocks, flying machines, automatons; they had a monomania about tunnels, passages, conduits, aqueducts—termites subject to space neuroses, grip compulsions.

Mass in instincts. Brain bubbles into the sink, germ layers into the flower bed, yolk sacs in the thrust of distance. Heritage of exaltation and intoxications, astral conflagration, transoceanic decay. Crises, mixtures, third century: Baal with the lightning and scourge of the Roman god, Phrygian hoods along the Tiber, Aphrodite on Mount Lebanon—realities in balance, tides in transformation.

Age-old drives of ageless masses in the sound of oceans and in the plunge of light. Life seeks to preserve itself, but life seeks also to perish; urge and denial—games of night. Lost is the individual; down with the ego. Through an indifference of high degree, through a fatigue born of character, a somnolence born of conviction—ah, work: a phantom for the shrunken; greatness: a spectacle for oglers, râles for gold dentures—via science, the commonplace method of veiling facts, and religion, the invective one—dithyrambics of youth, down, down!

I saw the ego, the look in its eyes. I dilated its pupil, looked far into it, looked far out of it; the gaze from such eyes is almost expressionless, more like scenting, scenting danger, an age-old danger. From disasters that were latent, disasters that antedated the word, come dreadful memories of the race, hybrid, beast-shaped, sphinx-pouched features of the primal face. I recalled the dicta of certain profoundly experienced men, that evil would come of their telling all they knew. I thought of the strange adages, that one should give up searching for the ultimate words that need only be spoken to unhinge heaven and earth. I sniffed in masks, I rattled in runes, I dove into demons with sleep-craving brutality, with mythical instincts, in the anteverbal, instinctual threat of prehistoric neura; I began to grasp, I saw the vision: monism in rhythms, mass in intoxications, compulsion and repression, Ananke of the I.

A matchless clarity came over me as, in a way, I saw life conquered. "For this the fleet of a thousand ships?" I asked, like the dialogues of the dead in the late Roman era. In the nether world, bleaching before the observer, lay the bones of celebrated shades, the jaw of Narcissus and the pelvis of Helen—for this the fleet of a thousand ships, the untold deaths, the ruined cities? For this the heroes, the founders, the sons of gods, Tuisko and Mannus, and the songs men sang to them? None had left more than an outline and a breath. Life was a deadly and unknown law; today as ever, man could do no more than accept his own without tears. Once it was the green luxuriance of the anthracite forest, once the vertebrates' conquering drive into prehistoric seas—recurrence was all.

Recurrence, and this hour of the night. I stood and listened. For a long time I stood breathing the sound. Life sought to preserve itself, but life sought also to perish—long rhythms, long sound. Long was the breath of the night; in play it could gather and scatter. It gave, it streamed, hesitated, drew back. The gods were merely silent. Daphne quivered in the laurel, and by the sea of Amphitrite the hermes slumbered.

And above all: languor and dream. Something, we knew not what, stirred the logs: home fire, early coffins, chairs of old men to and fro. Age-old change, dusk and poppy, to the stairs, downward the purl of remote waters.

(1929) Translated by E. B. Ashton

THE NEW LITERARY SEASON

Behind the purely seasonal literature which will capture the market this winter, there is also a genuine literary and intellectual war at hand. There is a problem which especially concerns the serious younger literature, and will doubtless concern it more than ever this coming winter, in view of the state of affairs today. If we try to formulate this problem briefly, it can be said to consist in the contrast between pure and collectivistic art. The question at stake is the following: in view of today's social and economic conditions, has man any right to feel and describe his own individual problems, or should there be only collective problems? Is the writer justified in taking his individuality as a starting point and giving it expression? Can he still expect his individuality to be taken seriously, or is he entirely reduced to his collective status, only worthy of attention or interest as a social being? Do all his inner difficulties become solved, or should they be solved, as soon as he helps in the construction of the social collectivity?

This circle of problems was discussed in a very shrewd and polemically fascinating lecture given this spring by the Russian writer Tretyakov, a lecture which was attended by the entire literary world of Berlin. Tretyakov, who is also known here as a playwright, is, as regards his exterior and the manner of his descriptions, a literary Tcheka type—one who examines, judges, and sentences all unbelievers in Russia. It is worth while to scrutinize this burning question, which is so exciting for the young German writers of today. Tretyakov describes how in Russia, during the first two years of the Five-Year-Plan, there still appeared a few

This translation of an essay originally published in *Die Weltbühne* appeared in *transition*, 1932, as Benn's contribution to a symposium on "The Crisis of Man."

psychological novels, against which the Writers' Soviet took preventive measures. To give an example, one novel showed how, in a house which had been expropriated from a bourgeois and subsequently requisitioned for a higher Soviet official, the latter began to drink, neglected his duties, deteriorated, so that, finally, the former owner of the house reoccupied his rooms. This was described in a western psychological manner in the usual novel form, somewhat imaginatively and entirely unpolitically. Tretyakov ordered the author to appear before him. "Where did you experience this, Comrade?" he asked him. "In which city and in which street?" "I didn't experience it at all," answered the author, "it is just a novel." "Never mind," answered Tretyakov, "you have taken this from a reality that exists somewhere. Why didn't you report to the proper Soviet authorities that one of the officials, as a result of drunkenness, was carrying out his duties improperly, and that the bourgeois owner of the house had been reinstalled?" Again the author answered, "But I didn't see this in reality, I made this up, I just wrote a novel." Tretyakov: "Those are Western European, individual idiocies. You have acted in an irresponsible manner, with vanity, and as counter-revolutionary. The plates of your book will be destroyed, and you will march to the factory." In this way, according to Tretyakov, all individual-psychological literature has been abolished in Russia, every belletristic attempt has been disposed of as ridiculous and bourgeois, the writer as a professional has disappeared, he works like everybody else in the factory, he helps in the social construction and the Five-Year-Plan. And an entirely new type of literature is about to begin. Tretyakov brought a few examples along and exhibited them with great pride. They were books, or rather copybooks, each written by a dozen factory workers, under the direction of a former writer. Their titles, for instance, were: ESTABLISHMENT OF A FRUIT PLANTATION NEAR A FACTORY; further, HOW TO AIR THE DINING ROOM IN A FACTORY; something particularly important, written by several foremen, HOW TO GET RAW MATERIALS MORE QUICKLY TO THE LABOR CENTERS. This, then, is the new

Russian literature, the new collective literature, the literature of the Five-Year-Plan. German writers sat at Tretyakov's feet, and applauded enthusiastically. Tretyakov probably enjoyed this applause, perhaps he was also amused by it, this clever Russian who, of course, knew very well that he was developing here a propagandistic fragment for the new Russian Imperialism, while his simpleminded German colleagues accepted it as absolute truth. As what truth, I ask myself now? What psychology, I ask myself, is behind this Russian theory which finds so many disciples in Germany?

This Russian art theory, once you have studied it carefully, avers nothing more or less than that everything that exists in Occidental man as far as his inner life is concerned, in other words our crises, tragedies, our scission, our impulses, our enjoyment, is purely and simply a phenomenon of capitalistic decay, a capitalistic trick. And the artist moved by vanity and desire for glory, yea, Tretyakov added, with a truly infantile ignorance of conditions, especially by greed for money, works these "individual idiocies," as he called them, into his books and plays. According to Tretyakov's theory, however, as soon as man awakens to the Russian Revolution, all this falls from him, like the dew before the sun, and there stands before us the joyous collective being, wretched maybe, but clean and normal, without daemon or instinct, eager at last to be allowed to cooperate in social reconstruction, in the factory, especially in the strengthening of the Red Army, his chest swelling with joy. Into the dust with all enemies not only of Brandenburg but of Moscow!

I ask now, is this psychologically probable, or is it primitive? Is man, in the last analysis of his essence, rooted in a naturalistic, materialistic, economic condition, determined in his structure by hunger and clothes? Or is he the great involuntary being, as Goethe said, the invisible, the incalculable? Is he indissoluble despite all social and psychological analyses, does he also go through this epoch of materialistic philosophy and atomic biology on his destined way, closely bound to the earth and yet above the earth?

I read recently the following sentence, by one of the leaders of the young German literature: "We loathe the eternally human." Since he said "we," he spoke, probably, in the name of a group of similarly-minded people, perhaps in the name of the new German literature. He continued: "we" are for realities. "Let us organize life," he expounded, "let us leave the tragic problems to the 'profound' writers. So far as we are concerned, we want to live." This, I assume, is the Tretyakov group in Berlin, and it is against this group that I must maintain the thesis, oldfashioned and Western, that man is not changed in a fundamental way by the organization of his food and living conditions. By *fundamentally* I mean that he is not changed substantially in hereditary form or disposition. Even he who, not less radically than the official social writers, feels the destructive and almost incomprehensible character of our economic system, cannot, in my opinion, fail to recognize that in all economic systems man remains the tragic being, the divided ego, whose abysses cannot be filled with bread and woolen vests, whose dissonances cannot be dissolved in the rhythms of the *Internationale*. He remains the suffering being, he who wore hair shirts for hundreds of thousands of years, during which he struggled not less deeply and sorrowfully for his humanity than today in buckskin and cheviot. Even if we could extinguish the entire epoch of individualism, the entire history of the soul from Hellenic days to Expressionism, one experience would remain, opposite to the inner spatial void of this Tretyakov idea. It would remain a great truth through all epochs and all seasons, that he who would organize life will never create art, nor can he consider himself as belonging to art. To create art, whether it be Egyptian falcons or the novels of Hamsun, means from the standpoint of the artist to exclude life, to narrow it down, yes, to combat it, in order to give it style. And I would add something else, something historic, since its knowledge is obviously so lacking in those circles. The struggle against art did not start in Russia, nor in Berlin. It runs from Plato to Tolstoy. It always proceeded from the middle forces to the outside, but also from the artist against the higher ones. All the struggles with which today's season begins, everything the Tretyakov people say against the "profound" writers, was written a hundred years ago by Börne against Heine, by Heine against Goethe. Goethe: "The genius that rejected the age," as Heine called him. Goethe: "The stabilization fool," as Börne wrote of him. Goethe, the enemy of progress; Goethe, the lazy heart that never had a wretched little word for his people; Goethe, who asked a visitor on August 2, 1831, what he thought of the mighty event of the time—everything, he said, was in fermentation; the visitor answered with declarations about the July Revolution, which everybody was following with bated breath, whereupon Goethe turned aside, indignant and uninterested, for he had had in mind the scientific fight concerning the evolutionary theory. That was Goethe, the man of moderation, of self-protection, in other words, the man of Art, whom they blamed for not being the man of the *stammtisch*. Nor did Heine fare any better. Heine fights with flowers, writes Börne. He does not care whether he describes monarchy or republic as the better form of government, he will always choose that which, in the sentence he has just written, has the better rhythm. Heine of the esthetic titillation who asked eternally the same question, "But is it beautifully expressed?" Heine, who fought shy of tobacco smoke, of public meetings, of the sweaty odor of the subscription lists; Heine, who was then the enemy, the "profound writer," and Börne the Tretyakov disciple, the young man who loathes the eternally human. And a hundred years hence, when someone will stand in front of a Hertz-wave apparatus and speak as I am doing about the coming literary season, it will probably be the same thing again. But perhaps he will then ask a question about our season. Perhaps he will ask where, at that critical time, was there one among the young literary generation who did not proceed with theories and talk, but with substances and works? Where was the brain which absorbed all these moods, possibilities, convulsions, travails, and did not report in chitchat and feuilletons, but witnessed his time through his existence, creatively? Where was that one who did not always follow the crowd, but was aware that whoever runs with the time will be run over by it, that whoever stands still, to him will things come? Perhaps he will see somebody. I do not see him now. Indeed, his would have to be an exceptional character and brain, in view of the great force necessary for the abandonment of everything existing in our public life. He would have to abandon not only the author's fee and the admiration of literary people and the preparations for the "season," but would have to endure long silence, long waiting and looking beyond and above all places of ancient play and dream. Salzburg, Vienna, Kurfürstendamm, the entire diversion, amusement, impressionism of the eroticized profiteers of the last fifty years would have to be denied by him. Yes, however sad it may be to say the word, however much the world hesitates to do so, however much he might fear to be misunderstood, he would also have to abandon Paris. It can never be forgotten, we can never be grateful enough for the memory: the truly great Occidental attitude of Latinity which France developed and handed down to us in her finest dialectical work; the only autonomous intellectual space into which Europe has gazed since Hellenic days—Nietzsche and the literary generation of 1900 have saved it for us as an incomparable possession forever. But we have gone further, burrowed deeper into ourselves, conjured more out of ourselves and for ourselves, than to allow ourselves to borrow our expression from the traditionally bound form of the classical, pseudo-antique spirit. This great intelligence would have to go further, quite distinctly towards the new world feeling which is now announcing itself: man no longer the sturdy ape of the Darwinian era, but originally and primarily disposed in his elements as a metaphysical being; not the breeding steer, not the triumphant man, but he who was, from the beginning, the tragic man, yet always more powerful than the animals, and the cultivator of nature.

Out of this new sense of humanity the coming season will be made, but perhaps not this winter, and, as far as I can see, not in "literary" literature. But science takes our gaze ever farther back, to human races that lived on earth millions of years ago, races that at one time resembled the fish, at another the marsupials, and later the simians, but always remained the human being—creating dwelling-places, creating tools, creating gods, creating agelong cultural relationships which again vanished in catastrophe beneath heavens as yet unstarred and moonless. I believe that from this viewpoint, and not from the flim-flam of *littérateurs* or from social theories, the new sense of humanity will develop, and the psychological and intellectual individualism of our time will be demolished.

The age-old, eternal man! The human race! Immortal within a creative system which is itself infinitely subject to mutations and expansions. What an endless epic! Luna, flooding bush and valley, is the fourth moon which we see. Not evolution but perpetuity will be the sense of humanity in the coming century. Let us wait quietly for it to approach—we shall probably find it outside of the Literary Season.

(1931) *Translated by Eugene Jolas*

ANSWER TO THE LITERARY
EMIGRANTS

You are writing to me from the neighborhood of Marseille. In the little resorts along the Gulf of Lyons, in the hotels of Zurich, Prague, and Paris—you write—the young Germans who once admired me and my books are now sitting as refugees; from the papers you have to see that I hold myself at the disposal of the new state, that I defend it in public, and that as an Academy member I do not eschew its cultural plans. You call me to account, as a friend, but very sharply. You write: "What could induce you to make your name, which to us has been the epitome of high standards and of an all but fanatical purity, available to those to whom this very rank is denied by all the rest of Europe? What friends will you gain in exchange for the old ones you lose? Who will understand you there? You will remain the intellectual—that is, the suspect— and no one will welcome you." You call me to account, warn me, demand an unequivocal reply: "He who does not declare for us in this hour, will henceforth and forever cease to belong to us." So hear my reply, please, which must, of course, be unequivocal.

First, I have to tell you that many experiences in the past weeks have convinced me that German events can be discussed only with those who have witnessed them in Germany. Only those who have passed through the tensions of these months, who have experienced them continuously at close range, from hour to hour, from news item to news item, from parade to parade, from radio broadcast to radio broadcast—even those who did not jubilantly hail all this, but suffered it rather—all those can be talked with, but the refugees who went abroad cannot. For they have missed the opportunity to feel the concept of "the people"—a concept so alien to them—grow within themselves, not as a thought but as a living experience, not as an abstraction but as condensed nature. They have missed their chance to perceive the concept of nationalism—which your letter, too, employs so derogatorily and scornfully—in its true motion, as a genuine, convincingly expressed phenomenon; they have missed seeing history, form-laden, image-laden, at its conceivably tragic but surely fated work. And here I do not mean the spectacular side of events, the impressionistic fascination of torchlight and music, but the inner process, the creative impact that tended to cause a goading, human transformation even in the initially restive observer.

For this reason alone we shall hardly understand each other. But understanding founders also on another problem—for years a theoretical issue between your group and me—which has suddenly become so bluntly acute as to demand from everyone a direct, outspoken decision. Our best approach to it will be to consider the word "barbarism," repeatedly used in your letter and also in others that have come to me. You put it as if what happens in Germany now were threatening culture, threatening civilization, as if a horde of savages were menacing the ideals of mankind as such. But let me ask you in turn: how do you visualize the movement of history? Do you regard it as particularly active at French bathing beaches? How, for example, do you envision the twelfth century, the passage from the Romanesque to the Gothic way of life—do you think that was *discussed*? Do you think that in the north of the country from whose southern part you are writing, somebody *thought up* a new architectural style? That people *voted* on round or pointed arches, *argued* about apses, whether round or polygonal? I think you would get farther if you discarded this novelistic notion of history and viewed it more as elemental and impulsive, an inescapable phenomenon; I think you would come closer to the German events if you stopped looking at history as the bank statement rendered to creation by your bourgeois nineteenth-century brain—oh, it owes you nothing, but you owe it everything; it knows neither your democracy nor your perhaps laboriously maintained rationalism; it has no method, no style, other than at its turning points to emit, from the inexhaustible womb of the race, a new human type that has to fight its way, has to work the idea of its generation and its kind into the texture of time, unwavering, acting and suffering as the law of life commands. Of course, this view of history is not enlightened and not humanistic. It is metaphysical, and even more so is my view of man. And there we have come to the core of our old dispute—when you accuse me of fighting for irrationalism.

Your letter puts it this way: "First one professes irrationalism, then barbarism, and already one stands with Adolf Hitler." This you write at the moment when your opportunistic progressive concept of man has gone bankrupt far and wide, for all to see; when it is obvious that it was a vapid, frivolous, pleasure-seeking concept, that no truly great epoch of human history has ever interpreted the human essence otherwise than irrationally—for *irrational* means close to creation, and capable of creation. Will you not finally realize, on your Latin shore, that the events in Germany are not political tricks, to be twisted and talked to death in the well-known dialectical manner, but are the emergence of a new biological type, a mutation of history and a people's wish to breed itself? True, the view of man beneath this breeding idea considers him, though rational, primarily as mythical and deep. True, his future is contemplated in terms of grafting way down at the trunk—for man is older than the French Revolution and more stratified than the Enlightenment believed. True, he is felt largely as nature, as proximity to creation—after all, we are witnessing his being far less free, far more painfully bound to existence, than it would have seemed from the no more than 2000-year-old antithesis of idea and reality. In fact, he is eternal Quaternary, a horde magic feuilletonistically decking even the late Ice Age, a fabric of diluvial moods, Tertiary bric-à-brac; in fact, he is the eternally primal vision: wakefulness, day life, reality—loosely consolidated rhythms of hidden creative intoxications. Will you amateurs of civilization, you troubadours of Western progress not realize, at last, that what is here at stake is not forms of government but a new vision of the birth of man—perhaps an old, perhaps the last grand concept of the white race, probably one of the grandest realizations of the cosmic spirit itself, preluded in Goethe's hymn *To Nature?* And will you absorb this, too: no success, no military or industrial result, will decide about this vision—if ten wars should be unleashed from East and West to crush this German mankind, if the Apocalypse approached by land and sea to break its seal, we should still have this vision of man; and he who wants to realize it must breed it; and your philological inquiry into civilization and barbarism becomes absurd before so much legitimate historic existence.

But let us leave philosophy and turn to politics, let us depart from the vision and face the facts of experience. So you sit at your beaches and call us to account for our cooperation in building a state whose faith is singular, whose seriousness is stirring, whose internal and external situation is so grave that it would take Iliads and Aeneids to tell its fate. Before all foreign countries you wish war, destruction, collapse, downfall to this state and its people. It is the nation whose language you speak, whose schools you attended, to whose cultivation of science and art you owe all your intellectual property, whose industry printed your books, whose stages presented your plays, which gave you fame and reputation, by whose members you wished to be read in the greatest possible number, and which would not have done you much harm even now, had you stayed. So you cast a glance on the sea that stretches toward Africa—perhaps a battleship happens to cruise on it with Negro troops from those 600,000 colonial soldiers of the notorious French *forces d'outremer* that are to be committed against Germany; others may look upon the Arch of Triumph or Hradcany Castle as they vow vengeance to this country that has no political aims but to safeguard its future, and which the bulk of them, spiritually, have only exploited.

You write in your letter that you have become a "true Marxist" only now, but now wholly *—that no charge of "vulgar Marxism"

Klaus Mann, an outspoken anti-Marxist, wrote the very opposite: "How well I always understood your indignation at the 'Marxist' type of German literati—how often I shared it! What wicked stupidity of these gentlemen ... to test a poet's work for its sociological content! That was perfectly sickening, and no one suffered more than I did at or "materialism" can still keep you from fighting our "hysterical brutality"—that you are on the side of "the spirit" and going to war against "political reaction." I do not quite know what you really mean by these words, which sound to me as from another geological age; I might ask you, also, whether you spoke of hysterical brutality when the state in which your Marxism won out killed off 2,000,000 of its bourgeois intelligentsia. But I will assume that you mean socialism, and, indeed, in the past years the rights of German labor have often been defended by the foremost German intellectuals now living abroad—most sincerely, visibly, and repeatedly by Thomas Mann. To these, I would say that the German worker is better off now than before. You know that as a doctor I am in touch with many circles, as a social insurance practitioner with many workers, including former Communists and Social Democrats. There is no doubt—since I hear it from every one of them—that they are better off than before. They get better treatment in their shops; the supervisors are more cautious, the personnel chiefs more courteous; the workers have more power, are more respected, work in a better mood, a citizen's mood, and what they never obtained from the socialist party has been given them by this new national form of socialism: a motivating sense of life. Be sure, too, that the conquest of labor by the new power will go on, for the German national community is no chimera, and the First of May was no capitalist trick in disguise. It was most impressive, it was genuine: labor had suddenly shed the stigma of a yoke, the punitive character of proletarian suffering that it bore in the past decades; instead, it stood as the base of a newly forming, class-dissolving community. No one who saw it can doubt that this year of 1933 has put a new, definite face on a lot of the socialisms that have been in the European air for decades. This year has newly proclaimed a part of the Rights of Man, and in case your term "political reaction"

the hands of these characters. . . ." Only, Klaus Mann considered this no reason to embrace Nazism: "I know my place now as clearly as never before. No Marxist vulgarity can irritate me any longer. For I know I need be no obtuse 'materialist' to want what is rational, and to hate hysterical brutality with all my heart."—Ed.

means that you wish to fight for the rights of labor, you would have to join the new state, not to disparage it.

Lastly, however, you also address my own person. You ask me questions, warning, searching questions about the peculiarity of my radical sense of language that would earn me nothing but jeers and sneers on the other side, and about my reverence for certain literary figures who are now on *your* side. My answer is this: I shall go on revering what I have found exemplary and educational for German letters; I shall revere it even in Lugano and at the Ligurian Sea—but I personally declare for the new state, because it is my people whose trail is being blazed here. Who am I to exclude myself? Do I know better? No. I can try to guide it, as far as lies in my power, in the direction I should like to see followed; but if I failed, it would still be my people. People means much! My intellectual and economic existence, my language, my life, my human relations, the sum total of my brain—all this I owe to my people. From the people come our forebears; to the people our children return. And as I grew up in the country, with the herds, I still know what "homeland" means. Big city, industrialization, intellectualism, all the shadows cast on my thoughts by the age, all the powers of the century I met in my work—there are moments when this tortured life fades away and nothing remains but the wide plain, the seasons, the earth, simple words—: the people. This is how I came to put myself at the service of those to whom, as you say, Europe denies all rank. This Europe! It may have values—but where it cannot bribe and shoot it does look pitiful! Now it whispers in your ear that the people are not behind Hitler—only his "sheep," as Lady Oxford just wrote in the *News Chronicle*. A great mistake! It is the people. Just compare the two great minds, Hitler and Napoleon. Napoleon was surely the outstanding individual genius. Nothing drove the French as a people to conquer the Pyramids and cover Europe with their armies; they were driven by that immense military genius alone. But here, today, you hear the question time and again: did Hitler **create** the movement, or did the movement create him? The question is significant, for it shows that the two cannot be distinguished. They are identical. Here we really find that magical coincidence of individual and generality which Burckhardt, in his *World-historical Observations*, ascribes to the great men of the world's historic course. The great men—it is all there: the perils of the beginning; the appearance, almost always only in terrible times; the tremendous endurance; the abnormal facility of all functions, notably including the organic ones; but also the impression of all thinking persons that here is the one to accomplish what is necessary and yet possible to him alone. Note that I said: all thinking persons—and you know I place thought above all. "It is a great and creditable obstinacy to refuse ideological consent to anything not justified by thought"—with this word of Hegel's I have always tested my political emotions. Believe me, therefore, and do not deceive yourself, whatever Europe may whisper to you: standing behind this movement, loving peace, willing to work, but also ready to perish, if need be, is the whole people.

I close with something which you abroad, if you read this, will certainly want to know about: I am not in the Party, have no contact with its leaders, and do not count on new friends. It is my fanatical purity, which your letter honors me by mentioning, my purity of feeling and thought, that determines my attitude. Its foundations are the ones you find in all thinkers of history. One said, "World history is not the soil of happiness" (Fichte); another, "Nations must bring certain great living traits to the fore, regardless of individual happiness or the greatest possible collective happiness" (Burckhardt); a third, "Man's increasing diminution is the very force that makes him think of breeding a stronger race." And: "A masterly race can grow only from terrible and violent beginnings. Problem: where are the barbarians of the twentieth century" (Nietzsche). The liberal and individualistic era had completely forgotten all this; nor was it intellectually capable of accepting it as a demand and envisioning its political consequences. But suddenly dangers arise, suddenly the community tightens, and everyone, the man of letters included, must stand up and choose:

private hobby, or direction toward the state. I choose the latter, and I must accept it for this state if you, from your shore, bid me farewell.

(1933) *Translated by E. B. Ashton*

EXCERPTS FROM
THE WAY OF AN INTELLECTUALIST
RÖNNE

In war and peace, at the front and behind it, as an officer and as a doctor, among generals and profiteers, before rubber and jail cells, over beds and coffins, in triumph and decay, I never lost the trance-like feeling that this reality did not exist. A kind of inner concentration began, a stirring of secret spheres; and individuality faded, and a primal stratum emerged, intoxicated, image-laden, Panic. The times reinforced it: the year 1915-16 in Brussels was enormity. There *Rönne* was born, the physician, the flagellant of individual phenomena, the naked vacuum of facts—the man who could bear no reality, nor grasp any; who knew only the rhythmic opening and closing of the ego and the personality, the continual disruption of inner existence; and who, confronted with the experience of the deep, unbounded, mythically ancient strangeness between man and the world, believed completely in the myth and its images.

Benn published *The Way of an Intellectualist* in the spring of 1934, one year after Hitler came to power. The first chapter traced his family tree, to defend his "Aryanism" against suspicions of "racial impurity." The second attempted an explanation and ideological vindication of his previous writings, the poems of two decades and the two main characters of his prose: Rönne, the self-portrait, and Pameelen, the "measurement conductor" whose brain reflects "disintegration of the epoch ... cortical wilting of worlds, the bourgeois, capitalistic, opportunistic, prophylactic, antiseptic worlds knocked out by the cloudbursts of politics"—yet whose "basic feeling for anthropological redemption by form" inaugurates "the new epoch, the new necessity ... the world of expression." The third chapter dealt with the concepts of "art" and "intellectualism"; in the fourth Benn addressed "the new youth that has lined up under Hitler's star"; and the fifth (THE DOCTRINE - s. p. 60) summed up his personal creed. The 1934 volume was soon out of print, and in 1950 Benn republished *The Way of an Intellectualist* as Part One of *Double Life*—thus in effect combining his pro-Nazi and anti-Nazi apologias.

"I meant to conquer the city, now a palm leaf caresses me"—thus Rönne sums up his experiences. He could not conquer the city; his situation forbade it. Instead, "he burrowed into moss: at the stem, water-fed, my brow—a hand's breadth, and then it starts. Soon after, a bell rang. The gardeners went to work: then he, too, strode to a can and poured water over the ferns which came out of a sun where much evaporated." In other words, vegetabilia after central destruction.

"Rönne wanted to go to Antwerp, but how, without corrosion? He could not come to lunch. He had to say he could not come to lunch today; he was going to Antwerp. To Antwerp, the listener would be wondering? Contemplation? Reception? Perambulation? That seemed unthinkable to him. It purported enrichment and construction of the soul."

Enrichment and construction of the soul—that was what the old world was doing roundabout, unmoved by the far-reaching collapse of the times that enfeebled Rönne. The old world was still sitting in the officers' mess, eating—as we shall soon see—of a tropical fruit, and waging wars, but he could no longer take part in it. In an age of rockets casually refueling on stars, of Cook's paving the jungle for guided tours, of polar distance shrinking to short-haul rates and dowagers competing in Himalayan excursions, Rönne's travel urge met with an inner resistance.

In the following I have to quote a longer passage from the Rönne stories, though at this moment their implications are somewhat disreputable and bizarre. I must do it to be truthful, and to proceed from Rönne's type to certain historical and epistemological conclusions.

So Rönne wants to go to Antwerp, and "now he saw himself sitting in the train and suddenly recalling how his absence would presently be discussed at the luncheon table—off-hand only, in reply to an incidental question, but still to the effect that he, on his part, was seeking relations with the city, with the Middle Ages and the quays of the Scheldt.

"He felt stunned, breaking out in a sweat. A curvature befell him as he perceived his indefinite, still incalculable, in any case so trivial and meager actions comprehended in the terms of a gentleman's life.

"A rainstorm of inhibitions and weakness burst upon him. For where was assurance that he would be able to tell, bring back, enliven anything about the trip at all, that he would receive anything in the sense of experience?

"Great asperities—like the railroad, being seated opposite some gentleman, stepping from the station on arrival, purposefully headed for the place of business—all these things could happen in secret only, could only be suffered, deeply and disconsolately, in oneself.

"How had it occurred to him, anyway, to leave in order to fulfill his day? Was he foolhardy, to step out of the form that carried him? Did he defy the collapse and believe in amplification?

"No, he told himself, no. I can swear to it: no. Only in walking out of the shop just now—there was scent of violets again, and talc powder, too—a girl approached with white breasts. Aperture seemed not unthinkable. Flaunting and flowing seemed not unthinkable. A beach moved into the realm of possibilities, washed by the blue breast of the sea. But now, to make my peace, I will go to lunch."

The problem, therefore, which puts Rönne through these agonies is this: what is the origin, the real meaning of the ego? Does it take a trip to Antwerp, medieval studies, a view of the quays of the Scheldt? Does it depend on such impressions, are the potential impressions of the Matsys Fountain and the Plantin Moretus house its necessary components, are there inner, constitutive grounds for such trips—or yet a third motive, perhaps: hybris, intemperance, exaltation? If the ego is predestined, it must never leave its form, never transcend its circle of duties, never jeopardize its cast, nor reveal its features; then a trip is dissolution, peril, unbelief within the rigid query after freedom and necessity, and can lead nowhere but to proof of the deepest corrosion. *Is the individual case needed?* These period pieces can have no primary derivation, anyway, and on the other hand, Rönne's experience and disposition did not fit him for the historic approach. All of it swam past each other, merely tiring him with its forces. Something else had to happen, a minglement, and it was this he incessantly strove for—something that was annulment and amalgamation at the same time; but that existed only for moments, in critical plunges, in breakthroughs, and it was always near annihilation. But one was not always capable of it, and so, after this groping thrust into vagueness at an inauspicious hour of the forenoon, we see Rönne recoil, flee from himself, and make sure of normalcy once again. He goes to lunch at the officers' mess:

"His bow in the door acknowledged the individualities. Who was he? Quietly he took a seat. The gentlemen loomed large.

"Herr Friedhoff was telling of the peculiarities of a tropical fruit containing an egg-sized kernel. You ate the flesh with a spoon; it had the consistency of jelly. Some thought its taste was nutty. As for him, he had always found it tasted like eggs. You ate it with pepper and salt. It was a tasty fruit. He had eaten three or four a day and never noticed injurious effects.

"Here Herr Körner found himself faced with the extraordinary. A fruit, with pepper and salt? It struck him as unusual, and he made a point of it.

" 'But if it tastes like egg to him,' countered Herr Mau, stressing the subjective judgment somewhat slightingly, as if he himself could see nothing unbridgeable. Besides, it really wasn't so odd, Herr Offenberg led back to normalcy—how about tomatoes, for instance? And finally, what of Herr Kritzler's uncle, who had eaten melons with mustard at seventy years of age, and that at night, when such things are known to be least digestible?

"All in all: was it in fact an oddity? Was it, so to speak, an occurrence apt to attract widespread attention—whether because its generalizations might have caused alarming consequences, or because as an experience from the special atmosphere of the tropics it was liable to make one think?

"It was at this point that Rönne trembled, found suffocation on

57

his plate, and had trouble eating the meat. But, insisted Herr Körner, had not Herr Friedhoff meant a banana, rather—that soft, mellowish, and elongated fruit?

"A banana, bristled Herr Friedhoff? He, the Congo expert? The Moabangi navigator of long standing? The suggestion virtually made him smile. He soared far above the group. What were their means of comparison? A strawberry or nut, perhaps a chestnut here and there, somewhat more southerly. And he, the official representative in Hulemakong, who came from the Jambo jungles?

"Now or never, ascent or destruction, felt Rönne—and: 'Really never noticed injurious effects?' he groped his way into the whirl, his voice controlled, depicting astonishment and the doubt of the expert. Facing him was the void. Would there be an answer?

"Yet was it not he, after all, who sat on the wooden chair in a chaste aura of knowing about the perils of the tropical fruit—who sat as if pondering and comparing statements and reports of similar experiences, a reticent researcher, a physician of professional and temperamental taciturnity? Thinly, through his eyelids, he looked up from the meat, down the line, slowly aglow. It was not hope yet, only a breathing without distress. And now an affirmation: several gentlemen seemed, indeed, to set store by a reavowal of the fact, to settle doubts that might possibly have arisen. And now it was evident: some of them nodded, chewing.

"Jubilation in him, chants of triumph. An answer rang out, maintaining the claim against doubters, and it was addressed to him. Acceptance followed, evaluation took place; he was eating meat, a well-known dish; remarks were linked to him and he joined gatherings, under a vault of great happiness. For an instant even the thought of arranging to meet in the afternoon flashed through his heart, without tremors.

"Rocklike the men sat. Rönne savored the fullness of triumph. Deeply he felt how each of his table companions granted him the title of a gentleman, one who did not spurn a quick one after the meal and drank it with a light joke that was cheering to the rest, yet firmly refusing all alcoholic excesses, spreading a certain atmosphere of coziness. He was the impression of probity, of artlessly speaking his mind, though always glad to concede a measure of truth to different views as well. He felt his features in order; cool equanimity, if not imperturbability, had triumphed in his face. And that he carried as far as the door he shut behind him."

Here, then, we see a man no longer endowed with a continuous psychology. His existence, in the officers' mess and outside, is indeed one single burning desire for this continuous psychology—the psychology of the "gentleman," who "did not spurn a quick one after the meal and drank it with a light joke"—but for constitutional reasons he cannot find the way back. Or fitfully, at most, conjured out of abysses, in battles of annihilation. The naive vitality which enclosed and carried and pulsed as lifeblood in the psychological process also—in our century until a rather closely determinable time, and thematically to a rather precisely definable extent—will no longer suffice for the further degrees of psychological sublimation in Europe. In Rönne, the dissolution of this natural vitality has assumed forms that look like decay. But is it really decay? What is decaying? Might it not be only a historic overlay, an upper stratum uncritically accepted for centuries, with the other side of the coin the primary one? Intoxication, languor, unwieldiness—might not this be reality? Where does the impression end and the unknowable being begin? Here, we see, we are face to face with the question of anthropological substance, and this is identical with the question of reality. The immense problem of reality and its criteria opens before us. "Sometimes, for an hour, you are; the rest is what happens. Sometimes the two worlds surge * into a dream." Which two worlds? The ego and nature. What is the result? At most, a dream. Of course, this principle of Rönne's is a principle of irreality—and when is it operative, when is it "rustling"? "When you are broken." At another time he perceives: "What had been mankind's way thus far? An effort to bring order

Benn misquotes himself. The original sentence in *The Birthday* (s. p. 12) read: "*Manchmal die beiden Fluten*"—not "*die beiden Welten,*" as here—"*schlagen hoch zu einem Traum.*"

into something that should have remained play. But after all, it had remained play in the end, for nothing had reality. Did he have reality? No; all he had was every possibility."

Perception is a fine way to perish, and, indeed, from here it goes on to minglement again: "He bedded his neck deeper into the mayweed that smelled of thyrse and Walpurgis. Melting through the noonday, his head pebbled, brooklike. He offered it to the light: irresistibly the strong sun trickled into the brain. There it lay: scarcely a molehill, brittle, the animal scratching inside."

The animal, and the more and more nakedly sublimated thought: is there still a principle common to both? Does the Western world still have such a monistic principle for life and cognition, for history and thought? For movement and the spirit, for stimulation and depth—is there still a union, a contact, a happiness? Yes, answers Rönne, but from far away; there is nothing general; there are strange, all but unbearable regions to be experienced in loneliness: "In itself rumbled a river or, if it was no river, a cast of forms, a game in fevers, pointless, ending around every rim—": he beholds art.

THE DOCTRINE

If all that my generation—and I, as part of it—experienced, all that it expressed in its work and raised to a thesis, is henceforth to be called "formalism," so be it. Again and again I have shown the central significance of the problem of form to Europe, and especially to Germany. But it can also be defined as the very opposite: a hard-earned knowledge of a possible new ritualism. It is an all but religious attempt to shift art from estheticism to anthropology, to proclaim it as an anthropological principle. In terms of sociology, this would mean moving the anthropological principle of form— pure form, formal compulsion—into the center of cults and rites. One might even call it the immaterialization of matter, the obliter- ation of the object: appearances mean nothing, individual cases mean nothing, sensible objects mean nothing, but expression, the legislative transformation into style, means everything. "But if we were to teach seeing the cycle, and creative mastery of life, would not death be the blue shadow in which felicities stand?" This early doctrine of Rönne's would be the rule that never leaves the substance—be it stone, clay, or words—and yet heeds only creation and its transcendent call. It would be a principle canonizing a power that is inborn only to the loftiest nations of the human species; the power to detach themselves from their contrived and formally wrought product—to dissolve in it, resolve their agonies and urges in it, and then to take their departure, to leave it to itself but so charged with the tension of their kind and so far-reaching, indestructible a meaning that after thousands of years other generations of this kind will still use this product to measure the epochs, will still recognize themselves in it, their mysteries, their eternally veiled nature, and their whole disaster-based existence. Here is shudder and secret once more, before the final decay!

For it is not till today, in my opinion, that the history of man, his jeopardy, his tragedy, begins. Heretofore, the altars of the saints and the wings of the archangels have stood behind him, and his wounds and frailties were laved from chalices and baptismal fonts. Now comes the series of his own great, insoluble dooms. Nietzsche will have been a prelude only, the prelude of the new symbols, the new empires—"white earth from Thule to Avalon"—but also the prelude of the last nihilistic destructions.

Upward, downward, on and on, but where? *Amor fati*—but from which substratum of existence springs this last call? Where does it point, to which oblivion? "Life is a deadly and unknown law; today as ever, man can do no more than accept his own without tears"—a word from *Primal Vision*—but how long will he bear it without tears? On and on, but where? Man's rearward view is dimmed, his forward view non-existent. As a creature he is but half successful, a sketch, a shot at an eagle: the wings, the feathers are already brought down, but the entire figure has not yet fallen —will it ever fall entirely, resting its heart right on the heart of things? So, on and on—nations, races, geological ages—smell of stone and fern and beast: rising from dusk, firm in its kind, and yet in an inconceivable transformation in which this human Quaternary type will also pass away. But while it is here it is marked, strongly marked, imperialistically strongly marked—what is the sign? It is the unreal sign of Rönne, the constructive sign of Pameelen. It teaches: there is no reality; there is the human consciousness ceaselessly forming, reforming, earning, suffering, spiritually stamping worlds from its creative property. In this capacity there are degrees and steps, chiefly preliminary steps. But the uppermost says: there is only the idea, the great, objective idea. It is eternity; it is the world order; it lives by abstraction; it is the formula of art. Through it runs the chain of races and nations; it is the chain. It directs the course—and it will block it, too, before the abyss, over the abyss. If this is intellectualism I will serve it as a trial and a challenge, but its perfection alone lends greatness to the human race. All the corrosion it brings to the individual, all the sacrifices it demands, all the life it takes shall be offered in this time-bound clarity—blindly, that is—for where else should we offer them? There, with the anguish of the Hyperborean: "Dream is the world, and smoke in the eyes of one eternally dissatisfied"—there, in the silence of Tao that cultivates waiting and letting existence work—there, the utmost Oriental and Occidental depth of the great nations: yield thyself.

(1934) Translated by E. B. Ashton

WOLF'S TAVERN

A certain period of my life was spent in a middling-sized town, almost a city. Bad climate, boring surroundings, all flat, immensely dreary. My profession had never really meant anything to me, here least of all. Just at the point where the cultured, eminent sort of men were feeling the social implications of their profession, whether politically or in the sphere of *Weltanschauung,* and seeing themselves and their work becoming incorporated into a pattern of widely accepted general ideas, my interest in my profession snapped right off. Counting in years, the larger part of my life was over, and it was perfectly clear to me that only considerable charity could call it fruitful. The lapsing of most lives caused no hitch, and neither would mine—at most an incidental, or rather accidental, traffic jam; but all the forces of law and order were ready to forestall that. All crossing of the one-way streets in both directions, the oncoming and the vanishing stream, went on without a hitch.

I had taken an apartment at the back of a house, all the windows overlooking the court. On purpose! For one thing, I can't stand light, can't stand being drenched in strong natural rays; but then, too, in order to hide from both men and women. "Always polite" was my slogan, "but few appearances and never without preparation." I had no telephone either, to make appointments impossible. I went to the usual parties, clinked glasses with the men, ran through the standard gossip with the ladies, and never let the flower girl pass without buying the bunch in season for the lady on my right. I don't think anyone thought of considering me improper. Of course, there was a lot of calculation and super-structure in all this, yet that was my own business.

I started out in colonial and consular circles. I had spent the main part of my life in the great cities of the world, and a place like this now, with its hundred thousand inhabitants, its three main streets where everyone met, its half-dozen restaurants where everyone met again, its few grass-plots buoyed up with crocuses in spring, geraniums in the fall, struck me as particularly remarkable. My life had never brought me so close to the bourgeois and human core of a community, so close to the historical core—to introduce this expression—to which I then attached particular importance. And so I let all these impressions work on me thoroughly, ready to open my frontiers, to become a new man, to re-examine the fundamental problem of human existence, which—in view of the spiritual situation of the white peoples I had so monotonously encountered during my years of travel—had, I must admit, prepared a quite definite answer in my mind.

What gave these peoples the right to lead all others? This was what I wondered. What had they to show in that respect? What spiritual image of man had they evolved, to what depths of being and to what external outlines had they worked out the human idea? Where did their most unearthly, their purest, minds stand? To what coldness of judgment, to what severity of moral decision had their masses attained under their imperial leaders? Recently they talked much of their history. But there was greatness that had no history. Asia had no history. The decline of the Greeks began in the century when Herodotus appeared. They also pointed to their masterhood—master race—all right then, who were these masters?

I never tired of observing things from this point of view. Perhaps I may be more explicit, going off into detail. My evening walk often led me to a little tavern, a place for habitués—the proprietress knowing her customers, chatting with them occasionally—a pleasant woman. There I often sat, behind the mask of pictures and memories, memories of past years, memories of Tahiti's narrow beach, the cabins among the breadfruit trees, the kernels of the nuts so sweet and cool, and the never silent breakers on the reefs; pictures of Broadway, still lit by prairie fires, smouldering sunsets at the end of narrow streets; memories and pictures of worlds old and new, redskins, brown pearl-divers, yellow shadows.

It was far from being romanticism, a hangover from Rousseau, an esthetic lamento, that lay behind these pictures. No, on the contrary, it was the vision of the light-skinned race whose tragedy I bore within myself, whose abysses I had sensed, when I had represented it in all those places. Now my return to it, and to the concept of history it had come to stress so much, had made me consider it in evolutionary terms, codify its course, feel out its past; and many an evening a sort of revue rose into existence about me, a cultural revue of tolerable duration, the first act carrying the falcon on the gauntlet and the last, bird in hand, singing its praises to those in the bush.

A company of white men, historically post-Antiquity, bearing the cerebral imprint of Graeco-Latin humanism, mongrels sprung from the shattered Roman Empire, run-to-seed Merovingians, unleashed Christians, sensual Popes, lust-ridden monks, flaring Moors, attar-of-roses-importing, heron-hunting, luxury-oozing Persians—that's what paces down the untrodden path.

To admit no conviction unless justified by thought—thus the race later described it. No conviction, no art, no religion, no science. Everything must conform to the yardsticks of clear logic: premise, assertion, proof; everything is tested for its emotional content by the logical proposition of contradiction, passed as valid only if the concord between the whole and the parts is seen to be indisputable. The transcendence of an ascetic, self-purifying, eremitical harmony that has left detail behind and stripped itself of confusion and profusion. But also a transcendence by the aid of restrictive hauteur, progressive aridity, self-corseted humanity—and yet transcendent even where this mode of life has not reached its ultimate peak, even in its rudimentary stages and off-shoots. Everywhere patches of élan, self-stimulation, disembodiment: transcendence, extra-transcendence, sectors of upsurge:—sectors of the wheel of Sansara in the whirl of infinite possibilities, with interpretations in all the directions of everlastingly inscrutable creation and of dreams. Advance of Occidental sectors, of special combinations, West-Nordic; over against the gentle beach life of the South Seas, it is complicated and conceptually over-ramified; over against the agelessness, the deep-sea swell of China, it is unaristocratic and restless. This was it: this white race with its compulsive pursuit of a downward path of no return, a lost, icy, heat-baked, weather-ravaged *anabasis* not held in the embrace of any *thalassa*.

I was increasingly drawn to these things, to their atmosphere, their roots, their causality, their being. Many an evening I sat there gazing around: it was the same old tavern, yet it seemed to me the room had a heavy list, a suggestion of sinking; its shape and paneling were like the interior of a ship. A torpedo speeding into the depths—yes, that was the impression that thrust itself on me, something gliding away down, a community drowning, its pictures like oil slicks on the surface, stragglers above the chasm. Just as simple as that.

At a neighboring table sat three gentlemen eating mussel ragout, telling stories, exchanging banter with the hostess, a gay party. "I don't mind another year of it so long as it's good," they said, keeping their eating utensils on the move, forkfuls between biting into their rolls, raising their glasses, now and then bending their legs and kicking out. Their arms hung loose in the shoulder-joints; they wore spats. A dog called Krause, due for a bath, an operation indicated in view of the approaching festive season, kept turning up in their talk. Ash lengthened on cigars sucked between remarks passed back and forth—this was how their evening was spent, how uncertainty was distributed, how time took shape.

So these were three of the present-day elect, comrades, bearers of a historic mission, beacon-fires of passion, their faces endowed to express anything that life might throw in their way: relish, hilarious laughter, the finishing-off of competitors, commercial triumphs, and condolences to the widows of business friends.

Personalities! Orgasm at its appointed hour, subsequently incense, also participation in ceremonies and celebrations. Occupational categories! Taking an afternoon train, business trip, taste of stale smoke in the mouth, compartment a bit drafty, scenery flying past, dusk falling—days and lives! Parallel: blonde divorcée (innocent party), husband company director, earning her own keep now, a wife sucked dry.

Specters! Void! Unarticulated billowing! Caesar-like as to the tie; red checks, not dots. Own vintage in the rummer: fruit juice, not malt brew. Stimuli, habits, ill-humor—the ace of particularity! Fruitful, inwardly determined impetus—never.

A people's or a race's degeneration always seemed to me to imply a decline in the number of men born with the potentialities and the secure source of inner values that enable them to give legitimate expression to the essential nature of that last, late phase of their own civilization and to carry on, in spite of all obstacles, toward an undefined goal. There was no reasonable doubt as to what that essential nature really was; still, I'll put it here once again in the terms I used then. The essential nature of man lies in the sphere of formal creativeness. Only in that sphere does man become recognizable; only in that sphere do the grounds and backgrounds of his own creation become clear and with them his rank in the hierarchy of animal life. Transforming the plane into depth, organizing and correlating words so as to open up a spiritual world, linking sounds so that they last and sing of the indestructible—*this* is what that sphere does. Peoples whose spiritual message is the housewifely idea of a centrally supplied home-and-town-life are degenerate. Peoples who stand up to the spirit as an autonomous force that attacks, cleaves, decomposes life are racially on a high level. Peoples who see the spirit only in historic victories and successful frontier-crossings are of low race. Peoples who allow the spirit in all its manifestations to rise to the sphere of creativeness are high-bred. So what counts is the sphere of the creative! Of its temporal manifestations we had: individualism, intoxication with forms, tempests of differentiation. On all levels of civilization this has so far appeared only in hints, sporadically, in the great individuals, so it is still a force entirely and deeply veiled. Appearing late, in man only, its concentration for the re-creation of the world was scarcely at its rudimentary stage. On the one hand, life with all its manipulations, the so-called actions, and, on the other, the principle of the new reality. The latter was served by the integer of the great, often physically weak race that lies outside all epochs and all nations. Whenever that race died out in one nation, the torpedo plunged into the depths. Before the impact, however, there came, with oratory, the epoch of the urge towards totality, of parades and collective cults, the epoch of revivals, of turns to the past, the epoch of history. This was how Rohde, in the final pages of his *Psyche*, had described the decline of the Greeks. To me the white nations seemed again in the midst of such an epoch. They had all shunned the decision to adopt a new form of existence, i.e., this attitude to the spirit. For them spirit served life, and they wrote tragedies about the fact that here and there it did not seem to do so. In fact, the spirit was a sort of spoiled reality. Therefore, down with it—and before history, that is, in the next war, they would be victorious all right.

The proprietress got up from the business gents' table and came over to me. "Like something to read?" "No thanks, I don't feel like reading." I was lounging as usual with one arm stretched out along the back of the seat. "Don't talk much, do you?" "Habit!" I relaxed a group of muscles in the shoulder region. "Don't you ever do anything?" I did my job during the day; was I supposed to do some special work on behalf of the universe after hours? "The gentlemen over there meant it in a quite particular sense." I held my own in the world I lived in, so what business was it of theirs? I must say, it was a bit thick. If those gentlemen's views tended toward the universal when they left home—all right, but without me, please. Frankly, I was amazed. The fact was I didn't like walking and I always tried to rest my arm on something. I often refrained from a purchase because at that moment my own shape under my hat-brim struck me as too weird. So perhaps I really did have a morbid streak. Originally I had meant to be a writer, too, but to become a writer you have to be able to read your own handwriting, and that was something I'd never been able to accomplish. For a novel, besides, you must acknowledge the idea of time; but the word was timeless, and I liked putting things into words. So I became a consular official, took jobs abroad, and Tahiti and the Azores slid behind me. Could they read that, by any chance, in my face?

It gave me a start. Supposing they could see deeper? Doing nothing, under favorable material living conditions, was, if I may put it so, in fact my ideal. Doing nothing in a general sense: no office, no definite working hours, no references top-left in the files. No roaming about the countryside—I was no dowser or wolf of the steppes, rather one for a quiet hour with worm and rod, waiting for a bite, impressions, dreams—a vast squandering of hours. Goethe's and Hamsun's praise of manual labor on the soil as the ultimate wisdom did not seem especially compelling, since they personally had spent seventy years feeding witches' milk to the entire range of terrestrial and supraterrestrial daemons, at all glands and by all channels, till at the end they felt like nibbling their supper rusks in the arbor once again—which struck me as not so much wisdom as fatigue, a fit of yawning. It went with the style of the *Novelle*, that celebrated work of Goethe's old age: a menagerie catches fire, the booths burn down, the tigers break out, the lions are at large—and everything works out beautifully to a happy end. No, that epoch was over, the earth was scorched, flayed by lightning, sore all over. Today the tigers bit.

The hostess moved as if to sit down with me, but I refrained from showing delight at the prospect. Was I disturbed? Busy? Not busy? All these tables and faces suddenly seemed to pose one definite question. These conversations, gestures, exhalations—was it all just by the way? The age that followed on Goethe, my own age, was Manfred's, not Faust's: "I did destroy myself and will myself destroy." Art: no remedy for scabies, but the human manifesto, existence balanced daily on a poisoned arrow, man's capital being disease, his essential nature incurability. "The damage done to the good is the most damaging damage."— "Suffering is the sole cause of consciousness"—nihilism—and: "Nihilism is a sense of happiness"—all the dissolved substances and contents that had been washed through the brains of my generation and kept on washing through them, this delta, these cleavages—and then, if one looked at these heads: immaculately padded tissues; cheekbones, teeth, no irregularity there; posture, expression, grimaces, all upward movements—whose thick skin was it that all these bankruptcies squatted on? Obviously it was all just by the way.

The hostess observed my reluctance, sensed something, turned her attention to other guests, and now our glances passed together, though in different moods, over the various groups and tables in the room. The eminent gray head over there belonged to an aged colonel, the direct descendant of that regimental commander at Malplaquet who took his troops across three deep canals and with soaked ammunition fell upon Villars' exposed, sensitive flank, to be rewarded by Marlborough with a snuff-box—this descendant was now waving his clenched fist as though giving the order to attack. The quiet man over the bottle of Burgundy spent his days insuring lives, demonstrably with success, a thoroughly conclusive man, known to impress the hesitant with Goethe's dictum, which had a place of honor in his firm's prospectus: "What is not done today will be still undone tomorrow." Filling an armchair was a personage from the realm of scientific thought, one known to specialize in derivations: butterflies from caterpillars, colonnaded temples from Indonesian pile-buildings—a specific mode in which a more exalted sphere of life expressed itself. All these were the authentic elect of our age, types whom a later era could not reproach with having unheedingly passed by such new, marvelous, and great events of our time as, for instance, the modern method of transmutations of matter (air and wood into transparent sheets, blocks, fibers), all complete personalities in whom each turn of life, vocation, inner transformation had taken the straight, direct route and always would. Compared with that, what was the sphere in which a life would have been passed by my standards?

Nothing against the order of the world—but merely uttering the word "life" condemns one—there's no getting out of this dilemma, the hostess was obviously telling herself as she took off for the other half of the tavern. Yet if I went on thinking, making straight for my goal, without ado: what these people here called action, activity in which I should be involved, according to the hostess, and miles deep in sociology, if possible—if one deducted all that was merely business, there remained only reflexes, or something like the stuff a shellfish grows to protect its jelly body against its environment. I can see no necessity for it. I can see necessity in all that an age thinks and in the way it links its own thought to that of the past epoch. In Nature itself there is obviously no such thing as necessity; it is only in the dissolution of Nature, that is to say in the mind, which is subject to constraining forces. But action —that is just vagabondage, *plein-air* stuff.

He who rides a tiger cannot dismount. Chinese proverb. Applied to action: what you get is history. Action is capitalism, the armaments industry. Malplaquet—Borodino—Port Arthur—150,000 dead, 200,000 dead, 250,000 dead—no one can now see history as anything but the justification of mass murder: rapine and glorification —there's the mechanism of power. And what history records is not the nations' folk-memory of themselves, but their funny papers. If you look at them twenty years later, you recall the fashions for war-widows, but not a word of what the battles were about. A shrapnel splinter on the watch-chain draped over the belly of the good-time boys, the sharks, the profiteers, while they bait a chippy at a thé-dansant—that's what remains, that is the *aere perennius*, that outlasts the general staffs, that's the nail that holds history's flag to the flagpole. All that travail brought forth a stone—that's history: a legend, a dream! Think of all that is now growing a beard in some Kyffhäuser: the Manchus and the Hohenstaufens, the Tennos and the Shoguns and the Lancashire woolmongers—the beard growing without hairtonic through all those table-tops, and the ravens have croaked themselves hoarse and are sick and tired of it and have gone flapping off over the hills: history, much too classical for these down-and-out nations, pinchbeck offspring of the Titans, more heroin than heroism, froth on their lips from talking platitudes—counter-jumpers of history!

Anyone who has nothing at all to offer the present day talks history! Rome, the Rubicon. The jaws of Caesars and the brains of troglodytes, that's their type! Wars, knouts, tyrants, plagues to keep the masses in check, there you might see a touch of the grand manner, but history, no, that's nothing for—heroes! À propos, victories and mis-victories, will and power—what labels for these broth-cubes! On the table free groceries and under the table looted Persian carpets: there you have the cold facts of history. What history destroys is usually temples, and what it loots is always art. Everyone gets his turn among the firms and the Pharaohs. The sapphires from Amphitrite's eye-sockets find their way on to the Madonna's mantle of beaten gold, then on to some imperial Colleoni's sword-knob. Malplaquet—Borodino—Port Arthur—in the mollifying light of cultural philosophy: states of levitation, that's all. Yet behind it all there stand, calmly and collectedly, the missionaries of formal reason, the leisurely collectors and artificers of decisions.

When I look back on that series of evenings extending through one particular spring of my life, it seems it was then that an odd summarizing tendency developed in me; I saw more clearly a phenomenon that had been a process for centuries but scarcely ever before raised to the level of conscious formulation. It was this: in the white peoples there were two classes of men, the active and the profound, and art was nothing but the making of a method for putting the profound man's experiences into words, and only in it did he come to fulfillment and to utterance. There were—it was necessary to add—two classes capable of vocal expression within the white race, and owing to a weird biological oversight both largely used the same words and ideas, only filling them with two kinds of blood unthinkably alien to each other, mutually hostile, never to be mixed. Just as now male and now female individuals resulted from the same act of procreation, so from the germ, the Creation, the ineffable distance, what sprang was now historical man, now central man, now the active and now the profound man, now life and now the spirit. Sometimes I occupied myself with working out morphological variations on this theme and giving it a point. The superstructure of the higher centers upon the lower was the path of organic articulation; externally that meant the development of the axis, the ever-increasing erectness of the spine, the transmigration of the living essence into the head. Inwardly it meant the ascending hierarchy of nervous function; intellectually it meant consciousness; and for the scale of values and a perspective of the future, it meant a definite and unassailable articulation no longer susceptible to anything except mutations. Both experience and methodically acquired material pointed to one and the same thing: the mind and its anti-naturalistic function. Variations and fugue on a springtide theme! Not that it eased my mind; there was no longer anything that eased my mind, any more than an uncompleted train of thought made me uneasy. It might have bothered me at the next sip of *Spätlese*, but it would have been washed down, submerged, and I would have gone home ready for the hour. I had seen the finishing and re-opening of too many things, and for a long time now I had slept with all doors open, or rather lain there dozing, counting the chimes and the hours.

An odd spring! I remember some of its peculiarities. A slowly yielding winter. A sort of weight lying on everything. It was almost a haze I passed through once on my way to the outskirts of the town, before going to the tavern. Warmth rising darkly everywhere. An usually overcast afternoon. Everything looking down upon the earth with an infinitely mournful, lingering gaze, hardly able to detach itself; almost no difference between leaves and moist ground. Somewhere near where I was walking there was, I gathered, an institution whose inmates gave a sort of extra depth to all this. Lots of cripples on the road, hunchbacks, freaks, also blind men. They crept along everywhere with timid steps, stammering, fumbling with their crutches. The chestnuts were almost in bud. There was this tropical sultriness hanging silently between all shapes, an indissoluble silence linking these figures; all that had risen sank back, all spellbound to what was below—"mingle!" It called me, too, singeing my eyes with salt and fire:

give of your bread—diminish the suffering—sacrifice your own flesh against tears and curses—yet if a man bows down, what more can he bear, bowing down before *this*? It is only the highest spheres that count, and the human sphere is not among them. A merciless height, where the undeflectible arrows fly; it is cold, deep blue, only rays prevail here, only one thing prevails: recognize the situation, use your means, you are in duty bound to your method, you can't retreat from what you have created. What you stand for is realms defying interpretation, realms in which there are no victories.

Evening again in the tavern. I sit listening. Listening to the strange life and being emanating from these people's voices. In Tibet it was the wind, in the jungle the insects, here it's the vowels. One was going to the Rhineland—haha, went the rest, he's full of plans, seems out for pleasure. Another had a visitor from America in October—from the USA! rang out from the rest, obviously regarding this as a clarification. Incomprehensible why they sat there so taut with interest, when their talk led simply nowhere at all.

The cloth-covered seats, intimately two and two in each compartment, faced each other with the mistrust of strangers. Fully loaded, they held their occupants as though on hinges, youth with debility, doubts with conclusions, business with love—natural needs meeting, blown together by chance.

How odd it all was! They keep their cities free of mosquitoes, at any rate I never encountered one either in Irkutsk or in Biarritz. Ingeniously, by pneumatic post, they frankly send each other their ideas on certain occasions: the East the machine-gun, the West the tank, and the New World the dew of death, the gas that smells of geraniums. The mind is there to serve life. Cultivation they call it. Later they exchange visits again. In the beginning was lust, later it scarcely had reason to put in an appearance. Women clinging to the jacket of the male, stylized on a titanic scale, demanding and granting; objectively regarded: embracing pug-dogs. The jacket-wearers: knobby, no concessions to form—"empty formulae"—realities!—the whistle blows: Ring clear!

This was what had chased me through all the countries that this race inhabited, through all its social stratifications and professions. I surveyed their current cultural values, their so-called theaters, and the lobbies alone condemned the whole epoch. An audience that has to recuperate from the terrors of tragedy by strolling for twenty minutes among counters laden with ham sandwiches and brandy bottles and then goes back to carry on, is ripe for the guillotine. By their metaphors ye shall know them! I eavesdropped on their minor characteristics, on what sufficed to satisfy their minds: a pilot is a Marshal Blücher of the air; a Pomeranian backwoods village with a duck-pond at the back of a stable is a Venice of the North. Then, too, I heard their songs—yes, the linden is their tree all right, sweet and heartfelt and, what's more, you can make tea from its flowers.

What speaks out of me is disintegration, I was often told. No, I answered, as long as I went on answering, what speaks out of me is the spirit of the West, which is admittedly the disintegration of life and Nature, their disintegration and re-integration by means of the law of man, that anthropological principle which separated the waters from the dry land and the prophets from the fools. But that's just it, my opponents said. You're trying to disintegrate Nature—that's the limit! The blood and soil of us all. And is this Nature of yours, I could not help retorting, really natural? Can one make it one's point of departure? I can prove that it is unnatural, a thing of leaps and bounds, indeed the very textbook example of what one means by "contrary to Nature." It begins something and drops it, makes a great stir and then forgets. It is unbridled, it exaggerates, it produces fish in incredible shoals off the Lofotens, or rolling swarms of locusts and cicadas. Or there is peace on earth, everything has the temperature of the stones, one can truly give one's attention to the climate, and then the Aaron's rod shoots up in flower at forty degrees Centigrade, everything is thrown into confusion and the gods insist on warm-blooded animals —is that Nature's doing, or whose is it? Or take geological folding, densification, unimaginable concentration—one of its methods—is that a simple and natural thing to do? Or it takes a fancy to send immense tensions charging across microscopically tiny spaces—is that now the thing to expect? Come to think of it, was the phenomenon of life not nicely looked after in plant form? Why set it in motion and send it out in search of food—is that not a model of uprooting? As for its creature, Man, does it not plunge him headlong into anti-Nature, hurling bacteria to destroy him, diminishing his sense of smell, reducing his sense of hearing, denaturing his eye by means of optical lenses, so that the man of the future is the merest abstraction—where are the workings of natural Nature? No, it is some other face that peers out everywhere, sleeping in the stones, blossoming in the flowers, making its demands in all late forms—a very different face, and the result I arrive at is an alien one.

If I wanted to work out a theory, I should refer you to the way biology is at this very moment busy demonstrating that the inorganic and the organic are two retrospectively associated forms of a higher unity, with no transitions or derivations between them, no "evolution" of life "out of" the inorganic now or ever; they are two independent realms, two modes of expression. Today you may say this scientifically—I mean, you won't lose your chair at the university, with attendant benefits, and the specialist journals will publish papers containing this sort of statement. It is not yet the established view, but there are signs that it is coming. Until recently you would have lost your chair at the university. But nobody is allowed to say that a Third Reich claims the same rights to its point of view. The Third Reich "serves" the Second and has spontaneously wangled its way up from it. Millennia are based on this theory. But it is not a theory, it is a procedural code that can be used for acts of power. In graphic terms, its results for the tavern are: steel chairs, Reich Number One, laden with Reich Number Two; the load enjoys mussel ragout and talks as vowel-bearers of the category "Life"; if they burp on bicarbonate, it is done scientifically, revealing Reich Number Three. Signed: Historical World. Point of departure. Departure not by any means in the tragic sense, quite the contrary: historical man is supposed to act, and the man of action is what history wants; let them act and trade and pile things up till they rupture themselves—let them fulfill themselves, manifest themselves—only one more hour to nightfall—then glow-a-low, high-low, hell-hello-low!

If one casts a glance at the leaders of the nations, all of them and in all their respective forms of government, one must imagine them standing in time on the brink of one or the other of the great movements of mankind, with the power to suppress it. What would they do? About Christianity, they would ask if the budget could stand it. About Buddhism, how it would affect the phonograph record and flag-making industries. About Mahomet, would it not hurt the banana crop? About art, would it not undermine the demand for new housing? About every religion, would it not hold up potato exports? About abstraction, summarizing thought, might it not dent the little man's watering-can? Multiplication of protoplasm and raw materials are their standards, everything else is agitation and calls for suppression—and that goes even for Plato. But always, at all times, every one of them has claimed to be the creative fulfillment of cosmic reason. Obviously there are contradictions involved—glow-a-low, high-low, hell-hello-low!

If now the tables themselves were to try persuading each other that it was consoling and elevating to each—giving it a deeper significance, in fact giving it all the significance it has—for others to live just this way in the future and for ever new figures to be born into the same environment, crawl around the same tables, go on living for centuries in the same flats, a so-called posterity that cannot be or become anything but the recurrent embodiment of the same nullity: publicly trying to persuade each other of this, proclaiming this as doctrine, strikes me as a spiritual perversity compared with which the worst monstrosities of scorched earth, fakirs' tricks, religious belly-dancing, Indian bowel-and-liver-exercises are like the pure breath of umbelliferous blooms.

In the tavern I beheld a dream. A very quiet animal-keeper led white-skinned human creatures around in a circle until they became discolored. Then he pried open their jaws and yelled: "Spirit or life! There's no more realizing the spirit in life."—"Who's of the spirit?" one gasped.—"This one talking!" was the answer.—No, we do not want to go that far; there is some truth in it, but it provokes justifiable opposition. Shut the jaws—there, there's the world looking natural again! Then one of them called out through teeth once more safely clenched: "Haven't you any mercy, any human feelings? Don't you know everyone wants to be better and more beautiful?" The answer came: "Mercy is not mine to give. Crave mercy from those who have brought you where you are, crave mercy from yourselves, you who let yourselves be led, crave it from your own baseness and greed. Time and again words have been uttered, warning you against life. Time and again the Other Thing came and set up its images before you—in human form, yes, even in human form! Set up before you the images of that force to which it would be too little to ascribe a religious or moral nature; it is the universal challenging, uplifting force, the entelechy—admittedly the very force that comprises heaven and hell within its infinity and yet gazes so visibly upon all man's damming and regulating characteristics and casts so strange a light on all heaven's slowly accumulating and always so hard-won achievements.—Did you ever worship it? Did you keep watch over it? All you wanted was to live your life, your white, fulfilled life, realized in Derby glitter and yachting spray—no, there's no more mercy. Now comes nightfall."

Everyone sees that the truth looming up among the vats here in this tavern is an extra-human truth. It is, besides, in a peculiar position, for it should most passionately combat its own generalization, should condemn its own projection into time, its own testing for realization, as the most decisive blunder. Realization is a concept that this truth excludes, one that it deliberately eludes; wherever it catches a glimpse of it, it lowers its gaze. Is it then a truth at all? Is it not perhaps an untruth for all; in other words, a prematurely dispatched message written in a code intended only for a certain few?

For a certain few? That is to say, for initiates of esotericism, for decadents, cliques, destructionists, divisionists, anti-social types, lone wolves, intellectualists, marked men? Let us consider this question in the twilight of truth among our vats. If one surveys the white nations in the course of the last five hundred years and looks for a yardstick to assess their great minds, the only one to be found is the degree of ineradicable nihilism they bore within them and spasmodically hid under the fragments of their works. It is quite obvious—all the great minds among the white nations have felt only one inner task, namely the creative camouflaging of their nihilism. This fundamental tendency, interwoven with the most varied trends of the ages—in Dürer with the religious, in Tolstoy with the moral, in Kant with the epistemological, in Goethe with the anthropological, in Balzac with the capitalistic—was the basic element in all their works. With the utmost gingerliness it is brought up again and again. On every page, in every chapter, in every stroke of the pencil or brush they approach it with ambiguous questioning, with turns of the most exquisitely groping, equivocal character. Not for an instant are they unaware of the essential nature of their own inner creative substance. It is the abyss, the void, the unsolvable, the cold, the inhuman element. Nietzsche's place in their ranks is for a long time that of an idealistic Antinoüs. Even his Zarathustra—what a child of Nature, what evolutionary optimism, what shallow utopianism about the spirit and its realization! Only in the last stage, with *Ecce Homo* and the lyrical fragments, did he let that other datum rise into his consciousness, and that, one may suppose, brought about his collapse: that brown night when he stood on the bridge staring down into the abyss, beholding the abyss—late—too late for his organism and his role as a prophet. On that bridge, in that night, a twilit form soared up on bat's wings, the earth gaped open, one age wrested its symbols from the other, and there came about that antithesis of life and spirit which we bore within us so long and now see again beyond the confines of Earth.

What is it that we see beyond the confines of Earth? Taking a closer look for a moment at the last hundred years, the century around Nietzsche, the laboratories and the prisons from Siberia to Morocco, we see the spirit from Dostoievsky to Céline in an attitude of sheer despair, its screams more terrible, more agonized, more evil than ever were the screams of men condemned to die. These screams are of a moral nature, definite in meaning, they are substantial and always "against" something, at war "with" something, struggling "for" something, trying to include "everything" and to remain honest, to improve, to complete, to purify, to deify. They are Lutheran screams in a Faustian skirmish. Mythopoeic puberty and prometheid biology extend right into their orbit. Only today, before so much absurdity and torment, we dimly sense that life is not meant to gain possession of knowledge, and man, at any rate the higher-developed race, is not meant to struggle for an explanation of the material world. It all looks more like an experimental step taken by that remote distance which yielded the formula for some monstruous alkaloid but withheld the substance itself in all its purity. And which still preserves it unchanged, in all its purity, not intending any such struggle or any further surrender in terms of temporal knowledge. The experiment was meant to indicate delimitation, abstractive elimination, formulae directed against Nature. The aim was not to intensify life biologically and to perfect it racially by means of stimuli to knowledge, but to set the formative, formula-wielding mind against life. Hence it is not the Faustian-physiological, but the anti-naturalistic function of the mind, its expressive function, that we see holding sway over the earth today.

This is the point of departure. We have to trouble history and the times for this assertion. We are no longer concerned with breeding for a future we can neither await nor utilize, but with our own bearing in an eschatological present that has become an abstract experience only. Thus reads the coded message. Here the certain few come to a halt: before the remote signs that are drawing steadily nearer, the invisible protagonists of the impending transformation.

This is said by a life-long, case-hardened expert in realities, one well acquainted with the body, with war and with death, skilled in several occupations, all of them carved out of the abdominal fat of capitalism and each one refined to ultimate craftsmanly finesse by the personal necessity of turning them into a living. It is said by one who always lived under the pressure of specific tasks, deliveries, contracts, market conditions, without room for romanticism or time for illusions. One who lived in the social style of his century, at times in tails and at times in dress uniform, traveling by the Blue Train and by caravan in the company of a Rurik and a Rochefoucauld (only recently on a ferry-boat he found himself sitting next to the last Romanov princess). One who loved an Austrian girl and a Czech one, a Rumanian, a Belgian, a Dane, a woman from Cape Town, a halfbreed from the South Seas, Russian girls on shores, fjords, salt lakes, in many landscapes and from many tribes, in Ritz Hotel suites and in tents. Let's call it an average life, with work and toil and the sort of understanding that a man's own time allows him—which says: No propaganda can turn excrement into lilies-of-the-valley. The white peoples are on the way out, no matter whether or not the theories about their doom are now accepted. Decomposition is palpable, a return to earlier conditions impossible, the substance spent; this is where the Second Law of Thermodynamics applies. The new power is there, holding the cigarette-lighter to the fuse. Whether by moon plunge or atom-smashing, by entropy or incendiarism, by whatever method it prefers, it is the transformation, the eternal element, the spirit, the antagonist of dreary rationality and mere consumption—in short: the end of the natural view of the world.

So let them try regenerating things by economics and biology and vegetarianism—all these are specters of annihilation. The race is more intuitive: it will no longer adapt itself, it has grown inert, it lies immobile round its core, and this core is the spirit—that is to say, nihilism.

He who cannot bear this thought stands among the worms that breed in the sand, and in the moisture that the earth has given them for their own. He wo still boasts of hope, gazing into his children's eyes, tries to hide the lightning with his hands but cannot escape the night that blasts the nations from their dwelling places. This is the law: Nothing is, if anything ever was; nothing will be. The fairest and profoundest of all gods is passing us by, the only one who bore the mystery of man: the greater the knowledge, the more infinite the grief.

There is nothing that can be turned into reality. The spirit hovers in silence over the waters. A road has come to an end; here is the sunset of a cosmic day. Perhaps it bore within it possibilities other than this gloaming, but now the hour is upon us—ecce homo—this is how man ends.

Such were my thoughts in that spring. I knew there would be other springs, and perhaps I myself would see another, whole weeks of beauty, in the multiplicity of unfolding leaves and petals, and roses would bloom for this man and for that, but one thing I knew: history had lost its power over man. His inner core had once more begun to glow, had written a word on his garment and a name upon his hip.

They will keep coming, but he will melt them down. They are approaching with nails, with knives to stab him in the back, and all he raises is a twig of hyssop and a cup of hemlock. A vast, millennial battlefield, and the victory is his. Only no action! Know this and be silent. Asia is deeper, but hide that! Face things in the spirit; it will be carried on, it helps to shape existence. Open your eyes only to the night; by day clink glasses with the men, run through the standard gossip with the ladies, and never let the flower girl pass without buying her posies. Live and observe to the end. Think always: transformation! We too have signs! One must be much, to cease expressing anything. Be silent; pass away.

(*Written 1937, published 1949*) *Translated by Ernst Kaiser and Eithne Wilkins*

ART AND THE THIRD REICH

1. GENERAL SITUATION

Life is beyond doubt inextricably bound up with necessity, and it
does not release man, the attempted deserter, from the chain; but
the chain need not clank at every one of his steps, need not drag
its whole weight on every breath. Such a moment, when the chain
temporarily loosened, came at the end of the last century, when,
for instance, the English Queen's Diamond Jubilee in 1897 gave
the whole rest of the world a chance to see the immense riches of
the Empire. The white race's two continents were both enjoying
a high degree of prosperity: new oil fields, depth-drilling in Penn-
sylvania, forest conservation, winter-hardened wheat—all this had
brought it about. Those who organized and enjoyed this prosperity
had for years been in the habit of meeting for the Season in
London, the Grande Semaine in Paris, the salmon-fishing in
Canada, or in the fall in the valley of the Oos. Some events over-
lapped in the calendar: on the first of September the bathing
season began at Biarritz, lasting till exactly the thirtieth of that
month, followed by the after-cure at Pau in the gigantic hotels on
the Boulevard des Pyrénées with its incomparable view over the
panorama of the Monts-Maudits, or in the shadow of the sixteen
rows of plane trees bordering the avenues at Perpignan. In England
the thing was to go North on August 12th, to shoot grouse in
Scotland, and to return South on September 1st, for partridge-
shooting. In Germany those were the great days of Baden-Baden,
which came alive in Turgeniev's *Smoke* and a remarkably large
number of other Russian books. There were certain families from
the old nations, and the intruders from the new ones. The Ritz
concern had a special card-index to deal with them. Such items as,
"Herr X sleeps without a bolster. . . . Madame Y takes no butter

on her toast. . . . Lord G. must have black cherry-jam every day," were telegraphed back and forth between London, Lucerne, and Palermo.

The modern nomad was born. About 1500, painting conquered landscape, the day in the country and the long journey. The voyages around the world had begun, and with them came the sense of distance and vast spaces. The religious and eschatological hue of man's sense of infinity was overlaid by the geographical and descriptive. Now, about 1900, the luxurious note was added, and what had sprung from necessity was turned into a source of sensory experience and enjoyment. How much history there is in the Blue Trains and the Golden Arrows! Those luncheon-baskets, a specialty of Drew's at Piccadilly Circus, with their little spirit-stoves, those flasks for distilled water and boxes for meat and butter, were now transformed into the dining-car; the luggage-racks, where for several decades the children had been put to sleep, into Pullman cars and *wagons-lits*. The hotels far surpassed the town halls and cathedrals in significance, taking on their century's identity as the town halls and cathedrals had betokened theirs. At the laying of the foundation-stone for Claridge's in the Champs Elysées, Lady Grey performed the symbolic ceremony with a silver trowel. When the Ritz was furnished, the artistic legacy of Mansard and his masons—which the Place Vendôme still exemplified, uniquely undisturbed from the 18th century down to the present day—was faithfully preserved in months of inventive toil by a staff of architects, interior decorators, artisans, art historians, and other experts. The differences between *petit-point* and tapestry, between porcelain and *faience*, between the styles of the Sung and Tang dynasties had to be no less precisely observed than the subtle distinctions between the Italian and the Spanish Renaissance. It took careful research to discover and select the right shop for silver, for glass, for carpets, brocades, and silks, for table linen, sheets, and pillowcases. In Rome there was a first-rate place for Venetian lace and embroidery, and as for lighting, the novelty was indirect light, casting no shadow. How many tones were compared until it was settled at last: a muted apricot in alabaster bowls, the beams cast up onto the warmly tinted ceilings. A Van Dyck portrait in the Louvre, in which luminous brown tones contrasted with a matt turquoise, served as the model for harmonizing the color scheme of blinds, carpets, and wallpapers. Escoffier, the chef, did not permit gas in the kitchen: "A faultless pie can be baked only with the old, tested fuels." Coal and wood were vastly superior to gas, in the opinion of Escoffier, who was Sarah Bernhardt's sole guest at a birthday party she gave at the Carlton in London—Escoffier, who named his creations after Coquelin and Melba.

It was the age of the great dinners, meals of fourteen courses, with the sequence of wines following a tradition that went back four hundred years to the pheasant banquets of Burgundian days, of the fleur-de-lis princes. A banker who had successfully brought off an important transaction handed the paladins of the Ritz a check for 10,000 francs for a meal with a dozen friends. It was in winter, and fresh young peas, asparagus, and fruit were hard to obtain; but it was done. The Jeroboam de Château Lafitte 1870 and the Château Yquem 1869 were brought from Bordeaux by a special messenger, who had to make the night-long journey with the priceless casket on his knees lest the sensitive old wine should suffer any jolting. Among the 180,000 bottles the house had in its own cellars, of which 500 different varieties could be ordered from the wine list every evening, there was nothing fit to go with the *bécassine* and the truffles *en papillottes*.

The restaurant trade becomes out-and-out aristocratic and industrialized. The inaugurators and main pillars of the "Ritz idea" are Colonel Pfuffer of Altishofen in Lucerne, Baron Pierre de Gunzburg in Paris, Lord Lathom in London, the last board chairman of the Savoy Company. Marnier Lapostolle, an industrialist in St. Cloud, concocted a cordial whose march of triumph, under the name of *Le Grand Marnier*, doubled its inventor's fortune. Apollinaris was to start on its career with a celebration at the new spring, the Johannisbrunn. Among the guests were the Prince of Wales, who happened to be in Homburg, Russian grand dukes and

Prussian princes, twenty in all. A special freight-train had to transport food-stuffs, plates, cups, glasses, potted plants, armchairs, ice, and a kitchen-stove from Frankfurt am Main to the remote valley of the Ahr. The twenty covers cost 5,000 Swiss francs, but the Derby victory of his horse, Persimmon, combined with the presence of attractive women, put the prince in one of his most charming moods. Socially and, as the concern foresaw, commercially, it was a great success.

The second third of the last century had witnessed the rise of the great gambling casinos—forever linked with the names of the Blanc brothers from Bordeaux—above all in Homburg and in Monaco. *Grand joueurs* like Garzia, Lucien Napoleon, Bugeja, and Mustapha Fazil Pasha lost or won half a million in a few hours: dangerous people, the terror of the management that had to keep in constant telegraphic communication with three big banks while they stayed. *Trente-et-quarante* was the game for high stakes; they played with a cool million in cash piled before them on the table. But also playing were Adelina Patti, by marriage Marquise de Caux, Madame Lucca, Madame Grassi, and Jules Verne. Rubinstein scarcely stopped to bow to his audience after the last notes had faded away at his concerts, so eager was he to get back to the tables. Paganini gambled away two millions. Dostoievsky at roulette—probably the most famous and most incomprehensible of gamblers, a gambler to the point of degradation, a real addict. The Rothschilds, Bismarck's son, Gortschakoff, Gladstone, gambled at Homburg. Then, for political reasons, Homburg had to close down, and the last game was announced: "Messieurs, à la dernière forever."

On July 1, 1869, an edict was issued, declaring that henceforth the district of Saint-Devote on the cape of Monaco, Les Speluges, was to be known as "Le Quartier de Monte Carlo." A quay was built, the harbor of Condamine enlarged, the Hôtel de Paris smothered in flowers. The railway and the road from Nice were completed, the Casino was built. As early as 1869 all taxes were abolished in the territory, and made up by the gamblers. In 1874 the fourth roulette table had to be set up. When Saxon-les-Bains in Switzerland was closed, too, the only casino left in all Southern Europe was this one at "the Dives," Les Speluges, on the Côte d'Azur. Secure in its monopoly, it could now afford to admit only gamblers holding tickets made out in their names, to permit only play with *refait*, to present building-plots to newspapermen, and to hand considerable sums and a railway ticket to suicide suspects. The environs were organized: golf matches at Cannes, horse-racing at Nice, pigeon shooting. One Blanc was dead, the other, François, was the main shareholder; out of his private fortune he lent the city of Paris five millions to restore the Opéra, for which the Ministry of Transport gave him faster trains to the Mediterranean. One of his daughters married a Prince Radziwill, the other a Bonaparte, and her daughter a son of the King of Greece. Blanc's godfathers back in Bordeaux had been a stocking-weaver and a shoemaker. He left his family eighty-eight millions, made in Homburg and Monte Carlo and soon to be squandered on racing stables, yachts, castles, hot-houses for orchids, and *bijouterie*. What is remarkable is how little the persons of this circle and their institutions were moved by the events of the time. It is known that the last Czar did not break off his game of tennis when he received the news of the fall of Port Arthur. The day after Sadowa there was an open-air masquerade in the Prater, with a Venetian *corso*; beer-gardens and wine-gardens were filled to overflowing, and in the Volksgarten, where Strauss was conducting, all seats were sold out. The Casino of Monaco kept open during the war of 1870-'71, and its profits were only two millions less than in the preceding year of peace; it still paid out a dividend of five per cent. In Homburg the profits were lower, but exceeded half a million even during the year of war.

One can look at world history from inside and from outside, as a sufferer or as an observer. Art is expression, and since its last stylistic transformation, it is more so than ever. It needs means of expression, it goes in search of them, there is not much can be expressed by potato-peelings—not so much, anyway, as a whole life tries to express. More can be expressed by gold helmets, peacocks, pomegranates; more can be associated with roses, balconies, and rapiers; princes can be made to say what coopers cannot, and the Queen of the Amazons what a factory-girl cannot; people who have had the experience of Antiquity, who have spent years observing forms and styles, people who travel, whose nerves are sensitive and who have a weakness for gambling, may well be more complex and more fractional than savages, and with their modes of expression they will do more justice to their era than the partisans of Blood and Soil, who are still close to totemism. The more austere the artist is, the deeper is his longing for finesse and light. His participation in an era of squandering and sensual enjoyment is existentially moral; Balzac could write only within the daemoniacal orbit of high finance; Caruso's voice became perfect only when he sang before the Diamond Horseshoe at the Metropolitan. Thus we see the artist play his part in the epochs we are concerned with, and the public, in its turn, took note of the things that art produced, including their peculiarities and their inner meaning.

2. ART IN EUROPE

Those were the decades of Duse as Camille, of Bernhardt as l'Aiglon, of Lily Langtry as Rosalind, and large sections of the nations shared in that. Remember, there is the press, criticism, essayism. Capitalism can afford a public; it does not compel valuable components of the nation to emigrate, its *Lebensraum* has not been limited to torture and extermination. When Zola entered the dining room of the Grand Hotel in Rome and a puritanical Englishwoman jumped up indignantly at being expected to lunch in the same room with the author of *Nana*, there was a public to notice it, full of alertness and warmth and that fluid which goes to create the flair of an era—undoubtedly trivial things, too, at times, but how deep a background it built for achievement and rank to stand out against! How much brilliance it cast round Kainz, for instance, not because he hobnobbed with a king, but because by giving a word the right emphasis he could make people feel the powers of the deep, could make men and women, lemurs and masks, grow pale merely by the way he descended a flight of steps or slung his arm round a pillar! There was one nation in which literature had long been a public power that even the government had to reckon with: the French. Now they had created a new rank, that of *grand écrivain*, successor to the great *savants universels* of the 17th, 18th, and 19th centuries, and socially the successor to the *gentilhomme*—a blend of journalism, social criticism, and autochthonous art: *grandseigneurs*, marshals of literature: Balzac, the Goncourts, Anatole France; in England, Kipling. A new form of modern creativeness. In Germany the type was largely rejected, the musical-metaphysical factor remaining the core of the "unreal" German endeavors. In Norway, by contrast, Björnson same close to becoming king.

An age in motion: inflation of themes, chaos of stylistic attitudes. In architecture: glass and iron displacing wood and brick, concrete displacing stone. The age-old problem of rivers was solved by the suspension-bridge; hospitals abandoned the palatial style for that of the barracks. Public gardens, Boy Scouts, dancing schools.

The Third Estate at the zenith of its power: the bourgeoisie advancing into rank and title, into commanding positions in army and navy. The great cities: the proletariat lives in them, too, but did not build them. Modern international law, the mathematical sciences, biology, positivism—all this is bourgeois; so is the counter-movement: modern irrationalism, perspectivism, existentialist philosophy. The white bourgeois colonizes, sends the sahib to take charge of the yellow, brown, and black riff-raff. European art turns in the opposite direction, regenerating itself in the tropics: Gauguin on Tahiti, Nolde in Rabaul, Dauthendey in Java, Pierre Loti in Japan, Matisse in Morocco. Asia is opened up mythologically and linguistically: Wilhelm devotes himself to China, Lafcadio Hearn to Japan, Zimmer to India.

A spiritual intensity pervades Europe; from this small continent a spiritual high tension makes the unspeakable, the undreamed-of, take shape. It is hard to say which is more remarkable, the way the public follows and takes an interest, or the harshness, the dedication to truth—brutal, if necessary—on the part of its creators, those great intellects which bear the responsibility for the race's destiny. Immensely serious, tragically profound words about that work: "To say Poetry is to say Suffering" (Balzac); "To say Work is to say Sacrifice" (Valéry); "It is better to ruin a work and make it useless for the world than not to go to the limit at every point" (Thomas Mann); "Oft did I weary wrestling with Thee"—the line that a galley-slave had carved in his oar, now carved by Kipling in the table he worked at in India; "Nothing is more sacred than the work in progress" (d'Annunzio); "I would rather be silent than express myself feebly" (Van Gogh).

Cracks in the positivist picture of the world; influx of crises and menaces. Postulation of the concept of the bio-negative (intoxication, the psychotic, art). Doubts about the meaning of words: for instance dissolving and destructive; and for a substitute: creative and stimulating. Analysis of schizophrenia: in the oldest evolutionary centers of the brain, there survive memories of the collective primal phases of life, which may manifest themselves in psychoses and dreams (ethnophrenia), primal phases! Pre-lunar man comes upon the scene, and with him the ages of geological cataclysm, world crises, doom by fire, moon disintegration, globe-girdling tides; secrets from the beginning of the Quaternary: enigmatic similarities between the gods, the world-wide legend of the Flood, the kinship between linguistic groups in the Old and the New Worlds—problems of cultures, prehistorical cultures, pre-Atlantean links; the complex of problems posed by Negro sculpture, by the cave drawings of Rhodesia, the stone images on Easter Island, the great deserted cities in the primeval forest near Saigon.

Deciphering of the Assyrian clay cylinders; new excavations at Babylon, Ur, Samara; the first coherent presentation of Egyptian sculpture—an analysis of composition methods in the reliefs leads to the surprising perception that they correspond exactly to the theories of Cubism: "the art of drawing consists in establishing relations between curves and straight lines." Promiscuity of images and systems. Forming and re-forming. Europe is on the way to new glory, the shining examples from the past being the grandeur of the fifteenth and the fulfillment of the eighteenth century. Germany hesitates, for here intellectual talents are few and far between, yet an élite answers across the borders, stirred by the truth of an ethos now revealed, manifest for the first time in this insistence on clarity, craftsmanly delicacy, brightness, audacity, and brilliance—the "Olympus of Appearances"; within Germany it means discarding the Faustian urge in favor of work with defined limits.

Ever new throngs of ideas come charging in, the problems become inflated, remote distances draw nearer, displaying their miseries and their splendors, worlds lost and forgotten loom into view, among them some that are cloaked in twilight, equivocal, deranged. The amount of real intellectual discovery during these fifty years is unequalled, and, all in all, it really expands the pattern. Rembrandt, Grünewald, El Greco, long neglected, were rediscovered, the strange and disquieting phenomenon of Van Gogh was given a place in the world of the intellect; the riddle of Marées' Arcadian dream was solved, the unrecognized Hölderlin was conquered for that circle to which his bio-negative *problematik* was intelligible ("If I die in shame, if my soul is not avenged on the brazen . . .") Bertram's book appeared, and, in an unending sequence of analytical works transforming themselves in their own dialectics, Nietzsche was placed among the very greatest of Germans. Conrad's fascinating novels were translated. Hamsun became "the greatest among the living." The North had long established its supremacy with Ibsen, Björnson, and Strindberg; by producing Niels Lyhne the small provincial town of Thisted in Jutland had helped to form the taste of at least one of our generations. The New World came—Walt Whitman's lyrical monism had a great influence—and conquered; everyone knows the situation today; Europe's last great literary form, the novel, has largely passed under American control.

Diaghilev appears, the real founder of the modern stage. Composing music for his ballet are Stravinsky, his own discovery, Debussy, Milhaud, Respighi. His dancers are Pavlova, Karsavina, Nijinsky. His stage designers are Picasso, Matisse, Utrillo, Braque. Moving through Europe, he revolutionizes everything. The intellectual novelty of his ideas is the concentration and toughening of all the arts. This is how Cocteau put it: "A work of art must satisfy all nine Muses."

Slavonic and Romance elements combined here in a distinct trend: *against* mere feeling, against everything inarticulate, romantic, amorphous, against all empty planes, against mere allusions in punctuation; and *for* everything perfected, clarified, tempered by hard work; *for* precision in the use of materials, organization, strict intellectual penetration. What it comes to is a turning against inner life, mere good will, pedagogic or racial side issues, in favor of the form-assuming, and thus form-compelling, expression.

Everyone knows how this new style suddenly appeared simultaneously in all the lands of the white race. Today its implication is clear: producing art means purging the inarticulate, nationalistic inner life, dissolving the last residue of Post-Classicism, completing the secularization of medieval man. That is to say: anti-familiar, anti-idealistic, anti-authoritarian. The only authoritarian factor left is the will to express, the craving for form, the inner restlessness that will not leave off until the form has been worked out in its proper proportions. This will take absolute ruthlessness toward the beloved, time-tested, sacred things. But what we might then see is the epiphany of a new image casting its radiance over the anxieties of life, a new image of man's fate, which is so hopelessly, disconsolately laden.

These were not "artists of talent" tipping each other the wink; there was no conspiracy between Montmartre, Bohemian Chelsea, the ghetto, and the barnyard; it was a secular surging of life, racially and biologically founded, a change of style brought about by a mutational *ananke*. Scheler somewhere speaks of "feelings that everyone nowadays is aware of having in himself but which it once took men like poets to wrest from the appalling muteness of our inner life." Such wresters come to the fore now. After all, the whole nineteenth century can today be interpreted as an upheaval within the gene, which saw this new mutation ahead. Things had lost their old relevance, not only in morals but in physics; they even broke out of the mechanical world view that had been held inviolable since Kepler. When this happened the public realized that something had been going on secretly for a long time. For centuries all the great men of the white race had felt only the one inner task of concealing their own nihilism. This nihilism had drawn sustenance from a variety of spheres: with Dürer from the religious, with Tolstoy from the moral, with Kant from the epistemological, with Goethe from the universally human, with Balzac from the social—but it had been the basic element in the work of every one of them. With immense caution it is touched again and again; with equivocal questions, with groping, ambiguous turns, they approach it on every page, in every chapter, in every character. Not for a moment are they in doubt about the essential nature of their inner creative substance: it is the abysmal, the void, the cold, the inhuman. The one who remained naive the longest was Nietzsche. Even in *Zarathustra*, what meaningful disciplined élan! It is only in the last phase, with *Ecce Homo* and the lyrical fragments, that he admits it to his consciousness: "Thou shouldst have sung, oh, my soul!"—not: believed, cultivated, thought in historical and pedagogical terms, been so positive—: and now comes the breakdown. Singing—that means forming sentences, finding expressions, being an artist, doing cold, solitary work, turning to no one, apostrophizing no congregation, but before every abyss simply testing the echoing quality of the rock-faces, their resonance, their tone, their coloratura effects. This was a decisive finale. After all: artistics! It could no longer be concealed from the public that here was a deep degeneration of substance. On the other hand, this lent great weight to the new art: what was here undertaken in artistic terms was the transference of things into a new reality, a new, authentic relevance, a biological realism proved by the laws of proportion, to be experienced as the expression of a new spiritual way of coming to terms with existence, exciting in the creative tension of its pursuit of a style derived from awareness of inner destiny. Art as a means of producing reality: this was the productive principle of the new art.

Undeniably: this art was capitalistic, a ballet demanded costumes, a tour had to be financed. Pavlova could not dance unless she was lodged in rooms filled with white lilac, both winter and summer, whether in India or in the Hague. Duse suffered much, everything around her had to be hushed, far away from her, with the curtains drawn. For some of his paintings Matisse received sums in six figures. Some went to bathe at Lussin-piccolo even at the height of the season; composing a new opera paid for a new car. The high-tension, condensations, oscillations of intensified life were part of this order of things, but so were the sufferings, the hag-ridden dread of losing the inner voice, the vocation, the visions overbrimming with imagery. Exhibitionism and breakdown alike were filled with truth, they were sovereign. The intellectual nonsense about the esthetic sense of the common people had not yet been trotted out to idealize the microcephalic; Bronze-Age barter was not yet proclaimed an economic dream full of pos-sibilities for the future; people could travel, spend their money, take on the imprint of many skies, be transformed in many cities.

There were also some perfectly successful representations of the social milieu: Van Gogh's "Potato-Eaters," Hauptmann's *The Weavers*, Meunier's sculptures of miners, Käthe Kollwitz's drawings; and, for the rural milieu: Millet's "Sower," Leibl's "Forester." But compassion and an intimate sense of one's own country were not all the emotional content and formal motif, no more than "The Return from Hades," or a woman bathing or a jug filled with asphodels. The human and humane was only one of the currents flowing toward the distant shore. And what peopled that shore was goddesses or orange-pickers or horses, girls from Haiti, post-men, railway-crossings, also flute-players and army officers—but all craving for the life of shadows. A very selective, exclusive start. A vocation. A great peculiarity. It meant elevating everything decisive into the language of unintelligibility, yielding to things that deserved to convince no one. Yet art should not be said to have been esoteric in the sense of being exclusive; everyone could come in and hear, open doors and see, draw closer, join, or go away. The tragic distances between man and man are felt a thousand times more as a result of other phenomena: the cruel accumulation of power, justice corrupted by politics, unbalanced passions, senseless wars. This is, perhaps, the place to point out that we had successful novels that were German in the good sense, best sellers such as *Ekkehard, Debit and Credit, Effi Briest, Jörn Uhl*. There was nothing remotely like a bar to German production in any foreign or racially alien works. It is one of the countless political lies to assert that only now was there any guarantee that the true-blue German would get true-blue German books. Rather, what made certain groups loathe the modern style was its exciting, experimental, controversial quality—in short, the intellectual quality of what was going on, and what their own meager talents could not cope with. Besides, there was the hatred of seeing the public reached by anything at all, other than their own political and nationalistic belly-aching. Thus the intellect in itself became "un-German," and at its particularly abominable worst: "European." The rest of Europe thought that a general paganization of form might perhaps reconsecrate the race whose gods had died; it did not expect this from fairy tales and dialect and Wotanisms.

It was this concept of "Europe" that in 1932 gave birth to the notion of a Mediterranean Academy, the Académie Méditerranéenne which was to have its seat in Monaco. All the riparians of that "narrow sea," the directly and indirectly Mediterranean countries, were asked to join. D'Annunzio, Marshal Pétain, Pirandello, Milhaud took the lead. The Royal Italian Academy, the Gami-el-Azhar University in Cairo, and the Sorbonne were among the cooperating institutions. All that the pagan and then the monotheistic generations had produced in esthetic and conceptual values was here to be clarified anew, for the enrichment and edification of today's world. All that had created and formed us, too, up in the North: the enigma of the Etruscans, the lucid centuries of Antiquity, the inexhaustibility of the Moors, the splendor of Venice, the marble tremors of Florence. Who would deny that we, too, were formed by the Renaissance and the Reformation—whether in devotion or in battle—that the monks, the knights, the troubadours, that Salamanca, Bologna, Montpellier, that botanically roses, lilies, wine, and biographically Genoa and Portofino and the Tristan palace on the Grand Canal, down to this hour of our life—that by all this breathless creativity Rome and the Mediterranean left so indelible an imprint upon us that we, too, belonged to it? But the invitations sent to Germany fell into the hands of the Gestapo. Art was closed down. "Messieurs, à la dernière forever!"

3. ART AND THE THIRD REICH

It is only against this background situation that one clearly sees what was special about the "German awakening." A nation broadly speaking without any definite taste, as a whole untouched by the moral and esthetic refinement of neighboring civilized countries, philosophically embroiled in confused idealistic abstractions, prosaic, inarticulate, and dull, a practical nation with—as its evolution demonstrates—only a biological way to spirituality: i.e., by Romanization or universalization; such a nation elevates an anti-semitic movement that demagogically conjures up before its eyes the meanest of its ideals: low-income housing developments, with subsidized, tax-favored sex life, home-made rape-oil in the kitchen, self-hatched scrambled eggs, home-grown barley, homespun socks, local flannel, and, for art and the inner life, S.A. songs bellowed in radio style. A nation's mirror of itself. Parallel bars in the garden, and St. John's fires on the hills—there's your pure-bred Teuton. A rifle range and the pewter mug filled with bock, that was his element. And now they gaze questioningly at the civilized nations and wait with childlike naiveté for their amazement and admiration.

A remarkable process! Inside a Europe of high brilliance and joint intellectual endeavors there evolves an inner-German Versailles, a Germanic collective based on a society of criminals, and whenever there is a chance they belabor the Muses. They are not content with the big cars, the hunting lodges where the bison roar, the stolen island in the Wannsee—Europe has to marvel at their culture! Haven't we talents among us with the resonance of tin cans and the pathos of waterlogged corpses, and painters whom we need only show the direction: say, His Nibs at the end of a shoot, the gun still smoking, one foot on the felled sixteen-point stag, the morning mists rising from the ground, furnishing a touch of the primeval woodland murmurs? And the block warden goes in for colored saucers—they will make Europe sit up! But above all one must exterminate: all that is Eastern, or Southern, or Western, not to speak of what is Latin, Gothic, Impressionist, Expressionist, the Hohenstaufen, the Hapsburg, Charlemagne—till they alone are left, perhaps with Henry the Lion and Snow White thrown in. On these odds and ends they base their Chambers of Culture, their esthetic Sing-Sing.

The artist is reincorporated in the guild order from which he freed himself about 1600. He is regarded as an artisan, a particularly senseless and corruptible artisan, patronized by the cell leader or the Soldiers' Home. Artisans are not supposed to care about the era's political or social decisions; only Kultur-Bolsheviks and traitors do. Anyone daring to say that artistic creation presupposes a measure of inner freedom is called before the Chamber; anyone mentioning the word style gets a warning; mental hospitals and institutions are consulted on the question of contemporary art. As filling station attendant for vital contents, the Propaganda Minister is the authority on line and counterpoint. Music must be folksongish, or else it is banned. Only generals or Party officials are subjects for portraiture: in clear, simple colors; subtle nuances are discouraged. For establishing a bridgehead in the East you get an oil portrait, 8-12, rated according to defense value—*i.e.*, value in defending the boss's job. Genre paintings showing fewer than five children are not to be marketed. Tragic, somber, extravagant themes are matters for the Security Police; delicate, high-bred, languid ones for the Racial Health Court.

Personages one could never object to if they confined themselves to fattening pigs or milling flour step forward, hail "man" as ideal, organize song-fests and choir contests, and set themselves up as the measure of things. Lübzow, Podejuch County, disputes the alliterative laurels with Piepenhagen in Pomerania, while the hamlets with a population below 200 in the Schwalm valley vie for the jubilee song of the Xaver Popiol S.A. Brigade. "Terpsichorean," says clubfoot; "melodious," murmurs ear-wax; skunks claim to smell of roses; the Propaganda Minister takes up relations with poetry. "Strong outlines"—no truck with the sublime! Obvious! Compared with shooting people in the neck outdoors or chair-leg fighting indoors, sublimity has a sissified, un-German look. Of course, flattening is not quite formative, but the gas station attendant does not notice. What does not take on expression stays prehistoric. Art is a buoy marking deep and shallow spots; what the Minister wants is relaxation and dash. Art among all gifted races is a profound delimiting of enhancement and transition; here they order four new pirates à la Störtebeker and three freedom-fighters à la Colonel Schill. Whatever style and expression a few inspired individuals achieved, over slights and abuse, among these ponderous, divided people, they have debased and falsified in their own image: the jaws of Caesars and the brains of troglodytes, the morality of protoplasm and the sense of honor of a sneak thief. All nations of quality create their own élite; now it has come to the point where being German means being hostile to any sort of differentiation and, in matters of taste, betting always on the clumsiest horse; the sensitive are given the third degree by the Gestapo. It also looks after art studios: great painters are forbidden to buy canvas and oils, and at night the block wardens go round checking on the easels. Art comes under the heading of pest control (Colorado beetle). A genius is chased screaming through the woods at night; when an aged Academy member or a Nobel Prize winner finally dies of starvation, the culture guardians beam with glee.

Vengeful underdogs, perspectival *formes frustes*—but, although the occasion scarcely justifies it, one must look at it even more comprehensively. It is the centuries-old German problem that here has the chance to manifest itself so clearly, under the protection of the nation's armed criminals. It is the German substance, something outside differentiation and esthetic transformation. An historically not uninteresting, in spots even distinguished work about conditions in the pre-Reformation era points out that Dürer endangered his Germanness by turning to those mathematical problems in painting that Italian painters had formulated under the impact of the Renaissance. So Dürer was concerned with formal processes of orderly consciousness—studies in proportion—and this was already un-German, already too much. The clear sky of abstraction, which arches over the Latin world without any dehumanizing or sterilizing effect, is here unhealthy and harmful to production. This is the voice of an urge for illiteracy—but here it is genuine. It is part of their *"Lebensraum,"* their "evolution," their thought-shunning dash. The resolution of inner tensions by esthetic means is alien to them. The cathartic nature of expression in general they will always deny, for lack of any corresponding inner experience. What they lack is impressions of the constructive form of the sublime. Spiritually held down by low-grade ideas, such as that of a single, mechanical causality, they will never be able to grasp an essential, productive causality of the creative principle. What they can experience is history, a result of bacteriological research, an experiment, an economic process—they are incapable of experiencing the questing and agonized motions of a productive gene inherent even in the white race and that gene's escape into a structural element. That is why their writers wind up even short paragraphs, trivial dicta, on a moral, didactic, and, if possible, absolute note; they can find no other way of getting themselves off-stage. Their lack of any tendency towards artistic abstraction is complete—for that would require hard work, objectivity, discipline. Objectivity in turn demands decency and detachment, a moral, personal decency that is beyond riff-raff. So wherever they see things raised to the level of consciousness and find an artist revealing his own productive processes, they work off their feelings in hatred against "artistics," in rambling balderdash about formalism and intellectualism. For this people, uniovular twins are more important than geniuses: the former lend themselves to statistics, the latter contain lethal factors. This people spews out its geniuses as the sea spews out its pearls: for the inhabitants of other realms.

And so this people is caught up in the Awakening, in the "German miracle," the "recuperative movement," according to E. R. Jaentsch's book, *The Anti-Type*. (The anti-type consists not of the awakened but of the undaunted, those who go on striving for more refinement.) This movement would have us believe that the Great Migrations have just come to an end, and that we are now called upon to clear the forests. It is a miracle whose most unique and sincere quality appears when the cities have to be blacked out, when people fall silent, mists billow, and only they talk and talk and talk, until their stinking breath rolls like vast cow-pats over the suffocated fields. It is a rising, the essence of which—apart from their get-rich-quick schemes, which come so naturally to them —is a lie of lies and an anthropological unreality, excluding the achievement of any sort of identity with any age, race, or continent. This movement purges art. It does so by means of the same concept with which it glorifies and justifies itself and which thus looms gigantically, programmatically, into our field of vision: history.

Five hoplites armed with machine-guns attack a boy they had promised not to harm; then they march in somewhere—: history. Mahomet began as a robber of caravans; the ideology was a later addition. He even poisoned the wells in the desert—for centuries an unimaginable crime, but now ennobled by divine and racial needs: first theft, then religion, finally history. Under Nero, in 67 A.D., private correspondence in Rome had ceased entirely, since all letters were opened; the postmen came to the houses in the mornings bringing news by word of mouth about the latest executions: world history.

And this means: at breakfast, on mountain-tops, while breaking and entering, with filmstars—Colleoni! Before rabbit-hutches, cloakrooms, extra distributions of synthetic honey—Alexander! At mass murders, lootings, blackmail: geopolitics and fulfillment of destiny! Now, history may have its own methods, and one that our eyes can clearly discern is undoubtedly its use of microcephalics, but art has also proved itself in forty centuries. This essay is art's rejoinder; these are the expressions it has found to fit the epoch. It finds them as naturally and sharply as the Gestapo aims its shots. It collects them and hands them on to those who will always exist, during every historical victory and during every historical doom, and whose influence will outlast both victory and doom. Art now records these expressions in the belief that there will some day be a European tradition of the mind, which Germany will also join, a tradition from which it will learn and to which, having learned, it will contribute.

(Written 1941, published 1949) Translated by Ernst Kaiser and Eithne Wilkins

EXCERPTS FROM

WORLD OF EXPRESSION

Physics 1943

Classical mechanics are grouped with optics, or, in more general terms, with electro-dynamics; the ninety-two elements of the old physics that was valid up to 1900 are reduced to two, the electron and the proton. The elements are transmutable. Time is only a factor of measurement. All these are phenomena of what modern physics calls "ultimate reality" and "absolute reality": an x that becomes ever more enigmatic the more closely one approaches it methodically. Ever more clearly the two realms confront each other: the world of expression, the summa of all the concepts that have been worked out in generations of intellectual labor, and then this background which once upon a time was substance, later was Descartes' *ens realissimum,* and today is what they call "ultimate reality."

The world of expression, and reality! To assume that there are no compulsive relationships between the two, that there is no *Ananke* at work between them, would indicate a lack of profundity, even if *the actual transformation of reality by the intellect did not go on before our eyes.* The transmutation of atoms tells the whole story. Since the physicists achieved the fission of the uranium atom, we must reckon with the possibility that the continuous bombardment of uranium atoms with neutrons may initiate chain-reactions releasing such quantities of energy as to involve the planets in catastrophes. Form-creating intellect is beyond doubt in the position to play its part in a process that would dissolve matter. "Ultimate reality" brought forth this intellect at a late hour in Creation, to be fertilized by it and so to be destroyed.

Fertilizing and destroying—these are conventional notions, human conventions and the term "compulsive relationship" naturally cannot mean to convey any knowledge in the general sense, or indeed anything but a merely local identity. If we consider for a moment that the thing we call time—which we do taste and breathe, which goes with our thinking like the pain and love we feel—is presumably only a splinter of something utterly alien to us, a chip of veiled worlds drifting, a mere flash of mirrors and mirror-images, and if we then tell ourselves that it is from such chips and fragments that we read off and play our human environment, our unique score of terrestrial history and racial existence—then it will cease to matter that our sense of time, our experience of time as truth, will never let us see yesterday as today, and what will emerge more clearly are the innumerable other living worlds, the worlds before birth and the worlds after death, and all those immemorial and forgotten worlds that the eons, alternately sinking and enthroned, bestow as their gift.

In this human world of ours there is a species of ants whose characteristic is diligence and quiet industry. They are the scholars. One might marvel at them. Here the Commission for Solar Radiation and Solar Spectroscopy comes out with the following statement: "While the enumeration of the various aspects of our work appears to be comparatively complete, from a general point of view we have to consider whether we are as yet capable of answering the simplest fundamental questions about the sun, questions that are the actual purpose of solar-physical research. It will be evident how little real knowledge we possess and how difficult it is to make any progress." From the report of the International Astronomic Congress, Stockholm, 1938. The history of this hypothetical mode of thought, which finds it difficult to progress, is demonstrably more than a hundred years old. In 1814 Fraunhofer discovered the spectral lines named after him; in 1851 the solar prominences were discovered; in 1900 the temperature of the sun was calculated at 7,000° Centigrade. Yet in Stockholm, in 1938, after four generations of research-scientists, nothing is known about the sun.... Elsewhere there are the biologists. They think ecologically: what their particular termite-eyes are looking for is the conditions, the chemico-physical conditions, in which "life" evolves, grows, and changes. Even more generations of research-workers than in the astronomers' case, more working hypotheses, classificatory theories, principles of observation, and experiments—of course, sea-urchins' eggs are easier to vary than suns—more institutes, laboratories, guinea-pig and rat farms all over the world, mice bombarded with sub-atomic particles, newts whose genes are literally shot to pieces—but as for life itself and what it actually is, we have recently been informed that in another hundred years the preliminary work may have perhaps reached a stage at which it will be possible to consider the principles upon which to base a view of organic existence. Amazing! Ants! If you want to know about life in the next hundred years, you had better ask other animals of the woods....

But what will these other animals answer, even the best of them, the speckled ones, the gentle ones, the doves? Will they point out that this question has already been answered by Hegel, who declared it to be a creditable obstinacy on man's part to refuse to acknowledge any point of view not justified by thought? What is thought, when does anything become thought? How wide must a basis be, what gravity must fundamentals have, to give a looming notion or an observation the status of thought? A thought that darkens the sun has turned up in modern radiology. Microscopes are now abandoning visible light, liberating themselves from its limited wave length, and working with one thousands of times smaller: that of the artificially produced electron beam. Shadows are cast upon the sun. He used to blaze, and is 400 million years old, but in 1895 x-rays and gamma rays were discovered, in 1900 the radioactive rays, and in 1930 the cosmic rays—the two first-mentioned artificially produced and all three of them together incomparably greater in scope and effect than light. Gamma and radioactive rays bring about the artificial transmutation of elements; cosmic rays, not absorbed by the top layers of the earth, penetrate 300 meters into solid ground and 700 meters into water, while hundreds of millions of them shoot through human beings every day. Nobody knows where they come from, probably from unimaginably distant new stars; their effect has hardly been touched upon by any theorizing. The spaces dealt with by the new hypotheses grow ever vaster, and, oddly enough, the apparatus used becomes ever smaller and more expressionless. No more laboratories; the noisy machines fall silent, the great scintillations are exhausted and mute. In gas-tight vessels the size and shape of a tin can one observes the explosion of stars and measures the mass of nova systems that can no longer be expressed in any human numerical order. A capsule the size of an orange, dragged through the stratosphere in the gondola of a balloon, is used to produce and measure the shower of ionization, caused by rays utterly unknown ten years ago. The materialization of rays and the dematerialization of matter by means of rays. Nature turns into a network of concepts and symbols, and these in turn produce matter and Nature. The unification of matter and energy is completed, as is the unification of thought and motile Nature. Once, to be sure, God was the Creator of worlds, and doubtless there are things more ancient than blood, but for some time now it has been brains that keep the earth going, and the evolution of the world leads through human concepts—at present obviously its main and favorite way. So the animals of the woods do in fact reply with the Hegelian apotheosis that places God's body in Nature and his self-awareness in man and defines thought as the second world, the super-world, the formula world of a once inarticulate, fettered movement that is now becoming conscious and always unappeasably transforming itself?

Pessimism

Man is not solitary, but thought is solitary. True, man is densely cloaked in mournfulness, but many share in this mourning, and it is popular with all. But thought is ego-bound and solitary.

Perhaps primitive man thought collectively—the Red Indians, the Melanesians, most markedly the Negroes—here a number of things might be interpreted as an intensification of mass-participation; on the other hand, even on this level the figures of magicians, medicine-men, and saviors indicate the individually isolated nature of the intellectual manifestation. As for the white race, I do not know whether its life is happiness, but anyway its thought is pessimistic.

Pessimism is the element of its creativeness. Admittedly we live in an epoch when pessimism is considered degenerate. There have been times—for instance, in the fourth and fifth centuries, before the great migrations could have any influence at all—when pessimism was an almost universal, at least theoretically admissible, attitude. It was pessimism that created the monasteries of Egypt and Palestine. A mass movement, incidentally: at the time of Jerome, the Easter festival at Tabenna was celebrated by 50,000 monks and nuns, all from the Nile area. They lived in rocky caves, in tombs between the sea and the marshes, in wattle cabins, abandoned citadels, with snakes around them as they knelt, the mirages of the desert around them in their ecstasies—wolves and foxes went leaping by while the saint was at prayer. What impelled them was denial of the world, of the *saeculum*. The consequences are with us to this day: monotheistic religion at its purest, the literature of Antiquity, the philosophy of ideas and images; in short: the West would not exist without them.

Pessimism is not a Christian motif. The Choruses of Sophocles tell us that it is best never to be born, and that if you live, the next best thing is to go swiftly whence you came. That we are such stuff as dreams are made on was taught, 2,000 years before the Swan of Avon, by Buddhism—the embodiment of all that pessimism ever said and meant. Modern nihilism goes directly back to this, via Schopenhauer: "extinction"—"fading out," "a juggler's tricks" —"the starless void." It is very striking that this first authentic, one might even say popular, pessimism to appear in the history of the world as a system and a mass conviction, did not originate among India's oppressed lower castes, but among the mighty Brahmins. It was from a principality tropically luxuriant in pleasures and possessions that Shakyamuni came, the hermit "son of the Shakyas" (born 623 before Christ). But it is still more remarkable that his teaching did not set out to abolish any evils, any social, moral, or physical states of suffering but to abolish *existence itself,* the very substance of being. Life as such cast that handful of dust into the air, into the cycle of growth, before Sansara's wheel—so extinguish it—blow away all thirst of desire— no gods—the void. At the beginning there is a form of pessimism that denies all historical achievement, the state, any community—an *existential* pessimism frankly aimed at germ destruction.

And its germ-destroying trend culminates in *Schopenhauer's* dictum "Paederasty is a stratagem of Nature driven to the wall by her own laws—a *pons asinorum* that she has constructed in order to choose the lesser of two evils." And: "Life is continuous deception; it keeps no promise and gives so as to take." Here we have neither consciousness nor the unconscious, neither substance nor causality, neither reality nor dream, only fathomless, blind will, incapable of cognition. Behind this there stands *Schelling,* for whom the human head was only "Creation's tail-end," man "an amusing beast," death's-heads behind the ogling masks, even the stars full of bones and worms. He says: "It is all nothing, all choking and greedily gulping itself down, and this very self-devouring is the sly pretense that something exists—since, if the choking were to stop, nothingness itself would be so clearly manifest as to appall them." And *Byron* stands behind it: "Accursed be he who created life"; "the deeds of Athens' great men are the fable of an hour, a schoolboy's tale." *Stendhal:* "History is a collection of misdeeds; there is scarcely one virtuous act to a thousand crimes." *Diderot:* "To be born in helplessness and dependence, with pain and cries; to be the plaything of ignorance, error, need, sickness, of vileness and the passions; step by step from the moment when one begins to stammer to the moment of departure, when one raves; to live among rogues and charlatans of every kind; to pass away between one who feels our pulse and another who confounds us, not knowing whence one comes, why one has come, whither one is going—this is what is called the most precious gift we receive from our parents and from Nature: life." Here too are the Romans. *Pliny:* "Hence Nature has given man nothing better than brevity of life." *Marcus Aurelius:* "Man's nature is fluid, his feelings dim, the substance of his body tending to corruption, his soul comparable to a spinning top, his destiny hard to define, his reputation a matter of uncertainty." "Dream and rapture—war and journeying —his epitaph: oblivion." "Mayflies both he who remembers and he who is remembered." "Yesterday a bubble, tomorrow an embalmed corpse, then a heap of ashes." "Life is spent in bad company, in the frail body; what should deserve our love and striving in all the filth and corruption of circumstances, in the eternal interchange of essence and form, in the incalculable way things take their course, is more than man can see." "The sole consolation is going towards the dissolution of all things." *Septimius Severus,* gazing back over the road he had traveled from a low position in life up to imperial greatness, summed up: *"Omnia fui et nihil expedit*—I have been everything, and it was all for nothing." *Charles the Fifth,* on the road to St. Just, said that the greatest happiness he had enjoyed had always been associated with such manifold unhappiness that he must truthfully say he had never known a pure pleasure, never an unmixed delight.

These last three were emperors, wearing the diadem and wielding the power of the world. Evidently he who wants to accomplish things mistakes the action; in any case, the action takes a course different from that of their dream: *omnia fui et nihil expedit.* To be extinguished—to fade out—Hispanic monks, open the door for me! But what are we to make today of these words in *Wilhelm Meister's Travels:* "Once one knows what really matters, one tends to stop talking." Again a turn towards silence, away from participation and fellowship; words that are sheer rejection—was even he who wrote this, and who confessed to Eckermann that for him life had been the perpetual heaving of a boulder that had to be shifted again and again, that in seventy-five years he had not known four weeks of real ease—was even he *pre-nihilistic*? And what had happened to life's most strenuous glorifier, to that great prober and summarizer—what had Nietzsche lost that the world became a gateway to "a thousand deserts mute and cold"? Is there any possible interpretation of those weighty verses entitled "In Isolation," other than the assumption that their writer had lost all belief in fellowship, in the strong man's will to something higher and his ability to reach it, in biology, in race, in the "blond beast" ("Caesar with the soul of Christ")—was it perhaps here that the breakdown began, the fall into those ten years of sickbed-Nirvana after so many gigantic visions of a superior breed of men?

Omnia fui et nihil expedit. The game is not worth the candle. *Vulnerant omnes, ultima necat*—"All of them wound, the last one kills"—an inscription on the face of a medieval sundial, referring to the hours. And the ancient waterclock in the German Museum in Munich, the nymph weeping away the hours, the minutes, tear by tear—all this is the prelude to European nihilism. In a word, *pessimism is a legitimate spiritual principle,* a very ancient one which found genuine expression in the white race and which it will interweave with the future, supposing it still to possess the metaphysical power to incorporate and assimilate, the power of integration and of giving form. In this direction, too, points the strange passage in a letter of Burckhardt's, written in 1875, which says that the global battle between optimism and pessimism still remains to be fought. Victory, we may add today, can be won only in the sign of pessimism; negation alone will help to create that new world which not only man but Nature herself inclines to, in which she senses her transformation: the world of expression.

Profiles

THOMAS WOLFE

A new book by Wolfe, fourteen short stories, small-scale work, very instructive. Fourteen experiments in posing an ontological reality, outlining it, using it to work in a certain direction, rounding it out and giving it completeness. All things of the present; the situation is mostly as follows: first something that exists, a milieu, something that is already general, socially and individually typical, historically set, and secondly the other, that which still has lacunae and weaknesses and even childlike aspects, that which is still experiencing. This is not worked out into conflicts, problems, trends of development, and similar pretexts for books; rather, the contrasts result from the expression of the inner basis, the style. The way of writing results in the crisis—it *is* the crisis. The approach reveals the abysses of time and super-time; the method of writing, the sequence of the sentences, their repetition, their charge of energy, their exuberance—this in itself is repose and destruction.

In other words, Wolfe has the gift of producing art, and that in the epic realm—a gift that hardly anyone in Europe still possesses. The novel, Europe's creation, dating from about 1800 and descended from comedy, over there attains to the grand style once more with Faulkner, Dos Passos, Wolfe: every one of their pages gathers up the earth, the tissue of earth, and pulverizes it under high pressure, sends it flying up in high fountains, to float down again over graves, over moments of happiness, into the shadows.

Peculiar how poetry springs into existence in these novelists' work! In these novels with their urge towards norm and type, big-city novels, amid concentrated asphalt scenes, city realisms, matter-of-fact relations, virtual statistics: suddenly a sentence soars, becomes airborne, frees itself, floats, fades into silence and breathless profundity. Sentences of pure poetry! This in itself shows that these books do not set out to educate anyone, nor to entertain the middle classes. It is good that in one of the countries where literature is made it should appear again that art does not originate in bourgeois and communal strata. Everywhere in Wolfe's work the two worlds part: that of material gain, of status, of earthly beauty, of power; and that of the spirit. There are no transitions from one to the other except in the way they meet, look at each other, and then look away. This looking away does not yet have the acuteness of its European equivalent, it is still biologically softer, more youthful, also more romantic; it all still lies in the phase when social conditions color everything, not yet in the dialectical and antithetical phases which constitute the end-situation.

Anyone who thinks he must infer from the above that what we meet with here are complicated and intellectual things, is mistaken. Wolfe writes about simple things, easy to read about though difficult to create; they can only be created out of a sphere of solitary spiritual power, far removed from all that is declamatory and programmatic.

RIVERA

It is the storm against the white race. The face of God is black or *café-au-lait* color. Diego de Rivera, the great Indian painter in Mexico, depicts the situation most impressively. One cannot fail to see how much the rest of them long to be liberated from these pigment-deficient, irritated albinos. We are speaking of the murals in the Palace of Cortez at Cuernavaca, the Presidential residence, entitled: "The history of Mexico, in particular its conquest by Cortez" (1930). Four centuries of white overlordship, meaning murder, looting, torture, and rape. Fifty-five faces and bodies, acting and suffering, in several parallel bands one above the other à la Rubens, Grosz, Dix: Rubens, the oblique construction; Grosz, the mean vacuity of the faces; Dix, the taut, three-dimensional, bellying quality of cheeks, bosoms, naked or clad legs. It is all held together by a system of tubes, arboreal, perhaps rather like an internal-combustion engine, evidently steam, Diesel oil, compressed air streaming upwards in many ramifications. Unsurpassable the crouching potency of greed and cunning, whip, stake, rope, branding-iron, promiscuous cot—emanations of the white man. Bending over a freshly raped mestiza is the figure of Las Casas, that great friend and benefactor of the Indians, the dying girl drawing his head down towards her to kiss his brow. Las Casas' head is broad, bronze-colored, swollen with shame. This is clearly the work of one of the greatest painters of the century;

there is hardly a picture in Europe that equals it in expressive power.

The theme is colonization. The white sahib elevates and converts the redmen and the blacks. His ideas are more split and unfruitful than those of the natives, his creeds more colorless, the Protestant one quite impossible to visualize. In his own country some snow falls outdoors, here soldiers drill, there a child cries, here crusts of bread are bought up, there they traffic in pearls pierced for stringing—all this accidents and details—all this falls apart, there is no longer any collective center, nothing with a primitive animistic meaning. This is how the sahib colonizes, but his magic is losing its power. Wars as the ultimate destiny of the race, nations as cases of Darwinism—this is not archaic and mythical; it is bewilderment, it is the end. If we count Russia as Asian, the whites are already dying out.

RILKE

Granted, Rilke could still fill the pages of his letters with the names of noblemen owning a beautiful collection of—just think!—old *livres d'heures,* and country estates and castles in the Ukraine and stud-farms where they bred Arab horses. That did not sound too boring, even though it was all addressed to countesses and written from castles or at least from the Villa des Brillants, Meudon-Val Fleury (Seine et Oise), precisely dated, down to the hour of the day. Or the abundance of his nature, from which his correspondence was known to flow, could require such details as the following: "On Saturday, the first of June, I took my first Turkish bath, enjoying it to the full, without the slightest discomfort. It was glorious to soak in the good warmth of it, for which I was, indeed, prepared by the warmth we had down south; I wish there were some of it outside the Turkish bath as well." A warm bath, Meudon, and then even that is too rough—a little creative crisis, and three months in Viareggio or Capri materialize for the poet, who spends them in Tyrolean pants, that is, "in a fashion, bare-legged," and: "Then and there a little tune would ring in me, perhaps only a very little one after so long a time, and so it did not seem prudent to take this seed of melody into the big railway train with me and on to new impressions in Genoa and Dijon, but important to wait here for the confinement, however small." Only a very little one, and a good warmth—a blend of male dirt and lyrical depth, fondled by duchesses, poured out in letters to the broadhipped Ellen Key—there you have the giant of 1907. Lucky fatherland! All's well that ends well, and there is always yet another countess's castle, where one can poeticize the poor; God listens, and the pens start moving! This meager figure and font of great poetry, who died of leukemia and was laid to rest among the bronze hills of the Rhone valley, in earth fanned by French sounds, wrote the line that my generation will never forget: "Who speaks of victory?—survival is all!"

Pallas

Athena, who leapt fully armed and shining from Zeus's brow—blue-eyed, the motherless divinity. Pallas—delighting in battles and destruction, Medusa's head on her breastplate, the somber, joyless bird of night upon her helmet; she steps back a little and with a single movement lifts the enormous border-stone from the field against Mars, who sides with Troy and Helen. Venus bemoans her hand, wounded by Diomedes, and Pallas laughs at this blood: probably scratched herself on a golden buckle down there, fondling someone in armor. Pallas, beyond Sappho and Mary, once almost overpowered in the darkness of a cavern, always helmeted, never impregnated, a childless goddess, cold and alone.

Pallas protects matricides! It is her vote against the Erinyes that gains Orestes his acquittal. (Aeschylus, *The Eumenides*, 458 B.C., Theatre of Bacchus.) Athena says:

"Not the mother is procreator of her child,
she only bears and nourishes the newly wakened life."

With these lines the cataclysm sets in. Woman is dethroned as the primary and supreme sex, debased into an inseminable hetaera. The accursed age begins. Plato, Aeschylus, Augustine, Michelangelo

—all of the accursed age, some even paederasts. The modern champion of the maternal spirit declares: "A glorious victory, forsooth! Clytemnestra slew vicious Agamemnon, who had slaughtered her daughter Iphigenia—hers, the mother's daughter—on the sacrificial altar and who returned to Mycenae bringing his new wives along. Orestes, her son, thereupon slew Clytemnestra, his mother, who had killed his father. The Erinyes appeared to accuse the matricide, Apollo and Athena defended him and forced his acquittal. The speeches of both, in behalf of the father-idea and the permissibility of matricide, suffice to indicate the moral decline concealed by the ascendancy of the Apolline solar cult and the cult of paternity in Classical Greece." "A perverse poetic idea." "The poet-philosopher (Aeschylus) may be excused by his ignorance of biological facts." "The immoral and violent spirit of patriarchal ethics." "One of the most disastrous errors ever made by civilized man." For: "Matricide is much further beyond atonement than mariticide by a wife, which is frequent enough in Nature, as for instance among the bees."

Among the bees! The bee is the matriarchalist's favorite animal. "The religio-social miracle of bee-life." "A thousand meters above the earth, where the larks sing and the clouds drift, copulation takes place. There the strongest drone overtakes the queen, clutches her honey-scented body, and gives life to her womb, himself dying immediately afterwards. It is, as it were, heaven itself that fertilizes the queen in the solitude of blue space." Thus pleads our modern matriarchalist. After the bees come the ants. "Males survive only for a short time in the ant state. They take no part in community activities." And, finally, the aphids: "One might call it a law that all state forms not constituted in the matriarchal spirit will not rise above the principle of aphid swarms." The insects against Pallas!

Isis, Demeter—those were the days! Ishtar-Madonna, Our Lady with the cow, the milk-giver, as a symbol of maternity; and then the fatherless condition of all Near Eastern saviors—certain God-men were sent back into the womb five times. Yet even Diotima would comb her hair, using Socrates' bald head as a mirror; whatever he may have been thinking inside it, he held it still for her anyway. But then the cataclysm! Pallas! Now her great bronze statue stands in the open place between the two temples. And what was Socrates up to right afterwards by the Illyssus, with Phaedo? That did not please the Great Mother! The tide of procreative life, exclusively destined for her womb, dialectically frozen under the hands of philosophizing old men of pockmarked countenance! (Our matriarchalist!)

Pallas, man's protectress, Pallas the ever-clear, though all should remain primal ground, primal womb, primal darkness, and primal murmurings! Pallas, who brought Achilles, Theseus, Heracles to success, and likewise that potency with the lion's face, the roaring cosmic bull—if he does not get the heifer instantly, his vengeful cunning makes him think with horns and testicles! First he thinks as a scent-atomizer, a seducer by means of fragrance, an evaporator of cerebral perfume—all honor to him! If only he had remained a bull, a perfume, a peacock, a little monkey, a Josephean watcher by the crib! But he became this transcendental masculine subject, this androcratic heretic, this temple-paederast, unnatural, immoral, and the cause of all crime! *Cherchez l'homme!* Why does society let him carry on? In heat he is the most infantile and dangerous of creatures, one that still goes in for tongue-clicking and whistling, he is the caipercaillie revolving in love-play, and a moment later he loses his mind and kills. His thinking, primarily sheer hullabaloo, cooing, steering by tumescent organs, the paraphernalia of an exterminable species ordained to be nothing but the co-opener of the gateway of birth—this somber can-opener has made himself independent now with his systems, all negative, and his contrary delusions—all these lamas, buddhas, god-men, divine kings, saviors, and redeemers, none of whom has really saved the world—all these tragic male celibates, alien to Nature's primal material ground, averted from the secret maternal sense of things, unintentional cleavages in the formative power, impure rationality, dismal customers far inferior to the communal musical courtships of cicadas and frogs; in the highest animal societies, the lepidoptera states where everything ends normally in the act of copulation, they would be declared public enemies, to be suffered only for a while. All this was brought on by Pallas; from Pallas to schizophrenia is only one step—Pallas and nihilism, Pallas and progressive cerebralization—it all began under those plane trees, in Socrates' thick, disagreeable skull, with the first mirror-reflections and projections —ah, and once upon a time it reflected your hair and your lips, O Diotima!

What lives is something other than what thinks. This is a fundamental fact of our time, and we must come to terms with it. Whether it was ever different, whether some sidereal union glimmers upon us out of worlds to come, who knows? At this hour, anyway, it is not there. We must not only come to terms, we must acknowledge, defend the Orestean epoch, the world as a spiritual construction, as a transcendental apperception, existence as an intellectual edifice, the act of being as a dream of form. All this is the outcome of hard fighting and much suffering, this and much else. Pallas invented the flute—reed and wax—a little thing. Our brain also finds itself faced with a limitation of space. We can form only limited partial centers; it is not given to us to develop long perspectives horizontally and in time. Working within limited areas, chiseling planes no larger than the palm of one's hand, tight summaries, concise theses—everything beyond that lies outside the epoch.

A feast of Dionysus, wine against corn, Bacchus against Demeter, phallic congestion against the nine-month magic, the aphorism against the historical novel! A piece of writing is accomplished, paper covered with typescript, thoughts, sentences; it lies on the table. One returns from other realms, circles, professional spheres, the brain loaded with data, overflowing, repressing every flight and every dream—one returns hours later and sees the white sheets on the table. What is this? An inanimate something, vague worlds, things garnered in anguish and exertion, thought up, grouped, checked, revised, a pitiful residue, loose ends, unproved, weak—tinder, decadent nullity. The whole thing devious, a disease of the race, a somber birthmark, a confusion of connections? Then Pallas approaches, never perturbed, always helmeted, never impregnated, a slender childless divinity sexlessly born of her father.

What approaches is the law of frigidity, of minimum fellowship. It is through the blood that animals rejuvenate themselves, in the loins that Nature exhausts herself; after her—before her in the cycle of hours—the mind appeared, issuing forth for the first time in a created being and filling it with the dream of the Absolute. Dreams also generate, images weave, concepts burn things of every kind—ash the earth, cinders ourselves. Nietzsche says the Greeks were constantly regenerating and correcting themselves by way of their physiological needs; that preserved their vitality. It may have been so, but his own physiological needs were called knowledge—that was the new biology, which the mind demanded and created. Out of the futility of the material and historical process a new reality arose, created by the ambassadors of formal reason; the second reality, achieved by the slow gatherers and introducers of intellectual decisions. There is no road back. No invocation of Ishtar, no *retournons à la grand'mère,* no conjuration of the Realm of the Mother, no enthronement of Gretchen over and above Nietzsche, can do anything to change the fact that for us there is no longer any such thing as a state of Nature. Where man occurs in the state of Nature, he is of a paleontological character, a museum piece. The white, ultimate man is no longer Nature; he has taken the road he was shown by that "Absolute Reality," by gods, pre-gods, *prima materia, ens realissimum, natura naturans,* in short, by the heart of darkness—he has stepped out of Nature. His goal, perhaps only his transition, at any rate his existential mission, can no longer be called natural Nature; it is cultivated Nature, intellectualized Nature, stylized Nature—art.

The world of expression! In front of it Pallas stands, the childless divinity; Demeter's and all embryonic glutens' grandson keeps silence; let it all repose in primal darkness, on the knees of the gods. And the gods, eternal inspirers with breath and kneaders of clay, millepedes and multicolorists, will catch up again with time and space, and the fission-fungi and the spectra will give posterity plenty to play with and to suffer—some day! But I see the Achaeans around me. Achilles, his sword in its sheath: *not yet*—or I shall tear your yellow hair; Odysseus, man of many wiles, there the island lies, you will fetch the bow of Philoctetes. *Today! This!* Not Oceanus, not the barren waste of waters; where the ships sail, the Aegean and the Tyrrhenian Sea—*there*! Posterity! Already there are nourishing wellsprings from the Gulf Stream, the meteors provide us with savory and choice raw materials—the milk of the molluscs has been made sure of—do you now turn—fetch the bow —you alone!

Pallas pauses, it is evening, she loosens her armor, taking off the breastplate with the Gorgon's head upon it, this head in which the Babylonian dragon Tiamat and the serpent Apophis from Egypt live on, but stricken and vanquished. It is evening; there her city lies, stony land, the marble hill and the two rivers. Everywhere the olive tree, her handiwork, spreads in groves. She stands on what was once the place of judgment, the hill of Ares, the old Amazon castle that was destroyed by Theseus, lifter of stones. Before her are the steps of the altar on which sentence was uttered. She sees the Furies, she sees Orestes. She sees Apollo, her companion in the scene, and she recalls the remark of Proteus, ruler of the seals: that before long, reckoned by the hours of the gods, another would stand in this place, proclaiming the resurrection of the dead. Clytemnestra—Agamemnon; mariticide—matricide; patriarchal idea—matriarchal idea; the slain and the resurrected: all mere murmurs, mere ideas—ideas are as meaningless as facts, exactly as chaotic, regulating and illuminating no more than a fraction of the eon, either—nothing counts but the completed forms, the statues, the friezes, Achilles' shield. These are devoid of ideas, speak only of themselves, are perfect.

Among the constellations she saw the Horn of Amalthea, the Cretan goat that suckled her father as a child, as the doves brought him food and golden bees fed him with honey. Then he destroyed the amorphous, the unformed, the unlimited, along with the Titans and giants, the boundless element. This star had a bright green light, it was purer than Ariadne, next to it, whom Bacchus had flung up there in the transports of love. Pallas thought of her father. By means of a stone wrapped in goat's hair, Rhea, his mother, had saved his life, handing Saturn the stone to devour instead of the new-born divine child. That much-talked-of stone! The living, the formed had gained time to steal into the light! Then his reign began, and things moved in his course. This land, the home of poverty and the ancestrally inherited custom of acquiring advantages only by work and understanding—there now were the ivory and gold statues of the gods, there now the ghostly white colonnades of the Propylaea. In these things a nation saw itself, created itself. How long was it since Helios' rays struck not only the backs and fins of the downward-looking but an answering fire, since a mortal walking upright came to behold himself, interpreting himself and thinking and introvertly returning his own essence to himself in utterances and works: now—here? Pallas turned away and paced toward the city. And the city was a-glimmer with olive twigs and red thistles; tomorrow's players billowed through the streets, throngs of pilgrims and the crowd of onlookers. It was the evening before the Panathenaea. People came from the springs, from the terraced slopes of the mountains, from the sepulchral mounds in the marshes near Marathon; those who came from the sea had sailed for the flashing spear of Athena Promachos—that had been their beacon. Tomorrow they would step before the images and the statues and the masks made ready for the drama. All the Hellenes! The Hellenes of the plane trees, the chisel-wielding, the Orestean Hellenes! From among them Pallas now vanished, the motherless goddess, once more armored and alone.

(Written 1943-44, published 1949) Translated by Ernst Kaiser and Eithne Wilkins

EXCERPTS FROM

NOVEL OF THE PHENOTYPE

(A fragment from Landsberg, 1944)

The God of the Hour

Undoubtedly there is a sphere of existence, definable as to form and content, within which a man belonging to a certain generation seems to be authentic and representative and outside which he appears decrepit and drained of life. Wherever such a man finds his modes of expression, what he voices is the point of intersection between inherited function and his own silent but ever-present germ cell—or, to resort to the terminology of modern genetics: what speaks out of him is the phenotype, the relevant section of the genotype, i.e. the racial type. It is the phenotype that realizes the given germinal life in relation to changes and defects.

As for the present-day phenotype, its *moral* factor has largely been shed and replaced by the legislative factor and hygiene; the moral factor as genuine feeling, such as was obviously still present in Kant, is no longer there. Nor has *Nature* for him any longer the lyrical quality and tension that it had, to judge by the testimonies, for the representative men of the eighteenth and nineteenth centuries; it has been dissolved by the sporting, therapeutic medium: toughening of the body, ski slopes, ultra-violet rays on mountain peaks—and where it occasionally penetrates the defenseless ego with a sort of shudder, it lasts only for a very brief moment, unvisionary and tragic.

The same goes for all that might be called a *mood;* it's all over. Pillars of smoke rise, are lost in the infinite blue, brown pigeons soar, late sunbeams glide over lattice-work—"on sunlit twigs flash millions of bright drops"—that is accidental, is dragged in. *Existence* is the mood that moves the phenotype, which he insists on, harshly and unceasingly.

The destruction of space by means of aircraft and radio waves, its dissolution into the stratosphere, the possibility of touching Africa, Europe, Asia with one's eye and with the sole of one's foot in a single day, has caused a bizarre distortion of such concepts as nation, social community, and frontier; their tax-political aspect is too marked for any inner effect. Everyone is today aware that *politics*, revolutions, wars, even though they may ceaselessly harass a generation—and this generation has been very hard hit by them—will soon amount to half a page in a history book, or even just a footnote to the text. The migration of swallows and of seals is just as much politics and history, that is to say, the politics and history of particular species of fauna.

Love is the productivity of those who do not happen to be within the bounds of this sphere we are concerned with. It sets up the illusion of meaningful content, creating surrogates for an individuality that no longer exists. In it the phenotype will scarcely discover anything of intimate concern to him. To the question whether or no one ought to resist one's instinctual urges, he will answer: That's not so simple, resistance sets up neuroses, creates tensions that aren't worth while, crises that will probably end unproductively—one ought to live and turn it all into artifacts; if resistance is part of that, if it is existential, then one should resort to it. The goal is to equip the ego to have a form expressive of experienced life, standing up to intellectual tests, to have an attitude that conveys a considerate interest in beings outside itself, and conveys no fear of the end.

Existential—here is the new word that turned up a few years ago and is decidedly the most remarkable expression of an inner transformation. It removes the main weight of the ego from the psychological, casuistic sphere into that of the species, the dark, closed realm, the stem. It almost entirely deprives the individual of everything peripheral, giving him a gain in weight, gravity, and emphatic quality. Existential—here is the death-blow to the novel. Why bother to infuse thoughts into someone, into a figure, into invented personalities, now when there are no longer any personalities? Why invent persons, names, and relationships, just when they begin to be of no account? Existential—the word aims backwards, veils the individual in a backward direction, binds him, makes demands that neither the past centuries nor the generations descending from them were equipped to fulfill. Manuscripts, ribbons from a wreath, photographs—all that is already too much. Existential—this word operates in the phenotype.

He sees a picture of the Repin school, a wonderfully fat and beautiful woman, a landlady gorging at the breakfast table—that's first-rate! All ready to hand, simultaneously produced by virtue of pictorial composition, no trace of any living context, no sequence in time, nothing relating to cause and effect—a drastic, massive statement of the case, but optically cumulative. Color interestingly distributed over grapes, hairnet, tabby cat, the bulbous cupola of the church in the background, the samovar in the foreground. The wonderful fat woman—a veritable whirl of biscuits, jam, tea, rum, melon, preserved fruits, all somewhat melancholy and, as was already been pointed out, very voluptuous, with the heaviness of a vast Eastern country, very sensual, superabundance—"on the Black Sea the roses bloom thrice."

Or he gropes his way through space at noon, leaving his house. A town allotted to one as a place of residence, to live in, is a datum; one is at liberty to interpret its landmarks. A modern school-building, imposing, of a pinkish tinge. The tax office on a gentle slope. The municipal lake with willows trailing into the water, with swans. A fireman walks along carrying helmet and smoke-mask, representative of an emergency service, an operative value. Karl Karczewski's car lot and repair shop. The Office of Weights and Measures. A dilapidated club house bearing the name: "Eagle's Eyrie"—("this is what love must be like"). What does it all mean? Either there's no such thing as the existential, in which case all these things ought to have turned out to be much more majestical, or there is, and then it is all garbage and damnation! These Eastern towns, so gray on days in March, so veiled in dust—no, they cannot be interpreted this way!

Then he looks around somewhere else. He sets up to be really eager. At the foot of a flight of steps, a group of gentlemen stand about after luncheon. He enters into the circle of their chat, gravely but firmly associating himself with their conversational communion, submitting to the semi-official, semi-social jargon: "Started at three—thought it was at five; what a mess!" Talking, he sees himself: an aging man, not very impressive, physically not a perfect specimen, intent on speedy escape, thoroughly equivocal, with a deeply pervious feeling in the small of the back, or a kind of mesencephalic failure—he sees it all as a shadow-play—himself, him, the phenotype, the existential man—silhouette of the god of the hour.

Ambivalence

The phenotype of the twelfth and thirteenth centuries celebrated courtly love; that of the seventeenth century, spiritualized osten-tation; that of the eighteenth, secularized knowledge; and the phenotype of today integrates ambivalence, the fusion of every concept with its opposite.

On the one hand, he is sold out and out to the mind and its standards, down to the very marrow of his bones—*on the other hand,* his attitude towards this mind as a regional geographic-historical freak product of the race is skeptical. On the one hand, there is his struggle for expression, which leads him into torment-stigmatized eccentricities and to a destruction of forms that extends to bizarre playing on words—on the other hand, there is the bitter smile with which, even in the very act of creating, he regards his handiwork with all its random and transitional qualities. On the one hand, he occasionally feels his dependence on powers that act upon him from afar, spinning the threads of his allotted destiny (Moira), and on the other hand, he cannot help denying this and thrusting it away from him, as though he were himself the master of all things, standing outlined against the sky, yawning and chewing even as he pedals away with his heel, keeping the spindle revolving. On the one hand, in fear of the dead and their eternally continuing scrutiny, their almost tangible gaze, being to some extent convinced of the power and terror of the psyche, even that of the past, even that of the shades—on the other hand, needing for his fulfillment the acclamation of the press, white spats, grand prizes, chamois-hunting. On the one hand, tradition—on the other, his congenital self-will. On the one hand, moved by whatever is gentle and bowed—on the other, full of hatred for his neighbor there at his side. On the one hand, seeing the universe as the pompous subduer of all evolved forms—on the other, seeing eye and nose, forehead and eyebrow, mouth and chin as the one and only form known to us. On the one hand, casuistic and subtle—on the other, with an inkling of the ultimate interconnection of all causes in realms of an utterly different kind. On the one hand, profoundly conditioned by his knowledge of the last four thousand years as a new historical sense reserved for his own generation, and continuously flooded with a sublimely sensual wallowing in time, a sense of the ephemeral, of the fragmentary nature of time, which in turn feeds upon his historical awareness. On the other hand, with a weakness, at once public and secret, for everything imperialistic and Caesarean, everything that to a middle-class eye looks gigantic and "global"; the loss of his sense of space being compensated by a longing for validity in all that is connected with time and duration. On the one hand, glassy—on the other, bloody. On the one hand, tired—on the other, yearning for ski jumps. On the one hand, archaic—on the other, the man of today with his hat from Bond Street and his tie-pin from the Rue de la Paix. On the one hand, bright, for no reason, at evening—on the other, broken up, without cause, the next morning. Thus, half play-acting and half suffering—forty per cent Adam and Eve, thirty per cent Antiquity, twenty per cent Palestine, ten per cent Central Asia— thus, on the whole, euphoric, the phenotype strides through the hour of the great battles, the hour that will destroy continents.

Geographical Details

Comparisons, studies, geographical details! How quietly it all rests within my mind: *Canal du Midi*—not a sail to be seen, the water motionless, brown, with rushes growing by the banks, water no more than six to ten meters wide, on each side a tow-path flanked by towering poplars, where the draft-horses plod along— what a contrast to the Belomorski Canal linking the Neva and the White Sea, which cost three million human lives to build, its waters ceaselessly whipped by storms and convoys of motorized cutters racing towards Onega Bay—there in the Midi they also have those big white oxen drawing the plows, moving slowly.

All set then for the resurrection! Pour out over vast areas! Pontine marshes, poisonous swamps, the rack and debris of tombs, hills with ruins on them—realm of fever and death, where the lime crumbles from Doric columns. Deep dark thickets, macchia, Phoe- nician elder extending from the Appian Way to Circe's Cape, sleepy water buffalo, flocks of purple gallinules against the clematis-blue sea on which the sails from Barbary appeared, coming to raid Fondi and vanish again!

From high snow-fields a torrent rushes down, disappearing among cones of fallen rock—this is the Styx. The red and blue rocks of Delphi, the shining rocks, a grove of gray olive trees melting upward out of the depths of the great valley. But how much else there is also awaiting expansion! Sarmatian country! It fulfills the hours! Winter of the steppes, terrible blizzards, the air quite dense, no visibility at all, a wind-witch heralding their approach: clumps of withered stalks, a sort of thistle, roll into a ball, grow to gigantic size, come rolling and jumping along, every- one is in full flight, no wolf now thinks of its prey! After this the spring seasons, a super-abundance of water, that unruly element, repulsive, dirty, bubbling puddles in the swamps, and then, it's true, crocuses and tulips, but all the plants will be crude, big, thick-stemmed, and at a closer look one will see how far apart they grow, no comparison with Surrey and Argolis.

Soft white air cloaks you like warm snow, the bark and the early buds are secretly sprouting; then everything is suddenly there, and then the fading summer with the purple of thistles, the sulphurous yellow of the hot sweet rose, Diane vaincue—this is the way the years proclaim their arrival and pass away. Whichever way you incline your ear, what you hear everywhere is the dying fall, the end always, the final rapture, from high snow-fields a torrent plunges down, a grove of gray olive trees melts upward out of the depths—sadness and light—how quietly it all rests within your mind—and then the fading summer, with the purple of thistles, the sulphurous yellow of the hot sweet rose, Diane vaincue.

The Town Park

On another plane there is the town park. It appears without more ado within your line of vision (without more ado?), whether seen from the arched bridge or from one of the benches with which the local improvement society horticulturally supplied various vantage points. There is a sky over it, too, not the bright blank pale-blue sky of Texas, and not the cloudless sky of the Midi, which is a vault above the pines, but still a sort of upper limitation for experimental glances. Various paths lead toward it, that is customary, but what is immensely striking is the *swan-motif*. Swans—there you have stylization! How senselessly high these water birds' heads are poised above the surface of the mirroring pool, on necks as though of blown glass! There is no causality in that, it is purely expressive composition. The same goes for the willows that droop into the water, inserting something insatiable and mournful and bio-negative into this town of soil-tillers—directly aimed, as anyone sees, at expression.

A world of contradictions—but, after all, the world has seen a lot: the coronation of boy-favorites, divine honors paid to a white horse, a mausoleum built to the memory of a goblet, a beautiful tree tricked out with jewelry—and now this dismemberment! However, our situation is not favorable. All one hears about life, about the mind, about art, from Plato to Leonardo to Nietzsche, is not crystal-clear, contains dodges—are we not publicly discussing non-objectiveness? Yes, indeed, we doubt the very substance that has given rise to these words, we doubt its experiences and forms of happiness, we doubt its method of presenting itself, we doubt its images. We have scarcely more than a few paces ahead of us on earth and little of what is earthly; everything is a tight fit now, everything must be very carefully weighed, we gaze pensively at the veined chalices of big flowers into which the butterflies of night sink in their rapture. Our realm is never larger than a page, no wider than a painted hat with a feather in it, or a fugue—and beyond is billowing chaos. It is March, there is a touch of the insalubrious about this park; even in this plain, in this depression, the irises look tense, open too suddenly, yesterday mere buds, they burst out in a sort of self-defloration, in a blue leaping towards the light, young and hard like sword-blades—and beside them more weapons: bell-buds, catkins swollen to bursting-point, certain and smooth-formed right to their purple or bee-brown rim—weapons of a hostile power, a superior force shattering all resistance—Nature herself. Faced with this, one has to summon up all one's strength.

Our situation is not favorable. Our senses are in retreat. Has anyone ever reflected on the fact that Nietzsche wore fourteen diopters, mostly two pairs of spectacles, had boys guide him down the mountain trails? Nor have we very acute hearing any more; the great Alpine hunters could hear over much greater distances. So what it comes to is letting one's own fountains spring up high, and building one's own echoing walls! Cassandra's snake has never licked our ears, opening them to the voices of the air and the melodies of earth; we have never slept on the marble over which that reptile wound its way. But there are millennia living in our souls, lost things, silent things, dust. Cain, Zenobia, the Atrides brandish their thyrsi at us. And yonder the pool! Water! Water is darker than earth, and one could go on looking at it for hours, lingering on its banks: to *become* water—to be transformed, transformations and depths beneath the ripples—oh, for an hour on *one* plane, on *one* plane of happiness!

History

History in its wonderfully equalizing justice: it sends off Mithridates to Tigranes, and Alaric to live in a rose-hedged cottage near Bordeaux. Cicero is first allowed to reveal the conspiracies; only later is he banished to a distance of four hundred Roman miles from Rome. It operates in fur barter and on the salt roads; it works with a grain of dust that blinds an eye, and it burdens five hundred camels with fragments of a toppled colossus. Down below it still allows digging and scraping around the remnants of white statues in a grove that happens to have been spared: Sol, Hecate, Zeus, the symbols of life for sixty generations—up above it is already forming the Byzantine mosaics—mosaics do not set out to tell stories or to edify, merely weaving the soliloquy of their coloristic ritual.

History in its wonderful monotony, in its regular and fruitful rhythm: downward taxes are raised, the grain on the stalk and whole forests sold by profiteers, one or more classes exploited, and up above the gentlemen wield lorgnettes and the ladies carry pompadours filled with candy. The ladies wear olive velvet trimmed with lace and feathers; the young Viennese countesses are dressed in white, have their fair hair plaited over their brows, and fresh roses at their bosoms, meet their visitors with welcoming smiles. The latest thing is bicycle-riding: the government-advising counts from the Ministry at the Ballhausplatz go pedaling along; the older men have bowling alleys built for themselves; in their gardens they arrange Italian Nights; it is the fashion to give bonbonnières as presents; orangeries with small faintly tinkling fountains are built into drawing rooms. This is the epoch of the bazaar: in the booths princesses masquerading as Columbines offer marionettes for sale, and Viennese songs, and champagne; in an arbor of stephanotis and gardenias Madame Recamier distributes autographs of famous artists in little baskets of Parma violets; Baron Bernsteiner casually drops a thousand-guilder note into the gold bowl for large sums of money. A she-devil in black and red sells ice cream and wafers; the whole coterie takes part in *tableaux vivants*, for the *haute gomme* a treasure of *sottises* and delicate, sentimental adventurings. And from below, through the senses and the brain, through acquired vices, inherited weaknesses, black days on the stock exchange, and deceases *mal à propos*, history burrows through the strata that make it up, just as it always does in its wonderful pageant of recurrence of the same, carefully digging away into the state-owned factories and the galleys. State factories for public bread distribution, with profitable inns and brothels attached, and from there straight ahead to the galley benches with the leg-irons. Down below savage penalties for crime, and up above monuments purchased with tips; down below the mines, and up above colossal sarcophagi of porphyry. Down below the calluses from chains worn on some island in the Aegean Sea, up above garlands and peacock feathers. Down below brickwork, the slums flooded by the Tiber, tufa caves; up above arches built of jasper and agate, and the villas in the cool of Tivoli.

History! Hireling slaves, field slaves, baggage slaves, these down below; and up above fanatical enthusiasm for circus horses, for water organs, monotonous but loud and as big as stagecoaches. Then a few lost battles, or the innumerable multitudes kill off a few tyrants, and it is all over for a while. Only for a while—history in its regular and fruitful rhythm goes on building one epoch out of another, building the Parthenon out of the rubble of the Persian empire, turning the temples of Antiquity into quarries for the Quattrocento, and under its outspread wings the Fora survive as hills for goats to graze on and the Capitols as pasturage for cows, the she-wolf lies down in the sheepfolds and suckles lambs—and so one has to stand up and hold one's own where the gentlemen wield lorgnettes and sink into the colossal sarcophagi of porphyry. One has to stand and look on, and then the rhythm becomes grandiose; one must look, step back a little, be amused, and then the galleys burst into leaf, wounds are healed by the maggots they breed, and world history becomes miraculous.

Blocks

What then is the ego's standpoint? It has none. May everything come storming in upon it? It may. Is a church banner or a child's kite veritably a Gaurisankar by comparison? Indeed, indeed. Flitting past as an adventure of the soul's, arisen from the void we are all rushing to escape, dissolving in the void that closes over us—arising like a blues and vanishing like a ray of light or a magnolia—a mere mayfly, ephemeral: this is the profound symbol of his soul! A quid of chewing tobacco under the tongue, a little quince-jelly on a pisang leaf means everything to the Javanese—so light, so limitless—and so clumsily a mere nothing: this is his doctrine!

"Come out to sea! Be broken, broken! The fortress still stands —yours is the gaze—: this is a tide flowing in to break in a splintering, a lingering, a few Pan-like hours, a piping from the reeds, a querying, breaking note. Come out to sea! Seen from the sea the land is at rest, hearts are at rest"—a verse from his song. Continents seen in projection, centuries as a shifting of clouds, destinies reduced to a formula, self-supporting blocks—an architecture with its own equilibrium.

Cities arise. At the foot of a giant obelisk, reminiscent of some ancient Egyptian monument, a black insect like a flea buzzes about on its hindlegs—a human being, and there is another, and yet another. They leap into apertures in the base of the walls, are shot upwards in vertical tubes inside the buildings, are unloaded, rush through the air, are plunged into the darkness underground, wedded to cranes and united with dynamos, among buildings shaped like pilasters and delicate as nude statues, gray or rosy and illumined by floodlighting. Bells peal, horns blare, whistles shrill—the cities swell up red, are inflated, wear scarlet, walk clothed in silk, tremble with lights and love-making. From high buildings one can see the bay, the waves round Long Island and all the sails of their pleasure boats, the weekend houses lying in the sunlight; the women are flights of white birds making for polo fields and long-drawn golden coasts; at night the glasses clink—: summer days, embroidered with flips and the great Beauty roses.

Broadway stars: brought up by a Negro washerwoman in Harlem, now earns 50,000 dollars a year. On waking, orange juice and black coffee to the accompaniment of the latest slow fox trot, while the maid collects the flimsy shreds of chiffon strewn all around; fifteen years of training in order to be able to revolve lightly, three hours' somersaulting daily to keep the joints supple, handstands in order to be able to climb like a monkey, and by night tearing at the heartstrings with a voice first bass and then high as a nightingale's, in songs about ukelele-babies and pickaninnies, evoking shudders of awe with that entirely personal style which consists of leaning backwards and waggling the knees. Everyone shudders, everything is whipped up: the shore, the land cleft by the Hudson and Lake Champlain, the East River, Sandy Hook, Shem's posterity, Ham's posterity, whites, mulattoes, half-castes, lip-laps, the bosses of the Federal Reserve Buildings who hoard the gold. After the song the ice-soufflé and the soup made from the jelly with which the rare Javanese salangane makes its nest.

Or yonder: the big brown horses with cockades of violets on their forehead, standing outside the palace, all correct, their four legs stretched out as far as possible, four forelegs and four hindlegs aligned, the hooves clean and shiny, the groom standing at the shaft under the horses' noses. Dina Grayville gets into the brougham, leans back against the padded cloth, going out to buy dresses and suits and children's underwear for an orphanage, going by way of the Longchamps promenade, the road where, once upon a time, exquisite voices from the Abbey could be heard during Holy Week—and afterwards she will go to Potin's, the strawberries from Hyères having arrived.

Hotels amid the roar of waterfalls, palace in the Pekin Road (more fort than bungalow), the President—exports: musk, gallnuts, wool from Tung-Chow—sits in the armchair in which Essex died. Blocks—: centuries as a shifting of clouds, continents in projection —come out to sea, in the reeds a piping, a querying, breaking note.

Summary
The preceding consists of the phenotype's impressions, memories, and actions during the three months from 3-20-1944 to 6-20-1944

—a span of time sufficient for description of his attitude. He was lodged in barracks somewhere in the East, lived on military rations, with two loaves of army bread twice a week, adequate margarine, and a bowl of soup or cabbage twice a day, so that he was well provided for, and his room overlooked a drill ground, where the generality pursued the trend of their ideas.

Old age was drawing on, bringing the days of stocktaking, the hours of certainty that nobody would now come any more to interpret and advise, nothing more would come to explain what one could not explain oneself. Everything was brightly illumined, in properly defined relation, the connections valid within the framework of their situation—only of their situation: for in the background lurked the great disharmony that was the law of the universe.

Into these projections of an abstract intellect, alien and suggestive of one of those mutations in which the inscrutable, what modern physics calls "Absolute Reality," occasionally chooses to advance; into these tensions, these splits in the zone of transformation, something now came from a long way off, something of those vast plains that flow on into Asia and in which he was then living, something of their forests and bleak rivers, the former with a whitish-blue buzzing at the edges, the latter with rushes at their banks, deep and monotonously staring—the young corn revealed to him something of their recurrences, so old and yet never tiring. Something immobile entered into him and became manifest, having probably been there always; an invisible god, not to be named, who belonged to the rustics, for he stayed in the fields, the harvest fell upon his shoulders without his stirring, his caverns lay near at hand, and the entries to nests and ravines were not inaccessible. And that mythical vanishing in streams, the enchantments of naiads, foam-births, tombs under water—these, too, he had leisure, had the measure, to reflect on. Then he paused, no longer casting his hook, and the waters drifted on, whole days went their watery way in enchanted silence, without impatience, and in their hours there was that honey which comes after blossom-time, after many blossoms, from snowy and scarlet fields.

And in Normandy the great battle began that was to restore his liberty—not the only true liberty, the absolute one, but that in which he had grown up, he and those with whom he had set out upon the road of life. Nevertheless, he saw no Ararat or rainbow when he peered out of the ark. Regarding the future only one thing struck him as certain: that in 1948 there would be a jubilee for the fiftieth year of the machine-gun's existence, the Sudan would be in the forefront, the dervishes would make an onslaught, a wonderfully brilliant target for the Maxim-Nordenfeldt guns, the black flag sinking, the light-green one, the dark-green one— now the moment for the famous charge of the 21st Lancers under Major Kitchener's command—spring 1898—and now the lions and eagles of all the great wars, victors and vanquished, would come streaming together to celebrate and be celebrated, all those experienced pioneers of rocket construction and incendiary bombs, all agog for weak links and gaps in the enemy front, and there would be no end to the *Vivats* and *Evvivas*. Once again he entered into the ambivalence of things that had revealed themselves to him so decisively. On the one hand, the mind set free as a result of battles, and on the other, the mind tidily classifying all such processes among animal developments, among geological events— it was an antinomy without end. This gearing of history to the world of the mind was one of the problems to which his age had no answer; even Nietzsche, in his remark about the mysterious hieroglyph linking the state and the genius, had refrained from giving any further definition of that hieroglyph. It was a question that was left open, and would remain open until it answered itself and sank into oblivion.

But some day it would supply its own answer in that circular motion which could never end and which never touched anything but itself. He regarded the question as one of those remote encounters. And once again it came into his line of vision: from high snow-fields a torrent rushing down, a grove of gray olive trees melting up from the depths—sadness and light, and both adored, how quietly it all rested in his mind, and then the summers coming to their end with the purple of thistles and the sulphur-yellow, the hot, sweet rose, Diane vaincue.

(Written 1944, published 1949) Translated by Ernst Kaiser and Eithne Wilkins

EXCERPT FROM
DOUBLE LIFE

BLOCK II, ROOM 66

This was the designation of the quarters assigned to me for many months. The barracks lay on high, fortresslike above the town. "Montsalvat," said a first lieutenant who evidently had heard operas; and, indeed, the place was inaccessible to loafers at least: 137 steps had to be climbed after making one's way from Bahnhofstrasse to the foot of the hill.

Nothing dreamier than barracks! Room 66 faces the drill ground; before it grow three small rowan trees, their berries without purple, the leaves as though stained with brown tears. It is late August; the swallows still fly, but already are massed for the great passage. A battalion band rehearses in a corner, the sun sparkling on trumpets and percussives as they play, "Die Himmel rühmen," and "Ich schiess den Hirsch im wilden Forst." It is the fifth year of war, and here is a completely secluded world, a kind of béguinage. The shouts of command are external; inwardly all things are muffled and still.

An eastern town topped by this high plateau, and that in turn topped by our Montsalvat with its bright yellow buildings and vast drill ground, a kind of desert fort. The immediate vicinity also full of oddities. Unpaved streets running half on low ground, half on hillsides; isolated houses without road connection—inconceivable how the occupants get in; fences as in Lithuania, low, mossy, damp. A gypsy wagon fixed up as a dwelling. At dusk a man comes carrying a cat on his left shoulder; the cat wears a string round its neck, stands askew, wants down; the man laughs. Low drifting clouds, black and purple light, scarcely a bright spot, eternal threat of rain, many poplars. At the wall of a house three blue roses grow lyre-shaped, horticulturally unmotivated. Mornings, the settlement is bathed in a peculiarly soft, aurora-like light. Here, too, universal unreality, a sense of two-dimensionality, a stage-prop world.

Around the drill shed the garrison blocks: dreams. Not the dreams of fame and victories, but dreams of loneliness, of transience, of shadows. Reality is far removed. Over the entrance block, the so-called hall of honor, stands a general's name in large letters: "General von X Barracks." A general of World War I. For three days, each time I passed, I would ask the arms-presenting sentry: for whom were the barracks named? "Who was General von X?" Never an answer. General von X was unknown, unremembered. In oblivion his standard, his auto pennant, the swarm of staff officers in his retinue. It has no effect over two decades. Strongly you feel the mortar, the ephemerality, the false values, the distortion.

Flowing through the blocks are waves of conscripts. There are two kinds: the sixteen-year-olds, underfed, slight, miserable Labor Service types, scared, submissive, assiduous, and the old codgers of fifty to sixty, from Berlin. On the first day these are still gentlemen, wear mufti, buy papers, walk in strides that say, We're corporation lawyers, business representatives, insurance brokers, have pretty wives and central heating; this temporary situation can't affect us, it's rather funny, in fact. ... On the second day they are in uniform, and their name is mud. Now they must flit through the halls when a non-com barks, jump in the barracks yard, lug boxes, press on steel helmets. Training is short, a matter of two or three weeks; interesting that they take target practice from the second day on—formerly this came after four or six weeks only. Then, one night, they line up with full pack, rolled-up mantle and pup tent, gas mask, machine-pistol, rifle—almost a hundred pounds of weight—and off they go to be shipped out, into darkness. This departure in the dark is weird. An unseen band leads off, playing marches, gay tunes, trailed by the soundless company that heads for permanent oblivion. The procedure is swift, a mere crack in the black silence, then the plateau lies in the dark, earthless, skyless night again. New ones come in the morning. They also leave. It gets colder outdoors, during drill. Now they are ordered to rub hands and slap their knees with their fists to stimulate circulation, keep life awake—militaristic biology. The blocks stand, the waves roll. Successive waves of men, new waves of blood due to trickle into the Eastern steppe after a few shots and manipulations in the direction of so-called enemies. The whole would be unintelligible if the general were not so impressively behind it, standing fascinatingly in his purple and gold, firing and commanding to fire; there is as yet no direct threat to his retirement pay.

At noon the officers meet at table. Since the start of the war there has been no distinction in fare between officers and men. A colonel, like a grenadier, gets two loaves of kommissbrot a week, with margarine and artificial honey on paper strips to take out; lunch is a deep dish of cabbage soup or a pile of boiled potatoes that must be peeled on the table (covered with oilcloth, if available, otherwise with "organized" bedcloth)—you put the peeled potatoes to one side and wait for the soup or the gravy. One day the colonel commanding my unit appears—unshaven. There are no more blades, nor any honing implements. Someone knows a place in Berlin that will "organize" things in that line. An Austrian ally contributes the story that in the Austro-Hungarian monarchy only the Windischgrätz Dragoons had the right to go clean-shaven—in memory of Kolin, the battle that was decided by the arrival of the new, young beardless recruits. A stick of shaving soap must last four months. Enlisted men are forbidden to shave, to save matériel. In America they shave lying down—typically lazy plutocratic rabble.

The conversations are those of nice, harmless people without an inkling of what threatens them and the fatherland. Badoglio is a traitor, the King of Italy a rickets-shrunken crook. On the other hand, a burial mound in Holstein has yielded a Teutonic ceremonial cap testifying to the highly developed cap-making art of our ancestors, 3,500 years ago. The Greeks, too, were Aryans. Prince Eugene of Savoy outlived his fame; what he finally did in France was nothing to brag about. Wearers of the newfangled short dagger are demimonde—cavalry still wears the long saber—cavalry! Now it's a bicycle squadron.

All these, no matter how sharp in demeanor, think fundamentally only about bringing the wife a dish of mushrooms when they go on furlough, about the boy's marks in school, and how not to land in the street again as in 1918, in case—this is the term heard at times, the term they permit themselves—in case of "a wash-out." Almost all are officers of the old army, around fifty, World War veterans. In the interim they have been cigarette or paper salesmen, farm supervisors, riding instructors, all with a hard row to hoe. Now they are majors. Not one speaks a foreign language or has seen a foreign country, except in wartime. Only the Imperial-and-Royal ally, ever alert and suspicious of being looked down on, has a somewhat broader outlook, probably because of Old Austria's Adriatic and Balkan ties. Even though there was no great spiritual world to be discovered, I tried attentively to penetrate my environment. Who did not constantly turn it over in his mind, the single question how it had been and still was possible for Germany to stick unswervingly to this so-called government, this half dozen loudmouths who for ten years now had been periodically reeling off the same twaddle in the same halls, before the same howling audiences? Those six buffoons who thought they alone knew better than the centuries before them and the rational rest of the world? Gamblers setting out to break the bank in Monte Carlo with a shady system, con-men dumb enough to think their fellow players would not notice their marked cards—saloon-fighting clowns, chair-leg heroes! This was not the Hohenstaufen dream of uniting North and South, not the idea behind the eastward drive of the Teutonic Knights, who were colonizers at least—it was sheer dross in concept and form, primary rain magic celebrating nocturnal torch fumes before requisitioned caskets of Henry the Lion.

This, plainly, was the government; and now we have the fifth war year, somber with defeats and miscalculations, evacuated continents, torpedoed battleships, millions of dead, bombed-out giant cities, and still the masses go on hearing and believing their leaders' twaddle. There can be no mistake about it: outside the bombed cities, at least, they firmly believe in new weapons, mysterious engines of vengeance, imminent, dead certain counter-blows. High and low, general and soldier on KP make a mystical totality of fools, a pre-logical collective of gullibles—something doubtlessly very Germanic and centrally explicable only in this ethnologic sense. Of peripheral ethnologic explanations two come to mind. First, war today is not felt so much by people in smaller towns and in the country itself: they have to eat, can "organize" what is lacking, have not been bombed, are supplied by Goebbels with all the emotion required for stable and house—and the weather always plays a larger role in the country than any train of thought. Second, family casualties are far easier to get over than the nation would have it. The dead die quickly; the more die, the sooner they are forgotten. Between fathers and sons there is probably as much basic antipathy as its opposite; the tension of hatred links them as strongly as the bond of love. Fallen sons can help materially, bring tax relief, make age important. Teaching this to the young would be most educational; then they would know what to think later, when the immortality of heroes and the gratitude of the survivors are served up again.

The following particulars were noteworthy: two ranks carry the army in the fifth year of war, the lieutenants and the field marshals —the rest is detail. The lieutenants, products of the Hitler Youth, have received an education whose essence was the systematic uprooting of any mental and moral content of life from books and actions, and the substitution of Ostrogoth princes, daggers, and haymows to spend the night in after a forced march. They have been insulated from parents who still may be cultured, from educators trained in the old sense, from clergymen and humanist circles—in short, from culture carriers of any kind—and that in peacetime; thus well equipped, they consciously, purposefully, and deliberately set out on their Aryan mission of destroying the continent. Just one word about the field marshals: it is not well known that they get their marshal's pay for life, tax-free, plus a permanent staff officer as aide-de-camp, and a country estate or a fair-sized Grunewald property on their retirement from active service. As the marshal-maker under our government of laws is also the marshal-breaker, and as in his latter capacity he vigorously wields the clubs of withdrawing titles, medals, pension claims, and holding the next-of-kin responsible, the marshals, as good family men, stand virtually exonerated—as demons they will have impressed nobody, anyway.

In looking at this war, and at the peace that preceded it, one thing must not be ignored: the vast existential emptiness of today's German man, stripped of whatever fills the inner space in other countries—decent national contents, public interest, criticism, social life, colonial impressions, genuine traditions. Here was nothing but a vacuum of historic twaddle, crushed education, bumptious political forgeries by the regime, and cheap sports. But to wear an eye-catching uniform, to get reports, bend over maps, trot with retinue through enlisted men's quarters and across squares, to announce dispositions, make inspections, talk bombast ("I command only once"—the subject was latrine-cleaning): all this creates a space-filling impression of individual expansion and supra-personal effect, in short, the complex which the average man requires. Art is forbidden, the press exterminated, personal opinion answered with a bullet in the neck—to gauge the space-filling by human and moral standards, as in civilized countries, was no longer possible on the premises of the Third Reich. What prevailed here was space-shamming; pontoon-bridge crossings, blasts about to go off, telescopic gunsights made the individualist feel like an immediate cosmic disaster.

Autumn around the blocks was dangerously dry, as throughout the Reich. The fields are mice-eaten, the potato crop is catastrophic, the beets contain too little sugar. The loss of the eastern areas curtails the food supply by two months' bread, one month's fats, one month's meat. Rations are cut. There are no more high boots, for want of leather; there are no more artificial limbs for the handicapped; the materials are at an end. There are no more shoelaces and no more dentures, no gauze bandages and no urinals. There is a shortage of doctors. Entire divisions take the field without a surgeon; of the civilian population, 25,000 may depend on one woman doctor, and she without gasoline. But the Führer awards chevrons, sets the width of ribbons on military funeral wreaths, forbids the soldiers to marry foreign girls, even Scandinavians: "the noblest Nordic woman" remains "racial driftwood" by the Great German yardstick. Putrefaction in every pore, but the propaganda runs at top speed. We look at magazines: Nera and Sehra, the "elves of Mostar," are so glad to be allowed at last to work in the great Organization Todt; Goebbels blinks his white teeth at the wounded; Goering comes as Father Christmas—the fairy tale entwines us.

One day in November I had to go to Berlin, on duty. It was the time when travel ranked with the most arduous sports. Regular rail service was a thing of the past. At 2 a.m. a marvelous train pulled into my station: eight sleeping cars, four practically empty first- and second-class cars, at the rear end a car with a flak crew. I got on. An SS man promptly hauled me back. I did not understand. He reported that this was the train from the Führer's headquarters, only for gentlemen of the top staffs. I realized that my brief case might well have held a hand grenade. I boarded the next train, i.e. I squeezed myself into a third-class toilet—I in a colonel's uniform, between East laborers. The toilet stood open. Women and children had to use it, the door was not to be closed, shifting was impossible, but no one minded. I had to change trains. In the next, I stood in a second-class compartment while three young louts in party uniform, stout fellows, sprawled on the cushions. White-haired women, women with children stood in the aisle with me. The master race produced a bottle of brandy and a few packs of cigars (the "people's community" got one cigar a day, at the time, and no brandy) and spent the three hours to Berlin fortifying itself for the party tasks to come. On the same day all the papers carried an article to the effect that the party's percentage of Knight's Cross winners and casualties was far higher than that of the rest of the people, and that home duty for party members did not exist. There was a sentence: "The contrary optical picture that occasionally presents itself is definitely misleading." Evidently my three fellow travelers were part of this optical picture.

Block II lets one understand the misty Niflheim of Germanic mythology, the eternal fog and fumes and the need for bearskins of those "splendid old Germans," as the radio just described them. From here, Taine would geophysically deduce the primary national estrangement from clarity and form—and, one might say, from honesty. In December, 1943, when the Russians had driven us back a thousand miles and punched dozens of holes into our front, a lieutenant colonel, small as a colibri and gentle as a rabbit, says at lunch, "Main thing, the pigs don't break through!" Break through, roll up, clean up, mobile tactics—how potent these words are, positively for bluff, and negatively for self-deception! Stalingrad: a tragic accident; the rout of the U-boats: a chance technical discovery of the British; Montgomery chasing Rommel 2500 miles from El Alamein to Naples: treason of the Badoglio clique.—At the same time, a party boss has business with our command. He eats with us, and my colonel, a cavalryman of the old school, a Knight of St. John who wears his monocle on steeplechases and to bed, exchanges it for black, horn-rimmed glasses, lest he offend the big shot's sense of the people's community and jeopardize his own future. ("Fearless and faithful"—"*Semper talis*," it said on the helmets of the old Prussian Guards. . . .)

Meanwhile, Christmas approaches. There is a special issue of four ounces of mettwurst and 25 per cent Bratling powder on the weekly meat ration. Moreover, anyone willing to give up an ounce of margarine and four ounces of sugar may order a stollen. I put my name on the list. Christmas songs are forbidden, winter solstice reflections in line of duty desired, with emphasis on the renewal of light from the womb of All-Mother Nature—commanding officers

are to proceed accordingly. For the present, no renewal is noticeable. I stand by the window of Room 66; the drill ground spreads
in a gray light, a gray from the wings of seagulls that dove into
all oceans. The feast has come. In the morning there was a big
raid on Berlin; you wonder if the apartment stands, and what is
left of the few acquaintances still living there. Then it is evening,
and the rations are brought up. I ask the orderly about his asthma;
he is hard of hearing; communication is difficult. I look farther
over the ground and beyond it, at the lowlands, the steppe, the
East—everything so near, everything so present, all these horrible
hosts of generations that failed to obtain clarity about themselves.
And then it descends, the Holy Night of the year 1943.

Soon after Christmas orders came to evacuate the blocks, to
make room for troops flooding back from the East. We move, I
go along. Actively, passively—the louse in the fur, the wolf in
sheep's clothing, the goat as cultivator of sprouts and shoots: do
they move, go along? What a bloated concept: action! To be
under duress and obliged to draw subsidies—it may be action; but
to want to unify action and thought—what a backwoodsy notion!
Imagine a modern physicist trying to express his calculations, his
professional work, in his life, to harmonize them with his life, to
"realize" them—or Bachofen, his matriarchal theories; or Boecklin,
his "Isle of the Dead"—how comical! If chance, the events of his
time, compel a man to live in the historic world, among sharp-
shooters and profiteers, trappers and rabbit thieves, should that
cause him to step out of himself and forcefully to voice opinions?

Is there an idea of mankind? There may have been times when
one existed in the universal consciousness. But today opinions are
constitutional, like fits of migraine—a hereditary ailment. One
might have the opinions of a prophet and still would not need to
raise a green flag and take to the high hills with snake and eagle.
That men are not changed, not improved, not reformed by prophetic opinions has been shown by the failure of the most recent
Dionysus; the "blond beast" has raved itself out. Opinions—just
to stimulate the peristalsis of the historic world, as a lubricant—

what man of mark today would make a public appearance for that reason? Historic world—brazenly grown and devoured off-hand; the potbellies sit in a box with their paramours and parasites, and violins play winged music for the killers, but in the darkness nameless victims trickle their life-blood away, and the strangled are hidden. . . . No, there is nothing to step out and nothing to fight here, neither with a small slingshot nor with a big trumpet. Let them run their thresher over the corn!

That which lives is something other than that which thinks—we must accept this basic fact of our existence. It may have been different once upon a time; it may be that a sidereal union will dawn in some unimaginable future—today the race lives in this form. What thought in me was moving in a realm of its own; what lived of me was considerate, well-bred, and sincerely comradely in my allotted environment. That which thought was guileless, cross-questioned no one, insinuated nothing to anyone, did not come to light at all; it was relaxed, and could be, it was so sure of being right and possessing the truth against all the facts of life within the barracks we inhabited together. "He that believeth shall not hasten," says Isaiah. Of course, one might say that this belief must be made known—that one who thinks, who sees things as I have just stated them, must act, oppose, make a revolution, or let himself be shot. I do not share this view. These matters are not susceptible of general proof; there are existential reasons only. For me these reasons lie in my personal disbelief in the significance of the historic world. I have not managed to be more than an experimental type that turns certain contents and complexes into closed formal structures, a type that can see the unity of life and spirit only in their common secondary results: in a statue, a verse, a structure worth leaving behind—I touch life and finish a poem. Whatever else affects life is dubious and indefinite. We no longer feel a religious link as a fact, to say nothing of the so-called national link; as a fact we only feel their incorporation in some expressive esthetic work. Biologic tension ends in art. Art, however, is no motivating force in history; it cancels time and history, rather, to work on the gene, on the internal inheritance, on substance—a long inner road. The entertaining and political aspects of a few specialties such as the novel are deceptive; the essence of art is infinite reserve. Its core is crushing, but its periphery is narrow; it touches little, but that with fire. Existential reasons are not causal but constitutional, obliging no one, valid only for those in whom they prove to be facts; they may be mutational variants, attempts that thrive or vanish again, or, as I said, experiments. They are not transferable, nor can we test them; they seek substantiation in the irrepressible world of expression that does not fail to encompass even these blocks—in which, in fact, these blocks seemed to create a special need for reviewing its own foundations.

The blocks will firmly reject this relationship. Such talk, the blocks will reply, comes from thought, from the cold, barren thought that threatens warm, natural life, from a roving intellect antagonistic to the patriotic impulse, to the idea of the Reich, to harvest festivals and Snow White and the Seven Dwarfs. Didn't we see today in the paper for the pretentious a photo, "Creative art at the front," with the caption, "Fleet commander gives morale officer his critique of picture, 'At the foe!'"—so? Yes, the fleet commander! An admiral, to be sure—and the gale lashes the wave, and the lighter or the freighter and the minelayer or the destroyer rolls or steams, and there's no lack of foam, either—at the foe, at the friend—this whole groveling historic victory craze—yes: compared with this, the thought represented by me is relentlessness—without asking where it may lead, this is my cruise at the foe, at the friend; this is my primary humanity, all else is crime!

True, it has already occurred to thought itself that Something came into the world to redeem the absolute, something called love, and that the Gentle one was sent to make thought bow down voluntarily—but, as I said: love, not obtuseness. Whenever there is interplay and counterplay of love and thought, there will be the higher world for which man also struggles in his striving for expression. Yet this is the terrestrial age of thought: thought works out the measure of things, the expression, the features, the mouth

—and that ends its mission on earth. True, love is said to be even the criminals' due, but not, I suppose, at all hours. It was Rodya's due, when he took Sonia and suffered—Rodion Raskolnikov who first dared all, dared to spit in the faces of all, dared to seize all power, dared even to kill—it was his due when Sonia said, "Go at once, this very minute, stand at the crossroads, bow down, first kiss the earth which you have defiled and then bow down to all the world and say to all men aloud, 'I am a murderer!' Will you go? Will you go?"—And this one went.

(Concluded for publication in 1950)

And then came the end in the East. If you called the garrison command on January 27, 1945, to ask, "What about the stuff we've taken so much trouble to bring here from Berlin—what do we do with it when the Russians come?" you were told by the adjutant, an SS captain: "Anyone asking that is going to be stood against a wall! The Russians won't get through! Maybe you'll get a look at some tank patrol in the distance; but the town will be held—and anyone who thinks of sending his wife back to Berlin will be shot, too." At five o'clock the following night there was alarm, artillery fire, and we ran home in a blizzard at 10 above zero, on foot, carrying a briefcase, over icy highways clogged up with the endless rows of refugees in covered wagons from which dead children fell. In Küstrin we were loaded on an open cattle car that took twelve hours under airplane strafing to bring us the twenty-five miles to Bahnhof Zoo in Berlin. Thus the end came all along the East, town by town. In the apartment were strangers; the rooms were bare; we covered ourselves with my uniform cloak and newspapers, to wake up when the sirens screamed. Thus it faded out—the block life in Room 66.

In these barracks I wrote *Novel of the Phenotype* and many parts of *World of Expression*, including "Pallas," and of *Static Poems*, e.g., "September" and others.

(Written 1944, published 1950) Translated by E. B. Ashton

A CHAPTER FROM

THE PTOLEMEAN
(A story from Berlin, 1947)

Winter is coming again, the color and the stillness of bronze lies over the city, and the spiders are creeping out. The light glides away on the swallows' feathers, anyone who has a plot of earth now harvests his garden, all the streets smell of tuberous plants, and the tobacco leaves are hung over the balcony railings. Soon the gales will come, there are the first touches of frost, hunger and plague will tread us under their hooves, the city council in its perspicacity has already taken on extra gravediggers, and the flower shops are hoping for a brisk trade in wreaths.

"A stork in the heaven knoweth her appointed times"—I don't mean to know less than that fugitive; "and the turtle and the crane observe the time of their coming"—I don't mean to observe less exactly than the fowls of the air. Therefore I say that the only thing that keeps us going is the black market; it is brilliantly organized and prices are almost stable, it is monetary reform both in a speculative and in a moral sense: looking at a pound of sugar or a tin of coffee, one knows what one is working for, *ora et labora*. Among my clients there is not one who does not get one thing or another and does not think the same way, but even my employees pretty regularly produce a bit of something extra out of their pockets. The only ones living on their allotted rations are evidently the civil servants, the local councils and the price-control agencies.

The material bases of our existence are of recent date. Chesterfields came on the market only between the two world wars, made by Liggett and Myers; the first blended cigarette appeared in 1913 in the shape of the Camel—the Duke Trust. It was the same year in which Bohr's sensational new atomic theory was published. On

June 20, 1920, the Panama Canal was opened, sixty kilometers long, a hundred meters wide; the level of the Atlantic is 20 meters above that of the Pacific, and the tide rises fifty-eight meters at Colon and only six at Balboa—hence the difficulties. Fifty ships have to pass through the canal every day if it is to pay its way, but then, pineapples from Honolulu and pearls from Macassar come to the banks of the Seine two months earlier now. 1922 brought insulin, 1935 the sulphonamides. In 1925 numerous Negro bands migrated from New Orleans, starting a sort of Alexandrine march of jazz right to our own gates. Since Caesar wrote *De bello gallico*, all blue dye in Europe had been derived from woad, cultivated mainly in Thuringia, and it was only indigo that drove it off the market, the first aniline dye to be used in dyers' vats; that was in 1900. My father used to recount that when they went visiting in the country in the old days the ultimate finesse in food was rice; that was the latest *gourmandise*, and those were the days when mail came to the villages once a week—today it is much the same, so there is a certain world-wide uniformity on earth, and sociology and the philosophy of civilization die like premature babies. 1947: while the gypsy tribes of the two hemispheres were choosing a new ruling family at the shrine of St. Sarah in Sainte-Marie-de-la-mer, the two ancient royal houses of the Kviek and the Sarana having exterminated each other, the four goats that had survived Bikini were kept under observation in Chicago. When I emerged from the void, the Manchus were still ruling China, and in Berlin the shops still kept open on Sundays; there were already three dozen cables linking Europe and the U.S.A., but someone returning from the Russo-Japanese war mentioned that the Kirghiz and the Tartars were still singing songs about Tamburlaine. What I'm getting at is that we're in a state of flux, in a slowly moving, largely opaque river, which is today going round a psychic bend: no causality, no psychology and no pensions, even the animals react perversely: the cats are sick of rats, and the buntings are horrified by worms. On the other hand, there is a certain agreement regarding shades of cinnamon, ginger, and amber for scarves and handbags in this little season, the lobes of the ears are adorned with enormous trinkets, and *rouge baiser* and after-shave lotion flourish again in adequate quantities among the ruins.

It was in these critical autumn weeks that I, influenced by certain states of suspension and a large bed of zinnias in the Botanical Gardens, came to think of selling my institute, changing my mode of life, and moving to some lake, to some plane of dark waves, big enough to carry my gaze, to bear it until it landed on distant shores. Man wants to see everything at once—to hell with the propaganda-ridden fragmentation of the towns, the everlasting boosting of the stuff in show-windows, hock shops, insolently impressive kiosks; to hell with the bother of turning corners and the perpetual compulsion to dodge those fish-faced, bull's-eyed, shark-finned limousines! Man wants to feel the unity of consciousness, to live in it and revel in it, for that alone gives him a sense of confirming his origin and his hour. All this the country promised; for days on end I saw the lake before me, its incorruptibility, its simplicity, its quietude, its colors. This was my mood, but there were syntactic-semantic motives in addition. Whenever I surveyed my nation's words, I had found many that I myself could never have created: holy, peak, starry—nothing vertical would have occurred to me. For plain, water, and horizontal situations I might have contributed a few things, and likewise for the unconscious, for somnolence, for everything to do with Pan, for honeycombs, gardens, the noon hour. Words from the steppe had always touched me closely. The sky is a drawn bow and fate an arrow, Allah the archer, as the saying went in Islam—altogether there was much of the Asiatic that very often cut across the insistence of my own nature, the most authentic element of which I had always felt to be the amorphous, the ambivalent.

Asia, the East, its cruelty and its ineffable splendor, its lust for power and its resignation, its dust, swirling across deserts as expansive as the sea, and the white stone with which the palaces of the Moguls were built long ago—were built and then crumbled away—yes, ruins everywhere, a submersion, an introspective bowed posture tending forgotten wisdom (in my own field yoga techniques, Chinese acupuncture, which was familiar with the age-old solar plexus therapy bearing on those secret centers and points of the body that determine the physiological tone of our life, from a vitalistic point of view in advance of modern European reflex therapy, which aims primarily at working capacity and is consecrated solely to raising industrial output)—there the Jordan flowed, from which other sacraments rose, and there the Ganges, on whose banks other pilgrims knelt—on all these waters did my lake border, expanding into the distances of Mongolia, seldom ruffled, only in autumn flinging a little foam among the reeds, and those who owned fishing-rights rowed out upon it, slowly sinking their eelpots.

Allurements, and everywhere water lilies that are almost fishes —the Titan submerged in his dream! What decided me to stay on in the city nevertheless, is something I can only explain in a roundabout way. The point of departure was the Zoological Gardens; the great cities positively compete with one another as regards zoos, aquaria, insectaria, and everyone can observe at leisure, impartially, what goes on from day to day in organic life. But inside the conscious mind, I had found, things were different—but why was consciousness itself so set on veiling, concealing, and denying this? I had studied the most important modern novels, in which Europe sought to discover itself and did recognize itself: *Growth of the Soil*, and *The Great Rain*, but the conclusion was always the same as in *Faust*, Part II: plain, straightforward work and service to the community, there in Norway, here in Ranjipur. Marvelous to have such heartfelt sentiments and not to have to suffer the problems of our time; there was idealism hidden behind that line of approach, and faith in the future, faith in life—that was the borderline concept, the water, the outline of palm trees in the desert. But some groups had emerged for which life no longer had any central, existential weight, for which it was not fulfillment; no longer the fairest of the greatest father's daughters, it no longer had wings to bear it either upward or downward. These groups were self-supporting—they had to be, that was their weight; that was the ultimate and only thing for which they still felt deeply, and it was clear to me that this was modern Europe, and this was where I wanted to stay.

This was to be my sacrifice in the place of many others I could no longer make. Anyone with any self-respect lays his own hour upon the altar; borrowings from other men's property are not acceptable to the gods. In this I followed Lord Ascot: a gift is to have something in you, morality is to express it, talent is to find an interesting way of expressing it—I knew of no other cosmic conditions. This limitation was, of course, essentially time-bound; perhaps there will be other times, or elsewhere, perhaps, there are times, capable of greater vision, with enormous radiations flowing to and fro, vast vaulted edifices; but not today and not here. Smyrna was Homer's birthplace and the grave of Tantalus, but in different generations—the second was later, and the devil take the hindmost.

Business, skyscrapers, the metropolis blocking out lakes and woods: here I had laid the foundations of my life, here I meant to determine its end with the precise stipulation that half my ashes were to be scattered on the September wind and the other half to be preserved in an empty Nescafé tin! An enhanced, a challenged life—tensions, condensations! Holding on to things, recognizing them exactly, and then blowing them sky-high—and at certain hours this struck me as very easy. It was a fountain of notes about things, details I had studied, only to fling them away. That was life! And here on the spot, in the rigidity of space, amid clerks and customers, everything was unfolding! Within the social world —good Lord, this social world—anyone who could juggle and disguise himself could still slip through its meshes! I kept salving and massaging, but I looked around me, I filled my eyes, saturated my hours, always transforming myself. A lady in black, proposing to go abroad, wants her hair done in an American bubblecut, the dryer-helmet is already being lowered—*tel est mon plaisir*—manicure is in progress, preparations for the honeymoon, but the mind tramples the biological horse-pond, ravages what has congealed, and the embers begin to glow. What are the doctrines, what is history—*bon mots*, arabesques, little eddies in the *panta rhei*! Little twists and turns. Kublai Khan moves his capital from Karakorum to Pekin, the Mongols are absorbed by the Chinese, observatories and cultivation of the silkworm win over the nomadic tents made of panther-skins, and grandfather Genghiz Khan turns in his grave, his grave in the brittle grass of Tartary! Little twists and turns: shades of the Battle of Plassey, which Clive fought in 1757, driving the Gauls out of Bengal once and for all—these shadows, stretching from the Khyber Pass across the homeland of snow and down into the tiger-ridden jungles of the South, dissolve into uncertainty, and the great ruby from the last Imperial crown returns to Rangoon, where it came from. Here a successful adventure and there an order misunderstood—patrols, squadrons, divisions of ghosts, generals, governors, Knights of the Bath, wearers of the Golden Fleece, Knights Commander of the Maltese Order, all bow, salute, fall *à toutes les gloires*, and finally two civilians slowly descend a flight of steps, the great staircase of a great castle, walk into the park, linger before the heliotrope beds and the trout pools, stand in silence—two Englishmen, alone and tired.

No, not the lake—here the veils lift, here the curtain rises over riddles and night. The peoples migrate, and the gods with them: from his African Olympus in the rainy forests of the Sudan, Wodu moves to Haiti, and the Madonna from Rome becomes Maîtresse Etilée in Port au Prince. Crossing the Kashmiri passes the Indians mingle with the Hellenes; through the defile of the Isère the Carthaginians come to conquer the Seven Hills; up mountains and down slopes there is always élan and radiation, then skull-smashing, strewn bones—indeed, only the vultures are constant! The Roman emperors flit straight out of life; the Yuan dynasts are soft-boiled with poison and dagger; the Merovingians tattoo each other with murders and vengeance; the Romanovs positively go out of their way to be bombed in carriages and shot at in opera-boxes—: only the vultures!

Yet it was by no means an arena for macabre moods that I worked up in myself. Observations on sport and business also went their quiet way, the whole of reality rising and settling again, and going on its rounds. India, which had hitherto held a world championship only in hockey, was considerably weakened by partition. The Great Salt Lake in Utah, on which some 3-liter and 550 HP contraption had managed to polish off all national and international records, could be reached quickly by the Yankee Clipper, the new three-story bus with the so-called Astrodome. The new golf-bag with a pocket for the caddy came into fashion. The Kentucky Derby, that celebrated race for the roses—whose winner is bedecked with a large garland of the flowers—put a sudden end to the career of Assault, the little wonder from Texas; and who owned that star of the Churchill Downs track in the land of the Blue Grass?—Elizabeth Arden Graham, the cosmetics queen from New York, whose products I sold in large quantities.

It is nine o'clock in the morning, my glass doors begin to revolve, my clients arrive, I conduct them to their chairs, they ask for their favorite attendants, male or female, who always serve them. I arrange it. This is craftsmanly work, work with the hands, but even if one leaves Hans Sachs out of it, Spinoza ground lenses, worked with forge-bellows and yet created a philosophy that moved the Olympian. My line is an ancient one. Job's third daughter was called Keren happuch, which means Little Jar of Face-Cream—a glorification of cosmetics. Nero's wife Poppaea always traveled with a hundred she-asses, in whose milk, mingled with myrrh and corn—what the eighteenth century called *lait virginal*—she bathed every day. Alcohol was at yet unknown; one perfumed milk, and wines were given an admixture of aromatic herbs. The kohl used by the modern Egyptian woman is the *mestem* of her ancestress, black antimony of sulphur: a little stick was dipped in the paint, then put between the eyelids, and the eye was gently closed. So the same old things recur! In materials there is always association, always recurrence of motifs; in commerce there is the eternal buying and selling, and social ideas rule as a retrospective myth:

after all, the masses have long constituted the Third Estate everywhere, if they have not long formed the government—in short, far and wide there was justification and scope for the expressive-archaic sphere, its autolysis, its maceration in the void, after which it would reach out with new brilliance for the images in the memory of plane trees.

In a city where there is nothing but strip-tease and nudity, where crimes become plausible and prison cells become scarce, the mind develops needs different from those in countries where the Shah sips nectarine-syrup in a red velvet chair among the sage bushes in his garden, or where Sir Something-or-other raises his dress-shirted arms behind his head to fasten the clasps on the blue and scarlet ribbon of the C.M.G., or on the beach of some scabious-colored sea, where the green parasols unfold and glamor girls, unclad save for a G-string, gaze through jeweled sunglasses at the water-skiers flashing behind the yachts—there the twittering of the wearers of purple and here the groaning of the damned. In a country where thoughts are safeguarded by lead mines and underground jails, where thoughts are revealed by subcutaneous injections, the mechanisms evolved for the ideation process are different from those in regions where psychologists hold meetings in spas and philosophers assemble at banquets so decorative that the florists rejoice. A sort of non-evolving consciousness will be at work here, steep and inert, introverted among squalls from Nirvana.

In a brain that feels this state of affairs to be neither tormenting nor morbid, there may then come impulses that bear it up into those spheres, those shuttlecock spheres, where a fragile net defines the ball's direction—up into the badminton game of things. Fluttering of lemon-yellow silk, of apple-green silk, of cucumber-colored silk, or the doe-brown traveling-rug that envelops the knees of the Secretary of State on motor rides in the leafy month of June in Nordic and breezy countries, or white hyacinths, or lilies-of-the-valley—these are not the only sources of feeling. Even from palpable, even from craftsmanly things, many a drop of honey drips onto the spoon for such a brain.

Remaining noncommittal, absorbing impressions from the reposeful earth, separating and reuniting components—the principle of those active on Olympus, of Mahadöh, and of the Norns—combined with the feelings of transformation held by ancient peoples to whom we are kin—the ideational method of *tat twam asi*: abasement into things, and then, after the anguish of unproportionate chaos, renewal in a grasp, a glance—all this takes just one stride into the Ptolemean landscape. It takes these ravishing, rich hours; for it is not work, not the load on the shoulders nor the oars of the galleys that make us so tired and wear us out—it is life itself, this hard, opaque condition of fate that brings us so close to the unbearable and can be met only for hours at a time, out of its own totality. But now I shall leave these generalizations and slip back into the current of my private notes, in which I am still heading for a quite definite subject.

For, frankly, there is one thing one has to reckon with: there is no stopping on this road, it's all or nothing—the All in nothingness. Even humanity can be held up for contemplation only by artistic means; for contemplation, after all, is the road to the esthetic world. To make up for that, this road makes lies impossible: it is based on the assurance of the body and on the ghostliness of the mind, which is variable in its materializations. This road is real, that is to say, it lacks the glossy finish, the swindle of padded substitutes for substance; I am speaking of our continent and its renovators, who keep writing that the secret of its reconstruction lies in "a profound inner change in the principle of the human personality"—not a morning passes without this whimper appearing in print! But wherever rudiments of such a change appear, they instantly start applying their extermination methods: snooping in the past and in private life, denunciation as a security risk, a menace to the West, a saboteur of humanity—denunciation as a form of revolution, this whole, by now classic system of an ideology of bureaucrats, half-wits, and licensees, compared with which Scholasticism looks ultra-modern and the witchcraft trials like world history. Well, let's forget that, it is no longer my field. I embrace the future, and even that does not affect me any more; I gaze impartially on the artificial rainfall induced by the Squire Kraus cloud-tickling process—150 pounds of dry ice on cumulus formations—the 200-inch telescope at Mount Palomar may register twelve more extragalacteal nebulae, for all I care—Greenwich moves house, to Tahiti, and the Arctic air bases communicate with each other by means of transmitters the size of lipsticks—and they are right, not only because Napoleon said the last comer is always right, but within their own competence they really are right.

No, there remains only vision, the style of seeing. Optimism-pessimism—: that would presuppose the fact of opposites or the wish to be someone particular. Far from it! There some Navy-Cut trickles out of a Russia-leather pouch, and there a citrous pellet with a betel-leaf rolls out of a jade box. Admittedly there are standpoints and vistas in which the whole world disintegrates, paralytic views, but those are not mine. I am no optimist, except for the optimism of the businessman who hears something tinkling into the till every day—no optimist, for I am getting on in years, and with age comes the great freeze, the retreat over the Berezina, the army defeated, the flag lowered, a handful of tattered troops in bearskin caps get as far as Poland, only the Emperor reaches Paris, and I am no emperor. Of course, there are also a few pleasant points, such as the birth of new concepts, *rhizosphere*, for instance—it was sent to me only today: it's the top layer of humus in which the fauna is classified into edaphodous, hemi-edaphodous, euedaphodous, and so on, according to depth level; the latter include chiefly springtails and other aptera, and the whole proceeds step by step into "The Fauna of Damp Soil." And where does all this originate? Not in the damp soil, not in im-pressions in the humus, no, in a wild grab, in predestination—and that, after all, is my doctrine: man's unsusceptibility to experience. One only needs to relax, to put one foot a bit forward and stand at ease, and already the weight on the chest changes. I, for one, find many things looking at me; for instance: minus times minus equals plus—how can minus times minus make a plus? What does it mean? Who hit on that idea? Who suddenly sniffed this lunacy? It is neither logic nor psychology, neither causality nor calculation; true, it is an inseparable part of mathematics, but pure phantasmagoria all the same, a surreal game, intelligible only as its own isolated expression. So here, too, are features of my type that never leaves itself, is always introverted, breathing these squalls from Nirvana.

Pessimism, that is a complicated affair—but what does pessimism mean when everything is so obvious? Doom—a nation in decline, Sparta in the past, the Sioux in the future; they will spend the next hundred years casting spells and standing in line, with some firewater from the rising victors. Doom—well, then one may surely play one's own game, let one's clouds pass over, garland one's windows, and lean out once more to hail the whole of the West, imposing in its multiplicity and profundity. They have specialists for everything, for galaxies and for Swahili dialects and for sharks— I have learned that to catch sharks you drag them by the tail, then the water pours into their gills in the wrong direction and they have to surface.

Pessimism—that is the deck-chair of the unproductive type, who trundles it down to the lake. I am an artist, I'm interested in countercurrents, I am a prismaticist, I work with lenses. As regards, for instance, my way of writing, anyone can see that it is prismatic infantilism. It doubtless stirs everyone's memories of childhood games; we ran around with little pocket-mirrors, caught the sunlight in them, and flashed it on shopkeepers standing outside their shops across the street, which caused annoyance and bad blood, but we kept in the shade. All we got out into the light was, of course, just skin, stucco, patches, moles on the surface of things, warts on the Olympus of appearances, nothing essential—which is why, confronted with anyone who would rather read historical novels and see whole epochs of civilization spread before him, I will fold my hands and wish him many sons to light his opium pipes and serve him bird's-nest soup with bêche-de-mer and turtle eggs, and that together they may go on playing fan-tan or mah-jong in peace to the end of their days.

Yet there are standpoints and vistas in which the worlds unite: the delirium about reclamation, the rock with the splinter, the jungle with the stone garden in its depths—Gretchen joins Lachesis, the Epiphany converses with the last hour of summer, and Bonaparte's mausoleum sinks silently to the brink of a mass grave. Ptolemean earth and slowly revolving heavens, the repose and the color of bronze under soundless blue. Ever and ever by nevermore, instant and duration in one—the glass blower's motto, the lotus song, playing the tune of its hopes and its oblivion. No, I am no pessimist—where I come from, where I shall fall, all that has been overcome. I spin a disc and I am spun, I am a Ptolemean. I do not moan like Jeremiah, I do not moan like Paul: "For what I would, that do I not; but what I hate, that do I"—I am the man I shall be, I do what appears to me. Nor do I bear within me any knowledge of having been "thrown," as the modern philosophers do; I am not "thrown," my birth set my pattern. I do not consist of "fear of life," nor, I admit, do I clutter myself up with wife and child and summer cottage and white tie. I wear inconspicuous ties but my suit is impeccably tailored: outside an earl, inwardly a pariah, base, tough, untouchable, and such may eat any flesh whatever, clean or unclean.

Coming to terms, and occasionally gazing out over water. Motions, lotions, customer service for the sake of the psycho-physical ideal—on top of the heap: a much-traveled and now self-employed beautician. The experiences of a lifetime, and then in certain hours this continent's last dream. Vultures and water-lilies, business and hallucinations, intersections and then final doom—that is how I face the rising nations.

I bring with me the brittle tautness of Nefertiti and flocks of memories from wonderfully complete vaults: *la Romanité* and Christendom, which this continent gathered out of sum totals, universals, and then scattered again. Traditions from Cordova and Montpellier, gifts from apostles, troubadours, and monks, seeds of suffering and ideas, bondage to mechanisms and idols, to experiments, cuneiform decipherings, theses and statistics—on the human, mass-determined scale a weighty brain, a heavy-laden *Pathétique*.

"Lotus"—who will inherit my business is not my concern; whether I shall be rembered is beyond me. From foreign papers I see that a single *maison* offers sixty-seven different brands of hair lotions and cosmetic waters, so *that* is not dying out—but when it is all up, they'll find something else, oil for robots or salve for corpses. Everything is as it will be, and the end is good.

(Written 1947, published 1949) Translated by Ernst Kaiser and Eithne Wilkins

LETTER FROM BERLIN, JULY 1948

to the editor of a South-German monthly

Berlin, Summer 1948

... In answer to your suggestion that I send a contribution to the *Merkur*, I should like to make the following remarks: I am in the peculiar position of having been banned and excluded from literature since 1936, even today remaining on the list of undesirable authors. Thus I cannot bring myself to come before the public after so long with some contribution that might, perhaps, fit into the framework of a periodical with a set policy and accord with the taste of an editor licensed ° within certain intellectual limits. I would have to insist on myself deciding exactly the nature and scope of the contribution, and make a point of its representing my new ideas. ...

For in the past years I have written several new books that have widened my own experience, but which would not meet with approval in the German literary and cultural arena. ... Lest this give you mistaken ideas, I add that my *Fragebogen* is satisfactory; as countless inquiries and investigations into my professional record have shown, I did not belong either to the Party or to any of its subsidiary organizations, I am not affected by the law—which makes it all the more grave that certain circles argue against my readmission to literature.

I do not know who belongs to these circles, and I have not taken any step towards getting in touch with them. The wings of fame are not white, as Balzac says; but if, like myself for the last fifteen years, one has been publicly referred to as a swine by the Nazis,

This refers to the Military Government licensing of publishers in occupied Germany.

a halfwit by the Communists, an intellectual prostitute by the democrats, a renegade by the emigrants, and a pathological nihilist by the religious, one is not particularly keen on pushing one's way out in front of that public again—all the less if one does not feel any inner bonds with it. For my own part, I have, as a matter of fact, not failed to keep abreast of the literary productions of the last three years, and my impression is this: here in the West, for the last four decades, the same set of brains has been discussing the same set of problems with the same set of arguments, resorting to the same set of causal and conditional clauses and arriving at the same set of either conclusions, which they call synthesis, or inconclusions, which they call a crisis—the whole, by now, seems pretty well worked to death, like a hackneyed libretto; it seems petrified and scholastic, a stereotype of stage-props and dust. A nation, or a West, hoping for a new lease on life—and there are signs pointing to the possibility of such a new lease on life—cannot be regenerated by these means.

A people is regenerated by an emanation of spontaneous elements, not by conservative care and chinstraps applied to historicizing and descriptive elements. Among us, however, the latter fill the public space. And as the background to this process I see something that, if I put it into words, you will regard as catastrophic. The fact is that in my view the West is doomed not at all by the totalitarian systems or the crimes of the SS, not even by its material impoverishment or the Gottwalds and Molotovs, but by the abject surrender of its intelligentsia to political concepts. The *zoon politikon,* that Greek blunder, that Balkan notion—*that* is the germ of our impending doom. The primary importance of these political concepts has long ceased to be doubted by this brand of club-and-congress intelligentsia; its efforts now are limited to tail-wagging and making itself as acceptable as possible. This applies not only to Germany—which even in this respect is in a particularly difficult, almost excusable position—but equally to all other European intelligentsias; only from England one occasionally hears a different tune.

Let us now cast a brief glance at these political concepts, and what they contain by way of degenerative and regenerative substance. Democracy, for instance—as a principle of government the best, but in practical application absurd! Expression is not achieved by majority vote, but, on the contrary, by disregarding the election returns; it is wrought by the act of violence in isolation. Or humanitarianism, an idea that the public invests with a positively numinous character—of course, one should be humane, but there have been great civilizations, among them some very close to us, which did not put this idea into practice at all: Egypt, Greece, Yucatan; its secondary character within the framework of productivity, its anti-regenerative trend, is obvious. All that is primary arises explosively; the leveling-off and the final polishing come about later—this is one of the few indisputable findings of modern genetics. The mutations of the entelechy are discontinuous, not historical. This is a universal law. But among us, wherever in the sphere of the mind a sign appears of anything primary, any volcanic element, the public intervenes with abortion and destruction of the germ-cell; the above-mentioned set appears with its club debaters, its round-table chairmen and members, its stump orators, issuing manifestoes, collecting signatures in the names of past and future, of history, of provision for grandchildren, of mother and child. The social philosophers, the interpreters of cultural values, the phenomenologists of crisis flock together, denouncing, eliminating, exterminating—and of course the editors-in-chief in their big press limousines, the professional patchers-up of perineal ruptures, which now, as usually, unfortunately occur before parturition—and all this in defense of democracy and humanitarianism. So why all this claptrap about the West and its rejuvenation and crisis, when all they want renewed is what has long been there—useful within its limits, but as a regenerative principle in terminal or crucial hours portending only atrophy and slackened forms?

The situation is deplorable, for there are new elements in existence and the West would like to take a bold new plunge. For me there is no doubt that a cerebral mutation is going on, held down

by all that is called public, guided by the state-controlled extermination of all entity. And here the tragedy begins. The public
is right, it is historically right. For the elements indicate an entity
that has destructive new features, always new and frightening
features of the depigmented Quaternary—man is something different from what the past centuries believed, from what they assumed,
and in his new intellectual constructions he will allot the Western
idea of history the same place as Voodoo or the black magic of
the shamans.

It is not my job to bring my own tragic ideas forward against
this public. I bear my thoughts alone; according to their law, one
who oversteps his own inner frontier in search of universality will
in this hour seem uncalled for, un-existential, and peripheral. The
objections to these thoughts I also bear alone. Estheticism, iso-
lationism, esotericism—"the migration of the intellectual cranes over
the heads of the people"—indeed, I am a specialized ornithologist
for this sort of migration, this migration that harms no one, which
everyone can look up to, gaze after, and yield his dreams to. So
they turn against that bestial monism which insists that everything
must fit together, that everything must be there for everyone without inner effort, without setbacks, without the experience of failure,
without the sort of resignation that determines one's bearing. And
then they aim at a process that seems to me to be drawing near:
the coming century will exert a compulsion on the world of men,
will confront it with a decision one can neither dodge nor emigrate
from—it will permit no more than two types, two constitutions, two
forms of reaction: the active and ambitious and those waiting in
silence for the transformation, the historical type and the profound
type, criminals and monks—and I plead for the black cowls.

And so ends my letter, for the length and nature of which I
apologize. You gave me a friendly wave of a glove, and I have
replied with something like a sjambok. But let me repeat: I do not
generalize, I do not extend my own existence beyond my constitution. I simply want you to gather from these lines that my fear
of not being published again cannot be great. My nihilism is

universal, it carries—it knows of the unfathomable transformation.

And so farewell, and greetings from this blockaded city without electric power, from the very part of the city which, in consequence of that Greek blunder and the resulting historical world, is on the brink of famine. Written in a room of many shadows, where there is light for two hours out of twenty-four; for a dark, rainy summer, incidentally, robs the city of its last chance of brief happiness, and the spring lays autumn over these ruins. But it is the city whose brilliance I loved, whose misery I now endure as that of the place where I belong, the city in which I lived to see the Second, the Third, and now the Fourth Reich, and from which nothing will ever make me emigrate. Yes, now one might indeed prophesy a future for it: tensions are developing in its matter-of-factness, changes of pace and interferences are developing in its lucidity, something ambiguous is starting up, an ambivalence such as centaurs or amphibia are born from. Finally, let us thank General Clay, whose Skymasters will, I hope, convey this letter to you.

(1949) Translated by Ernst Kaiser and Eithne Wilkins)

EXCERPT FROM
THREE OLD MEN
DIALOGUES

I

In a bachelor's den, not opulently but attractively furnished—indicating that its occupant considers comfortable armchairs, a large desk, soft carpeting, bookshelves, and a few prints on the walls as desirable—three gentlemen of about the same age are seated, dressed well but not alike. First class crystal and decanters on the table, fine china, whisky, vodka, black coffee, sugar bowls. All smoke. It is evening.

In addition: a young man.

ONE: No results, no perceptions—simply downhill—impossible! We must discuss that. Avalanches of shapeless existences roll into my field of vision—who, for instance, knows the birthday of his grandmother, a person so close to us? Who ever knew it? Dates! Dates missing all over! Letters without dates, documents without dates, on postmarks they are undecipherable—hence the trouble with horoscopy; that takes even the hour of birth—but we lack the dates for a good view of the whole nonsense. (*Fumbles about his jacket.*) Farsightedness is the end of happiness. I used to catch the fine print of the stock market quotations with the naked eye while running up Kurfürstendamm at night, on the double. Nowadays you spend all day rummaging in your coat pockets for your optics. . . . Young man: according to Tao, "a son is older than his father," so you know more than I do—where are my glasses?

THE YOUNG MAN: To begin with, I'd use the monocle that's dangling on your vest.

ANOTHER: Same vibrations here! Thinking in dates, in the center of gravity! If it were a fact that the stars are heavenly bodies, everything would be clear. We'd be mooncalves to think, then; we'd all be just so much applesauce. But as we do think, that star business can't be quite true—or things would certainly have stuck together, and we would not be the scum that sits here, drinking whisky. By the way, I've no desire to open any eyes. I'd rather shut some.

ANOTHER: From chair to chair, and then the three steps to the newsstand—that you can keep up in spite of economic crises. When we were young there were still scandals—spectacular! Remember the serenade whose author got a crown princess to run off with him from her husband and children? After a year he was pounding the ivories in a honky-tonk, and she was wading in the gutter. Themes, topics, excitements, continents aflutter—the serenade lives on, by the way; I recently heard it fiddled by a beggar near Trieste at midnight, and it was as gorgeous as on the first day.

ANOTHER: Cerebration and serenade! While the seducer was at work, a man in his forties figured out the law of quanta, one of the great theoretical structures of modern physics. The world of music and the world of atoms, where do they overlap? Did you personally suffer from classic causality, did you require a connection of the discontinuous energy quantum with the continuous wave, did you feel any need at all for a change in the physical *weltbild*, for a view of the world in which the concept of a constant distribution of energy would be invalidated? *Weltbild!* Always that word! What is there but fairy tales? Moment by moment—that is the world. Here a sip of coffee, there a red vest; now a sinking feeling, then an offering of honey—reminiscences, prophecies, and preludes—and then everything dissolves in an August night smelling of wreaths and stubble.

ANOTHER: There is nothing but fairy tales. I'll tell you one. I sat by an old woman's bedside during her last hours; she was freezing, had no cover but a folded sheet; on the table was a box of half-rotted Gravenstein apples from her father's estate, sent to her in secret by her brother's manservant. As a girl she bore one of the nation's proudest princely names; her husband represented his country at the court of Egypt. When the first railway ran in pomp and circumstance from Alexandria to Cairo, she raced it with four stallions and beat the governor. When her husband was transferred to Lisbon, a Dutch express firm undertook to move the household. There was a mover—well, to make a long story short, they, too, got married; it lasted six months. She had since been getting sixty marks a month from her family, and now the box of rotting apples. I asked her, "What do you think of the four stallions now, and of racing across the Nevsky Prospect in an open sleigh, on the way to the Czar's ball? The ambassador asks your husband, 'What's this Uhlan uniform you have on?' 'Second Brandenburg Nr. 2.' 'Impossible,' says the ambassador. 'Crown Prince Rudolf is titular chief of that regiment; would be a flagrant *faux pas* in the present political situation. Tell the Czar some other regiment.'—You arrive; the fires blaze before the palace; the *gorodovois* keep throwing logs into the flames—the Czarina in a glittering *kokoshnik,* diamonds trickling from her pearl earrings over the satin robe, down to the tips of her toes—tuberose fragrance and caviar as it's supposed to be eaten: on a hot *kalazh,* a roll with a handle like a small basket——what do you think of it now?" She was silent for a long time, looking in front of her, and then, in deep earnest, she said, "But he had such a lovely mustache!"—The mustache was some fifty years in the past, but she still saw it in her dying hour. It was the last thing she said—the end of her fairy tale.

YOUNG MAN: Disgusting dotards with their nihilistic prattle! "At the court of Egypt"—I guess that's over now, but we still have the Egyptian camels.

ONE: Ah, we have much more! Enter Pierino, the child prodigy. Listen to this, young man— (*picks up a newspaper, reads*): "Pierino Gamba, the ten-year-old Italian prodigy, conducted the Liverpool Orchestra at the Harringway Arena, before an audience of then thousand. In a black velvet jacket with ruffled collar and cuffs and white socks, he conducted Schubert's Unfinished Symphony and Beethoven's Fifth. Before the last tones had faded away, the audience was on its feet, showering Pierino with prolonged applause." Observe the appearance of the prodigy, the precocious pianist, the parental sacrifice to the platform—once his name was Mozart, then Liszt, now Pierino. He joins the round, he upholds the succession, the cycle expands, centuries pass, but these remain, civilization breathes—and you, young man, will not outbreathe it—ever!

YOUNG MAN: That's what you think. What I'm breathing, sniffing, actually inhaling is that your fairy tales will pop, and you'll have to face naked reality like all of us.

ONE: I've had my realities. First a village halfway in Lithuania, barefoot nine months of the year, the other three in clogs. My father was born in the year of Donati's comet, but he couldn't make much of it—kept busy with potato bags, rather. It was also the decade when lupine was introduced from Sicily, and he had to lug that. I went on the bum in America; the premises of my crossing are immaterial, but reality was represented by a landed proprietor and a gendarme. As a hobo you walk the tracks with steps of a certain length, and at curves you jump on the coupling and get in the open freight car. A job with a labor agent, selling glass eyes, but the first customer says, "You don't carry Negro eyes? They're most in demand," and the second wants eyes with tiny red veins—local problems. Stamping out the toes of shoes, three thousand a day, and selling sausage in the evening, gobbling the dried slices and hard butts yourself; turkey-killer, well paid, slaughtering turkeys but plucking them first, mean job—nix very nice, or very beautiful. From the latitudes of blubber to the lands of thick, slimy *pulque*—realities *en masse*, but I couldn't make head or tail of them.

ANOTHER: Go forth again, and come home. As far as I know, none of us stayed much at home; having no money, we forged the passports that got us across the dark and the yellow rivers. The century spread before us with pampas and savannahs. Lassoes thrown among gauchos, herds tended with the vaqueros—I once pulled the thorns out of cacti to feed the cattle. That year, '15, when one thought the sun was coming too close—140 under the tootsies, the hoofs sparking fire, the cows' udders eaten by ticks and getting hard as rocks, the sky transparent to infinity, the land a symphony of ashes.

Then I played White Man, beating the cotton-niggers over the head with a hickory cane so that the dust flew. But I had to; my employers in the civilized countries wanted their yachts modernized and their grooms assured of a higher standard of living. Then into the rice paddies, into the indigo fields, to the markets: I bought many a good set of hands—if they balked, they got the cat-o'-nine tails across their backs and pepper tea on the welts later. A queen in one civilized country got an orchid bouquet that flowered for six weeks under special Brazilian care; I had a part in this, though on the lowest level, where the panthers and rattlesnakes strike.

All realities—but what did they affect? The bones, the muscles, including dyspnoea and spirochaete. Where have they gone, what did they leave behind? Looking back now, all of it seems incredible, wholly imaginary; we are an ego but we perforate it hourly; we are heirs but we break the line of inheritance; we wreathe our heads in pampas fires and vanadium dust, sleep on camel dung and llama skins, and survice it all, until one night we sit and talk into the dark—

ONE: But we're quite off the track! What I said was: no results, no perceptions—simply downhill—impossible; we must discuss that. Once upon a time all things looked first-rate: youth, manhood, silver anniversaries, everything so organic; but when you get inside yourself now, it's all cuckoo-flowers. There has got to be something, though—there is something, an interior; are we not wandering restlessly in it, up and down, testing, listening, getting directions—or do I fool myself? No, there has to be something!

ANOTHER: You shouldn't be so Faustian about it. Your coffee is so good, and soap bubbles can substitute for the whole upper Peneus. What should there be, my friend? You know how hard we worked in business, and in between we drank fermented plant stocks and drifted on the tides of intoxication. The skies changed, the images fell. It was not the best of me that would remain archetypical. To know much, you must play much.

ANOTHER: Or do you think that intellectual pursuits might yield your result? Well, in Pasadena I was office boy to Johnny Macpherson who polished the big telescope with special rags; there I found out a lot. You know how many animal species there are on earth? It's not directly pertinent, but there are three million, and up to 1930, 750,000 of these were insects, the main contingent of which were 250,000 beetles, among them 35,000 weevils—that's a result. Or it might help you to learn that the reduction of metallic copper from its unmetallic-looking ores was one of man's most tremendous technical triumphs, his emergence from the Stone Age. These ores melt at 1083 degrees Centigrade, a heat that took some producing—2000 years before Christ, by means of bellows—surely one of the greatest jubilations of all time in the upper Nile valley! Or intellectual affinities between Montesquieu and Sun Yat Sen, and between the British Civil Service and the Chinese Examining Yuan—in Pasadena these were spiritual results, but if they can yield the result that you have in mind, only you can tell.

ONE: No, by interior I mean something else; I mean what forces us to be what we have become. To paint the Gioconda for five years, sit bent over it for five years, say nothing, show it to no one, not sell it—that's more than Raphael riding to court each morning with sixty pages. In the room where Leonardo worked were fragments of Greek statuary, dog-headed Egyptian gods of black granite, cameos of the Gnostics with magic inscriptions, Byzantine parchments as hard as ivory, with fragments of Greek poetry that had been considered lost forever, shards with Assyrian cuneiform, iron-bound scripts of the Persian Magi, papyri from Memphis, as fine and transparent as rose petals. This he had to transform himself by, this to pursue, this, perhaps, to succumb to—and there he lived for five years with his one inner vision.

ANOTHER: Splendid! But you're speaking of the Middle Ages—and, after all, the well-known study of Faust with its flasks and phials belongs there, too. It has often been said that all this no longer exists. We keep saying, Man, but we forget his mutations. Today the interior looks like this: a series of methodically determined categories such as zoology, physics, genetics. Then the organizations of uplifting and contrition: Salvation Army, Christian Science, Mormons, temples in the desert—plus, in the Western world, the gentle ventriloquists of synthesis—but all these are large fossils, standardized comforts, bleached slipcovers. Your remark on Leonardo makes me ask if you've ever considered the one alarming phenomenon of our time, and its significance: productivity? Doubtful conditions—to be moved and yet detached—do you know what osmosis is? That's what you must keep in mind! To be permeated with the vapor of the gods, with Pythian smoke, with the emanations of inconceivable manifestations; to watch the smoke as soberly as a tobacconist hawking papyri with and without tip—and even to cheat the while. Doubtful conditions, but no more so than all human tissue.

Moods, this or that, and the language beyond. Impressions, from within and from without, and in between the thrill of putting them into words. Thought that rests on observations, serial figures, statistics, percentages—trained thought, yes, but moving in what doesn't exist yet, in the world of imagination: expressive thought—this, and then the distortions and the dreams.

So, language arose from animal sounds, and now we face a mankind afflicted with word-making spasms, first epileptoid ones, then of a distinctly catarrhal type. Style is hyperbole; expression is usurpation and tyranny—by such evil methods is the spirit moved. It seems vain and idle as soon as your earnestness or your grief, your ancient hours, desert it. Behind it lies probably something that favors silence, as suggested by the verse from Revelation: "Seal up those things which the seven thunders uttered and write them not." Thus all basic questions of the soul are reopened, and now for its relationship to the body: *mens sana in corpore sano;*

the legions rattle and the eagles flash! Point Two: you can swim the Channel with cancer of the stomach; you can die of tuberculosis of the lung at 6 p.m. and make love to your heart's content from 2 to 2 : 15 on that same afternoon. Deviations always are already at work. But this is still perfection compared to Point One. There we're up against Beauty, Virtue, and Truth. One man regards a landscape of a heath in oil as beautiful, another a government proclamation as true, and a third thinks an establishment is good if it can advertise itself as "one of the few hotels where the meat is carved before the eyes of the guests. No northern exposure!"—That's how relative we have made the old Roman *virtus*.

YOUNG MAN: Tell me, are you making conversation, or whatever you call this, in Berlin or in a calligraphic vacuum? What is the difference between a phallus and an air-pump? According to you, none!

ONE: Yes, let's devote ourselves to the youth that sounds so open-minded. Look, young man, if I ruled the continent, I'd start by banning the double names that are so widespread in so many countries. One short word is enough for these stumps of individuality. Then I'd go back to the archaic time system: twice I-XII; in the railway schedules we could underline the minutes for nighttime, as we used to. Then, spats! Plenty of sleep—incomprehensible and meaningless in itself, but the most enduring beauty treatment known to biology. Not too much sun—we overrate the light; twilight is the proper human illumination. Furthermore: constant environment. There you last longer; in the marine depths we still find the paleozoic world surviving. And finally: avoid anything apocalyptic. The sevenheaded beast from the sea and the two-horned one out of the earth have always been with us.

YOUNG MAN: Sometimes I read foreign magazines and understand everything but the jokes. Same here. The dateless grandmother, the grandfather with the unknown shoe size, the grandchildren with brain mutations, the interior on the way outside, the soul getting epileptoid—just why are you still staying around your sugar bowls?

ONE: I don't think I was speaking only for the Middle Ages, or that you, in behalf of the present *pandaimion*, were charging me with considering the mutation thesis as another orthodoxy and an intellectualistic effort to disguise the current imbalance of causality and depth. But the young man is right: why are we staying around? As far as I know, all of us are pretty well removed from family and mankind. We lay wreaths on graves and escort the dead. Sometimes we may still be visited by one of those dearly bought mixtures of intellect and sensuality; she relaxes with us—the current has been turned off, she fingers the set, puts the earphones over her hair and a rose into her mouth—she's in repose, beautiful and deadly, and for a moment you see the position in which Zeus approached Leda, but you no longer overestimate it so.

Of course, we could leave. But should one make death appear so violent? It should belong to the serenities of the spirit, and well it might. The feast is over, you look at the bouquets, at the stiffening roses, at the relaxing gladioli that allow themselves to droop. And just as the whole banquet was improvised, so is the end. We lived something other than we were, we wrote something other than we thought, we thought something other than we expected, and what remains is something other than we planned.

ANOTHER:—or the times of remembering how much that is dead we carry around in ourselves—brows, sweet, tender, childlike words—sufferings that were in vain—tears that ran beside us—happiness, grief, everything down the drain. So many hours that are already unknown again, that go on living only in me, while I am—in my thoughts, in my eyes—hours I can't let fall, and for which I keep bearing the inability to know.

ANOTHER: A Greek reminiscence, to love light so much, and a Christian one, to obligate yourself to shadows.

ANOTHER: And beyond it the finale of the West: to believe that there is something. To keep rushing away from this something, rushing off time and again into veritable cavalry campaigns, mammoth *mêlées,* pachydermatous cataclysms—piling negation on annihilation, demolition on destruction, pestilence on poisons—just to sit here again one night and to believe *that there is something.* It's an inconceivable, incomprehensible, tragic, profound way, and it can't be cut short; the race will go it to the end.

YOUNG MAN: It's so dark—which of you is speaking now?

ONE: Everyone could speak everything. Individualities are no longer distinguished by their sentences. The collective feels, the lip speaks.

YOUNG MAN: I guess that's the mythical collective of the primitives?

ONE: Yes, there is something in the air, and it finds a voice.

YOUNG MAN: And the whole, I take it, is an autumn evening and becomes symbolic?

ONE: Indeed, at a rendezvous you won't get around certain premises.

YOUNG MAN: Say on, collective, the gaslight appears in the sky!

ONE: The collective will go to bed. And you, my friend and host, must you really go down the drain? The century spread pampas and savannahs before you, lifted your eyes to cedars, let you look deeply into gardens. You tied your sail to the mast and beat your sickle against the earth—don't you sense what word the seven thunders uttered: Go forth again and come home?

(1949)

DOUBLE LIFE

FUTURE AND PRESENT

The way of an intellectualist. ... An intellectualist, I take it, is someone rather cool in human affairs, someone who loves clear words and defends himself with concepts sharper than bread knives. He may be a still unbalanced rudiment of a *sapiens* type whose later forms will no longer have affective or humane or even historic problems, because he thinks in terms of order and regulation, feels his mission in those, and fulfills it under the aegis of great, supranational complexes that will be comparatively just but unsentimental. All this has yet to grow, and I hope that Europe will then be in on it.

The past century was bursting with the notion, and the word, "collective." The paleologists taught that the mythical collective was at an end; the social scientists opined that the social one was beginning—"no, the racial one," snarled the Third Reich, and the Eastern office neon-lighted the active, quota-fulfilling, progressive, constructive one; you could not make head or tail of all the collectives. This dream is finished. Collective—that was sheer illusion, a fable to fill the ineffable emptiness of our robot existence, and the explanation of our inability to put a modern state conception into practice. Now the states have broken down under the joint pressure of victories and defeats, and the new, supranational complexes no longer need this auxiliary construction; they drain and involve the individual in other directions and replenish it with other necessities.

But these questions more or less concern the future, and the future, as I often wrote, is not important to the living. Their serious concern is with the present, with their own inner being, their self. So I will take another look at my circles, and do so in aphorisms.

1. My generation still had certain literary residues from earlier ones to latch on to: father-and-son problems, Antiquity, adventure, travel, social issues, *fin de siècle* melancholia, marital questions, themes of love. Today's generation has nothing in hand any more, no substance and no style, no education and no knowledge, no emotions and no formal tendencies, no basis whatever—it will be a long time until something is found again.

Addendum: confusion and bad writing alone does not make one a surrealist.

2. Actually, what my generation discussed and excogitated— what, one might say, it suffered or, one might also say, it harped upon—had all been already expressed, exhausted, definitely phrased by Nietzsche; what came after him was exegesis. His dangerously stormy, flashing manner, his restless diction, his renunciation of idyls and universal reasons, his establishment of instinctual psychology, constitutional motivation, physiology as dialectics—"cognition as affect"—the whole of psychoanalysis, the whole of existentialism, all this is his work. More and more clearly we see in him the far-reaching giant of the post-Goethean epoch.

Addendum: after Nietzsche, Spengler. Not because of his assumption of decline, but because he propounded the concept of a morphology of cultures, a not only interesting but guiding and regulating idea in the confused historic world.

3. One may doubt and ridicule science, including genetics and paleontology, but the sciences are telescopes; now and then we put our eyes to them, and then we see that there have been infinities of human and extra-human development and formation before us, without us, far from us. Our bit of latitude, our bit of climate, our clothing, the nutrition of our momentary little continent, and our evaluations, moods, tendencies, ideals, philosophies—what does it all amount to? What I miss is a treatise on the domesticity of axioms, a geography of apriority, the climatical excuse for so much dust.

4. Estrangement from nature. Nature is a strange milieu; if you leave your room, even the ordinary air feels alien. A flowering shrub in a city street will do it, or again a look at the sky, a gray sky with a bird flying in it—no special bird, just a starling—and then the night begins. We are creatures of giant cities; it is in the city, and there only, that the Muses exult and grieve.

5. In the beginning was the word. It is amazing and has cost me a great deal of thought that this was in the beginning. In the beginning, when animism and totemism and cave-scraping and beasts and magic masks and rain-rattles kept the field and the world—the Jews were probably very old when they said this, and knew much. Truly, it is in the word that the earth centers; there is nothing more revealing than the word. It has always fascinated me to see experts in their fields, even profound philosophers, suddenly faced with the free word—the word that yields no tirades, no systems, no facts of external, historically buttressed observation, and no commentaries; that produces one thing only: form. How they operate there! Utterly at a loss. Little idyllicists, crickets, small boys. In the beginning, in the middle, and at the end is the word.

Addendum: there really are now only two verbal transcendencies, the theorems of mathematics and the word as art. The rest is business speech, bar parlance.

6. How many good starters were seen to fall by the wayside! At first, big avant-garde, some indeed divinely gifted—and at forty they take the family tramping through Andalusia and detail the bullfights, or they discover Hindu introversion on a Cook's tour. What breaks them, according to my observations, is premature fame, allowing themselves to be typed by critics and admirers. Only if you break yourself again and again, if you forget yourself, go on and pay for it, live under burdens, let no one talk you into occasions to write, but make your own reasons for writing—then, perhaps, then, if a great deal of disappointment and self-denial and forced abandonment is added—then, eventually, you will perhaps have advanced the Pillars of Hercules by a few worm-lengths—perhaps.

7. No work can come to be save in a closed space. What people call dynamic and imagine as being revolutionary, tempestuous, frontier-smashing belongs to other realms of existence. Those are premises, and art is static. Its content is a balance between tradition and originality, its procedure the equilibrium of mass and point of support. This fact explains the peculiar proximity of everything artistic in the cycle of civilization, from early Egyptian sculpture to Picasso drawings, from the hymns of the Middle Kingdom and the Hebrew psalms to the poems of Ezra Pound. Yet this fact separates art from all other realms—a thesis that we see ever more plainly emerging, a thesis that cannot be made plain enough, in order to take in what follows.

What follows came out of an interview with a gentleman from the radio and a gentleman of the press. They both asked what I had to say about the numerous reviews of my new books. "What are the objections of your critics, and what is your position?"

My first answer was: I greatly admire my critics, when they agree with me as well as when they object, since hardly any of them fails to grasp the essence of my literary manner, to set his sights in the direction of my style, and to digest my opinions. From this I infer, to my own surprise, that the inner currents I am trying to express are much more widespread in European letters than is casually assumed—that certain tensions in the productive sphere of present Western man have built up to a degree of condensation and have created pressures for discharge that will soon make undreamed-of psychic transformations understandable, even to those who are more remote and not artistically active.

As for the rest, I'll summarize that in aphorisms again. I am aware of the peculiar acuity of my phrasings, also of reiterating things already said in the first part of this book, that of 1934. As for the acuity, I think that in the intellectual world more damage has been done by flabbiness than by rigor.

1. *The Crisis of Foundations*
Thought clashes with thought—Marxist with Western, Faustian

with Mediterranean, collective with isolationist, biological with psychological, critical with empirical, social with aristocratic. These encounters can be most exciting, suspenseful, and moving, but they all occur in the same setting of dialectics, ratio, and ideology. The thought that advances today will be beaten tomorrow; the idea we identify with our time will be obsolete and void after the next counter-movement; some motifs last for hundreds or thousands of years, like those of Nazareth or of Antiquity, but the dialectic defensive-offensive milieu remains. The feeling of this actual or potential relativity of the world of European thought, the loss of certainty and absoluteness, is the present stigma of our civilization. It is an immensely widespread and general, an already popular, feeling. Everywhere you see societies that discuss it, circles which some city pays to reason about it; academies mushroom; clubs debate the hopeless situation—there is a rabbit warren of analyses and prognoses, a rabbit warren of introversions and incantations as well as evasions and blights all over the continent. Can you blame a man for saying: Fine, all right, I guess it must be that way, but without me, please—for the brief span of my days without me, please—for I know a sphere without this sort of mobility, a sphere that rests, that can never be set aside, that is conclusive: the esthetic sphere.

2. *Artistics*

When you announced your visit, you promised not to ask me if I am a nihilist. The question is, indeed, as immaterial as it would be to ask whether I skate or collect postage stamps. For the point is *what you make of your nihilism.* Sonia Henie and Maxi Herber doing *pas des patineurs,* the golden Suaheli in philately, and expression in the world of the mind: always the purest, always the nearly perfect. Style is superior to truth, for it carries the proof of existence in itself. Form: in form is distance, is duration. "Thought is always the scion of want," says Schiller—in whose work we see, after all, a very conscious shift of emphasis from ethics to esthetics; he means that thought is always close to utility, to the satisfaction of urges, to axes and clubs, that thought is nature. And Novalis goes on to speak of "art as the progressive anthropology."

The epochs end in art, and the human race will end in art. First came the saurians, the lizards, and then the species with art. Love and hunger—that's paleontology, and even insects have all kinds of government and division of labor; but our species made gods and art, and then art alone. We live in a late world underset with preliminary stages, early forms of existence; everything ripens in it. All things are reversed, all concepts and categories change character as soon as we view them as art, when it faces them, when they face it. A novel attitude, a novel affection. It is an hour from Homer to Goethe, and twenty-four hours from Goethe to this day—twenty-four hours of change, of dangers that only he who acts according to his own legalities can meet. People now ask often for a "correct" image of Goethe, but there will be no such thing; we must be satisfied with the knowledge that here something was launched that confuses, that is incomprehensible but scatters seed on barren shores—and that is art.

3. Religion and Humility

A great new tide of piety engulfs the continent. Doeblin, once avant-garde, Franz Biberkopf of Alexanderplatz, is now a strict Catholic proclaiming *ora et labora;* Toynbee is Christian, so is Eliot; Jünger plays the Christian humanist—all of them reach backwards. Fine pose, but style relaxation, conformism. I forego this reaching; it is another question I can only view artistically. "God is a bad rule of style," I once wrote, and, "Gods in the first verse is something other than gods in the last verse"—meaning, I either turn myself inside out or someone else does; I can't have it both ways. If you were to ask me whether I believe, I should say that believing would already put me outside the substance I work in, would separate me from the essence of my mission and my involvement; the nature of this mission and involvement is more obscure to me than it has ever been. I regard prayer and humility as arrogant and pretentious. Their premise is that I am anything at all—which is just what I doubt; there is only something that goes through me. A Catholic newspaper, after praising me highly in detail, concluded, "Out with this man; he derides God and despises the religions." What misjudgment! I despise humans who cannot handle their own affairs and therefore ask help from another quarter—a quarter that can scarcely know them, these shadows of nothing, these rabbits, these wormwood drops left in the dregs, who reform for ten cents and whose main hope should be to go to their graves before long and get out of the sight of the Great Being. This Great Being—a subject by itself! Consider what is has done to us: it certainly has not endowed me well enough to find my way; it has veiled much that would matter to me; I must take plenty and end up knowing no more than when I started. Result: I must go through everything alone, through my breakdowns, through the study of myself, through the phenomenology of my remaining ego—should I then suddenly grow humble at the decisive moment and say, "I'm sorry, I didn't mean it?" Where would that leave the individualism our West is said to live by, if it suddenly sawed off and threw away its façade and humbled itself? Humility as a broadening motif, a mood, a vacuum for lock-opening and novelty-admitting purposes—all right; but as a moralistic and religious overcast it merely confuses the style. This Great Being certainly should have elaborated its situation more distinctly before making precise claims.

4. *Principles of Art*

cannot be publicly and politically generalized. It is provincial immaturity on the artist's part to expect the public to care about him, to support him financially, and to celebrate his sixtieth birthday with banquets and floral tributes. He rampages within himself —who should thank him for it? Remember, too, how many "Egmont" and "Leonore" overtures have thundered over the average politician's head at inaugurations and other festive occasions, without effecting a change in him. I agree, therefore, with Monet's maxim, *"Il faut décourager les arts,"* and with James Joyce's paraphrase of a Talmud saying, "We Jews are like the olive, giving our best when we are crushed, when we collapse under the burden of our labors"—in Joyce's view this applies to artists. Those are healthy ideas! Let us at last distinguish between art carriers and culture carriers, as I proposed in one of my books fifteen years ago. The art carrier is statistically asocial, living only with his inner material, utterly disinterested in expansion, broad effect, increased reception, and culture. He is cold; his material must be kept cold, since his task is to chill and harden the idea—the warmth to which others may humanly yield—so as to give stability to softness. He is mostly very sober and does not even claim to be anything else, while the idealists sit among the culture carriers and money-makers. Thus I wrote some fifteen years ago; and it is not half of what will be revealed by the future.

(1950) *Translated by E. B. Ashton*

ARTISTS AND OLD AGE

Last winter in Berlin I went to a lecture at the Kant-Gesellschaft given by a Kant scholar on Kant's posthumous work. This work, the *Opus posthumum*, the original of which was lost in Northern Germany during the last war, exists in the form of transcripts which, with notes and commentary, were made available to the limited public of the philosophically interested about twenty years ago; it is apparent that Kant never got to the point of working it over and finishing it completely. The *Opus posthumum* was written during the years 1797-1803; Kant's great earlier works had been published some twenty years before that time. It has now become evident that some of his fundamental theses look very different in the light of the later work, which contains passages in contradiction to the *Critique of Pure Reason*, and the lecturer raised the question which propositions were to be considered valid, the earlier or the posthumous ones; for the two were scarcely reconcilable. The lecturer did not attempt to settle the question, but suggested that some of the earlier theses were cancelled out by some of the later. Behind this question of the comparative validity of Kant's earlier or later work, there looms up the problem of early and late works in general, the problem of the continuity of the creatively productive personality, of the transformations it undergoes and the breaks that occur. The particular case is that of a philosopher, but the problem is one that occurs in the case of artists, too.

It was about the same time that I read in a newspaper a review of an exhibition of the work of Lorenzo Lotto that had been held in

This translation of an essay originally published in *Merkur*, April 1954, appeared in *Partisan Review*, Summer 1955.

Venice the previous summer. In this review was the sentence: "The works of the last decades strike one as being unsure, in the same marked way as one notices it in the German artists Baldung and Cranach." So these great masters became unsure of themselves in their last period of creative productivity. While I was pondering on this, I came across the following dictum by Edward Burne-Jones in a work on the history of art: "Our first fifty years are squandered on committing great errors; then we grow timid and scarcely dare to set our right foot before the left any longer, so well are we aware of our own weakness. Then there follow twenty years of toil, and only now do we begin to understand what we are capable of and what we have to leave undone. And then there comes a ray of hope and a trumpet-call, and away we must go from the earth." Here then is the opposite of Lotto's case; here it is youth that is uncertain, and certainty comes with old age, when it is too late. This is reminiscent of the scene from "Titian's Death" by the twenty-year-old Hofmannsthal, where Titian lies on his death-bed, but still goes on painting—I think the picture was "Danae"—and suddenly he starts up and asks for his earlier pictures to be brought before him.

He says that he must see them,
Those old, and wretched, pale ones,
must now compare them with the new ones he is painting;
for now, he says, things very hard to grasp are clear to him,
he understands, as earlier he never dreamt he could,
that up to now he was a feeble blunderer.

So here, too, we have it, seen through the artist's own eyes: only in his ninety-ninth year does he cease to be a feeble blunderer.

To my surprise, I found similar trends of thought in the East. Hokusai (1760-1849) says: "I have been mad about drawing since I was six years old. By the time I was fifty I had given the public a vast number of drawings, but nothing of what I did before my seventy-third year is worth mentioning. At about the age of seventy-three I had come to understand something of the true nature of animals, plants, fishes, and insects. It follows that by the age of eighty I shall have made further progress, by the age of ninety I shall see into the mystery of things, and if I live to be one hundred and ten everything I do, even if it is no more than a stroke or a dot, will be alive." Here we come up against the question that has occasionally been aired in literature—what would the world have thought of certain men had they died earlier than they did in fact? In this particular case it is the question what would have been left of Hokusai if he had died before his seventy-third year.

"All Eastern and all Western lands/Tranquil lie within His Hands"—so I took counsel with our Olympian great-grandfather, Goethe, and studied his *Maxims and Reflections*, a book that everyone who has his troubles should dip into for a few hours each week. There I found the following aphorisms:

1. Growing old means entering into a new business; all the circumstances change, and one must either entirely cease to act or take over the new role with purposefulness and deliberation.
2. When one is old one must do more than when one was young.
3. On the guillotine itself Madame Roland asked for writing materials in order to write down the quite special thoughts that had occurred to her on her last journey. What a pity it was denied her—for at the end of life there come to the resigned and courageous soul thoughts that were hitherto unthinkable, and they are like blissful spirits, settling radiantly on the peaks of the past.

Blissful spirits—on the way to the guillotine! Very Olympian, very gigantic!—and indeed this great-grandfather of ours, with his many talents and possessions of every kind, was quite the man to start upon a new business at any moment. All the same, this was scarcely of a generally illuminating nature. However, in the same volume there was the fragment *Pandora*, and I found myself considering the strange figure of Epimetheus:

> *"For Epimetheus I was called by my progenitors,*
> *he who muses on things past, and traces back,*
> *in the laborious play of thoughts, the quick deed*
> *to the dim realm of form-combining possibilities."*

To muse, to trace back, in the laborious play of thoughts, to the dim realm of form-combining possibilities—perhaps this Epimetheus was the patron of old age, a twilight figure, sombre, backward-glancing, in his hand the torch already lowered.

At this point you may, perhaps, say to yourself that you are listening to someone making extensive use of quotations, alert for whatever he can pick up, on the lookout for advice and information, like a young girl travelling alone, and you may ask yourself: What is he after, what is he getting at? Is there something personal hidden behind all this? Yes, indeed, that is precisely the case, there *is* something personal behind it all, but it does not take up undue space in what is to follow. All the same, just for a moment, if you please, imagine a writer with an unquiet past, unquiet times, who began his vocation together with a whole circle of others of the same age from all countries of the world, and who also underwent that same stylistic development which was known by various names —Futurism, Expressionism, Surrealism—and still keeps discussion alive today, since it is a stylistic development of decidedly revolutionary character—admittedly, and let us get this said once and for all—no more revolutionary, in our author's opinion, than such earlier stylistic developments as Impressionism, Baroque, or Mannerism—but still, for this century, it certainly was revolutionary. This author sailed under various colors in his life: as a poet and as an essayist, as a citizen and as a soldier, as a hermit in the country and as a man of the world in this or that great metropolis—and for most of the time under criticism and attack. Well, now this writer is getting on in years, and he still goes on publishing things. And if he has not entirely quenched the volcanic element in himself, not entirely lost the dash and vigor of youth, what it comes to is that the critics nowadays exclaim: "Good heavens, why can't the man be quiet? Isn't it time he got down to writing something classical and preferably with something of a Christian tinge? Surely it's high time for him to ripen and mellow as befits his years!" But if, for once, he does write something rather more mellow and glowing and, so far as he has it in him, classical, the cry is: "Oh, the fellow's completely senile! He was moderately interesting when he was young, in his storm-and-stress period, but now he's a mere hanger-on desperately trying to keep up with himself. He hasn't anything to say, so why can't he have the decency to shut up?"

So far, so good. When an individual book of a writer's is reviewed, whether it is panned or praised, he can feel proud or annoyed, according to his mood. But the situation changes when the writer has got on so far in years that books begin to appear about him, when the younger generation begins to write theses on him for their doctorates, at home and abroad, analyzing him, classifying him, cataloguing him—theses in which a comma that he put in thirty years ago, or a diphthong that he produced one Sunday afternoon after the first World War, is treated as a fundamental stylistic problem. The studies in themselves are interesting, the linguistic and stylistic analysis is superb, but for the writer under discussion it is like watching himself being vivisected. Others have seen what he is like, and so now he himself sees what he is like. For the first time in his life he recognizes himself; up to now he was utterly a stranger to himself, and he has had to grow old in order to see himself.

·And supposing that this writer has at some time in his life uttered opinions that are later considered impossible, then good care is taken that these opinions should drag along behind him like the harrow after a farm horse, and everyone is delighted to see them continually hitting him on the heels. Well, that's part of the game—the writer says to himself—nothing can be done about that. If one were to write nothing but what turned out to be opportune fifteen years later, presumably one would never write anything at all. One little example of what I mean, and then I shall leave this writer of ours for some time. In a conversation, a very serious conversation between three old men, this writer once wrote the sentence: "To be mistaken and yet be compelled to go on believing what one's own innermost being tells one—that is man and his glory begins yonder, beyond victory and defeat." From our author's point of view this declaration was a sort of anthropological elegy, a cyphered melancholy; but his critics thought differently. It

187

shocked them to the core. Here they said was a blank check for every conceivable political crime. At first the author did not know what these critics meant, but then he said to himself: Oh well, in the nineteenth century the natural sciences made an onslaught on poetry, Nietzsche was fought by the theologians, today it is politics that gets mixed up with everything—all right, let's leave it at that— dim realm of form-combining possibilities. But all this together, the theoretical and the practical, caused our author to look into the question of how other old men had fared and what old age and the process of aging mean for the artist.

First of all, my inquiry is not concerned with the physiology of aging. What medicine has to say on this subject doesn't amount to much. Its current formula is that aging is not a process of wear-and-tear but of adaptation, and I must say this doesn't convey much to me. It goes on, as I have discovered from its journals, to deplore the lack of unprejudiced, systematic psychological examination of old people who are not in psychiatric clinics. I don't know how many of you will also deplore this. Nor am I going to say anything about rejuvenation cures, or about the celebrated Bogomoletz serum either. What I am more concerned with is the question at what age aging actually begins.

The forty-six years after which Schiller died, the forty-six years after which Nietzsche fell silent forever, the forty-six years after which Shakespeare had done his work and retired for five years more of life as a private citizen, or the thirty-six years after which Hölderlin became insane—such, surely, is no great age. But mere arithmetic will, of course, get us nowhere. There can be very little doubt that foreknowledge of an early death compensates, in terms of inner life, for decades of physical life and the process of aging that goes with them. Such seems to have been the case with those who suffered from tuberculosis, for instance Schiller, Novalis, Jens Peter Jacobsen, Mozart, and so on. The early death of so many men of genius— something that the bourgeois-romantic ideology likes to connect with the notion of the consuming and devouring character of art—

will have to be looked at a little more closely in each individual case. Some of these young men died of acute diseases. Schubert and Büchner died of typhus. Accident or war caused the deaths of Shelley, Byron, Franz Marc, Macke, Apollinaire, Heym, Lautréamont, Pushkin. Kleist, Schumann, and van Gogh committed suicide. In short, the ranks become thinner in relation to a direct causal connection between art and death. And looking at the dates when men of genius died, one makes a very odd observation of an entirely different kind, which I pass on to you, not as the result of deep thought or as something of a metaphysical nature, but simply because it is interesting. It is this: it is astonishing, indeed quite amazing, how many old and even *very* old men one finds among the famous. Let us take as our basis the figures that Kretschmer and Lange-Eichbaum give for those who have been regarded as people of genius or of extraordinary gifts during the last four hundred years in the West; there are between a hundred and fifty and two hundred of them. Now it turns out that of these men and women of genius almost half have lived to be very old indeed. Our lifespan is seventy years, so let us waste no time on that. Let us begin straight away with those who lived more than seventy-five years. I think you will be surprised, as I was. Here now is a list, merely with the names and ages, beginning with painters and sculptors:

Titian ninety-nine, Michelangelo eighty-nine, Franz Hals eighty-six, Goya eighty-two, H. Thoma eighty-five, Liebermann eighty-eight, Munch eighty-one, Degas eighty-three, Bonnard eighty, Maillol eighty-three, James Ensor eighty-nine, Donatello eighty, Tintoretto seventy-six, Rodin seventy-seven, Käthe Kollwitz seventy-eight, Renoir seventy-eight, Menzel ninety, Matisse eighty-four.

Among poets and writers: Goethe eighty-three, Shaw ninety-four, Hamsun ninety-three, Maeterlinck eighty-seven, Tolstoy eigthy-two, Voltaire eighty-four, H. Mann eighty, Ebner-Eschenbach eighty-six, Victor Hugo eighty-three, Tennyson eighty-three, Swift, Ibsen, Björnson, and Rolland seventy-eight, Ricarda Huch eighty-three, Hauptmann eighty-four, Lagerlöf eighty-two, Gide eighty-two, d'Annunzio seventy-five, Spitteler, Fontane, and Freytag seventy-nine, Frenssen eighty-two, Isolde Kurz ninety-one, Claudel eighty-five, and among the living: Thomas Mann, Hesse, Rudolf Alexander Schröder, Alfred Döblin, and Hans Carossa over seventy-five.

There are, admittedly, fewer great composers. Let me mention Verdi eighty-eight, Richard Strauss eighty-five, Pfitzner eighty, Heinrich Schütz eighty-seven, Monteverdi seventy-six, Gluck and Handel seventy-four, Bruckner seventy-two, Palestrina seventy-one, Buxtehude and Wagner seventy, Georg Schumann eighty-one, Cherubini eighty-two, Reznicek eighty-five, Auber eighty-four; and among the living: Sibelius eighty-eight.

My list is by no means complete. I did not set about compiling it systematically, but only picked up whatever I happened to come across when I was looking into this matter in general. I am convinced the list could be extended further. If one wanted to explain this phenomenon, there are two points one could bring up. First of all, there is the sociological point that it is primarily those who live long who become great and famous, because they have a long time in which to produce their works. Secondly, there seems to be a quite reasonable biological explanation: regarded from one point of view art is, after all, a phenomenon of liberation and relaxation, a cathartic phenomenon, and such phenomena are closely associated with the physical organism itself. This assumption accords quite well with Speranski's theory, now finding its way into pathology, that both the state and the threat of illness are regulated and warded off by central impulses to a far higher extent than was hitherto supposed. There can scarcely be any doubt about it that art is a central and primary impulse. In saying this I don't want to make far-reaching assertions, but it does seem to me that such great age is particularly remarkable in view of the fact that so many of these people lived in times when the general expectancy of life was far lower than it is today. As you know, the expectation of life for new-born children has almost doubled since 1870.

Now the question what aging means for an artist is a complex one, in which subjective and objective elements cut across each other; on the one hand, we have moods and crises, on the other, history and description. Never again to be able to reach the height once attained, in spite of struggling for decades, is one fate. It was, for instance, Swinburne's; at the age of twenty-nine he was a sensation, and from then on he went on writing, ceaselessly, until when he died at the age of seventy-two he was a fertile, stimulating man, writing poetry. Something similar could be said of Hofmannsthal: the way from the poems written by the twenty-year-old Loris to the political confusions of *Der Turm* was the way from the feeding of the five thousand to the gathering up of the crumbs. It is the same again with George and Dehmel. All these men are lyrical poets in whom hard work and determination took the place of the intuitive glimmerings they had known in youth. Now I shall turn from these introspective allusions to an entirely concrete question on the objective side of our problem, namely: what do art history, literary history, and art criticism generally mean by a "late" work? How do they define the formal transition from an artist's youthful work to the style of his "late" period?

It is difficult to get a straight answer to this question. Some critics resort to such terms as gentleness, serenity, toleration, a noble mellowness, liberation from the vanities of love and passion; others speak of weightlessness, a floating beyond the things of earthly life—and then they come out with the word "classical." Others again see the characteristic of the artist's old age as lying in ruthlessness, in a radical honesty—which makes one think of Shaw's dictum that old men are dangerous because they don't care about the future. Commenting on a painting by Franz Hals, Pinder introduces a new concept by saying that the style is recognizably that of an eighty-four-year-old painter, for only such a man could produce this petrified superabundance of experience and history, this conscious awareness of the proximity of death. Petrified—here now is a contradiction to "weightless" and "floating." Someone else writes of Dürer that he died too early, for one feels a downright need of a loosening of the formal power through the workings of a broad, gentle spirituality. At this point analysis of works of art becomes nothing less than wishful thinking, the desire to see a confirmation of the idea that broad, gentle spirituality is what constitutes a late style.

And now to take an example from literature, where the word "late" has become very fashionable—one is always reading articles about the late Rilke, the late Hofmannsthal, the late Eliot, or the late Gide. I am thinking now of a book by a well-known literary historian who specializes in the late Rilke. His book contains excellent, even profound observations, but the tendency is clearly as follows: phase 1: the phase of experiment, effort, and beginnings, then phase 2: "fulfillment" and "the true form." It is only in phase 2 that Rilke really became "what in the beginning he believed he was but in fact was not." What then is "the true"? There is too much eschatology, too much ideology, too much old-fashioned evolutionary theory, behind this term for my liking. Our friend the literary historian insists on seeing Rilke striving towards an ideal state, that is, his own, the literary historian's, ideal; but this seems to me particularly inappropriate in the case of Rilke, from whose early phase we have poems of such perfect beauty that no "true" anything can outshine them. I sometimes think that the urge, to be found among the learned, to see and represent the artist in "phases" must be one that is specifically German-idealist.

One of the most important books on our subject is Brinckmann's *Spätwerke grosser Meister*. Brinckmann tries to define the structural changes in creative minds by the aid of his antithesis between relation and fusion. These two concepts are the grappling-irons he uses in dealing with the problem. Relation, which is the first phase, means seeing and representing the relations between people, actions, objects in space, and colors. Fusion, the later phase, is that in which the colors fuse into one ground-tone and the elements that were previously treated individually and contrastingly are subordinated to the structural totality, often becoming elusive and intangible—and now Brinckmann speaks of "the abandonment of a state of tension in favor of a higher freedom." Wherever the word "freedom" crops up it all becomes obscure, and at this point I have difficulty in following him. However, Brinckmann has made an extremely fascinating analysis of several painters who painted a subject first in their youth and then again in old age. He places the periods of change in the structure of productivity in the thirty-fifth and sixtieth years, and in this claims to be following Freud. Brinckmann is, furthermore, the only writer who, still following Freud, touches on the relationship between sexuality and artistic productivity. Although this problem is, at this moment and at this point, rather a digression, I should like to mention it. Such a relationship does undoubtedly exist, although it is extremely obscure. Everyone knows there are a great many artists of the first rank who are homoerotic and in whose work this divergence from normal sexuality does not become apparent. Take four of the greatest minds in all Western culture, say Plato, Michelangelo, Shakespeare, and Goethe: two were notoriously homosexual, one may have been, and only Goethe seems to have been free from abnormality. And then, on the other hand, there is the asexual type of genius: you may remember Adolf Menzel's celebrated testament, from which it appears that in all his ninety years of life he never once had intercourse with a woman. We still know nothing about the link between the lessening of the sexual urge and the falling off of creativeness. We all know that, at the age of seventy-five, Goethe fell in love with Ulrike and wanted to marry her. Or there is the almost grotesque situation that Gide describes in his journals: in Tunis, at the age of seventy-two, he fell in love with a fifteen-year-old Arab boy, and he describes the rapturous nights that reminded him of the fairest years of his youth. There is something positively embarrassing about his enraptured confession that when he first saw the boy, who was a servant in his hotel, he was so overcome by his exquisiteness and shyness that he did not dare to speak to him. Gide at seventy-two in a Gretchen situation! The problem is interesting, but there is as yet no way of deciding whether the fading of the sexual urge paralyzes the mind or, as others contend, lends it wings.

A special case, and one that I was continually coming across in these investigations, is that of Michelangelo's Rondanini "Pietà," which he produced at the age of eighty-nine, but did not finish. Eminent art historians hold such conflicting views about this "Pietà" that one is forced to assume that here is a case of decisive structural change in the artist. One art historian writes of the work's sublime inwardness and spirituality. Another says it radiates a deep emotion that cannot be gainsaid, something spiritualized and ethereal, a sort of floating upwards in which a last sigh mingles with the first faint glimpses of redemption. The other school of thought asserts that in this work of his old age Michelangelo turned his back on all that had constituted the fame of his youth. Simmel goes so far as to say: "In this work Michelangelo disowned the vital principle of his art; it is a betrayal, a tragedy, the final proof of his inability to reach salvation by the road of artistic creation, which is centered in the vision of the senses. It is the ultimate tragic failure." Here, it seems, we have a case in which a great man abandoned his former methods and techniques of controlling his mode of experience, unable to make any further use of them, presumably because they had come to seem obsolete and conventional, and who nevertheless had no new mode of expression for his new mode of experience, and so gave up, let his hands sink. Perhaps this is an example of what Malraux means in a deeply significant passage in his *Psychology of Art*: "First they invent their language, then they learn to speak it, often inventing another one as well. When they are touched by the style of death, they remember how in their youth they broke with their teachers, and now they break with their own work." And Malraux goes on: "The most complete embodiment of the artist is based equally on rejection of his masters and on the destruction of all that he once was." These are weighty words, and I should like to apply them to a man who carried a whole century upon his shoulders and whose fame is a meridian in our scheme of values.

In conclusion of this section I should like to speak of a book that confronted me with another question arising out of the subject. It is Riezler's book on Beethoven, the final chapter of which is called "The Last Style." The description of this last style is fascinating, convincing, and imbued with tremendous knowledge. But—I said to myself—first of all, the writer of the book has to translate his musical impressions and analyses into language, expressing in words something that the music itself, by its very nature, does not contain. These words, which are intended to embody the essence of Beethoven's last style, are notably "authority," "power," "monumentality," "gigantic," "tectonic solidity," and, on the other hand, "weightless," "floating," "ethereal," "ultimate spirituality"—i.e., all words belonging to the emotive vocabulary we found in descriptions of the late works of painters and which we should presumably also come across now and then in descriptions of great works by younger men. Riezler begins this last chapter of his with the assertion that it is possible to find general terms for the description of a characteristic late style in all the arts throughout all periods, since "the modes of expression used in the various arts are all subordinate to the supreme fact of the 'universal artistic principle.'" And what is this universal artistic principle, this final hieroglyph? Would it not be just as easy to say that, quite apart from music, painting, and poetry, there is a linguistic medium that serves the purposes of criticism, providing the learned with the terminology they need in order to set up their systems?

But now another question—what is it like for the artist himself to grow old, to be old? How does he experience it himself? Take Flaubert—there in his house on the high ground, in Rouen, not leaving his room for days on end, and night after night the light from his windows shining out on the river, so that the Seine boatmen take their bearings from it. He is not old, he is only fifty-nine, but he is worn out, he has bags under his eyes and his eyelids are wrinkled with bitter scorn—scorn of the *gent épicière*, those shopkeepers, the middle classes—to be sure, the court did not pronounce *Madame Bovary* immoral, but it did recommend him to exercise his gifts of observation on nicer people, people with more goodness of heart. And did that make him write about goodness of heart? When his *Education sentimentale* was published, they wrote: A cretin, a pimp, one who dirties the water in the gutter where he washes.

In his youth he wrote that anyone who wanted to create something permanent must take care not to laugh at fame. But how was it later on? Was there anything he did not laugh at? And most of all it was himself he laughed at; he could not look at himself in the mirror while shaving without bursting into laughter. And now he was drawing up a list of follies of those of the dead whose names constitute what we call humanity. Should he put on yet another record? Sit yet again in the *bistro* downtown, tense with concentration visually and acoustically, in order to penetrate into the object, to slip behind those faces? Should he once again make that superhuman effort of observation, an effort so tragic in every instant, picking up expressions, collecting phrases, things one could take one's stand on?—For there they all sit in the bar, all after money, all after love, while what he is after is *expression*, a sequence of sentences, and these two worlds must embrace. Put on another record? Realism, Artism, Psychologism—they say I am cold—well, coldness is not such a bad thing, I'd rather be cold than go in for singing and interpreting—for whom? For what? So do you believe in anything, Flaubert? Come on, say yes or no. Yes, I do believe, for after all believing only means being made in a particular way so that you can accept this and that. No, I don't believe, *je suis mystique et je ne crois à rien.*

Such was Flaubert when he was old.

And there's Leonardo in the little chateau of Ducloux on the Loire, when Italy was no longer a place for him, all his patrons dead or imprisoned. What does he think of in those evenings? The king is out hunting, and all is still, there is nothing to be heard but the metallic clang of the clock on the tower called Harloge and the cry of the wild swans on the water. By the river there are poplars, like those in Lombardy long ago. The king has offered him four thousand guilders for the "Gioconda," but he cannot bring himself to part with her. The king goes on insisting, and the old man throws himself at the king's feet, weeping, making himself a laughing-stock before the guests, offering the king his latest picture, a "St. John the Baptist," but not the "Gioconda," not that, that picture is his life. Five long years he worked at it, five years he bent over it, silent, growing old, not letting anyone see it. In the room where he painted it there were fragments of Greek statues, dog-headed Egyptian gods in black granite, Gnostic gems with magical inscriptions, Byzantine parchments hard as ivory, lost, clay potsherds bearing Assyrian cuneiform script, Persian magical writings bound in iron, papyri from Memphis, transparent and delicate as the petals of flowers. ... He had had to transform himself into all that, to lose himself in it, perhaps even to succumb to it. And in this way he lived for five years, dedicated to his inner vision, his one vision. The king and the court thought him a poor fool, but still, he had managed to keep the picture in his room. The spiral staircase up to his bedroom was narrow and steep, and as he climbed it he suffered attacks of dizziness and breathlessness. Then his right side became paralyzed, and though he could still draw with his left hand, he could not paint. Then he spent the evenings with a monk, playing games with little blocks of wood, or cards. Then his left side became paralyzed, too. And he had just managed to say "Arise and cast yourself into the sea" when he died and lay there, at rest, like a weight that has fallen. After his death a Russian ikon-painter who lived nearby came and stood before his easel and exclaimed: "What unheard-of shamelessness! Can this debauched fellow who is naked like a whore, and beardless, be the forerunner of Christ? Diabolical sight, away, sully not my eyes!"

Such was Leonardo da Vinci when he was old.

Evenings of life—oh, these evenings of life! Most of them are spent in poverty, coughing, crook-backed—drug-addicts, drunkards, some even as criminals, almost all unmarried, almost all childless— the whole bio-negative Olympic assembly, a European, cis-Atlantic team of Olympians that has borne the glory and the sadness of post-Classical man for hour hundred years. Those born under a lucky star managed, perhaps, to get themselves a house, as Goethe and Rubens did, and those whose lot was meager went on painting to the end of their days without a penny in their pockets, painting their wavy olives, and those who live in the age of the conquest of space look out of a back-room window on a rabbit-hutch and two hortensias. Making a survey of them all, one can discover only one thing—they were all under some compelling urge that they could not escape from. "If I don't tremble as the adder does in the snake-tamer's hand, I am cold. Anything I ever did that was any good at all was done in that condition," Delacroix said. And Beckmann wrote: "I would gladly live in sewers and crawl through all the gutters of the world if that were the only way I could go on painting." Adders, gutters, sewers—that is the overture to life's evening.

I am not wallowing in the macabre for its own sake, nor amusing myself with an obsolete picture of things dating from the days of the *poètes maudits*. These psychopathological and sociological studies of the lives of men of genius, and of their last days, are none of my making; they are the work of others. The trend of thought may seem a little disconcerting nowadays, when the artist has acquired some of the outer trappings of the solid, respectable citizen and adopts the airs of a functionary; and indeed he feels that he *is* a functionary, in a definite position, which forces him to seek government commissions and external security. Routine criticism, the reviewing of exhibitions and books commissioned and paid for by newspapers and publishers, has dragged the artist into public life, into the general hotch-potch in which individualism is coming to an end in our epoch. But let there be no mistake about it: he who is under that compelling urge remains inwardly untouched. In a helicopter painted arsenic-green he goes on climbing back into his esoteric studio. It is only a short while since the eighty-three-year-old Degas said: "A picture is something that needs just as much smartness and viciousness as crime does—forgery with a dash of Nature thrown in."

Perhaps the image of the arsenic-green helicopter is a trifle banal. All the same, let us get into that helicopter for a moment so that we can look down on what we can't take with us of mankind and the earth.

It is not an ascent that is made with very much love for humanity. Think, for instance, of that self-portrait of Tintoretto's, a late work (I don't remember where it hangs, I only know it from reproductions)—there's a thing one can't forget, and there is only one word for it: rancid. Or think of Rembrandt's last self-portraits—reserved, wary, and as though they were saying: count me out. None of the great *old* men was an idealist. They got along without realism. What they could do and what they wanted were the things that are possible. It is only dilettantes who dream of the impossible.

Art—these men say—art *must* put into the picture the relationship there is between the world and the absolute. Art must restore the center, but without losing in depth. Art must represent man as being made in the image of God—and is there anything at all that is not made in the image of God?—for if there is, I haven't heard of it—and I don't exclude even the tiger. And what it comes to finally is that there is no "must" where art is concerned. There's a radio in this helicopter of ours, and right now it's playing a hit from the film *Moulin Rouge*. It makes me shiver with excitement. For a first-rate dance-tune sometimes has more of the century in it than a motet, and a word may weigh heavier than a victory.

Ah, these old men! What I see is not so much something lofty, but simply the century and the compulsion. A rose-pink century—right, then, let's paint pastoral idylls, and above all let us stick to the center. But supposing it's a black century—what do we paint then? Something technical perhaps, in keeping with our habit of holding conferences? After all, it's technical things that people sit round talking about; "technology" and "integration" are the watchwords. Everything must be in keeping with everything else: poetry with the Geiger-counter, inoculation-serums with the Church Fathers, and so on, and don't leave anything out or global coalitionism is endangered. Language must be assimilated to the technical, too—though I must say this is an idea I should never have had on my own. The only sort of language that bears, that grows, that works, is the language that lives on its own resources, spontaneously procreating, absorbing, but integrating according to its own immanent law, the few expressions it takes over from physics and the automobile industry. These few miserable splinters it absorbs into its body, and the place heals over; the transcendence of language is never disturbed.

Up and up we go in our helicopter—earth dwindles away, but we can still make out those colossal complexes, those collectives, those things called institutes and institutions. "I made my way through them, too," one of the old men might say nowadays. "I suffered from depressions, I entered an institution and went to a psychoanalyst. And he said: 'You are suffering from oral-narcissistic deficiency, you lack an adequate intake of external objects. You are introverted—I suppose you know what I mean by that!' I replied that introverted and extroverted seemed pretty crude basic concepts to me. There are those who bear a hereditary burden and those who bear none. There are those who are fettered and those who are free. And the first are the more interesting. 'Contactual insufficiency,' the therapist said, pressing into my hand a booklet entitled: *You and the Libido*, and thereupon fell into a trance."

"Then I heard," one of those old masters would say today, "that thought makes you free, thought makes you happy. And so I entered another institution and went to the thinkers. But sociology, phenomenology, and the theory of types—it all sounds just like Puccini. Ontology—where, I ask you, is there any existence of anything outside my pictures? And what is all this stuff about things, anyway? Things come into existence because one admits their existence, that's to say, one formulates them, paints them. If one doesn't grant them their existence, they vanish into the realm of unreality and insubstantiality. These thinkers with their grounds of existence that no one can see, which is utterly formless—all these contributions and contributors—they turn on the faucet and what comes out is generally a spurt of Plato. Then they take a quick shower, and then the next one steps into the tub. None of them ever finishes anything. *I* have to finish *my* things! They're all idealists, and they think the whole thing only starts with them. They're all optimists, and at the age of seventy-five they go and have a new jacket made to measure. Schopenhauer was a well-off man, I believe, independent, and did some real thinking all the same—his thought was interesting, it was sublime, it was far-reaching. But none of these gentry nowadays really *thinks*—unless one excepts Wittgenstein, who said: 'The limits of language are the limits of my world,' and 'What the picture represents is what it means.' There's sound thinking, there's concrete thinking! No loose ends there! There is a systematic self-limitation to the thinking of propositions. That is painterly thinking, that is Lethe, and there myth comes to an end."

And so what is the situation like? Desperate? Send me up some fresh supplies of libido and a guaranteed pre-Spenglerian civilization. The exploration of outer space hasn't yet reached the stage where we could start to feel something again at the sight of the stars. Oh, why didn't I become a landscape-painter, professionally busy dashing from the Teutoburger Wald to Astrachan, and all by aid of the Volkswagen that we have these days? Then I could have some springy woodland earth underfoot!

"How queer the nations are," our old man goes on thinking. "They want interesting minds, but they also want to be the ones who decide what the interesting minds are to be interesting about. They want internationally famous names, but anyone who writes a word against their pet ideas is instantly crossed off the list. They want to be delivered of works of universal significance, but it is they who organize the midwives and provide them with textbooks on confinement. Kleist's *Penthesilea* would never have been written if a vote had been taken on it first. Strindberg, Nietzsche, El Greco would never have appeared on the scene. But conformism would have existed all right! It has always been there, only *it* would never have created the four hundred years of Western civilization." Surely there's no writer who hasn't often envied painters: they can paint oranges and asphodels, pitchers, even lobsters and other crustaceans, and nobody reproaches them with not having got in anything about the housing problem. But obviously the trade unions have their rights in the case of anything written. Anti-social is the word. "Art *must* . . ." It's probably a waste of time pointing out that Flaubert gave us a description of the artist's predicament, of his inability to express all he feels and yearns for, and how he can only express what it is given to him to express within the limitations of word and form.

Only one kilometer more and we shall have reached the ceiling. The traveler glances down. When the diamond-dealer Salomon Rossbach jumped off the Empire State Building, he left a mysterious message: "No more above, no more below, and so I leap off." A good message, the traveler says: no more above, no more below, the center is damaged, the compass-needle and the quarters of heaven are no longer valid, but the species is rampant and keeps going by means of pills. The body has grown more morbid, with modern medicine positively offering it thousands of diseases, and they break out of it with scientific vigor—oh, no slur on the doctors, a very fine lot of men, I only mean that in the old days if you were bitten by a mosquito you scratched the place, but today they can prescribe a dozen different ointments and not one of them helps— still, that's life, it keeps things moving. Our bodies are more morbid than they used to be, but they live longer.

The brain lives longer, but where there was once power of resistance there are now empty places developing—or can you, down there on the earth, look out of your window and still imagine a God in it all, a God who created anything as gentle as plants and trees? Rats, plague, noise, desperation—yes—but flowers? There is a fourteenth-century picture called "The Creation of the Plants," with a small, crooked, black-bearded figure of God standing there, his right hand, which is much too big for the rest of him, raised as though he were pulling the two trees out of the ground, and there they are beside him—apart from them the whole place is still pretty empty. Can you imagine that kindly Creator today? Vice, worms, maggots, sloths, and skunks—that, yes; masses of it, ever new installments of it, fresh deliveries every day, 100 per cent genuine, continual new editions—but an affectionate little God who pulls two trees out of the ground? No trees, no flowers—but electronic brains, artificial insemination for cows and women, chicken farms with music laid on to increase productivity, artificial doubling of the chromosomes bringing about giant hybrids, deep freezing, over-heating—you've sown a seed, have you? Well, jump, quick! Else the shoot will get you in the leg!

Well, so here we are. The old man enters his studio—a bare room, a big table covered with slips of paper and sheets of notes. He goes up to it, saying to himself: "Now what shall I do with this?—essay, poem, dialogue? The notion that the form is born together with the content is just another illusion hatched by philosophies of art—I can use this here or there, coloring, weaving, fixing it up, all just as I feel like it, I went through my beginning and I am going through my end, *moira*, my allotted part. Only one thing is certain: When a thing's finished it must be complete, perfect. Though of course there's the question: And what then?"

Take another look at the most famous "late" works—what are they like? For instance, there's Goethe's *Novelle*—a menagerie catches fire, the booth burns down, the tigers escape, the lions are loose! And it all works out harmoniously. No, this earth is scorched and bare, flayed by lightning, and today the tigers bite. Or what about the second part of *Faust*? Undoubtedly this is Germany's most mysterious gift to the world. But all those choruses, gryphons, lamias, pulcinellos, ants, cranes, and empusæ, the whole thing humming and buzzing away, singing to itself, away off to where the fairy rings are and the crowns of stars and the angelic boys—where does it all come from anyway? Let's face it, the whole thing hovers in the realm of pure imagination, it's all table-rapping, telepathy, hocus-pocus. There's someone standing on a balcony, unreal, motionless, blowing bubbles—some bright, some dark—conjuring forth more and more clay pipes and straws to blow his iridescent bubbles with—oh, a magnificent God on the Balcony, inoculated with the spirit of the Classical and the Baroque, with miracles and mysteries dangling from his coat tails. But in our day the eye is slightly moist when one looks that way, and that's all there is to it. That's how it stands with such works nowadays.

Around the greatest of all, the translators and interpreters keep on circling for a few centuries, but soon there is no one left who understands their language. What then? Primitives, the Archaic, the Classical, the Mannerists, the Abstractionists, in a word, the Quaternary Period. But what then? Spaces that are much too big have been opened up to us, and too many spheres, and feelings too weighty—perhaps the making of art is, after all, a rather shallow reaction? Isn't it perhaps *profounder* simply to suffer the human substance in silence? What was it the Lord Jehova put into our essential nature, what was the fate he gave us? Was creative salvation to be our lot, or were we meant to go for the still point, to sit under the Bo-tree, immobile, waiting to meet Kama-Mara, the god of love and death? How many hours of my life I have spent pondering on a certain saying of the Balcony God's, turning it this way and that—the saying that: "On its highest peak poetry seems to be completely external. The more it withdraws inwards, the further it sinks." What does that mean? Am I supposed to disown my inner being, cheat it, make a fool of it—is *that* the precondition for poetry? And what else is it? A conjuror's act, the rope-trick, mere nothingness with a glaze over it? And from the East I hear them harping on the same tune. The Master Kung Dsi, speaking of painters, says: "He is crude in whose work the meaning has more weight than the line." In other words, for him, too, the higher thing is the manipulated thing, the manufactured thing, style. On the other hand, there's Guardini saying that "behind every work of art, as it were, something opens up. . . ." Well, and what is it that as it were opens up? After all, we are supposed to cover it up with paint and hide it. Or what of a great philosopher's dictum that "art is the self-manifestation and operation of truth"? What truth, anyway? A truth made up of sketches and designs, a manufactured truth? Or is truth only mentioned in order to let philosophy make a showing, for of course art isn't concerned with truth at all, only with expression. And then finally we come to the question: What is this expression that thrusts its way in in front of depth? Is expression the same as guilt? It might be.

Still, I dare say I'm too old to unravel these problems. Mists of weariness and melancholy cloud my mind. I can remember having heard Pablo Sarasate playing his fiddle and Caruso singing at the Metropolitan Opera House, with the Astors sitting in the diamond horseshoe. I have watched Bergmann operating, and I stood on parade before the last Emperor. I began studying by the light of an oil-lamp, with Haeckel's *Riddles of the Universe* for my forbidden reading. I have ridden and I have flown, but I have also seen the great sailing-ships upon the seas that no man had ever yet flown across—but that's all past and gone—all over now. And today I say it was all much more heavily charged than one thought at the time; everything was much more predestined than it seemed. And the oddest thing of all is that one was much more *in the air* then than one dreamed, believing as one did in one's autonomy. To take just one example: there were painters who spent their whole life painting in tones of silver or of yellow, and another one who always stuck to brown, and there was a generation that wrote poetry mainly in nouns. It wasn't a literary caprice, it was in the air—in the air of entirely heterogeneous dimensions. A short time ago I read the following story about Clemenceau. He had just engaged a new private secretary, and on the first day he was showing him what the job consisted of. "Some letters," Clemenceau said, "you will have to draft by yourself. Now listen: a sentence consists of a noun and a verb. If you want to use an adjective, come and ask me first." Come and ask me first! It's exactly the same advice that Carl Sternheim gave me when we were both young. "When you've written something," he said to me, "go through it again and cross out the adjectives. Your meaning will be much clearer then." It turned out to be true. Indeed, the leaving out of explanatory, padding-out adjectives became a sort of compulsion-neurosis with my generation.

My generation! But of course the next one is here by now, the young people, the youth of our time! God preserve their imitative urge for them, and then it wouldn't be long before the whole thing stops of its own accord. But supposing they were to produce a new style—*evoe*! A new style is a new type of man. Now, though genetics haven't produced very much that is clear, one thing seems to be certain: a new generation means a new sort of brain, and a new sort of brain means a new sort of reality and new neuroses, and the whole thing is called evolution, and that's the way civilization goes on spreading. If I were to give this younger generation of ours some advice, talking down to them from my pulpit of old age, it would be this: "When you have published four of those rhymed or unrhymed things that are called poems, or have drawn a goat more or less true to nature, don't expect that from now on every time you have a birthday the Mayor of your town will call to wish you many happy returns. After all, it's only human handiwork you're doing. You would do well to think occasionally of how when Schubert was twenty-nine someone advised him to buy unlined paper and draw the lines himself, since that was cheaper. What impudence! everyone says nowadays when they hear of it, but of course the same thing keeps on happening all over again, and it isn't everyone who by the age of thirty-one has reached a stage where he doesn't need to spend money any more."

Gentlemen of the rising generation, allow me to be provoking. I do it in the hope of making you tough. Toughness is the greatest blessing an artist can have—the ability to be hard on himself and on his work. Or as Thomas Mann said: "It is better to ruin a work of art and make it useless for giving to the world than not to go all out at every point." Or as I tried to put it a moment ago: One thing is certain, when a thing is finished it must be complete, perfect. And in this connection don't for a moment forget the questionable and devious nature of your undertaking, the dangers and the hatred that surround your activities. Don't lose sight of the cold and egotistical element in your mission. Your art has deserted the temples and the sacrificial vessels, it has ceased to have anything to do with the painting of pillars, and the painting of chapels is no longer anything for you either. You are using your own skin for wallpaper, and nothing can save you. Don't let yourself be tempted by "security"—312 pages, cloth-bound, price 13 marks 80.

There is no turning the clock back. The things of the mind are irreversible; they go right along their road to the end, right to the end of the night. With your back to the wall, care-worn and weary, in the gray light of the void, read Job and Jeremiah and keep going. Formulate your principles without regard for anything else, because there will be nothing left of you but your words when this epoch comes to an end, making an end of all singing and chanting of poetry. What you don't say will not be there then. You will make enemies, you will be alone, a tiny boat on the vast ocean, a tiny boat in which there are dubious clatterings and clankings going on and a shivering that comes from your own dismay at your undertaking. But don't send out an SOS. First of all, there's no one to hear you, and secondly, after so many voyages your end will be a quiet one.

Ladies and gentlemen, the portrait of old age is finished. We have left the studio. The helicopter is about to land. Out of the cabin there steps an *homme du monde,* wearing a gray tie and a black homburg, who disappears in the hustle and bustle of the airfield. The airfield is out in the country, and this gentleman strolls up to the edge of it, where he sees poplars like those on the banks of the Loire and like those long ago in Lombardy, and sees the river a ribbon winding away into the distance like the Seine, where once the bargemen looked out for that lighted window in the dark. The same things recur for as long as there is sameness. And when some day nothing is like anything else any more at all and the great rules change—even then some kind of order will persist.

"To be mistaken and yet be compelled to go on believing what one's own innermost being tells one—that is man, and his glory begins yonder, beyond victory and defeat. ..." Yes, he would write that same sentence yet once again, if he had to start all over again, even if it were misleading, even if it were a falsification. After all, what dictum is blameless? Face to face with the Western world, I did my work; I lived as if the day had come—my own day. I was the man that I shall be. And so at the end I take my

stand on all the Church Fathers, all those ancient men with
centuries behind them: *non confundar in aeternum*—I too shall not
be condemned eternally.

(1954) *Translated by Ernst Kaiser and Eithne Wilkins*

208

NIHILISM OR POSITIVISM?

ON THE POSITION OF MODERN MAN

We may as well delete the word "nihilism." For the last two decades it has lost virtually all meaning. To use another modern expression, we have "integrated" this concept into our thinking. Modern man does not think nihilistically; he puts order into his thoughts and thus creates a basis for his existence. For many of us today this basis is rooted in resignation, but resignation is not nihilism; resignation carries its philosophical implications to the brink of darkness, but upholds its standards of dignity even in the face of the darkness.

Pessimism is another story; this seems to be an ineradicable traumatic experience of human thinking. In a village in the Pyrenees I stood in front of a sun dial and read on its large face a Latin proverb: *vulnerant omnes, ultima necat,* which means, all of them wound, the last one kills; this refers to the hours—a bitter adage which stems from the Middle Ages. In the German Museum at Munich there is a water clock in the shape of a nymph who weeps off the minutes and hours with her tears; you read the time from her tears—this goes back to Antiquity. Or let us think of Asia, of Buddhism, which was the very incarnation of pessimism both in form and content: extinction— a drifting off—starless nothingness— a pessimism of an existentialist kind with the declared aim of destroying man's identity. Against this background, it must be admitted that today there is no real pessimism among humanity in general; humanity in general, it must be emphasized, is positive in its outlook. In spite of war and battles, in spite of the damaged

Radio Zurich had turned to Gottfried Benn as the "representative of pessimistic if not nihilistic literature" to ask his opinion about the position of modern and, specifically, creative man. This is his answer, given in an essay originally published in *Neue deutsche Hefte*, April 1954.

capacity for thought and the political hopelessness, humanity as such lives today in a state of euphoria. From all sides emerges the picture of a humanity which believes that in the final analysis it can lose nothing at all, and this belief is neither religious nor cynical; rather, it has the characteristics of self-confidence and vitality, which is astounding.

So much for generalities. Now as to the emotional state of the writer, or, more specifically, of the creative personality: it seems to me self-evident that such a man, even if personally and privately afflicted with the deepest pessimism, would rise from the abyss by the mere fact that he works. The accomplished work itself is a denial of decay and doom. Even if creative man realizes that cycles of culture must end, including the one to which he belongs —one cycle ends, another reaches its zenith, and above everything floats infinity whose essence is probably not accessible to human comprehension—creative man faces all this and says to himself: weighing on me in this hour is the unknown and deadly law which I must follow; in this situation I must assert myself, confront this hour with my work and thereby give it articulate expression.

I think that here something is happening that is beyond the personal sphere. To do justice to the transcendence of this process, one must quote Malraux' magnificent phrase from his *Psychology of Art*—that on the Day of Judgment, statues rather than past ways of life will represent mankind before the gods.

(1954) *Translated by Therese Pol*

POETRY

KLEINE ASTER

Ein ersoffener Bierfahrer wurde auf den Tisch
                                                gestemmt.
Irgendeiner hatte ihm eine dunkelhellila Aster
zwischen die Zähne geklemmt.
Als ich von der Brust aus
unter der Haut
mit einem langen Messer
Zunge und Gaumen herausschnitt,
muß ich sie angestoßen haben, denn sie glitt
in das nebenliegende Gehirn.
Ich packte sie ihm in die Brusthöhle
zwischen die Holzwolle,
als man zunähte.
Trinke dich satt in deiner Vase!
Ruhe sanft,
kleine Aster!

                                                1912

SCHÖNE JUGEND

Der Mund eines Mädchens, das lange im Schilf
                                                gelegen hatte,
sah so angeknabbert aus.
Als man die Brust aufbrach, war die Speiseröhre
                                                so löcherig.
Schließlich in einer Laube unter dem Zwerchfell
fand man ein Nest von jungen Ratten.
Ein kleines Schwesterchen lag tot.

LITTLE ASTER

A drowned truck-driver was propped on the slab.
Someone had stuck a lavender aster
between his teeth.
As I cut out the tongue and the palate,
through the chest
under the skin,
with a long knife,
I must have touched the flower, for it slid
into the brain lying next.
I packed it into the cavity of the chest
among the excelsior
as it was sewn up.
Drink yourself full in your vase!
Rest softly,
little aster!

—*Babette Deutsch*

LOVELY CHILDHOOD

The mouth of a girl who had long lain among the reeds
                    looked gnawed away.
As the breast was cut open, the gullet showed full of
                    holes.
Finally in a cavity below the diaphragm
a nest of young rats was discovered.
One little sister lay dead.

Die andern lebten von Leber und Niere,
tranken das kalte Blut und hatten
hier eine schöne Jugend verlebt.
Und schön und schnell kam auch ihr Tod:
Man warf sie allesamt ins Wasser.
Ach, wie die kleine Schnauzen quietschten!

1912

KREISLAUF

Der einsame Backzahn einer Dirne,
die unbekannt verstorben war,
trug eine Goldplombe.
Die übrigen waren wie auf stille Verabredung
ausgegangen.
Den schlug der Leichendiener sich heraus,
versetzte ihn und ging für tanzen.
Denn, sagte er,
nur Erde solle zur Erde werden.

1912

The others thrived on liver and kidneys,
drank the cold blood and
enjoyed a lovely childhood here.
And sweet and swift came their death also:
They were all thrown into the water together,
Oh, how the little muzzles squeaked!

—*Babette Deutsch*

CYCLE

The solitary molar of a whore
who had died incognito
wore a gold filling.
(The rest had decamped
as if by silent agreement.)
That filling was swiped by the mortician's mate
and pawned, so he could go to a dive
and dance, for, as he put it:
"Earth alone should return to earth."

—*Francis Golffing*

MANN UND FRAU GEHN DURCH DIE KREBSBARACKE

Der Mann:
Hier diese Reihe sind zerfallene Schöße
und diese Reihe ist zerfallene Brust.
Bett stinkt bei Bett. Die Schwestern wechseln stündlich.

Komm, hebe ruhig diese Decke auf.
Sieh, dieser Klumpen Fett und faule Säfte,
das war einst irgendeinem Mann groß
und hieß auch Rausch und Heimat.

Komm, sieh auf diese Narbe an der Brust.
Fühlst du den Rosenkranz von weichen Knoten?
Fühl ruhig hin. Das Fleisch ist weich und schmerzt nicht.

Hier diese blutet wie aus dreißig Leibern.
Kein Mensch hat so viel Blut.
Hier dieser schnitt man
erst noch ein Kind aus dem verkrebsten Schoß.

Man läßt sie schlafen. Tag und Nacht. — Den Neuen
sagt man: Hier schläft man sich gesund. — Nur sonntags
für den Besuch läßt man sie etwas wacher.

Nahrung wird wenig noch verzehrt. Die Rücken
sind wund. Du siehst die Fliegen. Manchmal
wäscht sie die Schwester. Wie man Bänke wäscht.

Hier schwillt der Acker schon um jedes Bett.
Fleisch ebnet sich zu Land. Glut gibt sich fort.
Saft schickt sich an zu rinnen. Erde ruft.

1912

MAN AND WOMAN GO THROUGH
THE CANCER WARD

The man:
Here in this row are wombs that have decayed,
and in this row are breasts that have decayed.
Bed beside stinking bed. Hourly the sisters change.

Come, quietly lift up this coverlet.
Look, this great mass of fat and ugly humours
was precious to a man once, and
meant ecstasy and home.

Come, now look at the scars upon this breast.
Do you feel the rosary of small soft knots?
Feel it, no fear. The flesh yields and is numb.

Here's one who bleeds as though from thirty bodies.
No one has so much blood.
They had to cut
a child from this one, from her cancerous womb.

They let them sleep. All day, all night.—They tell
the newcomers: here sleep will make you well.—But Sundays
one rouses them a bit for visitors.—

They take a little nourishment. Their backs
are sore. You see the flies. Sometimes
the sisters wash them. As one washes benches.—

Here the grave rises up about each bed.
And flesh is leveled down to earth. The fire
burns out. And sap prepares to flow. Earth calls.—

—Babette Deutsch

NACHTCAFE

824: Der Frauen Liebe und Leben.
Das Cello trinkt rasch mal. Die Flöte
rülpst tief drei Takte lang: das schöne Abendbrot.
Die Trommel liest den Kriminalroman zu Ende.

Grüne Zähne, Pickel im Gesicht
winkt einer Lidrandentzündung.

Fett im Haar
spricht zu offenem Mund mit Rachenmandel
Glaube Liebe Hoffnung um den Hals.

Junger Kropf ist Sattelnase gut.
Er bezahlt für sie drei Biere.

Bartflechte kauft Nelken,
Doppelkinn zu erweichen.

B-moll: die 35. Sonate.
Zwei Augen brüllen auf:
Spritzt nicht das Blut von Chopin in den Saal,
damit das Pack drauf rumlatscht!
Schluß! He, Gigi! —

Die Tür fließt hin: ein Weib.
Wüste ausgedörrt. Kanaanitisch braun.
Keusch. Höhlenreich. Ein Duft kommt mit. Kaum
                                          Duft.
Es ist nur eine süße Vorwölbung der Luft
gegen mein Gehirn.

Eine Fettleibigkeit trippelt hinterher.

1912

NIGHT CAFÉ

824: The Love and Life of Women.
The 'cello has a quick drink. The flute
belches throughout three beats: oh, lovely supper.
The drum reads on to the end of the thriller.

Green teeth, pimples in his face,
waves to conjunctivitis.

Grease in his hair
Talks to open mouth with swollen tonsils,
faith hope and charity around his neck.

Young goitre is sweet on saddle-nose.
He treats her to three beers.

Sycosis buys carnations
to mollify double chin.

B minor: sonata op. 35.
A pair of eyes roars out:
Don't splash the blood of Chopin around the place
for this crowd to slouch about in!
Hey, Gigi! Stop!—

The door dissolves: a woman.
Desert dried out. Canaanite brown.
Chaste. Full of caves. A scent comes with her.
                              Hardly scent.
It's only a sweet overarching of the air
Against my brain.

A paunched obesity waddles after her.

                              —*Michael Hamburger*

D-ZUG

Braun wie Kognak. Braun wie Laub. Rotbraun.
Malaiengelb.
D-Zug Berlin-Trelleborg und die Ostseebäder.

Fleisch, das nackt ging.
Bis in den Mund gebräunt vom Meer.
Reif gesenkt, zu griechischem Glück.
In Sichel-Sehnsucht: Wie weit der Sommer ist!
Vorletzter Tag des neunten Monats schon!

Stoppel und letzte Mandel lechzt in uns.
Entfaltungen, das Blut, die Müdigkeiten,
die Georginennähe macht uns wirr.

Männerbraun stürzt sich auf Frauenbraun:

Eine Frau ist etwas für eine Nacht.
Und wenn es schön war, noch für die nächste!
Oh! Und dann wieder dies Bei-sich-selbst-Sein!
Diese Stummheiten! Dies Getriebenwerden!

Eine Frau ist etwas mit Geruch.
Unsägliches! Stirb hin! Resede.
Darin ist Süden, Hirt und Meer.
An jedem Abhang lehnt ein Glück.

Frauenhellbraun taumelt an Männerdunkelbraun:

Halte mich! Du, ich falle!
Ich bin im Nacken so müde.
Oh, dieser fiebernde süße
letzte Geruch aus den Gärten.

1912

EXPRESS TRAIN

Brown as cognac. Brown as leaves. Red-brown.
          Malayan yellow.
Express train Berlin-Trelleborg and the Baltic
           Sea resorts.
Flesh, that went naked.
Tanned to the very lips by the sea.
Deeply ripe, for Grecian pleasure.
And yearning for the scythe: how long the summer
            seems!
Almost the end of the ninth month already!

Stubble and the last almond thirst in us.
Unfoldings, the blood, the weariness,
The nearness of dahlias confuses us.

Man-brown hurls itself upon woman-brown:

A woman is something for a night.
And if it was good, for the next night too!
Oh, and then again this being by oneself!
These silences! This letting oneself drift!

A woman is something with fragrance.
Unspeakable. Dissolve. Reseda.
In her the south, shepherd and sea.
On every slope a pleasure lies.

Woman-light-brown reels towards man-dark-brown:

Hold me, dear; I'm falling.
I'm so weary at the neck.
Oh, this feverish sweet
Last fragrance blown from the gardens.

—Adapted by Michael Hamburger
from the Lohner-Corman translation

VOR EINEM KORNFELD

Vor einem Kornfeld sagte einer:
Die Treue und Märchenhaftigkeit der Kornblumen
ist ein hübsches Malmotiv für Damen.
Da lobe ich mir den tiefen Alt des Mohns.
Da denkt man an Blutfladen und Menstruation.
An Not, Röcheln, Hungern und Verrecken —
kurz: an des Mannes dunklen Weg.

1913

HIER IST KEIN TROST

Keiner wird mein Wegrand sein.
Laß deine Blüten nur verblühen.
Mein Weg flutet und geht allein.

Zwei Hände sind eine zu kleine Schale.
Ein Herz ist ein zu kleiner Hügel,
um dran zu ruhn.

Du, ich lebe immer am Strand
und unter dem Blütenfall des Meeres,
Ägypten liegt vor meinem Herzen,
Asien dämmert auf.

BEFORE A CORNFIELD

Before a cornfield he said:
The loyalty and etherealness of the cornflowers
is a fine motif for daubing ladies.
I prefer the deep contralto of poppy.
It makes you think of caked blood and menstruation,
of stress, wheezing, hunger and kicking the bucket—
in short, of the murky path of the male.

—Francis Golffing

NO CONSOLATION

No one shall be the brink of my abyss.
Leave your blossoms to wither.
My path flows and runs alone.

Two hands are much too small a vessel.
A heart too small a hill,
To rest on.

I only live at shores
And under the blossom fall of the ocean,
Egypt is spread before my heart,
Asia is dawning.

Mein einer Arm liegt immer im Feuer.
Mein Blut ist Asche. Ich schluchze immer
vorbei an Brüsten und Gebeinen
den tyrrhenischen Inseln zu:

Dämmert ein Tal mit weißen Pappeln
ein Ilyssos mit Wiesenufern
Eden und Adam und eine Erde
aus Nihilismus und Musik.

1913

UNTERGRUNDBAHN

Die weichen Schauer. Blütenfrühe. Wie
aus warmen Fellen kommt es aus den Wäldern.
Ein Rot schwärmt auf. Das große Blut steigt an.

Durch all den Frühling kommt die fremde Frau.
Der Strumpf am Spann ist da. Doch, wo er endet,
ist weit von mir. Ich schluchze auf der Schwelle:
laues Geblühe, fremde Feuchtigkeiten.

Oh, wie ihr Mund die laue Luft verpraßt!
Du Rosenhirn, Meer-Blut, du Götter-Zwielicht,
du Erdenbeet, wie strömen deine Hüften
so kühl den Gang hervor, in dem du gehst!

Dunkel: Nun lebt es unter ihren Kleidern:
nur weißes Tier, gelöst und stummer Duft.

One of my arms always lies in the fire.
My blood is ashes. And I always moan
Past bones and breasts
Toward the Tyrrhenian isles:

A valley with white poplars is dawning
An Ilyssus with meadowy banks
Eden and Adam and an earth
Of nihilism and of music.

—*Richard Exner*

SUBWAY TRAIN

Lascivious shivers. Early bloom. As if
from warm furred skins it wafted from the woods.
A red swarms up. The great strong blood ascends.

Through all of Spring the alien woman walks.
The stocking, stretched, is there. But where it ends
is far from me. I sob upon the threshold:
sultry luxuriance, alien moistures teeming.

Oh how her mouth squanders the sultry air!
You brain of roses, sea-blood, goddess-twilight,
you bed of earth, how coolly from your hips
your stride flows out, the glide that is your walking.

Dark: underneath her garments now it lives:
white animal only, loosed, and silent scent.

Ein armer Hirnhund, schwer mit Gott behangen.
Ich bin der Stirn so satt. Oh, ein Gerüste
von Blütenkolben löste sanft sie ab
und schwölle mit und schauerte und triefte.

So losgelöst. So müde. Ich will wandern.
Blutlos die Wege. Lieder aus den Gärten.
Schatten und Sintflut. Fernes Glück: ein Sterben
hin in des Meeres erlösend tiefes Blau.

1913

GESÄNGE

I

O daß wir unsere Ururahnen wären.
Ein Klümpchen Schleim in einem warmen Moor.
Leben und Tod, Befruchten und Gebären
glitte aus unseren stummen Säften vor.

Ein Algenblatt oder ein Dünenhügel,
vom Wind Geformtes und nach unten schwer.
Schon ein Libellenkopf, ein Möwenflügel
wäre zu weit und litte schon zu sehr.

A wretched braindog, laden down with God.
My forehead wearies me. Oh that a frame
of clustered blooms would gently take its place,
to swell in unison and stream and shudder.

So lax, adrift. So tired. I long to wander.
The ways all bloodless. Songs that blow from
                                        gardens.
Shadows and Flood. Far joys: a languid dying
down into ocean's deep redeeming blue.

—Michael Hamburger

Note. In the original version of the poem, as published in *Söhne*, the last
word is not 'blue' but 'blood'.

SONGS

I

O that we were our primal ancestors.
A little clump of slime in a warm bog.
Then life and death, then pregnancy and birth
From our dumb lymph would issue for that quag.

A leaf of alga or a simple dune,
Windshaped yet weighted by its rooted clutch.
A gull's wing, the head of a dragonfly
Were all too long and suffering too much.—

Verächtlich sind die Liebenden, die Spötter,
alles Verzweifeln, Sehnsucht, und wer hofft.
Wir sind so schmerzliche durchseuchte Götter
und dennoch denken wir des Gottes oft.

Die weiche Bucht. Die dunkeln Wälderträume.
Die Sterne, schneeballblütengroß und schwer.
Die Panther springen lautlos durch die Bäume.
Alles ist Ufer. Ewig ruft das Meer —

1913

IKARUS

I

O Mittag, der mit heißem Heu mein Hirn
zu Wiese, flachem Land und Hirten schwächt,
daß ich hinrinne und, den Arm im Bach,
den Mohn an meine Schläfe ziehe —
o du Weithingewölbter, enthirne doch
stillflügelnd über Fluch und Gram
des Werdens und Geschehns
mein Auge.
Noch durch Geröll der Halde, noch durch Land-aas,
verstaubendes, durch bettelhaft Gezack
der Felsen — überall
das tiefe Mutterblut, die strömende
entstirnte
matte
Getragenheit.

II

Despicable, the lovers and the mockers,
Despair, longing, the hopeful, all are vile.
We are such sickly, such corrupted gods,
Yet our thoughts turn godwards every little while.

The gentle inlet. The woods' darkling dreams.
The grave stars, huge as blossoming snowballs.
The panthers leap soundlessly through the trees.
And all is shore. And always the sea calls.—
                                    —*Babette Deutsch*

ICARUS

I

O noon that with hot hay reduce
my brain to meadow, shepherds and flat land,
so that I flow away, my arm immersed
in the stream's water, and to my brow
draw close the poppies—noon that's vaulted wide,
now mutely winging above the curse and grief
of all that is and will be,
unbrain my eye.
Still through the hillside boulders, still through
                                    land-carrion,
turning to dust, through beggarly sharp shapes
of rocks—still everywhere
deep mother-blood, this streaming
deforeheaded
weary
drifting away.

Das Tier lebt Tag um Tag
und hat an seinem Euter kein Erinnern,
der Hang schweigt seine Blume in das Licht
und wird zerstört.

Nur ich, mit Wächter zwischen Blut und Pranke,
ein hirnzerfressenes Aas, mit Flüchen
im Nichts zergellend, bespien mit Worten,
veräfft vom Licht —

o du Weithingewölbter,
träuf meinen Augen eine Stunde
des guten frühen Voraugenlichts —
schmilz hin den Trug der Farben, schwinge
die kotbedrängten Höhlen in das Rauschen
gebäumter Sonnen, Sturz der Sonnen-sonnen,
o aller Sonnen ewiges Gefälle —

II

Das Hirn frißt Staub. Die Füße fressen Staub.
Wäre das Auge rund und abgeschlossen,
dann bräche durch die Lider süße Nacht,
Gebüsch und Liebe.
Aus dir, du süßes Tierisches,
aus euern Schatten, Schlaf und Haar,
muß ich mein Hirn besteigen,
alle Windungen,
das letzte Zwiegespräch —

The animal lives only for the day
And in its udder has no memory,
the slope in silence brings its flower to light
and is destroyed.

I only, with a sentry between blood and claw,
mere brain-devoured carrion, shrieking and cursing
                                        plunged
into annihilation, bespat with words,
aped by the light—

O noon that's vaulted wide,
but for one hour infuse my eyes
with that good light which was before eyes were—
melt down the lie of colors, hurl
these cavities pressed by filth into the roar
of rearing suns, whirl of the suns of suns,
o everlasting fall of all the suns—

II

The brain eats dust. Our feet devour the dust.
If but the eye were round and self-contained
then through the lids sweet night would enter in,
brushwood and love.
From you, the sweetly bestial,
from out your shadows, sleep and hair,
I must bestride my brain,
all loops and turns,
the ultimate duologue—

So sehr am Strand, so sehr schon in der Barke,
im krokosfarbnen Kleide der Geweihten
und um die Glieder schon den leichten Flaum —
ausrauschst du aus den Falten, Sonne,
allnächtlich Welten in den Raum —
o eine der vergeßlich hingesprühten
mit junger Glut die Schläfe mir zerschmelzend,
auftrinkend das entstirnte Blut —

1915

KARYATIDE

Entrücke dich dem Stein! Zerbirst
die Höhle, die dich knechtet! Rausche
doch in die Flur! Verhöhne die Gesimse —
sieh: Durch den Bart des trunkenen Silen
aus seinem ewig überrauschten
lauten einmaligen durchdröhnten Blut
träuft Wein in seine Scham!

Bespei die Säulensucht: Toderschlagene
greisige Hände bebten sie
verhangenen Himmeln zu. Stürze
die Tempel vor die Sehnsucht deines Knies,
in dem der Tanz begehrt!

III

So near the beach, so much embarked already,
dressed in the victim's crocus-colored garment,
and round your limbs the light and delicate down—
O sun, you rustle forth from out your folds
each night new universes into space—
Oh, one of these, obliviously scattered here
with its young glow is melting down my temples,
drinks my deforeheaded blood.

—Michael Hamburger

CARYATID

Leave stone behind, rise higher! Burst
the socket that enslaves you! Rush
out to the meadows! Mock the cornices—
look at the drunk Silenus: through his beard
from his loud blood forever drowned in roars,
shivered by alien music and unique,
wine drips into his sex!

Spit on this column mania: done to death
mere senile hands they trembled
towards cloud-covered heavens. Tear down
the temples to the longing of your knee
which prisoned dance desires!

Breite dich hin, zerblühe dich, oh, blute
dein weiches Beet aus großen Wunden hin:
Sieh, Venus mit den Tauben gürtet
sich Rosen um der Hüften Liebestor —
sieh dieses Sommers letzten blauen Hauch
auf Astermeeren an die fernen
baumbraunen Ufer treiben; tagen
sieh diese letzte Glück-Lügenstunde
unserer Südlichkeit
hochgewölbt.

1916

AUFBLICK

Heimstrom quillt auf zu Hunger und Geschlecht.
O Mühlenglück! O Abhang! Glutgefälle
stürmt noch die alte Sonne; schon verhöhnt
Neu-Feuer sie und um Andromeda
der frische Nebel schon,
o Wander-Welt!
Vermetzung an die Dinge: Nacht-Liebe, Wiesenakt:
Ich: lagernd, bestoßen, das Gesicht voll Sterne,
aus Pranken-Ansprung, Zermalmungsschauer
blaut küstenhaft wie Bucht das Blut
mir Egge, Dolch und Hörner.
Noch Weg kausalt sich höckrig durch die Häuser
des immanenten Packs, mit Fratzen
des Raums bestanden, drohend
Unendlichkeit.

Spread out your limbs, oh, bloom to death
                              and bleed
your gentle bed away through gaping wounds:
Look, Venus with her doves is twining
roses around the love-gate of her hips—
look how the summer's last and hazy blue
drifts over seas of asters to the far
fall-foliage-colored shores; and look:
now dawns the last glad lying hour
of our southernness
vaulted high.

—Michael Hamburger

LOOKING UPWARD

Homestream wells up to hunger and to sex.
O joy of mills! Declivity! Decline
of heat pours from the old sun yet; new fire
derides it now and round Andromeda
the fresh-formed nebulae,
O wander-world!
To things their whoredoms: night-love and meadow-
                                            flesh:
I: bedded, tupped, vision full of stars,
at flash of claws and shudder, pulverized,
the blood as coastal as a bay goes blue,
my harrow, stabber, horns.
Path runs still causal, rugged through abodes
of rabble immanent, lined all along
with caricatures of space that threaten
with infinity.

Mir aber glüht sich Morgenlicht
entraumter Räume um das Knie,
ein Hirtengang eichhörnchent in das Laub,
Euklid am Meere singt zur Dreiecksflöte:
O Rosenholz! Vergang! Amati-Cello!

1916

PAPPEL

Verhalten,
ungeöffnet in Ast und Ranke,
um in das Blau des Himmels aufzuschrein —:
nur Stamm, Geschlossenheiten,
hoch und zitternd,
eine Kurve.

Die Mispel flüchtet,
Samentöter,
und wann der Blitze segnendes Zerbrechen
rauschte um meinen Schaft
enteinheitend,
weitverteilend
Baumgewesenes?
Und wer sah Pappelwälder?

But round me prostrate morning light
from despaced spaces falls aglow,
a walk of shepherds squirrels through the leaves,
and Euclid sings to panpipes on the shore:
O rosewood! Deliquescence! 'Cello Amati made!
　　　　　　　　—Christopher Middleton

POPLAR

Restrained,
with branch and young shoot undisclosed
to cry the louder out into the blue of sky—:
trunk only, all enclosure,
tall and shivering,
a curve.

Medlar is fugitive,
killer of seed,
and when have blessing clefts of lightning
roared round my shaft,
disuniting,
casting far and wide
the thing once tree?
Who ever saw a wood of poplars?

Einzeln,
und an der Kronenstirn das Mal der Schreie,
das ruhelos die Nächte und den Tag
über der Gärten hinresedeten
süßen aufklaffenden Vergang,
was ihm die Wurzel saugt, die Rinde frißt,
in tote Räume bietet
hin und her.

1917

PALAU

„Rot ist der Abend auf der Insel von Palau
und die Schatten sinken —"
singe, auch aus den Kelchen der Frau
läßt es sich trinken,
Totenvögel schrein
und die Totenuhren
pochen, bald wird es sein
Nacht und Lemuren.

Heiße Riffe. Aus Eukalypten geht
Tropik und Palmung,
was sich noch hält und steht,
will auch Zermalmung

Individual,
restless at night and through the day
over the gardens' mignonetted
sweet deliquescence gaping wide
that sucks its root and gnaws its bark
insignia of cries on its crowned brow it offers
dead space opposing,
to and fro.

                              —*Christopher Middleton*

PALAU

"Evening is red on the island of Palau
and the shadows sink—"
sing, from woman's chalices too
it is good to drink,
deathly the little owls cry
and the death-watch ticks out,
very soon it will be
Lemures and night.

Hot these reefs. From eucalypti there flows
a tropical palm concoction,
all that still holds and stays
also longs for destruction

bis in das Gliederlos,
bis in die Leere,
tief in den Schöpfungsschoß
dämmernder Meere.

Rot ist der Abend auf der Insel von Palau
und im Schattenschimmer
hebt sich steigend aus Dämmer und Tau:
„niemals und immer",
alle Tode der Welt
sind Fähren und Furten,
und von Fremdem umstellt
auch deine Geburten —

Einmal mit Opferfett
auf dem Piniengerüste
trägt sich dein Flammenbett
wie Wein zur Küste,
Megalithen zuhauf
und die Gräber und Hallen,
Hammer des Thor im Lauf
zu den Asen zerfallen —

Wie die Götter vergehn
und die großen Cäsaren,
von der Wange des Zeus
emporgefahren —
singe, wandert die Welt
schon in fremdestem Schwunge,
schmeckt uns das Charonsgeld
längst unter der Zunge.

down to the limbless stage,
down to the vacuum,
back to the primal age,
dark ocean's womb.

Evening is red on the island of Palau:
in the gleam of these shadows
there issues rising from twilight and dew:
"Never and Always";
all the deaths of the earth
are fords and ferries,
what to you owes it birth
surrounded with strangeness—

Once with sacrificial
fat on the pine-wood floor
your bed of flames would travel
like wine to the shore,
megaliths heaped around
and the graves and the halls,
hammer of Thor that's bound
for the Aesir, crumbled, falls—

As the gods surcease,
the great Caesars decline,
from the cheek of Zeus
once raised up to reign—
sing, already the world
to the strangest rhythm is swung,
Charon's coin, if not curled,
long tasted under the tongue—

Paarung. Dein Meer belebt
Sepien, Korallen,
was sich noch hält und hebt,
will auch zerfallen,
rot ist der Abend auf der Insel von Palau,
Eukalyptenschimmer
hebt in Runen aus Dämmer und Tau:
niemals und immer.

1925

WER BIST DU

Wer bist du — alle Mythen
zerrinnen. Was geschah,
Chimären, Leda-iten
sind einen Kniefall da,

gemalt mit Blut der Beeren
der Trunkenen Schläfe rot,
und die — des Manns Erwehren —
die nun als Lorbeer loht,

mit Schlangenhaar die Lende
an Zweig und Thyrsenstab,
in Trunkenheit und Ende
und um ein Göttergrab —

Coupling. Sepias your seas
and coral animate,
all that still holds and sways
also longs to disintegrate,
evening is red on the island of Palau,
eucalyptus glaze
raises in runes from twilight and dew:
Never and Always.

—Michael Hamburger

WHO ARE YOU

Who are you—all the legends
are vanishing. What was—
chimeras, Leda's kindred
in genuflecting pass,

painted with blood of berries,
the scarlet drunkards, she—
the masculine-defying—
a fiery laurel tree,

with serpent hair the haunches,
by branch and thyrsus staff,
in drunken fit, finale,
and round a holy grave—

Was ist, sind hohle Leichen,
die Wand aus Tang und Stein,
was scheint, ist ewiges Zeichen
und spielt die Tiefe rein —

in Schattenflur, in Malen,
das sich der Form entwand —:
Ulyss, der nach den Qualen
s c h l a f e n d die Heimat fand.

1925

QUI SAIT

Aber der Mensch wird trauern —
solange Gott, falls es das gibt,
immer neue Schauern
von Gehirnen schiebt
von den Hellesponten
zum Hobokenquai,
immer neue Fronten —
wozu, qui sait?

Spurii: die Gesäten
war einst der Männer Los,
Frauen streiften und mähten
den Samen in ihren Schoß;
dann eine Insel voll Tauben
und Werften: Schiffe fürs Meer,
und so begann der Glauben
an Handel und Verkehr.

What is, are hollow corpses,
the rock and seawrack screen,
what seems, eternal token
that plays the whole depth clean—

in phantom fields, portrayal
inhabiting no form:—
Odysseus past affliction
who sleeping found his home.

—*Christopher Middleton*

QUI SAIT

Yet mankind shall mourn
while God—if that exists—
moves ever newly born
brain waves into the lists
from the Hellesponts
to Hoboken's quay,
opens ever new fronts—
what for? *Qui sait*?

Spurii: being sowed
used to be men's meed;
women stripped and mowed,
into their womb the seed;
then came an isleful of pigeons
and wharves: ships for the sea,
and thus began the religions
of commerce and industry.

Aber der Mensch wird trauern —
Masse, muskelstark,
Cowboy und Zentauern,
Nurmi als Jeanne d'Arc —:
Stadionsakrale
mit Khasanaspray,
Züchtungspastorale,
wozu, qui sait?

Aber der Mensch wird trauern —
kosmopoler Chic
neue Tempelmauern
Kraftwerk Pazifik:
Die Meere ausgeweidet,
Kalorien-Avalun:
Meer, das wärmt, Meer, das kleidet—
neue Mythe des Neptun.

Bis nach tausend Jahren
einbricht in das Wrack
Geißlerscharen,
zementiertes Pack
mit Orang-Utanhauern
oder Kaiser Henry Clay —
wer wird das überdauern,
welch Pack — qui sait?

1927

Yet mankind shall mourn—
masses; muscular mark;
cowboy, Centaur reborn;
Nurmi as Joan of Arc—:
sacred arenas of speeding
with DeVilbiss spray;
pastorals of breeding—
what for? *Qui sait?*

Yet mankind shall mourn—
cosmopolitan styles,
temple walls adorn
Pacific power piles;
eviscerated oceans,
calorific Avalon:
sea heat, costuming lotions—
Neptune's new pantheon.

Until a thousand years later
rabidly penitent
gangs invade the crater,
rabble cast in cement,
ape fangs dripping saliva
or Emperor Henry Clay—
and who'll be the survivor?
Which gang—*qui sait?*

—*E. B. Ashton*

DURCH JEDE
STUNDE

Durch jede Stunde,
durch jedes Wort
blutet die Wunde
der Schöpfung fort,

verwandelnd Erde
und tropft den Seim
ans Herz dem Werde
und kehret heim.

Gab allem Flügel,
was Gott erschuf,
den Skythen die Bügel
dem Hunnen den Huf —

nur nicht fragen,
nur nicht verstehn;
den Himmel tragen,
die weitergehn,

nur diese Stunde
ihr Sagenlicht
und dann die Wunde,
mehr gibt es nicht.

Die Äcker bleichen,
der Hirte rief,
das ist das Zeichen:
Tränke dich tief,

THROUGH EVERY MOMENT

Through every moment,
through every word
out of creation's wound
the blood is poured,

changing the earthly,
its nectar flows
on the heart of Become and
then homeward goes.

Winged all those beings
God has begun,
for the Scythian stirrups,
hooves for the Hun,

only no questions,
nor claim you know:
shoulder the firmament
who onward go,

only this moment,
fabulous dawn,
the wound hereafter,
no more is known.

The cornfields whiten,
the Shepherd has called,
that is the token:
drink deep unstilled,

den Blick in Bläue,
ein Ferngesicht:
Das ist die Treue,
mehr gibt es nicht,

Treue den Reichen,
die alles sind,
Treue dem Zeichen,
wie schnell es rinnt,

ein Tausch, ein Reigen,
ein Sagenlicht,
ein Rausch aus Schweigen,
mehr gibt es nicht.

1933

EIN WORT

Ein Wort, ein Satz —: Aus Chiffren steigen
erkanntes Leben, jäher Sinn,
die Sonne steht, die Sphären schweigen
und alles ballt sich zu ihm hin.

Ein Wort — ein Glanz, ein Flug, ein Feuer,
ein Flammenwurf, ein Sternenstrich —
und wieder Dunkel, ungeheuer,
im leeren Raum um Welt und Ich.

1941

look where the blue is,
vision outgone:
That is true loyalty,
no more is known,

loyal to the kingdoms
that are and are all,
loyal to the token
though fast it fail,

interchange, ringdance,
fabulous dawn,
rapture of silence,
no more is known.

—*Christopher Middleton*

A WORD

A word, a phrase—: from cyphers rise
Life recognized, a sudden sense,
The sun stands still, mute are the skies,
And all compacts it, stark and dense.

A word—, a gleam, a flight, a spark,
A thrust of flames, a stellar trace—,
And then again—immense—the dark
Round world and I in empty space.

—*Richard Exner*

WENN ETWAS LEICHT

Wenn etwas leicht und rauschend um dich ist
wie die Glyzinienpracht an dieser Mauer,
dann ist die Stunde jener Trauer,
daß du nicht reich und unerschöpflich bist,

nicht wie die Blüte oder wie das Licht:
in Strahlen kommend, sich verwandelnd,
an ähnlichen Gebilden handelnd,
die alle nur der eine Rausch verflicht,

der eine Samt, auf dem die Dinge ruhn
so strömend und so unzerspalten,
die Grenze ziehn, die Stunden halten
und nichts in jener Trauer tun.

1943

WELLE DER NACHT

Welle der Nacht — Meerwidder und Delphine
mit Hyakinthos leichtbewegter Last,
die Lorbeerrosen und die Travertine
wehn um den leeren istrischen Palast,

Welle der Nacht — zwei Muscheln miterkoren,
die Fluten strömen sie, die Felsen her,
dann Diadem und Purpur mitverloren,
die weiße Perle rollt zurück ins Meer.

1943

A WEIGHTLESS ELEMENT

When like wistaria against this wall
around you rings a weightless element
then is the time that you lament
being not rich and inexhaustible,

not like the blossom, or like the light:
in rays arriving, changing its design,
acting on forms akin to it
that, ringed in single ecstasy, entwine,

the single velvet ground where things repose,
so lush, so undivided, and
with time according, self-confined,
go not the way lamenting goes.

—Christopher Middleton

WAVE OF THE NIGHT

Wave of the night—sea-ram and dolphin seen
with Hyakinthos' airy weight borne high,
where laurel roses and the Travertine
around the empty Istrian palace sigh,

Wave of the night—two chosen shells it bore,
in tidal stream from cliffs incessantly,
then, diadem and purple lost once more,
the white pearl rolls into the sea.

—Christopher Middleton

NACHZEICHNUNG

I

O jene Jahre! Der Morgen grünes Licht,
auch die noch nicht gefegten Lusttrottoire —
der Sommer schrie von Ebenen in der Stadt
und sog an einem Horn,
das sich von oben füllte.

Lautlose Stunde. Wässrige Farben
eines hellgrünen Aug's verdünnten Strahls,
Bilder aus diesem Zaubergrün, gläserne Reigen:
Hirten und Weiher, eine Kuppel, Tauben —
gewoben und gesandt, erglänzt, erklungen —,
verwandelbare Wolken eines Glücks!

So standest du vor Tag: die Spring-
brunnen noch ohne Perlen, tatenlos
Gebautes und die Steige; die Häuser
verschlossen, du erschufst
den Morgen, jasminene Frühe,
sein Jauchzen, uranfänglich
sein Strahl — noch ohne Ende — o jene Jahre!

Ein Unauslöschliches im Herzen,
Ergänzungen vom Himmel und der Erde;
Zuströmendes aus Schilf und Gärten,
Gewitter abends
tränkten die Dolden ehern,

RETROSPECTIVE SKETCH

Oh, the green light, the mornings of those years,
the pleasure pavements before the sweepers came—
the summer cried of plains within the city
and sucked a horn of plenty
replenished from above.

Hour without sound. Watery colors
of a pale-green eye's diluted ray,
images out of this magical green, dances in glass:
shepherds and ponds, a cupola, pigeons—
woven and vouchsafed, flashed out or intuned—
mutable clouds of a happiness!

So you stood before daybreak; the fountains
still without pearls, constructions
raised without effort, the steps; the houses
still locked, it was you *created*
this morning, syringa time of the day,
its jubilation, pristine
its beam—without end as yet—oh those years!

A sense of inextinguishable things,
completions of heaven and earth;
encroachments from reeds and gardens,
thunderstorms nightly
watered the umbels to brass

die barsten dunkel, gespannt von ihren Seimen;
und Meer und Strände,
bewimpelte mit Zelten,
glühenden Sandes trächtig,
bräunende Wochen, gerbend alles
zu Fell für Küsse, die niedergingen
achtlos und schnell verflogen
wie Wolkenbrüche!

Darüber hing die Schwere
auch jetzt — doch Trauben
aus ihr,

die Zweige niederziehend und wieder hochlassend,
nur einige Beeren,
wenn du mochtest,
erst —

noch nicht so drängend und überhangen
von kolbengroßen Fruchtfladen,
altem schwerem Traubenfleisch —

o jene Jahre!

II

Dunkle Tage des Frühlings,
nicht weichender Dämmer um Laub;
Fliederblüte gebeugt, kaum hochblickend
narzissenfarben und starken Todesgeruchs,
Glückausfälle,
sieglose Trauer des Unerfüllten.

that darkly burst, held taut by their sap;
and sea and beaches
with their streamers, their tents,
pregnant with glowing sand,
sun-burning weeks tanning all
to fur for kisses that descended
heedless and briefly felt
as summer cloudbursts.

Over it all there hung sadness
even then—but grapes
out of it,

dragging the tendrils down and releasing them,
only a berry or two
when you wanted it,
then—

not yet so urgent and overhung
with bunches of fruit as big as clubs,
heavy old grape-flesh—

Oh those years!

II

Dark days of Spring,
half-light clinging to foliage;
lilac blossom that dropped, hardly glancing upwards
narcissus-colored and strongly scented with death,
cessations of gladness,
unavailing gloom of the unfulfilled.

Und in den Regen hinein,
der auf das Laub fällt,
höre ich ein altes Wälderlied,
von Wäldern, die ich einst durchfuhr
und wiedersah, doch ich ging nicht
in die Halle, wo das Lied erklungen war,
die Tasten schwiegen längst,
die Hände ruhten irgendwo,
gelöst von jenen Armen, die mich hielten,
zu Tränen rührten,
Hände aus den Oststeppen,
blutig zertretenen längst —
nur noch ihr Wälderlied
in den Regen hinein
an dunklen Tagen des Frühlings
den ewigen Steppen zu.

1943

MONOLOG

Den Darm mit Rotz genährt, das Hirn mit Lügen —
erwählte Völker Narren eines Clowns,
in Späße, Sternelesen, Vogelzug
den eigenen Unrat deutend! Sklaven —
aus kalten Ländern und aus glühenden,
immer mehr Sklaven, ungezieferschwere,
hungernde, peitschenüberschwungene Haufen:
Dann schwillt das Eigene an, der eigene Flaum,
der grindige, zum Barte des Propheten!

Ach, Alexander und Olympias Sproß
das wenigste! Sie zwinkern Hellesponte

And into the rain
that falls on leaves
I hear an old woodland song
about woods I once drove through
and revisited, but I did not go
to the hall where the song had sounded,
the keyboard had long been still,
the hands were resting somewhere
detached from those arms that held me,
moved me to tears,
hands out of the Eastern steppes,
long ago bloodily trampled—
only her woodland song
into the rain
in the dark days of Spring
towards the undying steppes.

—Michael Hamburger

MONOLOGUE

Their colons fed with mucus, brains with lies
these chosen races, coxcombs of a clown,
in pranks, astrology and flight of birds
construing their own ordure! Slaves—
from icy and from burning territories,
gross with vermin more and more slaves come,
hungry and whiplash-driven hordes of them:
Then all that's personal, the downy cheeck,
with scurf and scab, swells to a prophet's beard!

Ah, Alexander and Olympia's offspring,
that least of all! They wink whole Hellesponts,

259

und schäumen Asien! Aufgetriebenes, Blasen
mit Vorhut, Günstlingen, verdeckten Staffeln,
daß keiner sticht! Günstlinge: — gute Plätze
für Ring- und Rechtsgeschehn! Wenn keiner sticht!
Günstlinge, Lustvolk, Binden, breite Bänder —
mit breiten Bändern flattert Traum und Welt:
Klumpfüße sehn die Stadien zerstört,
Stinktiere treten die Lupinenfelder,
weil sie der Duft am eigenen irremacht:
Nur Stoff vom After! — Fette
verfolgen die Gazelle,
die windeseilige, das schöne Tier!
Hier kehrt das Maß sich um:
Die Pfütze prüft den Quell, der Wurm die Elle,
die Kröte spritzt dem Veilchen in den Mund
— Hallelujah! — und wetzt den Bauch im Kies:
Die Paddentrift als Mahnmal der Geschichte!
Die Ptolemäerspur als Gaunerzinke,
die Ratte kommt als Labsal gegen Pest.
Meuchel besingt den Mord. Spitzel locken
aus Psalmen Unzucht.

Und diese Erde lispelt mit dem Mond,
dann schürzt sie sich ein Maifest um die Hüfte,
dann läßt sie Rosen durch, dann schmort sie Korn,
läßt den Vesuv nicht spein, läßt nicht die Wolke
zu Lauge werden, die der Tiere Abart,
die dies erlistet, sticht und niederbrennt —
ach, dieser Erde Frucht- und Rosenspiel
ist heimgestellt der Wucherung des Bösen,
der Hirne Schwamm, der Kehle Lügensprenkeln
der obgenannten Art — die maßverkehrte!

Sterben heißt, dies alles ungelöst verlassen,
die Bilder ungesichert, die Träume
im Riß der Welten stehn und hungern lassen —

and skim all Asia! Puffed up, pustules
with vanguard, covert squadrons and with minions
that none may prick them! Minions: the best seats
for wrestling and in court! Let no man prick them!
Minions, joyriders, bandages, broad streamers—
broad streamers fluttering from dream and world:
the clubfoot sees the stadiums destroyed,
skunks trample underfoot the lupin fields
because the scent makes them suspect their own:
Nothing but excrement! The obese
course after the gazelle,
the windswift one, the lovely animal!
Inverse proportion enters everything:
The puddle plumbs the source, the worm the ell,
toad squirts his liquid in the violet's mouth,
and—hallelujah!—whets his pot on stones:
The reptile horde as history's monument!
The Ptolemaic line as tic-tac language,
the rat arrives as balm against the plague.
Most foul sings murder. Gossips wheedle
obscenity from psalms.

And this earth whispers discourse with the moon,
then round its hips it hangs a Mayday feast
then lets the roses pass, then stews the corn,
forbids Vesuvius erupt, won't let the cloud
become a caustic that would prick and shrivel
the beasts' base form whose fraud contrived this state—
oh, all the play on earth of fruit and rose
is given up to evil's usury,
brain-fungus, and the gorge's speckling lies
of the above-named sort, proportion inverse!

To die means leaving all these things unsolved,
the images unsure, and hungry dreams
abandoned in the rifts between the worlds—

doch Handeln heißt, die Niedrigkeit bedienen,
der Schande Hilfe leihn, die Einsamkeit,
die große Lösung der Gesichte,
das Traumverlangen hinterhältig fällen
für Vorteil, Schmuck, Beförderungen, Nachruf,
indes das Ende, taumelnd wie ein Falter,
gleichgültig wie ein Sprengstück nahe ist
und anderen Sinn verkündet —

— Ein Klang, ein Bogen, fast ein Sprung aus Bläue
stieß eines Abends durch den Park hervor,
darin ich stand —: ein Lied,
ein Abriß nur, drei hingeworfene Noten
und füllte so den Raum und lud so sehr
die Nacht, den Garten mit Erscheinungen voll
und schuf die Welt und bettete den Nacken
mir in das Strömende, die trauervolle
erhabene Schwäche der Geburt des Seins —:
ein Klang, ein Bogen nur —: Geburt des Seins —
ein Bogen nur und trug das Maß zurück,
und alles schloß es ein: die Tat, die Träume ...

Aus einem Kranz scharlachener Gehirne,
des Blüten der verstreuten Fiebersaat
sich einzeln halten, nur einander:
„unbeugsam in der Farbe" und „ausgezähnt
am Saum das letzte Haar", „gefeilt in Kälte"
zurufen, gesalzene Laken des Urstoffs:
Hier geht Verwandlung aus: Der Tiere Abart
wird faulen, daß für sie das Wort Verwesung
zu sehr nach Himmeln riecht — schon streichen
die Geier an, die Falken hungern schon —!

1943

but action means: to serve vulgarity,
aid and abet iniquity, means loneliness
and dropping furtively the great solution
that visions are and the desire of dreams,
for gain, for gold, promotion, posthumous fame,
while giddily like a moth, indifferent
as a petard the end is near and bodes
a meaning that is different—

A sound, a curve, a chink of blue almost,
reverberated through the park one night
as I stood there—: a song,
only an outline, casual, three notes heard,
and occupied all space and made the night
so full, the garden full of apparitions,
created so the world and bedded me
prostrate within the stream of things, the sad
sublime infirmity of being's birth—:
a sound, only a curve—: but being's birth—
only a curve, proportion it restored
and comprehended all things, act and dreaming . . .

A garland intertwined of scarlet brains
whose flowers grown from scattered fever-seed
shout to each other, keeping separate:
'the coloration form' and 'edges frayed,
the last thread snapping' and 'a hard cold contour,'
these spicy pickles of the protoplasm,
Here transformation starts: the beasts' base form
shall so decay the very word corruption
will smell for it too much of heaven—the vultures
are gathering now and famished hawks are poised!
                              —*Christopher Middleton*

EINSAMER NIE —

Einsamer nie als im August:
Erfüllungsstunde — im Gelände
die roten und die goldenen Brände,
doch wo ist deiner Gärten Lust?

Die Seen hell, die Himmel weich,
die Äcker rein und glänzen leise,
doch wo sind Sieg und Siegsbeweise
aus dem von dir vertretenen Reich?

Wo alles sich durch Glück beweist
und tauscht den Blick und tauscht die Ringe
im Weingeruch, im Rausch der Dinge —:
dienst du dem Gegenglück, dem Geist.

1948

CHOPIN

Nicht sehr ergiebig im Gespräch,
Ansichten waren nicht seine Stärke,
Ansichten reden drum herum,
wenn Delacroix Theorien entwickelte,
wurde er unruhig, er seinerseits konnte
die Notturnos nicht begründen.

NEVER MORE LONELY

Never more lonely than in August: 'tis
a time of plenitude—of lands
ablaze with red and golden brands—
and yet, where is your garden's bliss?

Lakes shine, soft is the heavens' roof,
the fields are clean and gently lambent,
yet in the realm you represent,
where is the triumph and the proof?

Where luck alone proves all mankind
and glances are exchanged and rings
in wine smell, in the lust of things:
you serve the counter-luck—the Mind.

—*E. B. Ashton*

CHOPIN

Not very forthcoming in conversation,
opinions were not his forte,
opinions don't get to the center;
when Delacroix expounded a theory
he became restive, he for his part was unable
to explicate his Nocturnes.

Schwacher Liebhaber;
Schatten in Nohant,
wo George Sands Kinder
keine erzieherischen Ratschläge
von ihm annahmen.

Brustkrank in jener Form
mit Blutungen und Narbenbildung,
die sich lange hinzieht;
stiller Tod
im Gegensatz zu einem
mit Schmerzparoxysmen
oder durch Gewehrsalven:
Man rückte den Flügel (Erard) an die Tür
und Delphine Potocka
sang ihm in der letzten Stunde
ein Veilchenlied.

Nach England reiste er mit drei Flügeln:
Pleyel, Erard, Broadwood,
spielte für zwanzig Guineen abends
eine Viertelstunde
bei Rothschilds, Wellingtons, im Strafford House
und vor zahllosen Hosenbändern;
verdunkelt von Müdigkeit und Todesnähe
kehrte er heim
auf den Square d'Orléans.

Weak as a lover;
shadows at Nohant,
where George Sand's children
would not accept
his pedagogic advice.

Consumptive, of the kind
with hemorrhages and cicatrization,
the kind that drags on for years;
quiet death
as opposed to one
with paroxysms of pain
or one by the firing-squad:
They moved his grand piano (Erard) up to the door
and Delphine Potocka
sang for him at his dying hour
a violet song.

To England he went with three pianos:
Pleyel, Erard, Broadwood,
played for twenty minutes
at Rothschild's, the Wellingtons, at Stratford House,
and to countless garters;
darkened by weariness and approaching death,
he went home
to the Square d'Orleans.

Dann verbrennt er seine Skizzen
und Manuskripte,
nur keine Restbestände, Fragmente, Notizen,
diese verräterischen Einblicke —
sagte zum Schluß:
„Meine Versuche sind nach Maßgabe dessen
vollendet,
was mir zu erreichen möglich war."

Spielen sollte jeder Finger
mit der seinem Bau entsprechenden Kraft,
der vierte ist der schwächste
(nur siamesisch zum Mittelfinger).
Wenn er begann, lagen sie
auf e, fis, gis, b, c.

Wer je bestimmte Präludien
von ihm hörte,
sei es in Landhäusern oder
in einem Höhengelände
oder aus offenen Terrassentüren
beispielsweise aus einem Sanatorium,
wird es schwer vergessen.

Nie eine Oper komponiert,
keine Symphonie,
nur diese tragischen Progressionen
aus artistischer Überzeugung
und mit einer kleinen Hand.

1948

Then he burnt his sketches
and manuscripts;
no residues please, no fragments or notes,
they grant such revealing insights—
and said at the end:
"My endeavors are as complete
as it was in my power to make them."

Every finger was to play
with the force appropriate to its structure;
the fourth is the weakest
(mere siamese twin to the middle finger).
When he began they rested
on E, F sharp, G sharp, B, C.

The man who has ever heard
certain Preludes by him,
whether in country houses or
in a mountain landscape
or on a terrace, through open doors,
a sanatorium's for instance,
will hardly forget it.

Never composed an opera,
no symphony,
only these tragic progressions
out of artistic conviction
and with a slender hand.

—Michael Hamburger

SEPTEMBER

I

Du, über den Zaun gebeugt mit Phlox
(vom Regenguß zerspalten,
seltsamen Wildgeruchs),
der gern auf Stoppeln geht,
zu alten Leuten tritt,
die Balsaminen pflücken,
Rauch auf Feldern
mit Lust und Trauer atmet —

aufsteigenden Gemäuers,
das noch sein Dach vor Schnee und Winter will,
kalklöschenden Gesellen
ein: „ach, vergebens" zuzurufen
nur zögernd sich verhält —

gedrungen eher als hochgebaut,
auch unflätigen Kürbis nackt am Schuh,
fett und gesichtslos, dies Krötengewächs —

Ebenen-entstiegener,
Endmond aller Flammen,
aus Frucht- und Fieberschwellungen
abfallend, schon verdunkelten Gesichts —
Narr oder Täufer,
des Sommers Narr, Nachplapperer, Nachruf
oder der Gletscher Vorlied,
jedenfalls Nußknacker,
Schilfmäher,
Beschäftiger mit Binsenwahrheiten —

SEPTEMBER

I

You leaning there over the fence with phlox
(splintered by rainstorm,
with a strange animal smell),
who are pleased to walk over stubble
and to accost old folk
gathering balm-apples,
breathe with joy and sadness
smoke over ploughland—

rising walls want there
roof before the snow and winter come,
to shout a "You're wasting your time"
at lime-slaking laborers,
but, hesitant, restrain yourself,

thickset rather than tall in build,
with dirty pumpkin also bare at your shoe,
fat and faceless this toady growth—

Descender from the plains,
ultimate moon of all flames,
from tumescences of fruit and flower
dropping, darkened your face already—
fool or baptist,
summer's fool, echoer, necrologue,
or foresong of glaciers,
anyway nutcracker,
sedge-cutter,
ponderer of platitudes—

vor dir der Schnee,
Hochschweigen, unfruchtbar
die Unbesambarkeit der Weite:
Da langt dein Arm hin,
doch über den Zaun gebeugt
die Kraut- und Käferdränge,
das Lebenwollende,
Spinnen und Feldmäuse —

II

Du, ebereschenverhangen
von Frühherbst,
Stoppelgespinst,
Kohlweißlinge im Atem,
laß viele Zeiger laufen,
Kuckucksuhren schlagen,
lärme mit Vespergeläut,
gonge
die Stunde, die so golden feststeht,
so bestimmt dahinbräunt,
in ein zitternd Herz!

Du: — anderes!
So ruhn nur Götter
oder Gewänder
unstürzbarer Titanen
langgeschaffener,
so tief eingestickt
Falter und Blumen
in die Bahnen!

Oder ein Schlummer früher Art,
als kein Erwachen war,

Snowfall ahead of you,
high silence, barren
the far unplantable distance:
that far your reach extends,
but, leaning over the fence,
throngs of beetles and plants now,
all life-desiring things,
spiders and fieldmice—

II

You, rowan-veiled
by early autumn,
stubblephantom,
cabbage-whites in your breath,
let the hands of many clocks revolve,
clamor with vesper bells,
gong
the golden persistent hour
that so firmly continues to tan,
into a trembling heart!

You:—world of difference!
Only gods rest thus
or the robes
of untoppleable Titans,
long-created,
embroidered so deeply
the butterflies and flowers
into their orbits!

Or a slumber of pristine kind,
when no awakening was,

nur goldene Wärme und Purpurbeeren,
benagt von Schwalben, ewigen,
die nie von dannen ziehn —
Dies schlage, gonge,
diese Stunde,
denn
wenn du schweigst,
drängen die Säume herab
pappelbestanden und schon kühler.

1948

FRAGMENTE

Fragmente,
Seelenauswürfe,
Blutgerinnsel des zwanzigsten Jahrhunderts —

Narben — gestörter Kreislauf der Schöpfungsfrühe,
die historischen Religionen von fünf Jahrhunderten
                              zertrümmert,
die Wissenschaft: Risse im Parthenon,
Planck rann mit seiner Quantentheorie
zu Kepler und Kierkegaard neu getrübt zusammen —

Aber Abende gab es, die gingen in den Farben
des Allvaters, lockeren, weitwallenden,
unumstößlich in ihrem Schweigen
geströmten Blaus,
Farbe der Introvertierten,
da sammelte man sich

only golden warmth and purple berries,
nibbled by swallows, eternal ones,
that never fly away—
This note strike, gong
this hour,
for
when you fall silent,
downward the forest-edges press,
thick with poplars, already cooler.

—Christopher Middleton

FRAGMENTS

Fragments,
Refuse of the soul,
Coagulations of blood of the twentieth century:

Scars—interrupted cycle of early creation,
The historic religions of five centuries pulverized,
Science: cracks in the Parthenon,
Planck with his quantum theory merging
In the new confusion with Kepler and Kierkegaard—

Yet there were evenings that went in the colors
Of the Father of all, dissolute, far-gathering,
Inviolate in their silence
Of coursing blue,
Color of the introvert;
Then one relaxed

die Hände auf das Knie gestützt
bäuerlich, einfach
und stillem Trunk ergeben
bei den Harmonikas der Knechte —

und andere
gehetzt von inneren Konvoluten,
Wölbungsdrängen,
Stilbaukompressionen
oder Jagden nach Liebe.
Ausdruckskrisen und Anfälle von Erotik:
das ist der Mensch von heute,
das Innere ein Vakuum,
die Kontinuität der Persönlichkeit
wird gewahrt von den Anzügen,
die bei gutem Stoff zehn Jahre halten.

Der Rest Fragmente,
halbe Laute,
Melodienansätze aus Nachbarhäusern,
Negerspirituals
oder Ave Marias.

1951

With the hands caught up round the knee
Peasant-wise, simple,
And resigned to the quiet drink
And the sound of the servants' concertina—

And others
Provoked by inner scrolls of paper,
Vaulted pressures,
Constrictions in the building of style
Or pursuits of love.
Crises of expression and bouts of eroticism,
That is the man of today,
His inwardness a vacuum;
The survival of personality
Is preserved by the clothing
Which, where material is good, may last ten years.

The rest fragments,
Half tones,
Snatches of melody from neighbors' houses,
Negro spirituals
Or Ave Marias.

—Vernon Watkins

IDEELLES WEITERLEBEN?

Bald
ein abgesägter, überholter
früh oder auch spät verstorbener Mann,
von dem man spricht wie von einer Sängerin
mit ausgesungenem Sopran
oder vom kleinen Hölty mit seinen paar Versen —
noch weniger: Durchschnitt,
nie geflogen,
keinen Borgward gefahren —
Zehnpfennigstücke für die Tram,
im Höchstfall Umsteiger.

Dabei ging täglich soviel bei dir durch
introvertiert, extrovertiert,
Nahrungssorgen, Ehewidrigkeit, Steuermoral —
mit allem mußtest du dich befassen,
ein gerüttelt Maß von Leben in mancherlei Gestalt.

Auf einer Karte aus Antibes,
die ich heute erhielt,
ragt eine Burg in die Méditerranée,
eine fanatische Sache:
südlich, meerisch, schneeig, am Rande hochgebirgig —
Jahrhunderte, dramatisiert,
ragen, ruhen, glänzen, firnen, strotzen
sich in die Aufnahme —
Nichts von alledem bei dir,
keine Ingredienzien zu einer Ansichtskarte —
Zehnpfennigstücke für die Tram,
Umsteiger,
und schnell die obenerwähnte Wortprägung:
überholt.

1951

IDEAL SURVIVAL?

Soon
a sawed-off, out-of-date
man who died early or maybe late,
of whom one speaks as of a singer
whose soprano is worn out
or of poor little Todhunter and his handful of verses—
even less: average,
never flew in a plane,
never drove a Borgward—
pennies paid out on the tram
a return fare at the most.

Yet daily so much passed through you
introverted, extroverted,
money troubles, marriage vexations, tax morality—
with all these you had to concern yourself,
a full measure of life in many a shape.

On a postcard from Antibes
which I received today
a castle looms over la Méditerranée,
a fanatical object, that:
southerly, snowy, marine, alpine at the edges—
centuries, dramatized,
loom, rest, gleam, glaze, swell
into the photograph—
Nothing of all this about you,
no ingredients at all for a picture postcard—
pennies paid out on the tram
return fares,
and quickly then the above-named caption:
out of date.

—*Michael Hamburger*

– GEWISSE LEBENSABENDE

I

Du brauchst nicht immer die Kacheln zu scheuern,
Hendrickje,
mein Auge trinkt sich selbst,
trinkt sich zu Ende –
aber an anderen Getränken mangelt es –
dort die Buddhastatue,
chinesischen Haingott,
gegen eine Kelle Hulstkamp,
bitte!

Nie etwas gemalt
in Frostweiß oder Schlittschuhläuferblau
oder dem irischen Grün,
aus dem der Purpur schimmert –
immer nur meine Eintönigkeit,
mein Schattenzwang –
nicht angenehm,
diesen Weg so deutlich zu verfolgen.

Größe – wo?
Ich nehme den Griffel
und gewisse Dinge stehn dann da
auf Papier, Leinwand
oder ähnlichem Zunder –

Resultat: Buddhabronze gegen Sprit –
aber Huldigungen unter Blattpflanzen,
Bankett der Pinselgilde –:
was fürs Genre – !

THE EVENINGS OF
CERTAIN LIVES

I

You needn't always be scrubbing the tiles,
                              Hendrickje,
my eye drinks itself,
drinks itself dry—
but then it has no other liquor—
the statue of Buddha over there,
Chinese god of the bosk,
as against a good tot of Hulstkamp,
I ask you!

Never painted a thing
in frost-white or skater's blue
or in Irish green
with the purple flickering out of it—
only my own monotony always—
my coactive shadows—
it's not pleasant
to follow this bent with such distinctness.

Greatness—where?
I take my pencil
and certain things emerge, stand there
on paper, canvas
or similar tinder—

result: bronze Buddha as against hooch—
all those obeisances under indoor plants,
banquet of the dimwit daubers' guild—:
give it to the genre painter!

... Knarren,
Schäfchen, die quietschen.
Abziehbilder
flämisch, rubenisch
für die Enkelchen —!
(ebensolche Idioten —!)

Ah — Hulstkamp —
Wärmezentrum,
Farbenmittelpunkt,
mein Schattenbraun —
Bartstoppelfluidum um Herz und Auge —

II

Der Kamin raucht
— schneuzt sich der Schwan vom Avon —,
die Stubben sind naß,
klamme Nacht, Leere vermählt mit Zugluft —
Schluß mit den Gestalten,
übervölkert die Erde
reichlicher Pfirsichfall, vier Rosenblüten
pro anno —
ausgestreut,
auf die Bretter geschoben
von dieser Hand,
faltig geworden
und mit erschlafften Adern!

Alle die Ophelias, Julias,
bekränzt, silbern, auch mörderisch —
alle die weichen Münder, die Seufzer,
die ich aus ihnen herausmanipulierte —
die ersten Aktricen längst Qualm,

. . . Rattles,
lambs bleating,
transfers,
Flemish, rubenesque,
for small grandchildren—
(likewise idiots!—)

Ah—Hulstkamp—
midpoint of warmth,
center of colors,
my shadow brown—
aura of unshaved bristle round heart and eye—

II

The fire is smoking
—the Swan of Avon blows his nose—
the tree-stumps are wet,
clammy night, emptiness suffused with draughts—
have done with characters,
earth overpopulated
by copious fall of peach, four rosebuds
pro anno—
strewn far and wide,
thrust on the boards
by this hand,
with its wrinkles now,
and its exhausted veins.

All the Ophelias, Juliets
wreathed, silvery, also murderous—
all the soft mouths, the sighs
I manipulated out of them—
the first actresses long since vapor,

Rost, ausgelaugt, Rattenpudding —
auch Herzens-Ariel bei den Elementen.

Die Epoche zieht sich den Bratenrock aus.
Diese Lord- und Lauseschädel,
ihre Gedankengänge,
die ich ins Extrem trieb —
meine Herren Geschichtsproduzenten
alles Kronen- und Szepteranalphabeten,
Großmächte des Weltraums
wie Fledermaus oder Papierdrachen!

Sir Goon schrieb neulich an mich:
„Der Rest ist Schweigen": —
Ich glaube, das ist von mir,
kann nur von mir sein,
Dante tot — eine große Leere
zwischen den Jahrhunderten
bis zu meinen Wortschatzzitaten —

aber wenn sie fehlten,
der Plunder nie aufgeschlagen,
die Buden, die Schafotte, die Schellen
nie geklungen hätten —:
Lücken—?? Vielleicht Zahnlücken,
aber das große Affengebiß
mahlte weiter
seine Leere, vermählt mit Zugluft —
die Stubben sind naß
und der Butler schnarcht in Porterträumen.

1952

rust, lixiviated, rats' pudding—
even the heart's Ariel off to the elements.

The age takes off its Sunday best.
These duke and desperado skulls,
their trains of thought
I drove to the extreme—
my history-making gentlemen
all illiterates of crown and sceptre,
major powers of space,
like flittermouse or paper kite!

Sir Goon recently wrote to me:
"The rest is silence."
I think I said that myself,
nobody else could have said it,
Dante dead—a great emptiness
between the centuries
up to the quotations from my vocabulary—

but if they were missing,
if all that stuff had never been turned out,
the booths and the gallowtrees, if the bells
had never jingled—:
gaps then? Gaps possibly in the teeth,
but the ape's great jaws
would go on grinding
their emptiness the draughts suffuse—
the tree-stumps are wet,
and the butler snores in his porter dreams.

—*Christopher Middleton*

WAS SCHLIMM IST

Wenn man kein Englisch kann,
von einen guten englischen Kriminalroman zu
hören,
der nicht ins Deutsche übersetzt ist.

Bei Hitze ein Bier sehn,
das man nicht bezahlen kann.

Einen neuen Gedanken haben,
den man nicht in einen Hölderlinvers einwickeln
kann,
wie es die Professoren tun.

Nachts auf Reisen Wellen schlagen hören
und sich sagen, daß sie das immer tun.

Sehr schlimm: eingeladen sein,
wenn zu Hause die Räume stiller,
der Café besser
und keine Unterhaltung nötig ist.

Am schlimmsten:
nicht im Sommer sterben,
wenn alles hell ist
und die Erde für Spaten leicht.

1953

WHAT'S BAD

When you do not know English
and hear of a good English detective novel
that has not been translated into German.

To see when you're hot
a beer that you can't afford.

To have a new thought without being able
to make it sound like a line by Hölderlin
as the professors do.

On a journey by night to hear waves beating
and to think: they do that all the time.

Very bad: to be invited out
when at home it is quieter,
the coffee is better,
and you've no need to be amused.

Worst of all:
not to die in summer,
when everything is bright,
and the earth is easy on the spade.

—*Christopher Middleton*

MENSCHEN GETROFFEN

Ich habe Menschen getroffen, die,
wenn man sie nach ihrem Namen fragte,
schüchtern — als ob sie garnicht beanspruchen könnten,
auch noch eine Benennung zu haben —
„Fräulein Christian" antworteten und dann:
„wie der Vorname", sie wollten einem die Erfassung
                                    erleichtern,
kein schwieriger Name wie „Popiol" oder
                    „Babendererde"—
„wie der Vorname" — bitte, belasten Sie Ihr
                    Erinnerungsvermögen nicht!

Ich habe Menschen getroffen, die
mit Eltern und vier Geschwistern in einer Stube
aufwuchsen, nachts, die Finger in den Ohren,
am Küchenherde lernten,
hochkamen, äußerlich schön und ladylike wie
                    Gräfinnen —
und innerlich sanft und fleißig wie Nausikaa,
die reine Stirn der Engel trugen.

Ich habe mich oft gefragt und keine Antwort gefunden,
woher das Sanfte und das Gute kommt,
weiß es auch heute nicht und muß nun gehn.

1955

PEOPLE MET

I have met people who, when asked what their names were,
Apologetically, as if they had no right to claim one's attention
Even with an appellation, would answer,
"Miss Vivian," then add, "Just like the Christian name";
They wanted to make things easier, no complicated names
Like Popkiss or Umpleby-Dunball—
"Just like the Christian name"—so please do not burden your
                                        memory!

I have met people who grew up in a single room together with
Parents and four brothers and sisters; they studied by night,
Their fingers in their ears, beside the kitchen range;
They became eminent,
Outwardly beautiful, veritable *grandes dames*, and
Inwardly gentle and active as Nausicaa,
With brows clear as angels' brows.

Often I have asked myself, but found no answer,
Where gentleness and goodness can possibly come from;
Even today I can't tell, and it's time to be gone.

                                        —*Christopher Middleton*

EPILOG

Die trunkenen Fluten fallen —
die Stunde des sterbenden Blau
und der erblaßten Korallen
um die Insel von Palau.

Die trunkenen Fluten enden
als Fremdes, nicht dein, nicht mein,
sie lassen dir nichts in Händen
als der Bilder schweigendes Sein.

Die Fluten, die Flammen, die Fragen —
und dann auf Asche sehn:
„Leben ist Brückenschlagen
über Ströme, die vergehn."

1949

EPILOGUE

The drunken torrents are falling—
the blueness is dying now
and the corals are pale as the water
round the island of Palau.

The drunken torrents are broken,
grown alien, to you, to me,
our only possession the silence
of a bone washed clean by the sea.

The floods, the flames, the questions—
till the ashes tell you one day:
"Life is the building of bridges
over rivers that seep away."

—*Michael Hamburger*

BIBLIOGRAPHY

Selected from *Gottfried Benn Bibliographie 1912-1956* by Edgar Lohner, Limes Verlag, Wiesbaden, 1958

A. Pre-World War II publications by Benn, reprinted in volumes:
   Frühe Prosa und Reden, Limes, 1950
   Essays, Limes, 1951
   Frühe Lyrik und Dramen, Limes, 1952
   Gesammelte Gedichte, Limes, 1956 (also contains post-war poetry)

B. Post-war volumes:
   Drei alte Männer, Limes, 1949
   Der Ptolemäer, Limes, 1949
   Ausdruckswelt. Essays und Aphorismen, Limes, 1949; 2nd ed. 1954
   Doppelleben. Zwei Selbstdarstellungen, Limes, 1950
   Probleme der Lyrik, Limes, 1951
   Die Stimme hinter dem Vorhang, Limes, 1952
   Altern als Problem für Künstler, Limes, 1954
   Über mich selbst, 1886-1956, Langen-Müller Verlag, München, 1956
   Ausgewählte Briefe, Limes, 1957

C. English prose translations not included in this volume:
   "The Island"—*transition* 2 (1927)
   "The Structure of the Personality (Outline of a Geology of the 'I')"—*transition* 21 (1932)
   "After Nihilism"—*Origin* X (1953)

D. English poetry translations, not included in this volume, in *Contact* (Canada) Vol. I Nr. 3; Vol. II Nrs. 5 and 9

New Mexico Quarterly, Summer 1952

Origin VII and X

Poetry, August 1952

Quarterly Review of Literature Vol. VII

E. English publications about Benn:

Eliot, T. S.—*The Three Voices of Poetry*, Cambridge University Press, London, 1953

Exner, Richard—"Gottfried Benn (1886-1956)"—*Books Abroad* XXX, 4 (1956)

Frank, Joseph—"The 'Double Life' of Gottfried Benn"—*New Republic*, October 12, 1953

Golffing, Francis—"Note on Gottfried Benn"—*Poetry*, August 1952

Hamburger, Michael—*Reason and Energy. Studies in German Literature*, Grove Press, New York, 1957

id.—"Art and Nihilism; the poetry of Gottfried Benn"—*Encounter*, October 1954

Jolas, Eugene—"Gottfried Benn"—*transition* 5 (1927)

Lohner, Edgar—"Gottfried Benn: German Poet"—*Western Review* XVII (1953)

Roditi, Edouard—"Gottfried Benn"—*Partisan Review* XVII, 4 (1950)

Seyppel, Joachim—"A Renaissance of German Poetry: Gottfried Benn"—*Modern Language Forum* XXXIX, 2 (1954)